Jo Spurrier was born in 1980 and has a Bachelor of Science, but turned to writing because people tend to get upset when scientists make things up.

Her interests include knitting, spinning, cooking and research. She lives in Adelaide and spends a lot of time daydreaming about snow.

D1650215

014180995 4

# JO SPURRIER

## WINTER BE MY SHIELD

CHILDREN OF THE BLACK SUN
⇒ BOOK ONE ⇐

**HARPER Voyager**
*An Imprint of HarperCollinsPublishers*
voyageronline.com.au

**HarperVoyager**
An imprint of HarperCollins*Publishers*
First published in Australia in 2012
This edition published in 2013
by HarperCollins*Publishers* Australia Pty Limited
ABN 36 009 913 517
harpercollins.com.au

**HarperCollins*Publishers***
Level 13, 201 Elizabeth Street, Sydney NSW 2000, Australia
31 View Road, Glenfield, Auckland 0627, New Zealand
A 53, Sector 57, Noida, UP, India
77–85 Fulham Palace Road, London W6 8JB, United Kingdom
2 Bloor Street East, 20th floor, Toronto, Ontario M4W 1A8, Canada
10 East 53rd Street, New York NY 10022, USA

National Library of Australia Cataloguing-in-Publication entry:

Spurrier, Jo.
  Winter be my shield / Jo Spurrier.
  ISBN: 978 0 7322 9253 9 (pbk.)
  Spurrier, Jo. Children of the black sun trilogy 1.
A823.4

Cover design by Darren Holt, HarperCollins Design Studio,
adapted by Alicia Freile, Tango Media
Cover images by shutterstock.com
Map by Jo Spurrier
Author photograph by Alex McDonald
Typeset in Goudy Old Style by Kirby Jones

*For my mum, Stephanie*

## Acknowledgements

I owe a great many thanks to the following people. Simon, problem solver and brainstormer extraordinaire. My parents, Stephanie and Rod, Auntie Pip, Mike and Jan. Toby and Katie, for happily talking books at all hours and for demonstrating the combat scenes. Fiona McIntosh, for her unfailing support and encouragement of emerging writers. Special thanks to Jane, Janos and Kate, and to Nikki, who gave me encouragement when I needed it most.

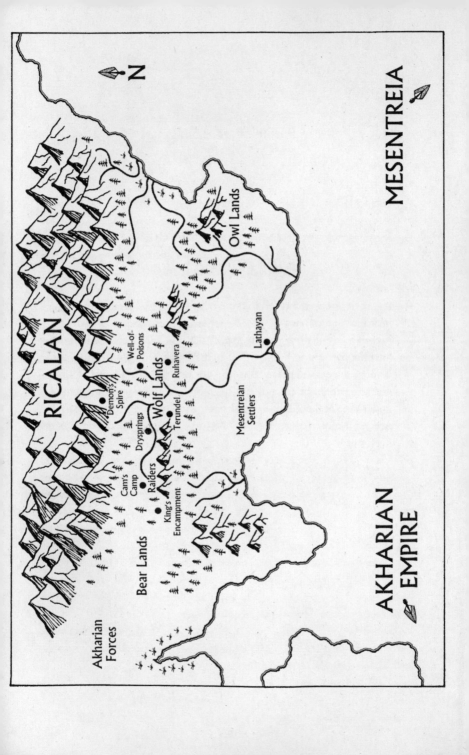

# Prologue

At the foot of the temple steps Isidro bowed his head into the icy wind and turned back towards the village. There were two figures huddling in the lee of the temple wall as they shared a wineskin and it struck him as odd that anyone would choose to wait out here, rather than in the warmth of the shrine. One of them had a thick, tawny beard beneath the shadow cast by the hood of his coat. Mesentreians, then. Probably soldiers. This region was crawling with the king's men, soldiers sent north to meet the invaders from the Akharian empire.

Once he passed through the gates, Isidro heard the faint crunch of boots on snow as the men pushed away from the wall to follow him.

He carried a sword beneath his heavy winter fur. Perhaps if he led them behind the temple and its outbuildings, he could deal with these two before they caused him trouble. But if he had truly been found out, it was likely there were more than just them watching him. It would get him nowhere.

With a silent curse, Isidro gritted his teeth and trudged on through the snow towards the village. How in the Black Sun's name had they found him? It had been ten years since he'd last been at court and then he'd been nothing more than a stripling boy. They couldn't have recognised him — he wasn't like Cam, with fair hair and green eyes that made him stand out amongst the black-haired Ricalanis. If they'd found him after all this time it could only be because they'd known where to look. Maybe Charzic or one of the scum who followed him had told the Mesentreians he would be heading this way and they'd taken advantage of the lull before the storm to track him down.

The wind was turning his face numb, but the hood would only restrict his vision so Isidro left it down. If they knew who he was why hadn't they jumped him yet? This path would take him to the market at the centre of the village but he was still far enough away from the crowds that a scuffle wouldn't draw much attention.

He'd come here to deliver a message to the ruling clan, to warn them Charzic had discovered their spies and was plotting reprisals, but he couldn't help but wonder if the clan would have bigger problems to deal with by the time it reached the Chieftain. Rumour had it the legions had already reached the north, but Isidro had been out of contact for too long to know if it was anything more than idle talk. He'd hoped to gather more information along with the supplies the women wanted from the market, but there was no time for that now — he'd settle for getting out of this cursed village alive. He'd left his horse at a house on the eastern side and if he could make it back there, he might have a chance.

His mind was racing. The only reason Isidro could imagine might make the Mesentreians hold back was the chance that he hadn't come here alone. It wasn't him they wanted, after all — it was Cam. They wouldn't take the risk that someone might slip away and warn the prince that the king's men were finally closing in on him.

There was a shout in Mesentreian, off to his left. Isidro was reaching beneath his coat for the hilt of his sword when a dozen men spilled out of the lane between two houses, pushing and shoving in a drunken brawl. As Isidro skirted around them one of the men lurched into his path. 'Fucking flea-herder,' the soldier slurred, and threw a clumsy punch. Isidro stepped aside, grabbed the man by the front of his jacket and shoved him against another soldier who was doubled over, puking at the edge of the fight. With a roar they turned on each other, dragging the brawl further across the path of the men who had been trailing him. In a brief moment Isidro saw their faces — annoyed and sober — despite the near-empty wineskin.

*Bright Sun help me,* he thought. *This is not going to end well.*

It was just past midwinter and the snowdrifts on the leeward sides of the houses were piled nearly to the eaves. In the dim light the drifts blended together in a wall of blue shadows. While the soldiers were still trying to shove their way past the brawl, Isidro turned down between the houses and out of sight.

The Ricalani houses were massive log-built structures with a barn in one half and a dwelling in the other, divided by a central aisle. The lower storeys were mostly buried under snow, but the entrance was on the upper level, reached by a wooden ramp that opened onto the aisle so stock and sleds could be driven in and out, however deep the snow. The doorway at the top of one such ramp had been propped open.

He had to act quickly — he had only moments before the soldiers caught up with him. Isidro climbed the ramp in a few long strides and ducked inside.

Two young women were sitting there, sewing in the meagre daylight with a brazier between them for warmth. They yelped in surprise as he barged in between them and dodged around behind the door where he would be concealed from the path below.

A low, deep-throated growl rippled through the sudden gloom. A great black and white dog had been lying at the girls' backs, near the brazier. Isidro hadn't noticed it at first and now it rose as though weightless, the sound swelling to a full-throated snarl. They were known as bear-dogs here in the north, because a pair of them could drive one of the great beasts away from a kill. The dog stood as high as a woman's waist and probably weighed as much as Isidro did.

Isidro raised his hands in a gesture of peace, but he kept moving slowly away from the doorway and deeper into the house. From outside there came the sound of boots crunching over the snow. 'That was Balorica, I'm sure of it,' a voice said in Mesentreian, drifting up from the street. 'Go look up there — I'll check around the side.'

Someone started up the ramp and one of the girls grabbed the dog's collar and turned it towards the door. As a soldier's shadow fell over the threshold the dog lunged at him, hackles up and snarling, and the soldier stumbled back with a curse.

The other girl darted forward and caught Isidro by the arm. 'You must leave,' she hissed and tried to pull him towards the door.

Instead, he seized her wrist and started down the stairs to the lower level, pulling her with him, as he reached into his coat for the leather case tucked away there. 'Show me to your stove. Then I'll go.'

Scowling, she followed him down the stable stairs and into the stone-floored dividing corridor where the boiler melted ice and snow to provide water for the household. An older woman must have been tending it when she heard the dog bellow and snarl — she met them at the foot of the stair with an axe in her hands. 'What's all that noise?' she said in Ricalani and then looked Isidro up and down. 'And who in the Bright Sun's name are you?'

3

'The southerners are chasing him,' the young woman said. 'We have to get him out without them seeing or there's going to be trouble.'

The older one narrowed her eyes and shifted her axe to one hand. 'This way,' she said, pointing with the silver-lipped head.

'One moment,' Isidro said. He tore the documents out of the leather case and crumpled them into a ball, which he threw into the open door of the stove, followed by the case itself. The papers identified him as a servant of the Wolf Clan and while they'd saved him in the past, if they were found on him now it would only cause trouble for his allies and for Cam.

The women led him across the aisle and then back up another set of stairs into the dwelling-half of the house. From there they shepherded him to a hatch that led onto the upper walkway, an outdoor space partially screened with a lattice of carved wood.

The young woman cracked the door open to look outside. Below on the snow a soldier peered around the edge of the house but after a moment he headed back around to the entrance where the dog was still barking and men were shouting. When he was gone, two pairs of firm hands shoved Isidro out onto the walkway. The door closed behind him and he heard a bar slot into place to keep him from forcing his way back in.

He'd expected nothing less. Helping him, even unwillingly, would only cause them trouble.

Only a man's height above the snow, Isidro slipped out of the covered walkway and dropped down to the ground. As he trudged away from the house he pulled his hood up to hide his face and slouched in an effort to disguise his height. If he did nothing else to attract attention he might just be able to escape with his hide intact.

As he skirted around the market Isidro heard voices shouting in Mesentreian as men searched between the houses. It took all of his willpower not to turn around and he strained his hearing to pick up any footsteps that kept pace with his.

When he reached the house where his gelding was tethered he was trembling with relief. There was no one around as he scrambled up the ramp and ducked into the gloom, not even a dog to guard the stock. Isidro tightened the girth and swung into the saddle and was turning the horse towards the entrance when he saw a door on the dwelling-side was open by a crack, and one frightened eye looked out at him. There was a scuffle of movement behind it and then the door slammed shut.

They knew.

Isidro opened his coat and loosened his sword in its sheath. He had no armour, but the thick fur of his coat would offer him some protection. Casting around for any other weapon, his eye fell on the spear rack on the wall. While the horse stamped and tossed its head, sensing its rider's tension, Isidro selected one with a broad head of polished steel and gave a silent prayer of thanks that he'd managed to acquire a battle-trained horse before Charzic had turned them out. Isidro took a deep breath, turned the gelding's head towards the door and drove his heels into its flanks.

With two powerful strides the horse leapt from the top of the ramp and landed amid a group of a dozen men gathered at the foot. One of them went down under the gelding's hooves and another dropped beneath Isidro's spear as he slashed and stabbed at the men crowding around him. For a brief moment he thought he might be able to break free of them, then he saw more soldiers running from the village, while mounted men circled around to cut off his escape.

When the spearhead snagged on bone Isidro abandoned it and drew his sword, but there were too many of them dragging on his coat and his sleeves as they tried to pull him from the saddle. With a sudden sick feeling, Isidro realised they weren't aiming to kill him. If they wanted him dead, he'd have a knife in his back by now. They wanted him alive. It strengthened his will as he hacked and killed and the gelding trampled the snow to a bloody churn. His only hope now was to goad them into killing him. He wouldn't, *couldn't*, let them take him alive.

The horse screamed and reared with a sword-hilt jutting from its chest. Its legs buckled, and as the gelding crumpled beneath Isidro, hands closed around him, dragging him from the saddle and wrenching the sword from his fingers. He fought for all he was worth but something struck against his skull and for a moment he was aware of nothing but a cold and echoing blackness. When he came back to himself he was pressed face down into the bloody snow while someone bound his hands behind his back.

'Back off,' a voice snarled in Mesentreian, speaking with an accent Isidro remembered well. 'Keep those blades away from him. Any man

5

who draws blood will be handed over to Lord Rasten.' A hand grasped Isidro's hair and wrenched his head back. The man looking down at him had an uncanny resemblance to Isidro's foster-brother, Cam — the same jaw and mouth, the same high forehead and yellow hair. He hadn't laid eyes on Osebian in ten years but there was no doubt that this was him. Osebian was Cam's cousin, brought here from Mesentreia by the queen when she realised her younger son was beyond her control.

'That's him,' Osebian said. 'That's Balorica.' He let Isidro's head fall back and kicked him solidly in the ribs. 'Where is the prince, flea-picker? Where's Cammarian?'

'Dead,' Isidro said. 'He's dead and gone.'

Osebian kicked him again. 'You lie about as well as you fight, Balorica. Lord Kell will have the truth from you. Get him on his feet! And make sure he's shackled properly — if he loses his hands to frostbite before the king's torturer gets to him I'll see that every man here pays for it.'

*Black Sun give me strength.* He'd never particularly believed in the Gods, but Fires Below, no one else could help him now. As the soldiers hauled him to his feet Isidro glanced up at the sun, hanging low in the eastern sky. It would be hours before Cam and the others expected him back and longer still until they realised something had gone wrong. By then the king's torturer would have him. Kell and his apprentice Rasten could make a dead man talk … He could only hope that Cam had the sense their father had drummed into them both and would be long gone by the time they wrung the knowledge from him. *By the Black Sun, brother, don't do anything stupid.*

# Chapter 1

*One month later*

Sierra turned her face towards the blizzard. Needles of ice stung her skin and blasted tears from her eyes and strands of black hair lashed around her face, stiff as a whipcord with frost. Huddled deep within her stolen fur she forced her way through the drifts, as the wind howled and shrieked in her ears.

'Spirit of storm defend me ...' She muttered the ancient prayer like a mantra and glanced back towards the tents and horse-lines she had left behind. The blizzard was her shield — without it she would never have come this far. She could see for perhaps thirty paces around her, but everything beyond was lost in a swirl of white. The men searching for her would be just as blind, but that was scant comfort. She was as likely to stumble into them as they were to find her.

As she turned back the wind caught her hood and swept it away. Without thinking Sierra snatched for it and the movement snagged her sleeve on the rag-wrapped bracelet around her wrist. It tore the cloth loose from her blistered skin and she bit back a yelp of pain. Her stride faltered and she tripped over her snowshoes and fell, sinking to her waist in the snow.

She bared her teeth to the storm in a wordless growl of frustration. She wanted to shriek and scream out all her rage and fear, to beat her fists against the shifting snow. But she dared not take the risk, not even with the roar of the wind to drown her voice.

Her power pulsed within her, struggling like a beast in a snare. Her fear had riled it; it would fight against her control until the pain and her tight-strung nerves eased and let it settle. The burns around her wrists were throbbing and with a sob of breath Sierra shuffled around until the

7

wind was at her back. She couldn't afford this time, but unless she did something her power would spill and spark again, drawing the hunters to her with light and noise. Carefully she eased the mittens off and rolled her gloves down over the backs of her hands to expose the smears of dried blood on her skin.

The rags around her wrists were dry and stiff, except for spots of dampness where the blisters had burst. She'd soaked the cloth before she left the tent — it was the only defence she had against the shackles Kell had locked around her wrists — but the water hadn't lasted long.

Blood-red stones gleamed at her through the rags and she sifted a little snow in to cover them. Whether it melted to soothe the burns or froze her hands to numbness she didn't much care. Prying the suppression bands off had taken too long — she'd had no time to work on the punishment bands as well. If she'd waited any longer Rasten might have found her before she even left the camp.

A distant shout made her freeze like a startled hare and she hastily pulled her mittens back on and clambered to her feet. They couldn't have found her tracks — in a storm like this the snow covered them in moments, but the swirling whiteness played tricks on the eye. One of the men must have seen a shadow and shouted before it melted away. It was sheer bad luck but it would end her brief freedom all the same.

Sierra leaned into the wind and set off again. Her only hope was to put as much distance as possible behind her. By now Rasten knew she was gone and if he grew close enough to sense her …

Kell had been treating his new apprentice gently for fear of crippling her growing power, but all that had ended the moment she stepped out of the tent. *It wouldn't have been much longer before he started the training, anyway*, Sierra told herself. Beneath her fur the hilt of her stolen knife pressed against her belly. If Rasten did find her, she had no intention of being taken alive.

She'd killed a dozen men in her escape — torn them apart with the power that lurked beneath her skin and slipped away in the confusion that followed. She'd stolen enough gear to have a chance of surviving outside in a Ricalani winter — a white coat that camouflaged her against the snow, boots and snowshoes, gloves, cowl, hat and dagger; all the things Rasten had kept locked up out of her reach, using the winter as another jailer. She'd found a little food — a meagre pack of emergency rations she'd snatched up from a tent. It wouldn't feed her for long.

Power brushed against her mind like the tickling caress of a feather and Sierra faltered, nearly stumbling again.

*Sierra* ... The voice came as a whisper. It sounded as though Rasten were standing right beside her and murmuring in her ear. *Sierra, where are you going to go? Don't do this, Little Crow. There's nowhere for you to hide — we found you once, we can do it again.*

His voice seemed to echo inside her skull. Sierra screwed her eyelids closed and for a moment she saw a ghostly vision through his eyes. He was sitting on a horse with men ranging ahead of him like a line of beaters as he gazed at a forest half shrouded in blinding snow. The Akharian army was drawing near, but Kell would turn out the entire camp to hunt her down if he could, despite the threat of southern soldiers and mages.

A band of searing heat encircled each of her wrists and with a sob of pain Sierra broke the contact. Her power was rising again and, as it neared the surface, Kell's shackles awoke in a bloom of heat to punish her lapse in control.

*Spirit of storm* ... With the wind howling in her ears Sierra tried to empty her mind. It was no easy thing while the power leapt and surged within her. For two years the suppression stones had kept it caged and without those bonds it was like a wild beast, snarling and bristling with every surge of pain and fear. She imagined her thoughts whipped away like smoke on the wind, but it was some time before it grew quiet once again. Rasten couldn't have expected her to reply — he must have been trying to frighten her into giving herself away. He was surely growing desperate. If he failed to find her, Kell's rage and frustration would fall on him instead. Kell wouldn't permanently damage his apprentice, but he knew how to inflict enormous suffering while still leaving his victim whole — Rasten knew that better than she did. He'd do anything to find her and avert Kell's rage.

*You have no food, no shelter and no one to take you in. You don't even know where you are, Little Crow. Come back and beg Kell for mercy and he'll grant it, I promise. There's no life for you without us, Sierra.*

She pushed his words from her mind — he was probably right, but at this point she didn't care if she survived the storm, so long as she died free of her chains. The Black Sun claimed everyone in the end and it would be a kinder fate than the one Kell had in store for her.

The wind eased, and Sierra glanced up to see dark shapes looming ahead. Trees, their branches sweeping low beneath their burden of ice and snow. Her blind flight had taken her into woodland, where the huddled trees gave some defence against the wind. It was an unwelcome sight — in the shelter of those trees, the snow would hold her tracks longer. Visibility was greater, too, and once inside she would be unable to move quickly amid the powdery drifts.

Sierra had turned away from the woods, aiming to lose herself in the driving snow, when she heard a horse snort behind her. She hurried for a clump of small trees buried beneath a mound of ice and ducked behind them just as a figure on a horse emerged from the swirling snow, skirting along the edge of the forest and heading in her direction.

Hunching down until she was a shapeless white lump against the snow, Sierra shuffled to a denser stand of trees, hoping they would be enough to block the light if she had to resort to her power.

The horse was a Ricalani pony, a small, shaggy beast, and it trotted along in the peculiar shuffling gait the ponies adopted with the willow and rawhide snowshoes buckled around their hooves. The rider, crouched low in the saddle, had his hood thrown back and was looking around keenly as he rode.

Sierra felt her stomach tighten. He was Ricalani, one of her own people. She should have expected it — Rasten would spare no effort in the search and the native-born scouts were the best in the army, trained since childhood for hunting in the snow. Hooded and shrouded in white as she was, a Mesentreian soldier might walk right past her, but a Ricalani would almost certainly spot her here where the snowfall was lighter. She had no choice but to kill him.

Slowly she backed away from the tree that concealed her, moving with care to keep the snowshoes' long tails from digging into the snow. A moment's clumsiness would finish her here.

The rider, still some distance away, turned his head in her direction and Sierra held her breath. He would have been told it was too dangerous to approach her, that once she was spotted he must retreat and report the sighting. She waited for him to turn and ride away but though he slowed the horse momentarily, he nudged it on again, still scanning the woods around her. With the barest sigh of relief, Sierra ducked back behind a young pine where she pulled off her mittens and her gloves and tucked them into the sash binding her coat. It was too cold for anyone but a mage to leave skin bare for long, but her power would keep frostbite at bay for a few moments. With her heart pounding, Sierra tried not to think about the pain the punishment bands would bring, the searing flash of heat that would come with her rising power.

The horse slowed to a walk as it approached. Sierra pictured the rider peering between the trees, uncertain now that he'd seen anything at all. She heard him rein in and turn the horse, its snowshoes crunching over ice as he moved towards her.

*Black Sun forgive me. I wouldn't do this if there was another way.* Sierra closed her eyes and loosed the beast within her.

# Chapter 2

The snow beneath the snare was churned and scuffed where the hare had struggled, but the dangling thread of wire was empty. Cam jammed his fists against his belt and glared at it in disgust. 'Son of a bitch.'

One stiff and frozen hare dangled from his pack. Of the six snares he'd visited today, only one had been successful. The first had been buried beneath a snowdrift before it could catch anything and the others had all been raided, by foxes, wolves and, in one case, a leopard — a big one, judging from the tracks it left behind. That couldn't be helped, but *this* one hadn't been broken, nor was the prey dismembered within the noose. The wire had been deliberately untwisted and then left that way, with no attempt to set the snare again and perhaps replace the stolen catch. The prints around it left no doubt. Someone had raided his snare.

'Black Sun take you, you miserable bastard!' Cam made a careful sweep of the hillsides through the narrow slit of his snow-goggles before he rested his bow against the sapling and crouched down with a muttered curse to undo the snare and recover the wire. He paid more attention to the silence at his back than the frosted steel. The armies gathered to the west were far too close for comfort. Perhaps it was foolish to run a trap-line out here, but they were near enough to starving as it was, and this way he might get at least a little warning when trouble began to head their way.

When he picked up his bow again, Cam scowled at the prints. They were old, with the surface frozen hard and the edges rounded by the wind. It was the first sign of people he'd seen in weeks, apart from his ragged little band. The king's army was perhaps as little as a few dozen miles away. The invaders from the western lands must be drawing near by now, but it had been weeks since he'd heard any word of the coming battles.

After the gut-wrenching weeks following Isidro's capture, Cam had barely given a thought to the brewing war. His mad, desperate scheme to ambush the guards taking Isidro south for his execution and then the days huddled by his brother's bedside as he hovered near death had become Cam's sole focus. It was only now that Isidro was past the worst and growing stronger that the greater threat snapped into sharp focus and Cam realised how much time had passed and how much the threat to the west must have grown while he was unaware.

No honourable man would raid another's snare, but there was more at stake than the matter of a stolen kill. Anyone desperate enough to steal so brazenly was a threat. It might be a deserter or another bandit kicked out of Charzic's band, or a foraging party from the king's camp. By the Black Sun, it might even be an Akharian scout, searching for a way past the king's forces. Either way, he had to know. Keeping his camp safe and undiscovered was of the highest importance. His tiny band ought to move on from these hills as soon as possible, but for the moment Isidro was still too weak to be subjected to the hardships of winter travel.

Cam followed the tracks away from the snare and around the thicket, where he found another surprise. The thief had tethered a horse there while he stole the kill — another worrying sign. The common folk of Ricalan rarely bothered with horses. Those who could afford a beast of burden preferred the *yaka*, which provided milk and fleece as well as strength for hauling and were hardier even than the native ponies; but most folk simply did without, packing their gear on a toboggan and hauling it themselves. Here in the north, only three sorts of folk kept horses — the ruling clans, the army and the Raiders who lived in the no-man's-land between the settlers and the native folk. Having Charzic and his men find them would be just as bad as if the Mesentreians did, but Cam had seen no sign of them since Isidro was taken. They'd heard the talk of war as well and he suspected they'd retreated to the east, where the villages wouldn't be full of soldiers itching for a fight.

But there was only the one set of prints: if the thief was alone it would be a simple matter to deal with. Once his pack was settled on his shoulders again, Cam set out to follow him.

The trail was perhaps a day old, but it led him back towards his own camp. The horse had been moving slowly, meandering really, as though the rider had dozed in the saddle and woken only when the horse stopped to graze. Cam relaxed a little as the tracks grew steadily more erratic. If the thief was that far gone with hypothermia, chances were that he wouldn't be a threat to anyone by now.

Every mile or so, Cam stopped to search for signs of pursuit. If the thief were a deserter, surely someone would come searching for him — unless the battle was already met and the king's men were too hard-pressed to worry about such losses.

There was no sign of other men, but as the sun passed its zenith an odd noise reached his ears. It was a low rumble like distant thunder, but the sky was clear, with only a few high mare's-tail clouds drawn out by the wind.

Cam veered from the track and ducked into a patch of cover. He'd heard something like that before, only the last time it had been far more distant, carried in snatches by the wind. The rumble died out after only a short time, but with his heart pounding in his throat, Cam scrambled up a nearby ridge to see if he could spot the source of it. The noise had seemed to come from the west, but it was hard to tell with the echoes rolling around the hills.

The last time he'd heard a sound like thunder out of a clear sky, he and Isidro had been watching Kell and his apprentice tear apart the fortress of a clan that had defied the king. From their vantage point on an overlooking mountain, they'd seen unearthly swathes of blood-red light and seething flame crawl over the ancient stone and consume it, with the sound reaching far further than any mere storm. By morning there had been nothing left but a blackened scar.

By the time he reached the ridge the noise had stopped. Cam searched the horizon, but there were no flickering lights or blood-red gleam — and in the low winter daylight, surely he would see the lights if they were there…

After a long moment he spotted a haze of ice forming a low cloud beyond hilltops to the north and breathed a heavy sigh of relief. It was only an avalanche, not mages doing battle in these hills after all. Of course, for all he knew Lord Kell and the Akharian mages were already squaring off to the west — with these steep hills to break up the sound he might not hear it until it was too late.

This war had been brewing for decades. The first Mesentreian settlers had come to Ricalan nearly a century before in the early days of the alliance with the southern isles, boatloads of starving and land-hungry people from the overcrowded islands. By the time Cam's elder brother Severian took the throne, the Mesentreians controlled the south of Ricalan, providing safe harbours for ships to strike at the Akharian Empire. They seized Akharian grain ships, their mundane cargo worth a fortune in Mesentreia, and landed to raid and burn Akharian farms. The empire lacked Mesentreia's mastery of the sea, and even their military mages could do little to stem the piracy or turn back the swift-striking raiders who plied their vast coast.

Even here in the north, Cam had heard tales of riots in the south over the price of grain. A bad harvest in the empire seemed to have been the final straw. The legions marched north, crossing the frozen fens that marked Ricalan's western border and aiming for the harbours to the south. Severian had brought his army and his sorcerer north to meet them at the boundary between the settlements and the tribal lands. But the king's goal was to protect the southern holdings — he would sacrifice no men to defend the tribal north and the clans who only tolerated his rule for fear of the sorcerer he commanded. The Akharians were slavers and Cam knew Severian would count it a favour if they thinned the ranks of those who despised their foreign king.

Cam had hoped he and his people would be gone from here by the time this came to a head, but he was afraid it was already too late for that. Somehow, he had to find a balance between giving Isidro time to heal and herding his little band out of here before the soldiers — any soldiers — found their camp and slaughtered them all. With one last sweep of the horizon, Cam slipped and skidded back down the slope to collect his pack and pick up the trail once again.

He spotted the horse as the sun was sinking. It was tethered in a stand of trees where it had scraped the snow away with its hooves, searching vainly for any grazing buried beneath. Cam set his pack down and took out his white war-coat, wrapped in a bit of oilcloth to protect it from blood and stains. The effort of walking had made him warm enough to shed his heavy fur in favour of a windproof buckskin parka and trousers. He pulled the white leather coat over it, buckled his quiver at his hip and nocked an arrow to his bow, then circled around to approach the copse from the other side.

The surface of the snow was smooth and unbroken apart from the tracks of small animals and the mark of an owl's wings, where it had swooped on some small creature beneath the snow. A tethered and unguarded horse would be fine bait for an ambush, but if there was anyone hiding in wait the snow would have betrayed them. Cam approached slowly, placing each foot with care to lessen the noise of his snowshoes. With shallow breaths he tasted the air, but all he could smell was stale smoke and the sharp scent of snow.

He was perhaps a dozen paces away when the horse finally noticed him. It threw its head up with a nicker of fright and jerked back on the tether.

'Whoa, lad,' Cam said, softly. 'Easy there. What's happened to your master, then?'

His voice soothed it and when he came close enough to rub its nose the beast lipped at his sleeve. 'Hungry, aren't you?' Cam said.

The horse was tethered beside a large spruce, its lower branches bowed down by the weight of ice. There was usually a space beneath the lowest boughs and in an emergency it made a good shelter, insulated by the airy bulk of the snow. Cam could see a place where the snow had been trampled and the branches pushed aside, but there was no sound or movement from inside.

The horse seized his sleeve in its teeth and Cam grabbed its nose to make it let go. 'Hello, the camp!' he called. 'Anyone in there?'

No response. The air was cold, with no hint of warmth from a fire, and the only sound was the moaning of the wind through the needles of the trees.

Cam took the arrow from his bowstring and returned it to his quiver. He sunk the end of the stave into the snow and crouched at the entrance, reaching inside his war-coat for his knife.

The thief had wedged the saddle into the entrance he'd created; as Cam shoved it aside, the disturbance sent a cascade of snow over his back. He ignored it and leaned into the gloom.

The ashes of a cold fire rested atop a platform of green twigs. The bones of his hare lay beside them, picked clean and heaped in a haphazard pile. *You poor sod*, Cam thought. Fresh hare was as tough as old boot leather. It had to hang for a few days in a warm tent to be considered edible.

The thief was curled up beyond the cold ashes, so bundled up in wool and fur that only his eyes were visible, peacefully closed as his head lolled against the trunk. Frost spangled the cowl that was pulled up over his mouth and nose and glittered on his eyelashes and finely arched brows.

Cam crawled into the narrow space and pulled the cowl down with a flick of his fingers. Not a man after all, but a woman, scarcely more than a girl, and of Ricalani blood too. This was no deserter. 'Hey,' he said, and shook her gently. 'Hey, can you hear me? Wake up!'

Her head slumped forward onto her chest, but she didn't stir. Her lips were blue with cold, but at least she wasn't frozen solid.

'Bright Sun, help me!' Cam pulled off his mitten and the glove beneath and held them in his teeth as he felt for a pulse in her neck. Her skin was so cold that his heart sank, but there was a rule for those who fell prey to the cold — *no one's dead until they're warm and dead*. He'd seen children pulled stiff and lifeless from beneath the ice, only to be running and playing with their siblings the next day.

'Come on,' Cam said, shifting his fingers to try again. His heart was beating harder and all he could think of was Isidro, deathly white and lying on a slab of river ice with water freezing in his hair.

They'd ambushed the caravan taking Isidro to Lathayan for his execution, but the man driving the sled had been determined not to let his prisoner be rescued. With an arrow in his back he'd driven the sled and its heavy bronze cage onto ice too thin to hold its weight. Chained and helpless, Isidro had been held under the black water for an age before they'd managed to cut through the wagon gate and pull him free, moments before the sled crashed all the way through and sank beneath the ice, dragging the screaming horses with it. Rhia had brought him back, but only just, and pneumonia still rattled and burned in his chest almost a month later.

A flutter beneath Cam's fingers brought him back to the present. Her blue-tinged lips parted and when Cam heard the faint whisper of her breath he wanted to laugh with relief. 'Ha! Well, my little thief, you'll answer for my hare after all!'

There was a tickle in his throat. Isidro tried to keep his breathing shallow to avoid another bout of coughing, but he knew he was fighting a losing battle with the dry winter air.

The sun had set and deep blue shadows were spreading over the snow. An owl called from somewhere among the scattered trees. He had been standing here long enough for a cloud of mist to gather around him, a haze of ice crystallised from the moisture in his breath.

Rhia came to stand at his side. 'Isidro, you should come in out of the cold.'

'In a moment,' he said. His voice was hoarse and rusty. Rhia said it was just the pneumonia, but he wasn't so sure. Many things had been damaged beyond repair during his time in Kell's tent.

He felt her eyes upon him and tried not to show his irritation. Most southerners were small but Rhia was slight even for them, due to the years she had spent as a slave. Only a fool mistook her stature for weakness, though — he'd seen her pull arrows and spears from struggling warriors and set enough broken or dislocated limbs to be sure of that. She'd been born in the empire, but had spent half her life in Mesentreia after being captured on a raid and then given in payment to a physician, who taught her his craft.

'Issey …' Rhia began again. Isidro smiled faintly. She was as protective as a tiger of her cub when it came to her patients, but he was in no mood to be mothered. Since he'd finally found his way back to consciousness he'd spent a week lying in his furs, too ill to get up but in too much pain to escape into sleep. This was the longest he'd spent outside since the day he'd been captured.

'Cam will be back soon, whether you watch for him or not,' Rhia said. 'You will only make yourself ill again by waiting out here.'

'Where did he say he was going?' He turned to face her, and that shift of weight was enough to set his right arm to throbbing again. Isidro laid his left hand gingerly over the limb, held in a sling across his chest beneath his coat. It had woken him again in the middle of the night and Rhia had given him a dose of poppy to let him sleep. Cam had set out before he'd woken.

'He went to check his snares,' Rhia said, showing no impatience, even though she'd already answered the question several times.

'It shouldn't be taking him this long.' Isidro winced at the petulance in his voice. *He's probably just taking the chance to get out on his own for a while*, he told himself. *With the way he and Brekan have been at each other's throats, I can't blame him.* Eloba and Lakua, the sisters who shared Brekan as their husband, had just taken their tent down for repairs when the weather worsened, so all seven of them had been crammed into a single tent while the storm howled around them.

It was dangerous for a traveller to be out alone after dark, and not just because of the threatening war. Aside from the soldiers, the Mesentreians still hunting the fugitive prince and his tiny band, and the Slavers striking from the west, wolves, leopards and tigers roamed these hills. With their normal prey frightened away or hunted out by foragers, they might be desperate enough to stalk one man alone.

'If he cannot return safely, Cam will take shelter for the night and find us in the morning,' Rhia said. 'The weather is good and he knows how to stay out of sight and cover his tracks if there is danger. He will be fine.'

She was soothing him like a fractious child. Isidro drew breath to reply, but he inhaled just a little too deeply. The cold air hit his lungs and a spasm clenched like a fist in his chest and doubled him over in a fit of coughing.

Rhia drew his good arm over her shoulder and turned him back towards the tent. 'Inside, quickly. You need warm air.'

The fit of coughing was so severe that he couldn't draw breath. With his head swimming and bright spots dancing before his eyes, Isidro didn't resist as she propelled him towards the larger of the two tents, the sisters having set theirs up again at first light.

Garzen appeared in the doorway just as he and Rhia reached it. With the lamplight behind him and thick black lines of mourning tattoos carved into his face, he would be a fearsome sight to anyone who didn't know him. He held the flap open with one hand and steadied Isidro's shoulder with the other as he stumbled through the doorway and into the spruce-scented warmth of the tent. Garzen started to let the flap fall behind him, but then stiffened and raised it again. 'Who's that?'

Isidro turned, but his vision was too blurred to see.

'It must be Cam,' Rhia said, but there was a note of uncertainty in her voice.

His face grim, Garzen ducked out through the doorway, snatching up one of the spears driven into the snow outside as he went.

'What's wrong?' Isidro wheezed, still out of breath.

'Cam left on foot,' Rhia said, peering after Garzen with a frown creasing her brow. 'Someone approaches leading a horse.'

\* \* \*

Cam ducked through the doorway with the limp figure slung over his shoulder.

'Set her down here,' Rhia commanded, spreading her own furs out to receive the girl.

'She was alive when I found her, but that was hours ago,' Cam said. 'I didn't want to take the time to stop and check on her again.'

Rhia eased off the girl's cap and cowl, lifting them carefully away from nose and ears that might be damaged by frostbite. 'We shall see. Where are the hot stones? I need them now!'

'Just wrapping them up,' Eloba said from the stove. She and Lakua had answered Rhia's shout for help without needing to be told what to do — every Ricalani knew the procedure when someone was brought in unresponsive from the cold. Smooth, round pebbles of soapstone were kept in the stove for just this purpose. Lakua lifted them from the coals with a pair of bone tongs and Eloba wrapped them carefully in scraps of cloth and fur.

Isidro sat cross-legged on his bed, trying to stay out of the way. Rhia always slept near him in case he needed her during the night, so the girl's head lay only a foot away from his own pillow, with frost melting in her hair and her lips a pale and bloodless blue.

Rhia opened the girl's coat. Beneath it, her clothes were Mesentreian, fastening up the middle with a row of silver buttons. Rhia ripped them open without ceremony and packed the hot stones around her torso, testing each one against her lips first to make sure it wouldn't burn. One of the buttons rolled over to Isidro's blankets and he picked it up with his good hand to examine the crest stamped into the metal.

Once all the stones were packed around her body, Rhia covered her with a pile of furs. Then, while she gently pulled off the girl's mittens and gloves, Lakua did the same with her boots and boot liners and pressed the girl's bare feet against her belly to warm them.

Cam had shrugged off his coat and stood in the cool spot by the doorway as he gulped down a bowl of lukewarm tea. Isidro tried to speak to him, but barely got the first word out before the cough took him over again. Each racking spasm sent searing needles stabbing through his shattered arm. Rhia glanced at him over her shoulder and said, 'Eloba, brew tea for Isidro —'

'I'll do it,' said Cam, crossing the tent to the stove and the low table behind it, where the medicines Rhia had ground and mixed were waiting in a bowl ready to be steeped. Cam filled it from the kettle on the stove, added a generous dollop each of butter and honey and brought it to Isidro, who was still struggling to catch his breath. Cam tried to hide it, but Isidro could see the worry in his face.

'Go ahead and say it,' he rasped. 'I look like crap.'

'You look as bad as she does,' Cam said, nodding to the patient in Rhia's furs. 'She has an excuse. I thought you were getting better.'

'He was out in the cold waiting for you,' Rhia said without looking around. 'I tell him to go in, but your brother is more stubborn than any mule.' She was still not quite fluent in Ricalani and her grasp of the language always suffered when she was under stress. Cam and Isidro both spoke Mesentreian, her preferred language, but the others did not, and the language of their enemies made them uneasy.

'Any sign of danger out there?' Isidro said as he sipped the brew.

Cam shook his head.

'Where did you find her?' Isidro nodded towards the woman.

'I tracked her to her camp after she raided one of my snares,' Cam said. 'But where she came from?' He shrugged. 'She had a Ricalani pony, but she was wearing a Mesentreian uniform under that coat.'

'Not just any uniform,' Isidro said, and nodded at the button lying on his furs.

Cam raised one eyebrow and then leaned across him to pick it up. The silver button was stamped with the sigil of a flaming torch. 'The Angessovar crest,' he said, rolling it between his fingers. 'That's odd.' Only someone attached to the royal household would wear that crest.

The inner clothes she had worn were made of the soft black wool used by the king's household guard, but it lacked the frogging and insignia Isidro remembered from his time at court.

'Interesting,' said Cam, and tucked the button away into his sash. 'So what do you think? She could be a concubine who took advantage of the bad weather to slip away.'

'Maybe,' Isidro said. The coughing fit had left him exhausted, and the soporific in Rhia's brew was taking effect. He was finding it hard to focus on the girl's face — it wavered and blurred before his eyes. 'Whoever she is, she must have been desperate, to leave without shelter or supplies.'

'Hmm,' Cam said. 'Well, I hope she can give us some word of what's going on out there.'

Rhia twisted around to face them. 'If she wakes, you may ask her,' she said, and levelled one finger at Isidro. 'You rest now. Cam, I want more wood for the fire. She must be kept warm.'

'As you command,' Cam said with a mocking bow. He took Isidro's empty bowl away with him as he left.

'Lie down,' Rhia said to Isidro, and began to pull off his boots.

'I can do that,' he protested, but she ignored him, setting the boots neatly at the foot of his bed and then twitching the furs up to cover him. 'Do not argue,' she said, and pressed her hand against his forehead. He closed his eyes against the coolness. 'You are feverish again, Isidro. Rest. Your curiosity will wait until you wake.'

'Will it?' he said. 'Will she live?'

Rhia turned back to the slight figure occupying her furs. 'I think so. But we shall see.'

# Chapter 3

*Sweat prickled on his skin and stung like acid on the searing wounds on his back. The burns reached from the nape of his neck down to his buttocks. Naked, he knelt on a blood-splattered carpet of spruce with his hands tied behind his back and the end of the cord that bound them thrown over a beam overhead and pulled tight. All the weight of his torso rested upon his shoulders, twisted as far as they could go: they felt as though they were slowly tearing free. Blood dripped from his mouth to the spruce beneath him. He'd bitten his lip to keep from screaming.*

*Rasten held the poker beside his face. Wisps of smoke wafted from the scraps of charred skin encrusting the iron. The heat of it dried the sweat on his cheek and Isidro closed his eyes to keep from flinching until it touched.*

*'Rasten,' a soft voice said from across the tent and a moment later the heat was gone. Isidro turned his head and could just see the two men standing with heads together, talking in low voices.*

*Another figure knelt at Kell's feet, her bound hands fastened to a block of lead too large for one man to lift. For a moment, Isidro caught sight of her face between strands of black hair that clung to her sweating skin, like the heavy black lines of mourning tattoos. He met her eyes for only an instant before she looked away.*

*'But the queen wants him whole.' Rasten's voice drifted across the tent.*

*'She wants to watch him die, like she did his father,' Kell said. 'But we progress too slowly. Much longer and the prince will be beyond our reach. Do as I say, boy.'*

*From the corner of his eye Isidro saw Rasten take a serrated knife and a bowl of liquid from the row of implements laid out on the table. The girl at Kell's feet huddled closer to the ground, as though willing herself to sink into it and vanish. Isidro steeled himself as Rasten came to his side again.*

Rasten threw the knife into the ground, where it lodged point first, and hunkered down by Isidro's head. 'Do you know what this is?' He dipped his thumb in the liquid and wiped it across Isidro's bitten lip. The salt-laden water bit like barbed needles and Rasten laughed at Isidro's grunt of pain.

Then he tipped the bowl over the ravaged skin of his back.

Isidro kicked the covers off and sat up, too quickly. It set his head spinning and he had to swallow hard against the gorge that rose in his throat. The beast in his arm flexed its claws.

Drenched with sweat, Isidro reached for the collar of his shirt and peeled it away from his skin, letting the cooler air flood in. The scars on his back prickled. When his fingertips brushed against one he flinched reflexively, even though all but the worst of them were healed. The burns had been the least of his troubles.

Rhia had strung an old blanket across his bed to keep the light from disturbing him, but it also isolated him from the radiant heat of the stove. The cool air chilled his skin and soon turned his damp shirt cold and clammy. Isidro pulled the furs up around his shoulders again and lay back until the world remained still once more.

His arm rested in its sling over his chest, a heavy and awkward weight across his ribs. Isidro gingerly slipped his good hand under it to move it to a better position. No matter how careful he was, any movement sent ripples of fire through the limb. The bones were broken in too many places for anything as simple as splints and birch bark to hold them in place. If he hadn't been so cursed sick for the last few weeks, Isidro knew Rhia would have cut it off.

At first, he'd tried to convince himself it would heal and that eventually he would be able to use his hand again. Over the last few days, though, as he had recovered enough to remain awake for a few hours at a time, he had come to understand how bad the damage was. His arm was beyond repair, a useless extremity of battered flesh and ragged bone.

Isidro hadn't imagined for a moment that he would survive Kell's treatment. His only goal had been to hold out long enough to allow Cam and the others to get away. It was past sunset when they finally broke him. Rasten had nailed his hand to a log and then set about breaking every bone from wrist to forearm. Once it was done, Rasten explained that they could start the whole process over again with his left arm. He'd run his fingertips over the ruined limb and murmured in Isidro's ear what

24

lay in store for him. He was to be taken to Lathayan for his execution, to be cut apart and slaughtered on the palace steps like his father before him. A man could survive the journey with one shattered limb, so long as he had the Blood-Drinker's enchantments to keep the wounds from turning septic. Any more and even Kell's powers wouldn't help him survive the journey — after each limb was shattered, they would have to cut it off and cauterise the stump. Rasten gave Isidro a choice — he could walk to his execution like a man, or be carried to the palace steps as a limbless, sexless lump. Worn down by pain and exhaustion, Isidro had surrendered, and told them where to find Cam's camp.

By the time they'd reached it, Cam was gone. In the days afterwards, while Duke Osebian and the king's men searched for the prince, Kell and Rasten had set about punishing Isidro for costing them their prize. Isidro remembered little of it, only snatches viewed through a fevered haze. He had escaped further maiming, probably because Kell didn't want to anger the queen by denying her the chance to witness the torture herself, but that still left a whole world of torment within his reach.

Isidro never imagined that he would survive the ordeal. He'd given himself up for dead the moment the soldiers closed around him in the village. Ever since he and Cam had fled the palace nearly ten years ago, they'd been well aware of the likelihood that one or both of them would be captured and brought back to face Valeria's wrath. It had never occurred to Isidro that one of them could be left crippled, unable to fight or fend for himself. Now he was a millstone around Cam's neck, an unbearable burden that could not be laid down. They were still here in the shadow of the army and the invasion because he was too weak to leave, Isidro knew. If he'd died in Kell's chains, or never awakened after sinking under the black water, they'd all be safely away from here. If they fell afoul of the Mesentreian soldiers, or were captured and enslaved by the Akharians, it would be because of him.

Murmuring voices reached him through the curtain and Isidro sat up again, suddenly craving company and conversation, anything to distract him from the memories and the despair. He kicked the covers back and ducked under the rough curtain, crawling awkwardly with one arm and blinking in the sudden light.

Rhia and Garzen were both kneeling beside the girl's bed, their heads bent over one of her small hands. A golden bracelet set with red stones encircled her wrist and beneath it was a wide burn, raw and weeping. It cut across the kinship tattoo graven into the delicate skin of her inner wrist. The blistered and scorched skin was so badly damaged he couldn't make out the symbol identifying her lineage and her clan. The sight of the burns made his stomach twist and he had to look away.

Rhia looked up, and read his distress in a glance. 'Isidro —'

'She's alive, then,' Isidro said, and forced himself to look at the wound. 'What's happened there?'

Garzen answered after a moment's hesitation. 'She needs the bracelets off to treat the burns, but there's no clasp. Can't pry the links open. Looks like pure gold, but it ain't. Not soft enough, see? We'll have to cut it, and hope we don't do more damage than we have to.' He gestured at his leather tool roll laid out beside him, a haphazard collection of scavenged equipment.

'There's a small chisel in my old carving set that will do it,' Isidro said. His gaze fell on the girl's face — her lips were pink now, but most of her face was hidden beneath a cowl Rhia had folded over and pulled down to cover her eyes. What little of her face he could see was puffy and swollen. 'Snow blindness?' he said.

'Yep,' said Garzen. 'Got herself frosted, too, but it don't look like it'll go to frostbite.'

'Lucky,' Isidro said. Frosting was the mild stage of frostbite, where ice crystals formed in the skin, but didn't do enough damage to turn it black and necrotic.

Isidro swayed and had to put his left hand out to catch himself. 'The tools are in my kitbag; would you mind finding them yourself?'

Garzen looked him up and down and nodded. 'I'll see to it. You sit yourself down, lad.'

Cam was sitting beside the stove with an empty satchel and an odd selection of gear spread out around him. He half rose when Isidro settled clumsily beside him. 'Are you hungry? We kept a bowl for you.' He picked it up from where it had been keeping warm beside the stove — fish fried in butter with yesterday's soggy beans. 'Garzen and Eloba had more luck with their lines than I did with mine.'

Isidro looked at the greasy mess and shuddered. 'Later, maybe,' he said and put it out of sight. 'Any sign of soldiers out there?'

'None, either southern or Slaver. I heard an avalanche and thought it was the cursed sorcerer for a moment …' Cam shook his head with a wry grin. 'The hills are quiet as a tomb and the only sign of people I found was her.' He nodded to the sleeping figure. 'This is her gear. I'm trying to work out where she's come from.'

'Leave it be,' Garzen said from across the tent. 'It's cursed rude to go through a stranger's gear — and her a guest at that.'

'Well, of course it sounds bad if you put it like that,' Cam said. 'It might be days before she can talk. We know she's on the run and we've taken a risk by taking her in. We've got every right to find out who she is and what she's running from.'

Garzen looked unhappy, but he didn't argue.

'Well, Issey, what do you make of this?'

The bag itself was nothing more than a scrap of blanket cinched into a pouch by the carrying strap. Cam had spread the contents out beside it — an empty water-skin and a tinderbox with a few charred scraps of birch bark that looked as if they might once have wrapped bars of pemmican. It grew stranger after that — two mismatched daggers, a pair of bracelets set with ugly green stones wrapped in a bit of rag, a book held closed with tooled leather straps, and two swords in their scabbards, an awkward shape and bulk to be carried easily in the bag.

'Loot, maybe?' Isidro suggested as Cam picked up one of the swords and slid it out of the sheath.

'Difficult to sell,' Cam said, examining the blade by the light of the stove. 'It's good Mesentreian steel, hard to come by out here. You'd get some awkward questions when you tried to get rid of it. What do you make of the pommel stones?' He turned the hilt with its polished cabochon towards Isidro and raised one eyebrow in a silent question.

Isidro glanced around to make sure no one was watching and pressed his palm against the stone, closing his eyes to block out any distractions.

It was no secret that he carried the taint of power; it was a matter of public record. His name and lineage were inscribed alongside those of other tainted children in the records of the temple where he'd been tested as a boy, there for anyone who cared to seek out the information. He preferred not to advertise the fact. Cam knew, and so did Rhia, but they would no sooner mention it than they would bring up any other shameful episode from a friend's past. The others tended towards superstition and Isidro was far from sure they would treat the matter with the same discretion. Especially now that it seemed bad luck dogged their every step.

Isidro dismissed those thoughts and emptied his mind. There was a tiny pool of energy within the stone: it fluttered and prickled against his palm, like a moth cupped in his hands. The dull grey stone flickered with minute iridescence at his touch. 'This one's a witch-stone,' he said. It was a common enchantment, meant to detect folk like him. He leaned over to touch the other, and found it cold and dead. 'The other's a fake.'

Cam held the two side by side and examined them closely in the meagre light. 'I'll never understand how you can tell. They look the same to me.'

Isidro shrugged. 'It's probably just as well. If you'd shown the taint, Valeria would have had you drowned like an unwanted pup.'

'No doubt you're right,' Cam said. He set the swords aside and picked up the book. 'Now this is odd. If you're escaping from a Mesentreian camp into the worst blow we've seen this winter, why would you pick up something like this? It's too cursed heavy to carry far, if nothing else.' The book was as long as his forearm and as thick as the breadth of a man's palm. The spine and cover were unmarked and it was closed with leather straps and clasps that wouldn't come loose, no matter how Cam pried at them. That was a disappointment: he would have welcomed the distraction of a book — or anything, really, to pass the time.

As Cam gave up and set the book aside, Isidro looked over the rest of the gear and picked up the bracelets. The dull green stones were set in gold in the Mesentreian style, with stylised leaves forming the settings and the links. They were jade, and good quality despite their murky colour.

The stones were lens-shaped and the setting left the reverse faces uncovered, so the gems would always be in contact with the wearer's skin. Isidro turned the bracelet over in his hand and the polished surface of the stone brushed against his palm. It stung like a fly-bite and he dropped it, biting back a curse.

Across the tent, Rhia glanced up from tending to the girl's burns and frowned with concern. His hand numb from the shock of contact, Isidro shook his head and waved her back to her patient.

Cam had seen it all. Cautiously, he picked up the other bracelet and turned it over in his hands, looking from Isidro to the links and back again. 'What is it?'

'Warding-stones,' Isidro murmured. 'Cursed strong ones, too.'

Everyone who carried the taint was required by law to wear one. Humankind was never meant to possess this kind of power, or so the lore said. It was an accident of nature and of the Gods, a corruption of the natural order. Folk like him were said to have brought the power with them by accident, when they journeyed from the realm of the spirits to be born into flesh. Those born with power couldn't help the way they were made, but they were dangerous, whether they meant harm or not. Left unchecked, their power would cause havoc and destruction, spread disease and bring disaster down on the people around them. If worn for long enough and paired with the rituals and prayers prescribed by the priests, the warding-stones were supposed to extinguish the spark of power entirely.

It had never worked for Isidro, but then he'd never worn the stone willingly. His first one had been presented to him at the Children's Festival, an event held every year in the spring, when every child between the ages of six and twelve was tested for the taint. In every temple in Ricalan, the priests marked out a ritual circle with lines of coloured chalk and set the sacred stones around it, while all the children living under the temple's remit would take their turn standing at the centre of the circle. If he or she carried the taint, the stones would light up like candles, the child's name and parentage would be marked in the temple records, and the child would be given a warding-stone, with the command to wear it until death.

Isidro was eight winters old when the stones lit up in his presence. It had come as no surprise — his birth mother carried the taint as well. In the home temple of his father's clan, Elza had always gone first into the circle, both to test the priests' preparations and to demonstrate to that year's crop of children there was nothing to fear. She had worn her stone until the day she died in a hunting accident, when Isidro was twelve.

Isidro set the stones down and unconsciously wiped his hand against his thigh. Just holding the things made him feel as though he was suffocating, as though his mouth and nose and ears were stuffed with wool that threatened to choke him with every breath. As a boy, he'd taken the wretched thing off at every opportunity, until his kin, in desperation, had tied the cord so tight he couldn't slip it over his head. Once his father had died and there was no one left to enforce the rule, Isidro had thrown the cursed thing away for good.

Cam knew all this. The nursemaids who had raised him in his mother's court used to threaten him with sorcerers if he misbehaved. He had grown up with a Mesentreian's attitude towards mages, but he set that aside when it came to Isidro.

'Valeria had a set like this,' Cam said, examining the gilded links. He only ever referred to his mother by her name. If pressed he would grudgingly acknowledge their kinship, but nothing more.

Garzen stood, stretching his back, and then came over to them with the two ruby bracelets dangling from one hand. 'Ye Gods, but they're ugly things,' he said, squinting at the murky jade. 'These aren't much better.' He held up the bracelets he had cut free. 'They must be worth a cursed fortune, but I can't say I care for the taste of him what made 'em. Well, at least they'll be worth a bit to sell. Put them with the others, will you, lads?' He dropped them into Isidro's palm and turned back to help Rhia finish cleaning and binding the burns.

When the stones touched his skin they flashed with a sudden, vicious heat; it took all his will not to curse and drop them. The enchantment inside the stones was a fierce, angry thing, and it lashed out at his touch. For an instant, it felt as though he'd grasped a live coal, but only for an instant, and then it was gone. His skin felt scorched. It left no mark, but Isidro had a fair idea of exactly where the girl's burns had come from.

'Those burns on her wrists ...' he said. 'Any idea what caused them?'

Garzen cleared his throat. 'Well, it's a funny thing, but looks like those bracelets did it. Couldn't have, of course — there's no way to heat them up that wouldn't have burned her worse. Maybe they'd tied her up with rope and she held it over a flame to free herself? That's probably it.'

That wouldn't match the pattern of the burns. Isidro caught the end of one of the bracelets between his thumb and forefinger and let it dangle, glowing sullenly in the lamplight. This was an enchantment he hadn't come across before. A Mesentreian priest could have made them, perhaps. Or maybe the one who locked them around her wrists had enough power and influence to convince Lord Kell to make them.

He handed the bracelets to Cam, who took them with a low whistle.

'Someone's going to be spitting that she walked away with these.' He put them with the others, all wrapped up in the scrap of cloth, and began to pack everything back in the bag, but when he went to put it at the foot of the newcomer's bed, Rhia waved him away. 'Not there. She is still weak. I don't want those cursed stones near her.'

'They're just witch-stones, Rhia.'

'No matter! Put them over there.' She pointed to the part of the tent where the miscellaneous gear was stacked. 'You have few mages in this country, Cammarian. You are lucky to have so few. I have seen strong men die of trifling wounds because they would not let their curse-stones be taken away. Even witch-stones sap strength.'

Cam shrugged and put the bag as far away as he could from the sick beds laid out head-to-head. 'Is that far enough?'

'No. Throw them into the sea. That will be far enough.' Rhia gave a weary smile. 'That will do, though. For now.'

Sierra held herself perfectly still. The soft noises of night were all around her — the sighing breaths of people asleep in their furs and the comforting crackle of the fire within the stove; but her heart was beating fast and she had to work hard to keep panic from taking her over.

She couldn't see. That was the worst part. A thick blindfold covered half her face and she didn't dare raise a hand to explore it. Her hands were by her sides, pinned down beneath a weight of fur, and the burns around her wrists kept a dull throb in time with her pounding heart. Her whole right arm throbbed from knuckles to elbow, as though she'd sprained or wrenched it.

The last thing she remembered was huddling beside the tiny fire in the rough shelter beneath the branches of a spruce. With hot food in her belly she'd been warm for the first time in days and had fallen asleep not caring that she would probably never wake. Better to die free than spend the rest of her life as Kell's pet and Rasten's plaything.

But now she was alive, warm, awake … and what? A prisoner? She'd thought she was heading east when she left the king's encampment, but in the midst of the blizzard the blasting wind was her only sense of direction. The fact that she was still alive told her she hadn't stumbled across an Akharian legion. The Slavers didn't tolerate mage-talent among their captives. They would have cut her throat at once.

31

She was too far north to have strayed into settlers' lands, and if the king's men had tracked her down she'd be back in Kell's hands already. What did that leave? She could have been found by the outlaws who haunted these hills, or by the men the Wolf Clan sent to hunt them. Or perhaps some country folk had come across her while checking their trap-lines ...

If she'd been brought in from the cold by ordinary Ricalanis, they'd feel duty-bound to hand her over to their ruling clan once they found out what she was. If she'd been picked up by one of the outlaw bands, they'd likely try to keep her for themselves, as they did with the women they captured on their raids. By the Black Sun, she ought to hope it was the bandits who'd found her — so many had died at her hands already that it seemed foolish to have qualms against spilling more blood, especially that of the murderers and thieves who made up the outlaw bands.

If an ordinary family had picked her up, she might have to shed blood to escape them anyway. *Stop it*, Sierra told herself, *just stop thinking like that. I'll cross that river when I come to it.* All her dreams and hopes had been focussed on escape for so long — now that it had come, she didn't know what to do next. All she knew was that she had to keep moving. If Rasten didn't track her down, then it would be the Akharians snapping at her heels soon enough. They couldn't be far away — she'd escaped while Kell and Rasten were attending upon the king in a discussion of strategy while the invaders massed on the far side of the river valley. For all she knew, the legions and their mages had already met the king's men. What if the Akharians came upon her before Rasten hunted her down? Sierra clenched her fists at the thought, but then with a shuddering breath forced herself to relax them before her power could spill. If they came, she would fight with all she had, but the Gods alone knew if her power would be enough. She was untrained — Kell had seen to that — and if they were anything like her old master they would flatten her with one blow. But Kell only spoke of the empire's mages with disdain, so perhaps she would stand a chance. Only by meeting them would she be sure, but she'd rather be well away from here by the time the Slavers came. Wherever *here* was.

Supposing she *could* avoid Rasten and the Akharians, she had no one to turn to, no family and no kin. For all she knew, her parents were dead, and had been for two years, ever since the night Kell had tracked her to the ruined temple where they'd taken shelter and pinned her there with Rasten and a contingent of the king's guard.

Her family had sacrificed all they had to protect her, giving up their kin, their lands, their herds, *everything*. When stories began to spread of the herder-girl's strange powers, they picked up what they could carry and moved along again, uprooting seven adults and half a dozen children, all for her sake.

Kell would have found them no matter what; Sierra knew that now. Her mothers and fathers had thought they were protecting her from the priests, or from a mob that would tear her apart for what she could do. It had never occurred to them that Kell himself would come for her and by the time they realised the danger, it was too late. Two of her fathers had died that night in the ruined temple — and after all this time, she still wasn't sure *which* two — and one of her mothers was bleeding to death when Kell sent Rasten to deliver his ultimatum: surrender now, and he'd spare the rest; resist, and he'd slaughter the lot of them.

Even then, she'd had no faith that he would keep his end of the bargain. But what else could she do? If Rasten outmatched her, Kell was a god compared to her fledgling powers.

Once she was in chains, Rasten had drugged her to keep her from giving them any more trouble, so for all she knew, the rest of her family had been put to the sword the moment she was too insensible to feel it. If they had survived, they would have gone into hiding to protect the children they had left. Everyone knew the taint of sorcery ran through families and there would be some who thought it best if the bloodline that produced Kell's new apprentice ended there. Even if they had survived, and she was able to find them, she couldn't bring herself to seek them out. They couldn't protect her and they'd suffered enough for her sake.

Thinking of them brought tears to her eyes; they stung beneath the mask. Sierra bit her lip to keep from sobbing. *Don't think about that*, she told herself. *Just focus on the problem at hand.*

Slowly, slowly, she eased one hand out from beneath the heavy furs and raised it up her face, expecting at any moment for it to be halted by chains or rope, but nothing checked the movement as she lifted her hand from the blankets. In the months that had passed since Kell left his dungeons to travel with the army, she had never been free of the chains for so long. Without them, she felt strangely light, as though she could just float away.

Sierra slipped her other hand out and explored the blindfold with her fingertips. It was a band of cloth folded over several times and without even a knot to hold it in place. She slipped it off and, as it unfolded, she identified it at last — her cowl, the soft knitted tube that could be worn loose around the neck or pulled up and over the head for another layer of warmth.

Her eyelids felt hot and tight. With great effort she could open them, but all she could see was a blur of grey. *Snow blindness.* Everyone who lived in the north experienced it at some point. It would heal within a few days, but she would be highly sensitive to light for weeks. Sierra mouthed a silent curse. It was a complication she could do without.

Her face felt tight and swollen. She'd got herself frosted, either while she'd been freezing to death during the night or in the days before, she wasn't sure. None of it had the icy-hot burning sensation of true frostbite, so she counted herself lucky.

Whoever had brought her here had stripped her to her underwear, a sleeveless vest and knee-length britches of soft *yaka*-hair cloth, tucked into socks knitted of the same. That seemed a good sign. In Kell's dungeons, prisoners were kept naked. Perhaps she was clutching at straws, but right now she'd take any reassurance she could get.

Her wrists were neatly bandaged and, as she felt her way over them, Sierra realised the punishment bands were gone. For a moment, she was shocked to stillness, but then she had to bite back quickly on a giggle of hysterical relief. The last thing that bound her, gone! Her powers had grown since Kell had first captured her, grown more than she ever dreamed they could. She was no longer a terrified girl of sixteen, hoping that something could be salvaged from this disaster. When they came for her again, she would give them no quarter. This time, she had nothing to hold her back, nothing to lose.

Sierra sat up and something soft yet firm brushed against her head and cheek. She flinched away violently with a small cry of surprise. She caught herself on her right hand and it was then that she realised the ache in her arm was not truly hers. Beneath the relentless throb a soft, spreading warmth was seeping into her body, a steady trickle of energy feeding into the store of power that coursed along her spine.

Nearby, someone sighed and shifted beneath their furs. Sierra froze, waiting until they settled again. After a moment's thought she knew what she'd brushed against — the shaggy fur of a reindeer-hide tent, spread taut between the poles. The air was full of the smell of smoke and spruce. She forced her eyes open again, but it was no good, she couldn't see a thing between the darkness and the snow blindness. Everything was silent and still.

'Are you awake?' a hoarse voice whispered. Taken by surprise, Sierra gasped aloud.

It was a man's voice, dark and rasping, and speaking in Ricalani. The sound of it almost made her weep — Ricalani had been forbidden in Kell's dungeon; for the last two years she'd spoken only Mesentreian, the language of the invaders.

There was a rustle of furs as the one who had spoken sat up. As he moved, the throb in Sierra's arm became a ripple of fire and the stream of power swelled to a river. There was something horribly familiar about it, something she'd felt before. *No, it can't be. He died, surely he died.*

'I know you're awake,' the man whispered. 'There's nothing to fear here. We know you escaped from the Mesentreians; we won't try to send you back.'

Sierra pressed herself against the wall of the tent, her fingers digging into the shaggy fur. 'How do you know where I came from? Who are you?'

There was a pause and then he explained patiently, as though speaking to a child. 'You were wearing a Mesentreian uniform, carrying Mesentreian swords and wearing Mesentreian jewellery.'

She twisted the coarse fur once more and then let it go. 'Oh.' *Stupid girl.*

'And as for us … well, we have our own reasons for staying out of the army's way. Do you have a name?'

Sierra was a common name, but that was no protection. Rasten would seize upon any clue that might lead him to her. 'Kasimi,' she said, picking the name of her next-youngest sister. She'd been a wretched little brat, always stealing and breaking and losing things she ought never to have got her hands on. Sierra would have given almost anything to know if she still lived.

'Kasimi,' the man repeated. Sierra bit her lip. She'd hesitated a moment too long, but if there was any doubt in his voice he'd hidden it well. *If you're going to have any chance of surviving you're going to have to learn to lie better than that*, she told herself. She could still feel the fiery ripples in her arm and the part of her that stored the power was soaking it up like a hearthstone absorbs heat. That could become a problem. The warding-stones kept her power in check. Without them she would have to rely on her own meagre skills to keep it under control. If they found out just what she was …

'Well, Kasimi, I'm Isidro.'

*Isidro …*

She remembered him. Most of the faces and voices from the dungeons blended together, but he had been different. Making a man spill secrets wasn't hard, nor was making him confess to something he hadn't done. After an hour with Rasten they would say whatever Kell wanted. But to make a man give up a loved one — a wife, a child, a brother — under an ordinary torturer, a strong man could take such secrets to the grave.

Kell was a Blood-Mage, though, and that made all the difference. A Blood-Mage gave his victim no respite. Kell could keep a man conscious through pain that would make anyone faint and keep a man's heart beating once he lost all will to survive. A Blood-Mage trapped his victims and then slowly tore them to shreds, until they were so delirious with exhaustion and pain they would do anything to make it stop. Oh yes, she remembered this one. The arm had been Kell's idea, but Rasten's precision in carrying it out had been a pinnacle of cruelty.

'Kasimi?' he whispered again; she felt a faint motion of air, as though he was reaching out for her in the darkness. Sierra recoiled, shrinking back against the wall of the tent. She was already drawing more power from him than she could easily contain. Rasten had warned her not to touch any of the prisoners — she was too powerful, he said, too uncontrolled. Her touch would drain a man of the strength that kept his heart beating — that was why they always kept her chained during the rituals, because her touch would destroy the victim and turn all their preparation to waste. Sierra wasn't sure if she believed it, but it was better not to take the chance and find out.

There was another rustle of movement and she thought she felt his proffered hand withdraw. What was he thinking? She was clearly shaken — her panicked and rapid breath was enough to tell him that. He probably thought her a fugitive like him, panicked to find herself helpless among strangers. Well, that was good enough. She could work with that.

36

'Where … where are we?' she said, her voice hoarse in her dry throat.

'Where? That I can't say. I don't exactly know.'

'But the soldiers! The armies must be close …' she couldn't have travelled far with short rations, no map and a mind muddled from cold.

'I'm told we're safe, for the moment,' he said. 'Are you hungry? Rhia is asleep, but she left food and water in case you woke.'

'I … I am a little thirsty.'

He knew the darkness far better than she, but the movement sent ripples of fire through his arm again. When she heard the water slosh, she groped blindly for it, keeping her hands low so that they wouldn't touch his. She found it by the base, a water-skin nestled in a pouch of fur to keep it from freezing. There was a leather stopper in the horn spout, and Sierra pulled it free and drank thirstily in the dark.

Her hands shook as she remembered how he had screamed.

Once she'd had her fill, the stopper eluded her, but finally she found it swinging on its cord and fumbled it back into the spout. She went to set the still-bulging skin down, but it knocked against something unseen in the gloom. There was a rattle of pottery and wood, and both she and Isidro reached out to catch it. Before she could stop herself, Sierra felt her fingers brush against his.

A spark of energy jumped between them, a glowing thread like a miniature lightning bolt, casting an eerie light over this tiny corner of the tent. With one blurred glimpse through watering eyes, Sierra saw the worn blanket that screened them, the rumpled furs and the wooden camp-stool she'd upset. She saw his face, pale and gaunt with hollow cheeks and dark eyes — just one glimpse and then the light blinded her, sparking a fierce pain behind her eyes and an almighty thump within her skull. Within moments, the great pulse of power that flowed into her from that touch washed all that discomfort away.

All at once, she was within him, wearing his skin and feeling the bones of his arm grinding beneath the splints. She felt the healing burns itching on his back, the thumping of his own head and the flush of fever in his cheeks, and the weary ache of his lungs as the pneumonia still battled within him. He was exhausted by it all, utterly worn down by pain that would not let him rest and would not let him heal. The lingering infection was still there: as he neared the end of his reserves

37

it would rise up again to finish him. She could feel it festering away, a mindless enemy lurking within his flesh.

For one moment, she was aware of every inch of him, then the rising tide of power flooded her with warmth. His pain was ebbing away, coming to her in a rush of power. His muscles went lax and she felt him slowly collapse even though he fought it, struggling to hold himself up and resist the outgoing tide that would leave him empty and dry.

Sierra felt him struggle, but with the power shimmering in her mind it seemed only a curiosity, something pretty to see, like sunlight on water. Of course it would fade as the sun set, the light dwindling to a few pale flecks.

But the power was coming so fast she couldn't drink it in quickly enough and it spilled over in a flood of light as multiple strands of energy burst from her hands, minute bolts of lightning that flickered and rippled ceaselessly, questing for some anchor. The light stabbed at her blinded eyes and with a yelp of pain Sierra broke the contact and quenched the light, pulling it back beneath her skin with a wrench of effort.

The tent was still and quiet once again, except for the pounding in her head. *By the Black Sun herself, what just happened?* 'Isidro?' she whispered.

There was only silence — silence from him, and silence beyond the curtain that screened them. The flood of energy had lasted only a moment and the burst of light even less, not long enough to wake the people who slept beyond the barrier.

'Isidro!' she hissed again, groping her way across the floor of trodden spruce. She found him sprawled face down, just as she realised that the echoed throb in her arm was gone. Her stomach lurched within her as she remembered how he'd fought against that tide of power, and in a near panic she rolled him over and pressed her ear to his chest. *Black Sun help me.* After a long agonising moment, she found the slow thump of his heart — too slow, but at least the beat was steady. Sierra wept with relief, a few stinging tears. Quickly, she gulped them back, listening for any sign of stirring from the rest of the tent. Once she was certain that no one had woken, she carefully dragged him back to the warmth of his furs.

He was far lighter than a man of his size should be. Sierra remembered when the guards had brought him in and stripped him — he'd been a warrior then, a man to be reckoned with, but in the weeks since all his flesh had melted away. With her fingertips she could count every one of the ribs standing out through his skin.

Once she had his blankets wrapped around him once more, Sierra felt her way down to the foot of his bed, where the kitbag was usually kept. Kell had dispatched Isidro to Lathayan with a set of enchantments to keep the wounds from sickening during the journey. The people who had cared for him must have taken them off. Most folks were suspicious of enchantments, but Sierra could only hope they hadn't been thrown away. She had stopped herself before draining all his strength, but the power she had taken had left him even weaker than before.

She could sense the enchantments in there somewhere, sending minute ripples of power through the air, but hampered by the need for silence, it took her some minutes to find them. Each one consisted of a few lumpy stone beads, threaded onto a bit of leather that had been tied around his wrists. They were most effective worn next to the skin but even at the foot of his bed they had probably done him some good. After weeks without wear their power had run right down but the enchantments themselves were still intact. All she needed to do was recharge them.

Sierra felt her way back to her bed and buried herself beneath one of the furs, trusting it to hide the light she made. She charged each of the stones in turn, clenching it within her fist as she trickled the finest stream of power she could manage into the stone. Too much would overwhelm the enchantment and corrupt it, or even destroy it entirely.

By the time she was done, Sierra's head was pounding so badly that she felt ill. It was all she could do to crawl back to his bedside and tuck the renewed enchantments inside his shirt next to his skin on either side of his chest, where they wouldn't be found until he woke and noticed them himself. Then, all she could do was hope he wouldn't remember what had happened here in the dark.

# Chapter 4

Days were short in a Ricalani winter. Everyone awoke while it was still full night, and when Cam and Garzen went out to check on the horses all the stars were out and there wasn't even a hint of dawn in the sky. They lacked the numbers to keep a proper watch, so first thing every morning and often several times during the night as well, either Cam or Garzen would leave the tent to check on their little herd. That morning, Garzen opened the water-hole with the ice chisel while Cam led the horses down to drink. He met Eloba there when she came down to fetch water for the tent.

'Cam, are you sure there's no sign of danger?' she said, glancing to the west. 'The cursed Mesentreians are so close and the Slavers must be drawing near ...'

'There's neither hide nor hair of them, Eloba, I swear. Charzic and those other wretches have made themselves scarce and the only tracks I saw belonged to the woman I found. Besides, you've heard the tales of what Lord Kell and his cursed apprentice can do in battle. We'd hear it and see the storm long before it comes upon us. We're safe for now.'

'But for how long?'

Thinking of it made him frown and echo her westward glance. It made little sense to think the Akharians would focus on the harsh and unforgiving north. It was a hard place to live for those not born to it. They would have an easier time of it if they concentrated their efforts on the settled lands to the south. Sometimes, when he lay awake at night worrying about what would come, Cam tried to convince himself that the Akharians would destroy Lord Kell, and the king, and destroy the foreign lords who held such a strangle-hold on Ricalan. It was a pleasant thing to consider, but he more wished than believed it could be true.

Cam shook his head. 'I don't know. We need to give Isidro as much time as we can, but if I see any sign of soldiers heading this way, we'll pack up and run, I promise. I didn't go to so much trouble to get Isidro back to let the king's men get their hands on him again.' They would retreat to the east and hope the Wolf Clan would shelter them.

Eloba bit her lip as she rested the full bucket on the tips of her snowshoes while she filled the other. 'I'll pray you're right. Well, the girl is up and about. Calls herself Kasimi. By the Black Sun, I hope no one comes out here looking for her ...'

'Calls herself?' Cam said. 'You think it's a false name?'

Eloba shrugged. 'Well, if I were some Mesentreian lord's concubine escaped with a king's ransom of his jewels on my wrists, you can bet I'd not be using the name he knew me by. That's all I'm saying.' With both buckets full, she started up the slope towards the tent.

'Is breakfast ready?' Cam called after her.

'Yes, but don't rush. It's nothing worth hurrying for.'

A light scatter of snow began to fall as Cam led the horses back up the hill and returned to the tent. Inside, Lakua was stirring the pot of barley porridge that had been soaking overnight. Behind her, Brekan was peering into Kasimi's satchel. Cam began to say something, but changed his mind and turned away with a shake of his head. Every one of them was weary of their arguments. Better to just let it pass.

Cam turned towards the section of the tent screened off for Isidro's sickbed. 'Rhia? Can I come in?' he said, just as the curtains twitched aside and Rhia guided Kasimi out. She wore Eloba's spare jacket and her face was still masked by her folded cowl. As Rhia guided her past the curtain, Kasimi stumbled and Cam reached out to steady her. 'Careful! The last thing you need is another burn from falling into the stove. I'm Cam, by the way. It was me who found you.'

'Cam,' she said, with a tremor in her voice. 'Yes, Rhia told me. Look, I want to apologise for taking your hare.'

'Don't worry about it,' Cam said, and he turned to Rhia. 'Is Isidro up?'

Rhia shook her head. 'No. He sleeps. Look in on him, but do not wake him.'

Cam waited while she guided the newcomer away and then ducked under the curtain. Isidro lay calm and still beneath his blankets and Cam knelt beside the bed to watch him. In weeks past such stillness had terrified him. More than once, he had sat up with Rhia through the night, certain that it meant the end was coming.

Cam sat back on his heels to watch the slow rise and fall of Isidro's chest. Isidro was the elder by a few months — enough that he'd had seven summers to Cam's six in the year Cam had been sent to Isidro's clan for fostering. He'd been looking out for Cam since they were boys.

Cam had spent his early years spoiled and cossetted by his nursemaids and ignored by his mother, Valeria, a minor southern princess brought north to marry Queen Leandra's brother. That sheltered and isolated life had come to an end — a fact for which he would be forever grateful — when Queen Leandra suffered another miscarriage and accepted she would never bear a living heir.

Ricalan's alliance with Mesentreia would never allow Leandra to adopt a sister or daughter to continue her line. So long as she remained barren, the throne was poised to fall into Mesentreian hands. In desperation, Queen Leandra turned her attention to her young nephew.

Cam just barely remembered the day the Queen's guards broke down the nursery door. The nursemaids had screamed and panicked, but they hadn't been harmed. The guardsmen who carried him away had tried to reassure the frightened little lad, but as a boy Cam had never even heard Ricalani spoken. He knew only Mesentreian and had never set foot outside of the nursery.

Looking back, he could see just how desperate Leandra must have been. Cam's elder brother Severian took after their Ricalani father, with dark hair and northern features, but Cammarian had inherited his mother's blonde hair and green eyes. There was only the barest hint of Ricalani blood in his features — it showed in the high, prominent cheekbones and wide-set eyes, with only a hint of the epicanthic fold common to his father's people. At first glance most folk took him for Mesentreian and it would have taken some hard talking to have the clans accept him as Leandra's heir.

Queen Leandra sent the young prince to be raised by her most trusted advisor, Drosavec, Chieftain of the Owl Clan. The Owl was a tiny clan, neither rich nor powerful, but its chieftain was a man of uncommon intelligence and the queen valued him highly, even ratifying Drosavec's only son as his heir despite the taint of power the boy inherited from his mother and against the objections of the priesthood.

Drosavec had turned the bewildered prince loose into his clan's flock of children and assigned his son, Isidro, to watch over him; and set about turning the brat into a man the clans would consent to have as their king.

It could have worked. Drosavec was a brilliant man and the queen was clever and shrewd herself. The pair had won the grudging support of the clans against the threat of a foreign ruler. But that all came to an end when Leandra miscarried once again and died amid blood-soaked sheets, along with her malformed child, when Cam was just fifteen and his brother, Severian, twenty. Leandra's will was clear: Cammarian had been named as her heir, with all the clans and the temples in support.

But somehow, Valeria had found a Blood Mage and smuggled him into Ricalan. Kell changed the game entirely. Where he had come from and just how long he had been hidden among Valeria's retinue remained a mystery, but what was clear was that Valeria had no intention of letting the laws against sorcery stand in the way of securing power for herself. When Drosavec entered the Great Hall to place Cam on the throne, Kell was waiting for them.

The rebellion, as Severian now referred to the events of that night, had ended in moments. In the aftermath Cam and Isidro had been smuggled out of the palace in one last effort by Leandra's loyal men, while Drosavec and the other nobles involved were captured and publicly executed on the palace steps. The foster-brothers had been on the run ever since. The longest they had ever stayed in one place was in these last two years, when the Wolf Clan had offered their patronage and protection.

In return, Cam and Isidro had infiltrated the Raiders who roamed the no-man's-land between the Wolf territory and the settlements to the south, to spy on them and steer them away from the lands belonging to the Wolf.

'It was a game at first,' Cam murmured to Isidro. 'We were playing at soldiers, playing at spies. But you were the strong one, Issey, and I always knew you had my back. Well, now it's my turn to look out for you and by the Black Sun herself, I swear I'll see you through.'

'Our biggest problem — apart from the cursed war — is the matter of supplies,' Cam said once they were all seated around the stove and the meagre ration of the morning meal had been doled out. 'We're nearly out of flour, butter, beans, meat ... well, everything, really. And there's only about four days' worth of grain left for the horses — five if we cut their ration again.'

'It'd help if we moved camp,' Garzen said. 'They do well enough on graze, but they've cleared all the snow they can here.' He turned to Rhia. 'Is Isidro strong enough to move a little way?'

'Perhaps, but not today,' Rhia said. 'He finally sleeps. I will not have him woken.'

'I still say we should get rid of the horses,' Brekan said. 'Their grain costs a fortune and we can't even use them so long as Balorica keeps to his bed.'

Cam rubbed a hand across his eyes. 'I've told you, Brekan, we can't get rid of the horses — especially not with the soldiers nearby. We'll need them come spring, if not before.'

'Spring's a long way off. A lot could happen by then.'

'You want to sell the horses now and hope we'll have the coin to buy more in a few months' time?' Cam didn't bother to keep the scorn out of his voice.

Eloba scowled at both of them. 'Don't start this again. We're *not* selling the horses ... unless you want Cam beheaded and me and Laki and Rhia passed around between the soldiers when they finally catch up with us,' she said as her gaze settled on Brekan.

'I've told you before, the horses make us a target,' Brekan said. 'The Mesentreians don't look twice at peasants travelling on foot, but once you're on a horse they get suspicious.'

'We've been over this,' Garzen said. 'I call a deciding. Raise your hand if you think we should sell the horses.'

Brekan immediately raised his hand. When no one else followed, his face darkened until Lakua hesitantly raised hers.

'Anyone else? No? Two for, four against. The horses stay.'

Brekan's face was thunderous, but Lakua looked faintly relieved. She leaned over to stroke her husband's knee, but he studiously ignored her.

'Well, there's nothing for it,' Garzen said. 'We'll have to head to a village and restock — I think we should have enough time and perhaps we can get some news, as well. It does leave the question of how we're going to pay for everything. How much coin do we have?'

'Not a lot,' said Eloba. 'Eight or nine silver crowns; that won't go far.'

'There's more in the cache we left at the start of winter,' Cam said.

'But that's a good six days' ride away, though at least it'll take us away from these cursed armies.'

'It's a pity you didn't start riding two days ago, then,' Brekan snarled. 'We wouldn't be in this situation if the hunting hadn't been so bad. Something's made our luck go sour, I swear it.'

Cam swallowed hard on the urge to call him a superstitious prick.

'I've got a few ermine furs set aside I can throw into the pot,' Garzen said.

Kasimi, who had been listening in silence, hesitantly cleared her throat. 'May I speak?'

'Of course,' Eloba said.

'I have a few things that might be good for trade. Two swords, a knife, and perhaps the horse — I don't know how to ride the beast anyway. It'll be a few days before I'm able to move on and I'll need some clothes and supplies — and I owe Cam for the hare … How much is a sword worth?'

'Those two you have are good Mesentreian steel,' Cam said. 'But they're military blades. This part of the country is crawling with soldiers — if we try to sell them people are going to want to know where they came from. Unless we take them to the sort of folk who don't ask questions, in which case we'll get only a fraction of the value. And I'd advise against selling your horse. If you're on the run you'll need it just as we need ours.'

'But your sword doesn't have a military mark,' Garzen said to Cam. 'If you were to trade Kasimi for one of hers, you could sell your old one and keep the new.'

'Well, that's a thought,' Cam said, scratching his chin. His weapon was a nondescript piece from the time they'd joined the raiders. 'If anyone asked I could say it was booty from a skirmish with the outlaws.'

'Problem is,' Garzen said, 'the old one isn't going to fetch anywhere near the value of one of those new blades.'

'From what I'm hearing, those blades wouldn't fetch their true value anyway,' Kasimi said with a shrug. 'We need the money now, so we may as well take it where we can.'

'That's all well and good, but what about the rest of it?' Brekan said. 'I saw those bracelets you were wearing. Those red stones would fetch a good price.'

Even around the mask, Cam saw the colour drain from Kasimi's face.

'No! The … the people I escaped from will be looking for me. If they find the stones …'

'We won't be going to a village nearby,' Cam said. 'It's too dangerous, what with Isidro still too weak to travel. We'll pick one that's a good day's ride away. By the time anyone recognises the stones, we'll be long gone, and they'll have no idea where to find you.'

Kasimi was shaking her head. 'No. Believe me, it's not worth the risk. I'll trade you anything else I have, but not those stones.'

Had he been able to stare her down, Cam might have been able to winkle some more information out of her, but that blindfold was as good as a shield. His curiosity prickled him like a burr beneath his shirt, but this was not the time to try to tease it out of her. The questions he itched to ask — *who are you?* and *what are you running from?* — would have to wait.

Eloba was keeping a tally of the things they needed on one side of a set of waxed tablets and on the other she was totting up the value of the goods they had to trade. 'Rhia, you're running low on some medicines? Is that right?'

'Yes.'

'Well, with those as well, this isn't going to be enough. We'll have to find something else to sell or trade.'

'But we've *been* through this,' Brekan said. 'We've already traded away everything of value we have. There's nothing left.'

Lakua raised her hands to the neck of her shirt. 'Well, actually, I do have one thing.' She produced a golden brooch that had been pinned to an inner seam of her shirt. 'It was Markhan's bride-gift. It's the last thing of his we have. Eloba's was stolen, back in the Raiders' camp, and Markhan died before he could replace it …' Tears welled in her eyes as she spoke.

'Lakua, no, keep it. We can find something else.' Even as he said it, Cam knew Brekan was right. They'd been counting on the fur and meat of a winter harvest to see them through the cold season, but that was before the soldiers began pouring into the region, before Isidro had been captured and left an invalid.

'No, Cam,' Lakua said. 'I've held on to it because I knew the time would come when we needed it. If it weren't for you and Isidro, Markhan would have been killed months earlier. I know how sick Isidro is — we'd have to turn it into coin sooner or later and where better to spend it than on the man who avenged my husband? I'll come with you and sell it myself, for Isidro's sake.'

Cam bowed his head. 'Thank you, Lakua.'

'Then I'm coming too,' Brekan said. 'All the villages around here are crawling with Mesentreians. I'm not going to let my wife walk among them unprotected.'

'That'd probably be for the best,' Garzen said. 'I'm likely to stand out if I show my face and as far as I know the Mesentreians still want to hang me.'

'Well,' Eloba said, straightening. 'The three of you should take our tent. I'll move my gear in here for a few days.'

Cam nodded. 'We'll ride out today, camp near a village tonight and do our trading first thing in the morning. That will give us time enough to confuse our trail on the way back, so if anyone does follow us, we won't lead them here. And maybe once we get back, Isidro will be strong enough for us to break camp and head east. Is there anything else to be settled?'

No one spoke: there was silence in the tent apart from the scraping of spoons on the breakfast bowls. Lakua swallowed her last mouthful and got to her feet. 'I'll start taking down the tent.'

Eloba rose as well. 'I'll give you a hand.'

'I'll get the horses ready,' Garzen said.

'Where is the wax tablet?' Rhia asked. 'Cam, I will make you list of medicines Isidro needs.' Eloba handed her the tablet and stylus as she left.

As Rhia turned away to assemble her list of supplies, Cam turned his attention to the newcomer, raising her fingertips to her blindfold again.

'Kasimi,' he said; she startled at the sound, turning her blind face towards him. 'How long ago did you leave the army? Do you have any news of what's going on out there?'

She grew suddenly tense, her lips pressed together and her hand still raised to her face, but after a moment she settled them in her lap, as though trying not to show her unease. 'The Akharians have taken the Bear lands. Some folk managed to flee ahead of the invasion, but not many. Not many at all.'

'Are they moving quickly?'

She shook her head. 'Not now. They're taking their time. Some folk said it's to accustom themselves to the northern winter before they met the king's men. They're digging in, too, building ditches and ramparts and making sure they have good fortifications at their backs —'

'Digging? In winter?'

'They have mages,' she said. 'Cutting through frozen earth is simple enough for them.' Her tone was flat, as though mages were utterly commonplace, not creatures of legend or demons walking the earth. Before the Lord Magister had come to Ricalan, no mage had been seen in the north for nearly a century. Just how much exposure to Lord Kell had she had, to speak of them so routinely?

'Do you know how far away they are?'

She drew a shaking breath. 'They're close. Very close. I only know what I overheard, but I think they're expecting to meet them soon — in days, maybe.'

Cam drew a sharp breath. 'They're as close as that?'

Kasimi nodded. 'The captured scouts were given to the Lord Magister for interrogation and I heard they said one of the legions is preparing to march east.'

'East?' Cam frowned. 'That can't be right. They wouldn't dare strike past Severian's main force like that — his men would cut off their retreat, and they'd be trapped in hostile territory with no supply line and no reinforcements.'

'The commanders said so, too, but there's no doubt that's what the Akharians are doing. They seemed to think the Slavers are looking for something.'

Cam fixed his gaze on her. 'You managed to overhear the king's counsel? Just who did you escape from, Kasimi? We won't sell you back to them, I swear it by the Twin Suns.'

She stammered then, and blanched, winding her fingers into a knot within her too-long sleeves. 'It's not important. As soon as my eyes are better, I'll ride on. But if you are where I think you are, it's not safe to stay here long. The Slavers are heading this way.'

'It doesn't make any sense. If it's slaves they're after, they'll have richer pickings near the coast and better loot, too ...' Villages were scattered in the north, where the winter lasted longer and mountains and forest seemed to battle for control of the land. The longer growing season and better farmland in the south supported far more people. The Akharians would probably try their luck anyway — they'd investigate the tribal lands eventually, but Cam couldn't believe they would split their forces until the king's men had been beaten back.

'Do the clans know any of this?' Kasimi said. 'Or the local people? Maybe I'm wrong — I hope I am — but if I'm not, the Slavers will rip through the village folk like a hot knife through fat. Our people won't stand a chance against their mages.'

Winter was the time for warfare in the north, when packed snow and frozen rivers let men move more quickly than the bogs and sucking mud of summer. Fighting was a matter of strike and retreat, of ambush and traps set for men instead of beasts. The northern people were masters of it, but were the Akharian mages enough to tip the scales back? Ricalan had battled mages before and won, but it had come at a high price. And besides, it had happened a century earlier — all those who knew how to fight sorcerers were long dead.

If the rumours *were* true, the Wolf Clan would send men to help defend the region — but did they have any to spare after meeting the king's demand for warriors? As a last resort, the village folk could flee into the forests, scattering the stock and burning the houses behind them. They'd done it in the past, in the old days of war between the clans, but folk would suffer from cold and hunger, the old and the young in particular, and if the fighting lasted into the brief summer there could be famine to follow.

'I don't know,' Cam said. 'But when we reach the village I'll see what I can find out. When we get back, we can try a short journey to see how Issey fares. We ought to move on anyway; we're too close for comfort as it is. Is there anything else you can tell me?'

She bit her lip and shook her head, but she was still so tense that Cam had no doubt she was hiding something. Well, whatever it was would have to wait. Right now, keeping Isidro alive and his tiny band safe and fed was more important.

'Cam?' Rhia looked up from her tablet and beckoned him over. 'I want to be sure you know all these names.'

The list she had written in the soot-stained wax was alarmingly long, and Rhia switched to Mesentreian, her preferred language, to make sure he understood it. 'These ones are most important,' she said, marking perhaps half a dozen out of a list twice that length. 'But get a little of the others too if you can.'

'Rhia, tell me —' A movement caught his eye and Cam looked up. Brekan hadn't left with the others — he was still sitting in his place, scraping up the last of his porridge with exaggerated care. When he saw Cam's gaze upon him Brekan slipped out of the tent with a pointed sniff, leaving his dirty bowl on the spruce behind him.

Cam just shook his head. Markhan had been a good man and a friend and he'd thought Brekan the same, but after his brother died Brekan had changed. He had never forgiven Isidro for avenging Markhan's death when Brekan didn't dare try, and now that Isidro was ill ... Ricalan had scant room for those who could not provide for themselves and Cam wondered how long it would be before Brekan started making snide comments about idle hands and useless mouths. When he did, Cam knew it wouldn't be much longer before it came to blows.

Rhia was still waiting patiently and Cam shook his head to clear it. 'Rhia, tell me truly,' he said in Mesentreian. 'Will Isidro recover?'

'You mean will he be the man he was before? I'm sorry, Cam, but no. His injuries are too severe and his arm ... It will never heal well.'

'But how do you know?'

'Here,' Rhia said, taking the tablet from him and reaching for his wrist. 'I will show you ...'

She pushed his sleeve up to his elbow. 'A single break, here,' she laid the edge of her hand halfway along his forearm, 'can be straightened and splinted to keep the bones still. But Isidro's arm is not broken once — they struck it many times ...' With a chopping motion of her hand, she gestured to his wrist, his forearm, and up along to his elbow. 'Two or three pieces, you might be able to put them back together, but what if you have dozens? The bones cannot be splinted firmly enough to hold them still and every time he moves they shift and grate. This is why he must have poppy. Pain will wear a man down and kill him as surely as any wound.'

'So it won't heal at all?'

Rhia waved her hands. 'It may, if he lies very still and has rest and good food. If it does, the bones will be crooked and they will ache always, and he will not be able to turn his hand. But it has been a month and they have not healed, so I do not think that will happen. If the bones do not knit, in time scars will grow between them and keep them from rubbing together, but that can take years. He will have to wear splints always and he will be in pain until the scars form. He would be much better off if I took his arm.'

'Took ... you mean cut it off?'

'Yes. If I amputate at the elbow,' with her index finger she drew a line across the crease of his arm, 'it will heal clean and his pain will be gone.'

'Amputate! He'll be crippled!'

'He is already. He will never use the arm again. All it will bring him is pain.'

Cam scrubbed his hands over his face. The sun wasn't even up yet and he felt weary. 'Have you mentioned this to Isidro?'

'He would not let me say it, but Isidro is clever. He understands.'

Cam threw up his hands. 'If he says no, then that's it.'

'He is frightened. Torture costs a man a great deal and he is afraid this will mean giving up even more. Of course I will not do it without his consent. But unending pain will drive him to despair and he is already afraid of being a burden upon you. I know that among your people, it is considered to be an honourable thing among the elders to give one's life to the winter rather than become a burden on one's family ...'

Cam felt his stomach turn to ice. 'He wouldn't.'

'Isidro is a proud man,' Rhia said. 'If he feels he can still serve some purpose, I think he will not. But the pain clouds his judgement. If he believes himself to be useless and a danger to you as well ...'

Cam sunk his head into his hands. 'I have to think about this.'

'That is why I am telling you now. You must decide what you think is best for him. Perhaps both of us can convince him, where one cannot.' She laid a sympathetic hand on his shoulder.

Cam took a deep breath and raked his fingers through his hair. 'I'll think it through.'

Behind her, he saw Kasimi, sitting with her head bowed and her back turned to them, the nearest to privacy that could be achieved when everyone lived in such a small and communal space. As his gaze fell on Kasimi's back, he idly wondered if she knew enough Mesentreian to understand a word of what they'd said.

Outside, Brekan glanced around to see if anyone was watching and pulled out the little bag hanging on a string around his neck. He slipped the red-stoned bracelet inside and, whistling, strode across to the smaller tent.

Eloba met him in the doorway with her arms full of furs and her bag slung over her shoulder. 'Here,' he said, reaching for the heavy bag. 'Let me carry that for you.'

'I can manage,' she said, leaning away from him. 'Look, Brekan, don't give Cam a hard time. He's got enough troubles as it is and the least you could do is show the man a bit of respect.' She turned on her heel and stalked away.

Brekan clenched his fists as he watched her go. Cam and Isidro had trained as warriors since they were old enough to walk. They'd been born to it, whereas he and Markhan had grown up chasing after a handful of skinny goats and spent their summers scratching in the meagre plot of ground the Mesentreian settlers let their family have.

Inside the tent Lakua was snuffling as she rolled up her furs. She glanced up as he came in, her lip trembling.

'Oh here, my love, don't cry …' He dropped to his knees beside her and wrapped his arms around her shoulders. 'Please don't cry. Here, Laki, let me tell you a secret. You don't have to sell Markhan's brooch. I've got a little something I've been hiding away, something left over from when we were with the Raiders.'

Lakua sniffed and straightened. The hope in her face made his heart swell. 'Really?'

He held a finger to his lips. 'Just don't tell anyone, alright? I've been saving it for an emergency, but I can't stand to let you lose your bride-gift.' As Brekan held her close, he felt the hot, hard lump of the bracelet between them and for a moment he was able to convince himself that he really had kept something aside — just once, he could be the one to save her.

# Chapter 5

The heavy book lay open at Rhia's side, the musty pages stained with mould. Isidro reached for one corner and tried to pull it around so he could see the text more clearly. Rhia swatted at his hand. 'Sit still, Isidro.'

'That's the Akharian text, isn't it? I'd forgotten you had that —'

'Be quiet, Isidro! I need to listen to your breath and I cannot hear if you talk!'

With a sigh, Isidro obeyed. It was too cold to sit around shirtless for long, anyway.

He and Cam first met Rhia among the outlaw bands. Unlike her other masters, the physician who trained her had been a kindly man. She'd set out to impress him and instead of selling her on for a profit the doctor kept her, first as an assistant and later as an apprentice. On his deathbed, the physician freed Rhia and bequeathed her his shop and his trade, to the fury of his nephew, who had expected to inherit. The old man's will had been clear but that was no protection for Rhia, who knew any magistrate would overturn it for a suitable bribe. She sold the shop, packed up all the books and medicines she could carry, and bought a place on a ship heading north to the new world, with no real plan in mind other than making a life for herself far away from the nation of her captivity.

The settlements on the southern coast of Ricalan were little different from the towns she had left behind. A woman travelling alone was an object of contempt, doubly so when people realised she was a foreigner and a freed slave. She had wandered north, vaguely aiming for the tribal lands, when she had been snatched by the Raiders.

There her knowledge and skill made her valuable, but in those lawless bands she was a resource to be owned and controlled. When Cam and Isidro met her she had been on the verge of sharing one man's furs just so that she would have someone to protect her from the rest of them — a nightmare for her, given the abuse she had already suffered as a slave. It had taken Cam and Isidro some time to convince her that their offer of protection came with no such expectations.

During the years he had known Rhia, Isidro had badgered her into teaching him the language of her birth. He had already known a little Akharian — before the alliance with Mesentreia that had brought Cam's mother to Ricalan, there had been some small trade with the Akharian Empire and Isidro's paternal grandmother had learned a smattering of the language, as well as picking up several books. She passed them on to her son, who passed them on to his, although until he met Rhia Isidro had no way of knowing if what he had learned was even remotely accurate.

Rhia pressed her ear to his bare chest, listening for the rattle in his lungs. He could feel it himself whenever he drew breath too deeply. Once Rhia straightened Isidro reached for the book again.

Rhia sat back on her heels with a sigh. 'You should try to sleep, Isidro. You need to rest.'

'I've been asleep for weeks. You want me to stay in the tent? Fine, but if you don't give me *some* way to pass the time I'm going to go out of my mind with boredom.'

He cast around the tent and narrowed his eyes. Something was out of place. The baskets stacked at the back of the tent were undisturbed, as was the low table behind the stove where bowls and jars were set out and food prepared. His and Rhia's furs were still laid out, but the rest had been rolled up and set along the tent wall where they served as bolsters folk could lean against while they ate or worked inside. He, Rhia and Kasimi were the only ones here, but that was usual during daylight hours. It was the stack of horse gear just inside the entrance that had changed since yesterday. Cam's saddle and harness were gone.

His hand still on the book, Isidro turned to Rhia. 'Where is everyone?'

Rhia glanced away from him. 'Cam and the others went out for a while. They'll be back soon.'

'Cam's saddle is gone.' Isidro craned his head to look past the stove to the gear along the far wall of the tent. 'So is his kitbag. You're a rotten liar, Rhia. He wouldn't take a horse if he was just gone for the day.'

'He went to get supplies,' Rhia said. 'Issey, your fever is down from last night and your breathing sounds clearer, too.'

'Supplies?' Isidro eased the sleeve of his shirt over his splinted arm and then groped behind him for the other. 'Where? Who went with him?'

'Brekan and Lakua. They will be back tomorrow.'

Isidro gave up for a moment on the second tie and held Rhia's gaze. 'Where did they go?'

'Northwest,' Rhia said with a shrug. 'Not far.'

'Rhia …' he began.

Kasimi, who had been lying in Rhia's furs as though asleep, propped herself up on one elbow and turned her blindfolded face towards them. 'They went to a village about a day's ride to the northwest. They'll camp near it tonight and do their trading in the morning. They should be back tomorrow evening.'

'Thank you,' Isidro said with a wince. He'd forgotten she was there and had neglected to keep his voice down. 'I'm sorry if we woke you —'

Kasimi was shaking her head before he finished. 'You didn't. Like you, I think I've slept enough.'

Isidro turned back to Rhia with a scowl. She at least had the grace to look ashamed. 'I did not want you to worry.'

'Really?' he said. 'That might work better if you don't make it quite so obvious that you're keeping something from me.' He looked down, fumbling with the ties of his shirt, and wrenched the cords into some sort of knot. 'I know you mean well, but keeping me in the dark is not the way to get what you want.'

She nodded, but he thought he recognised the expression on her face. He was a patient in need of care and for Rhia that took precedence over everything else. She would say whatever he wanted to hear so long as it kept him calm.

Isidro reached over to haul the book onto his lap, but as he leaned over, something hard and knobbly pressed against his thigh. He straightened with a wince and pulled it from the rumpled furs — three large and lumpy beads, knotted together on a leather thong. They tingled with power against his skin. 'What on earth is that?' he said, holding it up to the light.

Rhia made a small sound of disgust. 'What is that doing there? I told Cam to throw those things away!'

As he shifted, Isidro felt a similar lump against his other leg. He pulled it out as well and laid the pair of them across his knee. 'Where did they come from? I've never seen them before.'

'You were wearing them when Cam pulled you out of the water,' Rhia said. 'Filthy sorcerous things.'

Isidro rolled the lumpy beads between his fingers. The stones hummed with energy, but unlike the stinging, numbing hum of the witch-stones this was a pleasant, soothing buzz — like the comforting hiss of a kettle simmering on the stove.

'They came from Kell, so they must be tainted. Give them to me. I will throw them in the lake, as Cam should have done.'

Isidro thought of the witch-stones, with their awful leaden weight, and the rubies they had cut from Kasimi's wrists, each one bearing a touch of fire within its heart. Had they been his to dispose of he would have handed them over without a second thought. Most enchantments made his skin crawl, but these felt different. 'No,' Isidro said, closing his hand around them. 'I'll keep them for now. They're ugly things, but they might be worth something to sell.'

Rhia's face darkened. 'You should be rid of them. They will do you no good and the demons that they draw will make you ill.'

'Superstition, Rhia.' Behind her, Isidro saw Kasimi tilt her head as though listening, although her face was turned away. It was impolite to listen to a private conversation between others, even if they were sharing a tent, but she was alone and helpless among strangers — in her place he'd do the same thing. He tucked the bracelets into the pocket created by the wrap of his tunic and felt a suffusing warmth seep through the fabric and into his skin.

Rhia sniffed and turned away, more than a little put out that he wouldn't heed her advice.

'Rhia,' Isidro said. 'You've been cooped up in here for days, looking after me and Kasimi. Where are Garzen and Eloba? Fishing through the ice again?'

'They are down at river, yes.'

'Well, why don't you go and join them? It's not good for a body to spend all its time under a roof. Just because the two of us need to stay inside doesn't mean you do, too. Go and get Garzen to bait you a hook.'

'But you might need me ...'

56

'If we do we can shout from the door. The river's not far. You'll hear us well enough.'

Rhia's temper was as frayed as his after spending days and weeks trapped inside. It didn't take much persuading to convince her to pull on her wind-proof buckskin trousers, her boots and her heavy fur; and with snowgoggles to protect her eyes from the glare, she trudged down the slope to where the others were sitting around a hole chipped through the ice.

Once she was gone Isidro set Rhia's book aside. It would keep and there was another distraction drawing his attention now. 'I think I'll have a bowl of tea. Do you want one?'

Kasimi raised a hand as though to tug down her blindfold, checked herself and nodded. 'Please.'

It was a relief, he thought as he shook a pinch of herbs into two bowls, to be able to do something for himself for a change, without having someone jump up to do it for him. He was too weak and too clumsy with his left hand to trust himself to lift the full kettle or pour it without spilling, so he used the ladle to dip out the simmering water and carried the bowls one at a time to their portion of the tent.

Kasimi was sitting very still, but she'd plucked a spruce twig from the floor and twirled and twisted it between her fingers with nervous energy. When he brought her bowl, she dropped the twig and clasped her hands around the chipped pottery for warmth.

'Did we speak last night?' he said to her as he fetched his own bowl and sat opposite her. 'I seem to remember … something.' Waiting out in the cold for Cam to return had roused his fever again — if his memory of speaking to her was this faint, he wondered whether what he'd said to her made any sense at all.

'Yes,' Kasimi said. 'We spoke a little before you fell asleep. And I spoke to Cam this morning before he left.' She shivered and took a sip from her cooling bowl. 'I only hope he takes care when they reach the village.'

'You know who we are, then?' Isidro said. Perhaps they should have taken more care in speaking around her, but it was unlikely she'd try to sell their whereabouts to the Mesentreians, not after she'd taken such risks to escape. 'Well, if nothing else, that should reassure you we won't go trying to sell you back to the men you escaped from.'

She gave a tight little half-smile at that, but with her eyes covered he couldn't tell if it was real or false.

'To tell the truth,' she said, 'I was surprised to see you alive. Rumour around the camp had it that the king's advisors were certain you were dead.'

'Good,' Isidro said. 'Then they won't come hunting for us.' A wisp of smoke from the stove caught in his throat and sparked a cough. Though he tried to suppress it, the spasm shook him to the bone and stirred the fire in his arm.

Thankfully, the bout of coughing was short-lived. The stones in the front of his tunic seemed to be leeching warmth into his body, curling in soothing tendrils through his aching chest.

Suddenly alarmed, Isidro pulled them out. Rhia was right. Kell had made these with his foul and cursed magic — surely he was mad to put any trust in them. The Black Sun only knew what they might do. They could have been intended to keep him weak and docile, to sap his will to resist. Perhaps that was why they felt so good to hold and keep near his skin, and why he was so reluctant to hand them over when Rhia spoke of dropping them under the river ice.

The moment he pulled them out of his shirt, Kasimi lifted her head. 'Don't throw them away.'

Isidro stiffened. 'Why not?'

'I've seen them used before,' she said. 'Last summer, Duke Osebian was wounded — it was a hunting accident, or so they said … Anyway, the king had Lord Kell make a charm of healing for him. It keeps wounds from turning foul, it strengthens the heart and the blood. You were a valuable prisoner; they would have wanted you strong and well to make a good show at the execution. It stands to reason they'd give you a charm as well.'

Isidro stared at her, wishing he could see her face under that blindfold and pick up some hint as to whether she was telling the truth. 'You put these in my bed.'

She nodded. 'And today your fever is down. But don't let them out of sight — your healer will throw them away if she gets the chance.'

Isidro weighed the charms in his hand and then slowly tucked them away again. 'She means well,' he said. 'She spent half her life in Mesentreia — she couldn't help but pick up some of their ways.'

Mesentreians hated mages and their craft even more than the Ricalani priests did. Even as he said it, Isidro found himself thinking of the witch-stones Kasimi had been carrying. She must have found the charms herself — no one could have told her they were hidden in his packs. Perhaps she was like him, sensitive to the energies trapped in the stones. He thought of the red stones and the matching burns encircling her wrists. Clearly, she was no stranger to mage-craft and yet she didn't have the usual abhorrence for it, despite the way it had been used against her.

'You took a great risk, running like you did,' Isidro said. 'You could have died in the storm. You *would* have died if Cam hadn't found you. What was so bad that you risked death to flee it?'

She turned his way, her chin set in a firm and stubborn line. 'I thought you people already decided I was the concubine of some Mesentreian lord, making a desperate bid for freedom — at least, that's what Eloba told me.'

'I understand that was the leading theory ... but I'm not sure it's the truth. I don't see why a concubine would wear a uniform of the royal household. Let's see, you know enough of the king's matters to know the Duke was given enchantments to wear — and enough to recognise these as the same sort of stone. How did you find them? They can't have been easy to spot in my packs if Rhia thought they'd been thrown away already.'

He couldn't read her face beneath the bandage, but Kasimi stiffened with sudden tension and closed her mouth with a snap.

'Never mind,' he said. 'I don't mean to pry, I'm just so cursed bored. No doubt you have good reason to keep your secrets. But can you tell me anything of what's happening in the west? I haven't heard any news since before ...' He trailed off, glancing down at his splinted arm. 'Well, for weeks, and Cam and the others don't tell me anything they think would make me worry.'

She laughed, a brief, humourless sound that seemed born more of nerves than anything else. 'I heard about you,' she said. 'Back in the king's camp. I'm glad you survived; it's heartening to know Kell and the king aren't as all-powerful as they'd have us believe.'

Isidro glanced down at the splints again. *Glad, are you?* he thought. *I'm not, at times.* What tales had spread through the camp of his days of torment? He winced at the thought of it, but then Kasimi went on, giving him something to focus on and drive those unwelcome memories away.

'The fighting has probably begun by now. The Akharians were close when I left, digging in on the far side of the river valley. They have control of the Bear Lands — a few made it out, but most are slaves now, heading to the markets in Akhara.'

'How many men do the Slavers have?'

She shook her head. 'No idea. I never saw them and the men I overheard didn't say. But I think it's a lot. More than the king has, maybe.'

'The numbers don't matter as much if he has the advantage of terrain,' Isidro said. 'The pass where the river cuts through the ranges is good ground — I'd say Severian could hold it for years, if it weren't for the mages. Can you tell me anything of them?'

'Not much. From what I heard, the king isn't worried. Kell and his cursed apprentice are sure they can deal with them … the ones marching south, that is. The ones who head this way aren't likely to meet anything that gives them pause.'

Isidro frowned. 'The Akharians are heading east?

She nodded. 'I tried to tell your brother, but I don't think he believed me.'

'But why? Surely they'll be heading south to sack the harbours and burn the ships.'

'I can't explain it, but that's what I heard,' Kasimi said. 'And from more than one man, all of them well up in the chain of command.'

'That can't be right,' Isidro said. 'Even for slaves, it wouldn't be worth it. It would be easier to round up people living in towns along the coast than to seek out the villages at the foot of the mountains.'

'No one in the camp understood it either,' Kasimi said. 'The Black Sun only knows what they're looking for. What are you and the prince doing in this part of the land, anyway? The Mesentreians have been gathering for months — you must have been aware of the danger.'

'Mmm. We knew, of course, but at that point there wasn't much we could do about it.' He hesitated, unsure of the wisdom of telling her, but she seemed to relax as he spoke. The knowledge she hinted at intrigued him and perhaps sharing his tale would encourage her to spill hers. 'There aren't many places left where Cam and I could stay without drawing attention — the Raiders bands were one of them.'

In brief terms, he told her how he and Cam had come to this part of the country. Outlaws existed across the whole of Ricalan to some degree,

60

but there were perhaps a thousand of them on the border between the Wolf Clan's northern holdings and the new Mesentreian provinces to the south. Before the king's muster had called the bulk of their warriors away, the Wolf Clan would have just wiped them out, but they served as a protective buffer against the war-bands of the Mesentreian lords, who saw anything in Ricalani hands as theirs for the taking, especially towards the end of a long winter when stores set aside by those unfamiliar with the northern seasons began to run out.

The outlaws were displaced people of one kind or another — in the early days the settlers had lived side by side with the natives in an uneasy tolerance, but as the population grew the Ricalanis who held their ground found themselves treated as aliens in their own land. Some, like Eloba and Lakua and their husbands, simply left. Others resisted and found themselves attacked, either legally under the new Mesentreian laws or out of simple greed for their land and their herds. If any children survived the attacks, they would be fostered among the families in the district — which in practice meant they became the indentured servants of those who had slaughtered their parents. Some died, but still more ran away.

The lucky ones found their way to the seat of a ruling clan and claimed sanctuary, but many of them drifted into the bands of the lost and dispossessed wandering along the border, living with no real aim or goal other than to take revenge on those who had destroyed their lives. Half starved, untrained and with stolen or improvised weapons, they were not much of a threat when their numbers were small, but when enough of them came together, leaders emerged, and a good leader could turn fifty broken men into a force to be reckoned with.

Charzic was just such a leader. His arrival had stirred chaos within the band as he turned his supporters against those who resisted his leadership. It was one of those early battles that had resulted in Markhan's death. He had been cut down in the middle of the camp as he tried to defend Lakua from a warrior who was determined to possess her. Brekan was never the warrior Markhan had been: he would have been killed if he'd gone to the warrior's tent and tried to rescue his wife. It had been Isidro who had called Markhan's killer out and slain him in single combat. Lakua had already been beaten and raped, but at least Isidro had recovered her before she'd been passed around among the rest of the men.

That fight had been the beginning of the end, the first link in the chain of events which eventually saw Charzic force them out.

Isidro left out the Wolf Clan's role in setting him and Cam up as spies. If Kasimi were captured again, he doubted she would speak of it willingly, but he know that a desperate person could clutch at any offering that might turn a tormenter's wrath aside. If word reached the king's ears of the Wolf Clan's involvement, either with the Raiders or with hiding Cam and Isidro, it would be disaster for the most powerful clan left in Ricalan.

'But why head west?' Kasimi said. 'You must have known there was trouble brewing here.'

'We didn't have a choice,' Isidro said. 'We left one step ahead of Charzic's men, but they wouldn't dare follow us too close to the army. Our plan was to come west, then turn north and skirt around the edge of Charzic's territory as we headed back east. But then the king's men found me and put paid to all that.'

'I see,' she said. 'And now we're stuck here, more or less, until the others get back and you and I are well enough to travel.' She raised a hand to the blindfold again, her face still swollen with frost.

'I hope it won't take long,' Isidro said. 'If what you say is true, we'd best get out of here as soon as we can.'

# Chapter 6

Cam muttered a curse when he saw the soldiers gathered on the path at the edge of the village, stopping those who passed while an officer mounted on a pony watched over the operation.

'Cam — ' Lakua began.

'Don't stop. If we turn back, they'll wonder why the sight of all these soldiers put us off.'

'It's enough to put anyone off,' Lakua said. 'I wouldn't go past them if I could avoid it.'

'We should go somewhere else,' Brekan said.

'It's too late. They'll think we've got something to hide. Just let me do the talking and, by the Twin Suns, don't argue if I give you an order.' He'd hoped to gather more information of what was going on in the west, but faced with these soldiers Cam wasn't sure he dared ask too many questions and draw too much attention. Shoving down his misgivings, he nudged his horse on.

The Mesentreian division was camped between the village and the walled grounds of the temple, but they were preparing to move on. Tents were being taken down, bulky furs folded up and packed on sleds and black iron stoves set out on logs to cool above the snow. It seemed strange, then, that a dozen or so soldiers were gathered on the path leading into the village, searching anyone who entered or left.

A trio of country folk were also heading for the village and they reached the checkpoint before Cam's little band. There was one woman in the party and a soldier grabbed her by the arms as another snatched the knitted cap from her head, pulling a hank of hair out with it. When she cried out in protest, the soldier slapped her. One of her companions objected and the other soldiers swarmed on him. With a punch in the gut that doubled him over, they surrounded him and dragged him away.

Meanwhile, the soldier examining the woman wrenched her gloves off to show the tattoo on her wrist. Whatever it was they were seeking she did not appear to have, because they shoved her to the ground and turned their attention to the sled. The load it bore was covered with a sheet of oilcloth to protect it from the snow and tied down with twine. One of the soldiers cut through the cord to expose the load and pawed through it, scattering bundles into the snow. When the three were allowed to head on into the village they didn't pause to load their goods back onto the sled — they gathered the scattered bundles into their arms and hobbled on quickly, dragging the sled with its trailing cover and cords behind them.

The soldiers' attention turned to Cam's little band and one of the men gestured for them to approach. 'Laki, you stay by me,' Cam said over his shoulder and nudged his horse forward.

Cam was posing as a noble servitor of the Wolf Clan, with the others as his personal servants. It would draw more attention than appearing as country folk, but the papers Cam carried meant that he and Brekan were safe from being conscripted, would keep their horses from being commandeered and meant the soldiers wouldn't dare assault Lakua.

In order to fit the role Cam rode without packs or panniers; Lakua's horse carried bulging saddlebags slung over the saddle and Brekan's had been pressed into service to haul the sled. Riding never kept one as warm as walking, so both Cam and Lakua had their hoods drawn up, but Cam pushed his back as the soldiers surrounded them.

'What's going on here?' he said in Mesentreian. 'I don't care what you're looking for; I won't have you handle my servants and mangle my gear as you did with those country folk.'

'Hold off there, lads,' the officer said, guiding his mount towards them. 'Sorry to trouble you, y'honour, but we're searching for an escaped convict.' He carried a quirt with a gilded handle and gestured with it towards Lakua. 'If you'll oblige me, sir, have your servant show her face and her clan tattoo.'

Lakua knew only a scattering of Mesentreian, so Cam translated the command for her and with a wide-eyed look she shook her hood back. She and her sister had been born in the south with mixed blood in their ancestry. Lakua's hair was brown and wavy, unlike the woman who had been accosted before, who had the straight black hair of an old-blood Ricalani. When Lakua took off her glove to show the stylised elk tattooed on the inside of her wrist, one of the men stepped forward to examine it, then turned back to his commander with a shake of his head.

'Most obliged, sir,' the officer said. 'Now, if your man will let my lads see your sled, I'll send you on your way.'

'Take the cover off,' Cam said to Brekan in Ricalani. 'Show them whatever they want to see.' He turned back to the officer. 'What is this about?'

'Just trying to recover some property stolen from one of the king's advisors, y'honour; we won't hold you long.' The officer had sharp eyes, and Cam could feel him taking in every detail of his fair hair and green eyes, so unusual in Ricalan. He couldn't miss the traces of Ricalani blood in his features, though. To Mesentreian eyes Cam was a mongrel. 'Forgive my curiosity, y'honour, but what clan do you belong to?'

'Red Fox,' Cam said. The Red Fox was one of the southern clans, their lands broken up and shared among Mesentreian lords for decades now. The clan still existed, but only just, and those who were left were dispossessed and destitute. It would be more remarkable if one of the Red Fox didn't show mixed blood and the clan was so scattered it would take months to prove he wasn't one of them. 'The head of my clan has me on loan to the Wolf.'

'Wolf Clan, eh? Have any documents to prove it?'

'Of course,' Cam said, and reached into his saddlebags for the leather document case. It was just as well that Isidro had burned the other set — if he'd been captured with the papers Cam couldn't use his set without rousing suspicion.

He handed the case over and waited as the officer took his time thumbing through the parchments. They were impeccable — they'd been written by the Wolf Clan's own scribe, once in Ricalani and again in Mesentreian, with both sets signed by Lady Tarya herself.

'Camdaric of Red Fox,' the sergeant read. 'Just what service is it that you provide for the Wolf Clan? I'd have thought a fit young man like yourself would be under War-Leader Dremman's command — and his men are stationed in the south.'

'Lady Tarya has me bringing her news from the front,' Cam said. 'Her unranked servitors kept having their horses commandeered for the war effort.'

The officer shrugged. 'Oh? Odd that they didn't mention they were in the Wolf's service.' He handed the sheaf of documents back and pulled a piece of rag-pulp paper from inside his coat. 'As I was saying, y'honour, we're searching for an escaped convict, a girl of about eighteen summers. Killed her own suckling babe, she did, strangled it with her bare hands and then ran away for fear of the king's justice. Maybe you've seen her, travellin' round as you do? The king and his Lady Mother are anxious to see the little bitch brought to justice.'

He handed Cam the sheet of paper, printed with a simple wood-cut portrait of a young woman with straight black hair, a narrow face and wary eyes. 'Never seen her,' Cam said. 'With the war coming to a head and the Slavers running rampant through the Bear Lands, the finest men in our king's army are searching for a runaway girl?'

'The king and Lord Kell have the matter well in hand, I'm sure, y'honour, and there's nothing more impious than a mother who kills her own child,' the sergeant said. 'Surely you don't think the monster should be allowed to go free?'

Cam gave the man a humourless smile. There was no evidence, but he suspected that Valeria had killed the man who sired her sons and it was she who had written out the warrant ordering Cam's death. Clearly killing blood kin was only impious if someone else did it. 'Of course not,' he said. He offered the portrait back, but the sergeant waved it away. 'Keep it, y'honour. Mayhap you will run across her in your travels. If you do, keep in mind that the king has offered a reward of ten thousand gold crowns for information of her whereabouts.'

'Ten thousand?' Cam said. 'Really?' Ten thousand was a fortune — half that much was enough to buy letters of nobility and set oneself up as a minor lord.

'Indeed,' said the sergeant. 'There's a lot of folks as are keeping a sharp eye out for that little sweetheart.'

The men who had been searching the sled stood back and with a salute one of them told the officer the sled was clear. The officer backed his horse from their path and gestured for Cam and his companions to pass.

Once they were out of earshot of the guards, Brekan, leading the sled-horse, said, 'I don't suppose —'

'Of course not,' Lakua said. 'I got a good look at her when I was warming her feet. There's no way Kasimi had given birth or nursed a babe — Rhia would have picked it if I hadn't. I'd wager anything she's never been pregnant, or at least not for long enough for it to show.'

'Ten thousand crowns is a lot of money —'

'Yes, and you can be sure they'd find a way out of paying it to the likes of us.'

'It's a moot point, anyway,' Cam told him with a warning glare.

It was a great deal of money — far more than was justified by an infanticide. Cam glanced at the portrait again before tucking it away in his saddlebags. Her face had been too swollen and distorted from the frosting to be sure. It might be her, it might not … in a few days, he would know. Either way, Cam was as sure as he could be that the story the sergeant had told him was an outright lie.


It was a typical Ricalani village, much like the ones Cam knew from his fostering with Isidro's clan. The day was still early — the sun had not yet risen — but there was a steady bustle of activity as folk carried in blocks of ice for water and carried out nightsoil and animal muck to be buried in the snow over the plot of land each family used for their summer vegetables.

Those folk with wares to sell loaded them onto toboggans and dragged them to the trampled clearing in the centre of the village, where they were laid out on groundsheets spread over the snow.

Alongside them lay the fancier offerings of the Mesentreian merchants who pitched their tents on the village grounds. The merchants were preparing to leave as well, with their stoves cooling above the snow and the bare, skeletal frames of their tents still standing as the hides were folded away. Cam found a family willing to earn a few coppers by watching their horses and gear and then double-checked the cord that bound the cover over the sled, adding his own knot so he would know if it had been disturbed. He asked, but none of them had heard any rumours of an Akharian legion heading this way.

Cam took his battered old sword and Garzen's ermines from his packs and said to Lakua, 'Do you want me to handle the negotiations for your brooch? Those Mesentreian merchants will have more coin to spend than the local blacksmith —'

'Not for the likes of us, they won't,' Brekan said. 'You can negotiate with the southern pigs if you want, but I prefer to deal with a man of my own people.' He took Lakua by the arm and steered her away.

'We won't be long,' Lakua called back over her shoulder to Cam and let herself be pulled away.

The blacksmith's house was marked with a black hammer and anvil painted on the wall beside the upper entrance, barely visible beneath a rime of ice. Two massive black and white dogs guarded the doorway, so Brekan and Lakua stood at the foot of the ramp and shouted for attention rather than risk stepping past them. When someone came to order the dogs down and invite them in, Brekan went off to the forge with a wink and Lakua followed to the kitchen for a bowl of tea, where she asked the wives if they had any old clothes and bedding they were willing to sell.

'I've lost my kitbag,' she told the women. 'It must have fallen off the back of the sled and his lordship wouldn't give me any more time to look for it. I lost everything but what I had on my back. Do you have any gear you're willing to part with? I don't have much money, mind, but I don't need nothing fancy, just something to keep me warm.'

She asked for news from the west as the women hauled a basket chest out of a storeroom, but they knew no more than she did. By the time Brekan returned from the forge, whistling and with a bounce in his step, Lakua had a set of worn but functional gear picked out for the newcomer. Brekan handed over the price she'd agreed on without protest and when it was all stowed away in a sack he slung it over his shoulder and draped his other arm around Lakua's neck. Once they were down the ramp of the blacksmith's house he pulled a handful of coins in a fraying pouch from the sash of his coat and handed it to her. 'You can pass that lot on to Cam.'

She quickly tucked it out of sight inside her own coat. 'Is that all of it?' she said. He was still warm from the heat of the forge — he'd folded his coat open and she could see the lump made by another pouch around his neck, bouncing against his chest with every step.

Brekan noticed her gaze and quickly reached up to hide it with his hand. 'Well, there might be a little bit more, but let's not tell him about it, eh? The Black Sun knows it won't be long before another emergency comes up — let's save it until then.'

She leaned into his embrace and smiled. He had his faults, her Brekan, but at the end of the day he was a decent man and that was all that mattered.

The merchant looked over Garzen's pelts with a disparaging eye. 'Well, sir, I'm afraid I can't do much for you. There's no market for these at the present. I'd like to take them off your hands, but it's hardly worth the trouble for me to haul them south.'

Cam suppressed a sigh. At least the merchant hadn't tried to tell him the furs were poor quality. Garzen was a meticulous workman and the pelts were faultless. 'Just what kind of fool do you take me for?' he said. 'Of course there's a market —'

'Those as want fur out here go and catch it for themselves. Coin's tight all over, yer lordship, what with the war and all.'

'Here, perhaps, but not in Mesentreia,' Cam said. 'Fifteen, no less.'

With a heavy sigh, the merchant ran his hands over the thick white fur. 'I suppose I could stretch to nine — and that's out of respect to you, m'lord.'

'Then I'll take them elsewhere,' Cam said, reaching for the pelts.

'Well, I could make it eleven, though that's beggaring myself, m'lord.' The merchant's tone was obsequious, but his eyes were flinty.

'Thirteen,' Cam said. 'Or I take them to your neighbour. With trouble brewing in this part of the world it might be some time before you see their like again.'

The merchant gave Cam a narrow look through watery eyes, but he said nothing, and after a moment Cam started gathering up the pelts again.

'Twelve, then,' the merchant said. 'Twelve, and that's the last offer. I'll be lucky to fetch even that much for them on the docks in Lathayan.'

They'd fetch twice the price on the docks and twice that again in Mesentreia. 'Let's see your coin, then,' Cam said.

Once the coins were counted and weighed Cam slipped them into his pouch, along with the money he'd got for the sword and the little they'd had in camp. Altogether, it would feed the people and the horses, but it wasn't enough to cover Rhia's list of medicines.

He'd rather starve than skimp on those. The thought of Isidro dying now, after all they'd been through to keep him alive, was more than he could bear. The grief welled up so strong that for a moment he found it hard to breathe. They'd been a team for as long as he could remember.

He'd never been worried when Isidro had his back — even the best of Charzic's men had been wary of taking on the pair of them. Cam could still feel the fear that had gripped him the day Isidro hadn't returned. As the hours had slipped by with no sign of him, Cam felt as though he'd been gutted, all his innards dragged out, leaving him hollow and empty. He'd insisted on waiting long after the others had packed up the tents and saddled the horses. They'd had to drag him away in the end. Lakua had been in tears. Cam had never felt so lost, not knowing what had happened and fearing the worst.

Cam tossed his head like a fly-stung horse, and turned his face to the rising sun. *Bright Sun, watch over him,* he thought. *Just let my brother live.*

Lakua and Brekan caught up with Cam just as he was going over Rhia's list with a clerk and he made an excuse and moved away so they could talk in relative privacy. Lakua gave him the purse and he tipped the coins out into his palm to count them. 'Rations for us aren't so bad but grain is in short supply — and I hate to think how much Rhia's list is going to cost. The clans and the army have been buying up all they can get their hands on and it's driven the prices right up …' He paused as he counted up the coins that would be left once he'd paid for the grain and other goods.

'It's not enough, is it?' Lakua said.

'Nowhere near. I'll have to cut some of the grain.'

Lakua turned to Brekan. He avoided her gaze until she elbowed him in the ribs. 'Give him the rest of it. Cam, we got more than we thought we would for the brooch. We were going to save it for an emergency, but Isidro needs it now.'

Glowering, Brekan pulled out his pouch and shook the coins carelessly into Cam's hand then turned and stalked away as they spilled onto the snow. Lakua scrambled to pick them up. 'I'm sorry,' she said, tipping the coins back into the purse. 'He doesn't mean it … It's just that ever since Markhan died …' Tears welled up in her eyes.

'Don't worry about it,' Cam said as he counted through the coins.

'Is it enough?'

'I think so. Fires Below, Laki, I can't thank you enough for this.'

Cam went back to the clerk to finish the deal. While the fellow weighed out the herbs and powders, the merchant's servants were loading everything else onto the sleds. Cam watched them all with narrowed eyes. He hadn't bothered to speak to the soldiers — they were all busy with their tasks and wouldn't answer a mongrel like him in any case. He'd asked some village folk if they'd heard anything about legions marching this way, but none of them knew what he was talking about. 'Moving on, are you?' Cam said. 'Getting out before the Slavers march in from the west?'

The clerk glanced up sharply. 'I'm not permitted to speak of it, m'lord.'

'You're heading south, though? Travelling with the regiment?'

'I really couldn't say, sir. Now is there anything else you require?'

Since Brekan had vanished, Cam wrangled the loan of a couple of servants to carry his purchases back to the sled, where he found him in sullen conversation with the officer Cam had spoken to at the checkpoint.

'Get this gear stowed,' Cam told him. 'It's time we moved on and I'm not paying you to stand around and gossip.'

Brekan tossed his head and for a moment Cam thought he would refuse, but he turned his back on the man and began to untie the load.

Cam turned to the Mesentreian. 'Is there a problem?'

'No, no problem, m'lord. I just came to ask which way you were riding. If you were aiming for the army, my lord, you'd do well to ride with my men. It's dangerous for a small party to ride so close to the Raiders' haunt.'

'Thank you, captain, but that won't be necessary.'

The officer rubbed his chin. 'Tell me, my lord, have you ever been to Lathayan?'

'I haven't,' Cam said.

'Only you look cursed familiar — I'm sure I've seen you before, m'lord.'

'You must be mistaken,' Cam said. 'I've never been to Lathayan.' He glanced over his shoulder and saw Lakua pulling the last knot tight. He caught her eye and tossed her the purse containing the last of the coins. 'Pay the good folk for watching our gear, will you? It's past time we left.'

# Chapter 7

It was well after dark by the time Cam and the others returned to camp. Every hour past sunset, Garzen climbed to the saddle of the hill behind their camp to look for sign of their return. On his fourth trip, those still in the tent heard his shout of welcome and Eloba and Rhia both hastily dressed for the cold and went out to meet them.

Moving more slowly, Isidro shrugged his good arm into the sleeve of his coat, but he had yet to work out how to tie the sash that held it closed with his one good hand.

'Can I help?' Sierra asked after watching him fumble for a few long moments. Once the sun had set Rhia had let her take the blindfold off, so long as she sat with her back to the lamps. She had spent most of the last few days listening to the physician hover over Isidro, offering to do almost every little thing for him and hearing his mood range from patience to anger and back again.

He stiffened slightly at the offer and then turned to her with a sigh. 'Would you mind?'

She stood to wrap the strip of fabric around him. He was taller than she remembered — taller than Rasten and perhaps even Kell. His eyes were dark as he watched her with a warrior's face: impassive, it gave nothing away, but she knew he was in pain. Power was pouring off him like heat from a glowing coal. If she closed her eyes, Sierra could feel it like a physical warmth bathing her face.

'With a couple of rings sewn on the end here, you'd be able to do this with one hand,' Sierra said, turning her attention back to the knot. 'And a few loops on your coat to thread it through would keep it in easy reach.'

'Just a loop on the end would do,' he said. 'I could tie a slip knot with one hand.'

Once she found her own gear they both stepped outside to see the returning party making their way down the slope.

Outside Sierra hung back, staying beyond Isidro's line of sight. She ought to be avoiding him, not drawing his attention. As far as she could tell he hadn't recognised her. Or at least he hadn't yet — there was no telling if or when that memory would arise. He'd seen her face during his long day of torment, she was certain. If he did learn who she was ... She didn't want to hurt anyone, least of all these folk who were hiding from the same forces hunting her, but if they found out who she was, she might not have any choice. *Best just to go*, she thought. *Go as soon as you're able.*

When the sled and the horses reached the foot of the slope, Isidro started towards them, picking his way across the broken surface of the snow. Sierra stayed where she was and watched, trying to match faces to the voices she'd heard the previous morning. Eloba was arm in arm with a smaller and prettier version of herself. Brekan, who was leading the horse pulling the sled, had his hood drawn up so she couldn't see his face. The one who drew her eye was the man who strode out to meet Isidro, caught him by his good arm and clapped him on the back in welcome. Even at this distance, Sierra felt the shock it sent through his ruined arm, the needle-stabs as the bones shifted beneath the splints, but Isidro showed no sign that it hurt. Sierra saw him toss his head and turn to walk with Cam back towards the tent.

Her first proper look at the man who had rescued her made Sierra's breath catch in her throat in sudden panic. The prince was the spitting image of his cousin, the Duke Osebian Angessovar, who had been brought from Mesentreia to serve as the king's heir. It was only as he came closer that Sierra saw the difference in his eyes and cheekbones that betrayed his Ricalani blood.

During her time in Lathayan Sierra had glimpsed the king only from a distance, but she had seen his mother, the queen, several times. The first had been shortly after Kell had brought her to the dungeons, when the queen had descended for the sole purpose of viewing his new apprentice. Rasten had brought her naked and shivering out of the dark cell in which she'd been confined and had her kneel on the bare stone floor so that the tall, haughty woman wrapped in a leopard-fur robe could look her over. The family resemblance was so strong that no one could doubt their kinship, but where Valeria's cold, tight smile had chilled her, Cam seemed all warmth and good nature as he waved and called a greeting.

Garzen and Brekan led the horses away while the others set to unloading the sled, stowing the supplies and setting up the tent again. Once the reindeer-fur cover was lashed into place over the poles Sierra helped Eloba set the iron stove onto three notched posts driven into the snow and then tramp down a fresh bed of spruce. Working alongside another woman with the scent of crushed needles and wood-smoke swirling around her lifted her spirits and gave her a moment of pure contentment — a glimpse into a life she'd never dared think she might live again.

While Eloba was laying out their bedding and furs, Lakua came to fetch Sierra to the other tent to see the gear she had found for her, chattering nonstop as she laid it all out to show her. The clothes were worn and much-mended, but they were serviceable. Once she'd seen them all Sierra and Lakua laid them out on the snow, weighed down with firewood, to freeze and kill any lice they carried.

Back inside, as Garzen and Eloba reheated the stew they'd saved for the others, Sierra fetched her makeshift pack and moved all the contents to the new kitbag, a sturdy leather case specially constructed to keep out water and snow. She stowed Kell's book away quickly, hoping no one would notice the wretched thing. Isidro had mentioned it briefly, hinting that he would like to see it, but Sierra had fobbed him off with a hasty excuse and then ignored it, grateful for his good manners in not pressing the matter. If he'd simply taken it out and tried to open it she would have faced awkward questions of where it had come from and why no one else could loosen the straps binding it.

Right down the bottom of her old bag, she found the bracelets wrapped in a bit of rag. Sierra pulled them out gingerly, trying to keep the stones from touching her bare skin, but the rag came unwrapped beneath her fingers and she balanced it on the palm of her hand to close it up again. The green stones had an oily gleam in the light of the lamps hanging from the tent poles, and the rubies winked at her with vicious fire. Sierra quickly covered them over again but something made her hesitate as she went to put them away. Later, she was never sure just what it was that drew her attention — perhaps her instincts told her the weight wasn't right, or that there wasn't enough red mingled in with the green; but something made her stop and tweak the cloth open again for a closer look.

She spread the bracelets out on the crumpled rag and then numbly turned them over again as though doing so might magically turn three into four. The warding-stones were all there, two thick and ugly strands of them as heavy and lifeless as lead, but only one strand of rubies coiled across her palm, glowing with all its wicked fire.

The tent had fallen quiet and in the lull someone rose and slipped outside with a muttered excuse and a swirl of cold air.

Sierra closed her hand over the bracelets and took a deep breath, trying to stay calm and ignore the sinking feeling in the pit of her stomach. It must have slipped out of the wrapper. Surely that was all. She tucked the bracelets into the front of her jacket and steeled herself to reach into the bag, groping into the folds and wrinkles of the cloth with her fingertips. The first touch of those stones felt like grasping a hot coal. Sierra hated them as much as she'd loathed anything in her life — as much as she'd loathed the crows that attacked newborn kids too weak to defend themselves and pecked out their eyes. As much as she loathed Kell and what he did to Rasten and his other boys, and what he forced Rasten to do. But in that moment she would have welcomed a touch of that fire — she closed her eyes and prayed to the Black Sun to let her find it snagged on a loose thread.

Sierra searched every corner of the bag but there was nothing there. She upended and shook it, and then turned it inside out. Nothing. With growing desperation she emptied her new kitbag and laid all the gear out on the spruce, all pretence at secrecy forgotten. She checked everything, even though she'd handled each item only moments before. No rubies, no fiery glow. Lifting the rag out of her jacket, she teased the bracelets apart again, hoping against hope that she'd been mistaken.

There was a rustle of clothing as someone stood and then a shadow loomed over her. Sierra glanced up, but she'd guessed who it would be. Isidro was too clever by half, and too observant for his own good. He missed nothing, and had seen her distress.

He crouched before her, reaching down with his left hand to steady himself. 'What's wrong?'

'One of the bracelets is missing,' she muttered, shoving everything back into the new bag. All the contentment she'd felt had vanished like smoke in the wind; her muscles had drawn tense and tight and her stomach had clenched into a knot. The smell of bannock sizzling in fat on the stove was suddenly nauseating.

'Are you sure? I saw Garzen cut them off the first night you were here. Cam put them both in with the witch-stones.'

Sierra turned away from him and shuffled to the storage section where her bag had been sitting, running her hands over the prickling spruce and searching for any glint of red or gold. Eloba, prodding at the bannock with a peeled twig, peered at her over the stove. 'What have you lost?'

When Sierra didn't answer, Isidro told her. 'One of the ruby bracelets is missing.' The tent fell silent and Sierra felt all their eyes on her. She gritted her teeth and pulled her sleeves down over her hands. Her power had been feeding off Isidro's pain all day; it was as restive as a stall-bound horse and her nerves were whipping it up like a wind at sea. The last thing she needed now was for her control to slip and her power to spill.

Cam rose to help her while Isidro straightened the new bedding furs she had been sitting·on, in case it was hidden within a fold.

'I don't see it,' Cam said. 'Have you taken anything else from the bag? Before now, I mean? With your eyes covered you might have dropped it without noticing.'

'I haven't so much as touched it,' Sierra said.

'No one has,' Isidro agreed. 'Not since you lot left, anyway.'

'The last I saw it was when Brekan was poking around — ' Cam said.

Lakua gasped and clapped a hand to her mouth. As everyone turned her way the colour slowly drained from her face.

'Laki?' Cam said. 'What's wrong?'

'Nothing,' she said. 'Nothing, I just … I think I left something in the other tent.'

Lakua snatched up her coat on the way out, wrapping it tight around her shoulders as she crossed the snow to the other tent. Inside she found Brekan prodding at the coals in the stove. He glanced up as she entered and then quickly looked away.

'Brekan,' she said. 'What did you sell to the blacksmith?'

'What? Oh. Nothing. Just a bit of jewellery I took from the Raiders.'

'What was it?'

He hunched over the stove. 'A ring with a bit of blue glass.'

'He paid you well for it then, if that's all it was.'

She stayed where she was and after a moment he glanced up again. 'What's she gone and lost then?'

'A bracelet. One with red stones. Really, Brekan, a ring? From the Raiders? When did you get it?'

'Before we left, obviously.'

'But when? Because I remember when Elli lost her bride-gift. She was so upset and you and Markhan swore you'd find something to replace it … only we never saw any gold from the raids, did we? Charzic and his lot always got first pick of the loot and they could sell that stuff to the smugglers for armour and weapons. If you'd taken it while we were still with the Raiders, you'd have given it to her.'

'It was just a bit of tat,' Brekan said with a shrug. 'It wasn't good enough for that.'

'So the blacksmith overpaid you, then?'

Brekan stood. 'Laki, what do you want? Why are you asking all these questions? Aren't you glad you got to keep Markhan's gift?'

She raised a hand to the brooch, still pinned to the inner seam of her shirt. 'Of course —'

'Then leave it alone!'

She narrowed her eyes.

Brekan had always been a thief. Markhan had a warrior's heart, but Brekan lacked his size and was crafty rather than brave. He'd grown up surrounded by settlers who forced his family onto the poorest lands and forbade them from hunting in the best forests. And so he'd become a poacher. In the Raiders' camp she'd been proud of his light fingers and his ability to snatch something here or there from Charzic's stinking louts. But this was different.

'Brekan,' she said. 'Did you take the bracelet?'

'Of course not.' He was crouching by the stove again and didn't look around.

'Brekan! Will you at least look at me?'

Reluctantly, he raised his eyes. And flinched.

Lakua covered her face with her hands. 'Brekan, how could you? She's a guest! By all the Gods, I'm so ashamed …'

'Laki!' he hissed. 'Keep your voice down. And what's wrong with it, anyway? We saved her life. She *owes* us. Greedy little bitch, keeping them all for herself.'

'But she said —'

'Don't worry, I told the blacksmith he'd best break it up and sell the stones on the quiet. It's only fair that we get our share of it. And I don't see why you're complaining. You get to keep Markhan's brooch *and* your friend Balorica got his medicines. Where's the harm?'

'The harm? Brekan, you *stole* from a *guest*! Aren't things bad enough without calling the wrath of the Gods down upon us? Bright Sun have mercy, Brekan, we *have* to put this right!' She turned towards the door, and Brekan lunged forward to seize her arm.

'Fires Below, Laki, what do you think you're doing? You can't *tell* them!'

'They'll work it out —'

'No they won't! For the love of life, Laki, keep your wretched mouth shut.'

'If we don't put it right, we'll be cursed! Our luck has already turned bad, but with this as well … I've already lost Markhan, I couldn't stand to lose you or Elli as well.'

'So you'll betray me? You ungrateful bitch!'

Lakua closed her mouth with a snap, and Brekan's grip suddenly went slack.

'Laki, I'm sorry. I didn't mean it —'

Wrenching the door flap aside, she ducked out into the night with Brekan on her heels. 'Laki, wait! I'm sorry, please just let me explain —' He grabbed her by the shoulder, hard enough to wake the memory of the day Markhan was killed. 'Let go of me!' she screamed and wrenched away.

'Keep your voice down!' he pleaded. 'Laki, they'll hear you —'

Too late. The door of the larger tent lifted and Cam leaned out with Eloba right behind him.

'What in the Black Sun's name is going on?' Cam demanded.

In the main tent once again, Lakua blotted tears away with her sleeve and pulled her collar open to display the brooch. 'I … I didn't sell it,' she whispered. 'Brekan said he had some loot left over from when we were with the Raiders. I was so upset remembering Markhan that I didn't even think about it.'

Eloba slipped an arm around her sister's shoulders. Both of them were flushed bright red with shame. Sullen and indignant, Brekan sat across the tent from them, scowling at the spruce.

'I'm so sorry,' Lakua said to Sierra. 'He's not a bad man, I swear ...'

Sierra plucked a twig from the floor and began tying it in knots. After a moment, she realised that Isidro was watching her and she threw it down again and pulled her fists into her sleeves. Her power was pulsing within her, humming just beneath her skin. Rasten had taught her some tricks to keep it under control, but she'd never been all that good at them — that was why Kell had made the punishment bands, to give her an incentive to try harder.

'You're all jumping to conclusions,' Brekan said. 'I can't believe my own wives would accuse me of stealing from a guest!'

'You were poking through her bag yesterday morning before we left,' Cam said to him. 'I saw it myself, and no one's touched it since then.'

'But you were going through it before that. Garzen gave the bracelets to you when he cut them off. Seems to me that it could have gone missing then just as easily.'

'All four were there when I wrapped them up,' Cam said. 'Isidro saw it, too.'

'You've no right to be treating me this way,' Brekan said. 'You'd be starving if it weren't for me bringing in game and finding a bit of coin once you'd frittered all yours away. You ought to be thanking me for making sure we could afford all those medicines Balorica needs.'

There was a reek of smoke in the air. Eloba cursed and scrambled to her feet. 'By the Black Sun, the wretched bannock's burnt.' She snatched the pan off the stove and tipped it out onto a platter, charred and black. No one made any move towards it. There was no appetite left in the tent.

'We should do a proper search of all the gear and supplies,' Garzen said. 'And then everyone go through their bags. If we don't find it in the first round, everyone swap and search through someone else's kit.'

'I'll have no part in this,' said Brekan. 'You've all decided I'm guilty anyway.'

With a shake of his head Cam turned his back on Brekan and crouched down in front of Sierra. 'Look, are you *absolutely* sure?'

'You saw me go through it,' she said. 'I'll do it again if you like, but it's not here ...' Her hands were trembling so badly they looked palsied.

Cam raked his own hands through his hair. 'He could have sold the whole thing, I suppose.'

'If he did, he was cheated,' Isidro said, reaching over to pick up the bracelet resting on its bit of rag on Sierra's knee. 'These stones are worth a king's ransom. The things you bought and the bit of coin you had left would only make up a fraction of their value.'

'Don't bother tearing everything apart,' Lakua said. 'He as good as told me he took it.' She rose shakily and came to kneel at Sierra's feet, reaching inside her shirt to unfasten the brooch. 'I must apologise for my husband,' she said. 'With the Bright Sun as my witness, I swear I didn't know he'd stolen from you. Please let me make amends.' She placed the brooch in Sierra's hand.

'No!' Sierra closed her hand and pulled it away. 'No, I can't ... I mean, thank you, but I don't want it. I never cared about the stones, I was just afraid they'd use them to find me ...'

Lakua caught Sierra's sleeve and looked imploringly into her eyes. 'Please, you have to. He's my kinsman. If we don't help make atonement for his crime, the Goddess's curse will fall on us, too.'

Sierra kept her hands closed. 'By the Gods and all their children, I bear you and your sister no ill will. I'll swear it on the altar of the first temple I reach ... after all, the damage is done.' She pulled her hands away and stood to face Cam. 'We have to leave this place *now*.'

'We can't leave now,' Cam said. 'It's late, we're all weary and it looks as though the weather might turn. We were planning to move on in the morning and find fresh grazing for the horses. We'll leave as soon as the weather allows.'

Sierra closed her eyes and suppressed the urge to scream at him. 'Moving a few valleys over is not enough. If they find those stones they'll follow your trail back here. They'll hunt me down, however long it takes.'

'Who will hunt you?' Cam said. 'Look, Kasimi, I understand you're worried but they'll never trace us back here. The village we went to is a hard day's ride away. Even if the men hunting you do find those stones the trail will be long cold. Trust me, we've been doing this for a long time.'

His words did nothing to calm her. Her heart was pounding and her power was pulsing higher with each throb of her heart. It was going to spill over, and soon — she was past the point where she could call it back. 'I need to get out,' she said. 'I can't breathe in here.'

Cam snagged her coat off its peg. 'Don't go far. You don't want to get lost once the snow moves in.'

'Oh, go teach a crow to fly,' she snapped at him and blundered out into the cold.

Cam brought Isidro a chunk of torn bannock. Eloba had done her best to scrape off the char but it still tasted burnt. 'Nervy, isn't she?'

'Terrified, I'd have said.' Isidro rested it on his knee while he rubbed the back of his neck. His hair was still standing on end, his skin prickled with goosebumps, though it eased now that Brekan had taken himself off to the other tent and the tension in the atmosphere was going down. For a while there he'd felt as though there was a summer storm brewing around them, and the air was tingling with energy, though thunderstorms were rare in winter.

'Do you have any idea why she's so afraid?' Cam asked.

Isidro shook his head. 'She doesn't want to talk about it.' He lowered his voice. 'And I doubt that Kasimi is her real name. She jumps whenever you say it.'

'You noticed it, too?' Cam murmured.

'Did you see any sign of people searching for her?'

Cam straightened. 'They're definitely searching for someone …' He leaned over to his saddlebags. 'They were looking at every woman who came into the village and searching the sleds. The captain had some cock-and-bull story about a woman who'd killed her child —'

'Rhia would have said something if she'd had a child.'

'That's what Lakua said. Ah, here it is.' Cam passed him a folded and crumpled sheet of paper and Isidro smoothed it against his leg. For a long moment they both gazed at the simple woodcut portrait.

'Well,' Cam said. 'I guess it could be her. I didn't think so when I first saw it but now that the swelling's coming down …'

There was Mesentreian text printed under the portrait. *The woman, Sierra, may be using a false name. She can be identified by scars on her back and around her wrists. A reward of 10,000 gold crowns will be paid for information leading to her capture.*

The woman in the portrait stared out with wary eyes. As he studied it Isidro was certain he'd seen her somewhere before … but he couldn't pin down the memory. When he tried, it skittered away from him like a leaf on the wind, but he was certain it had nothing to do with the stranger Cam had brought to their tent.

Then it came to him in a rush — the heat, the smoke, the sickening stench of burning hair and skin, a jumbled memory of blood and sweat and pain. The girl huddled at Lord Kell's feet, her face hidden behind a curtain of tangled and sweat-streaked hair.

Isidro felt his good hand clench into a fist, crumpling the paper within it. Muscles twitched in his right hand, drawing a needle-stab of pain from the broken bones. With a deep breath he made himself relax and when he could trust his hand not to shake he folded the paper over and tucked it into his sash and then heaved himself to his feet.

'Where are you going?' Cam said.

'Out,' Isidro said, shrugging into his coat. He didn't intend to sound so short but he still couldn't bring himself to speak of what had happened while he was in chains.

Once again the belt defeated him and he had to let Cam knot it in place. 'We'll have to do something about that,' Cam said, and then he lowered his voice. 'What do you know, Issey?'

'Nothing, yet.'

Outside the wind was blowing steadily, stirring the loose snow so that the landscape seemed to be veiled beneath a seething mist. The moonlight that had helped guide Cam and the others home was gone — the sky overhead was a black void of low cloud.

Isidro buried himself within his cowl and hood and turned to the west, in the opposite direction from the tent Brekan shared with his wives, going slowly to let his eyes adjust to the night.

Out in the darkness a blue light flickered, casting deep bars of shadow between the trees. It caught the scatter of falling snow and lit the drifting flakes like a myriad of stars.

Isidro headed towards it, forgetting for the moment just how weak he was. Beyond the circle of trampled snow around their camp site the crust on the surface of the unpacked snow was too thin to hold his weight. Once his feet broke through he sank to his knees and within a few dozen paces he was out of breath and sweating despite the cold wind working its way in at the neck of his coat. When he stumbled again and began to cough he realised what a stupid idea this was; it sickened him that even the smallest of challenges was more than his weakened frame could bear.

Ahead of him the light flashed again. Isidro buried his chin in the collar of his coat, trying to breathe the air warmed by his body and calm the racking cough. Through watering eyes he made out a silhouette moving towards him in the midst of the flickering glow.

She dropped to her knees at his side, using her body to shield him from the wind as the cough raked claws through his chest. 'What are you doing out here?' she shouted over the wind.

Her face was red from the cold and still a little swollen from her brush with frost. In a few days she would have recovered enough that he'd probably have recognised her anyway. Face to face, there was no doubt left in his mind.

The light flickered again, a blue glow spilling around them, but all Isidro could see were her eyes, deep blue like the sky at a summer's midnight. In those oceanic depths, lightning struck, and for a moment he glimpsed the storm raging within her.

'Hello, Sierra,' he said.

# Chapter 8

There had been a time when Ricalan had mages of its own — once they had been the third part of the triad that ruled Ricalan, beside the ruling clans and the priesthood.

It was hard to know just how different life would have been in those days. The histories said only that mages were an evil influence, poisoning everything they touched. Isidro's mother had told him stories of life before the War of the Mages, tales told to her by her elders and handed down in secret to those who inherited the taint. She spoke of buildings and bridges built in a day, growing out of the ground like mushrooms; of floods and lava flows being turned away from villages, of fires extinguished and avalanches cleared. She told him that for centuries before the alliance with Mesentreia the mages had defended Ricalan's coast against Raiders from the south.

In those days there had been as many factions of mages as there were clans. The war had begun when some of those factions decided there was no need for them to accept the clans and the priests as equals and that mages, by grace of their power, were the rightful rulers of the land. While the factions squabbled over just which of the mages should rule, many people who had taken no part in the fighting were caught up in the skirmishes and killed. One of them was a young noblewoman by the name of Jenova, born of the Lion Clan and the daughter of Leandra the First, ancestor to Cam and his aunt, the second queen to bear that name.

At first Leandra had been interested only in finding and punishing the mages responsible, or so the histories said. But when all of the three factions involved turned her messengers away and refused to help her find the truth, her plans changed. Leandra entered an alliance with her neighbouring clans, and with one of the factions of mages, and led an attack against the other two, in which they were wiped out to the newest trainee. In the victory celebration that followed Leandra and her allied clans turned on the mages of their own alliance and slaughtered them as well.

It could have ended there, but Leandra was not content with avenging her daughter's death. After seeing what mages could do when they wielded their power in anger she was determined to destroy them all, even if it meant overlooking centuries of raids and depredations and allying herself with Mesentreia. After all, the Southern Isles had killed or expelled all their mages half a millennia before and an alliance would end the raids in a manner the mages had never managed to achieve.

It took years of bloody and brutal warfare but Leandra and her armies killed the last of the mages, led by the man now known as the Demon Vasant, at the foot of the northern mountains, where molten rock flowed from the ground like blood from a wound.

As a boy Isidro had been unable to comprehend how Leandra and her armies had been able to wipe out a class of people as powerful as mages were rumoured to be. Once he and Cam had been forced to survive on their own he had grown to understand. At least the two of them were able to ask for help either from the common folk for a warm place to spend the night or from the ruling clans, who in the early days had provided them with horses and weapons in honour of Drosavec and Leandra's memories. A mage's power might provide him or her with shelter and warmth but it wouldn't keep them fed and clothed through six months of darkness and snow. When the common folk turned against them, swayed by the stories Leandra and her allies spread of the atrocities carried out by mages, their power didn't protect them from poisoned food, arrows in the back or a knife across the throat as they slept, or from traps and snares. Ricalan was a difficult place for outright warfare and in winter guerrilla attacks and swift surprise assault were the only course. A mage who was cold, hungry and weary was as vulnerable as any other warrior under poor conditions — perhaps more so, as they were accustomed to their power providing them with every comfort they desired. Leandra's army simply wore them to exhaustion and killed them once their powers were spent.

Leandra wasn't content with wiping out the living mages of Ricalan — she set about making sure that in future generations, mages would never rise again. She destroyed their books and halls of study; she stripped the history books of any mention of mages and of any version of events but hers. At her order, the priests twisted the rituals used to identify children with a talent for mage-craft and used them instead to select those who were forced to wear the amulets that would suppress their power and mark them to be watched. Some of them were inducted into the priesthood itself — they needed some talent to perform the rituals and create the amulets in the first place, but all other use of power was forbidden on pain of death.

Nothing, however, could stop new babes from being born with the talent. Perhaps most of them were like Isidro, carrying only a feeble spark of power, but there had to be some whose power burned too bright and fierce to be extinguished by a priest's mumbled and half-understood rituals. Isidro had always dreamed of meeting one — but he'd never imagined it would happen like this.

Sierra slung his good arm across her shoulder, taking some of his weight as she guided him to the shelter of a copse of trees. It was only once he was leaning against the naked trunk of a birch that he was able to look at her properly.

Miniature bolts of lightning coursed over her with an unearthly blue glow, writhing over her skin and through her hair. Raw power hissed and crackled around her hands and sent long, questing tendrils to the ground where they writhed around her feet. When one flickered too close to her face she swatted at it with a mittened hand as though to shoo it away.

'You're the real thing, aren't you?' Isidro said hoarsely, and coughed again. 'A Child of the Black Sun.'

She gave him a wry smile. 'Something like that.'

A minor mage-talent such as the one he'd inherited from his mother was one thing — useless without training and easily contained by the warding-stones — but Sierra was in a different class entirely. A Child of the Black Sun was to him what a tiger was to a house cat. If he was tainted by the touch of power he carried, then she was nothing less than a demon in the flesh. When there had been mages in Ricalan, the Children of the Black Sun were their elite. Over time, his meagre talent would atrophy like an unused limb for want of training; folk like her would be consumed by the power that lived beneath their skin.

In Mesentreia, a child with the talent would be killed. Even if her family tried to protect her there was no defence against a mob prepared to beat a child to death in the street. The priests in Ricalan denied they would allow any such thing but no one ever said exactly what would happen if the Children's Festival discovered a child who had been touched by the Black Sun. They were every bit as dangerous as a rabid bear — anyone who doubted it had only to look at Lord Kell and his apprentice.

'I knew you'd recognise me eventually,' she said. 'You saw me clearly when Rasten brought you into the tent, but I wasn't sure how much you remembered.'

'It wasn't you I recognised — not at first, anyway.' He pulled the folded paper out of his sash and handed it to her. She unfolded it carefully, her mittened hands clumsy as the wind tugged and tore at the sheet. He watched her eyes rove over the printed text and realised she could read Mesentreian. 'I like this tale Kell concocted. Foul enough that no one would shelter me, but not so bad they'd want to kill me on the spot.' She gave a small sigh of resignation. 'If the clans knew what I am they'd kill me rather than let Kell take me back ...' She handed the paper back and met his gaze. 'I'm sorry, Isidro,' she said. 'I would have stopped them if I could —'

'Sorry for what?' he said. 'From what I saw you were as much a prisoner as I was.'

For a moment neither of them spoke and the only sound was the moaning of the wind in the pines.

'Who else knows?' Sierra said.

'No one, yet. I only picked the likeness because I'd seen you before. Cam will work it out in a few days — the others might, too, if they got a good look at that portrait.'

She took a step back, stricken, and her breath hitched in her chest. 'I'll leave,' she said. 'First thing in the morning. I've endangered you all enough already.'

'You can't,' he said. 'It'll be weeks before you can see clearly in daylight. If you leave now you'll be dead inside of two days — if the soldiers or Charzic's men don't find you first.'

'I can't stay,' she said. 'I can't hide what I am for long — I'll only give myself away. It's better if they never know.'

Isidro remembered the heavy green stones in her pack. 'The warding-stones — you could put them on again.'

She shuddered violently. 'I *hate* those things! They're not strong enough by themselves anyway. That's why Kell made the punishment bands.'

Isidro blinked. 'The burns ...' He remembered the blisters and her charred skin.

She looked away, fierce blue-grey eyes searching the darkness around them. 'They were supposed to teach me to control myself.'

All at once the thought of Rasten alone with her hit him like a punch to the gut. After that first day, once they knew Cam was beyond their reach, Kell and Rasten had shown him every way a man could be tormented, degraded and humiliated while still leaving him more or less in one piece. Isidro knew it was stupid, a worthless remnant of a pride he no longer had the right to claim, but the thought of someone else being forced to submit as he had filled him with rage.

Sierra frowned at him and he wondered if she could read the pain in his face. 'What's wrong?'

'Rasten,' he said. 'And you —'

'Ah,' she said, and shook her head. 'No, thank the Gods for small mercies, he never touched me. Kell made sure of that. Rasten was like me once, but Kell ruined him by taking him too hard, too young. He wanted to make sure the same thing didn't happen to me. If he finds me again, though, that will be the least of his concerns.' She bit her lip. '*When* he finds me. Will you tell Cam?'

'I have to,' Isidro said. 'He needs to know the danger we're in.'

She turned away with a snarl and kicked at a clump of snow. 'That wretched Brekan! He's got no idea what he's done.' The lightning bolts coursing around her had settled but now they sprang up again; a bolt as thick as his finger arced between her hand and the ground and coursed up her arm to her shoulder, crackling like dry leaves in a blaze.

'Do you have anywhere to go?' Isidro said. 'Anyone who will take you in?'

She shook her head. 'No. No one.'

'How badly will Kell want to find you? Once the Akharians meet the king's army surely he and Rasten both will be needed there — they won't have time to search the wilderness for you.'

'It's not as simple as that.'

'No? Why not?'

She bit her lip, and Isidro guessed she was debating just how much she should tell him. 'I'm a Sympath. Do you know what that means?'

'No. Is it an Akharian word?'

She frowned. 'I don't know. Kell came from there, so I suppose it might be. A Sympath is a mage who generates power from pain. Kell can raise power on his own with his rituals but it's nothing compared to what he can take if I'm there, too. He'll stop at nothing to get me back.'

He could still picture her, chained and kneeling on the floor. How many souls had suffered and died in front of her while she was powerless to prevent it?

'You must have kin somewhere,' he said.

She looked away. 'They're probably dead. When Kell found me, he had us trapped in a ruined temple. He said he'd spare them if I gave myself up. I had no choice.'

'I heard something about that,' Isidro said. 'There were rumours the king's torturer had a new apprentice.'

'A new slave, more like,' she said with a toss of her head. 'What else did you hear? Was there any word of survivors?'

Isidro shook his head. 'No. I'm sorry.'

'He killed Rasten's family. They tried to hide him and Kell slaughtered the lot of them. Rasten was twelve.'

She was looking away — she couldn't have seen the expression that crossed his face at the sound of the apprentice's name. Isidro screwed his eyes shut, fighting against the memories that welled up. Sierra had been there — she'd felt every moment of it. Isidro shoved the thought to the back of his mind. Better to forget.

'You should go back inside,' Sierra said. 'Come on, I'll help you.'

The energy spilling from her had died down, but whether she had brought it under control again or simply burned off the excess, Isidro wasn't sure. He didn't protest when she offered him her arm and they started back towards the tents.

'You know,' Sierra said. 'You're the only person who's seen me shed power like that who hasn't run like a pack of wolves was after him.'

'Really?' he said.

'Except for Kell and Rasten. Even my family were frightened of it. My fathers were furious every time I let it slip.'

'Well, I've never met anyone who carried the taint who was willing to talk openly about it,' Isidro said. He wanted to say more but between the cough and the cold he was still breathless and light-headed. His wits were sluggish enough that something she'd said earlier only struck him then.

'Wait a moment — Kell is *Akharian*?'

'Of course. He left their mage-school when he was young and found a master in Mesentreia to train him to the Blood Path. I think it happens a lot — many of the Blood-Mages in Mesentreia come from Akhara. Mesentreian children who show the talent tend not to survive, but sometimes the parents are tricked into handing the children over to a Blood-Mage, thinking the mage will keep them safe. The mages either use them up or turn them into apprentices if they're strong enough to survive. If their families knew what they were letting the children in for they'd smother them with pillows. It would be kinder.'

A tremor of unease ran through Isidro. 'How much was Kell relying on you to face the Akharian mages?'

She gave a small, tight smile, but it quickly faded. 'He's going to have to change his plans ... unless he finds those cursed stones and tracks me here.'

The more he heard, the less he liked the situation. If Sierra was so important to Kell's strategy, then he and the king would stop at nothing to get her back, even if it meant losing ground in the short term. The northern lands were all held by Ricalanis and the king would lose no sleep for holdings burned and villages enslaved north of the Mesentreian settlements. They had to get word of this to the Wolf Clan — and yet it was too dangerous now for them to dare show their faces in a village.

'I'll leave here as soon as I can,' Sierra said. 'I've put you in enough danger as it is.'

'You should talk with Cam,' Isidro said. 'We've been living on the run for a long time now. We might be able to come up with a plan for you.'

They were approaching the tent when the flap swung open and Cam ducked through, settling his coat around his shoulders. As soon as he straightened and saw them, he stopped. 'There you are, Issey! You were gone so long I was starting to worry.' He turned to Sierra with a frown. 'He's not strong enough to stand around out here in the cold.'

Isidro could feel Sierra bristle but he spoke before she could reply. 'The cough got me again, that's all. Sierra waited with me until it passed.'

'Sierra?' Cam said, raising one eyebrow. 'I thought you said your name was Kasimi.'

Isidro pulled the crumpled paper out of his belt and handed it back to Cam. 'It's her. I mean, the story's a load of horseshit, but it's her they're searching for.'

Cam tucked the paper away without looking at it. 'Now why is that?

I don't see how one woman could be worth a reward of ten thousand crowns; so just who are you, *Sierra?*'

'Cam —'

'She can tell me herself. Better yet, we can go inside and she can tell all of us.'

Isidro shook his head. 'Better to keep this quiet. Trust me, you don't want —' An odd sound reached his ears and Isidro broke off mid-sentence. It was faint, but he could have sworn he heard the whinny of a horse carried on the wind. Sierra caught her breath in a gasp and Cam raised a hand for silence.

'Did you hear that?' he said in a breathless whisper. Isidro pointed to their own horses huddled at their tether with their rumps turned into the wind. The lead mare had raised her head to scent the wind and pricked her stubby ears to listen.

Sierra had turned pale. 'Rasten —'

'No one could have recognised the stones so quickly,' Isidro said. 'Anyone who has found us now would have to have followed the others from the village. Cam, is there any chance you could have been recognised?'

Cam grimaced. 'The local commander was asking a lot of questions. I didn't think he'd come to any conclusions, so I didn't say anything. I didn't want to worry anyone.'

'Couldn't it just be a trapper?' Sierra asked.

'Trappers don't bother with horses,' Cam said. He ducked back into the tent and returned with his sword belt, which he buckled over his coat, and then reached for one of the spears standing upright in the snow outside the tent. 'Both of you go inside — tell Garzen what we heard. I'll go and check it out.'

'Take Sierra with you,' Isidro said. 'Cam, she's Kell's second apprentice — she fought her way out of the Mesentreian camp. If there's trouble the two of you are the best ones to face it.'

Cam blinked and then, as the information sunk in, he recoiled. 'Kell's apprentice? How — ' He broke off and shook himself like a dog. 'No time for that now.' He turned to Sierra. 'Are you with us?'

He didn't trust her. She could tell from the way he kept glancing back. Isidro's calm acceptance of what she was had come as a shock but this wariness and suspicion was something familiar and Sierra felt herself bristling in response. By the Black Sun, if the Mesentreians had found their camp, they were all in danger and yet Cammarian was watching her like an enemy. She wondered what he saw when he looked at her — was it a frightened herder-girl in borrowed clothes or a demon in the flesh, trailing destruction and despair in her path?

With the spear held low, Cam moved in near silence over the snow, any small sounds he made covered by the moaning wind. To her surprise Sierra found she slipped easily into the stalk she'd learned as a child during the long hours she'd spent watching over the goat herd, with nothing to break the boredom but practise with her leather sling and a handful of stones. She knew it was irrational, but she would have given anything to have her old sling again. The only weapon she had now was her power and if she was forced to use that it would be bloody. *Black Sun please let it be a false alarm. I don't want to kill again.*

Cam gave her a sidelong glance and she steeled herself to meet his gaze. 'How do we do this?' Cam murmured.

'I'm not much of a warrior, but I can watch your back,' she whispered. 'If there is trouble, it'll be messy, and it'll be bright. If I have to kill someone, *everyone* nearby will know something is going on.'

Cam nodded. 'Hang back then and let me go in first.'

Sierra mimicked Cam as they crossed the saddle, hunching low to disguise her silhouette until they were concealed behind a thicket of bare twigs. They were some distance from the camp now, moving into a small valley. It was sheltered from sight and sound, but cold air pooled in low ground, and it grew steadily colder as they descended.

Down on the slope below someone had lit a fire. A small cloud of mist had formed and the firelight reflected off the haze of ice crystals hanging in the air. There was a string of horses tethered to a line strung between two trees and a pair of laden sleds on the snow nearby. One man left to guard them sat huddled beside the small fire with a tea-bowl in his hands and a crossbow within easy reach at his side.

Cam was perfectly calm as he surveyed the intruders; Sierra envied him. She was shaking, certain that at any moment the guard would look up and see them.

'This isn't good,' Cam murmured. 'If they were travellers, they'd have unsaddled the horses, pitched their tents.'

'Should we kill him?' Sierra asked.

Cam shook his head. 'If we do, the others will know they've been spotted —'

A woman's scream pierced the air behind them, a high, thin sound, attenuated by distance and the cold. Sierra started and the man by the fire lifted his head. Cam swore under his breath and turned back in the direction from which they'd come. 'The camp,' he said. 'Go!'

Sierra had turned back the way they had come when a soldier lunged out of the gloom to block her path. He was shrouded in a white war-coat and only blue eyes and red cheeks were visible between his cap and his cowl. He feinted high with his short sword, making her reflexively raise an arm in a futile defence before he swung the blade low and thrust at her belly.

Without thinking, Sierra struck him with a lash of power. It leapt from her palm in a thick blue bolt, crackling like flame in dry grass, searing through the metal and down his arm and through his chest. A roar of fire speared through Sierra's right hand and arm, a flash of pain followed by a sumptuous wave of power that washed through her and filled her with calm, golden light.

The soldier gave a grunt of pain as the power struck and then went rigid. Paralysed, caught mid-swing and off balance, he collapsed.

'Crossbow!' Cam shouted, breaking the spell the power held over her. She turned away, not noticing that as her attention shifted it broke the contact of power that held the warrior immobile.

Cam was facing another man in white, parrying and thrusting with his spear against the Mesentreian's sword while the man beside the fire had snatched up his crossbow and was sighting down the quarrel towards them.

Gathering her power, Sierra threw up a shield to cover them both. It hung in the air like a glowing net of blue light. Kell and Rasten hadn't taught her much about using her power but Rasten had shown her this and drilled her on it until she could respond in an instant. Sorcerers were feared even in the king's own camp and there was always the danger that someone would try to kill her before her powers reached their full strength, even if it meant sacrificing his own life.

The bolt struck the net of power and shattered into splinters that rained, burning, onto the snow.

Distracted by the light, Cam's opponent fumbled a parry and Cam ran him through with the spear. The soldier crumpled, collapsing over the shaft and dragging it out of Cam's hands. He discarded the weapon and drew his sword instead. 'Don't let him reload!'

Before Sierra could respond she felt a hand close around her ankle. The man she had felled still had his hand locked around the hilt of his sword and he swung it at her knee.

Sierra threw herself down and the blade missed her by a hair's breadth. She kicked at the man's head and his grip slipped.

Cam hacked at his arm and Sierra scrambled away; a ribbon of fire seared across her forearm and then another across her throat as Cam slashed at the soldier's neck.

At the foot of the slope the third man had his foot in the stirrup of the bow as he hauled the string back. He had a bolt held ready in his teeth and as soon as the string slipped over the notch he slapped it into place on the stock and raised it to take aim again.

Sierra was a dozen paces away when his finger found the trigger. The two men behind her were dying — a furnace burned within her chest to match the line of fire across her neck, their nerves flooding her with sensation and power even as their blood pumped out onto the snow.

Shaking with terror, the crossbowman squeezed the trigger, but Sierra already had a shield in place. The quarrel shattered against it and Sierra's power tore loose from her grasp and swarmed over him, wrapping him in a seething cocoon of light. It bore him to the ground, thrashing and shrieking, while the horses screamed and reared, throwing themselves against the tether until it broke and they bolted into the night.

Sierra tried to choke the power off but it had a will of its own and refused to be called back, struggling against her like a leopard caught in a snare. A heart still beat within that tangled cocoon of light, feeding the beast: it was only once it faltered and stopped that the light died away and her power consented to be tamed.

She found herself standing amid a splattered circle of blood, but in the gloom of night it was black, not red. The corpse, too, was a black and twisted thing — all raw meat and yellow bone — while scraps of clothing flickered and rippled with flame.

Cam grabbed her by the arm and Sierra jumped, loosing a belt of nervous sparks that coursed over her body before earthing themselves in the ground.

'The camp,' Cam said. 'Hurry.'

# Chapter 9

Isidro lifted the tent flap enough to lean inside. 'Garzen,' he said, beckoning him outside with a jerk of his heads then dropped the flap and went to the other tent. Eloba heard the crunch of snow beneath his boots as he approached and lifted the flap before he reached it.

'What's going on?'

'Strangers nearby,' he said. 'We heard a horse off to the northwest. Cam and Kasimi have gone to check it out.'

'I'll tell the others,' Eloba said and ducked back inside.

Garzen emerged from the larger tent with Rhia on his heels and Isidro repeated what he had told Eloba. Garzen puffed out his tattooed cheeks at the news. 'That's all you heard? One horse could just be a deserter.'

'Or it could be that someone in the village spotted Cam and followed him back here,' Isidro said. Still a little light-headed from coughing, he turned carefully on his heel to scan the countryside around them. Their camp was pitched in a small clearing; the ground before them swept down to the frozen river while the slope above grew steeper up to the wooded crest. To the west there was the scattering of bare birches and snow-laden pines where he had confronted Sierra but to the east was a much thicker stand of trees sheltering the tethered horses. 'If I were raiding this camp I'd come from the east,' he said. 'There's cover enough there to let the men spread out to scout, and with the wind blowing from the west, horses and dogs won't catch your scent.' A pair of dogs would serve them well just now, if they'd had the means to feed them.

Eloba, Brekan and Lakua came out to join them, Brekan with his brother's sword and Eloba with her bow and quiver slung over her shoulder. Lakua had a hatchet and twisted her hands nervously around the oiled wooden handle.

'Laki, you and Rhia should go into the big tent,' Eloba said. 'There's no sense in all of us milling around like sheep.'

Her face pale, Lakua nodded and slipped past them to duck under the flap.

'Isidro, you too,' Rhia said, laying a hand on his arm. 'You have been out in the cold long enough.'

Isidro drew breath to argue, but he gave up before he'd even opened his mouth. He couldn't fight any more — couldn't even defend himself. A few months ago they would have turned to him for leadership but now he was just a distraction.

'As you wish, then,' Isidro said and lifted the tent flap for Rhia to step inside. The three standing on guard were still watching him with their backs to the western woods. Behind them, Isidro saw a movement at the edge of the trees. The lead mare threw her head up and backed away with a nicker of alarm.

Isidro cursed. 'They're here,' he said. 'Get on your guard; they'll break cover any moment.' The three finest warriors in the camp stared at him dumbly. 'We're under attack!'

Eloba was the first to turn and follow his gaze, just as the warriors broke from the woods, heading for them at a run. With a wordless cry of surprise she nocked an arrow to her bowstring and took aim. Shouting, Garzen and Brekan took up positions to either side of her, each armed with a long-bladed spear but with swords near to hand if the fighting pressed too close. Men were swarming out of the trees; too many to count at a glance. Before Isidro could take stock someone took hold of his arm and dragged him into the tent.

He spun around angrily and found himself face-to-face with Rhia, her hands locked around his good arm. In the past he could have shaken her off, but weeks of illness had robbed him of his strength. He tried to brace against her but Rhia was stronger than she looked and she simply pulled him off balance. 'Isidro, no! You cannot fight!'

'Black Sun take you, Rhia! Let me go!'

There was a scuffle and a shout from outside, and the point of a sword stabbed through the thick fur that covered the tent. A sweep of the blade cut a man-sized slit and a soldier shoved himself through.

Lakua screamed and dropped her hatchet. Rhia still clung to Isidro's arm but her eyes grew wide and her grip lax as she recoiled from the soldier, a Mesentreian man with ash-blond hair and pale blue eyes.

Isidro jerked his arm free of Rhia's grasp and bumped her out of the way with a quick shove from his shoulder. Lakua's hatchet had fallen at his feet and he stooped to snatch it up. The soldier was still only half in the tent, caught between two of the poles, and Isidro stepped around his flailing sword to swing the hatchet at his arm. The blade was sharp but his left arm was weak and clumsy — the hatchet cut through the thick leather and fur of the soldier's coat, carved through the flesh and then turned on the bone. If he'd been able to swing it with his right hand Isidro would have severed the limb. As it was the blade skidded down the bone, carving off a thick tongue of muscle and skin.

The soldier screamed and the sword slipped from his hand. Isidro stepped in front of him and swung the axe again, aiming for the neck, but between his own poor aim and the soldier's flinch as he saw the weapon swing towards him, the blade hit high and struck him in the face, biting deep into his cheek and his nose. With a choking cry, the soldier wrenched himself free of the tent poles and threw himself backwards.

Even dressed in his outer fur Isidro had lost enough bulk that he could slip between the tent poles with ease. He followed the soldier out onto the snow, dropped to his knees at the man's side and sank the axe into his throat.

With a bellow of rage, another figure lunged towards Isidro out of the darkness. The light spilling from the tent flashed bright along metal and Isidro threw himself back while the blade hissed through the air in front of his face. The soldier raised his sword for a second swing and an arrow hit his chest with a meaty thunk.

Isidro was already scrambling back when Eloba grabbed his arm and pulled him the rest of the way into the sheltered spot between the tents. The sleds and the stack of firewood made just enough of a barrier to give her a safe spot from which to shoot. Isidro scrambled to his feet with the bloody hatchet still in his hand and saw shadowy figures coming around from behind, seeking a way across the barrier.

Brekan and Garzen were hard pressed, and step by step the attackers forced them back between the tents. Eloba dropped another with an arrow in the belly, but it made little difference. There might be only a score of attackers, but that was more than enough. Even half that number could overwhelm them.

'Rhia! Laki!' Isidro bellowed. 'Get out here on defence!' They couldn't make it through the doorway — it was too close to the fighting, so instead they lifted the wall of the tent and scrambled out from underneath to snatch up the last of the spears still standing on end in the snow.

Isidro abandoned the hatchet — the handle was too short to be any good here — and instead he found the ice-chisel, a hardened iron tip fixed to a six-foot pole, used to cut through river ice to the flowing water beneath. It was a poor substitute for a spear but it would do.

While men pressed close around Garzen and Brekan, Isidro saw more shadowy figures rush around the back of the tents. As one of the men clambered up onto the woodpile Isidro couched it under his arm and rammed the blade into the soldier's chest, angling up beneath his sternum and into his heart. He fell and Isidro nearly lost the weapon as the weight of the attacker's body almost wrenched the shaft from his hands.

Beside him Garzen cried out and Eloba screamed. Isidro could spare only a glance in their direction before turning back to the men trying to breach their makeshift wall, but what he saw burned into his vision. He saw Garzen on his knees doubled over an enemy's hand, with a bloody swordpoint emerging from his back.

Rhia was already moving towards Garzen. 'Leave him, Rhia!' Isidro barked. 'Help Brekan!'

'But —'

'We'll *all* be dead if we can't keep them off! Take your spear and help Brekan!'

Her face drained of colour but she did as he said and Isidro moved back to take her place on the wall. Lakua was bloodless and trembling, her lips drawn back in a grimace as she jabbed and parried. Isidro risked another glance back to see Garzen crawling towards them into the meagre shelter and then turned back just in time to clumsily parry the sweep of a sword. The attackers were pressing closer — a few more moments and they would be overwhelmed.

A fat blue spark crawled over the iron point of the chisel and the metal began to glow with a nimbus of blue light. Isidro stared and his attacker was startled enough to hesitate. His sword glowed, giving off a faint, mist-like haze and a minute bolt of lightning crackled over the steel, as fine as a hair and as long as man's arm. It was Black Sun's Fire, a rare phenomenon of the summer storms — Isidro had seen it only once before, and had never heard of it appearing in winter.

The witch-stone on the pommel of the man facing him blazed like a falling star. 'Witchcraft!' the man spat in Mesentreian and swung at Isidro's head. Isidro ducked back and then lunged forward and jabbed with the chisel just as another bolt arced from the steel to flail in the empty air. As the warrior jerked away from it a figure loomed out of the darkness behind him and the pale blue light flashed over Cam's face.

The point of a sword burst from the soldier's chest, glowing blue and flickering with lightning like a distant summer storm. With a strangled cry, the warrior stiffened and Cam whipped the blade free and slashed at the last man striking the rear of the camp. While the soldier tried to parry Cam's glowing sword Isidro caught him under the ribs with the ice-chisel. As he fell, Cam leapt to the top of the woodpile and down the other side.

'Garzen's down!' Isidro said. 'Where's Sierra?'

'You'll see her,' Cam said, and took Rhia's place beside Brekan.

An eerie blue light was creeping over the slope down to the river, flickering like firelight and growing steadily stronger.

A man at the back of the crowd of attackers shouted a warning, but his cry quickly became a shriek as thick ropes of jagged light wrapped around him and lifted him bodily into the air. He kicked and thrashed and screamed as the writhing lights cut through clothing and armour, biting deep into his flesh. Blood spattered onto the snow.

Sierra stepped into view. She stood at the centre of a storm of power while lightning tore and writhed at the air around her with the roar of a wildfire.

The attack faltered as the screams rang out and then abruptly stopped and the man fell with a sickening thump. The men at the back of the crowd gaped in horror at the demon approaching them. The men facing Cam and Brekan couldn't look away without leaving themselves open — one of them tried it and Cam killed him at once, only to be forced back again as his fellows surged forward with a shout of rage.

All the while Isidro's skin was tingling. Every hair on his body was standing on end and he could feel the energy coursing over his skin, humming like a bell the moment after the ringer strikes.

A few men at the edge of the crowd of attackers turned and ran for the trees just as the hum of power reached a crescendo.

Lightning burst out of the ground at their feet, erupting up from the snow like a forest of glowing spears; each one a strangling vine that wrapped a jagged tendril around the men facing them, bearing them to the ground in a sudden gout of blood. Light swarmed over them all, wrapping each of the men in a shroud of power while he screamed and thrashed, heaving beneath a veil that obscured everything but a fine mist of blood settling over the snow.

Mesmerised by the sight, Isidro couldn't look away until Brekan, gasping for breath, stumbled against him with one hand pressed to a bloody rent in his jacket. Isidro grabbed Brekan's arm with his good hand and tried to steady him as he fell to his knees. When he looked back the light was gone and Sierra stood alone amid a ruin of bodies and bloody snow, her eyes wide and sightless. Pure energy crackled in the air around her, questing strands rising up out of the ground and reaching high overhead so that she stood amid a tempest of light and power that bathed her in a flickering and unearthly glow.

'Help me!' Rhia cried, her voice breaking the spell. She was kneeling at Garzen's side with his shirt open and her hand buried inside the wound beneath his ribs as she worked to staunch the bleeding. Judging from the trail of blood Garzen had left when he dragged himself back, she was fighting a losing battle. Isidro's makeshift spear fell from his numb fingers and he stumbled back and out of the way as the others swarmed around to help her.

'I need light!' Rhia shouted, with a sob in her voice. 'Bring blankets! Someone make a stretcher. As soon as the bleeding slows, we must carry him inside.'

Garzen was conscious, but beneath the tattoos his face was drained of blood and his lips were tinged with blue. 'Too late for that,' he whispered.

Light blazed over his body and Isidro glanced up, expecting to see Lakua with a lamp, but it was Sierra, her hand cupped around a glowing sphere the size of a child's fist.

'Demon!' Rhia spat at her. 'Get away from him! Haven't you taken enough lives for one night?'

Sierra ignored her. 'I can help you,' she said to Garzen.

Garzen shook his head. 'You can't, girl, I'm dying.'

'I know,' Sierra said. 'I can't change that. But I can take the pain. I can give you peace.'

'Don't say that!' Rhia said. 'You will not die! I will not let you!' Blood was welling around her hand and Garzen gave a low moan of pain. There was a sour, acrid stink in the air, the scent of vomit and bile, and Isidro had seen enough of war and butchery to know Sierra was right. The wound had pierced his gut — even if Rhia could halt the bleeding Garzen would still die a slow and painful death as it seeped poison into his body.

Sierra pulled off her gloves and laid her hands on Garzen's bare chest. He gasped at her touch and arched his back with a groan of pain, but then he relaxed and took a deep, shuddering breath. 'Ah ... by the Black Sun, it's gone,' he whispered, and laid his head back on the snow as all the tension and fear drained from his weathered face. 'The Black Sun, she calls to me ...'

Sierra backed away leaving room for Rhia and the other women to gather around him. Eloba cradled Garzen's hand between her own. 'The home-fires are lit to guide you,' she said through her tears. 'All your kin are coming to g-greet you ...'

Isidro waited for Garzen to speak and say the final part of the ritual for the dying. Some long moments passed before he realised Garzen had died.

Eloba threw her head back and wailed. Lakua, her arms around her sister, added her own voice to the keen.

'No!' Rhia dug her bloody fingers into the hollow of Garzen's jaw, and when she felt no pulse she rose to her knees to pound on his chest, as though she could pummel his heart into beating again.

'Rhia,' Isidro said, reaching for her arm. She slapped his hand away.

'Rhia.' Cam dropped down beside her, wrapped his arms around her shoulders and pulled her away. 'Rhia, he's gone. Leave him be.'

# Chapter 10

Taking hold of one of the warrior's arms, Cam dragged the bloody corpse to the edge of the woods where the dead were arrayed in a rough line. 'You should have told me.'

'I told you as soon as I'd worked it out myself.'

'Rhia swears she killed Garzen.'

'What do you think?' Isidro said. 'Maybe she could have stopped the bleeding, but you and I have both seen men die from gut wounds. There are some folk I might wish it on, but I'd rather see a friend die quickly than end his days screaming in pain.'

Cam didn't reply at once. He just looked over the line of dead men with his face blank and impassive.

It was an unnerving sight, even to men who were familiar with the aftermath of a battle. Some of the corpses looked no different than any other men who had fallen beneath swords in a battle, but others seemed to have been flayed and some were blackened and scorched as though a great fire had blazed around them.

Cam looked away from them. 'It's just ...' he began, but then broke off with a shake of his head.

'What is it?' Isidro said.

'When we pulled you out of the water, you were dead. Your face was blue, you weren't breathing and your heart had stopped, but Rhia wouldn't give up, and she brought you back. After that ... for the first week, you just kept getting sicker. We thought you'd never wake again, and we told ourselves at least he'll die among friends. But Rhia wouldn't give up. She sat up night after night, brewing her potions and making you drink them a spoonful at a time. She brought you back from the dead, Isidro.'

'She's probably the finest physician we'll ever meet,' Isidro said. 'But even the best can't save everyone.'

Cam sighed. 'I know that. I do.' He glanced in the direction Sierra had taken when she left the camp in a trail of sparks. 'I just don't trust her.'

'Trust her? By the Black Sun, do you think we'd be free right now without her? We'd either be dead or in chains.'

Cam grimaced, but didn't deny it.

'She's in the same position we are.'

'Except that she won't be killed if she's caught.'

'Kell won't kill her,' Isidro said. 'He'll give her to Rasten to break her will. He'll torture and warp and poison her until she's just like him. Can you blame her for doing whatever it takes to avoid that?'

Cam didn't reply, but turned to survey the carnage Sierra had left on the snow.

'I don't think she can control it,' Isidro said. 'From what she was saying, Kell was wary of her powers — he was careful not to teach her anything she could use against him and he relied on the enchantments to control her.'

'Is that supposed to be reassuring?' Cam demanded. He stared intently at the scattered trees opposite. 'Black Sun take her, she's coming back.'

With Brekan wounded and the women still overcome with grief, Sierra had volunteered to check on the intruders' camp where the horses had been tethered, to make sure the survivors hadn't retreated there to regroup, but also, Isidro suspected, to give her a chance to regain control of her power. There couldn't have been many survivors — a bare handful at the most.

'Cam,' Isidro said. 'There's an important thing I think you're forgetting here.'

'What's that?' Cam didn't take his eyes off the young woman heading towards them.

'The enemy of my enemy is my friend.'

Cam turned to him with a frown. 'What are you suggesting?'

'She's as desperate as we are. When the one who sent these men realises they're not coming back, she'll need us as badly as we need her. And then there's the Akharians to consider. We've no way to face their mages, but someone like her ...'

Cam grew tense as Sierra approached, even though she stopped a good few paces away, making an effort not to crowd him. 'They were there,' she said. 'It looks as if they took a few things from the sled and ran.'

'How many?' Cam said.

'Four, one of them wounded. It might be a good idea to take one of the horses and fetch what's left of their gear. They only took what they could carry — there might be things we could use.'

Cam nodded stiffly.

'Look,' Sierra said. 'I know you don't want me here — and I don't want to endanger your people any more than I already have. There's got to be a tent and a stove among the gear they left and I can cut down a sled to a size I can haul myself. I'll trade my horse for whatever supplies you can spare — the Black Sun knows I have no idea how to look after the beast, anyway.'

'That would probably be for the best,' Cam agreed.

'Don't be stupid,' Isidro said. 'She can't — ' He turned to Sierra. 'You can't head off on your own. You might be fine in the dark, but it'll be days before your eyes have recovered enough to see in daylight. And then there's the matter of the stones. If anyone does recognise them they're likely to send another division out to track us down.'

'What do you mean, *if* they recognise them?' Sierra said. 'Why else would they have come here?'

'There's a good chance someone in the village recognised Cam and *that's* what drew them here,' Isidro said. 'But sooner or later someone will either identify the stones or wonder where a score of soldiers have disappeared to —'

'Or the ones who fled will make it back to tell their story,' Cam said.

'Exactly,' Isidro said. 'They'll find the bodies — and our trail.' He caught Cam's eye. 'It's better for everyone if Sierra stays with us.'

Cam turned away, kicking idly at a clump of snow. 'Well, we can't go on like this,' he said to no one in particular. 'Isidro, once you were well enough to travel we were planning to get away from this thrice-cursed battlefield and head east to ask the Wolf Clan for shelter. At the moment we've got enough supplies to reach the cache we left at the beginning of winter, but if we divide them up now it'll be a close thing, especially when we don't know how fast you'll be able to travel. What say we travel together until then? If there's no pursuit, we'll have supplies enough to send Sierra on her way. Unless you'd rather try to claim sanctuary from the Wolf Clan?' He turned to her with one eyebrow raised. 'You could be of use in this war — if what you say is true and the legions do march this way.'

'Hah,' Sierra said. 'I can't see a noble clan jeopardising their position for a demon like me, however many legions and Akharian mages they face.'

'You may be right about that,' Cam said. 'I'll have to put it to Rhia and the others. I can tell you now they won't like it, but it's safer than parting ways right now.' He kept watching her with a steady gaze. 'So *that's* how you know so much of the king's plans and the enemy's movements. Were you at Kell's side the whole time?'

'Not exactly.' Sierra glanced away, her face neutral and impassive. 'I was there when they interrogated the captured scouts. The rest I truly did overhear.'

When Cam started back towards the tents, Isidro followed and Sierra started after them, but then she stopped, turning towards the trees. 'Wait,' she called after them as another bolt of light crackled through her hair. 'There's someone back there in the trees.'

Cam stopped in his tracks and laid a hand on the hilt of his sword. 'Where?'

At Sierra's side, Isidro could see nothing, but she led them into the stand of trees where a trail of blood on the snow brought them to a young soldier with one of Eloba's arrows in his belly. He sat with his back against a tree and one hand coiled loosely around the shaft.

Cam nudged him with his toe and the soldier roused with a shudder and a low moan. 'Well, what do you know?' Cam said, drawing his belt knife. 'He's still alive.'

'Wait,' Sierra said, and crouched down beside the soldier. A thin strand of lightning skittered across her shoulders. She lightly touched the boy's cheek but when that elicited no response, she slapped him, and his eyes fluttered open. She looked up at Cam and Isidro. 'We might be able find out why they came here and how long we have before anyone notices they're gone.'

Isidro felt his stomach lurch. Something must have shown on his face because Cam turned to him with a frown. 'Isidro —'

He shook his head. 'It's nothing.'

'But —'

'I can handle it, Cam. She's right — it's better to know exactly what we're facing.'

Cam watched him with narrowed eyes for a moment longer and then turned to Sierra. 'I'll get his arms, you grab his legs. We'll put him in the smaller tent until we're ready to deal with him.'

'Better get Rhia to have a look at him,' Isidro said. 'With an arrow in his ribs he might not last long enough to answer any questions.'

Sierra crouched down beside him and held one hand an inch above his chest. 'I'd say he's got a few hours yet, so long as we leave the arrow in place. Does Eloba use broadheads or bodkin-points?'

'Broadheads. Hunting arrows. If we remove it, it'll do enough damage to make him bleed out.'

Sierra nodded. 'Well, we won't have to worry about him escaping. The arrow lodged in his spine. He'll never walk again.'

'How do you know?' Cam said.

Sierra shrugged but she wouldn't meet his gaze. 'It's what I do.'

Together she and Cam hauled the moaning soldier into the smaller tent, where Cam found a leather thong and tied the prisoner's hands together behind his back and then tethered them to one of the tent poles. He bound a spare sash over the soldier's eyes for a blindfold, then they left him.

Inside the other tent Rhia was sewing up a long gash across Brekan's ribs. When he'd stumbled back, Isidro hadn't seen the extent of the wounds, but from the grimace of pain on Brekan's face and the way he held himself it was more than just a cut. Lakua was at the stove, stirring something in a pot. Eloba was doing her best to repair the slash in the tent, but her hands were trembling and she had to stop with every stitch to wipe tears from her eyes. She and Garzen had grown very close, fishing and trapping together often enough to make Brekan grow jealous.

When Sierra followed Cam and Isidro into the tent everyone fell silent.

'How bad is it?' Isidro said to Brekan, breaking the silence.

It was Rhia who answered. 'His ribs are cracked. It will take a few weeks for him to be fit again.' She craned her head to look him and Cam over. 'Is anyone else hurt?'

'No,' said Cam. 'Bright Sun be thanked.'

That was scant comfort. Brekan was an indifferent fighter but his injury left Cam as their only warrior. Eloba was skilled with a bow but she used no other weapons.

'We're going to have to leave here, and soon,' Cam said. 'A few men survived the battle and for all we know they've managed to track down their horses and ride for help. We have time for a few hours' sleep, but we need to be off and moving well before first light.'

'What about Garzen?' Eloba said. 'We need to build a pyre ... or dig up stones to cover him, at the very least.'

Cam scrubbed a hand over his face. 'We don't have time for either. The best we can do is build a cairn of branches over him.'

Eloba stared at him open-mouthed. 'That's *horrible*! How can you even suggest such a thing?'

'Eloba, this isn't over. The battle we fought tonight is just the beginning — time is against us, and now we have two wounded people to care for —'

'I don't need to be cared for,' Brekan spat. 'I'm not an invalid. I'll pull my weight, don't you worry.'

Cam ignored him. 'The needs of the living outweigh the needs of the dead. Garzen believed that too, we all know it.'

'Um ... may I make a suggestion?' Sierra said. 'There's a fair store of firewood behind these tents. We don't have time to let a pyre burn out, but we could start one burning. That would be better than leaving him in a cairn any beast could break into.'

Eloba narrowed her eyes. 'It'll go out if it's not tended. That's not a clean burial. Once the flames die down the foxes and weasels will eat what's left and scatter his bones.'

'Is there anything you can do?' Isidro said to Sierra. 'If the fire burns hot enough —'

'No!' Eloba shouted. 'Isn't it enough that you want to leave him without a proper burial? You want to desecrate him too? She's a monster! She brought this down upon us!' She turned to Sierra. 'Child of the Black Sun,' she spat. 'He would have lived if it weren't for you.'

Brekan cleared his throat. 'She made me take the stones,' he said. 'She put a spell on me. I didn't want to do it.'

'Brekan, shut your cursed mouth,' Cam said without bothering to look at him. 'I've no time for your horseshit right now. Eloba, it will have to be a pyre — we don't have time to go digging through the river ice for stones. Will you build it? Of all of us, you were closest to Garzen.'

Eloba blinked. 'Alright then. But she doesn't touch it,' she said, nodding to Sierra.

'I'll help you,' Lakua said. 'And we'll call the rest of you when it's ready to light.'

'Good,' Cam said. 'When we move out, we're heading for the cache we left in autumn. Sierra's going to travel with us that far.'

'I won't have it,' Brekan said. 'She's not staying in my camp.'

'When you have your own camp, you can make that decision,' Cam snapped. 'I say she stays. Issey's right — we'd be prisoners now if she hadn't been here and now we're down two warriors. Sierra was Lord Kell's apprentice before she escaped, and the men who survived tonight will report back that she was with us. Make no mistake, they will be after us.'

'But …' Lakua said. 'Even if she leaves us now, it'll be us they track, because we'll leave a clearer trail.'

'Yes,' said Cam. 'Once we reach the cache, we'll have to get a message to Ruhavera and beg the Wolf Clan for sanctuary. At this point, we have no other choice. Does anyone have any questions?'

When no one responded, Eloba stood and reached for her coat. 'I'll start stacking the wood. Laki, will you come with me?'

Lakua looked to Rhia, who nodded. 'Go. That hide will be soft enough by now and Cam can help me wrap it.'

Lakua nodded and followed Eloba to the door. 'Oh, and another thing,' Cam said before they left. 'One of the soldiers was still alive — we've got him trussed up in your tent.'

Eloba grimaced. 'Question him all you like, but I don't want to know about it. And bring him in here to do it, will you? I've seen enough blood for one day, I don't want it splattered over the walls where I sleep.'

'We'll bring him in here,' Cam agreed, and the women left.

Her stitching finished, Rhia turned away from Brekan and lifted the soaked leather from the pot with a twig. Her back was stiff as she wrung the water from it. 'So, Cam, you will become a torturer?'

'It was my idea,' Sierra said. 'I won't ask anyone else to do my dirty work.'

Rhia ignored her. 'I would have thought you had seen enough of the effects of torture to renounce its evils forever.'

108

'Rhia, there are things we need to know,' Cam said, his voice apologetic but unflinching. 'Our safety depends on it.'

Rhia wound a bandage over a padding of clean rags on Brekan's chest. 'Help me with this,' she ordered Cam as she began wrapping the damp leather. It would shrink as it dried, pulling tight over the ribs as they healed. 'And what of your prisoner, then?' Rhia said. 'Will you cut his throat and leave him for the crows, or will you just leave him in the snow to freeze?'

'He's dying anyway,' Cam said. 'Sierra thinks that the arrow pierced his spine. But we'd need you to look at him to be certain, of course.'

'Hmph,' Rhia said. 'I will stay. I will not look the other way and pretend I do not see evil when it is done in my presence. You are done,' she said to Brekan. 'Stay somewhere warm until the leather dries; it would not be wise for you to take a chill.'

Brekan dressed quickly and left without a word. More than anything, Isidro wanted to leave with him, but he would not let himself move. Panic was warring with his nerves, making his heart beat faster and squeezing his chest so tight it was hard to breathe. But he wouldn't let himself give in.

Desperate for some distraction he cast about the tent and his eye fell on Sierra. Her face was impassive, an expressionless mask, but it seemed that he could feel a force pulsing in waves over his skin, sending goosebumps prickling beneath his clothes. He'd felt it before, he realised, in those moments before she'd stepped out behind the attackers, and earlier still when she'd left the tent in distress. Was he sensing her power building in those moments before it spilled over? If that was the case then her calm was all an act and she was hiding some great tension beneath that impassive gaze. But after two years with Kell he couldn't be sure if it was excitement or dread she was hiding. *My power comes from the pain of others ...*

'Isidro? Do you hear me?'

Isidro shook himself, realising that Rhia had been talking to him. She pressed her lips together and gave him a look of such pity it made him grit his teeth in anger. 'Isidro, you should not watch this. Go sit with Brekan, or help Eloba with the pyre.'

'No,' he said. 'I'll stay.'

'Issey ...' Cam said with a frown.

'Oh, leave the man be,' Sierra said as she began clearing a space for their prisoner. 'He knows his own mind. Don't keep harping on at him like a child.'

Cam frowned at her back but all he said was, 'I'll bring him in then. Rhia, I'll need your help to move him, and Isidro, a word?'

Isidro followed him outside where the cold air hit him like a slap in the face. While he shivered, sweat was beading around the scars on his back. Even in the quiet and stillness of the night he felt as if the world was too loud, pressing so close he couldn't breathe.

'Issey, don't do this,' Rhia said. 'I know what you're thinking, but believe me, you have nothing to prove.' She laid a hand on his arm, but Isidro shrugged it off. He knew she meant him no harm, but in his mind he couldn't separate her touch from the memory of the leather cords they'd used to tie him down. *It's in the past*, he told himself firmly. *It's over. They did all they could to me, but I still won.* That was the reason Isidro had survived all they'd done to him with his mind and will unbroken — Cam was beyond their reach and that meant they'd lost.

'Issey …' Cam settled a hand on his shoulder, and Isidro flinched violently, stumbling back out of reach.

'Don't touch me!'

Cam pulled back, raising his hands in a gesture of peace. 'I'm sorry. By the Black Sun herself …'

Isidro turned his face into the wind and imagined for a moment that it could blow right through him and carry him away, scatter him across the sky like smoke from a fire. The pain would be gone and the memories of that time would no longer torment him.

'Don't worry about it,' Cam said. 'But stay out here, will you? You don't need to watch this.'

Isidro nodded. He couldn't bring himself to look his brother in the face. 'I'll stay with him while you see to the prisoner,' Rhia murmured to Cam as they headed into the tent where the dying soldier was waiting. 'Do whatever you feel you must.'

But Isidro left them behind and trudged down the slope towards the frozen river, where he hoped he'd be far enough away not to hear the sounds of what they'd do to make the soldier talk.

He'd been fearless once. No man could be master of the Ricalani winter but he'd been as much a creature of it as any beast that lived in the frozen north. He still knew the ways of the forest and the snow, but his life in Ricalan had ended with the first blow of Rasten's club. All his knowledge and experience was useless to him now. Rasten had left him as helpless as a babe in arms — there was no room for a cripple in this harsh world.

*Keep walking*, said a small voice in the back of his mind. *Just keep walking and let the winter take you. Cam will spend the rest of his life looking after you and it will doom you both. Just keep walking and it will all be over.*

Isidro pictured the water flowing beneath the ice. He could feel the world moving on around him, just like that water, but he was fixed in one place, rooted to the ice and unable to move with it.

Some moments later, a long scream of agony rang out, carrying clearly through the cold air. He turned without thinking and saw the tent flap swing open and a slender, dark-haired figure stumble out and stagger a few paces before she fell to her knees and retched into the snow.


The prisoner struggled as Cam drew the knife across his throat, throwing himself about with a strength he hadn't expected from a man paralysed from the waist down. The knife didn't bite quite deep enough and the prisoner got one scream out before Cam finished him off. He looked up just in time to see Sierra stumble out of the tent and double over to vomit into the snow. He followed her out to see the other women stopped in their tracks and staring at her with their arms still full of cut wood for the pyre.

Cam crunched over the snow to Sierra's side. The blood on his hands had already dried to dark smears, the moisture whipped away by the dry and icy wind. He gathered up her tangled hair and held it back from her face as she doubled over again. It was a peculiarly intimate gesture — he'd only ever run his hands through a lover's hair and that was a far cry from the stinking, visceral moment that had brought them together now.

Sierra spat and gathered up a handful of snow to wipe her mouth.

'All done?' he said.

She nodded. 'You might have warned me first.'

'Warned you?'

'Before you cut his throat.' She ran shaking fingers over the winter-pale skin of her neck. 'I don't just take power from it. I *feel* it, too.'

'Oh,' he said, and then he understood. 'Oh. I didn't realise. I'm sorry ...'

'It doesn't usually get me quite so badly, but you took me by surprise.' She brushed some loose snow over the mess and sat back on her heels, still too shaky to stand. Cam's hands had grown numb with the cold and he tucked them into his armpits as he crouched on his heels beside her.

'Tell me,' he said. 'Would you have done it? If you hadn't been able to just scare him into talking, would you really have tortured him?'

There were deep shadows under her eyes, so dark they looked like bruises. 'I don't know, Cam. I really don't know.'

# Chapter 11

The horse slipped and stumbled on the icy path. The movement ripped Rasten's shirt away from the wounds on his back and he snatched at the pommel of his saddle, biting back a curse. When the king's cousin had dragged him out to investigate this supposed sighting of the fugitive prince, Rasten had been torn between resentment that Osebian was pulling him away from the search for Sierra and gratitude for taking him beyond Kell's reach, even if just for a few days. Losing Sierra, together with the first skirmishes with the Akharians, had aroused in Kell a lust for blood and pain that would not be sated.

Somewhere behind him one of the men sniggered. 'Look at 'im squirm! Just like a virgin in a brothel! I 'eard 'is master sends 'im out with a broomstick up 'is arse, just to remind 'im who's bitch 'e is.'

Ah. A distraction — just what he needed. Rasten turned in the saddle, his aches forgotten. He knew which man had spoken by the way his comrades edged their horses away from him, steadfastly avoiding his gaze.

The man was drunk. His face was red and he listed in the saddle, leaning so badly it was throwing his horse off balance. Many of the men had brought flasks of strong liquor with them to stave off the cold, as they would be riding through the night to reach the village where Cammarian had been sighted, but most of them were wise enough not to get stupidly drunk in the presence of Lord Kell's apprentice.

Rasten wrapped a cord of power around the soldier's neck and lifted him from the saddle. The men around him scrambled out of the way and when the weary horse shied out from beneath his kicking legs, one of them caught the reins and led it quietly away. No one spoke or tried to come to the defence of their comrade, who was kicking at empty air and clawing at the insubstantial cord crushing his throat.

As the men milled around in the road those coming up behind had no choice but to stop. There was a commotion from the front of the line as well, as those at the head realised what was going on behind them.

The drunken soldier's red face was turning purple, his eyes bulging from their sockets. Rasten threw his head back as the power surged through him, flowing from the amulet the man wore on a leather thong around his neck. Before they had set out, every one of these soldiers had been issued with an amulet which allowed him to draw power from them without the preparation of a ritual. If by chance they did run across an Akharian sortie it would give him a distinct advantage, no matter how many of their Battle Mages were spread among the legionaries.

Having Sierra around had spoiled him with power — he and Kell both had grown too used to having her there, a seemingly endless reservoir of power to be tapped at will. The last few days had felt like a famine in comparison, even with the captured Akharians to feed upon.

With a clatter of hooves on ice the duke guided his horse into the circle of bare ground the men had left around Rasten and reined in sharply. 'Is there a problem, Lord Rasten?' Osebian said. He looked over the struggling, strangling man with no more concern than he would show for a horse that had slipped a shoe.

'You need to pay more attention to the discipline of your men,' Rasten said.

'I'll mention it to my captain,' Osebian said. 'What did he do?'

'Ask your men,' Rasten said. 'Let's see if any of them dare repeat it.'

Osebian turned to the man who had ridden to fetch him and raised one inquiring eyebrow. The soldier simply shook his head. 'Well,' Osebian said. 'If Lord Kell's apprentice believes the matter is important enough to warrant his concern, far be it from me to contradict him. But I will remind you, Lord Rasten, the trail grows colder with every moment. The king will be displeased if he hears that avoidable delays caused us to lose his trail.' He pursed his lips, watching the feebly struggling drunk. 'If it's his life you want, I'll have his head off for you now, so we may at least keep moving.'

Rasten released the man and he fell to the road with a force that cracked the bone of his thigh. Too winded to cry out, the soldier lay there gasping like a landed fish. 'That won't be necessary,' Rasten said. 'Take his weapons and bind him to a horse — but don't splint the leg.'

'See to it,' Osebian snapped to the nearest soldier and turned his mount. 'If we might press on, Lord Rasten?'

It was well past midnight by the time they reached the village. A handful of sleepy sentries stood watch around a signal fire to guide them in and, as soon as the duke's personal guard of fifty men appeared out of the darkness, one of the sentries ran into the village to tell the commander of their arrival. Now that the first clashes with the Akharians had begun, and it was clear that at least one legion was marching eastwards, the men stationed in this part of the country had been ordered to pull out and report to the king's encampment, but when Cammarian had been sighted, they'd had no choice but to pitch camp again and await further orders. As much as the king wanted the fugitive prince dead, he wanted Cammarian dead by his own command, not slaughtered by some nameless foreign soldier.

Osebian left his men at the Mesentreian camp and rode with Rasten into the village itself, escorted by a soldier to the house their commander had taken for his quarters. An aide was waiting for them at the door and he bowed deeply as he ushered them through to the chamber where Captain Corasan was waiting.

'Your grace, Lord Rasten,' Corasan greeted them, while a servant prepared mulled wine over a brazier. 'I am honoured by your presence. I wasn't certain until now, your grace, but seeing your face, I have no doubt. You do bear a striking resemblance to Queen Valeria, and I do say you look so like the man I saw today you could be his brother —'

The man droned on, but Rasten had stopped listening. There was something in the air here, a frisson of energy that skittered over his skin. He accepted the tankard from the servant and drained half of it in a gulp, then stalked around the room, searching for the source of the power. Usually only a powerful enchantment could be sensed from a distance, but one that he had made or participated in making always had a more powerful pull than one made by a stranger.

'Captain,' Rasten said, interrupting the man mid-sentence. 'You have in your possession a square-cut ruby the size of a fingernail —' He hesitated for a moment, frowning. 'More than one, I think. Show them to me.'

The captain's jaw dropped, but he recovered himself with a hasty bow. 'At once, my lord.' He barked a command to his servant, who opened the officer's campaign chest and took out a small parcel of silk. The officer unwrapped it, and placed it gingerly in Rasten's palm.

A dozen rubies were nestled in the square of silk and the deep red stones winked at him in the lamplight. Rasten brushed one with his fingertip and it sent a searing jolt of heat through his hand.

The enchantments were intact. It was only when he heaved a sigh of relief that Rasten realised he'd been holding his breath. The stones Sierra had been wearing were worth far more than the reward offered for her, more than enough to justify killing her to get at them. Killing a sorcerer of her calibre wasn't easy, but there were ways it could be done. But if Sierra *had* met a violent end the discharge of energy at her death would have destroyed the enchantments and could well have shattered the stones themselves. 'Where did these come from?' Rasten asked.

'It would appear that one of the men in the prince's company sold them,' Corasan said.

'He's not a prince,' Osebian growled. 'The king disinherited him; the dowager disowned him. He's nothing but an outlaw.'

'My apologies, your grace,' the captain said with a bow. 'As I was saying, my lords, Cammarian was travelling with two companions, a man and a woman. The man sold these stones to the village smith —'

'A woman?' Rasten said. 'What did she look like?'

'It was not the woman you are searching for, Lord Rasten,' Corasan said. 'My men checked every female who entered the village against the portrait that was circulated and I saw this one myself.'

'Go on, captain,' Osebian said. 'How did Cammarian identify himself?'

'He had papers identifying himself as belonging to a southern clan. They appeared genuine, my lord …'

'Forgeries,' Osebian said. 'It's known that he has sympathisers among the clans. No doubt one of them supplied him with identification.'

Rasten only half listened. The humiliation of coming so close to the prince only to have him slip between their fingers still stung, but Sierra was far more important. Clearly, though, they'd underestimated Cammarian — for years, they had all assumed he was as dull-witted as his brother the king and that Isidro Balorica was the brains of the pair.

'I do have a list of the goods he and his servants purchased — supplies and horse feed for the most part, but he also asked for a particular list of medicinals —'

Rasten's head snapped up. 'Let me see that,' he said and snatched the list from the captain's hands. They had believed that Balorica was dead — the remains of the caravan taking him to Lathayan had been found, along with the frozen-over hole in the river where the wagon had fallen through the ice. The enchantments Kell had left on him would have kept him alive long enough to reach Lathayan but they would do nothing to protect him against further injury. Even a mild bout of hypothermia on top of the injuries he had already sustained should have been enough to finish him. The list said otherwise. Rasten had studied enough healing to know the properties of the medicines and compounds on the list. 'Well, what do you know?' he said. 'It appears that Balorica is still alive — although judging from this list, not exactly well.' He kept reading and frowned. 'And what's this? Your report says the woman left the blacksmith's house with a kitbag, but there's no mention of what it contained.'

'Well,' Corasan said with a nervous smile. 'I don't see that it could have been important ...' He faltered at Rasten's black look.

'Imbecile,' Rasten said.

'Uh, if I may interrupt, my lords?' the aide said. 'I did speak to the women of the blacksmith's household. I'm sure it was simply an oversight that it was left out of the report —'

'Get to the point, man,' Rasten said. 'What did she get from the women?'

'Clothing, my lord. I understand she told them she'd lost a bag off a sled and needed to replace a full kit.'

Rasten closed his eyes. If he'd still had any faith in the Gods, he might have offered up a prayer of thanks, but as it was he merely held onto the thought in an ecstasy of relief. She was alive, alive and with people. Sorcerer or not, a person alone with only the clothes on her back could not expect to survive long in a Ricalani winter. It was nothing short of a wonder that she hadn't fallen into Akharian hands, or blundered into an outlaw camp — but it was sheer bad luck that she'd stumbled into the company of the one man in Ricalan who couldn't be tempted to turn her in for the reward.

If he could offer to commute Cammarian's death warrant into a sentence of exile, then he might be induced to cooperate and hand her over ... but there was no way he would agree to it without Balorica and they could not let a Sensitive like him live after being subject to the rituals. In any case, Valeria would never consent to giving up the spectacle of a public execution, not after the humiliation her younger son had put her through.

'I'm afraid it took me some time to put it all together and recognise the fugitive, but once I did I sent a score of my best men to bring him back. They had gear to make camp but I ordered them to ride straight back if the weather held. They can't have been more than a few hours behind the outlaw, so I expect them here by first light —'

'Your men are dead,' Rasten said, crumpling the report into a ball. 'I'll need pen and ink and one of your men to carry a message to my master.' Kell would punish him for failing to reach him directly with this news, but Rasten was too weary and too pained to make contact at this hour.

'We'll have trouble finding the tracks if we ride out now, as much as it pains me to stay away from the fighting,' Osebian said. 'The men have been riding through the night — they're as likely to trample the trail as follow it.'

'In the morning, then,' Rasten said. He truly didn't care about the war at their backs. It made no difference to him who ruled this country, or whose blood spilled over the snow. There was nothing here he would fight to protect, except Sierra. Ever since she'd fled, the concerns of the army and the king had seemed nothing more than a distraction, an annoyance sent to plague him. Even the brief battles as the Akharians tested the enemy's strength and the power he wrung from the prisoners to meet them couldn't draw his thoughts away from her, and the rage and despair that had overcome him when he found her gone. 'We'll need a couple of local men to help our trackers,' Rasten said.

'I'll see to it,' Corasan said. 'And I'll have one of the houses cleared for your men tonight, to spare them the trouble of setting up tents and stoves.'

'Very well,' Osebian said with a nod. 'You may go.'

Corasan hurried out, muttering orders to his aide.

There was a wicker chair padded with sheepskins beside the stove and Rasten gingerly eased himself into it. His back had stiffened during the ride and his muscles were rigid and throbbing.

'It's a great deal of trouble to go to for the sake of one barbarian girl,' Osebian said, his voice heavy with doubt.

'You've no idea what you're talking about, lordling,' Rasten said. He closed his hands around the rubies. The scrap of silk offered little protection and they felt like coals burning their way into his palm. 'No idea at all.'

The threatening weather had blown over with only a scatter of snow and it looked as though the day would dawn crisp and clear. Luck, Cam reflected as he squinted up at the stars, was not on their side. They needed low cloud and mist to shroud them and snow to bury their tracks. Still, what could he expect, when they had a creature like Sierra in their party?

He halted the horse he was leading and pulled his water-skin out from under his coat, where the warmth of his body kept it from freezing. As he took a swig the mare he was leading jogged his arm with her long nose and he spilled a stream of water over his cowl and into the furred front of his jacket. He snatched at her halter with a curse. 'Hold still, you wretched old cow, or I'll stake you out for tiger bait.' She bared her teeth to snap at him, then rolled her eyes and tossed her head when he took a swipe at her nose. The spilled water was already freezing in his clothes and with a shiver he tucked the water-skin away and took hold of the horse's halter again.

Rhia was standing on the trampled path ahead, gazing back behind them and squinting into the pre-dawn gloom. 'Watch yourself, Rhia,' Cam growled. 'If you're going to stand around, please make sure you're off the cursed path.'

She winced. 'My apologies, Cam. I was just checking on Isidro.'

'He can shout for help if he needs it,' Cam said. The restive horse pawed at the ground with one forefoot, flapping the snowshoe buckled to its hoof. 'Stop it, you miserable beast,' Cam said, and tugged on the halter rope. When he'd buckled the snowshoes on that morning he'd noticed they were showing signs of wear, but he wasn't sure how best to repair them. Garzen had been the one who understood such things.

The horse started forward again and Rhia hurried out of the way, turning a careful circle in her snowshoes. Within a few paces, the toboggan the mare was hauling ran up on something concealed beneath the snow and tipped, slewing down the slope towards the river. The ropes wrapped around the mare's hindquarters and she baulked, treading nervously in the twisted traces.

'Oh, for pity's sake,' Cam said. 'Rhia, hold her head.'

'I'll help you —'

'No, just hold her head! The wretched beast won't stand still for more than two moments together ...'

He'd gone up to his knees in the snow before he got the sled turned on its right side again, but it was still angled down the slope, with its tow ropes dragging across the horse's hocks. With a sigh, Cam pulled the brake rope out from where it had been tucked within the sled wrapper. He played the rope out and wrapped the end around his fist. A couple of the other horses could be guided by voice, but Cam had let Lakua and Eloba take those and kept the most difficult one for himself. They only had three sleds — the rest of the gear had been loaded onto packhorses, which were left in the charge of Rhia and Brekan. 'What happened to your horse?' he said as Rhia began to lead the stroppy mare forward.

'Brekan took him. He said he could lead two as well as one.'

By walking higher along the slope and keeping the rope taut, Cam could keep the toboggan from sliding downwards. The two of them got the mare moving again, but Rhia kept looking back, paying so little attention to her feet she caught her snowshoes together and stumbled and they had to stop again.

'Bright Sun, Rhia! Watch where you're going!'

She shot him a black look. 'Someone should be watching Isidro with that whelp of a Blood-Mage. Only a fool sets a fox to watch over the weakest lamb. We should not let them fall so far behind.'

'Isidro's not stupid,' Cam said. 'I spoke to him this morning, before we moved out. I told him to be on his guard.'

'He is weak and he is wounded. He is nothing but prey to her. Trust me, Cam. I have seen her like before. In Mesentreia, where I lived with my master, there was a lord who kept a mage, and the mage had an apprentice, a boy like her. The mage was a poor physician and my master was often called to attend to his victims when the lord wished to keep them alive. When we first met the boy he pleaded with us to help him escape and find his way back to his family. A few months later, he was begging for poison. Within a year he was wielding the irons and the knives beside his master. Their power consumes them, Cam. They are no more than beasts, enslaved by their lust for blood and pain.'

He'd heard such tales before. They were lucky in a way that Kell was so powerful. He wouldn't tolerate any other Blood-Mages in Ricalan. It meant they had only Kell and his apprentice to worry about: there were no other mages who would try to poach Sierra for themselves. 'What happened to him?' Cam said. 'The apprentice?'

'He turned on his master and the mage killed him,' Rhia said. 'This one is already far gone. You saw how she fed off the men who fell. Isidro would be a great prize for her — she will feed from him like a tick sucking blood. I am afraid for him, Cam.'

It was still dark enough to allow Sierra to ride with her eyes uncovered and she watched Isidro's back as he rode. He left the reins slack on his horse's neck, guiding it with his knees and heels while he kept his left hand wrapped around the pommel of the saddle. He rarely glanced up from the path, even when a snowshoe hare burst from a tangle of branches beside his horse's feet and bolted across the track. It was only when his horse snorted and tossed its head in sudden fright that he stirred himself to look around.

The path Cam had chosen was not an easy one. The smoothest route would have them following the frozen riverbed, which provided a flat and unobstructed road, but one that meandered back and forth across the countryside rather than cutting straight as a crow flies. Instead the path they took cut across the bends in the river, and every mile or so they had to scramble up or down a riverbank over jagged, slippery ice or a thin crust of snow that broke under their horses' weight, even with the snowshoes.

Every shift of weight, every awkward step, sent a jolt of pain through Isidro's broken arm and a ripple of energy along Sierra's nerves. If they were attacked, at least she'd have power to fight, but she carried so much that her mind was buzzing with it. She felt drunk on power, giddy with it and horribly ashamed that another person's suffering could make her feel this way.

When she couldn't bear it any more, she kicked her horse forward and rode up to Isidro's side. He barely acknowledged her, glancing up only briefly; his face incurious and his eyelids heavy with weariness and pain.

The events of that first night still weighed on her mind. Isidro didn't seem to remember it at all but to Sierra it was still vivid and fresh. She had come within a hair's breadth of killing him, but afterwards ... afterwards he had been free of pain for the span of half a day. And last night, when Garzen died she felt that flow of power again. He had been

121

only minutes away from death, but she had known even then that she could have killed him if she wished, could have drained him through the conduit of power created by the wound. That time she had known when it crossed the line into dangerous ground and she choked off the flow before she could drain the power that kept his heart beating. The last moments he had, though brief, had been free of pain and fear.

It was no wonder that Kell had always taken such pains to chain her out of reach of his subjects. He must have known what she could do, that with a touch she could render all his preparations and his rituals useless and end the pain of his victim, even if only temporarily.

'This must be good for you,' Isidro said after a long moment, glancing down at the bulge of his arm beneath his coat. 'A constant flow of energy, isn't that how it works?'

'More or less,' she said. 'Doesn't Rhia have some poppy? I'm sure I heard her mention it earlier ...'

'She's already given me as much as she dares.'

Sierra bit her lip. She couldn't let him go on like this, not if there was some chance she could help. 'Isidro, stop for a moment,' she said, reining in and pulling off her glove. She had to remind herself it was not *her* arm that was broken, that it was not *her* wrist that would explode into agony if she tried to flex it. 'I think I can help you. Give me your hand.'

He stopped, but did not lift his hand from the pommel. He merely sat and watched her with narrowed eyes. 'What do you mean? How can you help?'

'The night we first spoke,' Sierra said. 'Do you remember any of it?'

He began to shake his head, but then went very still. 'I remember that I slept for about a day afterwards. It was the first time since I came round that I slept without poppy ...' He leaned forward and fixed her with his piercing gaze. 'What did you do?'

'I-I'm not really sure,' she said. The tremor in her own voice made her wince. 'I didn't mean to do anything — but I know you had no pain for hours and it didn't come back completely until the next day.'

'Last night,' Isidro said. 'With Garzen. He was in peace before he died.'

Part of her wished she'd never mentioned it. Isidro was more forgiving of her than she had any right to expect, given what he'd suffered, but this might be more than he could take. Her power was a twisted thing and Sierra could understand why decent folk shied away from her. 'I ... I think I took you too far that night. I didn't understand what I was doing and I didn't know how to stop. It was better with Garzen, but he was so weak ... he would have died quickly no matter what I did.'

Isidro laid his hand on his ruined arm, bound to his chest beneath his coat. Sierra could feel it throbbing and the power pouring off it was like heat from a stove. 'What are you saying?' he said. 'You can make it stop?'

'I think so. And I'm almost certain I can do it without killing you.'

'Ha!' He smiled, but there wasn't much humour in it. 'If you put it that way, it seems I've not got much to lose. What do you want me to do?'

She tried to nudge her horse closer, but she wasn't much of a rider and she and the horse both knew it. The horse stamped a foot and refused to move, so using his heels and his knees Isidro coaxed his mount into sidling up to hers.

'Take off your glove,' Sierra said, removing her mitten and the glove beneath. It was another operation Isidro had not quite mastered with one hand, so he took the tip of the mitten in his teeth and pulled it off. The glove beneath presented him with more of a problem, but Sierra took hold of his wrist and peeled it off herself.

The moment their hands brushed, a blue spark jumped between them. Isidro hissed at the sting and pulled back. His horse twitched and stamped as though bitten by a fly, but Sierra's mount reared up and shied violently away. Sierra was already off balance and leaning towards Isidro and as the horse shied she slid from the saddle and landed in the snow with a whoosh of breath. Her mare leapt away with reins and stirrups flapping and bolted towards the rest of her herd. At the noise of it another beast grazing unseen on the slope above also took fright and ran, crashing away through the bare trees. In the gloom it was nothing but a dark blur, but from the sound it was large enough to be an elk or a reindeer.

'Are you alright?' Isidro asked, grabbing for the reins as his own horse danced away from her.

'No harm done,' Sierra said, picking herself up. 'I should have guessed she would spook. I killed the man who was riding her.' She brushed some snow from her coat and then reached out and took Isidro's bare hand.

The shock almost knocked her flat again, a sudden doubling of sensation as she felt his body overlaid on hers. She experienced the peculiar rush of her power just as he did, felt it as clearly as if it were her own nerves sensing it, an odd mixture of heat and cold that shot up his arm and earthed itself somewhere near his heart.

The pain drained from his arm like a water-skin punctured with a needle, to be replaced with an icy numbness. Isidro gasped and went rigid. She could feel his muscles clenching as he fought the drain of power. He had some talent for mage-craft himself but it was weak and utterly undeveloped and he lacked the strength to mount any real resistance.

Once his arm was numb, Sierra tried to withdraw. Her power flexed within her — it didn't want to let him go, but this time Sierra was ready and, when it rose up to try to take control, she forced it down and broke the contact with a wrench. Isidro's own latent power struck at her, a stinging slap that almost made her lose her grip, and for a long moment she could do nothing but focus on bringing all her raging energy to heel.

Once she was able to look up, Isidro was doubled over in his saddle, his left hand white-knuckled on the pommel, and he was drawing deep, shuddering breaths.

'How does it feel?' Sierra said.

'Well,' he said, and loosened his hand from the saddle with an effort. 'I won't say it was pleasant, but …' He ran a cautious hand over the bulge of his splinted arm. 'It seems to have worked. I don't feel a thing. It's like it's turned to wood.'

He reached inside his coat and through the layers of clothing, as though to reassure himself that his arm was still flesh and blood. Sierra took the horse's reins and waited, holding her breath, not entirely sure what she was afraid of. After a moment Isidro straightened and pulled all the layers back in place. 'It worked,' he said with a note of wonder in his voice. 'It doesn't hurt.'

There was the sound of hoofbeats on the track ahead and they both looked up to see Cam coming towards them at a trot, mounted on Sierra's mare. His frown of concern turned to exasperation as he saw them standing there together with a conspiratorial air. 'What's going on?' he said. 'I looked around and saw the mare careening towards us as if her tail was on fire. She almost knocked Rhia down.' He reined in and swung down from the saddle, but the mare began to pull away before he even touched the ground, snorting and tossing her head.

'She spooked when Sierra dropped a spark,' Isidro said. 'She's not spent much time on horseback and it looks as if the mare's set against her now. It might be wise to swap her for another.'

'The others are all well ahead of us,' Cam said. 'The only other horse nearby is the stroppy cow I'm driving and I doubt either of you could cope with her.'

'Then I'll swap,' Isidro said. 'Sierra's mare's not bad tempered, just a little witless. I'll take her and Sirri can have my gelding.'

Cam raised one eyebrow at the intimate form of her name. He hesitated for a moment before he spoke, reluctant, Sierra thought, to say anything that might imply he doubted Isidro's ability to handle the beast. In the end he shrugged and said, 'Well, it's worth a try. I'll walk with you until we catch up with Rhia. I don't like having you both riding so far back. If there was any trouble Brekan and the women wouldn't hear until it was too late. Best if you stay close now anyway — the sun will be up soon and Sierra will have to ride blindfolded. I want you both in easy reach from now on.'

Sierra stole a glance at Isidro, trying to read his face without being obvious about it. His loyalty was to his brother, she understood that, but he hadn't mentioned the experiment or its effect. Cam's suspicion of her the night before had hardened into outright antipathy today — if Isidro saw no reason to mention it she certainly wasn't going to bring it up and give him any more opportunity to take against her, but she couldn't help but wonder why Isidro chose to keep silent.

Isidro slipped down awkwardly, swinging a leg over the pommel and sliding down with his back to the horse, rather than dismounting normally and risk catching his splinted arm between his body and the saddle. Cam had one arm out ready to aid him, and Sierra felt a ripple of pain through his arm as his feet touched the ground and he staggered before Cam steadied him. The ripple died almost as quickly as it had come, but Sierra suspected that a more serious impact would override whatever magic it was she had worked.

'Let's get a move on, then,' Cam said, tossing the gelding's reins to Sierra. 'We've got a long way to go.'

The crystalline brilliance of the day was fading when Osebian's scouts led Rasten to the abandoned camp. The scouts were half-breeds, cautious, taciturn men made even more so by the fact Lord Rasten stalked behind them. Osebian's men were hand-picked, the best that could be enticed from Mesentreia to this barbarian land. They looked down on half-breeds as mongrels, but the truth was that no import could match those born and raised here when it came to tracking in the snow. Ricalani children were given white balls to play with in the winter to train their eyes to spot the slightest difference in shades of white. They spent their childhood following their parents trapping and hunting, and lived and breathed the world of winter until they were as much a part of it as any other creature of the wild.

Once, Rasten supposed, he must have lived a similar life, but he remembered little of the days before Kell had taken him, and after that it had been years before he saw the light of day. He could read a scatter of prints in fresh snow, but that was all.

He'd left his horse with the men at the same place Corasan's men had stowed their gear before the disastrous attack, while Osebian's men scraped and hacked at the snow to dig some semblance of a grave for the men who'd died there. Rasten went on ahead with the scouts. Sierra had been here — he wanted to put himself in her place, to imagine what she had been thinking and feeling while men bled and died around her.

'Two of 'em came this way, my lord,' one of the scouts said to Rasten. 'A man and a woman. They walked out towards the horse-line, moving carefully, and once the men there were dead, they ran back.'

'A woman?' Rasten said. 'How can you be sure?'

'Her tracks aren't as deep,' he said. 'She was lighter than the other one, and shorter, too, judging from the stride.'

'What proof is that?' Rasten said. 'It could have been a boy.'

'So it could, my lord,' the tracker said. 'But my gut tells me it's a woman.'

The scouts led him over the rise and down into the little valley where the camp had stood. Bloodstains kept fresh and bright by the cold were splashed across the snow. The tracks were still visible but in a week's time only the most experienced eye would pick them out. Within a month they would be gone entirely, covered by fresh snow, and any other remains would stay hidden until the spring thaw left them scattered on the bare and sodden earth.

To the west was an untidy row of man-sized mounds where the dead had been lined up. The snow drifted over them, but the scavengers had dug through to rip into the corpses and scatter the remains across the campsite. Foxes and wolverines had left tracks and bloody scraps as they squabbled over the bodies, but at the men's approach they had melted away. Only a pair of crows remained, perching on a frost-covered bone before finally flapping away with a hoarse complaint when they came too near.

'They had time to pick over the dead, then,' Rasten said.

'And go through the gear they'd left on the sleds,' the scout agreed.

Rasten grunted. 'And what's that down by the ice?' he said, nodding to a dark smear further down the valley, a mound of ash and charred wood. 'Looks like a pyre.'

'It is, my lord,' said the tracker. 'Lost one of their own, I'd say. There's some bones left.'

Rasten clenched his hands within his mittens. 'Man or woman?'

'Man, I'd say, and older. Past his prime.'

Rasten let out a breath. Not Sierra. 'How many?'

'My lord?'

'How many were here? How many people were living in those tents?'

The tracker blanched. 'Six or seven, perhaps. No more than eight.'

Just seven or eight, against the twenty men Corasan had sent out, and only a couple of them warriors of any skill. Those were pitiful odds unless they happened to have someone like Sierra with them.

'Uncover those bodies,' he said. 'I want to see them before the light's gone. And I want to know how long they were camped here and when they left. Find out how many horses they had and what direction they took.'

The scout bent low. 'At once, my lord.'

Rasten turned his back on him and pulled off first his mitten and then his glove, then reached into his sash where the parcel of rubies nestled beside a coiled braid of fine black hair. She'd been here; she'd killed and bathed in the power that spilled with the blood. 'And what did they say, Little Crow?' he murmured. 'What did they do when they saw just what you are?' They would blame her for the one who died and hold her responsible for bringing Corasan's men down upon them. Already they would be muttering about the folly of rescuing her from the snow and someone, very quietly for fear that she would hear, would suggest it might be best to correct the situation. A drug in her tea perhaps —

127

given the medicines Cammarian had purchased, they certainly had such a thing — and then, as she slept, a knife across her throat.

Rasten wound the black braid around his fingers, raised it to his face and caught a whisper of her scent. *You wouldn't let them,* he thought. She was too much of a fighter for that — too stubborn and wilful to bow her head and let anyone else decide her fate.

The rest of the men arrived with Osebian in the lead. Most animals were nervous around sorcerers and the duke's black horse snorted and fought the bit as Osebian forced the beast to approach him. 'I've ordered the men to pitch camp,' he said. 'Since you're intent on picking over the dead, I see no point in pushing on tonight. I take it you wish to pick up the trail again in the morning?'

'Early,' Rasten said. 'We're a full day behind them. We have more men, but they have to break trail as they go. It shouldn't take us more than a few days to catch them.'

'Very well,' Osebian said. 'About that fellow who insulted you —'

'He's mine,' Rasten said, narrowing his eyes.

'If you want his head, hurry up and take it,' Osebian snapped while his horse danced beneath him. 'It's bad for the men's morale to see their comrade dragged along like a cursed prisoner.'

Rasten carefully tucked the coil of hair away and pulled his glove on again. 'When we do catch up with Sierra, I'll need to work a ritual before I bring her down. I was planning to use the loudmouth. If you would rather I killed him now, I can, but you will have to provide me with another in his place. If you think morale is bad now, just wait until you announce the lottery to sacrifice one of their number who is blameless.'

Osebian's face darkened. 'Deal with him as you will, then,' he said, and wheeled his horse around to ride away.

The scout stood nearby with a flaming torch in his hand to ward off the rising dusk. 'The bodies are ready for your inspection, my lord.'

Rasten held his hand out for the torch and the scout handed it to him with a faint tremor in his hand that shuddered through the wood. *Well, Little Crow, let's see how far you have progressed.*

# Chapter 12

They travelled until well after dark. Isidro felt Sierra's touch wearing off before sunset and as the darkness encroached so did the pain, spreading through him like a thicket of thorns, the barbs jabbing deeper with every movement. When they paused just before sunset to debate pitching camp now or pushing on for a few more hours, Rhia poured him a dose of poppy and Isidro downed it without hesitation. What he needed most of all was rest, but the growing pain in his arm wouldn't allow it until the numbing dose of poppy swept it away.

When Cam led them on again, Isidro fell into a doze in the saddle, and the next thing he remembered was being steered inside a half-constructed tent and being told to lie down on a thick pile of spruce, while Lakua coaxed a fitful flame into life inside the stove. He felt as if he was floating as he watched the tent go up around him, Eloba lashing the shaggy cover to the tent frame and Rhia carrying in all the gear.

Once the fire was burning bright Lakua brought in the pot with the evening meal and set it on the stove to warm. Lakua and Brekan had set it going that morning before they took down the old camp — they had brought the pot to a rolling boil, then bound the lid in place and wrapped it well in blankets and furs, with stones that had been heated in the stove packed around. With enough insulation, the pot stayed hot and continued cooking well into the day. By evening it had cooled but by then it was cooked through and needed only to be heated again. While she waited for it to come back to the boil, Lakua mixed up a bowl of batter for a bannock and cooked it in a spluttering pan with plenty of butter. Cam came in several times with buckets of water dipped from a hole in the river ice and armloads of wood, and Brekan, who had been tending the horses, shuffled in and sat as near to the stove as he could, with his arm pressed tight over his broken ribs.

Isidro didn't realise Sierra was missing until she came in, pausing just inside the doorway to stamp the snow from her boots. Everyone fell silent for a moment when she appeared, but the noise picked up again, though lower than before. They were all somewhat subdued that night. Garzen's absence was keenly felt and not just because the loss of a pair of hands meant that those of them who were able were still working long after the camp chores were usually finished.

Sierra settled beside Isidro, sitting cross-legged so that her feet were out of the way of Laki and Rhia, who still fussed around the stove. The poppy was wearing off and Isidro sat up. 'Any trouble getting your tent up?' he said with a yawn and scrubbed the heel of his hand across his eyes.

'I worked it out,' she said with a small shrug. When they had stopped for the noon meal there had been a brief but terse discussion about where Sierra would sleep that night. None of the other women wanted her in their tent despite the fact that she'd slept among them before without any ill effects. Sierra had defused the situation by volunteering to use her salvaged tent, but only now did Isidro realise that no one had helped her — everyone had been occupied with their own tasks.

Isidro lightly touched her arm and offered her his left hand. No one was watching — Sierra was effectively being shunned, and it extended to Isidro by association. His first instinct was to keep quiet about this aspect of her power and this inattention was the nearest to privacy they would get.

Sierra took his offered hand in silence. Once again the initial contact was painful but this time he was ready and steeled himself against it. Within a few moments the blessed numbness had spread through his arm again.

Cam and Eloba returned not long after and Rhia and Lakua served up the evening meal, topping each bowl of stew with a torn portion of bannock. There was a little more in each bowl than usual — when Lakua had set the beans to soaking Garzen had still been alive. Isidro thought of him with every mouthful he ate. Gathered together like this, they felt his loss most acutely; the mood in the tent was heavy and subdued.

When everyone had eaten Eloba and Brekan took the bowls outside to scrub them clean with snow and Rhia called Sierra over to change the bandages on her burned wrists. The dressings had stuck to the burns and

Rhia had to soak them loose. He knew it was rude, but Isidro watched Sierra closely as Rhia worked. She didn't so much as flinch, although it must have been painful. Sierra had either trained herself or had been trained not to react to pain — and given the nature of her power, Isidro suspected it predated her capture by Kell. Her kin must have policed her mercilessly against showing any sign of her talent.

The only time Sierra showed any reaction at all was when she saw the damage the bracelets had done to the clan tattoo on her wrist. The burn had almost obliterated it, leaving only a few blurred marks on her skin. The only way a tattoo could be removed was with a hot iron and to have one's clan tattoo destroyed that way was a grave thing — if carried out in punishment for some crime, it meant the ancestral Gods of her lineage had removed their protection. The superstitious held that anyone so marked was cursed.

Rhia was fastidious as she cleaned the wounds and wrapped fresh bandages around them but the lack of warmth in her manner and her touch made it clear she was doing it solely out of duty. When she was done Sierra thanked her, shrugged on her coat and said her goodnights before ducking out of the tent with a flurry of cold air.

Now that the poppy was wearing off Isidro remembered the book Sierra carried in her packs. He hadn't given it a thought since he'd learned her true identity, but now that he knew, he realised there was only one place the book could have come from — she had stolen it from Kell.

The realisation left him torn. The thought of handling anything Kell had touched left him revolted, but if it was Kell's, then the book would contain knowledge of mages uncensored by the priests and the clans. Of course, Sierra might not be willing to let him see it — but there was no harm in asking. Isidro cast around, looking for his coat, when Rhia sat herself firmly down in front of him and told him to open his shirt and lie down so she could listen to his chest.

'But I feel fine,' he protested. 'Really. I've hardly been coughing all day.'

'Quiet,' she said. 'I cannot hear when you talk.' She listened to his lungs, felt his pulse, and went through an examination he thought unusually thorough, given that he was showing no real sign of distress. She took so long that Isidro wondered if she had guessed he meant to talk with Sierra and was trying to keep him here instead. 'You have done well today,' she said. 'I was worried you would be ill again. A day in the saddle is very straining for a man who has been as ill as you.'

'Strenuous,' he corrected her; she repeated the word with a smile.

'And now you should sleep,' she went on. 'I have more poppy for you if you want.'

'Not just yet,' Isidro said, sitting up and fumbling with the ties of his shirt.

Rhia tied them for him, then sat back on her heels with a scowl as he pulled on his jacket. 'Why must you get dressed? Everything you need is in here.'

So that *was* her game. For a moment Isidro considered offering some excuse, then decided he had no mind to lie to her. 'I'm going to talk to Sierra.'

Rhia's scowl darkened. 'I think you should stay here. You have spent too much time with her already. It is not good for you.'

'Rhia — ' he began, but before he could go on, Cam leaned in to interrupt him.

'Just what do you think she's going to do to him, Rhia?' he said in a quiet voice.

'Magicians work harm wherever they go,' Rhia said. 'Their power is a poison — it corrupts everything they touch. Isidro has been tainted by it once already, when Lord Kell had him captive. This woman can only do him harm. They cause fevers and madness. They weaken the blood, and turn wounds foul … I saw it happen, back in Mesentreia when I was serving my master.'

Cam and Isidro exchanged a glance.

'Those diseases all exist where no mage has been seen within living memory,' Isidro said. 'You might as well blame them on evil spirits.' He managed to get his jacket tied with a clumsy knot and reached for his coat. 'Consider this an experiment. Sierra will be with us for another week — we can see if I get sicker or not.'

Rhia turned imploringly to his brother. 'Cam!' she pleaded, but Isidro was already reaching for the tent flap and behind him he heard Cam say, 'Let him go. He's a grown man, not a child.'

Outside, with the cold biting down through his fur, Isidro shuddered. There was much about Rhia he admired, but this insistence on treating

132

him like a halfwit who needed to be watched over was grating on his nerves. He took a deep breath, trying to shake the feeling off, then headed for Sierra's tent, a low and dark silhouette pitched some way from the larger shelter.

Unlike the big conical tent, Sierra's salvaged shelter was wedge-shaped, with the hide suspended from a single pole supported by a pair of sticks driven into the snow. The ridge-line sloped down towards the back so the tiny stove didn't have to heat quite so much space, with more snow heaped up along the tent walls for insulation. The little chimney exited the tent wall through a pipe-thimble that protected the leather of the tent from scorching and every so often a drift of sparks wafted from the end of the chimney, released by the shifting of coals in the fire. From inside, he could hear soft noises as she moved around in the cramped space.

He announced himself. 'Sierra, it's Isidro.'

There was silence and then a hasty rustle of fabric and a moment later she peeled the door flap back enough to look out. Her face was guarded and tight and only when she saw he was alone did she relax a little. 'What are you doing here? Is something wrong?'

'No,' he said. 'I just came to talk to you. That book you've got — it was Kell's, wasn't it? I was wondering … would you let me see it?'

She pursed her lips for a moment. 'Can you read Mesentreian? Wait, that's a foolish question, of course you can. Come in — I'm afraid it's a little cramped.'

At the front of the tent the roof was just high enough to let them sit upright, but one had to enter it almost on one's hands and knees and Isidro had not yet learned how to do so gracefully with one good arm. Between his boots and his coat he brought in more snow and cold air than he intended and Sierra had to lean past him to fasten the tent flap closed again. Her hair brushed against him, tumbling over her shoulder in an inky cascade.

Inside, the tent was warm and cosy. The stove, resting on a tripod of notched green sticks inside the entrance, was just large enough for one small pot, which bubbled away at a merry simmer. A small pile of firewood sat next to it. Her furs were spread out within arm's reach of the stove, but with only a light blanket for a cover. The tiny stove would need to be fed throughout the night and with a light blanket the chill would wake her sooner than if she slept bundled in furs. If the fire died out completely, she would have to rouse herself to start it again from flint and steel, growing wide awake and thoroughly chilled in the process. By sleeping lightly and waking more often she could simply reach out and shove a few more sticks into the fire without ever properly waking, and get a better night's rest.

Already sweating beneath the weight of his coat, Isidro settled cross-legged on the spruce and shrugged it off, letting it fall in a puddle around him. The space was so small he sat very close to her, close enough to feel the warmth from her skin. The stove door stood open and in the ruddy firelight Isidro could see Sierra's shirt was loosely tied and unbelted, her skin damp and her hair freshly combed. He'd come upon her just as she had finished bathing, he realised, and the bustle of activity was her getting dressed before letting him in.

Sierra turned away, rummaging through her kitbag at the foot of the tent to find the book. In daylight, her hair was a lustrous blue-black, but now it reflected the firelight in a ripple of red. The curve of her neck and shoulder as it disappeared under the collar of her shirt was so exquisite it made his heart lurch and he tried hard not to think about what she might be wearing underneath.

*Stop it*, Isidro told himself, *just stop it*. True, she was beautiful and fascinating, but he was still a broken man, a cripple. Once he may have been a man with something to offer any woman who caught his eye, but those days were over. Now he was a liability, as helpless as a child and utterly unable to contribute to the daily life of his companions, let alone able to survive on his own.

But there was at least one thing he could offer her in return for what she'd given him. All the education and study that had seemed so useless in the past could at least be of some value.

Sierra set the book between them and then rummaged through the sack by the stove. 'I think I've got a lamp and a bit of oil here, too, somewhere ...' She spoke quickly, almost tripping over her words, and a fat blue spark spluttered to life in the palm of her hand and chased itself around her fingers for a moment before vanishing up her sleeve with a buzz, like an angry hornet.

His mind still full of hopeless longing, it took a moment for her words and their strangeness to sink in. The light from the stove might be enough to fumble around in, but any real activity in a tent after dark in a Ricalani winter required a candle or a lamp of some sort.

'Don't worry about the lamp,' Isidro said. 'Just use what you were using before I interrupted you.'

Sierra froze, and then very slowly turned back to him. Another miniature bolt of lightning burst from her fingertips, but this time it arced across to the stove and hung there crawling restlessly over the metal. Her eyes were narrow and suddenly wary. 'Most people are frightened of what I can do,' she said. 'You're not, and yet you have more reason than most. Why is that?'

Isidro shrugged. 'The priests keep saying that mage-craft is evil, but I've never seen evidence to prove it.'

'Kell and Rasten didn't convince you?'

'You can kill a man with a sword, too, but I don't hear people saying that everyone who can wield one ought to cut off his hand to keep from harming others. It's not the power that's evil, it's what you do with it.'

Sierra smiled. When her face was impassive it was an icy mask, but a curve to her lips gave her a wicked, mischievous grin that transformed her in an instant from ice to warmth. 'I bet the priests in the Owl Clan's lands are relieved not to have you as the head of their clan.' She cupped her hands together with a small frown of concentration and blue light streamed between her fingers. When she opened her hands a tiny globe of light floated above her palm. As soon as she released it, it began to drift as though it was dragged along by some ethereal current. With a waft of her hand, Sierra nudged it back, but it soon drifted again, bumbling along the roof of the tent like some ungainly insect.

'Pesky things,' Sierra said. 'Rasten can make his stay where he puts them, but mine always want to move.' She caught it again and brought it back, trapped between her thumb and forefinger.

Isidro couldn't keep from staring. He'd seen sparks created by rubbing a lump of amber with cloth or fur, just like the ones Sierra shed when she was nervous. It worked best during the driest days of winter, unlike real lightning, which usually came in the humidity of summer. One day one of the Owl Clan's grizzled old warriors had told him about balls of lightning that floated through the air just like this creation of Sierra's. 'Can I touch it?' Isidro said, leaning forward for a better look at the globe pulsing between her fingers.

'Ah … I'm not sure. Rasten always could, but anyone else who came too close to one would get zapped.'

'Zapped?' Isidro said.

Sierra just grinned. 'You'll see. Try it if you want — it'll sting, but it won't do you any harm.' She released it and the hovering ball floated to the roof before bumbling its way towards the foot of the tent again.

Isidro gingerly cupped his hand around it before steeling himself and closing his fist. The sphere hummed, a buzz so low and quiet it was barely audible but as his hand closed around it the sound swelled to a growl, an angry hum somewhere between the whirring wings of a large insect and the crackle of a fire, then it burst with a *zap* and sent a shock spearing through his fingertip and down his arm. Isidro yelped and the light vanished, plunging the tent into darkness.

Lost in the gloom, Sierra began to giggle. 'I'm sorry,' she said, 'I shouldn't laugh. Really, I thought you'd be able to touch it. You have an affinity for power.'

Isidro was sucking his finger when she made another light and she frowned at him. 'It didn't burn you, did it?'

'No, no,' he said. 'It just stung, like you said. Here, let me try again.'

'I don't think —'

Before she finished the sentence he'd closed his hand over hers and felt the glowing ball pulsing against his skin. It was neither warm nor cold, but had a peculiar sensation that was at once both prickly and slippery, and when he squeezed it, it yielded slightly before forcing his fingers apart again.

'Well that's odd,' Sierra said, sitting back on her heels. 'Usually people can either touch them or they can't. Mind you, only a handful of folk have ever tried.'

Isidro released the ball and caught it again, still with no reaction. Then, in the spirit of investigation, he touched the ball to the chimney pipe. It stuck there as though it had been glued in place.

Sierra gaped at him. 'How did you do that?'

'Well, I think it must be something like Black Sun's Fire. Last night it was crawling all over the spearheads and the swords. It must have an affinity for metal.'

Cupping her hands, Sierra made another sphere and stuck it beside the first. Laughing, she made another and another until the chimney was clustered with them like a branch crawling with fireflies. 'Ye Gods, you don't know how much easier that's going to make everything. Earlier, I was trying to hold one between my teeth just to keep the wretched thing still long enough to see what I was doing.'

'They never bump up against the chimney on their own?' Isidro said.

Sierra shook her head. 'Fire gives off some kind of power of its own. It's not something I can use, but it creates a current, of sorts. You saw it yourself. They always tumble away from it. If I release one outside, it'll float up like a spark from the fire until it gets out of range and winks out.'

'Fascinating,' Isidro said, and she shot him a sidelong glance, heavy with suspicion. 'No, really,' he said. 'It's fascinating. I never knew people could do things like this.'

She looked down and reached for the book. 'One day you might wish you'd never found out.'

Sierra felt a flush creeping over her face.

Isidro smelled of wood smoke, leather and spruce. The scent swept over her like an antidote to the foulness that had been ground into her senses in Kell's service, the stench of blood and shit and terror that filled the dungeons. It stirred a rising heat that seeped through her, feeding the crackling pillar of energy along her spine. All the loneliness, the fear and despair that had been dragging at her was swept away by a tide of … of what?

She'd felt lust before, of course she had, back before Kell had found her. Awkward fumblings with boys her age had left her perplexed — they seemed to bear no resemblance to what the other girls talked about, nor to the soft murmurs and moans she'd heard from her parents' furs in the night. She'd thought that was lust, but it was like a candle flame to the heat growing inside her now.

She wanted an end to the loneliness — a distraction, however brief, from the dread of knowing that Rasten was on her trail, maybe as little as a day or two behind. She wanted to feel in control and take something for herself, just this once. Most of all, she wanted to feel his hands on her skin, his lips against hers and the weight of him above her.

'Sierra?'

Sierra shook herself. He'd been speaking and she hadn't heard a word he'd said. Their eyes met and his gaze dropped to her lips, parted a little from her quickened breath.

Sierra leaned forward and kissed him. She wrapped her arms around his neck and clung to him, as though she were drowning and he was her air. His good arm found its way around her back and he turned to spare the broken one while still pressing her body against his. Where they touched, her belly to his, her breasts against his chest, Sierra felt the heat spread. Her power surged and erupted in a dazzling tangle that swarmed around them both and filled the tent with flickering blue light.

Surprised, Isidro broke away, and Sierra reluctantly let him go. He was aroused, though, she could feel it. Her power fed from pleasure as well as pain, though it was the latter she had grown most familiar with over the last few years. Kell was a sadist through and through and rape was a weapon he took particular joy in wielding. If this situation felt odd, it was because she was so used to experiencing pain mingled with Kell's perverted pleasure — to feel arousal alone seemed strange and unfamiliar, but to her it felt like the first gulp of fresh air after being locked in a room full of smoke and stench.

'Sierra,' Isidro whispered. His pupils had dilated to deep and gaping depths but his hand was on her shoulder, gently but firmly keeping some distance between them. 'Sirri, I —'

'Just kiss me,' she said, half demanding, half pleading. In a few days' time when Rasten found them, Isidro and his comrades would all be dead and she would be in chains again. Kell would have no fear now of breaking her with hard use as he had done to Rasten — she was already too strong to be easily controlled.

She couldn't speak of that, though — Isidro wasn't like Kell and Rasten, excited by such things, and she needed him too badly to risk turning him away. 'Just kiss me,' she repeated. 'Please, Isidro. I want something for myself, just this once ...' She leaned in again and this time he let her reach him. When he kissed her back, his hunger was equal to hers, so full of need it left her gasping. His frame was painfully lean, but as his arm pressed against her back, it seemed to her she could feel the memory of the man he had been, before Rasten and his club had brought him down.

He drew her forward into his lap and she wrapped her legs around him and ran her hands over his shoulders and down his back. He stiffened as she slipped her hands beneath his shirt, and when her fingers found the rough and tender scars she remembered why. 'I've got them, too,' she said, reaching for the ties of her shirt, 'though they're not as grand as yours.' She let the fabric slip from her shoulders and twisted around to let him see the neat row of white points marching in ranks across her shoulders and along the backs of her upper arms. Frowning, he ran his fingertips over them and Sierra shivered.

'How?' he said.

'On the rack, with steel needles,' she said. 'First time I broke Kell's rules.' She pressed herself against him, as much to distract herself as to divert him from her words. His arms tightened around her and when she felt the rigid length of him straining against the cloth between them she rocked her hips against him with a moan, letting her power spill in a swarm of lightning crackling over them both, covering them in a brilliant veil of light.

The tent had grown cold, but Sierra radiated heat like a hearthstone. All her lights had winked out once she fell into a doze, nestled into the crook of his good arm with her dark, lustrous hair spread out across his chest.

He was thirsty. Isidro knew there was a pot of water by her stove, but he didn't want to disturb her and make this moment end. It was, he had to admit, probably the last time a beautiful woman would ever invite him to her furs.

A narrow band of light from the stove door fell across her. Sleep softened the lines of her narrow face. The wariness, the hunted look that haunted her throughout the day were gone, and he was struck by how young she was. The world was cruel to take a woman so young and so perfect and leave her so devoid of hope she would bed a near stranger just to feel alive, to feel some human warmth. To not feel so lost and alone.

Isidro kissed her forehead and, as gently as he could, he eased himself from beneath her and left her on the folded jacket she was using for a pillow with the fur pulled up to her chin.

Shivering in the cold, Isidro found his shirt and wrapped it around his hand and then gingerly sought the stove door, meaning to build up the fire and give him enough light to find the water. Instead of the latch he found the handle of the pot and clumsy in the darkness he knocked it off the stove. It fell into the woodpile with a clatter and a hiss of steam as the water splattered over the hot metal.

With a gasp of panic, Sierra sat up, snatching the blanket around her as her power erupted, surrounding her in a nimbus of flickering blue light.

'Only me,' Isidro said, kneeling naked and shamefaced on the spruce. 'Sorry, I didn't mean to wake you.'

She pressed a hand to her chest and sagged with relief. 'I swear, my nerves are strung as tight as a drum.'

Isidro reached for the pot but all the water was lost, draining down into the snow beneath the spruce. 'I'll fetch you some more water.'

'You don't have to —'

'It's alright.'

Sierra opened the stove with a wad of rags to protect her hand and fed a few splints of wood into the flames. Isidro cast around for his clothes and reluctantly began to dress. Suddenly shy, Sierra huddled back beneath her blanket and watched him.

Isidro felt conscious of the scars on his back, prickling in the cold air, and gritted his teeth. They were ugly things. Rhia's skill had kept them from growing into raised knots of proud flesh, but even flat, they were livid and angry, as though they held some memory of the hot iron Rasten had dragged over his skin. He yanked his shirt over them and Sierra winced.

He pulled his boots on and shrugged his way into his coat, then took the pot and crawled awkwardly out of the tent. 'I won't be long.'

Outside it was so dark he almost went back for a lamp, but stopped himself when he remembered he had no way to carry it. Instead he huddled deeper into his coat and followed the trampled path past the horses and down towards the river where Cam had chipped a hole through the ice and down to the water beneath.

The horses raised their heads, and one nickered to him on the way past, but he didn't have a hand free to give them their usual scratch of welcome.

He thought of Sierra and the way she'd clung to him, the feeling of her hands on his shoulders and his back, the desperate hunger in her kisses. She'd been feeding off him, he was sure of it, but that wasn't all that had happened. He would have thought himself in no condition to satisfy a woman — he was too weak and too wasted for that. Even if he'd had the strength to perform, the exertion should have left him prostrate.

He felt a little weary, perhaps, a pleasant kind of tiredness, but nothing like the exhaustion it should have caused. He could have sworn that while she was feeding off him, she was also radiating that power back.

In a week she would be gone and he'd likely never see her again — and that was if everything went well. At the worst Rasten and Severian's men would find them and they'd all be slain or captured. Isidro knew he should walk away from her and let this first time be the last. He was crippled, a wasted man, and there was little room for someone like him in a world where a man's worth was in his hands and the strength of his back. Without a family to support him, the best he could hope for would be to live in a temple off the priests' charity, along with the halfwits and the mad and the other scraps and remnants of society. In another time he might perhaps have found a place serving one of the clans as a tutor or a clerk but that was impossible for a fugitive. The price on his head was higher than ever and no clan would risk its position to shelter him. He would end up little more than a beggar, counting out the days until Severian's men finally tracked him down. The memory of Sierra in his arms would be as much a torment as a comfort.

'Isidro?'

Isidro realised he was standing on the ice with the waterhole at his feet. The surface of the water had frozen over, and there were lynx tracks in the snow around it where the beast had come prowling to investigate the disturbance. Isidro turned and saw Cam a dozen paces behind him.

'What are you doing out here?' Cam said, his voice soft.

Isidro held up the pot. 'Fetching more water for Sierra.'

'Oh,' Cam sagged with visible relief. 'I was worried — ' He broke off abruptly and shook his head. 'Look, I'm glad you're getting along with her. Whatever trouble she brings us … it's worth it to see you showing some life again.'

Isidro started to smile, to make a joke and shrug it off, but stopped when he saw Cam's grave face. 'Have I been that bad?' he said.

'I've been waking up a dozen times a night to check that you're still in your furs. I've been having nightmares about waking up with you gone, and finding you in the snow. And when I heard you walking past …' Cam swallowed hard. 'This is where you're supposed to say you wouldn't do such a thing, you hadn't even considered it.'

Isidro set the pot down. 'I won't lie, not about that. If I thought I was going to be captured again, I think I'd cut my own throat. I don't think I'd survive another round and if they marched me into that tent again, I wouldn't trust myself not to beg to be allowed to do what they wanted. Cam, if they find us, don't let yourself be taken alive.'

'I've had much the same thought,' Cam said. 'By the Black Sun, brother, what are we going to do?'

Isidro just shook his head. Ever since he was taken prisoner, they'd all been living from one day to the next, with no chance to make a plan to weather the coming war, or even how to survive until the end of winter.

The future seemed hopeless no matter what came. If the Slavers defeated Kell and the king's men, the Ricalani folk would be helpless to resist being enslaved alongside the settlers. If the Mesentreians prevailed, they would continue their efforts to push the clans northwards and claim their land for the settlers. Either way, it would be a precarious existence for a wounded man and the fugitive foster-brother struggling to support him.

'Mira will help us,' Cam said. 'The Wolf Clan has spies all through the king's army. She knows the lay of the land better than we do.'

Isidro had his doubts, but he held his tongue. Mira — or Mirasada, to give her full name — was heir to the Wolf Clan, and every bit as cunning and scheming as her mother. She was genuinely fond of Cam, but she was also betrothed to the king's cousin, and he wasn't at all certain she would let sentimentality sway her if the association became inconvenient. Even if she did chose to help them, Isidro wasn't sure there was much she could do once the fighting began and the country descended into chaos. This would be a war not of sword and spear, but of mage-craft and power, and all of Ricalan had been raised on tales of the horrors that were born when mages fought. 'Do you think there's any chance Mira and her clan will take Sierra in to help fight the Akharians?'

Cam paused, surprised by the question. 'Honestly? No. The clans will never accept a mage, Issey, you know that.'

Isidro nodded, wearily. He did know it; he just wished it could be otherwise. What Sierra could do was remarkable and it seemed foolish beyond reason to throw away such a weapon in a time of such need. But when did folk ever let reason guide their actions?

'Are you coming back in?' Cam asked.

Isidro broke the ice with the heel of his boot and shook his head. 'No. I think I'll go back to Sierra, if she'll have me.' If he did end up on the headsman's block, he didn't want to regret turning down the offer of a night in her arms.

'Well, for the sake of my sleep, brother, will you promise me something? Will you swear that you won't go and kill yourself without letting me know and giving me a chance to talk you out of it?'

The water beneath the ice was black and oily, like the blood of the world oozing from a wound, and Isidro remembered how he'd longed to be carried away the night before. It was a distant thing now, but when Sierra was gone and the future felt bleak and empty once again, he knew it would return. 'I'll promise, Cam. If you promise that after we've talked it through, you won't try to stop me.'

# Chapter 13

'Sir?' Osebian's captain sat stiffly in the saddle, his eyes unreadable behind his wooden snowgoggles.

The duke shifted in his seat irritably. The ribs he'd cracked in a fall last summer ached fiercely, feeding Rasten a steady thread of power through the amulet he wore. 'What is it?'

'One of the men thinks he saw a man watching us from the tree line. I sent a couple of scouts out to investigate, and they found no tracks, but Drebian swears blind he saw it and he's a reliable man. Would you have us stop and search further, sir, or shall we push on?'

Osebian pursed his lips and twisted in his saddle to take a good look at the country around them. Sierra's trail followed the winding path of a narrow river valley, a ribbon of bare ground that wound between the hills. The spring floods kept the valley clear of vegetation and the wide northern bank was so exposed it carried only a thin cover of snow packed firm enough by the wind that the horses followed the trail without snowshoes. Here, the river channel was at the southern edge of the valley; in places it had carved deep cuttings into the earth and trapped windblown snow in the hollows. If man or beast veered off the trail and into the river channel, within a dozen paces he would find himself foundering up to his waist in soft, powdery snow.

'It's too exposed to stop here,' Osebian said. 'Tell the men to head for the trees. We'll find cover while the scouts take a closer look.'

Not for the first time, Rasten wished he had Sierra's powers. Her ability to sense the pain of others, even something as minor as a cut or a burn, gave her a good chance of detecting anyone trying to creep up on her. The Akharian legions had been only a few days to the west when they'd picked up her trail and now staying ahead of the invaders was as important as keeping on her heels. The delay itched at him — every halt meant they were losing ground, but Rasten couldn't deny that Osebian had more experience in these matters. The duke had been leading men into battle back when Rasten had just begun his training.

As he turned his horse, Rasten saw a flash of movement out of the corner of his eye. The winter sun hung low in the southern sky and the trees that stood on the southern bank of the river above the small cliff cast long shadows over the edge of the channel. It was the movement of a shadow that drew his attention, but it was gone too quickly for him to make out what it was.

Osebian's captain trotted back along the line shouting orders to his men, who obediently turned their horses towards the trees. When his mount went to follow, Rasten reined it in and the beast pawed at the snow, tossing its head in protest. Osebian's valet, who led the horse that carried Rasten's prisoner, skirted around him with a wary glance and prepared to follow the duke up the shallow slope.

A man cried out in a strangled shriek and a jangling barb of power speared into Rasten from the chain of amulets binding the men to him. A soldier was slumped over in his saddle with an arrow jutting from his back. The horse shied away, startled by his cry and the sudden scent of blood. The rider slipped from the saddle and landed heavily on the ice.

'Archers!' one of the men shouted as a rain of arrows fell. 'Archers to the south!' All around him men and horses alike screamed as the shafts found flesh.

Rasten cast a shield over himself, then activated the amulet Osebian wore, shielding him as well. None of the other men carried the same protective enchantments — it would have drained his power too quickly had he tried to shield them all.

The men at the head of the line spurred their horses towards the trees, but after only a few strides they reined in so sharply their mounts squealed and fought their bits.

'Riders to the east!'

'Form up!' Osebian bellowed as arrows flashed to ashes against his shield. 'Form up and charge! And you, mage, do something about those whoreson bowmen!'

Rasten was already on the ground with his knife in his hand. The mounted warriors were closing the gap with Osebian's men, and the archers had come forward to the edge of the cliff above the riverbed where they were silhouetted against the sky as they took calm, measured shots at the riders milling below.

Rasten ignored them. He cut the cords that bound his prisoner to the saddle and dragged him onto the snow. The man screamed and struggled as Rasten pinned him down with a knee across his throat and cut open his shirt to bare his chest and belly. He was already marked with the symbol that anchored Rasten's power, a brand he had burned into the prisoner's skin. The ritual words came to his mind unbidden, not a prayer as the priests chanted in their temples, pleading with gods and spirits who didn't listen and didn't care, but a ritual of the Blood, a set of key words to which his body and his power had been trained to respond. Almost at once he felt the calm detachment of the trance descend upon him, and then a great rush of energy as his power rose up and locked onto the man lying beneath him, feeding off the sacrifice like a leech drinks blood.

With a flick of his wrist, Rasten opened the man's belly from pubis to sternum. The prisoner arched his back and gurgled a scream, bucking beneath him, but Rasten was ready and looped cords of power around him to hold him down.

Glistening grey ropes of intestine spilled from the wound. Rasten pushed them out of his way and reached into the warm, sticky cavity of the prisoner's chest. His fingers found the heart and, when they closed around it, it pulsed and squirmed against his palm like a sack full of snakes. Rasten clenched his hands and with one practised movement he tore the man's heart from his chest.

The flood of power hit Rasten so hard and so fast that it knocked him back onto the snow. Colours burst in front of his eyes, vivid and bright. The sky turned to sapphire and the snow around him was as brilliant as crystal.

The ritual was a quick and clumsy one, but it served his purpose. It had taken only a few moments and, as he fell back onto the snow, Rasten saw the archers arrayed on the cliff above concentrating their aim on him despite his protective shield.

Rasten raised one blood-smeared hand and sent a wave of energy sweeping over them. It hit the bow-staves first, scorching them black, then it swept up the arrows, consuming the fletching in a flash of flame. Next the hemp bowstring caught and charred to ash, and then it hit the archers themselves, igniting their clothing and their hair, enveloping each man in a ball of flame and sooty smoke. The hail of arrows abruptly stopped as the archers blazed like bonfires on the edge of the cliff. One or two of them hurled themselves over, leaping down to the deep, powdery drift below in an attempt to quash the flames.

Drained and empty, Rasten slumped back onto the snow. It had taken most of the power he'd wrung from the sacrifice and he had no connection with the dying men through which to recover it, no amulets or ritual marks upon the ground he could use to draw energy from them.

While his attention had been on the archers, the mounted men had met on the snowy bank. The clash of swords surrounded him and men shouted and cursed while their horses squealed, kicking up sheets of snow while steam rose from their sweating bodies. Osebian's men had the worst of it — still milling under the rain of arrows, they had been unprepared when the enemy hit them, swinging around to come from the northeast to drive the horses and men back into the deep, soft snow that filled the river channel.

With his head swimming Rasten got to his feet with a hand still clenched around the heart he'd ripped from his prisoner's chest. One enemy rider spurred his horse towards him and chopped down with his sword. Rasten's shield, at rest a barely visible veil of flame-coloured light, caught the blow and flashed bright red as it absorbed the force of the cut. He dropped the ragged wet lump of meat onto the snow and summoned a claw of power that caught the warrior and dragged him from the saddle, the cords of his energy searing deep into the man's flesh as he screamed.

'Mage!' the cry went up around him. 'Battle-Mage here!' It took Rasten a moment to realise they were calling out in Akharian, the language of Kell's homeland and one he had insisted Rasten learn.

As the shout went through the Akharians they turned their horses towards him. Akharians had their own mages, but without one of them on the battlefield to launch a counter-attack they had another tactic for dealing with him. The riders mobbed him, trying to overwhelm him with sheer numbers and hammer on his shield until he grew too exhausted to hold it up any more. As they pressed in around him, Rasten threw the last of his strength into the shield and reached for the amulets Osebian's men wore. The enchantments they bore were forged with his blood, inextricably linked to the column of energy that coursed along his spine. If a man who wore the charm was wounded, the enchantment would channel the energy to him without him needing to do a thing. They delivered enough energy to keep his shield up, but now he needed something more.

Rasten drew himself up, still wrapped in the calm detachment of his trance. When he worked a ritual in the controlled space of Kell's camp, he would place the subject within a circle that would help contain and focus the energies produced, but in a battle it was not possible to choose one's ground and mark the sigil out. Instead, he used the amulets, each one a little node of energy with its own supply of power. With a word, Rasten summoned a burst of energy from each stone and linked them together in a net that covered most of the battlefield in a field of power. He felt a few of the men falter and some of the worst wounded collapsed and died as the amulets drained the last of their strength. Rasten didn't spare them a thought — he couldn't with this ecstatic pulse of energy thumping through him. It took all his training to maintain his focus and not lose himself in that rapturous flood of power. He had to hold it until the charge grew large enough, but each instant he waited was a temptation to give himself up and let the power consume him.

When at last he could hold no more, Rasten released it and let the energy burst from him with the force of a dam giving way. It swept through the men like a wave and everywhere it touched living tissue it ripped, tore, crushed, shredding muscle and splintering bone. The amulets worn by Osebian's men saved them, shielding them from its fury.

Within a few seconds, the wave broke and the energy scattered, leaving Rasten at the centre of a field of carnage. Men and horses had fallen where they stood, now little more than bloody, flayed lumps upon the snow. The damage grew less as the wave swept further away from Rasten — at the very edge some men were still alive, screaming in agony and terror. A few who had been outside the net of power had escaped completely, and in the sudden calm that followed the storm of power they wheeled their horses and fled. Osebian, untouched by the battle, barked at his men to go after them.

Rasten raised his arms over his head and stretched. He felt warm and languorous, just as he did after bedding a woman. Power hissed and crackled along his nerves. The net between the stones still held, and would for a while longer until all the energy contained within it dissipated. While it still stood, energy continued to flow into him from the wounded, Mesentreian and Akharian alike.

'Don't kill the prisoners,' he called to Osebian as he began picking his way across the churned and bloody snow. 'Line them up and let me look them over first. I'll need one to replace the man I sacrificed.'

Osebian frowned for a moment, but then nodded to one of the soldiers. 'See to it.' He turned back to Rasten. 'We've nine dead and four more badly injured. That's a quarter of my men lost.'

'Against what, fifty or sixty Akharians?' Rasten said with a grin. 'Have a care with your tone, your grace. Anyone would think you were ungrateful. Where's my horse? Did the beast survive?'

Still mounted, Osebian could see further than Rasten could on foot and he raised a hand to wave someone over. 'My servant has it. I must say, Lord Rasten, I am surprised to see you walk away from that mob. I wasn't looking forward to having to report to your master that he'd lost his second apprentice in as many weeks.' He nudged his skittish horse closer to one of the corpses. 'So these are the Akharian legions we've heard so much about.'

'Their scouts, anyway,' Rasten said.

'And they have mages of their own, or so Lord Kell informs me. Tell me, Lord Rasten, can their mages do this too?'

Rasten snorted. 'The Akharians are afraid of mages like me. That's why Kell left them to enter the queen's service. They treat their mages like slaves and kill any who grow too powerful for the state to control. Why? Does it offend you that they'll be making free with the land that will be yours within a year? I know it's the Wolf Lands you covet, not the girl you'll marry to get them.'

Osebian curled his lip at the mention of his betrothed. 'Let the Slavers come. They'll save me the trouble of clearing the land when the territory does become mine. No, I only ask because I don't want to see this weapon used against my own men. What about this girl your master has us chasing? Can she do it?'

Rasten threw his head back and laughed. 'You'd better hope and pray she never learns how. With a little more time to prepare I could kill perhaps a hundred on the first wave. Sierra could destroy ten times that number without breaking a sweat if she could control her powers. Don't worry about the Akharians. Once we have her back we'll tear their legions to shreds.'

* * *

Once again, Isidro and Sierra found themselves riding at the end of the line, following a path that by now was well trodden into the snow. Sierra's eyes, though much improved, were still too tender to stand the glare of daylight, so she rode blindfolded during the day while Isidro led her horse on a rope. He managed both horses by tying his reins in a knot he could hold with one hand, and by fastening the lead of Sierra's horse to his saddlebow with a slipknot, so that one tug on the end of the rope could free the knot if trouble arose.

'What time is it?' Sierra said again, turning her face around to try to catch some glimpse of light.

'Still early afternoon,' Isidro said. 'It'll be a good few hours before the sun is low enough for you to see.'

She slumped in the saddle with a sigh. 'This plan Cam has to seek shelter with the Wolf Clan — do you think it will work? Mirasada will be marrying Duke Osebian at midsummer and he'll flood the Wolf Lands with his own men. Surely you'd be better off finding shelter elsewhere.'

'Well, for one thing, neither Mira nor her mother will simply hand the Wolf Lands over to an outsider, no matter who Mira's forced to marry. But to be honest, Sirri, I don't know. There aren't many who are willing to take the risk of sheltering us. I think we'll have to take what we can get. If nothing else, the Wolf Clan will give us some time to work out just what other options we have — presuming we're not overrun by then.'

'Are there any other options?'

He sighed. 'There was a time we talked about heading west to the Akharian Empire, but I think that ship has sailed. Before the invasion, and before this wretched arm, we might have stood a chance, but now?' He turned to her, still a little unnerved at trying to have a conversation with someone whose eyes he couldn't meet. 'But you could ride that way. Would Kell chase you into the empire?'

'The Akharians kill mages like me — or so Kell says. I suppose he might have been lying. Their sorcerers are trained to serve the emperor. Kell says they are slaves — better treated than the brutes who work in the mines and the fields perhaps, but slaves all the same. Any who learn the ways of the Blood are slaughtered, no matter how many of their own men it takes to kill him. Even their generals won't tolerate a Blood-Mage, however useful they might find one in battle. I suppose —' She broke off just as Isidro felt a shiver run through his body, a tremor that rippled along his nerves and wrung a wave of pain from his ruined arm. Isidro grabbed for the pommel of his saddle as he felt himself sway. The hillside dipped and swung around them and he closed his eyes, gritting his teeth against a wave of nausea.

The moment his eyes closed a shadowy scene appeared in the darkness behind his eyelids. Isidro saw a knife in his right hand, which was whole and unbroken, and with the other he dragged a bound and gagged man from the saddle of a nervous horse.

Isidro shook his head, trying to force the picture away, but it stayed with him even after he opened his eyes again, a ghostly image overlaying his own vision. His horse, the mare Sierra had stolen during her escape, seemed to sense something was wrong — she tossed her head and broke into a nervous, jolting trot. Isidro gathered up the reins and tried to soothe her with his voice and his seat, but it only made the mare quicken her pace and fight the bit.

'What's going on?' Sierra said, groping for the pommel of her saddle.

'Something's upsetting the horses.'

She kicked her feet out of the stirrups. 'It's probably me. I'd better get down —'

'No, stay where you are. If they've caught wind of something stalking us, a leopard or a tiger, you'll be safer where you are.'

'I can deal with a predator, but I don't think that's what's bothering them.' She slipped down from the saddle and staggered as she landed in soft snow.

Isidro was about to reply when he blinked again; in that moment of darkness the shadowy vision suddenly resolved into a brilliant view as clear and crisp as a reflection in mirrored glass. He was looking down at the body of a man being butchered alive. He had been gutted like a hunter's kill, belly and abdomen laid open, ribcage cracked and wrenched apart to expose his beating heart. In that vivid glimpse, Isidro saw bloody hands reaching for it.

The next thing Isidro knew, he was stumbling through the snow with his heart pounding and his head feeling as if it was about to explode. Sierra was beside him with his good arm across her shoulders, bearing up beneath him to support his weight. She'd pulled her blindfold down and was squinting at him through reddened eyes. 'By the Black Sun,' she said through gritted teeth. 'You see it too, don't you?'

151

'What in the hells is happening?'

'It's Rasten. He forged a link with you when he worked the rituals. You're seeing through his eyes, but he can't see you. We're not in any danger.'

Blood and flame filled his vision. Eyes open or closed, it made no difference — he couldn't look away from the scene playing out before him. It triggered memories he did his best to keep buried and once again he could smell the hot iron and the sweet, foul stench of burning hair and skin.

'Isidro!' Sierra's hand tightened on his shoulder. 'Don't think about it! Stay here. Focus on something else.' He clenched his teeth and tightened the muscles of his wounded arm. It sent a spear of pain through him, enough to make him cry out, but it drove the other view from his mind. For a few seconds, there was no room in his mind for anything but pain.

Beside him, Sierra trembled. 'Not like that!' she gasped. 'Black Sun …'

'It's the only thing that works,' he said. Too weak to hold himself up, he dropped to his knees and slumped against Sierra, trusting her to support them both.

'Do you want me to get Cam?'

'No,' he said. Cam would only worry if he saw him like this. Another blink and the vision shifted. This time, he saw a wave of flame engulf men and horses in a sooty red haze. 'By the Fires Below, what's he doing?'

'He's killing them,' Sierra said softly. Then Isidro heard hoofbeats approaching them and felt Sierra stiffen. He looked up and saw Cam riding towards them with Rhia close behind.

Cam's face was a dark mask of anger and when he reined in he slipped down from the saddle before his horse had halted. He dropped the reins, trusting his horse's training to make it stand, and strode towards them. 'What in all the hells is going on here?'

Sierra straightened but before she could reply, Rhia drove her horse towards her. 'What have you done? Get away! Get away from him!'

Sierra raised a hand and Isidro felt her power prickle over his skin. A spark leapt from her hand and flickered up her arm, coursing around her shoulder and torso in a tangle of blue light. Rhia's horse shied violently and upset her seat so badly she had to grab for the mane to keep from falling.

With a snarl, Cam strode forward and seized hold of Sierra's wrist. 'Don't you threaten her —'

Sierra flinched as though expecting a blow, but then with a shudder she brought herself under control and met his glare with one of her own. 'Let go of me,' she said with deadly calm.

Cam released her wrist and took a step back, hands raised in a gesture of peace.

Rhia, her mount now under control, slipped from the saddle and went to Isidro. 'What did she do to you?'

'She didn't do anything —'

'Curse it, Isidro, don't give me that,' Cam said. 'I can see that something is wrong.' He turned back to Sierra. 'Why in all the hells didn't you call for help?'

'Because I asked her not to!' Isidro shouted. The effort left his head spinning and he slumped down again. Mercifully the visions of blood and flames had ended, but in their wake he felt some phantom force prickling through his flesh, jangling over his nerves and leaving them raw and frayed.

Cam took a breath through clenched teeth. 'Will one of you *please* tell me what's going on here!'

'It's Rasten,' Sierra said. 'He's on our trail with a couple of dozen men, and someone attacked him.'

'Who? Not Wolf men, surely?'

'No,' Sierra said. 'I heard them shouting and I think they were Akharian.'

'You *heard* them?' Isidro said, looking up at her. 'I couldn't hear a thing.'

'Well, no, but you've never dealt with a ritual link before — I'm surprised you saw anything more than a few flashes. But Kell and Rasten have been using me in rituals for years now and I've grown used to the echoes.'

'But how can you be sure they were Akharian? Do you know the language?'

'I don't, but Kell does. He taught Rasten and I've heard them use it.'

Cam was scowling at her with his fists jammed against his belt. Before he could speak again, Sierra turned to him. 'Look, the rituals Kell and Rasten use leave these marks behind, like scars. The lore calls them "wounds of the soul".'

'Wounds of the soul? What a load of rot —'

'Yes, I know it sounds stupid, but that's how Rasten explained it to me. The ritual forges a connection between the mage and the subject

153

and it remains for as long as they both live. It's kind of a … a conduit for energy, and it flows both ways. While Rasten was gathering power, some of that energy spilled back down the conduit to Isidro, carrying an echo of what Rasten was seeing.'

'Does that mean Rasten can see what I see?' Isidro demanded.

Sierra made a face. 'Under the right circumstances, yes, but it's unlikely. When I escaped, Rasten tried to reach me, to trick me into giving myself away. I could hear him but because I didn't reply he had no way of knowing if I had. You have an affinity for power, Isidro, but it is very weak. Even if you wanted to make contact, I doubt you could reach far enough for anyone to hear. We only heard Rasten because he'd raised more power than he could easily hold and some of the overflow spilled down the conduits to us.'

'But what if Rasten tried to reach him?' Cam said. 'If he traced me to the village, he could have found out what we bought, and from that he could guess that Issey's still alive. Could Rasten do the same thing and see through Isidro's eyes?'

'He can try, but unless Isidro returns contact, it won't do him any good. Since Isidro doesn't know how to raise power, there's no issue of him raising more than he can hold.'

'Not for him,' Cam said. 'But what about for you? If these echoes are unintentional, you could be sending them, too.'

Sierra shrugged. 'It's possible, but I'm not carrying that kind of power — not since that battle the other night. Even then, it wouldn't tell him where I am, not unless he recognises some landmark nearby. All you see is a picture: there's no sense of distance or direction. It can't put us in any more danger than we're already in.'

'Is this all in that book of yours?' Isidro said, looking up at her.

'I think so,' Sierra said. 'Not that I can understand the rotten thing. But I'll show you when we stop tonight. You might make more sense of it than I have.'

Isidro nodded. The stones set into the cover carried enchantments that preserved the parchment and the ink. He had realised when looking at it last night that the book was much older than he'd first thought. The language was archaic, and to someone like Sierra, who'd only learned Mesentreian when Kell had taken her prisoner, it was almost incomprehensible.

Cam hooked his thumbs into his belt and scowled. 'So Isidro's a sorcerer too, is that what you're saying?'

'Nothing of the sort. He's a Sensitive, but you must have known that already. What Kell and Rasten did blasted open the channels of his power, but he still can't use it any more than a child can swing a battle-axe. This is why Blood-Mages do their best to make sure no one leaves their dungeons alive — otherwise there would be dozens of folk like Isidro, able to spy on them whenever their power ran high.'

His head clearing now, and his heart slowing to a more natural rhythm, Isidro looked down at his ruined arm and suppressed a sigh. If he could wield power like Sierra … *And what difference would that make?* he told himself. He'd still be crippled, still be unable to tie his shirt or his sash, would never set a snare or lash a load down on a sled. 'They were Akharians?' he said to Sierra. 'You're certain?'

She bit her lip. 'As certain as I can be. It sounded like the language I've heard Kell and Rasten speak, but I don't know it myself.'

'Isidro would know,' said Cam, 'but you didn't hear it, did you? Did you see anything that would tell you who they were?'

Isidro shook his head. 'They were wearing war-coats with the hoods pulled up, with snowgoggles and cowls over their mouths as if they'd been lying in wait and wanted to catch the frost from their breath.' He glanced up at Sierra. 'I'm not saying you're wrong, just that I didn't see anything to identify them.'

'It could have been Charzic's men,' Cam said. 'I still think it's madness for the Akharians to come east. I don't see why they'd turn their backs on Severian's army to run around here in the north for the sake of a scattered handful of slaves. And if they were, we would have heard about it in the village — someone would have seen smoke from the burning buildings and there would be people fleeing ahead of the legions.'

'I know what I heard,' Sierra snapped. 'I told you about this days ago! If you still don't believe me, it's your cursed problem.'

'Look, either way we need to keep moving,' Isidro said as he rose shakily to his feet. Both Rhia and Sierra moved to offer him a steadying hand, but Rhia was closer and she warned Sierra off with a glare. 'Whoever they were makes no difference. Rasten tore them to shreds and there's no longer any doubt that he's on our trail.'

# Chapter 14

Sierra bent over the book with a frown creasing her brow, brushing the tip of her braid against her lips. When her eyes shifted back to the start of the passage she'd already read several times before, she bit the thick rope of hair in a sudden fit of frustration, and when she reached the end spat it out in disgust. 'Fires Below, I've read this passage five times and it still makes no sense!'

Isidro lifted his head from the pillow of his arm. 'Let me see?' Sierra shifted it around for him and then raised her arms above her head to stretch her back as best she could in the low-roofed tent.

Isidro scowled as he puzzled through the text. 'You're right,' he said after a few moments. 'It's nonsense.' He flicked back through a few pages of dense, crabbed script. 'Is this the only book Kell had?'

'It's *the* book,' Sierra said. 'Whenever Rasten gave me a lesson, it came from that. Not that it made any more sense then. He'd have me copy a page out, and then he'd go through it line by line and explain what the wretched thing meant. At first I thought it was just because I didn't speak Mesentreian well enough, but now I'm not so sure.' She lay down, rolling onto her back, and covered her eyes with one hand. The worst of the snow blindness had passed and she could open her eyes in daylight now, but only while she was wearing goggles to reduce the glare. At the end of the day when her eyes were tired, her vision tended to blur again.

'I don't think your Mesentreian is the problem,' Isidro said. 'I think it's written to be confusing.' He turned back to the frontispiece of the book, where a list of names had been scrawled with dates beside each one. 'Blood-Mages aren't known for treating their apprentices well, I take it?'

Sierra snorted. 'They're no better than slaves.'

'That's what I thought. So, no Blood-Mage would want his apprentice to learn something he wasn't ready to teach. And they definitely wouldn't want a runaway to steal the book and learn all his master's skills for himself ...'

Sierra held herself very still for a moment and then began to curse. 'May the Black Sun cut out his worthless heart and feed it to her hounds. I've been lugging that dead weight all this way for nothing.'

'Well, the real knowledge has to be in here somewhere,' Isidro said. 'It's probably a memory-aid of sorts, otherwise there'd be no value in keeping it. The challenge is just to separate the real mage-craft from the drivel. Which isn't going to be easy, given how little we know of mage-craft.'

There were a score or so of names on the list, with dates that spanned more than three hundred years. 'Were these apprentices?' Isidro asked, running a finger down the list. 'It looks as if some of them died before their masters.'

'The only way an apprentice can be free is if he kills his master,' Sierra said. 'Most of them die in the attempt. You see that name above Rasten's? Pendaran? He's the reason Kell walks with a cane. He tried to hamstring the old man.'

'You're not on here,' Isidro said.

'Well, I wasn't really an apprentice. More of a servant, I suppose. Kell used me to generate power. He never meant me to be able to wield it.' Sierra frowned at the tent roof. 'Do you know the stories of Vasant and his books?'

'Of course.'

While the most powerful and power-hungry mages aligned themselves with the factions fighting for survival against Queen Leandra's forces, there were other mages who wanted no part of the fight for supremacy — the scholars and tradesmen of the craft, weak in power for the most part. Some were rejected by their kin and driven away; others left voluntarily rather than expose their families to the danger of trying to protect them from an increasingly hostile population. While Leandra was hounding the last of the factions, in order to remain independent of the warring sides, these mages came together under the leadership of the most powerful, the scholar later known as the Demon Vasant.

Leandra had ordered the clans under her banner to destroy every book of mage-craft and every mage-crafted device they could find. As the order went out, these minor and independent mages preserved what they could of their history and their craft and, under Vasant's leadership, gathered together all the books and relics they could find. Vasant hid them in various caches and hoards throughout Ricalan until Leandra finally cornered him and his followers at the temple complex once known as Blood-of-Earth, but now called Demon's Spire. There, Vasant had made his last stand, and after losing fully half her men, Leandra wore the Last Great Mage and his followers to exhaustion and slaughtered the last mages of Ricalan, a rag-tag army of scholars, hearth-mages and wandering craftsmen.

'Do you think they still exist?' Sierra said. 'The books, I mean? When I was a girl I used to dream about finding them. I thought there must be something there that would teach me how to use my power. I've heard the tales the priests tell, that Leandra found them and had them all destroyed, but they might have been lying to keep people from searching for them.'

'I wouldn't put it past them,' Isidro said. 'According to the histories, Vasant was the greatest mind of his age — he knew Leandra would be searching for them. It's hard to believe he left them somewhere where people with no power at all would have been able to find them and destroy them.'

'But people *have* searched for them ever since Leandra the First sealed the caves. They've had a hundred years to find them,' Sierra said. 'If no one's discovered them by now they must be gone for good. Perhaps Vasant outsmarted himself and hid them too well.'

She frowned up at the roof of the tent and the globes of light clinging to the chimney. Ever since she'd come to realise just what she was, she'd wondered what it would have been like to be born a hundred years before, when mages where honoured for their talents, not reviled. None of this would be happening now if there were still mages in Ricalan.

Whenever Sierra could pull herself back from the immediate danger to see the greater threat that stalked the north, she felt overcome by a rush of fury. She was enraged that this invasion had occurred, and that their foreign king had brought this upon them and yet would not raise a hand to defend the people he ruled from being slaughtered and enslaved.

She wanted to fight — what use was this power she'd been given if not to defend the only home she'd ever known? But how could she, with Rasten snapping at her heels and Kell determined to reclaim her, no matter what it cost? But even if she could shake them from her trail, she knew the clans would never accept a creature like her, whatever the threat they faced. The clans had decided long ago that they would rather accept foreign rule than share Ricalan with mages.

Contemplating the greater threat left her feeling more dejected than before. The only people in the world who wanted her were the monsters she had fled from, Kell and Rasten — well, them and the warm, kind and quick-witted man who was sharing her tent for the last time. Tomorrow they would reach the cache and then go their separate ways, swept apart by the winds of fate as swiftly as they'd been brought together.

Sierra rolled over with a sigh and closed the book. 'Well, if the wretched thing is as good as useless, I won't waste any more time on it tonight.'

Seeming as pensive as Sierra felt, Isidro lay back beside her. He touched his fingers lightly to his splinted arm with a frown creasing his brow, and she wondered if he was thinking of the pain that would return once she was forced to leave.

'It'll get better,' she told him. 'Once you're in a safe place and have time to rest and heal it won't be so bad.'

'That's what Rhia tells me,' he said.

If Rasten found her Isidro and Cam would be safe for a while. Rasten would be fully occupied with containing her and bringing her back to Kell, with no time to spare to chase a pair of fugitives.

'Will you head north?' Isidro asked.

'And east, I think,' she said. 'Just because it's away from Kell. If I can stay ahead of Rasten until the fighting gets truly fierce, then Kell might have to call him back to help him ...' She took a handful of the blankets beneath her and crushed them in her fist until her knuckles turned white. 'I wish I could stay, I truly do, but I'd only bring you danger ...'

'I know,' he said. 'Sirri, do as you must. I'm just grateful for what you've given me, and the time we've had ...'

She squirmed closer and laid her hand on his chest. He was stronger than he had been the night she woke in a strange tent and he hailed her in the dark, even with the exertion of travelling. Was it just relief from the pain that had changed him, or was there something more going on within his lean and battered frame? Sierra supposed she'd never get to find out. 'I just wish that we could change this road we're on. There must be something that can be done — against Kell, against the Slavers — but I just can't see it.'

He said nothing and, as the silence grew unbearable, Sierra hauled herself up and kissed him, hungry and demanding. 'Make me forget,' she said. 'Please, Issey, one last time. Make me forget and I'll do the same for you …'

'The cache is just down in that copse,' Cam said. They stood in the shelter of a few trees, gazing across an avalanche-cleared slope. 'Looks like there's someone down there already.'

Sierra adjusted the twisted leather cord of her snowgoggles. They left welts in her skin, but she didn't dare take them off. Even a few moments of exposure would risk another bout of blindness. Once she was on her own that would be a disaster.

Through the narrow field of view the goggles allowed she spotted the figure Cam was talking about. He was wearing a white coat but made no other effort to conceal himself. His hood was thrown back and he held a spear in one gloved hand, gazing about the open slope with a mixture of watchfulness and boredom.

'Looks like a sentry,' Isidro said. 'You told Mira where our cache was, didn't you?' he asked Cam.

Cam nodded. 'She was going to leave some more medicines there.' In the first few days after Isidro's rescue, when he had been too ill to be moved, Cam had taken two of the horses and ridden hard for Ruhavera, the seat of the Wolf Clan, to beg them for the medicines Isidro desperately needed. 'She must be here,' Cam said, 'or one of her kin, maybe. I don't think they'd bother with guards for a mere messenger.'

Sierra shrugged deeper into her fur, but it did nothing to dispel the chill that gathered inside her. Cam had been cool but civil to her ever since the day of Isidro's vision. He'd not said one word to her about Isidro spending most of the nights since then in her tent, but Sierra had the impression that it was only because the arrangement was temporary. The previous night had been the last. She was leaving them today, probably within the hour. She had been doing her best not to think about it.

'I should go now,' Sierra said. 'Better if they never see me.'

'We don't have enough supplies left,' Isidro said. 'There's another day's worth for the lot of us, but that'll only keep you for a week.'

'There's the grain for the horses …' Sierra said.

'But you'll need more than grain to keep you fed.'

'With the Wolf men to help us dig, it won't take long,' Rhia said quietly from behind them. 'You will be able to go on your way while it is still light.'

Sierra tossed her head, about to reply when her eye fell on Isidro, standing by his horse with the reins held loosely in his mittened hand. For his sake, she wouldn't make a scene. Unlike Cam, the others had made no effort to hide their disapproval of the time he spent with her, and she had no wish to make things any more difficult for him.

Isidro turned his back on Rhia and caught Sierra's eye with a smile and half-shrug that made her stomach twist. She wasn't naïve enough to believe it was love they shared after knowing each other for little more than a week, but it was comfort and affection and a mutual regard. The others treated him like a child. Even Cam. They meant well, but it made her grit her teeth to see how they spoke around him and shared glances above his head, as though Kell had robbed Isidro of his wits as well as his independence.

Their pace had slowed considerably these last two days. They'd been pushing the horses hard and they were showing the strain. Cam had been planning to let them have a day of rest once they reached the cache, and Sierra had been half hoping, half fearing, they would reach the site so late in the day it would be too dark to move on once they did uncover the supplies. The thought of being on her own again filled her with dread. The night before, she'd dreamed of the dark, solitary cell where Kell had kept her for months after her capture. She'd woken sobbing at the memory, but couldn't bring herself to tell Isidro. He had enough troubles without bearing hers as well.

'Don't worry,' Cam told her. 'They won't hold you up for long. We'll have you on your way soon enough.'

Cam started across the slope, leading his horse behind him. As he stepped out onto the clear ground, the sentry barked a warning, bringing a few other warriors to his side at a run. But by the time Cam had covered half the distance across the bare slope, they were lounging against their spears again, so Sierra assumed they had recognised him, though no one shouted his name. She dropped back in the line, letting Isidro and Rhia go ahead before she led her horse across.

At the centre of the clearing, surrounded by warriors dressed in pristine white, was a young woman with bright red hair bound up in fine braids, each tipped with a blue glass bead. 'Mira!' Cam called; he strode over to engulf her in an embrace while the woman laughed in delight.

Even before Kell had taken her to Lathayan, Sierra had heard of Mirasada of the Wolf. The Wolf was the largest clan left in Ricalan, but even before the clans of the southern coast had been driven off their lands and scattered, they had been among the wealthiest, with a vast territory to their name. Mirasada had been the unofficial heir for years, but the king had only formally accepted her mother's choice of a successor a few months ago — and only then on the provision that she marry his cousin and heir, the Grand Duke Osebian.

Like Cam, Mira was of mixed blood — the colour of her hair was ample evidence of that. This wouldn't be the first foreign marriage in her clan. Her clothes were particularly fine — a lacy cowl hung around her neck in luxurious folds and at the open neck of her coat Sierra could see a flash of patterned fabric dyed in brilliant greens and blues.

Sierra realised she was staring and quickly looked away. She ought to be careful not to draw attention to herself — Kell might not have sent her portrait this far. Faced with proof of her identity, the clan wouldn't willingly hand her back to Kell to be trained as a weapon to be used against them. Instead they'd kill her as quietly and as swiftly as they could and bury her so deep Kell would never find so much as a trace. Or at least, they'd try.

*Black Sun*, Sierra prayed silently, *just let them send me on my way.* Cam and Isidro were depending on Mira and her clan for their safety — if she was forced into action, she would be endangering their future as well.

Mira's hazel eyes widened when she saw Isidro standing behind Cam and she held her gloved hands out to him in welcome. 'Isidro, it's so good to see you! After all I'd heard I was afraid I'd never lay eyes on you again!'

'Mirasada,' Isidro said. He took her fingers and bowed low to kiss the back of her gloved hand.

'Why so formal, Issey?' Mira said with a laugh. 'Ten years in the wild and you still have better manners than half the men at court.'

Isidro smiled faintly. Mira was every inch a politician, raised from birth to follow in her mother's footsteps and lead the clan. She never quite knew what to make of him. Too often he had failed to bounce in the precise direction she pushed him. For a while, he'd enjoyed sparring with her, but now he was too weary and too heartsick to take any pleasure in the game.

Mira frowned and quickly pulled her glove off to lay her hand on his forehead.

He pulled away. 'Mira —'

'You are ill, aren't you? You're so thin and pale. Here, you really ought to sit down. Someone fetch him something to drink!'

'Mira, it's not necessary.'

Cam came to his rescue, just as one of Mira's men hurried over with a flask wrapped in felt. Rhia pushed her way through the crowd to his side and tried to get him to sit, kicking off her snowshoes to make a platform in the soft snow. Isidro refused, even though he had grown dizzy. He felt helpless enough as it was without having to stare up at everyone.

All at once, Isidro felt the hair on his arms prickle and rise; he looked up quickly, catching Sierra's eye across the crowd. She was nervous and his discomfort was making her more so, feeding her restless power. Isidro turned to his brother. 'Cam,' he said in a low voice. 'Better get on with it.'

Cam understood him at once and nodded. 'Mira, we need to get digging.'

'No you don't, Cam. I was going to leave a message, but it's so much better to find you like this. I've arranged for the clan to shelter you and Isidro for as long as you need. Your companions are welcome to stay with us, or we can help them settle in another clan's territory if they'd rather be further away from the troubles here.' Mira scanned the faces of his companions. 'You told me of a man with mourning tattoos who might be recognised as one of the Raiders …'

'Garzen,' Cam said. 'He died. We had to buy supplies, but there were some soldiers in the village who recognised me and followed us back to camp. They took us by surprise.'

Mira's lovely face grew sombre. 'Oh, how awful! And I remember how much help he was when you were with Charzic's band. Did the poor man leave any family?'

Cam shook his head. 'They were all killed when the Mesentreians took their lands.'

'Black Sun rest him,' Mira said. 'But I see there is another addition to your group since I saw you last, Cam. You told me of Rhia the physician, as well as the sisters and their husband. But who is the other woman?'

Sierra had positioned herself on the other side of her horse, fussing with something out of sight as an excuse to hide her face.

'We only met her a few days ago,' Cam said. 'She was in some Mesentreian lord's retinue and slipped away when she had the chance.'

'Ah,' said Mira. 'That's a familiar story. Well, we can shelter her as well. What's her name?'

'You can offer, but I doubt she'll take it,' Cam said. 'Here, I'll call her over. Kasimi!' he said. When Sierra looked up, Cam beckoned her over.

She came warily. Isidro frowned, hoping her nerves wouldn't get the better of her. One wrong step would put all her plans awry.

Mira looked her over, taking in the worn and faded clothes Lakua had picked out for her. 'Cam tells me you've escaped from the army.'

'That's right,' Sierra said.

'Well, you're welcome to take shelter with the Wolf Clan. Do you have family who will take you in? We can help you find them.'

Sierra shook her head. 'No, no family. And thank you, but no. I can't stay here.'

'Why not?' said Mira. 'Who did you escape from? Will he try to hunt you down?'

Sierra shook her head again. 'He'll make things difficult for anyone who shelters me. It's better if I just keep moving.'

Mira hooked her thumbs into her sash and tilted her head to one side. 'The Wolf Clan is not easily pushed around,' she said. 'If he has no reason under the law to keep you, then you will be safe … unless he intends to bring some charge against you?'

Sierra looked away, casting around as though hoping to find a way to escape. It was the worst thing she could have done and told Mira clearly what she was really afraid of.

'Mira,' Cam said, 'Just let her go. It's for the best. The charge against her is false but there's no easy way to prove it; the taint will cling to her forever. It's easier if she just disappears.'

'Really?' This time, when Mira frowned it was in honest puzzlement. 'Well, now I *am* curious. But very well, you know your own mind best, I'm sure.'

'We promised her supplies from the cache,' Cam said.

Mira shrugged. 'Show the men where it is, then, and they can get digging.'

While Cam was getting his bearings on the trees surrounding the little clearing, Sierra turned away with an air of relief — but Isidro saw Brekan sidling towards Mira with a smirk on his lips.

Isidro went to head him off. 'Brekan —'

Brekan ignored him. 'They're lying to you, my lady! Cam and Isidro — they're hiding something from you.'

Mira turned to him with a small frown of confusion, but then she laughed, and Brekan flushed bright red.

'Oh, come now,' Mira said. 'I've known Cam and Issey for years. Why would they do a thing like that?'

'I'll tell you,' Brekan said. 'That woman —'

'Hold your tongue, Brekan!' Isidro said with a warning glare.

Mira turned to him, suddenly suspicious. 'Isidro,' she said in a low voice. 'Is there something to what he's saying?'

Brekan smirked.

'We'll explain later,' Isidro said. 'In private. Trust me, Mira, it's better to keep it quiet.'

Mira cast a narrow glance over at Cam and Sierra, who had once again ducked behind her horse and out of sight. 'Are my people in danger?'

'Not at the moment,' Isidro said. He laid a hand on Brekan's shoulder on the side of his broken ribs in an effort to steer him away from Mira.

'Well,' Mira said. 'I hope you know what you're talking about.' To Brekan, she said, 'Come and speak to me later this evening and I'll hear your concerns if you still have them.'

It took Brekan a moment to recognise the dismissal in her words, but once he understood his face darkened even further. 'What? No! My lady, you have to hear this! That girl —'

Isidro tightened his grip. 'Brekan, shut your mouth —'

'No! And don't you talk to me like that, you useless cripple! I've had enough of being treated like the lesser man when you're nothing but a traitor!' Cam was striding back towards them with a face like thunder. Lakua, standing by the sleds, hid her face in her hands. Eloba was furious, but Brekan ignored them all. 'You couldn't even last a day before selling us all out to the king's men! And what are you now? So worthless that the only woman who will take you to her furs is a cursed sorcerer! Get your wretched hands off me!' Brekan turned and shoved Isidro hard enough to send him sprawling in the snow.

For a moment the only thing he was aware of was the pain in his arm. Somewhere in the distance he seemed to hear a sound like the world itself was being ripped apart as the clearing erupted into light. Men were shouting in alarm as horses reared and screamed. Cam, a mere silhouette against the blaze of blue light, bunched one fist and swung at Brekan, but Sierra got him first.

She flung out one hand and a bolt of energy as thick as her wrist burst from her palm and struck Brekan like the lash of a whip. It caught him on the chin and whipped his head back so hard it lifted him into the air and threw him back and out of Isidro's line of sight.

The next thing Isidro knew, Cam and Rhia were kneeling beside him. Sierra stood a few paces away, still blazing with light, while Mira's men held her at the centre of a circle of spears.

For a few long moments it took all of Isidro's strength to keep breathing through the pain. Intentionally or not, when Brekan shoved him, his hand had pressed on the fingertips of the arm bound in the sling across his chest. Even with all the splints and wrappings intended to hold it rigid, that shove had forced his shattered wrist to flex. It was no more than a fraction of an inch, but it sent a spear of pain through his arm so intense that for a long moment he thought he was going to pass out. It seemed as though he was viewing the world through a long, dark tunnel.

Sierra had her hands in the air in a gesture of peace, but her attention was on Cam and Rhia, as though she wasn't even aware of the weapons ranged around her. 'I can help him,' she said.

'You've done enough damage!' Rhia spat.

All Isidro could think about was the pain in his arm. He would have crawled to her if he could and to hell with the shame of it, but Rhia and Cam both had an arm around his shoulders and he lacked the strength to shrug them off.

'Stay where you are!' Mira ordered, her voice hard and cold. 'I have bowmen on you, and they'll shoot at my order!'

'Let them!' Sierra shouted as the strands of power snapped and crackled around her head.

'Sierra,' Isidro whispered, but his mouth was dry and the words came out as a croak.

'What's that?' Cam said, leaning closer.

166

Isidro swallowed hard and tried again. 'Sierra … I need her, Cam …'

Rhia's hands tightened on his shoulders. 'No, keep her away. Cam, I warned you of this —'

Isidro clenched his good hand into a fist. The pain was a beast inside of him, trying to claw its way out. When it rose up like this, he couldn't talk, he couldn't think — it robbed him of his will and he hated it. His mind was the only strength he had left now and the pain and the drugs kept it caged.

'I need to get to Isidro,' Sierra said, her voice calm. 'Tell your men to get out of my way. I don't want to hurt anyone …' Her voice faltered. 'Anyone else.'

For a moment there was confusion and then Sierra was crouching beside him. Her bare hand, already cold in the winter air, brushed against his face.

This time he didn't feel the shock. Her touch opened a channel beneath his skin and a flood of cold carved a path through his flesh until it reached his hand and pooled there, turning bone to ice.

In a few moments the pain was gone and Isidro wanted to weep with relief. His head was spinning and his body trembled like a newborn foal, but he could think clearly again and the awful, devouring pain was gone. He tried to sit up and would have toppled to the side if it weren't for Cam's arm supporting him. 'Where's Brekan? Did you …'

'He's alive,' Cam said, looking past him. Isidro twisted around and saw Brekan sitting on the snow with a blood-soaked cloth pressed to his cheek.

'She's a mage!' Brekan said again, his voice strangely wet and thick. 'What are you waiting for? Kill her!' He spat a mouthful of blood onto the snow.

'Sierra,' Cam said softly. 'You should go.'

She looked from him to Isidro and nodded. 'You're right.'

Before she could stand again, Isidro caught her sleeve. 'Sirri!' he said. 'I …' He tried to speak, but the words wouldn't come. It wasn't supposed to happen like this.

She cupped her hands around his. 'Be well,' she told him with tears in her eyes, then gently pulled her clothing free and stood to face Mira. 'I'll leave,' she said. 'Let me take my gear and go and I promise you'll never hear of me again.'

'I can't let you do that,' Mira said.

Sierra gave a brief, humourless laugh. 'Just how did you plan to stop me?'

'She fought her way free of Kell's encampment, Mira,' Cam said. 'A few nights ago she killed a dozen armed men without raising a sweat. She's going to walk away from here no matter what you do — spare your men and give them the order to stand down.'

Mira was shaken and her carefully schooled calm was slipping. The men were loyal, they would do whatever she asked — Isidro only hoped she was not so afraid of losing face that she would order them to attack Sierra despite Cam's warning. He doubted that Mira had ever found herself in a situation like this before — she had been groomed to be a peace-leader, not trained as a warrior to lead men into battle.

Sierra, on the other hand, was deadly calm and utterly fearless. There was nothing Mira's men could do to her. Isidro had spent enough time with her to be certain she had no wish to harm anyone, but she would if she had to.

Sierra held Mira's gaze, but slowly raised her hands in a gesture of peace. 'I'm going to unhitch my sled.'

'I'll help you,' Cam said. He gave Isidro's shoulder a squeeze, then got to his feet and headed to Sierra's side.

'Cam!' Mira said in protest.

'Just let her go, my lady, please!' Eloba implored her. 'You have no idea what she'll do if you try to stop her. She's a Child of the Black Sun!'

'Kill her!' Brekan said. 'Kill the bitch! Can't you see she's an abomination?'

'Enough!' Mira snapped, and to Sierra she said, 'You will leave the Wolf Clan's lands at once and never set foot in them again on pain of death. Do you swear to abide by this?'

'Why not?' Sierra said. 'But let me say this. It would be better for all your people if Kell never hears of this. It won't matter how loudly you protest that you couldn't keep me. If he learns you had me and let me slip away, he will want blood.'

Sierra's sled was already packed and ready to go. While she spoke, Cam had gathered the last of their supplies and was shoving it beneath the wrapper covering the loaded sled. He held the trace-line while Sierra wrapped it across her chest, took hold of the poles and turned to face the north. The warrior she was facing shifted his grip on his spear and threw a nervous glance at Mira.

'Stand aside,' she ordered him. 'Let her pass.'

Mirasada unrolled the woodcut with shaking hands and took a single glance before letting it curl up again and shoving it back into Ardamon's hands. 'Yes, that's her. Oh, what did that writing say? I didn't even read it —'

'No point,' Ardamon said. 'It's just some story Kell made up to protect his lost rabbit from the baying mobs.' He tossed it down onto the low table behind the stove and stooped to pour a measure of mead into a bowl for Mira. When he pressed it into her hands she downed it with a gulp.

'Rabbit? You wouldn't say that if you'd seen her for yourself, cousin. She made my blood run cold. And that fool of a man who gave her away — she could have killed him for that.'

'Really? I heard all he had is a cut to his face.'

'A cut? Ardamon, she opened his cheek right down to the bone. I could see his teeth through the wound.' She shuddered and held her bowl out to him again. 'Pour me another, will you? Cam's physician is going to sew him up, so no doubt we'll hear the cries soon.'

Ardamon poured her another measure and settled in his chair. 'I should have gone with you. I'm supposed to be guarding you, after all. It was foolish of me to let you go off alone.'

'And how were you to know? In all my days, I never thought I'd meet one of *them*. Tell me, Ardamon, what would you have done?'

He propped his elbows on the carved armrests and steepled his fingers. 'The same as you, I dare say. The histories take great pains to point out the dangers of attacking a mage directly. Subterfuge, poison and ambush are the only way to remove them safely.'

'That's what I thought,' Mira said, and she flopped into the matching chair, its leather-slung seat and back padded with thick, soft furs. 'This way, she thinks she's got cleanly away.' She pulled her red braids back from her face and the beads clattered together with a musical chime.

'I can't believe Cam knew about it all along and lied to your face!' Ardamon said. 'Isidro, yes, he's always been the cunning one, but Cam?'

'Don't underestimate him, Ardamon. He pretends to be as slow as an ox, but there is a reason why Leandra named him as her heir — and why Valeria's so determined to have his head. Remember, the man who raised the Owl raised the prince as well, it's just that Isidro looks too much like his father for anyone to forget it. I only wish I could look as pure and innocent as Cam. I'd be well-nigh unstoppable if I could pull that off.'

'It's the hair,' Ardamon said. 'That red hair of yours makes people think you're up to something.'

Mira threw a cushion at him and Ardamon slapped it away with a grin. 'Speaking of the Owl,' Ardamon said, 'I saw him when you led them in. Our spies with the army are saying Severian's men are certain he's dead. It would be in our best interest if no one were to disabuse them of the notion.'

'Shouldn't be too hard,' Mira said. 'He's in a bad way — he wouldn't last much longer out here on his own. I must admit, after what Cam told me last time I was sure he'd be dead by now, but this works just as well …' She rolled the bowl between the palms of her hands. 'In fact, it should work out perfectly.'

'You're still going ahead with this plan of yours, then?' Ardamon shook his head. 'It's going to be incredibly dangerous, Mira. Once you're married, Osebian is going to flood Ruhavera with his own men and if any of them spot Cam it will all be over.'

'But they won't spot him, Ardamon. Once we dye his hair black he'll be another Ricalani. And anyway, it won't be for long. Severian is not a well man. The diseased whores his mother employs to entertain him have seen to that. All I need is one child, maybe two, with Cam's blond hair, and then we can arrange an accident of some sort for Osebian.'

'Presuming we all survive that long without the Akharians making slaves of us. Do you expect Cam to agree to this?'

'Of course he will. He needs to keep his brother safe and we have the means to do that. There are plenty of isolated temples where no one will notice another priest, crippled or not, and it'll only be for a few years. When Valeria is gone and I'm regent for the young king or queen, Isidro can come out of hiding. Cam will agree in a heartbeat, you wait and see. Oh, but don't you say a word of this to him, not until I bring it up.'

'Let me guess,' Ardamon said. 'First you're going to make him pay for lying to you.'

'Of course.'

The sound of voices outside made Mira sit up straighter. The sentry guarding her door was hailing the men she had summoned on her return to the camp. Ardamon rose to invite them inside.

There were three of them, all nondescript and weathered, the sort of men who would blend into a crowd and never be remembered. Mira knew the youngest was only a little older than her, though his face was scarred and spotted with frostnip.

'Gentlemen,' Mira said. 'I take it you have heard of the incident this afternoon?'

The men did not exchange a glance. 'We have, my lady.'

Ardamon brought out the portrait again and the men passed it around. Mira said nothing, letting them study it in silence. She had never had to order an execution before, though she had stood beside her mother when Tarya gave the command. These men had joined her retinue for another purpose, to find Cam and discreetly let him know that Mira had left her message and was waiting for a reply. She had never dreamed that this would be the first time she had to send her men out to kill another human being.

Mira had no doubt that her clan elders would support her decision. It was the sacred duty of the clans to protect their people from sorcerers. What worried her were the repercussions if her orders were ever found out. If Kell learned of what she had done, nothing would save her, not even her position in the clan or her betrothal to the duke.

As the third huntsman handed the portrait back to Ardamon, the eldest of them spoke up. 'You needn't say a word, my lady. We know what needs to be done. An arrow in the back will do the job and she'll never even see us. D'you want any proof that it's been done, my lady? The girl's head, perhaps?'

Mira swallowed hard. She'd butchered her share of animals, and had helped lay out the dead many a time, but the thought of receiving some grisly memento sickened her. Still, it was the custom — the huntsmen would consider their job unfinished if they didn't bring her some proof that the task was complete. 'Bring me her hands,' she said at last. Tarya preferred the head, to be sure the men had killed the right person, but Mira had seen what a heavy and bulky bundle it made. Cam was clever and Isidro more so — if they saw it they may well guess what she had done. Hands were smaller, more easily hidden and disposed of. 'Wait until dark and leave quietly. The fewer people who know about this, the better.'

The lead huntsman bowed. 'As you command, my lady.'

'I simply can't believe this, Cam — you looked me right in the eye and lied to me! I thought we were friends — I thought you trusted me! I just can't believe you would do such a thing!'

Cam sighed. 'I did it to protect you, Mira, and your men as well. If that lackwit Brekan had kept his mouth shut, Sierra would have gone quietly on her way and none of you would be any the wiser. As it is, everyone in the camp knows about her by now. You're going to have to swear each and every one of them to silence. If Kell hears so much as a whisper that she was here, he and Rasten will take Ruhavera apart stone by stone to find out where she's gone.'

Isidro was beginning to think he should have stayed in the tent Mira's servants had provided for them. Rhia had tried every trick of persuasion she knew to make him rest while Cam answered Mira's summons, but Isidro had refused to listen and now he was regretting it. He felt strange: light-headed and ill. Sierra's touch often left him feeling odd, but it had never been quite like this. His body knew it had been injured, but the absence of pain confused and confounded its response. While Cam and Mira argued, they both kept turning a worried gaze on him, too distracted for their argument to build up any real heat. For his part, Isidro just felt miserable. He was trying very hard not to think about how much his arm was going to hurt in a day's time without Sierra to ease the pain.

'Oh, for the love of light, Isidro, just sit down,' Mira said at last, propelling him towards her carved and padded chair. 'You look as if you're about to keel over. And ye Gods but you're cold. Fenari, pour him some tea.'

Cam hooked his thumbs into his sash and stared down at Isidro with a frown. 'You're not going to be able to keep up this pace much longer, are you?' he said, and turned to Mira. 'We're going to have to find somewhere safe to hole up for a few days and let him rest.'

'No time,' Isidro mumbled. 'Rasten is behind us, remember?'

'Lord Rasten?' Mira said. 'What are you talking about?'

'Whoever spotted me in the village sent a dozen or so soldiers after us,' Cam said. 'Sierra killed most of them, but a handful escaped. They'll have reported back by now and there's been no snowfall to cover our tracks, so we have to assume that Severian has men on our trail. Sierra was certain that Lord Rasten will be among them.'

'She's got more means of knowing that than any of us,' Isidro said. He caught Cam's gaze over the rim of his tea-bowl. 'Tell her about the Akharian forces heading this way.'

'By the Black Sun, Isidro —'

'The Akharian legions?' Mira said. 'Oh, we know about them.'

'What?' Cam burst out. 'Then why is this the first we're hearing of it?'

'Because we only got the word a few weeks ago and you've been camped in the middle of nowhere where I haven't been able to get a message to you,' Mira said. 'When War-Leader Dremman led the Wolf's contingent of warriors to the king's muster the king had him posted to the rear of the army with some nonsense about guarding supply lines —'

Cam frowned. 'That's odd.'

'That's what we thought. We'd expected him to use our men as crow-fodder, hoping uncle would be killed so that Osebian can take over as War-Leader for the clan once we're wed. Well, our spies in the king's camp have ferreted out the real reason. With the army encamped at Chain-of-Lakes, the Brokeridge Pass has been left unguarded. The legions can march east into Wolf Lands with no one but hunters and herders to stop them. If they enslave our people and take them back to Akhara, they'll have saved the king and his cousin the trouble of clearing the Wolf Lands — then they can move in another shipment of Mesentreian settlers.'

'Dear Gods,' Cam said.

'What are you intending to do about it?' Isidro asked.

'Dremman has defied the king's orders to hold his assigned position,' Ardamon said. 'He and the Wolf warriors are marching back to defend our lands.'

'Now there's a move with guts behind it,' Cam said. 'And everyone will get to see them when he's hung, drawn and quartered. How does your war-leader expect to escape a charge of treason?'

'The king doesn't have the power to carry it out,' Mira said. 'All Ricalan knows Severian and the queen favour the new southern lords over the clans, but if Dremman is punished for defending our lands when the king clearly intended to let the Slavers overrun them, it could quite likely be the shifting stone that triggers the rockfall. If the Wolf falls, every clan in Ricalan will know it could be them next. They'd all turn against him, and Severian can't afford that, not when he needs every man he has to defend his southern holdings.'

Cam stared at her incredulously. 'You really think that Severian and Valeria are going to look the other way while the Wolf flouts a royal command?'

'They don't have a choice,' Mira said. 'The king can't destroy us without destroying himself.'

'And your betrothal?' Cam said.

Mira sighed. 'Unfortunately, it stands. Valeria thought it a victory when she forced us to sign the contract but when the tables turn it will give us the advantage. Our clan is still the most powerful in Ricalan and if they break it they'll never have a chance to bring us to heel. As much as I hate the idea of having Osebian for a husband, that marriage contract means we have the Angessovars by the throat.'

'And what of the Akharians?' Isidro said. 'What's their goal? Slaves?'

'It must be,' Ardamon said. 'There's nothing else here that would have any value to them. With no warriors to defend the villages, they're easy pickings. But the war-leader and the army are due to return in ten days. There is a second muster under way and they'll be gathering men as they march north to meet the Slavers. Dremman is too far away to aid us against anyone following you, but if we can meet up with the men at one of the mustering points we'll have numbers enough to give them pause. The nearest one is Terundel. It's still a good few days away — we will have to ride hard.'

'We break camp early in the morning, then,' Mira said. 'Isidro, we can clear a sled for you so you can rest while we travel.'

Isidro raised his bowl to her in a mock salute. He had no intention of riding on a sled like an invalid but tomorrow, when Sierra's touch wore off, he would probably change his mind.

'Cam,' said Mira, 'there is something we need to discuss. The clan has agreed to shelter you and Isidro for as long as you need it but there are a few problems to be dealt with. Isidro is going to be difficult to hide — his wounds are distinctive and easy to recognise —'

Isidro handed his bowl back to the servant and heaved himself out of the chair. 'If you'll excuse me, I think I'll go back to the tent.'

Cam frowned, and Mira said, 'I'd have thought you'd want to have your say in the solution.'

'What's the point?' Isidro said. 'You've got us over a barrel — we need your clan's help and we're in no position to negotiate. Cam's still fit and strong — no doubt you've got some plan in mind for him — and I'm to be hidden away in some temple until Valeria gives up looking for me. I know you, Mira, and I'm sure you've got it all worked out.'

Isidro turned towards the door and swayed on his feet. Cam stepped forward and took hold of his shoulder to steady him. 'You made me a promise, brother,' Cam said softly.

'I did, and I intend to keep it,' Isidro said. 'But right now I'm too weary to pretend to be grateful for whatever hole Mira's found to stuff me into. Perhaps tomorrow I'll be more willing to dance to your drum. Mira, Ardamon.' Isidro bobbed his head in a sketch of a bow. 'I'll see you in the morning.'

As he ducked out through the tent flap, Isidro heard Cam speak softly behind him. 'I'll do whatever you ask if you keep him safe.' Isidro walked away before he could hear any more.

Night had come upon them and it was now full dark outside. Isidro felt utterly heartsick and the thought of Sierra walking alone through the chill night made his stomach twist and his throat close over, so that for a moment he couldn't breathe. He'd never fallen so hard for a woman before ... but he couldn't be certain how much of what he felt was for her and how much of it was fear of what would happen when the pain in his arm returned. He wanted it to be her but the memory of the agony, the awful grating of splintered bone, the helplessness and despair of it, filled him with such overwhelming dread that he felt awash with shame. He wanted nothing more than to go after her, to beg her to stay. After the long week he'd spent as Kell and Rasten's plaything, subject to every torment and humiliation they could contrive, why did his courage fail him now?

A fire had been lit in the centre of the camp and a few men were gathered beside the blaze, drinking and talking in low voices that were drowned out by the crackling flames. Isidro had intended to head straight back to his tent, but suddenly decided he didn't want to be alone with his hopelessness and heartache, and started towards the fire.

As Isidro came up to them they fell silent, but welcomed him with friendly nods. One of the men had a little ceramic jar, its lid sealed with wax, which he was examining in the firelight. As Isidro neared he unhurriedly tucked it away into the satchel slung across his shoulder.

'Evening,' Isidro said and held his good hand out to the warmth. All three men had satchels, as well as bows and quivers slung across their shoulders. 'Off on a hunt?' he said, thinking only of making some conversation, but once the words were out he realised the scene was odd. It was rare for hunters to go out in the evening when they were weary from the day. It was more common to take a few hours' sleep and head out in the early morning.

'Aye,' said one of the men. 'Folks hereabouts have a leopard stalking their goats. They're worried it'll take a child watching the herds next.'

Isidro nodded. That made more sense — the big cats preferred to hunt at night and the men could well have been resting through the afternoon in order to be fresh for the evening's hunt. 'Well, good luck to you,' he said as the last man drained his bowl and tucked it into his satchel.

'Thank ye, sir,' the hunter said, and without another word the three of them turned away from the light and melted off into the darkness. Isidro felt a prickle of regret as he watched them go — just as he had when he was a boy, watching his clan's retainers heading out for a hunt deemed too dangerous for the heir to accompany them.

The image of the wax-sealed jar rose in his mind again and Isidro felt himself go very still. He'd seen jars like that before, but rarely in a hunter's hand. Rhia had a few containing medicines too dangerous to allow any chance of them contaminating other preparations in her kit. Once, just once, he'd seen such a jar as a boy in his clan's lodge, a white glazed jar sealed up with soot-stained wax. He'd crept into his father's private chamber to retrieve a confiscated toy when Drosavec had come in with one of his huntsmen. Isidro had heard them coming and hid. That was when he'd first learned that some of the clan's huntsmen performed other, secret services for their patrons. His father had given the hunter a sealed pot just like the one he'd seen here, taking it from a locked chest to which his father possessed the only key. Once the hunter was gone, Drosavec had found him and, to Isidro's surprise, had explained what was happening. The son of a Mesentreian merchant had raped a girl and his father was protecting him from trial. Once it became clear that there was no way to bring the boy to justice, Drosavec dispatched his assassin with a stiletto and a jar of poison with which to anoint the blade. A fatal wound was too dangerous — the boy's father would want revenge — but a little knick with the poisoned blade would be enough to kill him with no real proof of the cause.

Those men were the Wolf Clan's assassins, with a pot of poison to anoint their arrows. There was no wounded leopard stalking in the night. They were after Sierra.

*I should warn her*, he thought. *I should go after them ...*

*And then do what, exactly?* Those men were professionals and loyal to the Wolf Clan. There was nothing he could do to sway them from carrying out their orders. But if one of the hunters was injured in some way, Sierra might just feel them coming — otherwise it was unlikely that she'd ever see the men who killed her. If it were Isidro following along behind her, though ...

There was no pain in his arm now — Sierra had seen to that before she left, but it would be a simple thing to change. It wouldn't even have to be his arm, a small cut would do if he were close enough. Then Sierra would know that *someone* was behind her and it would put her on her guard. It wouldn't be easy for him to match the pace Mira's hunters set — if he wanted to be close enough to do any good, he had no time to spare.

Cam left Mira's tent with defeat weighing heavy on his shoulders. Mira had invited him to stay the night with her, but he couldn't face it, not now. For the last week he had been a little jealous of Isidro's good fortune in finding a female companion, but now that his chance arose he found he had no heart for it. Cam left with the excuse that he didn't want to leave Isidro alone when despair was creeping up on him again.

It was the truth, but not the whole of it. Cam had spent the greater portion of his life as a political pawn, one piece among many in the game between Valeria and Leandra, his mother and his aunt. As a boy, he'd hated it from the moment he'd been aware of what was going on. When the chance came to loose his bonds he'd bolted for it like a wild horse and never once regretted anything he'd left behind. Ten years of freedom he and Isidro had had and, as he looked back on it now, Cam felt as though they'd been playing at warriors, at bandits, at spies. That was over now. For Isidro's sake, Cam would allow himself to be dragged back into the filthy games of politics and power. Mira was scheming twenty years into the future and, once again, Cam was a pawn in someone else's plan. Of course, he'd agreed to it — he had to, but still it tasted of bitterness and defeat.

The tent he shared with Isidro was silent. No light spilled out when he lifted the flap to duck inside. Well, it had been a long day, and Isidro was both physically exhausted and weary in spirit with the loss of a friend. Cam entered quietly, so as not to wake him.

Once inside, though, he knew something was wrong. The stove had died down and the air had the desolate chill of an uninhabited space. There were no soft sounds of breathing. The tent was too dark for him to see anything at all. Cam felt his way forward cautiously to find the stove, and then opened the door to light a candle from the coals.

Isidro's furs were empty. They hadn't been disturbed since Cam laid them out for him hours ago. His stomach lurched so violently that Cam felt as though he'd been punched in the gut. *No, he couldn't have.* Isidro had *promised*. If he'd left, then it was Cam's fault for letting him go off alone when he was so clearly overwhelmed with hopelessness and despair.

There was a note-tablet lying open on Isidro's furs: two flat plaques of wood joined together with a leather hinge. Cam held it up to the meagre candle-light with trembling hands. Scrawled with Isidro's left hand, the letters were child-like and shaky as they spelled out a message written in a code their father had taught them years before.

*Cam, I didn't break my promise. Mira sent hunters after Sierra. I'm going after them. I.*

Cam was familiar with the sort of hunters sent out on a human trail. 'Oh by the Black Sun, Issey,' Cam whispered. 'What were you thinking?' There was no telling what Mira's assassins would do if they discovered Isidro trailing them. *For the love of light, brother, don't do anything stupid.*

# Chapter 15

At the foot of a hill Sierra stopped to rest, letting the sled-poles drop as she reached inside her coat for her water-skin. There was only a few swallows of leathery-tasting water left and she allowed herself a scant mouthful before pushing the stopper back into the horn spout. Soon she would either have to stop and light a fire to refill it, or else resort to eating snow to quench her thirst. That was a bad idea — it would bring hypothermia on faster, just as it had before Cam found her. This time, she would most likely wake to find Rasten gazing down at her. *Better not to wake at all*, Sierra thought. *Cam should have left me where he found me.*

People rarely travelled alone in a Ricalani winter. It was something done only in desperation when there was no other refuge available. Alone there was no one to keep watch for leopards and tigers while she slept, no one to help her stay alert for the confusion and disorientation that were the warning signs of hypothermia. If she fell through the ice, there was no one to pull her out, to put up the tent and light a fire to help dry her clothes and warm her again. If she was injured, or fell ill, no one would cut firewood for her, fetch water or find food once her supplies ran out. No one survived alone for long in the Ricalani winter. If she grew too cold, too tired, or if she got frostbite, or snow blindness again, she would die — unless Rasten found her first.

Somewhere nearby, perhaps just a few hillsides over, a wolf raised its voice in a howl and after a moment another cried out in answer. Sierra froze for a moment before working the stopper back into the spout of the water-skin. Wolves were no threat to her at the moment. She could see off a whole pack of them if she had to, but once her power ran down it would be a different matter. She couldn't feed from animals the way she could from humans and she had no other weapon in her pack. That was another thing she would have to see to when she next met up with people.

Tucking the water-skin away again, Sierra took a moment to stretch her aching back. It was growing late and, wolves or no, she ought to pitch her tent and rest before she became too cold and weary to watch for danger. *But not yet*, she thought. Maybe after another hour or so, but now the thought of crawling into her cold furs alone was enough to make her stoop and pick up the poles again. It had been unwise to let herself get used to companionship. Loneliness had settled across her shoulders like a leaden yoke but as long as she kept moving, the ache in her back and her legs was enough to distract her. In time, she would get used to the solitude, just as she had before, but for now she wanted to be utterly exhausted when she finally crawled beneath her furs. Anything less and she wasn't sure she would be able to keep from weeping from the emptiness.

With a sigh, Sierra leaned into the harness buckled across her chest again. The poles were there to help her steer and check the sled's speed on a downward slope, but it was the harness that took the strain of hauling it. By tomorrow the points where the straps crossed her shoulders and rubbed on her collarbone would be tender and sore, even with the layers of clothing to pad the spots. In a few days' time when she found a house or a temple from which to buy food she might be able to afford a rest day to recover and let the blisters heal. Before then she would have to come up with a convincing reason as to why she was travelling alone and why she could not accept shelter in a temple or from the ruling clan. No matter what she came up with, any folk she met would probably assume she was a fugitive of some sort, a pariah and a law-breaker. Even the outcasts who roamed between the Mesentreian settlements and the Ricalani lands offered her no safety — once they realised who she was they wouldn't hesitate to sell her back to Kell.

An owl swooped across her path on silent wings and Sierra stopped in her tracks with a small gasp of surprise. She turned to follow its flight but the pale shape vanished as swiftly as it appeared, lost in the darkness between the trees. The woods were utterly silent and still and the only sound Sierra could hear was the faint, whispering roar as the steam in her breath froze in the air, forming a hazy cloud around her.

She should light a fire and make a hot drink to revive herself. She ought to pitch her tent and stop for the night. Pressing on like this when she was already exhausted was suicide.

Behind her the owl called, a low, mournful sound that drifted through the still air. Sierra turned and a movement caught her eye, a shifting blur of white-on-white.

Without thinking she threw up a shield, a glowing disc of flickering blue light that wiped out her night vision and blocked the woods beyond it from her view. For an instant Sierra thought she must have overreacted, her tired eyes playing tricks on her. The movement she had seen could have been just a clump of snow slipping from a laden branch.

The thought lasted for a bare instant, but no more, as an arrow struck the centre of her shield. Her quiescent power, stung into life by the impact, struck at it wildly and tore the shaft into myriad blazing splinters. The metal point turned molten and fell, the glowing gob of metal rousing an angry hiss of steam as it seared through the snow.

For a moment Sierra stood stunned — then she tore at the strap buckled across her chest. Her mittened hands could get no purchase and in a flash of rage she took hold of the buckle and cut through the leather with a flick of power. Shrugging free of the loops, she abandoned the sled and ran in the direction the arrow had come from with her power flickering and coursing around her. The light from her shield had as good as blinded her but the one who had loosed the arrow would be no better off.

At the base of a tree she found his tracks, the wide, scuffed marks of snowshoes and the slight haze in the air from his breath as he had settled himself and taken aim. He had dropped his bow there and stumbled away; blinded by the flash of light, his steps were weaving and uncertain. Sierra went to follow them when she heard a rustle of leather behind her and turned to find him lunging at her with a broad-headed spear.

She slashed at the shaft with a lash of power and sheared it off a foot behind the head. Then her power took over and with a will of its own it writhed up the shaft with a dozen rippling strands that swarmed over his hands and up his arms.

At the first brush of power against his flesh, the man began to scream. Wherever it touched, those strands of light cut like knives, slicing through leather, cloth and flesh and leaving gaping wounds behind. He screamed again, a deep and tearing sound that died in a gurgle as lightning crawled like worms out of his mouth. A gush of blood broke over his lip, flooding down his chin, and then he collapsed, falling face-first into the snow. His coat and clothing hung off him in strips, as though they had been shredded by a set of giant claws, and his back looked like a side of raw meat attacked by scavengers. It reminded her sharply of the final ritual, the one Kell used when his subjects were nearing the last of their strength. How many men and women had she seen in this state, a flayed and bloody mass of raw meat and yellow bone? Isidro would have ended up like that — still could, if Rasten found him again.

Breathing hard, Sierra steeled herself to hook a foot under the man's shoulder and turned him over to see his face. Her stomach churned, threatening revolt, and she swallowed hard, forcing it down again. She felt physically ill and not just from the sight and smell of the gore scattered around. This was *her* work; *her* power had wrought this horror — she couldn't blame it on Kell or Rasten, it was hers and hers alone. But who was he and why had he attacked her? She would be dying by now if the owl's call hadn't made her look around.

While she was still struggling to control her nausea, she heard a noise that had no place in this silent, frozen forest — the crackling of flames. Turning, she saw yellow light streaming between the trees from where she had left her sled. Feeling suddenly numb, she headed back, but she already had a fair idea of what she would see.

The sled was ablaze, flickering with yellow flames along its length and pouring off black and greasy smoke. Someone had cut the cord that bound the waterproof wrapper and doused the gear beneath with oil before setting it alight, while the wrapper protected the flames from the melting snow beneath. As she neared it, Sierra could make out her tent and her kitbag charring and twisting within the blaze. All the things she would need to survive on her own were being reduced to ash and char.

She drew a quick breath of air that stank of burning fur and held her hands out over the sled, pouring her energy over the flames to smother them. Before Kell locked the rubies around her wrists there had been a time when the spill of her power would light small fires a dozen times a day. Rasten had been run ragged trying to find them and put them out, but Sierra only stirred herself to extinguish them if the flames threatened something of hers — or if they came too close to the poor souls Kell kept for the rituals, who suffered enough without her adding to their pain. It was only once Kell locked the punishment bands in place that she'd had any incentive to keep her powers under control.

Even as the smoke cleared Sierra could see she'd come too late. Her tent, her spare clothes and her supplies were all ruined, either soaked with oil or charred beyond repair. Whoever lit this fire must have moved in the moment she left the sled behind.

Inside her, curling like a strangle-vine around her spine, her power pulsed and writhed. Provoked by the darker and more primitive of her emotions, it craved destruction and revenge. Slowly Sierra circled the blackened sled and found a set of tracks leading away. She'd been foolish to leave it unprotected — she should have known that anyone sent to kill her wouldn't have come alone.

Light still blazed around her: questing strands of power that crawled over the snow at her feet. As she set out to follow the trail Sierra called them in with an iron will, shoving them back inside her until no light showed. She didn't stop to think what she would do once she found the ones who had done this, or what she could hope to achieve now that all her gear was ruined. There was no thought, just a raw and furious thirst for revenge. All she had wanted was to be left in peace, and they couldn't even allow her that!

A figure loomed ahead of her, a vague pale shape in the darkness, moving with a hurried stride as though his only thought was to get away. He must have heard her behind him — it took more patience than she could currently muster to move silently over snow. The man glanced back and stumbled, tripping over his snowshoes and floundering in the soft and airy drifts. He threw his hands up in supplication, hiding his face in the shadows they cast. 'P-p-please don't hurt me! It was Nars who set fire to your gear, not me! Have mercy, I beg you!'

Her power pulsed within her, straining at the bonds she'd placed on it, but Sierra forced it back down. 'Who sent you?' she demanded. 'Why are you doing this?'

'Never meant no harm, I swear! Oh mistress, please, have mercy!'

His grovelling made her turn away, disgusted at the thought of what she would have done if he'd turned and fought, or waited in ambush as the archer had. Then Sierra heard the distinct sound of a twig snap behind her and without thinking she turned her back on the man floundering waist-deep in the snow to seek the source of the noise. She realised at once she had made a mistake, but by then it was too late. From the corner of her eye she saw him lunge at her with a dagger in his hand.

He stabbed low, aiming for her inner thigh and the enormous blood vessel there beneath the muscle. Sierra stepped back to dodge and tripped over the long tail of her snowshoe. She twisted as she fell and instead of her inner thigh, the tip of the dagger slipped beneath the thick leather and fur of her coat and dragged across her leg, slicing cleanly through leather and fabric and skin. If it stung for a moment, Sierra didn't notice — she was already swinging her hand at the man's knife-arm. It wasn't much of a blow. From any other person it would have been little more than a slap, but as she moved Sierra loosed the bonds that held her power in check. It roared like a dragon up her arm and burst from her palm in a brilliant spear of light. It struck his forearm with an audible crack, splintering the bones like dry twigs. The hunter screamed as his knife-hand went limp, dropping the dagger into the snow where it vanished in the powder. The man screamed again and kept screaming as tendrils of light crawled over his arm, his sleeve rapidly soaked in blood that dripped in a gentle patter onto the snow.

Sierra stopped the threads from reaching any further, but it took a moment longer for her to haul her power back. He lay sprawled across her legs, shaking; she shoved him off and stood carefully, wary of the knife that lay somewhere beneath her. Her leg stung where the dagger had sliced her — it was little more than a scratch, but it was bleeding freely, and her thigh felt wet with blood. Where it seeped into the cloth, dry snow clung to the moisture and froze it in a crust that looked black in the meagre starlight.

'Stay where you are!' a man's voice called out, and Sierra cautiously turned, wary of tripping over her snowshoes again. She saw him making a careful way through the trees, sighting at her down the bolt of a crossbow. She glanced down at the other warrior, but he was still lying in the snow and groaning as he clutched at his shattered arm. It was only then that Sierra realised she'd inflicted almost the same injury on him as Rasten had on Isidro.

The man on the ground seemed to be of little threat, but all the same Sierra moved to keep them both in sight. Backing up in snowshoes was a precarious manoeuvre but still safer than turning her back on the man with the crossbow.

'I said, stay where you are or I'll shoot!'

'Oh, come now,' Sierra said. 'Why would you do a thing like that? You've already seen me stop one arrow.' Once she could keep them both in view without shifting her gaze she stopped and relaxed all the bonds on her power, letting it spill around her in the form of a dozen writhing tendrils of light that stretched out into a sphere with her at the centre. With power flowing in from the man on the ground it was easier to let it have its head than keep it so closely contained.

The one still standing swallowed hard and shifted his grip on the bow. He was frightened, Sierra realised. He could have just left — he could have quietly slipped away while she finished the one who had attacked her. She wouldn't have bothered searching for any other attackers, even if it was unwise to leave enemies behind her. But instead he'd approached her, demon though she was, to save what was left of his comrade's miserable life. 'Drop the bow,' Sierra said, 'and you can take him and go. But tell whoever it was that sent you I won't be so merciful the next time.'

The warrior slowly lowered his weapon until it was aimed at the ground by his feet, then he pulled the trigger and loosed the quarrel into the snow with a heavy twang of the string. Then he let the weapon fall and raised his hands.

With a flick of power Sierra opened a shallow cut across his cheek. The warrior flinched, but made no other move. 'Don't think you can sneak up on me again,' Sierra said. 'I'll feel you coming.'

The warrior just bowed his head in reply and, as wary as a pair of spitting cats, he and Sierra moved in a slow circle until he was beside his moaning comrade and Sierra was on the path that would lead her back towards her sled. She stooped to pick up the fallen crossbow and then turned her back on them and walked away.

Back beside the sled, Sierra dropped to her knees to sort through what was left of her gear. No doubt some of it could be salvaged — the stove and pots at least, and probably part of the tent. It would still be more than she had when she'd left the army camp. As she began to pull it apart her eyes started to sting and she bit her lip to keep the tears from spilling. Those men were still close and she would not let them hear her cry.

This was the last night of his freedom.

Rasten checked his stride as he dropped below the crest of the hill. After this night he would have to return to Kell with all haste — keeping Sierra contained would not be easy and, once he was back within Kell's reach, his master would make sure that the memory of this brief respite was driven far from his mind. The night was peaceful and this moment of solitude was paradise. He would enjoy it while he had the chance.

*Little Crow, I could strangle you.* She could have ruined everything in her panicked flight from Kell and the king's army. She wasn't ready, and when Rasten brought her back Kell would set about breaking down her will and her mind until she was nothing but an obedient slave, too terrified to even think of resistance. After she had defied him so openly, Kell could do nothing else, and if he succeeded in breaking her they would both be condemned to a lifetime of this miserable existence.

What on earth had possessed her to take such a risk? She had no hope of remaining free, no resources to draw on and no friends to shelter her. What could she possibly hope to achieve? Rasten had done his best to protect her, convincing Kell she wasn't ready for the next phase of her training, that her power still had a way to grow. Now all of that was for nothing. Just another half-year might have let her powers grow enough that Kell's treatment would temper her instead of breaking her down. Even a few more months might have made a difference ...

Delaying her capture was not an option. She was simply too vulnerable. Alone in the Ricalani winter an accident or a miscalculation would kill her as quickly as it would any other person, and if she sought shelter in a village or a farmstead it would only be a matter of time before she gave herself away. Once the Wolf Clan caught wind of her they would finish her swiftly. She had power enough to defend herself against swords and knives, but she still had to eat and sleep. No, there was nothing for it now but to bring her in and hope he could keep her from being ruined as he had been.

At least she was alone now. That was a blessing on two counts. Rasten hadn't been looking forward to taking her from Cammarian's camp. Even as unskilled as she was, that handful of people would give her enough power to make the fight a vicious one, if she was desperate enough to turn on them to feed herself.

And then there was Isidro Balorica. The time she had spent with him in her furs had become a torment — and not just because it should have been Rasten making her sob and moan, not that wretched cripple. Of course he understood why she had wanted another warm body in her furs — they both knew what lay in store for her when Rasten brought her

186

back. What puzzled him was her choice. Why the weak and sickly Balorica and not the prince? Was it the power that drew her? It was the only reason he could think of, but it didn't ring true with the Sierra he knew. She hadn't yet learned that power was the only thing that mattered, and that everything else was a luxury people like them couldn't afford. *Black Sun, let me be mistaken — let her be using him for the power and nothing more.* If he was right, if she really had been foolish enough to develop feelings for Balorica, then she had handed Kell another weapon to use against her. Once he learned of it, Kell would spare no effort to track Balorica down and have him tortured to death in front of her. *You little fool, how could you not have known it would come to that?* But there was nothing to be done about it now. She would learn the folly of her ways soon enough.

She would hate him with every fibre of her being before it was over, but he could live with that. He would do whatever it took to make her strong enough to help him destroy their master.

A prickle of energy interrupted his trail of thought. Rasten stopped in his tracks and closed his eyes, emptying his mind so there was nothing to distract him from the echo of impressions that filtered through his bond with Sierra. In a ghostly vision he saw her running through the trees while the flickering light from her power cast thick black shadows over the snow.

A nagging thought told him he was breathless. Rasten ignored it. Years of experience had taught him to separate his own senses from those of the person bonded to him by ritual. As a flush of energy swelled within her, his body echoed it with a fierce tingling along his bones, and through her eyes he saw a spray of blood, colourless in the moonlight. Somewhere up ahead she was waging a battle and he was too far away to do anything but listen to the echoes that reached him.

For a moment Rasten warred with himself. He wanted to run after her and tear apart the ones who threatened the light of his life and his hope for the future. If he did he would lose these brief impressions, so if she was truly in danger, he wouldn't know until it was too late — but if it did come to that, there wasn't much he could do about it. She wouldn't let him help, however great the danger. All he would do was distract her.

He forced himself to stay where he was as another wave of power washed through him, tingling with such intensity it was painful. A stinging pain on his thigh like the bite of an insect made him slap at it out of reflex. For a few moments there was nothing but a constant pulse of energy, but then the tension within her eased, and he felt her walking away from the source of the power even though it was still pulsing with energy behind her. *Lackwit girl*, Rasten said to himself in silent disgust. *You'd better not have left a live enemy behind you.*

The next sensation confused him completely, as he saw a distinct vision of her weeping in frustration and rage although he knew she wasn't hurt beyond a scratch or two. As her heightened emotions sank back to normal, he lost the contact and found himself alone again. But she was close — so very close.

He set out again, moving silently and cautiously. It was only a short time later that he heard people moving clumsily towards him and ducked off the path to conceal himself behind a stand of trees and wait for them to approach. It was only when they came close that Rasten realised one of them was badly wounded and going into shock — one arm, crudely splinted, was bound across his chest, the other was slung around the shoulders of his companion, who struggled to keep him upright as they staggered through the deep snow.

As the men made their slow way past Rasten removed his mittens and tucked them away, then reached for his dirk. The long, slender blade never saw much use compared with his other tools, but he always kept it close to hand. If one of Kell's subjects began to feed Sierra more power than he and his master could control, the dirk allowed him to finish them quickly and with minimal pain to cut off the supply.

He waited silent and still until the men had their backs to him and then stepped out onto their trail and closed the gap between them with a few quick strides. He seized the wounded man by the shoulder to steady him and punched the dirk into the back of his skull with a crunch of steel and bone. There was no cry of pain or alarm — it was too fast for that. The man collapsed onto the snow with barely a sigh, with the hilt still jutting from the back of his head.

The other hunter turned, gaping at Rasten in a moment of stunned shock before fumbling for his knife.

Rasten threw a lash of power around his wrist and wrenched it away from the hilt. He caught the hunter by the throat and reached inside him with a tendril of power to crush his larynx and keep him from crying out.

In desperation the hunter struck at Rasten's eyes with his free hand, but Rasten caught his arm with another thread of power, locked his wrists together and shoved him to the ground. His lips moving with a hoarse whisper of sound, the man thrashed on the snow, writhing and kicking up clods of ice until Rasten bound his ankles as well and forced him to be still.

He cast a ritual circle around them both, building a wall of pure energy to contain the power and keep Sierra from sensing it.

'Now then,' Rasten said, squatting down on his heels at the prisoner's side. 'You can still talk if you keep it to a whisper and there's one thing I want cleared up before we begin. Who sent you after my Sierra?'

The hunter spat at him and Rasten deflected it with a shield that was little more than a blur of ruddy light in the air. He set his foot on the back of the dead man's head and pulled the dirk out with a low moan of steel. With the point of the blade, he cut a nick in the man's jacket, slicing deep enough to cut the skin beneath, and then ripped his clothing open to bare his chest. 'Let's try again,' Rasten said while the man struggled and writhed in the snow. 'Who sent you?'

Sierra stopped in her tracks with a shiver. The stream of power from the wounded man had stopped, snuffed out as suddenly and swiftly as a candle-flame. *Are you surprised?* she asked herself. *He was going into shock — he probably just fainted.* But her nerves wouldn't stop prickling and she felt a nervous crackle of energy swarm over her skin with an unpleasant tingle. Of course he could have collapsed from shock, but she couldn't sense the other man either and he hadn't gone far enough to be beyond her range.

*Rasten.*

Sierra struggled out of the mended sled rope and dropped it to the snow, then blindly walked away from the gear she had salvaged from the fire. What was the point of weighing herself down with it? If Rasten was within a few hours of her, he would take her, and that was that. Even with the power she had taken from Isidro and the hunters, she was no match for his years of training and experience. She would have been better off letting the hunters kill her.

Weariness and a deep-seated chill had settled into her bones and the pad of rags she'd bandaged over the cut on her thigh was wet and cold.

The wound was contaminated — Sierra suspected the knife had been smeared with a preparation of blood-root. It was a drug that prevented blood from clotting; hunters and warriors painted it onto their blades and arrowheads so that a wound that might otherwise staunch itself would see human or beast bleed to death. If the hunter had sliced into her inner thigh as he intended, then even if he had missed the vein Sierra would have passed out and bled to death on the snow. As it was, the wound might bleed enough to make her light-headed, but the drug would wear off before she lost enough to be truly in danger.

She'd thought herself lucky when she'd bandaged the wound, but now she wasn't so sure. If only she'd gone back and found the poisoned knife … One good cut on Rasten and even with all his power he would bleed out before he could reach help. Or, if all else failed, she could turn it on herself. But the knife was well behind her now, buried beneath the trampled and bloody snow.

Sierra turned her face up to the sky, blinking back tears that blurred the stars above her. Back when her powers first manifested, she'd overheard a priestess advise her parents to let the winter take her. *If she's truly a Child of the Black Sun*, the priestess had said, *then she was never meant for this world. The kindest thing you can do is send her back to where she belongs, before she brings destruction and despair down upon you all.* Get her drunk, the priestess had told them, drug her with poppy and strong wine, then take her far into the woods and leave her to the snow.

Her parents sent the woman away and began making plans to leave that very night. But her prediction had come true in the end — not just for her kin, but for Cam and his little troupe. Perhaps she should wait for Rasten to find her and let her curse bring destruction down upon them, too. Perhaps Kell would be persuaded to go easy on her if she gave herself up and came in quietly …

Sierra threw her head back and laughed, a near-hysterical giggle. No, she couldn't make herself believe that. Now that he knew she bore the seed of rebellion, Kell would stop at nothing to break her. She'd surrendered once in the hope that it would salvage a desperate situation, but never again. Vasant, the Last Great Mage, hadn't surrendered, even when he knew that death was inevitable — and he'd made Leandra pay for her victory with a river of blood. In her youth, Sierra had wondered why he'd drawn that last battle out in such a senseless display of waste and destruction, but now she was beginning to understand. She'd tried to do the right thing — she'd given up everything she'd ever loved to salvage some scraps of her life and her family — but it hadn't worked. Kell would never give up, not until he had what he wanted.

A strange kind of calm had settled over her and Sierra knew, at last, what she had to do. Rasten wouldn't take her alive, not again.

And by the Black Sun, if she could, she'd take him with her.

# Chapter 16

Isidro crouched leewards of a listing tree, trying to keep his teeth from chattering. The cold and his cramped position were taxing his strength, and the memories he'd done his best to bury threatened to overwhelm him.

Mercifully, the tree blocked his view, but he couldn't stop his mind from conjuring images of what could cause those soft, wet sounds and the desperate, panicked breath of a man who was being butchered alive. The victim was silent except for the low, scuffling sounds of a futile struggle. Rasten had done something to keep him from crying out, and that meant that Isidro couldn't move a muscle, not even to shift his weight. Any noise could be enough to give him away.

He should never have come here — Isidro knew that now. Exhaustion had made him unwary and he had come within a few paces of stumbling into Rasten's path. It was only a matter of luck that Rasten had come across Mira's men first.

More than anything else in this world he wanted to attack, to strike Rasten down and finish him then and there, but that was impossible. Even if he were fully whole and able, it would be suicide. All he could do, crouched there like a hunted beast, was separate himself from the part of him that was overcome with fear, lift himself out of this shell of trembling flesh and become a dry and distant observer. Sierra was right, he noted dispassionately — the ritual chant Rasten was murmuring as he worked was in Akharian. With each cycle of the chant, each rise and fall of the cadence of the words, Isidro felt a tingling current of energy sweep through his limbs and close in around his spine, helping to keep the chill at bay. There was no denying it — those hours in Kell's tent had bound him and Rasten together in some way. At another time the thought would have disgusted him, but now Isidro saw it only as a curiosity. If Rasten sensed he was losing even a minute portion of his power, Isidro would be the next one struggling in the ritual circle. So he kept his head down and stayed as still as a stone.

After what seemed like an age the ripples of power reached their peak and began to fade. When Isidro blinked, he saw a flash of vision through Rasten's eyes — a mutilated corpse lying in a circle of churned and bloody snow. The power he'd raised had made Rasten indifferent to the cold and he'd stripped off to his shirtsleeves. His arms were bloody to the elbows and he held the hunter's heart, steaming in the cold air.

The vision lasted for only a moment and then Isidro heard Rasten cleaning his hands with snow and dressing again. When he stamped his feet in the snowshoes to settle the straps and set off again, it took all of Isidro's will to remain unmoving as he heard the yss-yss-yss-yss of snowshoes as Rasten went on his way. Even after the sound had faded he kept his position, not quite daring to believe the danger had passed.

Presently, another sound reached his ears — it was an echo of the first, another pair of snowshoes moving towards him from the opposite direction. Isidro had been on the verge of easing his cramped position — now he froze where he was, though he took the chance of turning his head in the direction of the sound.

What he saw was another figure robed and hooded in white, holding a bow in one hand with an arrow nocked to the string. He stopped in view of the mutilated corpse lying on its bed of bloody snow and, after a moment of stillness, the figure raised a hand to sweep his hood back. It was Cam, his face white and bloodless.

Isidro stood. 'Cam!' he called in a hoarse whisper.

Cam started violently and dropped his bow. 'Issey? Oh, by the Black Sun ... I thought that was you! I couldn't get a clear shot —' He stared blindly at the corpse at his feet. 'I ...' Words failed him and he grabbed Isidro in a rough embrace, pounding him on the back hard enough to make Isidro cough. Cam broke away with a wince. 'Ah, sorry, your arm —'

'Never mind that,' Isidro said. 'Can't feel it at the moment, anyway. What are you doing here?'

'What do you think I'm doing? What in the hells were you thinking of? Have you gone mad?'

Isidro sighed. 'I must be. I couldn't just let her go, Cam.'

Cam shook his head. The remains of the corpse caught his eye again and he turned away with a whoosh of breath. 'And you were there the whole time, just on the other side of that tree?'

Isidro nodded.

'By the Black Sun, you must have the luck of the Gods. If he'd seen you —'

'But he didn't,' Isidro said. 'And now he's gone after Sierra.'

Cam went very still and then slowly straightened. 'There's two men here. How many did Mira send out?'

'Three,' Isidro said. 'Sierra killed the first one a little while ago.'

'How d'you know?'

'I felt it, the same way I did when Rasten was fighting a few days ago.' Cam was shaking his head with a frown, but Isidro went on. 'Look, I know you don't understand it. In your place, I wouldn't know what to think of it either. But I know what I felt.'

'If you say so,' Cam said. He circled around the corpse, searching out the tracks Rasten had left in the snow. 'Can she take him?'

'She didn't think so,' Isidro said. 'He's got ten years of training on her. We have to help her.'

Cam's head snapped up. 'Help her? How? He just made mincemeat out of two of Mira's finest men. By the Fires Below, Sierra can take on a dozen warriors all by herself — if she doesn't believe she can best him, how are we going to help? We couldn't even slow him down!'

'I can help her,' Isidro said. 'I can feed her power —'

'Can you? I saw what she did at the cache and from what I know it'll be hours before it's worn off enough to give her any real boost. It's likely all you'd do is distract her!'

'Well I'm not going to sit back and do nothing! By the Twin Suns, if Rasten takes her alive, we're finished. You know that, don't you? They've gone easy on her up until now, but once they really get to work, she'll tell them everything if it'll spare her a few moments of pain. Trust me, I know what I'm talking about. It'll be the end of the Wolf Clan as well as us.'

Cam heaved a sigh. 'I hadn't thought about that.' He fell silent, staring off into the night, and ran his hand over the stiff white fletching of the arrows in his quiver.

'Cam,' Isidro said.

'She didn't want to be taken alive. She said it herself, more than once. Kell and Rasten together are bad enough. If they bring Sierra around to their ways she'll be a horror like nothing we've ever seen.'

'Cam —'

'If she were here now what do you think she'd say? She's better off dead than in Rasten's hands. It would be better for everyone.'

The words struck Isidro like a blow to the gut. He'd known her only for a week. He couldn't have fallen in love with someone in a week, that would be ridiculous. And yet the thought of losing her struck him with a physical pain that made it hard to breathe. But Cam had it right. Every night he'd slept beside Sierra she'd woken in a cold sweat after dreaming that Rasten had found her.

Cam laid his hand on Isidro's shoulder. 'I'm sorry. You shouldn't be here to see it. Head back to the camp —'

'No.' Isidro drew himself up. 'Let's think this through. What happens if you succeed? If Sierra dies at Rasten's feet, there's no power in this world that will keep him from seeking revenge. The only upside I can see is that he'll be too far gone in fury to take you back to Kell — most likely he'd kill you on the spot.'

'It's got to happen sometime,' Cam said. 'The chance of us lasting a few more years is small; even if this grand plan of Mira's works, we're all headed for the next world. If I can tear Kell's ambitions to shreds on the way I'll consider my life well lived.' Cam shrugged. 'But there's a chance I can kill him too. It's unlikely anyone will ever find him such a good target as he is now. And if I put an arrow in Rasten's back early on, Sierra might well be able to finish him herself.'

'Well then,' Isidro said. He pushed his hood back to scrub his good hand through his hair. 'If Sierra puts up a fight we try to tip the scales in her favour. If Rasten takes her down quickly, we make sure he doesn't bring her in alive.'

'What's this "we"? You're no good to me out here. You're heading back to Mira's camp.'

Isidro shook his head. 'Mira's plan has me hiding out in a temple for the next ten years. I can just about do it if I know there's a chance of finding my way out again, but if Rasten does for you, then my value to Mira goes with you.'

'Mira wouldn't abandon you —'

'No, but without you I'm as good as worthless. I'm no help to Sierra back at the camp, but if I go with you I might be able to skew things in her favour.'

Cam thought it over with a frown. He still thought he was invincible, that he could clear any hurdle in his path. Isidro knew the signs well — he'd felt the same way not so long ago.

'Alright,' Cam said. 'But I want you to hang right back. If Rasten knows you can send power Sierra's way he'll kill you on sight.'

'Don't worry about that,' Isidro said, and ran a hand over his splinted arm. 'I'm well aware of what I can and can't do.'

Cam nodded and stooped to pick up the bow. 'Let's go then.'


Sierra felt elated and as weightless as a thought. At last, all the fears and worries she'd carried with her were gone, as though she'd set them down along with the useless gear she'd left behind. This must be how the elders felt when they gave themselves to the winter, leaving behind the restraints of failing sight and senses and the burden of stiff and painful joints.

When she walked away from the sled she had left the Ricalan of humanity behind her as well. Now she was walking through the Black Sun's world. If the Bright Sun watched over humankind, giving her warmth to the crops and the herds and melting the rivers so the salmon could spawn, then winter was the realm of the Black Sun, when the land was given over to those other children of the Gods, the wild creatures who lived in mankind's shadow. The Black Sun was their Goddess, the cold and indifferent queen of winter, and Her mercy was swift and final, the numbing and somnolent touch of ice.

She had pressed on without care for where she was headed and her feet had brought her to the bank of a river. An open lead of water stretched before her, a dark gash in the winter's pale skin where the ice had retreated from the surface. It was black and oily beside the snowy bank, the surface as smooth as a mirror and utterly silent, without the gurgle or chuckle of water one might hear if the water level had dropped below the skin of ice.

The black water stretched upstream, back into the lake feeding the river. The great weight of snow deposited in the storm that aided her escape had pressed the ice down into the water beneath. Insulated by ice and snow, the water was warmer than the air above, and had melted the ice away. In a few days the water at the surface would cool and the gash would heal over until the cycle started again.

On the far bank of the black river a hill rose up to command a view of the narrow valley she had crossed. Some years ago a wide swathe of the slope had been cleared of trees by an avalanche. The saplings that had sprouted in their place were all but buried, with only their tips peeking out from beneath the blanket of snow. If she could get across the water and wait for Rasten high on that slope, the mass of snow poised there would be enough to bury them both — and if that failed, there was always the black water waiting below.

Sierra turned downstream, aiming for a point below the tip of the lead, where the snow was stained grey by water flowing over the edge of the ice. As she made her way across, the ice beneath her rocked like a boat. While the water had seeped into the snow, a layer of powder over the top insulated it enough to keep the slush from freezing. As she crossed it, water wicked up into the prints of her snowshoes, leaving a stark grey outline against the clean white snow. If she stopped for even a moment, she would sink into the slush and the icy water would seep into her boots and liners, drowning her feet in a misery of cold. So long as she kept moving she stayed on the surface, but even then the wet snow clung to her snowshoes, weighing her down with a load of ice that grew heavier with each step.

Once she was on the other side, Sierra trampled a patch of snow and took the snowshoes off to brush the crusted ice from them with a mittened hand. Allowing herself a moment to catch her breath, she searched the bank across the black water for any sign of Rasten.

The hillside above her was bare, an ominous swathe of white reaching up towards the peak. The slope was relatively shallow when Sierra started up the middle of the white scar but as she gained ground it grew steadily steeper until she was ascending on her hands as well as her feet, each step displacing a drift of snow that dragged her back as far as she'd pushed herself forward. When she reached that point, Sierra kicked off her snowshoes and sat on them, burying her feet into the snow for warmth, and wrapped herself up in her fur to wait.

Cam set a cautious pace as they followed the tracks, wary of alerting Rasten to their presence. Even so, Isidro found it hard to match and Cam kept looking back to make sure he wasn't falling behind. Each time

Isidro gestured to Cam to go on, even though he was breathless and stumbling. His greatest fear was that they would arrive too late, when Rasten already had Sierra under his control.

They slowed briefly when they came across another corpse. Rasten had mutilated his victim with precision, each cut calculated and prescribed by ritual, but this one was like the other men Sierra had killed, butchered in a frenzy of wild, deranged slashes. 'That looks like Sierra's work,' Cam said.

'She can't control her power like Rasten,' Isidro said. 'She told me she'd never done anything like it before Kell took her. Being part of their rituals has made her that way.'

Cam snorted. 'Watching Rasten at work would be enough to warp anybody. But if Mira sees this, it's going to be impossible to convince her Sierra means no harm.'

A short distance ahead they found a scattering of discarded gear amid a circle of soot-stained snow, and some way beyond that, the sled itself, abandoned and forlorn. By now Isidro had to stop, feeling dizzy and light-headed from trying to match Cam's pace. 'She knows,' he said. 'She knows Rasten's behind her.'

The tracks took a turn there, striking a path through a bare wood and avoiding a ridge to the north. With a gesture Cam told Isidro to slow down and catch his breath, then forged on ahead to the edge of the trees to check the lay of the land. By the time Isidro caught up, he was off the edge of the path, shielded from the open land before them by a thicket of bare twigs. Still breathing hard, Isidro joined him, pulling the edge of his cowl up to catch the vapour in his breath.

There was a thread of ruddy light in the valley below, reaching across the dark gash of water. It was a bridge, a shallow arc of flame that spanned the open water with a figure in white halfway across.

'Can you see her?' Isidro murmured to Cam.

'I think there's something on the slope above him,' Cam said. 'It could be her.'

Isidro squinted at the distant slope, and after a moment he made it out — a smudge in the snow, with a faint scratch of tracks leading up to it. The white leather wasn't a perfect camouflage — without something to break up the outline, a figure sitting exposed on a field of snow wasn't hard to spot. Rasten, crossing the bridge, was heading directly for her.

While she waited Sierra had gathered her power, meditating as Rasten himself had taught her. It seethed within her like a storm in the summertime: a tower of black cloud, wreathed around with lightning.

Rasten crossed the open water and came to the foot of the slope to gaze up at her.

'Well, Sierra?' he called, and an echo of his voice boomed back at him from across the fields of ice. 'You've made a good play of it, but it's over now. Are you going to come down quietly, or do I have to come up there and get you?'

Her head was filled with lightning. Fire was a tame thing — men contained its hungers, used it and doused it at will, but lightning … lightning was a creature of the air and the storm — fierce, brilliant and pure. With storm clouds building behind her eyes, Sierra felt enveloped in an icy calm. She made no reply to Rasten, just watched and waited as he started up the slope.

He kept his eyes on her, wary for some trick, although that made it difficult for him to climb as the slope grew steeper. Once he was within a few dozen paces of her, Sierra stood, rising with a swiftness that made him hesitate — she wondered if he was afraid of her. When they first brought her in he had bested her easily, but the pool of power she could hold was much greater now.

Rasten stopped. 'I tried to tell you,' he said. 'I tried to explain, but you wouldn't listen. Every time you struggle, every time you resist, you're just making it worse. Once you give in and accept it, things will be better, Sirri. You have to trust me.'

'Better?' Sierra said. 'Really?' She hadn't intended to speak to him, but the words spilled out of her before she could stop them. 'I know what he does to you, Rasten. It's not enough that you'll kneel for him and bow down even though you hate it. I know he still makes you beg for mercy just to prove that he can, even though in ten years you've never raised a hand to resist him.'

'Because I knew what would happen if I did,' Rasten said. 'It's just the way things are, Sirri — pain is everywhere and it's better to give than receive it, believe me … But you'll learn that for yourself soon enough.'

Sierra wanted to weep for him. He was honestly trying to help her and it broke her heart. In many ways Rasten was still the stripling boy Kell had brought to his dungeons in chains. He was a monster, but it was Kell's training and his sadistic appetites that had made him this way.

'That's not the fate he has in mind for me,' Sierra said.

Rasten raised his hands: two cords of flame erupted from his palms and swept towards her.

All her energy was barely contained beneath her skin, just waiting for something to set it off. As Rasten reached for her, Sierra turned her face to the indigo sky and loosed all that power into the mass of snow beneath her.

Light erupted all around and with a deep and unearthly roar the ground around them heaved and began to slip. The slope gave way beneath them and hurled them both downwards in a sudden confusion of snow, air and rock. Rasten tried to catch her — Sierra saw the ruddy glow of his power — but then they were falling, surrounded in a deadly shroud of ice that was tumbling to the valley floor.

As the avalanche swept them down the slope Rasten snatched and tried again to hold her, but in the sudden confusion of light and darkness he couldn't hold her close and defend himself against her as well. He had one hand on her arm and the other twisted into her hair, but Sierra struck out with the heels of her hands, and when they hit something solid she loosed a bolt of power through them so fierce her hands tingled and burned with the force of it.

If he cried out, she couldn't hear it over the roar of falling snow, but she felt him spasm and go rigid beneath her hands. The ruddy light of his power died and after a moment the falling snow tore them apart. With an effort of will Sierra choked off the power that was spilling from her skin, and everything went black as she slammed into the ice over the lake and the snow buried her.

When he realised he had lost her, Rasten rolled into a ball and shielded himself with a mantle of flame. Sierra's blast had cut through the crust of snow and ice on the surface right down to the rock and scree that had been buried since autumn. Massive blocks of rock and ice crashed around him, but the shield protected him from impacts that should have crushed him like a dry leaf. When the avalanche hit the foot of the slope the force of it would pack the debris so dense a man with a pickaxe would find it difficult to break ground. If he was buried Rasten could blast his way to the surface, but it would take some time to find Sierra and pull her free, and every moment she was buried increased the chances she would suffocate before he found her.

Rasten gathered himself and pushed down with a thrust of power, reaching through the tumbling snow and ice to the solid ground beneath. The force of it threw him up and into the air before he fell back through the cloud of ice, but now he was on top of the slide, and the volume of the shield made him light compared to the other blocks falling around him. It all happened in seconds and the next thing he knew he was slammed into a plain of ice as hard as solid ground. The shield popped like a soap bubble and the impact knocked the wind from him. For a moment he lay there gasping for breath as the aftermath of Sierra's blast made his muscles twitch and spasm. He burned all over from the jolt she had channelled into him, but as soon as he could draw breath Rasten forced himself to his feet. His apprenticeship had taught him to function through much greater pain.

Rasten scanned the wedge of packed snow. The hillside above was a jagged grey face of exposed earth and stone and overhead there was a haze of ice, fine crystals thrown into the air by the force of the avalanche. With growing desperation, he turned towards the lake and the open water, roving over the flat plain of ice. A body buried deep by an avalanche might not be found for years — and when the snow thawed and the bones were picked clean by scavengers it was often only jewellery that allowed the remains to be identified at all.

The only thing he could see was a dark shadow on the ice, down near the open water. Rasten broke into a run, his heart pounding against his ribs. It was just a dark stain against the white, and for a moment he nearly gave up on it, thinking it to be only a smear of soil from the hill above. As he drew closer he saw it was too dark for that. It was black like the open water, black as soot — Sierra's hair, trailing like ribbons behind her. If she had been buried only a few inches deeper, he wouldn't have seen her all.

It was the cold that roused her, the icy touch of water wicking up through the snow. It was packed so firmly around her that Sierra couldn't move.

She could feel the bulk of her coat around her arms, but the sash binding it had come loose and the body of the coat was entombed away from her.

Her arms were spread, wrenched back at a painful angle as the force of the snow and the fall had almost stripped it from her.

As icy water seeped through her clothing, Sierra realised she had been vaguely aware of it for some moments now — it was only when the rising water touched her face that a sudden bolt of panic had roused her. If she didn't move, she would drown.

She tried to pull herself free but the ice held her as securely as chains drawn taut. To be true to the choice she had made she ought to stay here and drown, but as the icy water welled over her lips, panic won out over intellect. She didn't want to die.

Light flared around her before she had even mustered her thoughts. Lightning burst from her skin and thrashed against the snow like a wild beast. She felt rather than heard the ice crack, and the weight above her shifted.

Gasping for breath and soaked to the skin, she scrambled to her feet. There was a rumble beneath her and the ice groaned, the low, ominous sound punctuated with deep, percussive cracks. It trembled as though the avalanche was beginning all over again. It took Sierra a moment to realise it wasn't her that was swaying — the ground beneath her rocked like a boat on water and Sierra staggered to keep her feet. The impression of her body in the snow was turning grey, growing darker by the second as the water wicked up into the hollow.

Rasten was coming towards her, but as another muffled crack echoed around them, he hesitated. 'Sierra!' he called. 'Come to me!'

She was sinking into the slush. Water was bubbling and frothing up through the ice around her. The full weight of the avalanche, all that snow and ice and rock, had landed on the slab of ice reaching over the lake, and that weight was more than it could bear. The ice was breaking up.

'Sierra!' Rasten shouted, with a bark of command in his voice. 'Come here! Now!'

'Come and get me!' she screamed as the water reached the top of her boots and poured in. It was so cold it was painful, like needles in her flesh, and Sierra realised she was shivering and sweating at the same time.

Rasten started towards her, walking on cushions of power that kept him from sinking into the slush.

Sierra spread her hands and let her power spill. The avalanche had taken most of her strength — she was getting a small recharge from Rasten, his muscles still twinging from the bolt she had flung into him, but it wasn't enough. This was her last chance.

As he drew near, Rasten cast a shield to protect himself. 'Just give it up,' he said. 'You couldn't take me before; you can't do it now. It's over, Sierra.'

She stood her ground and waited — waited until he was close enough to touch, waited until he reached for her with cords of flame ready to enhance his strength — then she leapt for him, wrapping her arms around his neck and, with the last of her power, she shattered the slab of ice beneath them and dumped them both into the black water.

The shock of the cold drove the breath from them. Rasten tried to wrap his arms around her, refusing to let her go even as they shivered, but before he could take a firm hold Sierra twisted in his grip. She grabbed his neck with both hands and drove her knee into his crotch with all the force she could muster. With a grunt of pain, he doubled over, and Sierra pulled her knees up to brace against his chest and slammed her elbow into his face. She pulled back to do it again and with a roar of rage and pain Rasten struck her with a blast of power that lifted her out of the water and hurled her against the ice on the far side of the lead. Sierra had time to wrap her arms around her head to brace for the impact, but nothing more. She hit the edge, half in the water and half on the ice, and before she could recover she slipped back into the water. The impact knocked the breath from her body and, too stunned to fight it, she felt herself slip beneath the surface, where the current caught her and swept her away.

Cam grabbed Isidro's arm and cursed. 'By the Bright Sun Herself, did you see that? Who was it?'

Isidro staggered under his grip and Cam quickly released him. 'Where is she?' Isidro said, scanning the black water.

'I can see one of them,' said Cam.

'That's Rasten,' said Isidro, watching one small figure swim across the black water. 'Where's Sierra?'

For a moment, Cam didn't reply; when he did speak, his voice was hushed. 'She went under the ice.'

Her lungs burned as the current swept her onwards. It pulled her under then slammed her up against the ice again and again. She curled into a ball with her arms raised to protect her head, but knew she wouldn't have the strength to hold it for long. The cold was seeping into her muscles and sapping her strength. Her coat, floating free in the water, caught the current and pulled her along like a sail. The only thing that mattered was the need to breathe, but there was no air, only the cold and the dark and surging water all around. She was tumbling head over heels, so disoriented in the darkness she couldn't tell which way was up.

Ruddy light flared through the water — Sierra glimpsed it for only a moment before the current tumbled her away. It lit up the channel, illuminating boulders and dead-wood snags that stretched dark, skeletal fingers towards her. She saw a shape that might have been Rasten diving into the airless channel to follow her, but before she could take in anything more the Black Sun, the queen of cold and darkness, opened her arms and took her in.

Rasten saw Sierra ahead, her black hair fanned out around her as the current dragged her along. He saw her go limp, her body unfold from its tuck against the cold, and he cursed, kicking after her with all his strength. She had passed out and if he didn't get to her within the next few seconds she would begin to drown. In that moment, Rasten decided that if he couldn't save her he would join her in the indifferent cold. With her gone, there would be no other escape from Kell.

The current threw her limp body against the ice overhead; each time, it slowed her momentum and let him get just a little closer. Rasten's chest was burning and his head pounding with the need for air, but he braced himself against it. Kell's training had given him practice at withstanding pain, at focussing his mind even as it was failing and exhausted. Reaching out and kicking hard with feet made thick and clumsy with the heavy bulk of his boots, Rasten's fingers grazed the felt sole of her boot. He grabbed her, boot, foot and all, and yanked her towards him. Her limp body bucked in the water like a fish caught on a line, and he clawed his way along her, burying his hand in her tangled hair before she could float away again. She felt like a dead weight, her body as stiff and heavy as water-logged wood as he wrapped an arm across her chest, holding her to him. Her head turned towards him, her midnight-blue eyes wide open and her gaze as vacant as the night sky.

Rasten twisted around and dug his feet into the rocks on the floor of the channel. Withstanding the cold had been steadily eating into his power, but he had enough left to get them both to safety. He raised his free hand, summoned his power, and shattered the ice overhead.

Cam swore softly as ruddy light bloomed beneath the ice, illuminating the course of the river with an unearthly glow. 'He's going after her,' Cam said softly, and he glanced at Isidro. 'Stay here. I'm going to get closer.'

Hurling chunks of ice away from them, Rasten broke the surface with a desperate gulp of air. Black spots danced before his eyes and his limbs felt boneless and weak. His legs trembled violently as he half carried, half dragged Sierra to the edge of the channel, stumbling over rocks and boulders and jagged slabs of ice. She was stiff and still in his arms — all the water soaked into her gear seemed to double her weight. It took all his strength to haul her out of the water.

As soon as they hit the air the water began to freeze. By the time Rasten dumped Sierra face down on the snow her hair was a mass of glittering crystals and hoarfrost bristled on her sodden clothes. Panting, Rasten dropped to his knees beside her and cast a globe of flame into the air. Beneath its ruddy glow he pressed down on her back to squeeze the water from her narrow chest. It poured from her mouth, clear and sparkling, utterly unlike the black and oily face the river showed to the night sky.

When no more water came, he turned her onto her back. Her eyes gazed up at him, wide open and sightless, and her eyelashes glittered with frost. Rasten ripped layers of tunics and shirts aside to press an ear to her chest. For a long moment, he heard nothing, and his heart began to sink, but at last it came — a faint, tentative beat, irregular and faltering.

Rasten tore off his gloves, sodden and stiff with ice, and pressed his palms to her chest. Her skin was blue, and cold beneath his hands. He remembered how he'd felt when she was naked and bound, pale and trembling in anticipation of Kell's punishment — how badly he'd wanted her then. She was so cold now and so still.

Rasten flooded her with power, warming her from the inside out. He was shivering himself but his condition was irrelevant compared with hers. He knew the adage as well as any Ricalani — *no one's dead until they're warm and dead*. As long moments passed, he felt her heartbeat strengthen, until at last she took one rattling breath and began to cough as her body rejected the water still in her lungs. Rasten rolled her onto her side and kept channelling the heat. She couldn't move yet — the flow of blood to her limbs had ceased in the extreme cold and it would be a few moments yet before she had either the strength or the awareness to struggle. With a pulse of power, he dried her clothes, driving off the water and ice in a burst of steam, and then did the same to his own. After a few moments more, the flow to her limbs opened up again — when the cold blood in her arms and legs flooded back into her torso, Rasten was ready. The shock when that cold blood hit the heart was enough to kill a strong man, but with a steady pulse of power Rasten kept her heart beating evenly as she gasped and bucked beneath his hands. She blinked and her pupils suddenly shrunk to pinpoints in the flare of his witch-lights. Rasten brushed her hair back from her face and wept with relief. She was alive.

Cam left his snowshoes behind, moving cautiously over the packed snow with his sword in his hand. Perhaps it was foolish to come so close instead of hanging back to use his bow, but the sight of Sierra stopping a crossbow bolt was still vivid in his mind. Perhaps he would get lucky — perhaps Rasten wouldn't sense the arrow's flight — but if it did fly true, at the range at which he was sure of getting a fatal shot, the arrow would go right through Rasten and kill Sierra as well. Despite his words to Isidro, Cam couldn't bring himself to do it — not after the comfort she had given to his brother, not while Isidro watched ...

Sierra moaned, arching her back off the snow and dragging one heel towards her as though she was preparing to sit up. She looked straight at Cam, but her eyes drifted over him without recognition — awake, but not conscious. There was a chance that the long minutes she had spent under the ice had robbed her of her wits. It happened sometimes: a body pulled out of the ice and snow could be revived after the soul had flown, leaving a shell of a person with no more wit than a newborn babe.

As Sierra pulled away from him Rasten grabbed her wrist in one hand, rolled her onto her belly again and twisted her arm up behind her back. 'Be still,' he said to her, his voice a soft growl meant to carry no further than her ears.

Cam inched another step closer and raised his sword.

Sierra clawed at the packed snow with her free hand and cried out in pain as Rasten twisted her arm in an effort to make her stop struggling. He reached into his sash for a length of cord, preparing to bind her wrists.

Cam swung his sword, aiming for the base of Rasten's skull. Later, he was never sure if Rasten caught the movement in the corner of his eye or if some other sense alerted him — either way, Rasten glanced over his shoulder and ducked with a curse, throwing himself down across Sierra's body. He was not quite fast enough — the blow didn't fall squarely, but neither did it miss. The very tip cut a gash across his scalp. Cam pressed before he could lose his advantage, lunging forward to strike again but Rasten threw up a hand blazing with ruddy light and caught him with a lash of power that struck Cam full across the chest and flung him into the air.

The sword flew from his hand and Cam landed hard on the river ice, winded by the impact. He could feel something warm and wet against his skin, and when he raised his head to look Cam saw that Rasten's lash of power had cut his clothes to shreds and blood was seeping through from wounds beneath. His head spinning, Cam pressed a hand to his chest, forgetting for a moment that he wore gloves, and felt a sting as the coarse fibres brushed against raw and ragged flesh.

Rasten staggered to his feet, exploring the wound on the back of his head with one hand. He scowled at the blood on his fingers and took a step towards Cam.

On the ground at his feet, Sierra pushed herself up, and Rasten hesitated. Cam vaguely remembered what Isidro had told him — she drew power from those in pain. Gritting his teeth, he shoved his gloved fingers into the wound again. At the same time he heard Sierra gasp and saw her blue-white light spill out and cover her with a second skin composed of minute threads of lightning.

With a curse Rasten dropped to his knees at Sierra's side. He shoved her to the ground again and put his knee between her shoulders to keep her there. He grasped her hair and wrenched her head back hard enough to make her cry out. The light died as quickly as it had come and Rasten turned away from her, twisting around to fix his gaze on Cam. He held out one hand and Cam felt Rasten's power settle around him, pinning him to the ice with a heatless blanket of flame.

Then the pressure against him turned cold and, too late, Cam realised the danger he was in. He kicked and struggled, but couldn't move so much as a hair's breadth against that shroud of power. Within seconds, Cam began to shiver violently: as panic gripped he struggled harder and his body fought to curl up and conserve its heat. Rasten was stealing his warmth, chilling him to the temperature of the ice. Of course, Rasten couldn't kill him outright, Cam realised as his hands grew numb. Even a swift death — breaking his neck, cutting his throat — would give Sierra a boost of power and they must both be nearly spent by now. Cam was feeding her and so must be disposed of, but without sending her any more power. The creeping numbness of hypothermia would do just that.

As his shivering grew weaker, Cam felt a calmness sweep over him. The ice, hard and unyielding a few moments before, seemed to grow soft and paradoxically warm. He was so very tired and the soft gurgle of the running water was a soothing, drowsy sound.

Pinned as she was, Sierra struggled while Rasten fought to get hold of her other wrist. He twisted her arm so far that Isidro expected it to break at any moment and yet she would not give in. He could hear Rasten panting and cursing in frustration and at last he wrapped his free hand around her throat and slowly strangled her into submission while Sierra clawed and scratched at his fingers.

Isidro wouldn't let himself look at Cam. There was nothing he could do for him now. His eyes were on Sierra and Rasten and his left hand was clamped around the hilt of his knife while the palm of his glove grew damp with sweat.

Sierra sobbed for breath, feeling herself grow weaker with every moment. Rasten had given up on grabbing her second wrist for now — he just kept squeezing her throat, indifferent to her fingers plucking and clawing at his hand. She had lost her mittens somewhere in the water and wore only her thin inner gloves. They made her fingers slick, so she couldn't get a grip that would allow her to bend his fingers back and loosen his grasp. He would strangle her unconscious and then secure her before she regained her senses. He would have done it already if Cam hadn't interrupted him. She could no longer feel Cam lying on the ice. The small trickle of power he had given her was still there but she couldn't focus enough to use it while her lungs screamed for air. Even as she struggled for breath, Sierra felt despair clawing at her heart. She should have died twice over, once in the avalanche and then in the water but she had been cheated each time. Why had she fought so hard to stay alive when this was all that awaited her? A life of pain and degradation as Rasten's plaything and a weapon of pure destruction in Kell's hands. It seemed utterly futile to keep fighting when the darkness was rising up to swallow her. She could see it now, creeping in at the edge of her vision.

And then she felt a trickle of power flowing in to her, a little thread of light that reached through the creeping blackness. It grew steadily stronger and at once the burning in her lungs and muscles began to ease — or perhaps it just became unimportant next to the fire that awakened within her. Her right arm burned with a voluptuous heat, a rising tide of light and warmth that nearly swept her away. For a moment she stopped fighting and felt Rasten's hands tighten with anticipation of triumph. But then the knowledge of what she felt struggled up through her sluggish mind. *Isidro!*

She felt him clenching his right hand into a fist, the torn and battered muscles contracting around the jagged shards of bone.

Rasten dug his fingers harder into her throat. 'Where's it coming from?' he snarled in her ear. 'Don't tell me that wretch is still alive?' She felt him twist around to glance at Cam, but it had been some minutes now since she had felt anything from him. 'Well, he won't last long,' Rasten growled. 'Give it up, Sirri. You're only making things worse for yourself.'

With Isidro's pain sending a river of fire through her Sierra twisted and squirmed, kicking at him until he gave her arm a vicious twist to make her stop. She cried out and for a moment lost control of the power gathering within her so that it burst out in a brilliant flare of light that made Rasten wince and curse aloud. Sierra writhed hopelessly, trying to ease the strain in her arm and for a moment she saw a flash of vision — the two of them struggling while another man loomed above them with a shaft of silver in his hand.

Sierra raised her head and saw Isidro standing behind Rasten with a knife in his hand. His eyes were wide and blank and she knew in an instant the flare of light had blinded him, but he had one chance to strike.

He took it before Rasten had time to notice the shift in her attention and drove the blade into Rasten's unprotected back.

With a shout of rage and pain Rasten threw himself forward, crushing Sierra beneath him and pinning her right arm between their bodies. She barely noticed it. All her thoughts were on the searing touch of the blade as it parted skin and flesh and grated against bone. Momentarily blinded, Isidro's aim had been off and the blow had fallen more to the shoulder than the back, but the knife had cut deep. While Rasten clenched his teeth against the pain it sent a flood of power pouring into Sierra.

Rasten rolled off her, every movement twisting the blade within him. The pain didn't slow him down. He was conditioned to ignore it. Attacking a Blood-Mage was suicide unless one was sure of killing him quickly and Isidro knew enough to understand that. As soon as his weight was off her Sierra tried to push herself up but her muscles, still cold and starved of air, were too weak to obey. Her throat was burning and her right arm throbbed with a deep, tearing ache that told her Rasten had done some damage in his effort to pin her, but all of that was made remote and distant by the power that pulsed within her.

Rasten stood, breathing hard through the pain, and swept Isidro's feet out from under him with a lash of flame.

His lips twisted in a snarl, Rasten kicked Isidro in the ribs, slamming him back into the snow with a grunt. As he fell back Rasten stepped onto the elbow of Isidro's broken arm, pinning him to the ground. 'So, you're still alive!' Rasten said in a breathless growl, his face twisted in pain. 'I didn't think you'd have the balls to face me again. This time I'll skin you alive.' Rasten lifted his foot and stamped with all his weight on Isidro's broken arm.

Light flared over the riverbank as Sierra abandoned all restraint and erupted in a storm of power. The world seemed to pause and that one instant stretched out so that time appeared to move with glacial speed. Rasten couldn't take her now and he knew it — the pain of his injury would feed her power beyond his ability to control her. She might be safe for the moment, but Rasten would make Isidro pay for what he had done.

Isidro pressed his head back on the snow, bracing for the blow. He had made his decision and he expected to die here. The sight of it made Sierra's heart ache. Death had been her choice tonight, not his or Cam's.

She struck at Rasten just as his foot fell on Isidro's arm with a muffled crack. Isidro cried out, a low bellow of pain, and then Sierra's blast drove Rasten off him, leaving him staggering to keep his feet. It would have killed any other man but Rasten's power met hers head-on with a clash of brilliant light and crackling energy.

In the midst of it all Isidro curled around his ruined arm, his face an ashen grey. Rhia's splints and wrappings had given him some protection but they weren't enough.

The clash of power had also thrown Sierra back. Shakily, she crossed the snow to Isidro's side while Rasten turned to face her. With a rope of flame he reached over his shoulder to pull out the knife and dropped the bloody blade onto the snow.

Sierra wanted to drop to her knees next to Isidro and take his pain away, but she didn't dare take her eyes from Rasten. Instead she stayed where she was with Isidro curled and gasping for breath at her feet. For this moment at least, his agony was all that kept him alive. She needed the power his pain gave her and though she hated herself for it, she would leave him to suffer.

Breathing hard, Rasten backed away. 'This isn't over,' he said. 'Not by a long shot. You're a monster, Little Crow, and without someone to guide you your power will grow until you can do nothing to rein it in. You'll bring pain and destruction wherever you go. We're the only ones who can help you, Sierra. Remember that.'

'Just go,' Sierra said. 'Just go, Rasten, or I'll kill you where you stand.'

He laughed, a humourless chuckle, and cast a shield of flame over himself. 'If you could do that you'd have done it already,' he said. Veiled in flame he turned and walked away, blood seeping from the wound in his back and staining the white leather of his coat black in the moonlight.

# Chapter 17

Sierra crouched at Isidro's side but when she reached for him he pushed her hands away. 'Cam,' he said through bloodless lips. 'Help Cam.'

Still trembling she ran for the river, where Cam lay in a pool of icy water with his lips blue and frost glittering in his hair. Pulling off her gloves, Sierra dug her bare fingers into his neck to feel for a pulse. His heartbeat was a faint and irregular flutter, like a dying moth beating against her palm.

'Black Sun help me,' she muttered, hands hovering over his still form. Rasten had warmed her from this state but she had only a vague idea of how he had done it.

Isidro heaved himself up and staggered unsteadily towards her. 'Sirri.'

'Just let me think!' she hissed. 'I don't want to kill him!' Her forearm throbbed with a sympathetic echo of Isidro's pain. The burning in her wrist and shoulder where Rasten had locked her arm behind her back, however, was all her own.

Isidro sat heavily at Cam's head. 'He's already dead.'

Biting back on her snarled reply Sierra ripped aside the tatters of Cam's shirt, slapped her palms against him and loosed a bolt of energy into his chest. Jagged cords of power swarmed through him and Sierra felt them wrapping around his heart. He was cold, so very cold.

'Sierra — ' Isidro pleaded.

'Just wait!' Sierra snapped. 'I don't dare give him any more. I want to warm his blood, not boil it.' After an interminable moment his heart lurched beneath her hands and roused to a slow and erratic pulse.

A wave of pain swept through him as sensation returned and his nerves awoke with a rush that made Sierra's power spike. He moaned, and began to shiver violently, more alive now than dead.

'Cam!' Isidro said, reaching over to shake him. 'Cam!'

Cam opened his eyes, bleary and unfocussed with no hint of recognition. They were, Sierra realised, an extraordinary shade of green, quite rare in Ricalan. The strain of channelling the power and keeping it steady was draining her and as the adrenaline of the fight faded her muscles were trembling with fatigue.

Cam drew a deep, shuddering breath and tried to sit up. He pushed Sierra away and wrapped his tattered furs around him but not before she saw the red marks her palms had left on his chest and the smear of blood as his wounds began to seep. He made a groan of pain as his shirt rubbed against the burns and he hunched within the fur, still shivering.

She helped him shift away from the water and dried his clothes with a pulse of power and the sudden reek of scorched wool. Then she and Isidro pressed close around him, wrapping their coats over his to pool their warmth. Sierra kept channelling power into him but it was still a few minutes before Cam was recovered enough to speak through chattering teeth. 'W-where's R-Rasten?'

'Gone,' Sierra said. 'Isidro stabbed him in the back and he knows he can't take me if he's feeding me power.'

'F-f-f-fatal?' Cam stammered.

'Doubt it,' Isidro replied.

'It didn't feel like a mortal wound,' Sierra said.

'C-c-can he heal it? He's a s-sorcerer, after all.'

Sierra shook her head. 'It doesn't work that way. You can't heal a wound with power.'

Cam turned to Isidro and saw for the first time that his brother's face was white with pain. 'What happened?'

'Rasten stomped on his arm. The splints saved him from the worst of it, but ...'

'Can't you do something?'

'Better not,' Isidro said, his voice hoarse. 'She might need the power before the night is out.'

'Can you stand?' Sierra asked Cam. 'You'll warm up faster walking and you and Issey need to head back.'

Cam's hand tightened around hers. 'Not just us. You're coming, too.'

Sierra turned away. 'I can't go back. Mira —'

'I saw what Mira's hunters made of your gear,' Isidro said. 'You don't have any more choice than we do.'

213

It was pointless to argue. She knew he was right. Her chances of survival had been slim before, but now they were non-existent.

Once on his feet, Cam squinted through the gloom to pick out the trail of blood Rasten had left in his retreat. 'Seems a shame to let him get away,' Cam said. 'If we had the men I'd say we run him to ground and finish the job.'

'Don't think for a moment he's any less dangerous,' Sierra said. 'He won't risk facing me when he's wounded but he'd make short work of anyone else.'

'She's right, Cam.' Isidro turned to Sierra. 'Rasten killed the other two hunters, but he made one of them talk first. This will be a disaster for Mira's clan once word gets back to Kell. She needs to be warned.' His face was deathly pale: the pain was wearing him down swiftly. Sierra could feel his strength draining. She glanced at Cam and found him looking his brother over with the same critical eye. 'We should get moving. Sirri, where are your snowshoes?'

She jerked her head towards the site of the avalanche. The massive weight of snow and rock was still pressing the ice into the lake; at the site where Rasten had punched through the ice to drag her out the water level had already risen enough to spill over the top of the ice. 'Lost. I'll have to rig something to get back to the camp.' The cord Rasten had intended to use to bind her wrists lay on the scuffed snow and she stooped to snatch it up.

Cam went to a nearby pine to cut a pair of branches for Sierra to use as makeshift snowshoes while she stayed with Isidro, watching over him while he rested.

Crouched on his heels, Isidro scrubbed at his face with his good hand. When he closed his eyes he swayed dangerously and Sierra grabbed for his shoulder to steady him. 'Isidro, you have to let me help.'

'No,' he insisted with a shake of his head. 'You might need it.'

'I still get power from it, you know. Maybe not quite as much, but it'll be enough to deal with anything that comes up.' Even as she spoke the power she was taking from him was roaring in her ears. Her whole body ached from the effort of containing it. At this rate, by the time they made it back to Mira's camp she would be overflowing.

Sierra touched her bare hand to Isidro's cheek. 'You're cold, Issey,' she said and pulled the cowl hanging around his neck up to cover his ears. 'Don't you have a hat?'

He fumbled in the front of his coat. 'Somewhere. Couldn't get it on with one hand.'

Sierra put it on for him, pulling it down to his eyebrows and then settling the hood and wrap of his coat over it all. It reminded her keenly of doing the same for her younger brothers and sisters. Isidro would normally refuse this kind of fuss but now he just closed his eyes and submitted without complaint. 'Sirri?' he said. 'Don't let me fall asleep.'

She touched her face to his, forehead to forehead, nose to nose. The pain that refused to let him rest was no match for the creeping somnolence of hypothermia. 'We won't,' she said. 'I promise.'

When Cam returned Sierra borrowed his knife to cut the cord in half, and bound the branches to the soles of her boots. The bushy twigs would splay out to spread her weight over the surface of the snow.

'Come on, brother,' Cam said, taking Isidro's good hand and hauling him to his feet.

Sierra created a globe of light and held it up to light their path. 'I'll take the lead,' she said. 'Let's just hope there are no more surprises heading our way.'

Someone in Mira's camp must have realised Cam and Isidro were gone because her men met them on the trail near where Rasten had killed the hunters and herded the three of them back to the camp under a tight guard. A pair of crossbowmen took up position at Sierra's back, making the skin between her shoulder blades tingle with unpleasant anticipation despite the shield she cast beneath her coat.

At the camp they were whisked through the ring of sentries and into Mira's tent, but not before Sierra saw three sleds pulled up nearby, each man-sized load covered with an oil-cloth wrap.

Mira was waiting for them along with a man Sierra hadn't seen at the cache, a tall fellow with the typical black hair of a Ricalani, although his features showed some influence of southern blood. Rhia was also there and she immediately went to Isidro, helping him across the tent to settle into a chair. Still in her outer fur, the warmth of the tent made Sierra sweat but as Isidro collapsed into the chair he continued to shiver. Even as exhausted as he was, the awful, gnawing pain in his arm wouldn't let him be still.

The crossbowmen had followed them in and the anxiety of having them at her back was making it difficult to keep her power under control. She could feel it clawing at her skin, searching for any point of weakness in its cage. The men watching her were nervous. If she did spark they might well shoot at her out of reflex. If she had to use her power to stop the bolt it could trigger a chain of events that would end in disaster for everyone here.

'Issey,' Sierra pleaded, hunkering down beside him. 'You have to let me help you. We're safe here. Rasten won't dare come after me in a camp full of people.'

He swung his head her way and when he spoke his voice was a hoarse whisper. 'It's not Rasten I'm worried about now.' They were shielded from Mira's view by Rhia's hovering form but Sierra saw his eyes flick in her direction.

Sierra leaned closer and lowered her voice. 'I'm reaching the limit of what I can hold. I've got more than enough to deal with any other surprises that come my way. Issey, please, I can't bear this any longer!'

With a sigh he bowed his head and offered her his good hand. Sierra swiftly stripped off his mitten and glove and then bared her own hand to make the link. The numbness that swept through his arm was a relief for them both and Isidro finally slumped back in the chair and fell so still that Rhia quickly leaned forward to check his breathing. 'What happened to him?' she demanded.

'Rasten stomped on his arm. I heard something go crack. I hoped it was just the splints.'

Rhia gave her a hard look. 'Most likely it was. There's nothing left in his arm big enough to break.' She laid her hand against his pallid cheek. 'He should be lying down. Help me.'

Isidro caught her wrist. 'Not yet. There are things we need to talk about. Mira ...'

Mira had drawn herself up to deliver a blistering address but the sight of him had stolen her voice. When he said her name, though, she composed herself and came over to him. 'Hush, Issey, you should rest. What on earth possessed you to go off like that?'

'Trying to keep you from making a mistake,' he rasped. 'Too late. Rasten killed your hunters. He knows you sent them after Sierra.'

Mira gasped and clapped a hand over her mouth as the colour drained from her face. Behind her, the man Sierra didn't know swore beneath his breath.

'You've brought a whole new world of trouble down on yourself and your clan, Mira,' Isidro went on. 'If you've got any sense you'll call a truce with Sierra until you can set it right.'

In the stunned silence that followed his words Cam went to the table behind the stove, poured bowls of hot tea from the kettle simmering over the coals and handed them around. Sierra caught his eye and nodded her thanks, wrapping her cold hands around the bowl to savour the warmth.

'A truce?' Mira spluttered. 'That's out of the question! She broke her word never to return. She murdered my men!'

'Murdered? They were trying to kill me!' Sierra snapped. 'And believe me, I wouldn't be here if I had anywhere else to go. But your men settled that when they destroyed my gear!'

Mira gaped at her for a moment. 'What do you mean, they destroyed your gear?'

'One of the men doused her sled in oil and set it alight,' Cam said. 'She's got nothing now but the clothes she stands up in.'

That wasn't entirely true. They'd stopped by her abandoned sled and Sierra had picked up Kell's book and the enchantments she had been wearing when she made her escape, all of which had been protected from the flames by the power they held. They were hidden under her coat.

For the first time since their arrival, Mira's anger faltered and she turned to swap a glance with her companion.

'That wretched Pillepor always had a fondness for oil and tinder,' he muttered. 'The war-leader warned me about him when he left for the muster.'

With a shake of her head, Mira dismissed the matter. 'The laws are clear. A sorcerer who practises his power must be put to death and as a representative of my clan I'm bound to uphold them.' To Sierra, she said, 'It's nothing personal.'

'Nothing personal?' Sierra said incredulously. She clenched her fists, trying to keep control, but realised at once that it was a mistake. Her power leapt in response to her anger and it burst from her skin in a blaze of blue light, crackling like fire in dry grass and showering blue sparks onto the trampled spruce at her feet.

Startled, Mira jumped back while the man cursed and shoved her behind him as he drew the knife from his belt. Shouting, the two guards stepped forward with crossbows raised, while Cam pushed himself between them and Sierra. He grabbed her by the arm hard enough to make her realise just how much tension he was concealing. 'Stop it!' he shouted. 'For the love of life, get yourself under control!'

'I'm trying!' she snarled back. 'But by the Black Sun, you're not helping!'

Muttering, he let her go, but kept himself between her and the crossbows. With a wrench of effort Sierra pulled the power back beneath her skin, but it refused to stay there. With every beat of her heart fat blue sparks swelled out of her skin to writhe and course over her body. Sierra tried to calm and focus her mind the way Rasten had taught her, but it wasn't easy and she was getting tired of the way everyone stared at her.

In the shocked silence that followed, Isidro spoke again. 'Mira, Ardamon. Just think for a moment. Dremman might be able to buy himself and the clan out of a charge of treason, but when word of this reaches the king he won't accept any deal that doesn't include your head on a platter. Do you understand?'

Mira turned away, covering her face with her hands.

'Don't talk to my cousin like that, Balorica,' Ardamon snarled. 'Remember you're a guest of our clan —'

'Ardamon, no.' Mira laid a hand on his arm. 'He's right, as usual,' she said with a hint of irritation. 'But a truce? Impossible. It would violate the laws the Gods themselves set down —'

'Horseshit,' Isidro said. 'The Gods made Sierra the way she is — why would they condemn her for doing the very thing they created her for?' He scrubbed a hand through his tangled hair. 'But that's not important now. Mira, there's no way we can prevent word of this from reaching Kell and the king. You and Ardamon and your whole clan are screwed unless we can do something to change the state of play.'

'And do what, precisely?' Ardamon drawled.

'You have to kill Rasten,' Isidro said. 'You'll never get another opportunity like this. Rasten is wounded and on the run and here —' he gestured to Sierra '— is the one person in Ricalan, other than Kell, capable of bringing him down.'

The tent fell silent and Sierra shivered, wrapping her arms around herself. 'Issey,' she said. 'I can't … he would have had me tonight —'

'But you won't be meeting him alone,' he said. 'You can do this, Sirri.'

'You think killing Kell's right-hand man will make things *better*?' Ardamon said. 'It would be a declaration of war!'

'But it's a war the king doesn't have the men to fight,' Isidro said. 'Kell is the only thing holding the Akharian army and their mages back from the Mesentreian settlements. He can't turn his attention away from that or the kingdom is lost. With Rasten gone the king will have no choice but to forge a new treaty with your clan. He'll need the Wolf Clan's support so desperately he'll agree to anything you demand. Surely you can see that you and Sierra have more to gain as allies than as enemies? Removing Rasten will change everything ...' As he spoke, Isidro's face slowly turned grey but now he broke off abruptly and slumped forward in his seat.

Rhia lunged in to catch his shoulders. 'Help me!' she demanded. 'He needs rest. You must not tax his strength further!'

Together, Cam and Rhia laid him on the ground. Rhia shoved bundled blankets under his feet while Sierra brushed damp hair back from his forehead. 'What's wrong with him?' Cam demanded.

'I don't know! He's not in pain ...' That wasn't entirely true, but it wasn't the sort of pain she could help. There was a dull, leaden ache in every fibre of his body. His breathing was fast and laboured but there was no one cause, nothing that she could identify and relieve to spare him.

'He is not well and he has pushed himself too hard for too long,' Rhia said crisply as she loosened his sash, opened his coat and gently lifted his bound arm from the sling tied across his chest. 'He will not admit how weak he is.' Isidro's fingertips, just visible through the bandages and splints, were an unhealthy dusky shade. Rhia held her hand out to Cam. 'Give me a knife. Quickly. I must cut bandages off.'

Cam gave her his knife and she began cutting through the bandages. Without looking up, she said, 'He needs lots of rest. Somewhere warm and comfortable where he will not be disturbed.' When the bandages were cut away, Sierra quickly looked away from the ruin of his arm. It was swollen, turgid and black with spreading bruises.

Isidro shifted his head and his eyelids fluttered open. He turned towards it and Sierra quickly reached out to stop him. 'Don't look,' she said.

Somehow he managed a smile, a meagre quirk of the lips, but a smile all the same. 'It's alright,' he said. 'I've seen it before.' He lay back and licked his dry lips. 'Is there any water ...?'

Mira poured some from the kettle, cooled it with clean snow, and Sierra helped him lift his head enough to drink.

'We could stay here for a few days,' Mira began, but Rhia interrupted with a shake of her head.

'A tent is not good enough. Too cold, too much noise and disturbance. He needs to rest in a house, or perhaps a temple.'

'Drysprings Temple has a good healer,' Mira said, turning to Ardamon. 'It's only an hour's ride to the south.'

'A little more than that at an invalid's pace,' Ardamon said. 'But it's an easy journey.'

'It's not that bad,' Isidro said. 'I just need to sleep. I'll be well enough in the morning.'

'Hush,' Rhia said. 'He will manage that, but he must be carried in a litter. The bumping of a sled is not good. And there must be no more arguing or discussion,' she said, glaring at her patient.

'Well?' Isidro said, looking past Rhia to meet Mira's gaze.

Mira tossed her head with a rattle of beaded braids. 'Very well then, a truce — but only until tomorrow, to give us time to think it over and discuss the matter.' She fixed her gaze on Sierra. 'Do you think you can keep your word this time?'

'I can if you can,' Sierra said through clenched teeth.

Sierra rode close to Isidro's litter on the journey to the temple, in case some jolt disturbed him, but Rhia had prepared him well for the journey and the need for her help never arose. She had pulled his arm as straight as the swollen flesh would allow and splinted it again and had laid him on the litter well wrapped with furs and packed all around with hot rocks to ward off the cold. Isidro would have hated the very idea of being consigned to a litter but as near as Sierra could tell he slept the whole way.

Cam rode nearby and, although Sierra felt full to overflowing with fears and worries of what lay ahead of them, she didn't want to discuss it with him where they might be overheard. So she held her tongue and let her concerns bubble and ferment inside her.

Since she had escaped from Kell's camp she had never been able to form a plan that reached more than a few days ahead. She couldn't remember a time when she hadn't had a cold knot of fear lodged in her belly or a sound sleep that hadn't been brought on by sheer exhaustion.

Her only respite had been the time she spent with Isidro between the furs, lost in the shared sensation, but even that was only a brief release.

All the time she had been a captive, she had believed things would be different if she could escape. She had to believe it — that hope was all she had to sustain her. Now she was free — as free as she would ever be — but nothing had changed. She still lived from day to day with no control over the future and with allies whose lives were as precarious as hers. Out here her power counted for nothing. It didn't matter how powerful a sorcerer she was, she couldn't survive if the people of Ricalan closed ranks against her. Rejection by the common folk had doomed far more powerful sorcerers than her in the past — Vasant and all his followers had known they were finished when the common folk had begun to refuse them shelter and aid. What hope did she have, untrained and friendless?

And now Rasten had marked her trail and tested her strength. He would heal and once he did he would be better prepared for her the next time they met. When that time came she knew she could expect no mercy.

Isidro woke when the bearers set the litter down. Rhia appeared over him and pressed him back down onto the sling. 'No, Issey, lie still. It will not be long and they will take you inside.'

'Where are we?' he said, still trying to sit up, but despite her small size, Rhia was strong and he was forced to admit defeat.

'At the Drysprings Temple,' Rhia said, looking around with a frown. 'Lady Mira sent word ahead for the priests to expect us. I don't know what is causing the delay.'

'By the Black Sun, let me up. I'm not so far gone I can't walk a few paces to get inside.' He freed his left arm from the furs and levered himself into a sitting position. The effort set his skull pounding.

'Do not do this to yourself ... Limitations come upon us all and fighting them does more harm than good.'

Isidro shook his head. 'Don't treat me like a halfwit.'

'I do not!'

'Yes, you do!'

'No! I only tell you what I learned when I was a slave. There comes a time when we cannot fight any longer, when we bow our heads to fate and do what we must to survive.'

221

The world was swaying around him as though he was on a boat and the world around him was a stormy sea. 'So there does — but I'm walking inside.'

She sighed and offered him her hands. 'As you wish, then.'

Chilled after the inactivity of the saddle, Sierra stamped her feet on the packed snow and tucked her mittened hands under her arms as one of Mira's men took the reins of her horse and led the beast away. The entire complex of shrine, halls and outbuildings was surrounded by a high stone wall broached by a gate at each of the cardinal points, although the wooden doors that had once existed to close them off were long gone. Behind the drifts of snow and a rime of ice the walls seemed oddly flat and regular, just like the caverns Kell had carved out of the rock beneath Lathayan. Even without closer scrutiny Sierra would have been willing to wager the walls had been mage-built.

A fitful lamp flickered beside the entrance to the Priests' Hall. So weary she could barely think straight, Sierra had been about to create a globe of light before she remembered where she was. She hadn't set foot inside a temple in years, not since the last time a priest had realised just what was odd about the young Herder girl who seemed so nervous. Many folk with latent powers were admitted to the priesthood and Sierra wondered how far inside she would get before someone recognised what she was. And how would her reluctant hosts respond then? When she saw Isidro struggling to rise from his litter she went over to help him, smiling to herself with a kind of humourless mirth. She would find out soon enough.

When she came to Isidro's side Rhia gave her a noncommittal nod of greeting. Over the past week, Sierra had noticed that the physician's hostility towards her depended on how much pain Isidro was in. The more he needed her, the more Rhia tolerated her presence.

Isidro swung his head towards her, but it took a few moments for his eyes to focus on her face. 'Sirri …'

'Hush, Issey. Let's get inside.'

The steps leading up to the doorway gave them some trouble. Cam met them at the door and quickly backed up to hold the heavy draught curtain out of the way. On the wall opposite the entrance a mural of the Bright Sun gazed serenely down at them, bedecked with garlands of flowers and finished with gold leaf that glittered in the lamplight.

'The priests have a chamber ready for him,' Cam said. 'This way.'

Another curtained doorway admitted them to the common room, the gathering place at the centre of the Priests' Hall. Three sides of the large room were divided into chambers by partitions of wicker and carved wood. The remaining wall incorporated the furnaces that warmed the hall, a complex network of chimneys and chambers that trapped the heat in the stone and radiated it back to warm the air.

The chambers against the walls were raised above the floor-level of the common room by a platform that housed another set of furnaces, heating the floor from beneath. Off in one corner was a stairway that led to the second level, where the lower-ranking priests and temple dependants had their quarters.

At this hour the common room was empty except for a handful of priests wrapped in yellow robes, who gathered around Mira as she spoke to a stooped old woman with white hair and the red robes of the High Priestess. Most of the chambers were dark, but the one Cam led them to had lamps lit within, the glow filtering through the blankets hung across the latticed partitions. As they approached it a priest wearing a yellow robe trimmed with a wide green band detached himself from the others and gestured them into the chamber. 'In here, if you please. I've added a brazier, so it should be quite warm by now.'

Sierra fell in behind Cam and Rhia, letting them shield her from the gaze of the priests, but it seemed to her that she could feel hostile eyes upon her, and when she dared glance up she saw the High Priestess watching her intently. The old woman had a walking stick in her gnarled hand and she raised it to point at Sierra. 'That girl,' the High Priestess said. 'Who is she? Have her come here.'

Sierra stopped where she was, her weight balanced on the balls of her feet. Her weariness had lifted, blown off like a fog in a strong wind and her power was bristling within her like a dog with its hackles up. Kell walked with a stick and when he pointed with it like that it was usually a sign that horrible things were about to happen.

Sierra took a deep breath and forced her power down. Losing control now wouldn't help her one bit. Isidro must have sensed the flare of it because he stopped in his tracks and turned, reaching for the doorframe for support. 'What's the matter?' he said.

Sierra turned towards the priestess. 'You wish to speak to me, Honoured One?'

Mira frowned as the old priestess looked her up and down. 'You carry the taint, girl. You reek of it.' Her watery eyes fixed on Sierra's wrists and she reached out with one gnarled hand to seize her left arm. Sierra didn't resist when the old woman turned her hand over to reveal the mutilated remains of her kinship tattoo and the healing burns that encircled her wrists. 'Hah!' the old woman said. 'Even the guardian of your mothers' line has disowned you. What manner of demon are you? And what possessed you,' she said turning to Mira, 'to bring a creature like this into a holy place?'

'She is here as my guest,' Mira snapped. 'Whether she is a sorcerer or not, the laws of hospitality bind my hands. You may complain to my clan elders if you wish, but she will not be turned out.'

'You foolish chit of a girl! Do you have any idea what you've brought here? A weak taint can be contained, through prayer and the Gods' goodwill, but this one? She should have been sent back to the Black Sun the moment her feckless mother realised what she'd birthed! It's no wonder our people are being enslaved and our lands overrun when we've filth like this bringing death and destruction down upon us!' The priestess swung her stick at Sierra as though shooing away a dog. Sierra quickly stepped back out of range. She could have blocked it with a shield — Fires Below, she could have taken the blow; the old woman had no strength in her skinny arms and gnarled hands — but she didn't trust her power not to rear up and break loose.

'If you're going to blame anyone for the troubles we face, blame the priests and the clans who purged the mages a hundred years ago,' Isidro said from the doorway. 'If Ricalan had mages of her own, Kell would never have become what he is today and all those who have suffered at his hands would have been spared.'

'Enough of this!' Mira said, with a rattle of her beaded braids. 'Honoured Priestess, you will treat my guests as though they were my own kin, or I will tell my elders of this insult and advise them that the leadership of Drysprings should be reassigned.' She took a deep breath. 'Of course, I understand that Sierra's presence here is distressing to you and all those under your guidance. I will make a personal contribution towards the purification that must take place when we leave — but only if you leave me and my guests in peace tonight.'

The old woman frowned, her parchment skin settling into a landscape of creased folds. 'Will you swear to me on the honour of your clan that you'll leave in the morning? I have my village to think of as well. It's bad enough that she's brought her taint into the temple grounds — I don't want her contaminating those innocent lives as well.'

'We will be riding out early,' Mira said and then frowned at Isidro, still clinging to the doorway to keep his feet. 'With the possible exception of Isidro. If he is not strong enough to ride out with us, he may have to remain as your guest for a few days longer, until he recovers.'

'That won't be necessary,' Isidro said. 'I just need a few hours' sleep. I'll be fine in the morning.'

Grateful for the distraction, Sierra turned her back on the priests and went to his side.

Isidro let her and Rhia shepherd him through the doorway and into the chamber. It was small but well appointed — a wide stone platform running along the far wall was heated by flues beneath, well padded with mats of grass and felt to provide a warm bed. Without any prompting, Isidro lay down and covered his eyes with his good hand while Sierra sat by his feet to pull off his boots. 'I'll be alright in the morning,' he said again.

While Cam went to fetch their gear, Sierra shifted the lamps so they wouldn't shine in Isidro's eyes and Rhia ducked out through the curtained doorway to speak to the temple's physician. Heavy curtains sewn from layers of cloth hung over the lattice panels to keep noise and draughts out but Sierra could just hear their murmured conversation beyond the partition.

'Do you really think it's wise to let the sorcerer remain so close to a sick man?' the physician said. 'She seems to care for him, but surely there's great danger in letting her stay.'

'I'm not pleased by it either,' Rhia said. 'But he's fond of her and grows upset if anyone tries to separate them. Lady Mira has promised we will leave tomorrow and if he is not well enough to travel, well then, the parting will be unavoidable. Now, his arm is very swollen — you will have to replace the bandages and splints once it goes down …'

Isidro lifted his head. 'What are they talking about? I can't quite hear it from here.'

Sierra shook her head. 'Neither can I — it's too muffled. Here, let me help you take that coat off.'

He'd grown even thinner over the last few days and Sierra began to fear that Mira and Rhia were right and it would take much more than a night's rest to restore him. Earlier that afternoon she'd steeled herself to leave him behind, but now she couldn't bear the thought of riding away and leaving him so weak and defenceless.

Cam returned with their bedding and gear, followed by a temple servant bearing bowls of stew set out on a tray. She wore the plain grey wrap of a temple dependant and, though her eyes flickered to Sierra's face, she stopped short of meeting her gaze, instead thrusting the tray towards Sierra and retreating without a word, not responding at all when Sierra managed to stammer out some thanks.

Cam took the tray from her and set it down on a stool. 'I think she's deaf,' he said. 'The cook was talking to her like a halfwit when he told her to bring the food.'

Sierra kept herself from glancing at Isidro, hoping desperately that he hadn't noticed the woman. Becoming a temple servant was the last resort for the crippled and the destitute, those who had no families or whose kin lacked the means or the will to care for them. They were fed and clothed but it was a mean existence and one Isidro was destined for if the Wolf Clan didn't make good on their promise to shelter him — if the king's men didn't find him first.

Cam kept his eyes lowered as he examined the meal and Sierra had no doubt he was thinking the same thing.

When he passed the bowls around the scent of food made Sierra's stomach growl, reminding her she hadn't eaten since noon. Isidro accepted his without enthusiasm and when he smelled it he blanched and handed it back. 'I'm not hungry.'

'Eat it — for pity's sake, you're skin and bone.'

Isidro shook his head and pushed it away. 'Take it — the smell is turning my stomach.'

Sierra set the earthenware lid back on it to keep the heat and the odours in. 'I'll put it here by your bed,' she said, shifting a lamp along the shelf near his head to make room. 'So you can reach it if you get hungry during the night.'

He nodded once and then settled back into his furs. 'Will you sleep here tonight? I want you nearby, in case …'

'Of course,' she said.

'You might as well use Isidro's bedding,' Cam said, shoving a bundle of blankets and furs her way. 'We can find you some more in the morning.'

'I'm not sure how,' Sierra said. 'I've nothing of value to trade and I doubt that either the priests or the Wolf Clan will be moved to charity.'

'Oh, I'm sure I can convince Mira to replace it,' Cam said. 'Sirri ... there's something you should think about. You might be better off following your original plan and striking out on your own.'

Sierra paused with the spoon halfway to her mouth. 'Why?' she said. 'Because it worked so well the first time?' Then Isidro turned his head towards them and Sierra felt her heart sink. 'Is it because of Isidro? I know it's my fault he's hurt again.'

Cam raised his hands in a gesture of peace. 'That's not it at all. I'm talking about you. We pushed Mira into this truce, but there's no way of knowing how it'll end. The Wolf Clan is known for its intolerance of sorcery. Chances are the clan will turn on you again and this time they'll make sure you don't see them coming.'

Sierra looked from him to Isidro and back again. 'You think I should leave?'

'It's an option,' Cam said. 'I can convince Mira to give you the supplies and money you'd need and she's too spooked by all this to set someone on your trail again.'

'But ... Rasten knows where you are. The Wolf Clan can't protect you from him and if I disappear you'll be the first ones he hunts down ...'

Cam and Isidro exchanged a glance. 'To be perfectly honest,' Cam said, 'our chances of making it to midsummer were never that great.'

'We're dead men walking,' Isidro said. 'Have been for years.'

Sierra shook her head. 'No. I can't do it. You ... The two of you are the only friends I have and I won't abandon you again. If it comes to the worst we'll go down fighting together, I promise you that. But I won't leave.'


Cam slept poorly, even though he was weary to the bone. When he woke in the belly of the night to hear soft music playing, he knew he wasn't the only one failing to find any rest.

Music was a rare thing in his world. In the years he'd lived among the Raiders, singing came on the nights after a successful raid, drunken bawls of triumph as the spoils were shared out and any women taken

227

captive were passed around. This was different: a delicate and complex air plucked from the strings of a fine instrument. It was intriguing enough to make him pull on his clothes and seek it out.

He followed the sound out into the common room. After so many years of living rough in the wilderness, wandering alone through the Priests' Hall seemed surreal. The temple was by no means a rich one — the hot springs for which it had been established had dried up suddenly nearly a hundred years before. The temple had gone into a long decline but the stonework and the carvings within the hall were freshly painted and the embroidered blankets hanging across doorways and over the latticework were bright and clean. In his stained and filthy clothes Cam felt like a beggar in a palace.

The music led him through the doorway in the stove-wall and into the kitchen — and that was like kitchens everywhere. Shelves bolted against the walls held leaning stacks of bowls and wooden utensils, and blackened pots hung from hooks in the ceiling. Baskets of wood and kindling had been shoved against the wall to wait until morning and a couple of cauldrons bubbled sluggishly as tomorrow's breakfast simmered over dying coals. A collection of buckets had been left around the stove, each one containing a block of ice set out to melt overnight in the kitchen's lingering warmth.

Against one wall was a wide bench where the head cook could sit and oversee all the activity in the kitchen. Mira sat upon it with her legs crossed and her back against the wall. With her head bowed she held her setar nestled in her lap as her fingers danced over the strings. At the scrape of his boot on the stone floor she looked up with a little gasp of surprise and her fingers faltered.

'Cam! You startled me! I didn't think anyone would be able to hear me if I played in here.'

Cam shrugged. 'I was already awake.'

Mira shifted along on the bench and beckoned to him to join her. She had changed from her travelling clothes into garments more befitting a member of the ruling clans. Her jacket had wide, full sleeves embroidered in bright colours, the sort that would be ruined by heavy work like cooking or tending the fire but would hang gracefully from her wrist while she played. 'I couldn't sleep either,' she said as Cam settled beside her and stretched his feet out to the stove. 'I kept having bad dreams.'

'Rasten?'

Mira nodded, running her fingers nervously along the strings. 'I've really messed this up, haven't I?'

The quaver in her voice tugged something inside of him and Cam wrapped his arm around her shoulders and pulled her close. Isidro didn't get along with Mira. He thought she was too much a creature of politics, too steeped in a life of expediency and power-play to ever be trusted. And Mira, since she was a politician born and bred, sensed Isidro's distrust and was always on her guard around him, but with Cam she let her defences down. She'd invited him to her furs on a whim back when she first met the pair of fugitives and found a safe haven for them in the service of her clan.

Ruhavera was full of men vying for Mira's attention. As daughter of the clan chief, her favour was a prize the young bloods of Ricalan's nobility fought over. Prince or not, Cam had never expected to hold her interest, but the relationship had persisted even after he and Isidro took up their positions among the Raiders and was renewed every time they could snatch a night or a few hours together. Cam knew it was more friendship than love and had no doubt that Mira had other men back in Ruhavera. Fidelity was only expected upon marriage and perhaps not even then for someone so highly placed as the chieftain's heir, although it would be a different matter once she was married to Grand Duke Osebian Angessovar.

'Well,' Cam said. 'Sending those men after Sierra wasn't the best decision you could have made, but it's worked out for the best. If Isidro hadn't seen them and gone after her, there's a good chance Rasten would have taken her back tonight.'

'Ah, Isidro ...' Mira swept her braids back from her face. 'I still feel sick over what's happened to him. No matter what the elders say, he was wounded in our service and we're honour-bound to provide for him. But when they hear about this ... I'll have to be very careful how I explain it all. You know how they view sorcery. There were some who were dead against sheltering Isidro at all. Even with his father's bloodlines they would have excluded him because of his mother's taint. Rhia told me he's sleeping with her — if the clan hears of this everything I've put in place will come unravelled.'

Cam's heart sank. The Wolf Clan was his only hope of finding a safe haven for Isidro. If they turned him out no one else would dare take him in. 'By the Black Sun, is it as bad as that?'

Mira nodded. 'I didn't tell you earlier because I didn't want to worry you. I thought it was all settled, but now ... ye Gods, I always thought the priests were exaggerating when they said a mage can poison everything around them, just by being there, but it's true!'

'Mira, that's nothing but superstition —'

'Is it? Look at you. You found this little mage half-dead in the snow and carried her home. No one could blame you for that — anyone would have done the same — but within a few days a Mesentreian officer in the middle of nowhere recognises you. Next thing you know, one of your band is dead, another injured and you're running for your lives with Lord Rasten on your trail. Tonight Isidro set out to help her only to end up hurt all over again.' She gave him a sidelong look. 'And you're hurt, too, I know. I can see it in your face when you move.'

Cam remembered the dreadful cold as Rasten had pinned him down to the ice. The palm-sized welts on his chest throbbed and stung despite the salve Rhia had given him.

'And it's not over yet,' Mira went on. 'Once word reaches the clan that I called a truce with her, they'll turn on me. We have factions of our own and there are plenty who like to picture themselves in Lady Tarya's place. If I was there I might have a chance to make them see it my way but I can't go home now. We have to chase after Rasten. Our only hope is to kill him before he can return to his master.' Mira dropped her head into her hands. 'Perhaps you should have let Rasten take her. Let her bring disaster down upon them instead.'

'It's rubbish. Sierra didn't make any of this happen. She was Kell's prisoner for two years. Rasten's been Kell's apprentice for ten. No disaster has befallen them yet.'

Mira just shook her head. 'I feel sorry for the girl, really I do. I don't believe she ever wanted this to happen ... But what else could I do? She's no more to blame than a rabid dog but she's every bit as dangerous.'

'Mira, that's not true and it's not fair. You don't know her —'

'Of course it's not fair! Fires Below, I didn't want to give the order, but we can't pick and choose which laws we want to follow! In the morning I'll send a messenger to Lady Tarya to explain the situation here but I can guess what she'll say. She'll tell me to use Sierra to kill Rasten and then trade her back to Kell. If I'm careful he'll have no way to prove I had a part in Rasten's death and, even if he does suspect it, he'll have his hands too full dealing with Sierra and with the Akharians to follow it up.'

'You can't,' Cam said. 'Sierra doesn't trust you. If she had even the slightest suspicion —'

'I know, I know. I'm lucky she hasn't killed me for what I did today. Let us just suppose for a moment that we can kill Rasten. What then?'

'You'd be wise to keep Sierra around,' Cam said. 'She needs shelter and if you give her a place where she feels secure she'll fight to protect it.'

'We *can't*, Cam, the laws —'

'Fuck the laws! Where have they got us? I don't know if you've noticed, but we're the only ones obeying them! Mage-craft has been outlawed in Mesentreia for centuries, but they still keep them around — and the empire has a whole cursed army of mages! Fires Below, maybe we should just let Rasten run, let Kell demand our heads … chances are, by this time next year we'll all be slaves of the empire anyway! How in the Fires Below are we going to fight the Akharians when they have folk like her to call upon, and not just one, but hundreds, maybe thousands? Has it occurred to you that Sierra may be our only chance to keep from being utterly overrun? The way things are headed, soon enough there'll be no one left who even remembers the cursed laws!'

'I know the situation as well as you do! Our ancestors weren't stupid; they understood the dangers we'd face once they destroyed the mages. They knew it would leave us vulnerable and they did it anyway, at enormous cost to themselves. Thousands died at Demon's Spire! The flowers of a generation sacrificed themselves to destroy the Demon Vasant. And within less than a hundred years, will we forget their sacrifice and invite a sorcerer to join our ranks? It would be the undoing of everything they died to achieve! Our ancestors are not to blame for what is happening here. The fault is ours, because we knew this day would come and we failed to prevent it.'

'And so you'd throw away the only weapon we have? I've seen her fight, Mira, if the Akharians can manage even a fraction of it, we'll fall like grain under a sickle and the king won't turn out his pet sorcerer to defend us. Severian would count it a favour if the Slavers cleared the tribal lands.'

'We can deal with mages,' Mira said. 'We've done it before. The land itself will drive the Slavers back. Those who survive the winter will drown in the floods or fall to the spring fevers, and any who make it through the summer will likely starve before they freeze.'

'And what about the folk taken as slaves? What comfort will that be to them?'

Mira sighed and ran a hand through her clattering braids. 'Uncle Dremman has sent warnings to the western territory along with word of the muster; he's ordered folk to leave the villages and take shelter in the forests. I've told the priests here, too, though the legions are weeks away — the houses and herds are nothing, they can be rebuilt. Some won't heed it, of course, but there's naught we can do about that. We'll survive, though it'll mean hard years ahead.

'But if we accept Sierra, it will destroy us as well, Cam: it would be an affront to the ancestors and turn the Gods themselves against us. Sierra can't help the way she's made and she's suffered so much already — she and Rasten both. They were never meant for this world. I want to feel pity for her, but she is so angry and so cold, and she killed my men without any hint of remorse. It's the demon in her, I suppose, but if only she were more human it would be easier to have some sympathy for her.'

'She's not like that,' Cam said. 'I was raised in the clans, too, and I know what you've been taught. I thought the same thing when I found out what she is, but with Severian's men on our trail I had no choice but to keep her with us.'

'I understand that. But what about Isidro? I realise the two of you have been cut off from civilised society and forced to do whatever you can to survive, and I know Isidro's been through a lot, but what on earth possessed him to share his furs with a *sorcerer*?'

Cam looked away. 'You didn't see him before she came to us. He was in so much pain and he was losing the will to fight it … but when she came it was as if she brought him back to life.'

Mira narrowed her eyes. 'You can't tell me he's in love with her. He's only known her for a little over a week —'

'No, it's not that. She's given him a reason to keep living — some hope that the future might be different.'

'And I suppose he thinks no woman is going to want him now that he's crippled. But why would someone like her take such an interest in a sick and wounded man?' Mira frowned and sat up a little straighter. 'And that business in the tent, when you were telling me about Rasten … I was too preoccupied to take much notice at the time, but she was doing something to him, wasn't she? Just what in the Bright Sun's name is going on here?'

Cam cursed silently. He didn't want to have to explain this — but if he shied away Mira would only ask Rhia, who would tell her, and with a lot less concern for what it would mean for Sierra. 'Mira, I want you to swear that you won't repeat what I tell you.'

Mira frowned at him. 'I can't keep a secret from my clan.'

'I realise that, but I don't want you telling everyone in the temple, or announcing it to your escort. Things are bad enough as it is without making Sierra more nervous.'

Mira pursed her lips with a touch of annoyance and finally nodded. 'Very well. I'll tell only those who need to know.'

There was no way out of it now. Perhaps he should have refused to explain and instead woken Sierra so she could tell Mira herself ... or perhaps this was the better way, after all. He doubted Sierra would be able to keep her temper or her powers under check in the face of Mira's scorn. In the morning he'd apologise for spilling her secrets and, if he did it with Isidro in the room, he could be reasonably sure she wouldn't take it out on him too badly. 'Sierra's powers ...' he said. 'There's a reason why Kell went to so much trouble to track her down and why he's desperate to get her back. She's not just an ordinary mage: she's a Child of the Black Sun. She derives power from the suffering of others. Kell uses her to generate power from his victims.'

Mira's face drained of colour and she wordlessly covered her mouth with her hands, eyes wide with shock and horror. 'She's a torturer?'

'No! Kell never let her near his victims. From what I understand he kept her chained like a dog. She had to watch while he and Rasten did the work. She was there when they ... when they had Isidro. She was shocked that he was still alive.'

'So she ... she *feeds* off it? That's *foul!*'

'It saved our lives when the soldiers tracked us back to our camp. And tonight Rasten was forced to back down rather than face the power she raised from him and Isidro. But that's not all. She doesn't just feed off pain, she can take it away as well. Before Sierra came to us Rhia was giving Isidro as much poppy as she dared and he was still in pain. But with Sierra he says the pain vanishes completely and it's hours before it returns. That's what happened in the tent — Isidro wouldn't let her do it until we were back at the camp in case Rasten came after us again.'

Mira was staring into middle distance. 'Isidro's right, isn't he? Kell will do anything to get her back and he'll destroy us if we can't shift the balance of power. But do you really think she can kill Rasten? If she couldn't do it tonight, what makes you think she'll fare any better the next time?'

'She was alone,' Cam said. 'The moment people start dying, her power grows.'

Mira let out her breath in a heavy sigh. 'And you want to keep her around? Ye Gods, what happens the first time she needs a boost of power? We'd be lucky if she asked for a condemned criminal to torture instead of simply reaching for the nearest warm body.'

'Fires Below, Mira! Rasten might do a thing like that, but Sierra wouldn't.'

'How do you know?'

'Because I've got to know her! I told you: I felt the same way at first, but I've been watching her and Isidro. If I thought she was doing him the slightest bit of harm —'

'You'd have cut her throat while she slept. Do you think she didn't know that? She had no choice but to win you over. And Isidro wouldn't say anything and risk having her withhold the relief. How can you be sure she's telling the truth about how Kell treated her? You can't trust Isidro's version of events. You told me yourself he barely remembers his time there.'

Cam rested his head in his hands as he stared at the flagstones. 'He would never have made it through the last week without her.'

She fell silent at that and after a moment he felt her hands against his shoulders, trying to soothe away his weariness. 'Cam, I'm sorry. I've forgotten what all this must have been like for you. You must be exhausted and worried sick over Isidro. I don't want to argue. Just tell me what you want me to do about her. I'll think it over; we can discuss it again once we've both had some sleep.'

Cam sighed. Sleep would count for little when they had to mount up and ride on again in the morning. What he needed, what they all needed, was a few days' rest with nothing to do but eat and sleep and rebuild their reserves. But that was impossible. Time was a luxury they could not afford.

'Give her a chance,' Cam said. 'She's got no one and nothing in the world beyond us. If an alliance isn't possible then just give her what gear you can and send her on her way, because if she thinks you're going to send her back to Kell, she'll destroy you without a second thought. Whatever you do, Mira, don't make her into your enemy.'

Mira's hands tightened on his shoulders. 'I'm afraid it's too late for that.'

# Chapter 18

Rasten knelt, naked, on the floor of his tent. The trampled spruce prickled like needles against his skin.

His back was a mass of scars but one stood out among them all — Kell's sigil, a mark that had been branded into his skin but reached far deeper. Dried and flaking blood was smeared over it all and a fresh red trickle ran down over his ribs. His bloodstained clothes lay discarded in a heap and a bowl of steaming liquid and a pile of clean rags sat near him. He was close enough that Sierra felt she could reach out and touch him, as he soaked a rag in the liquid and reached over his shoulder with a gasp of pain to clean the wound. The shift in position pulled on the gash, sending another rivulet of fresh, bright blood trickling over his ribs. *What do you want, Little Crow?* he said.

*I'm dreaming,* Sierra thought.

*Are you? Not entirely, I'd say.* He squeezed the rag out over his shoulder and when the liquid ran down and into the wound, it stung like a lance of fire.

He was alone. Even if Kell had sent a servant with him Sierra knew Rasten wouldn't allow anyone to attend him in this state. She could see his hands shaking as he soaked the rag again — the shock of the wound had been held at bay until he'd returned to his camp, cushioned by the power he carried, but now that it had drained away he was paying the price.

For two years, Rasten had been her only companion. When she had been confined to a black and lightless cell he had been her jailer, bringing her food and water and emptying the waste bucket. Later, when Kell judged that the isolation had worn her down enough, Rasten had become her teacher. He gave her the training Kell deemed necessary to enable her to serve. When time came for the sessions with the poor souls Kell used to fuel his power, it was Rasten who had dragged her into the chamber and chained her hands to the floor, leaving her helpless to resist becoming part of the ritual. When she angered Kell enough to earn a session on the rack herself it was Rasten who had chained her down and it was he who had cleaned and bandaged the wounds afterwards and helped her drink the draught to let her sleep. Sierra had returned the favour sometimes, when Rasten was left weak and bloody from a session of Kell's pleasure. She feared him, sometimes she hated him, but she also knew he was as much Kell's victim as anyone. He was Kell's slave, too, but while she had been spared the worst of it Rasten had been subjected to every degradation and humiliation Kell could contrive. Rasten was as tough as a slab of granite, but she'd heard Kell make him sob and beg for mercy.

*Why don't you run?* she asked him. *Slip away, lose yourself in the mountains. Kell's tied down holding back the Akharian mages. He can't follow you.*

*If you think that, then you don't know him at all,* Rasten said. *If this king falls, he'll soon find another to accept his services. We belong to him, you and I, and he'll sacrifice everything he has to bring us back to heel. So long as he lives, we'll be his slaves.*

*Have you told him what's happened yet?*

*No. I thought I'd save that particular pleasure for later, when I have the strength to deal with it.* His power was probably too low to make the contact and Kell would not lower himself to lending any of *his* power to bridge the gap.

By stretching as far as the wound would let him, he could just reach the gash to clean it. It set Sierra's back afire, just as it had when Rasten turned the poker on Isidro. Somewhere, she felt her body twitch in response to the sensation, threatening to wake.

*Your powers have grown since Kell first brought you to us,* Rasten said. *I was afraid you would never reach this point — until a few hours ago, I was sure of it.*

*I'm sorry I didn't kill you,* she said to him in her dream. *It would have been better for us both, I think.*

*I felt that way once,* Rasten said. *But not any more. And I know you don't want to die either, Little Crow, despite sending us both beneath the ice.*

*I'll die before I'll let you take me back,* she vowed. *I'll kill us both rather than submit to that.*

She wrenched herself awake with a splutter of light. Energy hummed and buzzed along her nerves while her heart pounded in her ears and sweat trickled down her spine.

Her face was wet with tears. Sierra touched them incredulously, then quickly scrubbed them away with the blanket while a flush of shame crept over her cheeks. She didn't want to pity Rasten — she needed to hate him if she was going to have the strength and the will to kill him. There was no other option — if Kell ever took her back he would break her down and Rasten would be the tool he used to do it. It would be better for Rasten, anyway — a release at last from this life of torment.

Her heart still pounding, Sierra made herself lie down, willing sleep to return. In a few short hours they would be moving on again. She had just closed her eyes when Rasten's voice came to her again, weak with pain and fatigue.

*The first time I saw you, Little Crow, you gave me hope. Now I know, one day soon, you'll set me free.*

Sierra woke to a clatter of metal as one of the temple servants fed the furnace in the wall of Isidro's chamber and then shuffled away to his next task. The noise woke Cam as well and Sierra lifted her head to see him push his blankets away and sit up with a yawn.

Sierra shuffled down to the foot of the bench and raked her hair back from her face, only to have her fingers snarl in a nest of tangles. She hadn't combed it after her dive into the river and it was knotted with fragments of leaf and litter from the riverbed, while her comb was with the remains of her gear on the torched sled. All she had were the clothes she'd been wearing, piled in a rumpled heap at the foot of the bed. She'd been too weary to bother hanging them up the night before. When she reached for them the damp green smell of the riverbed wafted up from the fabric. They needed to be aired at the very least, washed for preference. Her winter fur needed attention, too — it was stiff from its dunking and the leather needed to be scraped and worked to soften it again, but there was no time. Rasten would be on the move and they would have to be mounted and riding out within the hour if they were to have a hope of catching him.

Sierra dropped the garments in her lap and turned to Isidro. He slept still, unmoved since she had woken in the middle of the night. But she could feel the pain in his arm returning. It would wake him before long.

'Best to let him sleep while he can,' Cam murmured and then he nodded to the kettle sitting over the brazier. 'Is that water still hot?'

Sierra licked her fingertips and gingerly tested the metal. 'Warm enough for washing.'

Cam rolled up his bedding and shoved the bundle against the wall and out of the way. 'Well and good,' he said and tossed her a lump of soap from his pack. 'You go first and I'll fetch our breakfast.'

It felt good to be clean, even though she had to dress in her filthy clothes again. While she waited for Cam to return, Sierra built up the fire, and she was just settling to work through the knots in her hair with her fingers when a tap against the doorpost startled her and brought her to her feet with a skittish burst of power that rippled over her skin in a lattice of light. With a deep breath to steel herself and force her energy down, Sierra went to the doorway and twitched the curtain aside.

Mira was there with a pack under one arm and her other hand raised to knock on the post again. At the sight of Sierra she faltered, her hazel eyes growing wide as she took a half-step back before she could stop herself. Her sleek red braids were twisted into a knot at the back of her head and jewels of jade and gold winked on her earlobes. 'Ah ...' Mira said. 'Good morning. Did you sleep well?'

'Well enough,' Sierra said, acutely conscious of her bird's-nest hair and her rumpled clothes. Behind her, Isidro sighed, and she glanced over her shoulder and stepped out, letting the curtain fall closed to shield him from the light.

As she did so, Mira leaned around the doorpost to peer into the gloom. 'How is he?'

'Sleeping,' Sierra said and wound her fingers together to keep from fidgeting. She didn't know what to say to this woman who had sent assassins to kill her. Part of her was still furious and that fury was feeding the crackling power coursing up and down her spine; but Cam and Isidro were depending on Mira's support for their safety and she didn't want to cause them any more trouble than she already had. So Sierra sucked up her anger and with clenched teeth put her power on a tight leash.

Mira hefted the pack under her arm. 'I had my women put a new kit together for you. I have them hunting down some bedding and there's a comb in there, too. If there's anything else you need, let Cam know, and I'll find it for you.' She passed the pack over and as Sierra took it the movement pulled back the cuffs of her sleeves to show the fresh scars encircling her wrists.

'Uh … thank you,' Sierra said, juggling the bundle to keep the scars and the mutilated remains of her kinship tattoo out of sight. 'I —'

'We —'

They both stopped. A nervous ripple of power slipped past Sierra's controls and flickered over her shoulder and she shifted the bundle again to swat at it.

From behind the curtain there came a thump and a hiss of indrawn breath and then what sounded like a shelf giving way with a crash and clatter of breaking crockery.

'Isidro!' Sierra and Mira both dived through the curtain to see Isidro on his knees on the floor, surrounded by the shards of broken bowls and a small puddle of burning oil from a shattered lamp that had spilled onto the grass mat on the floor.

Sierra dropped the bundle and smothered the flames with a blanket of power that manifested as a tangled net of lightning. Then she summoned a globe of light and tossed it into the air to illuminate the chamber. Mira had crouched at Isidro's side but as Sierra went to do the same Mira shot her a look of such ferocious hostility that Sierra hesitated and hung back.

'Issey, what happened?' Mira said.

Isidro shook his head and the movement made him sway so violently that Sierra steadied his shoulder in case he slumped onto the broken shards of pottery. 'Here,' she said, 'sit on the bench. We'll help you up.'

He was so unsteady that it was difficult to help him without jostling his arm and hurting him further, but after a few moments Sierra and Mira got him lying on his furs, only to have him try to sit up again.

'No, stay where you are,' Sierra said, catching his good hand in hers and setting the other on his chest to keep him down.

He tried to push her hands away. 'I'm getting up, curse it.'

Mira went to the door and leaned out past the curtain. 'You there!' she said to someone passing by. 'Find Rhia, the physician who came with us last night — the fair-haired foreigner. Have her attend upon us at once.'

'Yes, my lady.'

'And send someone in to clear up this mess!' Mira called after them as Sierra heard footsteps hurrying away.

A moment later Cam ducked through the curtain carrying a tray with an assortment of rattling vessels and bowls. 'What in the Black Sun's name is going on?'

'He is not well enough to ride,' Rhia said.

'Just tie me to the saddle,' Isidro mumbled. 'I'll manage.' He had covered his eyes with his good hand. Sierra moved her globe of light so that it didn't shine in his face, but even the glare of it sent stabbing pains through his head. She felt an echo of it in her own skull, diffused by power into a soft, golden fog.

'You will not,' Rhia said. 'You are feverish. Someone build up the fire. I need hot water and more light.'

Sierra created another small globe and held it out to them. Rhia and Mira both recoiled from it as though she were offering them a live wasp, but with a little growl of irritation Cam took it from her and held it so Rhia could see to rummage through her medicine chest.

Sitting back on her heels, Mira drew herself up. 'Can't *you* do anything for him?' she said to Sierra.

Sierra shook her head. 'All I can do is ease pain and that's not the problem here.' She saw Isidro's packs shoved back against the wall and pulled them over to rummage through until she found the enchantments Kell had made.

'He is exhausted,' Rhia said. 'There is no cure but rest.' She glanced up from mixing medicaments together in a bowl and curled her lip at the sight of stones in Sierra's hand. 'Not those wretched things again!'

'They'll help him,' Sierra said.

'What are they?' Mira asked, frowning.

'Enchantments Kell makes for his prisoners,' Sierra said. 'They make sure the wounds don't kill them before he's done with them.' Isidro raised his left hand so she could tie the cord around his wrist. His skin was cold and he trembled with the effort.

'Well,' Mira said, 'at the risk of sounding callous, we have to make a decision. Ardamon says the men are ready to ride and the demons-cursed apprentice is getting further away from us with every moment. Perhaps a sled —'

'No,' Rhia said. 'He must rest undisturbed and it will take some days for him to recover. He must stay here.'

'He can't,' Sierra said. 'It's not safe. The Akharian Legions are heading this way —'

'They're weeks away at the least,' Mira said. 'My uncle and his men will be here long before they will.'

'And we can't afford to let Rasten get away from us now,' Cam said. 'I'm sorry, Issey, but she's right. We'll have to leave you here.'

Isidro closed his eyes and nodded. The words must pain him, Sierra thought. He had been fighting since his capture to maintain his independence and keep his injuries from changing his life completely. To be told now he was too weak, too vulnerable, too much of a liability to go with them, must have burned like poison.

'So you will,' he said, after a moment. 'Do what you have to.'

Sierra shook her head. 'If the Akharians come he'll be defenceless.'

'But they're miles away,' Mira insisted.

'They've already come further than you think,' Sierra said.

'We've no proof of that,' Mira said. 'You may well have fallen asleep and dreamed the whole thing.'

Sierra clenched her fists as her power flared along with her anger.

'I saw it too, Mira,' Isidro said.

Mira tossed her head. 'Well then. I'll speak to Ardamon and leave a couple of men here with you. Once you're well enough to ride, they'll escort you to Terundel to meet up with us again.' She turned to Cam. 'Will that satisfy you?'

He gave a sigh of relief and nodded.

'But what if that's not enough?' Sierra said. 'Rasten ran into those scouts only a few days ago —'

Watching her with narrowed eyes, Mira cut her off. 'He's ill and in pain, and pushing on now could well kill him, but you want to take him with us anyway? Do you care about him at all? Or is it just that you don't want to lose this little feast of power?'

'Black Sun take you!' Sierra leapt to her feet and the sudden pulse of anger sent her power spilling over and erupting in a shower of crazed blue sparks that rippled over her skin and rained down from every movement she made. 'Do you think I'd do that to him? You think I'm no better than Rasten and Kell?'

'Aren't you? Cam told me what you are. He explained where your power comes from and why Kell lusts after you so badly. You couldn't have found a better place for yourself if you'd tried, could you? Not only do you have someone to feed your power but he's so desperate for the relief you give him that he'll do whatever you want to get it.'

'Mira!' Cam snapped. 'Sirri, I had to tell her —'

Sierra dismissed his words with a wave of her hand. 'She would have heard it soon enough from Rhia or the others. You listen to me, Mira of the Wolf. I have never caused anyone pain for my own ends and I've only ever used this power against another living creature in order to save my own life. I've never stood back and let a friend of mine be injured to protect my own interests and I've never withheld any help I could offer until I can get something else in return. By the Black Sun, I never chose this power, but it's all I have and I'll be cursed if I won't use it to help when I can!'

When she fell silent, no one spoke, but the chamber was full of the angry crackle of power that seemed to be seeping from her every pore. The grass mat at her feet was beginning to smoke.

'Sirri — ' Cam began and she backed off it onto the flagstones.

'I'd better go and cool off,' she said. 'Issey, I'll come see you again before we leave.' She strode across the chamber and ducked out through the curtain. Outside in the hall, a servant carrying a tray laden with bowls screamed and dropped it at the sight of her, but Sierra didn't pause. Still in her soft indoor clothes, she strode out into the cold and darkness of the early morning and wept until the tears froze in her tangled hair.

Heaving a sigh, Cam got to his feet and stamped out the small flames that flickered over the grass mat. In the sudden darkness he said, 'Well, that could have gone better. Anyone have a flint and steel handy? What happened to that lamp?'

'Mira?' Isidro said from the bed.

'What is it, Issey?'

'That was a cursed stupid thing to do.'

There was a scrape of metal and stone and Rhia held up a candle stub she'd had tucked away in her kit.

Pale and shaking, Mira raked her braids back from her face. 'I don't want to hear it, Isidro.'

'That's too bad. You're not going to be able to kill Rasten without Sierra and the less she trusts you the harder that's going to be. She's

243

*not* like him and Kell. Just because she's a mage doesn't make her your enemy.'

Mira stood with a toss of her head. 'I need to make arrangements with the High Priestess,' she said and swept out of the chamber.

Isidro lifted his head to watch her go and then lay back with a sigh. 'Rhia, I need to speak to Cam.'

Rhia hesitated, then nodded and set the candle stub on a shard of broken bowl. 'I'll go and speak to the temple physician. I wish I could stay here, Isidro, but Mira has no physician. If there is a battle they will need me.'

Isidro nodded and Rhia left.

Cam sat on the foot of the bench and wiped his palms against his thighs. Sierra's display had left him in a cold sweat. He only hoped Mira hadn't noticed.

'Cam, I need you to promise me something.'

'Of course.'

'Look after Sierra. You read Mesentreian better than she does and she'll need help with that cursed book. And don't let Mira and Ardamon drive her away. If she feels as if she's alone among enemies and that Kell and Rasten are the only ones who'll accept her ...' He trailed off and Cam felt himself go cold. Isidro's instincts had always served them well. He would be the first to admit they were only hunches, but every once in a while events would unfold in just the way he had predicted.

'I'll do whatever I can,' Cam said. 'On our father's grave, I swear it.'

Isidro lifted the hand that shielded his eyes and sought Cam's face in the gloom. 'Bring her back to me, Cam. Please, just bring her back.'

Cam found Sierra still out in the darkness, letting the pre-dawn cold burn off her nervous power. She had been watching as Ardamon assembled men, horses and sleds; she was beginning to shiver when he strode towards her through a scattered fall of snow with her coat hanging over his arm.

'Ardamon says we're ready to ride,' Cam said, holding the fur out to her. 'I told him you'd need a few minutes with Isidro.'

Sierra nodded. 'I'm sorry. I never wanted to put you and Isidro in this kind of danger.'

He folded his hands under his arms. 'Don't worry about it now. Once Rasten's disposed of we'll work it all out.'

Sierra pulled her hood up as she followed him back to the hall, letting it shield her from Mira's men as they stared at her with a mixture of fear and awe. She hurried up the steps, anxious to be beyond their gaze.

Inside there wasn't a priest in sight, but Sierra saw Brekan sitting on the common-room floor, sorting through his gear with the slow movements of a man in shock. On the far side of the room, Eloba was talking to Mira while a tearful Lakua embraced Rhia with the air of someone delivering her farewells. They all fell silent as Sierra entered the hall and crossed the floor to Isidro's chamber.

She dropped to her knees beside his bed. He reached for her hand and then winced at the touch of her skin. 'Sirri, you're cold.'

'I'll warm up,' she told him. 'Issey, I have to go.'

'I know,' he said. He caught her hand and brought her palm to his lips.

Her voice grew thick. 'I'll miss you.'

He began to speak, but the words died in his throat, and he simply shook his head. Sierra felt as if she couldn't breathe. What was coming over her? It couldn't be love. They'd known each other for so little time. It was infatuation, perhaps, and simple gratitude that they'd found a safe harbour in each other, just when they needed it most.

Isidro reached out and stroked a tear from her cheek with his thumb. 'You can do this, Sirri.'

She nodded, dumbly. She *had* to do it. Killing Rasten was their only hope for safety.

His pain was coming back, clawing at his arm as it throbbed and burned beneath the splints. With a breath to compose herself, Sierra opened the neck of Isidro's shirt and laid her palms against his chest. 'I'll come back to you if I can,' she murmured, and drew the pain from his body like the poison it was.

By the time she finished, he was asleep.

Cam was waiting for her at the foot of the steps, holding the reins of his horse and hers. Sierra let him keep them for a moment while she checked that the book and the enchantments she had worn during her escape were all still there. She swung into the saddle and pulled the hood up to hide her face. 'Let's go.'

# Chapter 19

The cut to the back of his head stung and his shoulder throbbed. When Rasten closed his eyes he could still feel the knife sliding in and grating over bone. Pain was a teaching tool for the fledgling mage — the rituals gave him an echo of the suffering of his victims and a blood-mage had to be able to focus and channel power despite it. Once, Rasten had dreaded it, had fought and pleaded to avoid it, but now he knew that pain was as inevitable as the sunrise and, in the subterranean world of his master, about as relevant. It came and went as it always did and the world carried on regardless.

Still, he hadn't expected such a simple wound to *hurt so cursed much.*

*You lost her?* Kell said through the connection. *How in all the hells did you lose her, boy?*

*It was Balorica,* Rasten said. *I nearly had her, master, but then he came up behind me —*

*Spare me your excuses! How bad is the wound?*

*It didn't sever anything important. It should heal cleanly enough.*

*If you lose any use of that arm I'm going to hunt Balorica down and skin him alive. By all the hells, boy, how could you be so foolish? Where is she now?*

*Back with the Wolf Clan, I believe, master.*

*After they already tried to kill her? Idiot girl!*

Rasten could feel Kell's rage burning through the connection. The sigil carved into his back was throbbing with it, as though the iron that had scored it was glowing still.

*Well, you can't do anything until that wound heals. How long?*

*At least a few weeks, master.*

*A few weeks? By all the Gods! Perhaps you'd better come back here.*

Thinking of the punishment Kell would exact for his failure made Rasten's control waver for a moment and with a flare of power flames

246

licked over the bare skin of his hands. *Master, I believe it would be better for me to stay here. Sierra must know she cannot trust the clan and she has developed a certain ... fondness for Balorica. I might be able to convince her she can spare him by giving herself up.*

*The little fool might even believe it. Well then, spin her whatever tale you like, boy, but do not move against her again without my command. If you fuck this up a second time, I'll cut the price of the failure out of your wretched hide.*

*Yes, master.*

Kell broke the connection, leaving Rasten shivering in his tent and trembling with the effort of maintaining the contact. He'd killed his last sacrifice in preparation for Sierra's capture and hadn't arranged another. It would have been too dangerous given she could derive power from a subject more quickly than he could.

When he closed his eyes Rasten could still see her on the riverbank, wreathed in a nimbus of lightning. She wasn't the same terrified girl who had surrendered in the ruined temple. Properly fuelled, if she tried again to kill them both with all the strength and determination desperation would give her, Rasten was far from certain he would be able to stop her. All his fears that she wasn't ready seemed laughable now. She'd grown so strong!

That didn't mean the danger was past. Kell was uncommonly brutal with his apprentices; he had been ever since one snapped and attacked him, delivering the wound that had left Kell needing a cane for support. Rasten himself had been a Sympath like Sierra, one of the rare breed of mages who could raise power without the elaborate rituals of the blood-mages, but Kell had crippled him with hard use. While Rasten was powerful compared to the charlatans who eked out a living in Mesentreia, he was still far less than he might have been.

It was Sierra's sex that had saved her from the same fate. By the time Kell had finally tracked her down, she was old enough to have a woman's body. A few years younger and Kell might have been able to convince himself she was boyish enough to arouse his desire, and she would have been ruined as he was. Now that her power had matured, Kell would set about breaking her down to a true slave, a living reservoir of power to be filled and tapped as required.

Rasten remembered clearly the day he realised she would one day outstrip him and had fully understood just what he'd lost to Kell's hands.

She'd awoken a dream Rasten had buried long ago; she'd let him hope that one day, perhaps, he could be free of Kell and his torments. Free of the dungeons and their stench and the perpetual cold and the gloom.

Rasten knew he couldn't kill Kell. He lacked the strength. Sierra, on the other hand …

He could use her power, but that alone wouldn't be enough. She had to be so powerful Kell couldn't break her. So powerful that his attempts would only make her stronger and bring her through torment and pain until she came into the full flush of her power.

And once she did they could turn on their master, the one who had slaughtered their families and stolen their innocence, murdering the people these stolen children would have become. Together, they could destroy Kell.

'Oh, Sirri, my love,' Rasten whispered. 'You're going to hate me before it's over, but in the end you'll understand. It's the only way.'

*Sirri.*

Sierra's eyes flew open and she stared up at the roof of the tiny tent Mira's servants had found for her. *Not him*, she thought. *Not now.*

*Sirri!*

She hated it when he used the intimate form of her name. There was nothing she could do about it — they were intimates, after all. It was only a matter of time before Kell captured her again and they would be as intimate as two people could be, entwined together in blood and pain.

*What do you want, Rasten?*

His reply, when it came, was hesitant. *I … I just wanted to know if you're alright.*

*I'm fine*, she replied. *How's the shoulder?*

*It'll heal. What about your lover's arm?*

A wave of anger sent the power breaking over her naked skin, filling the tent with rippling blue light. For a moment neither of them spoke, but Sierra could feel his attention still fixed on her. Pain was of no importance to Rasten. He thought nothing of inflicting or receiving it. Any normal person would want to spare those they loved, but to Rasten the concept was inconceivable. Pain was unavoidable.

More than anything else right now, she didn't want him thinking about Isidro. *What do you want?* she said again.

She felt him draw a breath, as though steeling himself for something difficult. *Little Crow, we need to talk.*

*I have nothing to say to you.*

*Perhaps not, but you do need to listen. Sirri, you have to know that Kell will never stop hunting you.*

Sierra pressed her head back against the furs. So, he was doing this to hound her, to keep her exhausted and fearful. *Anyone who shelters me will suffer and decent folk will drive me off with stones and spears. I know this tale, Rasten.*

*Good. Then you understand that you can't go on like this for long.*

Sierra laughed silently, but the giggle that echoed down the line to Rasten had an edge of hysteria to it. *You want me to give myself up? Rasten, you're either mad or you're desperately trying to avoid whatever punishment Kell will use to reward your failure —*

*I can take whatever Kell gives me,* Rasten said evenly. *Sirri, just listen. I've been watching you grow, but until last night I didn't realise how far you've come. I'm not sure I could take you alive and your power is still growing. But if Kell comes here it will be a different matter. You're powerful enough for his purpose — if he captures you again, he'll break you like he did me and he'll see to it that you're not capable of running again. You'll be a slave for the rest of your life.*

*And you woke me up to tell me this?*

*Just listen, Sirri. You've no shortage of power and it's growing every day you use it, but you lack the training and the skill you'll need to stand against Kell. For now he's pinned down by the Akharian army and he's given me permission to stay here in the east until this wound heals and I can bring you in. I can help you, Sirri. I can give you the training you've been denied. I can make you so powerful that Kell won't be able to break you down.*

*Rasten, I am not going to give myself up. I'd sooner die than go back.*

*Then Kell will hunt down and slaughter everyone you come into contact with. Your crippled lover and the prince will die slower deaths than you can imagine. He will keep them alive just to torment you, but if you come home, he'll be so focussed on you they'll be able to slip away.*

*And why would you let that happen after what Isidro did to you?*

*Because I don't care about them. There's only one thing I care about now and that's you. I need you. I can't do this on my own. I need you to help me destroy Kell. It's the only way, Little Crow. It's the only way we'll ever be free.*

Sierra lay awake for hours after Rasten left her in peace. It would be beyond foolish to trust him. It had to be a trap. He had never rebelled against Kell, not in all the months she had known him. Rasten loathed his master's lusts but he would not resist, no matter what Kell inflicted on him. It sickened her to think what he must have suffered to bring him to that point … and that he was right: Kell would subject her to the same treatment.

He had to be lying. There had never been so much as a hint of this plan, of such a deep thirst for revenge.

But there wouldn't be, would there? Kell punished any intransigence with swiftness and brutality. Rasten would have learned long ago to police his every thought and expression, but he couldn't trust her to do the same. Even with the restraints Kell had chained around her wrists she couldn't control herself. Every peak of anger and emotion sent her power roaring to the surface, overwhelming her control. And she had barely been tested with Kell's darker lessons. The few times she had earned a punishment on the rack had been minor compared to the rituals Kell performed on his sacrifices, but they had left her so traumatised that she had never pushed against his bounds again. The needle scars on her back prickled at the memory. He wouldn't have trusted her with his secret before she had been tested — so why trust her now?

If Isidro were here, she could talk it over with him. He would listen to her rambling fears and recollections and offer his own dry and detached opinion. Or would that be asking too much of him, to talk this way about the man who had tortured and crippled him? She had never told Isidro just what sort of life she had shared with Rasten, but not because he wouldn't understand what it had been like for her. She didn't want him to have to understand. His path was hard enough without having to muster compassion for the man who'd crippled him.

She couldn't tell Cam, either. His situation was difficult as it was, as he tried to walk the line of diplomacy between her and the Wolf Clan. She would not put him in a position of having information that would allow the Wolf Clan to condemn her.

Beneath it all, gnawing at her like a snake coiled amid her vitals, was the fear that Rasten was right. Kell would never give up. The only way she would be free was if he were dead.

Ardamon set a hard pace as they rode south from the temple and, within half a day, Sierra was forced to admit that leaving Isidro behind had been the right decision. Ardamon's men were all well rested, but she, Cam and Rhia had already spent the last week cramming as much distance into each day as they could. By the time Ardamon called a halt on the first evening, Sierra's head was swimming with exhaustion.

No one came out and told her she wasn't welcome in Mira's tent, where Cam and Rhia laid their bedrolls. One of Mira's serving-women simply came and said her tent was ready, guiding her to a tiny structure set up some distance from the rest of the tents of the heir's escort, where the sentries would be able to keep watch on her throughout the night.

Solitude was something most Ricalanis found uncomfortable. Everyone, from the poorest peasant to the chief of the wealthiest clan, spent most of their lives surrounded by friends and kin, and rarely went out alone even when hunting and trapping. Two wives and two husbands was generally considered to be the smallest stable family unit and Sierra had grown up with twice that number, as the eldest of nearly a dozen siblings.

Her first months of solitary confinement in Kell's dungeons had been an agony of loneliness and fear, but since then Sierra had grown accustomed to being alone. With her bedding laid out and coals glowing in the little stove, Sierra was simply too weary to care if she slept alone or with company.

Mira's women had left a dish of food on the corner of the stove to keep warm but she was also too tired to eat. Sierra managed to hang her socks and boot liners from the ridge-pole to dry before she wrapped herself in her furs and slept until Mira's servant returned to wake her in the morning.

If Ardamon was setting a hard pace, then Rasten was driving his men unmercifully. After the speed they'd been setting to chase Cam's little party, they would be feeling the effects by now, and Rasten himself was in constant pain. Sierra could feel it occasionally when exhaustion made his control falter and his senses spilled into her with a rush of heat and power. But when Ardamon's scouts returned to the main camp on the second evening of the chase their news was grim. Rasten and his men were still hours ahead and had maybe even gained a little time.

The problem, Cam explained to her, was that his horses were the best the king could provide, bred from a mix of tough little Ricalani ponies and the longer-legged, swifter southern breeds, whereas the Wolf's best horses had gone with the war-leader's army. Ardamon's men had been equipped for little more than a brief jaunt through safe territory, not a chase like this.

Sierra had another concern, one she hesitated to share even with Cam, now her only ally. Since they'd left Isidro behind she had no source of power other than the healing cuts and burns on Cam's chest. Rasten had no one to feed from, either — she could tell from the brief slips of his shields that his power was running low. He could take another sacrifice from among his own men if the situation demanded, but to do that too often would tempt mutiny. She knew he would be on the lookout for another warm body to bleed for power.

The thought was very much on her mind on the morning Rasten's trail led them to the doorstep of an isolated farmstead. The sight of it made Sierra feel sick to the pit of her stomach.

The house was ancient and run-down, almost buried beneath the drifting snow heaped against its walls. It was not abandoned, however. A flock of goats had run from the horses' path as they approached and a string of frozen fish dangled from the eaves. There was no smoke rising from the chimney, but the stove-wall that heated a Ricalani house was usually fired only twice a day.

As Ardamon led his men closer she saw the door was newly splintered and broken, but had been forced back into the frame and wedged closed. Ardamon's captain, Dreshavic, dismounted to knock on it with the hilt of his sword. For a long time there was no answer and Sierra began to fear the worst. No family would let one of their number be taken by Rasten and his men without putting up a fight. If he had been here, she doubted they would find anyone left alive.

While Ardamon and Mira conferred with their captain, Cam guided his horse over to Sierra. 'Can you sense anything from inside?'

'No. There's no one wounded in there, I'm sure of that.'

'But is there anyone alive?'

She shrugged, helplessly. 'I can't tell, not with all these people around ...'

Mira slipped down from her saddle and led her horse up to the doorway. 'Hello the house!' she called, her high, clear voice ringing through the cold air. 'Mirasada of the Wolf gives you greetings! Is anyone there?'

For a long moment, there was silence. Sierra held her breath. Then with a groan of rusting hinges the door opened just enough for a man to peer out. A moment later it opened fully and he came a few cautious paces outside with a spear in one hand and a battered old shield on his arm. 'It's the Wolf!' he called out to those inside. 'Bright Sun be thanked, the Wolf warriors are here!'

The chamber was warm, but the woman who spoke was wrapped in a heavy fur. She was still in shock, Sierra thought.

'He was here yesternight,' the woman said. 'Him and all his men.'

There were six adults living here and eight children Sierra could see, the eldest a sturdy boy of about twelve. The children were still pale and frightened and stared in silence at the newcomers.

Ardamon had wanted Sierra to stay outside but Cam insisted that she join them in the main hall. She knew Rasten best, after all, and she might be able to explain what had happened here.

'I was here on my own watching the children.' The children were lined up beside her on a bench, the nearest, a little girl of about three, huddling under her arm. The child carried the taint. Sierra could sense the power in her the moment she walked into the room, but it wasn't the sort she could draw upon for herself. It was a peculiar sensation to have a hint of power coiling around her but out of reach.

She carefully kept her attention on the woman. She was some years older than Sierra, her face lined and weathered, with a sprinkling of grey in her hair. 'The others were out trapping, or bringing in the goats, and it was just me an' the little ones when they broke down the door and charged in. The men threw me on the floor and tied my hands behind my back before I even knew what was happening.' She raised a hand to brush a strand of hair back from her face and Sierra noted the fresh red welts encircling her wrist. 'I thought it was the cursed Raiders at first, but once they hauled me up, I saw they were dressed too neat for that. Tems tried to fight 'em,' she nodded to the eldest boy, 'but they just knocked him down and one of them held him there at the point of a sword. I thought he was going to kill him, but one of the men said they ought to wait for Lord Rasten.'

'You understood them?' Mira said with some surprise. 'Were they speaking Ricalani, or do you know Mesentreian?'

'I know little of the southern tongue, m'lady, but I understand it better.' She dropped her gaze to the floor as she went on. 'Lord Rasten came in a few moments later and he just stood looking down at me, right where you are now, sir,' she said with a shy glance at Ardamon. 'I begged him, I said do what you want with me, but don't harm the little ones. He slapped me across the face and told me to hold my tongue ...' The woman raised a hand to her cheek but there was no bruise Sierra could see. With that wound in his shoulder he couldn't use his preferred hand, but Rasten could still do a lot of damage with his left. Rasten always hated it when a prisoner begged, but it seemed to her that he'd stayed his hand.

'He just stood there for a moment, looking around. The children were crying and making an awful racket. He just stared at them like a cat watches a mouse and then he shakes himself and says I was no good to him and orders his men to leave. Well, they were near as stunned as I was. For a moment, none of them moved. He bellows at them to get out and mount up again, and they all just trooped out and left me here. Tems had to run down to the kitchen and find a knife to cut my hands free and by that time they were gone.'

'And that's it?' Ardamon said. 'They didn't take anything with them?'

'Oh, they took some stores from the kitchen and a bit of cloth, and a couple of goats for meat we think, but that's all. My husbands and my sisters came back a few hours later and found us all barricaded in the furnace room with every weapon I could get my hands on.'

Ardamon turned to Sierra with a furious glare. 'What in the hells was he playing at?'

'Rasten was about Tems's age when Kell took him,' Sierra said. 'Kell had a band of the king's warriors with him. They killed his fathers and Kell let his mothers and his older sister be passed around among the men, then he made Rasten watch while he cut their throats. There were some younger children, I think, and Kell had them shut away in a room on their own before they all rode away.

'Rasten doesn't like to work with children. He wouldn't have touched them,' Sierra said to the pale and trembling woman. 'And you probably reminded him of his mothers. It's just as well your menfolk were away. He'd have had no hesitation in taking one of them.'

Ardamon folded his arms across his chest. 'Do you mean to tell me that raping, murdering monster has a conscience?'

'Of a sort,' Sierra said. 'Kell's the one without one.' Once again, everyone was staring at her. She knew there was no threat but her power responded to more base instincts and flared in response to her nerves. Fortunately, running as low as it was without anything to feed it, she could keep it contained beneath her skin.

The little girl sitting nearest the still-shaking woman tugged on her mother's sleeve and pointed at Sierra. 'Look, Mama. She's got all lights around her.'

The woman blanched. Stammering an excuse, she gathered the little girl up in her arms and fled from the room.

One of the men who had been standing with his hands folded behind his back took a step towards Sierra, glowering and with his hand hovering over the hilt of his belt-knife. 'I'd like you to leave now, miss.'

Cam settled a hand on Sierra's shoulder. 'Now wait just a moment,' he began.

'Cam, no, it's alright,' Sierra murmured. 'I'll go.'

He held her where she was for a moment longer. 'Do you think there's anything else here we should know?'

'No. They're safe enough. Rasten won't come back.' She pulled away from his hand and ducked back into the entrance hall and from there went down the ramp and outside.

As soon as she set foot down on the snow Sierra heard a cough off to her left. She turned to see the woman from inside peering around the corner of the house. With a wary glance at the men waiting some distance away she beckoned to Sierra and then backed away again, moving around the corner of the house and out of sight.

Curious, Sierra followed. The woman led her around to the back of the house. The household dogs had been tied up to keep them from harassing the horses and a pair of caribou had taken advantage of their absence to come down from the trees and pick over the snow for any feed that had been set out for the goats. They watched the women warily, but did not flee.

The woman was still holding the little girl on her hip. 'I didn't want to ask in front of the others,' the woman said. 'You have the taint, don't you? Like *him*.'

'Yes,' Sierra said. She took off her gloves and cupped her hands together to create a tiny globe of light. With Isidro as a willing test subject she'd finally learned how to make them without shocking a non-mage. She handed the ball to the little girl, who took it with a giggle of delight.

'This is Ricca,' the woman said, hitching the girl to a more comfortable position. 'I'm Marima.'

'Sierra,' Sierra said, and reached out to smooth down a lock of the girl's coal-black hair.

'There's something else. Something I didn't tell the others. You saw it in her, didn't you? Well, he did, too. I thought he was going to take her. Isn't that what the likes of him do, take mages and turn them into slaves? I know that's what she is. She's not even old enough to be tested in the temple yet, but there's no doubt in my mind.'

'She will be,' Sierra said. 'She's still too young — she's got the spark, but it won't develop into real power for a good few years. Maybe not until her menses start.'

'Will she ... Will she be like him?'

'No,' Sierra said. 'She's not a Sympath and she won't be a Blood-Mage unless someone forces her onto that path.'

'But is there anything I can do to stop it? What about a warding-stone? She throws a fit if I try to put one on her, but I could make her wear it if it would help ...'

'It won't. It won't do a thing and she'll never stop hating it,' Sierra said. 'Do the priests know about her?'

'Not yet. One of my husbands thinks we should give her to the priests to raise. He says maybe they'll be able to nip it in the bud ...'

'It won't help. Do you *want* to keep her?'

Marima squeezed the girl tighter. 'I'll kill anyone who tries to take her from me!'

'Then keep her away from the Children's Festival,' Sierra said. 'Once she's in their record book, it'll be too late to hide her. Here, do you have a warding-stone with you?'

Marima reached hesitantly for the neck of her coat. 'I … I started wearing one myself. I thought she must have got it from me, from *my* mother, you see? I thought maybe it would help …' She pulled the cord over her neck and handed it to Sierra.

The touch of it made her flinch, but Sierra steeled herself and wrapped her hands around the little plaque of jade. It couldn't do anything to her. The enchantment was a simple one, worked by rote by the priests who'd made it.

Sierra summoned the small amount of energy she had and shattered the enchantment within the stone. It made no noise, but the goats nearby startled and trotted away and the browsing caribou lifted their heads with a snort and wheeled to lope for the shelter of the trees.

As starved as she was, the effort left her momentarily dizzy and she had to steady herself against the wall of the house before she could hand it back. 'When she's of age for the test, take her on a journey. Tell the local priests that you had her tested while you were away and give her that stone to wear as a decoy. Don't let any priests get a close look at it or they'll know it's broken. Keep her away from temples, too. Priests are often Sensitives and they'll be able to feel the power in her. When she gets older see if you can find a former priest to teach her how to meditate and focus her mind. It will help her control it. Some of them will go and report her to the nearest temple, but if you're careful you'll be able to find one who is sympathetic. There are a few of us around, very few. If any of them feel wrong to you, be prepared to drop everything and flee with her. And if a Blood-Mage does find her, she'll be better off if you give her to the snow rather than let him take her.'

Marima stared at her, wide-eyed and speechless. From the front of the house came the sound of boots tramping down the ramp and people talking. One set of boots seemed to be heading their way.

'You should go now,' Sierra told Marima. 'It's probably better if you're not seen talking to me.'

Marima slowly backed away and turned and fled just as Mira came around the corner of the house, her eyes narrowed in suspicion. 'What are you doing over here?'

'Nothing,' Sierra said with a shrug.

'That was the woman from inside, wasn't it? With her little girl? What were you doing with them?'

'I told you, nothing,' Sierra said, pulling her gloves on again. 'Should we be riding on? You can bet that Rasten is.'

'Not until I hear the truth of this!' Mira demanded. 'What do you want with these people?'

With that, Sierra's temper snapped. 'What do *you* want with them?' she hissed. 'Your clan is known throughout Ricalan for harassing folk who carry the taint. Rasten never harmed a child if he had a choice in the matter and that's more than can be said about your clan. I've heard the tales of children with the taint who are fostered with the ruling clans and never seen again. I'd trust him with the child long before I'd trust the likes of you.'

While Mira spluttered, Sierra turned her back on her and stalked towards the horses. Cam was waiting, holding her reins as well as his, and when she took them from him Sierra warned him away with a shake of her head. 'You'd best keep your distance for a while,' she told him in an undertone. 'I'm well and truly in Mira's bad books now, but there's no need for the stench to rub off on you as well.'

# Chapter 20

Isidro tugged at the cord around his neck. He did it without thinking, as he had done hundreds of times over the last few days — so often the cord had rubbed a welt into his skin. The sting of it made him curse under his breath.

On the other side of the chamber the priest looked up from building the fire in the brazier and sighed. 'I'll find you some salve for that, but it won't get better unless you leave it alone.'

Isidro merely grunted in reply. He'd been trying to do just that, but it irritated like a thorn in his clothes.

As soon as he'd been strong enough to stand and walk a few paces on his own, the High Priestess had demanded that he present himself at the Shrine to be tested for the taint of mage-talent.

Isidro had gone along with the charade. There was nothing to be gained by arguing and once he'd done as they asked the physician, Jorgen, had promised he would not be disturbed further until Mira's escort arrived to take him away. He'd still been very weak — the exertion of walking across the temple grounds to the shrine had left him dizzy and exhausted, so he'd paid no mind to the ritual circle they'd drawn on the floor of the hall in coloured powder or the statues and carvings they'd placed around the perimeter of it under the blank gaze of the statues of the Twin Suns and the altar. He'd seen the ritual before and all he'd wanted was to return to his furs and go back to sleep.

It was only the fierce whisperings of the priests as the ritual reached its peak that made him pay attention to the skin-prickling energy around him. Each of the carved statues placed around the edge of the circle contained an enchantment and if a person carrying the taint of mage-talent stepped into the circle during a ritual those stones would light up like candles. The brightness of the light depended on how strong the mage had the potential to be — they glowed weakly for someone like him, but would blaze as bright as a star falling to earth for someone in Sierra's league.

Instead of the white light he'd seen at other performances of the ritual, this time the light spilling around his feet was a deep and sullen red wreathed through with darker streaks. It reminded him of nothing so much as Rasten's ruddy flare of power.

It was apparently as much a surprise to the priests as it was to him. Instead of being presented with a new warding-stone then and there as he'd expected, Jorgen had led him back to the hall and his chamber, while the priests gathered around the altar, with its sacred tiger skin, to argue over just what it meant.

Hours later, he'd been woken at the High Priestess's insistence and she'd presented him with the stone he now wore. The enchantment was as powerful as the ones in the bracelets Kell had made for Sierra and the stone itself was carved with the likeness of a tiger's snarling face. The tiger was the Black Sun's consort, just as the bear was the husband of the Bright Sun; and it was said that the tiger was the executioner of the Gods, delivering justice to those who broke the laws the Gods laid down.

If he took it off, the priestess threatened, the Gods themselves would punish him. They'd tied the cord tight enough that he couldn't slip it off over his head. That was probably for the best, he had to admit. If he had been able to take it off he would have done so, if only to be able to sleep without dreaming he was suffocating under the weight of the wretched thing.

The wide oval of stone never grew warm. It was always cold and somehow greasy and where it touched his skin it prickled unpleasantly. Whenever his mind wandered he would catch himself with his fingertips on the amulet ready to wrench on the cord again.

The priest watched him with his hand on his hips and shook his head with a sigh. 'I hate to think what Lady Mira's going to say when I send you back to her with another wound on top of what you've already suffered.'

Life in the temple must be a fairly sheltered existence, Isidro thought, if a bit of raw skin qualified as a wound.

'I really don't see why it bothers you so much,' the priest went on as he tidied away a stack of empty bowls. 'There are plenty of people here in the temple who wear the blessed amulets and they don't seem to be troubled by them.'

*How nice for them,* Isidro thought. 'A distraction would help,' he said. 'Perhaps a book, to pass the time?'

'Ah,' Jorgen said. 'I did ask, but I'm afraid the High Priestess has forbidden it. She says she cannot risk having the library contaminated. It's probably best for you to be resting, anyway ...'

When Cam and the others had left he had been too exhausted and too ill to think of asking them to leave him something to help pass the time. At first he had done nothing but eat and sleep but now he had recovered enough to lie awake for an hour or so at a time, boredom was taking hold.

He had no company other than the priest who tended to him. Earlier a few of the temple servants had found excuses to come into his chamber and ask breathless questions about Sierra, or Kell and Rasten, or about the men who had died when Mira set them on Sierra's trail. Isidro had refused to discuss any of it. Thanks to Brekan, he gathered, stories were spreading thick and fast.

Jorgen was shifting an empty tea-bowl from the shelf near Isidro's head when he hesitated and held up a tiny slip of parchment. 'Do you want to keep this, or shall I toss it on the coals?'

'I'll keep it,' Isidro said and took the note from his fingers. The ink from Lakua's childish scrawl had run and blurred on the old hide and her signature was blotted with tears. She and Eloba had left while he was sleeping, riding to Ruhavera with Mira's messenger to her clan. He held the note up to the lamplight to read it one more time.

*Issey,* the note read, *I'm sorry to bid you farewell in this way, but we cannot delay Lady Mira's messenger any longer. Eloba and me have severed the knot with Brekan. We're going to start a new life.*

*I know I wouldn't be here if it weren't for you. I'll never forget what you did for us and for my poor Markhan, and I'll pray that the Gods watch over you always.*

Both the sisters had signed it, though the words were Lakua's.

Isidro tucked the scrap of leather into the front of his jacket. He was keeping it only for sentiment's sake, but as long as he was here alone he couldn't bear the thought of throwing away anything that connected him to his old life. Markhan was gone, Garzen was gone, and now Cam and Sierra had ridden off and left him behind. It seemed that everything was slipping away from him. 'Is Brekan still here?' he asked the priest.

'Who? Oh, that fellow. He left a few days ago. I think he went east? Or maybe it was south ...' Jorgen dismissed the matter with a shrug and perched on the bench beside him. 'Let's have a look at that arm of yours. Has the swelling come down yet?'

With an effort Isidro lifted himself out of the fugue that was settling around him and gingerly moved his splinted arm into Jorgen's reach. 'It's getting there,' he said while the priest peered and prodded at the bandages wrapped over his hand.

'So it is. Tomorrow, perhaps, I'll re-wrap it. Once it's bound more firmly and with a few more days of rest I think you'll be well enough to travel.' The priest stood and gathered up his basket of dirty dishes and clothing to be laundered. 'Well, I've measured out your next dose,' he said, nodding to the little ceramic bowl he'd set on the shelf near Isidro's head. 'Don't take it until you've eaten — and don't let the meal get cold this time, will you? If you need anything else, ring the bell and someone will fetch me.'

Isidro nodded and then remembered a question that had been bothering him vaguely the last few times he had awoken. 'Can you tell me what time it is?'

Jorgen paused in the doorway with the curtain half drawn back. 'Evening. You slept through the dinner hour.'

As much as he was tempted to down the dose of poppy and escape into sleep, Isidro took only a few sips from the bowl Jorgen had left for him. The priest wasn't as careful of the stuff as Rhia had been and, unlike her, these folk didn't seem to care if he took so much that he began craving it. He'd seen where that path led. Valeria had plied her elder son with wine, drugs and women once he grew old enough to rebel against her meddling and control. Isidro had seen the effects of it himself back when his father was still alive and had brought his son and foster-son to court in Lathayan. Isidro was vulnerable enough as it was, without giving an enemy something else that could be used against him. As the heavy somnolence crept over him, Isidro tucked a fold of blanket under the cursed stone around his neck and waited for the refuge of sleep to settle over him again.

* * *

262

A bell rang somewhere in the night, an incessant jangling that echoed around Isidro's skull. Hanging near the head of his bed was a cord that rang a bell in the physician's chamber so he could call for assistance during the night. That was a tiny contraption, though, unable to produce the swelling sound that filled the temple — it could only come from the one attached to the bell-pull outside the temple door, to allow late travellers to gain entry to the shelter of the hall.

Isidro rolled over with a groan as he heard someone shuffle past his chamber. 'Alright, alright,' a woman grumbled beyond the lattice. 'Fires Below! Are you trying to wake the whole temple?'

The ringing continued, a cacophony of discordant noise. Something about it made Isidro kick his blankets off and sit up and he was reaching for his outer clothes before he even knew what he was doing. There was urgency in that frantic sound. Something was wrong.

In the act of reaching for his boots, Isidro froze. What use would he be in an emergency? What could he contribute, as weak as he was and with his sword arm ruined beyond repair?

The bell kept up its frenzied peal as the priestess hauled the door open with a scrape of wood over stone. Then she shrieked, calling for help, and Isidro heard a boy's voice babbling something unintelligible. He swept the curtain aside and saw a woman helping a boy of about twelve or thirteen into the common room. He wore only indoor clothes and was pale and shivering with cold. Blood was sheeting down his face from a wound to his scalp.

Her scream brought people running from their beds and chambers, rousing enough of a crowd that Isidro hung back to stay out of the way. There were more than enough able hands to help her as a pad of rags was pressed to the bleeding wound and a blanket wrapped around the boy's shoulders.

The boy's wound bothered him. The Gods knew that awful injuries could happen by accident, but that gash had cursed near scalped the lad — as though someone had swung a blade at him and he'd ducked, but not quite quickly enough.

His first thought was of the vision he'd seen on the journey, of the Akharian soldiers ambushing the Duke and his men. Isidro shook his head and tried to dismiss it. It could be a raid. Charzic had never led his men this far east before, but the king's army and the Akharian forces might have driven him to seek out new hunting grounds. That made more sense than the idea that a legion had slipped past the king's men, leaving their supply line vulnerable and their rear open to attack. Trying to convince himself it was only a handful of ragged outlaws, Isidro ducked back into his chamber for his coat and headed for the doorway while wrapping it around his shoulders.

The priests and temple servants ignored him as he edged past the crowd to the entrance, but there he met more people from the village, pale and shivering as they pushed past him into the warmth of the hall.

'What's going on?' he tried to ask one of them, a man, but he took one look at Isidro's face and must have realised who this stranger was, because he recoiled and blundered past, leaving Isidro staggering to keep his feet.

From the foyer, Isidro pushed through the heavy draught curtain. The outer door had been hauled open until it jammed on a drift of snow. Treading cautiously for fear his feet would slip out from beneath him, Isidro went out onto the landing to look over the temple wall and down towards the village.

More people were streaming in through the gates, stumbling in the soft snow, and down in the village there was a ruddy flare of light amid the houses. It gleamed like a beacon, illuminating a few scurrying forms before the gloom swallowed them again.

Someone grabbed his arm from behind. Isidro whirled, turning too quickly for his frail state, and would have fallen if Jorgen hadn't had a grip on his arm. 'I thought I saw you come this way,' the physician said. 'You're the only one in the temple with any experience of fighting. They say there's a raid on the village. What should we do?'

'Get your weapons and mount a defence,' Isidro said. 'There's a good wall around the temple grounds. Your village should have enough men to hold the gates.'

'We don't *have* any weapons,' Jorgen said. 'This is a *temple*.'

'What about the village militia?'

'Most of them are away at the Wolf Clan's muster. There's a handful of them left but they're mostly boys and greybeards ...'

'We need to know what we're facing,' Isidro said. While some of the folk streaming through the gates were heading to the hall, others milled around below with spears and shields. Isidro headed down towards them with Jorgen at his heels. 'Outlaws will be interested in food and women and not much else. They'll take what they can and torch the rest, but they don't have enough men to face an organised defence. Get everyone into the temple grounds and block up the gates any way you can. Put the women and boys there with shields and spears or axes and send any archers you've got there, too.'

'But the houses!' Jorgen said. 'If they put them to the torch we'll lose the stock and the winter stores —'

'You don't have the numbers to defend them. The stock will run and the houses are too laden with snow to burn to the ground. Save the people now; salvage what you can later.'

'And what if it's not Raiders? What then?'

Isidro scowled into the darkness. The attackers couldn't be Mesentreian. However much the king might want to punish the Wolf Clan's rebellion, he couldn't spare the men. A hard knot of unease formed in his belly. Why would Akharians come so far, so quickly? This wasn't how one conquered a country, by penetrating deep into enemy territory to attack a sleepy village and a dilapidated temple with no wealth or strategic value.

He'd felt so weak and ill he'd been happy to accept Mira's assurance the Akharian forces were still weeks away. Only Sierra had disagreed, but everyone had disregarded her concerns. Even Isidro had believed she'd exaggerated the danger, not deliberately but out of simple anxiety; it was only now that he considered what it would mean if they were wrong. If the attackers weren't simply Raiders snatching women and supplies and fleeing, then they could only be Akharian Slavers. If so, there was no defence the villagers could muster that would save them. Their best chance would be to flee into the countryside.

A woman at the edge of the crowd glanced at him as he approached, taking in his height and his build. She held two spears in one hand and clutched a wailing child to her hip with the other. Hovering behind her was a girl of about ten, pale and frightened, but with a hatchet in her hands. The woman peeled the child off her hip and passed him to the girl, then held a spear out to Isidro. 'Here, take this,' she said. 'You look like you know how to use it.'

Isidro held up his hand in refusal. 'I've only got one good hand,' he said. 'There are others who can use it better than me.'

The woman looked him up and down. 'So *you're* the one the gossips are talking about. You don't look much like a demon to me.'

'What's happening down there?' Isidro said, nodding to the gate. 'Who are the attackers? What do they look like?'

'I didn't get a good look at them,' the woman said, and for the first time her voice trembled. 'I was hiding the little ones when I heard them coming through the door, so I grabbed the spears and slipped out the back and we ran up here. My sisters and my husbands are still down there …' She looked around with tears in her eyes, as though hoping to spot them in the crowd that was gathering around them.

'They're wearing war-coats with the hoods pulled up,' someone in the crowd said.

'They're speaking Mesentreian.'

'No they're not. I know some Mesentreian and it wasn't that. Sounds a bit like it, though.'

The woman with the spear shook herself. 'Fessa, take Benri to the hall and do what the priests tell you.'

'Can't, Mama,' the girl said, hitching the boy up in her arms. 'They've closed the door.'

At her words, the people nearby turned to the hall. In the commotion Isidro hadn't noticed the folk gathering on the steps and pounding on the hall's bronze-bound doors.

'Black Sun take her!' the woman said. 'That toothless old bitch of a priestess has locked us out!'

'Take your children and run for the forest,' Isidro said. 'These aren't Raiders, they're Akharians! Slavers! Run while you can.'

The woman pursed her lips and tightened her grip on the spear.

'But we've no shelter,' someone else said. 'No food!'

The woman took the little boy from her daughter and swung him onto her back. 'Come with us,' she said to Isidro.

Isidro shook his head. 'I wouldn't make it.' The world was spinning around him and more than anything else he wanted to lie down and close his eyes.

The woman looked him up and down again and nodded. 'Spirit of Storm watch over you, then. Fessa, follow me!' Without another word she turned and strode to the far gate of the temple grounds with her daughter hurrying behind her, stretching her legs to match her mother's

266

stride. A few others followed her, carrying children on their backs and whatever weapons they'd snatched up. Those who chose to stay behind huddled close together in sudden shock.

'Don't stand around like a herd of goats waiting to be slaughtered!' Isidro shouted at them. 'Find some shelter!'

'Head into the shrine!' Jorgen shouted. 'Quickly, now.'

With a subdued murmur, the crowd obeyed and, with nowhere else to go, Isidro followed them.

As Jorgen guided him to the shrine the trickle of people coming in through the village-side gates suddenly swelled to a flood of bodies pushing and shoving, shouting in panic and terror. Isidro saw a flash of steel and heard a scream and then he was caught in a press of bodies. The jostling woke the fires in his arm and by the time he was able to think and see clearly again he was in the darkness of the shrine and men were heaving massive wooden bars into place across the doors. All around him people were wailing or raising their voices in prayer.

At first the temple was so dark, and those within packed so tight, he couldn't move without treading on the people huddled around him, but as people began to feel their way through the darkness the press of bodies eased a little. From outside came the sound of men shouting and the dull crunch of feet and hooves on the packed snow. A worried murmur rippled through the temple and then the crowd fell silent.

As his eyes adjusted to the gloom Isidro could just see enough to pick his way towards the doors and set his eye against the door crack, granting him a narrow view of the temple grounds.

Men in white war-coats, armed with swords and shields, were roaming through the grounds. A handful of mounted men rode into view and reined in to dismount. They tossed their reins to a soldier who came hurrying over to take charge of the beasts and split into two groups as the foot soldiers converged on them. One group headed towards the Priests' Hall, the other towards the shrine.

The far group reached their destination first, arriving at the steps while the nearer one was still milling around and talking in voices too low for Isidro to make out. Beyond them he saw two figures approach the steps of the Priests' Hall while the others hung back, arranged in neat ranks with their weapons at the ready. One of the figures raised his arms and summoned a nebulous wall of blue-white light between his comrades and the hall's massive doors. Even at this distance Isidro felt the power prickle against his skin and the warding-stone around his neck sent an icy tingle through his chest, a loathsome flicker of greasy cold that made him shudder and yank on the cord again.

Once the shield was in place the other figure stepped forward. Isidro felt power rise and the tingling of his warding-stone swelled to a stinging throb, making him curse and pull it away from his skin.

Then the mage loosed his power at the bronze-bound doors. It struck the wood with enough force to rattle the doors of the shrine and send a cascade of dust raining down from the rafters above.

In winter the sap within a tree could freeze, swelling until the pressure tore the tree apart, shreading it into splinters with a sudden percussive crack. The hall's doors made that same sound as the blast of power tore them apart and filled the doorway with fragments and rubble as it ripped away part of the wall as well. The shield deflected the splinters that were hurled towards the gathered men, and as soon as it was over, the wall of fog and light vanished. With a shout the men gathered below charged up the steps and into the hall.

In the foreground, Isidro saw the men gathered before the shrine come to some decision and turn as one towards the doors.

'Ah, shit,' Isidro said and backed away. 'Everyone get back! Towards the altar, as far as you can go!'

Perhaps a few others had seen what he had, watching through the cracks in the doors, because his cry was taken up by those around him as they herded the others to the rear of the hall. Outside, someone rattled the door, testing to see if it was truly barred, and the sound of it raised another shriek of terror from the people trapped within. 'Get back, all of you!' Isidro shouted, but the folk at the rear had no idea what was going on and like baulking *yaka* stood their ground and shoved back at those who shoved them.

A sudden flood of prickling power told him the shield was in place. The swell of energy in preparation for the blast made every hair on his body stand on end and his nerves shriek in a confused flood of sensation. Then there was a rush of air and light — something hit him very hard on the back of the skull — and everything went black.

# Chapter 21

The only sound was the crunch of snow under Sierra's feet, but it seemed to her she could still hear echoes of the screams and shouts of the attack.

'Can I help you, miss?' A pair of sentries had come from the edge of the camp to intercept her as she neared Mira's tent.

'I need to speak to Cam,' she said. 'It's urgent.'

'It's the middle of the night, miss,' one of them said. 'Perhaps it could wait until the morning?'

'It can't,' Sierra said, fighting to maintain a civil tone. 'Please let me through, or wake Cam and have him come out to me.'

The guards exchanged a glance. Sierra found her hands clenching into fists and made them relax. The delay didn't matter. Fires Below, the news didn't matter, not here, miles away from where they had left Isidro, thinking he would be safe. There was nothing they could do about it, but she had to tell Cam what had happened. 'Look,' she said, 'I need to talk to him. I'm not going to do your lady and her kin any harm —'

The tent-flap twitched aside and Ardamon looked out, frowning down his aquiline nose at her. 'What's the matter out here?'

'My apologies for disturbing you, sir,' one of the guards began, but Sierra interrupted him.

'I need to talk to Cam. It's important.'

Behind him, Sierra heard Mira say, 'Let her in, cousin.'

He considered for a moment and then stepped back, nodding a dismissal to the guards while he held the flap open for Sierra to duck through.

Inside, Cam was sitting up and scrubbing his hands through his hair, while Mira yawned sleepily with a blanket wrapped around her shoulders. Rhia was awake, too, as well as Mira's two servants, one of whom slipped out of her furs and went about lighting the lamps that hung from chains hooked around the tent poles.

269

'What is it, Sirri?' Cam said.

'Something's happened to Isidro,' she blurted. 'He's hurt and confused and … I don't know what's going on, but it's bad.' Sierra felt her face growing hot. She hated it when they stared at her like this, as though she was some freak, like a two-headed kid, some accident of nature that shouldn't exist. The control she'd fought for since waking slipped and sent a nervous ripple of energy coursing over her from head to foot.

Cam stood and took her arm. 'Here,' he said, 'sit down. Tell me what's happened.'

'There's been an attack on the village,' she said. 'Isidro's been hurt. I don't know how it started — I was asleep until the flood of power woke me. I think he must have passed out for a while, but he's awake again now. He's so confused … I think he must have been hit on the head.' Sierra closed her eyes and tried to summon the last image that had come to her. 'He's kneeling on flagstones with a lot of other men, and there are men in war-coats standing guard, and others coming and going …'

Cam fell silent, and Sierra stared at the ground, not daring to look at him. He wouldn't believe her, just as he hadn't when she had seen Rasten fighting the Akharian scouting party. Even Isidro had seen that and Cam still hadn't believed her.

'Did you dream this?' Mira said, her voice carefully neutral.

'No,' Sierra said. 'I saw it — some of it — though his eyes.'

'But —'

'It wasn't a dream,' Sierra said. 'If it was, I wouldn't have this power.' She held out her hands, letting her control relax, and the power burst from her skin and surrounded her hands with a flickering, dancing halo of light. 'I thought I *was* dreaming, until the power-spike woke me,' she said to Cam. She'd scorched the tent-poles again, and the reindeer-fur lining.

Cam rubbed the back of his neck, frowning. 'Mesentreian?' he said.

'I don't think so,' Sierra said. 'From what I saw they didn't look like southerners.'

'What about Isidro? Can he tell you anything?'

Sierra shook her head. 'His talent is weak and he's never had any training. If I had more skill I might be able to make a better connection, but …' She spread her hands and shrugged.

'Talent?' Mira said. 'You mean Isidro's a mage?'

'He carries the taint,' Sierra said. 'What did you think that means?'

'Forgive my ignorance,' Ardamon said with a touch of sarcasm, 'but I fail to see how this could be anything other than a bad dream. How can you possibly know what's happened dozens of miles away?'

'Because of Kell,' Sierra said. 'When he tortures someone, he uses a ritual to harvest the energy it produces. I was part of the ritual, too ...' Sierra looked around and saw a leather instrument case near Mira's bed lying open, with the gleaming, polished wood of her setar nestled inside. 'I'm like the sounding-box on the setar. The box captures the sound and makes it louder and more intense, you see? That's why I'm valuable to Kell — I can derive more power from the ritual than he can on his own.

'Anyway, I was there when he tortured Isidro. It forges a connection between all who took part, including the victim. It leaves a scar of sorts that binds us all together. That's how I know he's hurt and why I can sometimes see through his eyes.'

'The priests would have had to re-splint Isidro's arm once the swelling went down,' Rhia said. 'Could it not be that? They might have had to straighten it again, and it would have been difficult for him — is it possible that you have misinterpreted what happened?'

'In the middle of the night?' Sierra said. 'Without even a dose of poppy to numb the pain?' She shook her head. 'Cam, I wish I could tell you more ...'

Cam scrubbed his hands over his face. 'Alright. It can't be Charzic's men — they would have torched the place and fled, not lined up prisoners. That leaves Mesentreian or Akharian.'

'You mean you believe her?' Ardamon asked.

'Why wouldn't I?' Cam said. 'Sierra wouldn't lie, not about this. It's not likely to be the king's men. They were pulling out ahead of the Akharian forces heading this way, all except for the men Rasten brought to chase Sierra. It has to be Akharians.'

'But they couldn't have come so far so quickly!' Mira said and turned to Ardamon. 'Can we spare a couple of men to ride back and find out what's happened?'

'No,' Ardamon said. 'I can't allow that. If we're going to deal with Rasten we'll need every man we've got. I'm sorry, Cam, but there's nothing we can do. We need to keep our aim fixed on the stag we have, not the one we think is behind us.'

'I agree,' Cam said. 'There are fewer than thirty men in this escort. Whatever happened in the village, there's nothing we can do about it now.'

'There must be some folk who escaped, whoever the attackers are,' Mira said. 'Everyone in the Wolf Lands knows the meeting points for the second muster. Once this is settled we'll head to the nearest and wait there for my uncle and his men. There's bound to be some news by then.' She laid a hand on Cam's arm. 'We'll get him back, Cam. On the honour of my clan, I swear it.'

Cam looked stricken and ill with shock and despair, but he nodded and stood, casting around for his coat and his boots. 'I need some air.'

'I'll go with you — ' Mira said.

'No. No … thank you, Mira, but I need to be alone …' He snatched up the fur and was out of the door before he'd even settled it around his shoulders.

Sierra grabbed her own fur and went after him. Outside, snow was falling and the heavy clouds overhead had turned the world around them pitch black. As the cold air hit her Sierra's power flared and covered her in a halo of blue light until she had the fur settled around her. 'Cam!' she called. 'Wait!'

He glanced back, his brow furrowed and his green eyes glowering in the gloom. 'I said —'

'Just wait!' she snapped. 'There's something else I need to tell you.' He stopped, reluctantly, and let her catch up with him. She kept walking and drew him out beyond the circle of tents. 'Come on,' she muttered. 'I don't want to be overheard.'

He followed her out beyond the perimeter of the camp, where they disturbed a porcupine feeding from the branch of a yellow pine, bowed low under the weight of snow. When it chattered its teeth and turned its spines towards them, they moved away to talk rather than risk its quills.

'What is it?' Cam asked, as he pulled his hood around his ears.

'Rasten contacted me the other night.'

His eyes widened and he began to curse, lapsing into Mesentreian, the language of his childhood. 'That whoreson whelp of a scabrous pig … what game is he playing? Or was he just trying to terrorise you?'

'I thought so at first,' Sierra said. 'I have nothing to say to him, but … he has a connection with Isidro, too. I tried to make contact with Isidro and I couldn't … but maybe Rasten can.'

Cam stared at her for a long moment. 'May as well ask a wolf to track a lame calf,' he muttered. 'Why didn't you tell me about Rasten sooner?'

Sierra scuffed at the snow with the toe of her boot. 'I couldn't. You must see why.'

'Does he know we're following him?'

'He ought to,' Sierra said. 'We didn't speak of it, but he's not stupid.'

Cam turned away for a moment and frowned into the swirling snow. 'What good would it do? Even if we knew what Isidro was facing there's nothing we can do for him and the Gods only know what Rasten would want from you in return. There's nothing to gain there.' He drew a deep breath. 'If they *are* Akharians taking slaves ... well, what use is a one-armed man, especially one as sickly as Isidro? At best they might let him take his chances but they may decide he's not worth the trouble and just cut his throat. I've seen that sort of thing happen before.'

Sierra felt tears sting her eyes. Angrily, she wiped them away with the back of her hand. 'But Isidro will see the lay of the land and he knows some Akharian. He can make himself valuable.'

'Even if it means helping the enemy?' Cam said. 'He's an honourable man, not some coward who will do whatever he can to save his own life.'

'Of course not,' Sierra said. 'But he has to know we'll come for him. Doesn't he?'

Cam shook himself. 'You're right. Of course he knows that.' He pulled himself away from gazing into the night and fixed instead on her face. 'But Rasten ... Sirri, don't do it.'

'I have to know,' Sierra said.

'Even if it means giving Rasten an advantage over us?'

Sierra turned away and kicked at a clump of snow. 'Black Sun take him! I just hate feeling so helpless. You'd think I'd be used to it by now. You're right, though. But if Isidro does die, I'm as sure as I can be that I'll know it's happened.'

He looked away. 'That's a small mercy, I suppose.'

She left him brooding in the cold and returned to her tent, which was now thoroughly chilled, though the stench of singed hair still lingered. Sierra closed the flap and built up the fire, keeping her coat on until the stove was roaring again, then lay down beneath her furs with her chin resting on her hands. The night was only half gone, but she doubted she'd be able to get to sleep again. Instead, she turned her thoughts to Isidro, hoping she'd be able to pick up even a faint impression of what he was facing.

Instead of Isidro she found another awareness waiting for her and when she turned his way he latched onto her with a grip she couldn't shake.

*I thought you must be awake by now, Little Crow.*

She fought instinctively and as she twisted against his grip she managed to break his hold with a burst of power that left them both gasping.

After a moment, she felt Rasten laugh. The movement of it roused pain from the wound in his back but he didn't appear to notice. *You are growing stronger, Little Crow.*

*Must you call me that?* she snapped.

*Don't you like it? You thrive on battle and herald the coming of the storm … it fits you as well as a name could.*

*Why were you waiting for me?*

*I wanted to see if you knew what had happened to Balorica.*

*In other words, you came to gloat.*

*Actually, no …* he said, sounding puzzled. *I suppose I wanted to know why it was him that you chose. The prince I could understand, but why Balorica, the crippled and sickly one? Do you feel guilty for what we did to him?*

*I —* Sierra stopped herself before she could go on. This was unwise. Cam was right. Any information she gave to Rasten would eventually be used against her. Rasten had been her only companion for so long the line between friend and foe had been trampled to dust. If she had someone else to talk to it might be different but the only person in Mira's party who had a kind word for her was Cam, and he was risking his and Isidro's future by taking her side. At least, he *had* been risking Isidro's future. Tonight, everything had changed. *It's not that*, she told Rasten. *He's not afraid of me, and the things I can do. He doesn't condemn me for what I am.*

*Really?* Rasten sounded genuinely puzzled. *Even after we raped and tortured him?*

*Yes.*

Rasten was silent for a long moment. *You do know they'll probably kill him? Even if he weren't crippled, he carries a touch of power, and it will appear all the stronger for the rituals we used. Akharians don't tolerate mage-talent among their slaves.*

Sierra said nothing.

*If it's any consolation, it's a cleaner death than he'd get if the king got his hands on him again. I hear the queen is eager to stage a repeat of his father's execution —*

*Why have the Akharians come so far east?* she broke in, changing the subject. *If they're here to take slaves and sack the harbours, they've come a cursed long way out of their way.*

*Oh, they're probably looking for Vasant's books,* he said.

*Vasant's ... but they were all destroyed!*

*Little Crow, do you believe everything the ruling clans tell you? Vasant hid his treasures well and they weren't all found, not by a long shot. The Ricalani mages have always known things the Akharian school didn't. Back before Leandra led her people in the Great Purge, the Akharians would sometimes raid our coast for slaves and our mages had weapons to use against them. Now, it's the Akharian coast being raided by Mesentreian ships, and they could use those weapons themselves. They're probably hoping Vasant left some records that will let them re-create them.*

The news left her speechless. Vasant's books ... It could mean an unimaginable wealth of knowledge just waiting to be found. Or it could be just so much rotting paper, as much use as the decaying mulch revealed by melting snow. Not that it mattered either way — if the Akharians found the books they would be taken out of Ricalan before Sierra even heard of it. She had her doubts, too, regarding just how much one could glean from books alone. She'd been studying Kell's book daily but had not yet learned anything of use. *Will they find them, do you think?*

*Who knows? People have been searching for Vasant's treasure for nearly a hundred years without finding a thing. I think he hid it too well. But maybe the Akharian mages know something we don't. Sirri, there's something else we need to talk about. I know you're hunting me.*

Sierra made no reply.

*If you try to corner me I promise you won't like the results. It was unwise of you to leave Balorica behind. He would at least have given you a source of power. What have you got now to feed you?*

*He wouldn't have survived the ride.*

*How well do you think he'll survive as a slave? If you insist on following this path, you'd better start thinking about which one of your companions you intend to sacrifice to raise the power to face me.*

# Chapter 22

Delphine wrapped her arms around herself and bounced on her heels, hoping the movement would warm her a little. She had hand-warmer enchantments tucked into her sash, but she didn't want to use them just yet. She knew from experience she would need them later on. 'How much longer are they going to keep us waiting?' she muttered to Harwin, who stood beside her, hunched and miserable in his barbarian fur.

'Oh, we've hardly been here any time at all,' he drawled. 'If they want to break their previous record we'll have to be standing around for at least another hour.'

She sighed and the steam in her breath condensed into frost on her hair, where it glittered like diamonds in the light of her lamp.

The academics were only allowed into the village once all resistance had been quashed, but Delphine had seen no one move except soldiers in the entire time she and her colleagues had been kept waiting here. Early on in this campaign she had come to the conclusion that the soldiers liked to keep them waiting. Back in Akhara these soft civilian academics were their social superiors — this was one of the few occasions when the mages had to wait upon the pleasure of the rank and file, instead of the other way around.

Delphine's feet were numb inside her monstrous barbarian boots by the time a soldier wandered over to lead the Collegium mages up to the temple. They tramped through the village, weaving around the bodies that still lay where they had fallen during the fighting. Delphine carefully averted her gaze from the staring, sightless eyes and the brilliant stains of frozen blood. The soldiers were more interested in the business of taking slaves than in wholesale slaughter, but any who refused to drop arms and surrender when surrounded were simply cut down where they stood. The sight of the men didn't trouble her so much. They were tall, these barbarians, taller than most Akharian men, heavily built, and decidedly strange with the alien features of their race. The women disturbed her more but the ones who wrung her heart were the children — beardless boys and young girls who had snatched up weapons they didn't know how to use. If Delphine had borne a child when she was first married, the babe would be of an age with them now ...

And then there was the blood. Instead of seeping to a brownish stain on the soil it froze bright and vivid on the surface of the snow where neither time nor sun would fade it. She hated to think of the trail of blood her people had left across this land. *Good Goddess forgive me. I never imagined just what this would be like ...*

The new captives had been driven back into the houses where they were being divided up by age and sex. Other slaves, ones who had already learned their place, would be brought here to ransack the houses for gear and supplies. Slave-keeping was a more complicated business here in the north than it was back in the empire. There, slaves could be made to sleep on the ground with the privilege of a blanket for warmth if they were lucky, but here the new slaves couldn't be marched to the slave camp until tents and stoves had been found for them. In the meantime they would be kept in the houses that had until recently been their homes.

The temple lay at the far end of the village at the top of a small rise, surrounded by a stout stone wall. Once inside the temple grounds Delphine and her colleagues had to wait again while a soldier went to find Mage-Commander Presarius, the leader of the Battle-Mages and nominal commander of the Collegium contingent. In the meantime Delphine turned her attention to the wall. Though covered with a rime of ice it was so sheer and smooth it would have been near-impossible to climb. 'Those walls,' she said, catching Harwin's eye and nodding to them. 'What do you think? Mage-built?'

'Could be,' Harwin said. 'If they are, I'd like to know why they don't crumble under ice like sea walls do under salt spray. I wonder if the general will give us a chance to examine them before we move on?'

Presarius emerged from the great hall with her cousin Torren at his side, and Delphine nudged Harwin into silence as they stalked across the snow towards the dozen or so Collegium mages. 'Ah, so our flock of lost sheep has turned up at last,' Presarius said. 'The hall and the shrine are both secure, professor. You can take your people through, but first

I'll need some volunteers to look over the slaves.' Presarius's gaze swept over the academics before settling on Delphine. 'Madame Delphine, I understand you've served as a talent scout for the Collegium before. You should be well suited to the task.'

Delphine's stomach lurched and she gritted her teeth to keep from spitting out a refusal.

Every mage was trained at the empire's expense and had to serve the empire's needs for a certain length of time each year to repay the debt. For a time Delphine had served by searching for fledgling mages among the empire's children, both free-born and slaves, but that was a very different thing from what Presarius was asking now. A slave-child with the gift was granted his freedom, placed with a foster-family and destined for a life of honour and prestige. A fully grown slave with talent, however, whether enslaved as an adult or missed by the screening process, was a different thing entirely. Anything more than the weakest of mage-talents simply could not be tolerated in an adult slave. Any person she identified here with a spark of talent powerful enough to become dangerous would have his or her throat cut and be left for the crows.

By all the demons in hell, she didn't want to be responsible for any more deaths. But she'd fought tooth and nail for the right to be included in this expedition, while Presarius was one of those who expected her to wait at home and get on with her spinning. He expected her to protest and beg that this task be given to someone else — well, she wouldn't give him the satisfaction. 'Very well, commander,' she said.

'Now wait a moment, commander,' Torren said, glaring at her. 'I don't want my cousin traipsing around alone with a mob of soldiers and slaves. What would people say?'

Delphine rolled her eyes. Torren could always be relied upon to take any bait that happened to be waved in his direction.

'You are quite right, Mage-Captain Castalior,' Harwin said, stepping forward. 'I'll go with her.'

'Capital!' Presarius said. 'Are you satisfied, Castalior? Surely no one would imagine the Matron Castalior getting up to anything untoward with Master Harwin for a chaperon? Well, until it's time to look over the slave-boys, anyway, and then she'll have to chaperone him!' Presarius laughed and slapped his thigh at his own joke while Delphine tried to hide her disgust for Torren's sake. How a man like Dassenar Presarius had risen to the rank of mage-commander was beyond her. 'Well,' Presarius said, still chortling, 'the rest of you no doubt have your own tasks awaiting — get on with it, then, off you go.' He shoved his hands into his pockets and strolled away, whistling.

'Matron, my arse,' Delphine growled at his back. Then she saw the red flush creeping over Harwin's face. 'Oh Harwin, don't let him get to you.' It was the hypocrisy of it all that angered her the most. No one cared what a man did at home with his slave-boys, but because Harwin chose free men for his partners, rather than slaves, he was the one they called a pervert.

Harwin kicked at a clump of snow and shook his head with a chuckle. 'Never mind, Delphi. But by all the Gods — your language!'

'Oh, screw him —'

'Him? Not with a ten-foot pole. I do have standards, you know.'

Delphine laughed and linked her arm through his. 'By the hells, what a miserable job. Come on, then, best get it out of the way.'

Since Presarius had returned to the Priests' Hall followed by the other academics, the pair of them began with the shrine, a low, heavy-beamed building with a steep, shingled roof. The doorway was filled with rubble and splintered wood from where the battle-mages had blasted it down and one of the junior mages had hung lanterns inside so the soldiers could find their way around without tripping. The light was weak and Delphine was glad she had brought her own lamp.

The captives in the shrine were divided into two groups — women and children on one side, men on the other. The women, considered less of a threat, had been allowed to huddle against the wall, clutching their children close. A few of them were wounded, but other than being allowed to tear strips from their clothes for bandages, had been permitted no other means to tend their injuries.

'Let's start with the men,' Delphine said. That would be easier. The men were dangerous — even with the despair of defeat settling over them they would still be hoping for an opportunity to begin the fight again. They would kill her in a moment if they could and she could convince herself to feel less guilt if she had to single any of them out.

The men had been made to kneel in ranks on the far side of the hall. They were bent double with faces to the floor, hands bound behind their backs and their feet tethered.

It was easier if she couldn't see their faces. Delphine dropped her gaze to the floor and let herself slip into a partial trance. This was one talent she had inherited from her famous father, the skill that made her valuable as a talent scout and let her spend her months in service on a veritable jaunt, travelling the empire in comfort to reach out like some messenger from the Gods, lifting a select few from a life of poverty and servitude and giving them the gift of a future.

Of course, what she was doing now was exactly the opposite.

When a person had mage-talent, energy radiated from them like heat from a flame. Part of a mage's training involved suppressing this wanton seepage of energy but even the best of them could never contain it entirely and the untrained couldn't contain it at all.

She wasn't expecting to find much here. Without use and training a mage-talent would atrophy just like an unused limb and the enchantments these barbarians made their talented children wear would only make that happen faster. It was rare that she found anyone powerful enough to be considered dangerous, but it did happen. Delphine let down her own containing shields — because the same mechanism that held her energy in prevented her from sensing energy from outside — and opened her senses to the men lined up in front of her.

A flash of light blazed across her field of view. One of the men was glowing like a blacksmith's forge, radiating such a fierce and jagged aura of power it startled her out of her trance like a novice.

Beside her, Harwin swore. 'By all the boils on the arse of the king of Hell. Can you feel that?'

'I certainly can.' Suddenly Delphine's heart was beating hard. She wasn't feeling pity for these folk any more — that surge of power had snapped her out of it like the sight of a dog frothing at the mouth. She waved one of the guards over and pointed at the source of it. 'That one,' she said.

One of the soldiers strode towards the prisoner, drawing his knife from his belt.

'Not yet!' Delphine called after him. 'I want a look at him first. Bring him over here.'

Harwin's face had turned faintly green. 'Delphi, must you?'

'Bear with me, Harwin. There's something odd about that power. I've seen something like it before …'

'You have? Dear Gods, where?'

'Do you remember, oh, about fifteen years ago, one of the students at the Collegium stumbled onto the Blood Path?'

Harwin blanched and reeled back. 'Heavens preserve us, he's a Blood-Mage?'

'No, I don't think so. After the student was killed, the Watch thought he had another victim hidden somewhere in the city, but they didn't know where. My father spent the whole day riding around in a sedan chair, trying to find him.' It was the bravest thing he'd ever done. Delphine had gone with him, to hold his hand. Her father had been a Sympath, one of that rare breed of mages who could harvest power from others instead of merely generating it within their own flesh.

Sympaths were incredibly powerful, so long as they were treated with the delicacy their condition required. There were rarely more than half a dozen of them alive in the empire at any one time, although how many more were born only to have their powers snuffed out by the suffering of people around them no one could say. Most of their lives were spent living a pampered existence in the residence known as The Palace, where they were sheltered from the hardships of the common folk out in the city. The thought of some poor soul tortured and dying alone and by inches had driven Delphine's father, Ballenar, to use his remarkable senses to try and track him down.

'We did find him, though the poor lad died a few days later. I was there when they carried him out on a litter … the energy radiating off him was something extraordinary. He must have had a little power to start with and what that wretch did to him blasted all his channels wide open …'

While she spoke, a pair of soldiers had grabbed the prisoner by the shoulders, dragged him free of the others and dumped him sprawling on the flagstones at Delphine's feet.

The moment they dropped him on the ground, a wave of energy washed through her, tingling unpleasantly right at the edge of her range. Delphine shuddered profoundly and silently thanked the Gods she hadn't inherited all of Ballenar's powers. She could feel the energy but she couldn't touch it directly — and that was a welcome thing. If she were a Sympath, the sympathetic echo of that wave of pain would have brought her sobbing to her knees.

The prisoner moaned and opened his eyes with a brief flicker of awareness. There was a lump on his forehead and another on the back of his head where the skin had been split open. Drying blood was matting into his hair.

'Take off his jacket and his shirt,' she told the guards. They didn't bother to free his arms — they just yanked the garments open and pulled them down from his shoulders to bare the skin of his back.

Harwin gasped and covered his mouth with his hand. Delphine just bit her lip as her stomach lurched. The prisoner's back was a mass of burn scars, still tender and fresh, marching from his shoulders all the way down to disappear past his bound hands.

Delphine pulled off her mitten and her glove to bare her hand. She could feel the power radiating from him as a hot but insubstantial wind, streaming through her fingers rather than around them. In the centre of his back, hovering right over his heart, she could feel the rigid form of a sigil carved into the part of him that most folk called the soul. As she touched it, the prisoner gasped and shuddered as though he could feel it himself. Well, most likely he could. It probably felt as though she'd plunged her hand into his vitals. 'He's got the mark, right here,' she said. 'You can feel it.'

'Thank you, but I think I'd rather not,' Harwin said. 'Are you sure, Delphi?'

'As sure as I can be. He's been tortured by a Blood-Mage. What are the chances it's the same one who wiped out the scouting party a few weeks back?' Delphine circled around the slave and crouched down to look him in the eye. 'Why do you suppose they stopped where they did? You're surprisingly intact for one of their playthings.' The question was rhetorical. Of course the slave didn't speak her language, but his unfocussed eyes sharpened for a moment and flickered to her face.

Delphine leaned closer. 'Can you understand me?'

Nothing. He didn't respond and held himself perfectly still. 'You *do* understand me, don't you? You're just trying to pretend otherwise.'

One of the guards standing by drew a knife from his belt. 'He's concussed, madame. Best let us deal with him now before he comes to his senses and makes a fuss. We've just got the slaves settled down; don't want them getting stroppy again now, do we?'

'Put it away, you clot,' Delphine told him. 'And go and fetch Mage-Captain Castalior. Tell him we've found a prisoner who's survived a session with the Ricalani Blood-Mage.'

The prisoner drew a sharp breath and tossed his head — it was a small movement, but Delphine was watching for it. As the soldier left she crouched down again. 'You *do* understand,' she said and then switched to Mesentreian. 'How about this tongue? Do you know this one too?' He was ready for her this time and didn't respond.

There was no doubt he'd suffered a great deal — all these people had. And this was just the beginning; they still had the long march to the slave markets in Akhara ahead of them. She didn't want to add to his misfortune, but the Ricalani Blood-Mages had already killed hundreds of Akharian soldiers, and by defending the settlements that sheltered and supplied the Mesentreian raiding-ships they were implicated in the deaths of thousands more.

'Playing dumb will get you nowhere,' she said. 'You have information we need and we're going to get it one way or another. I can see you've survived torture before — do you really want to go through that again when you know full well we'll get what we want in the end? It will go much easier on you if you cooperate.'

The slave kept his eyes firmly fixed on the floor but as Delphine spoke he began to tremble uncontrollably. He was very thin — she could count every one of his ribs and even the knobs of his spine.

Torren arrived a few minutes later, looking annoyed, but his scowl lifted as he saw the prisoner kneeling on the flagstones, now shivering as much with the cold as from the strain of this examination.

'Here,' Delphine said, taking Torren's hand to show him the sigil over the prisoner's spine. Charged with all the energy he was giving off, it felt hot enough to burn.

'Merciful Gods,' Torren said.

'We've been hearing rumours about Blood-Mages in Ricalan for years,' Delphine said. 'Every Mesentreian trader who comes to port has some tale of the demons in the north.'

'How on earth did they let a survivor escape?' Torren said. 'It's a cursed shame he can't tell us anything about them.'

'Oh, but he can,' Delphine said. 'He understands Akharian, I'm certain of it. Mesentreian, too, I'd wager.'

Torren gave her a sharp look. 'What makes you so sure?'

'He reacted to what I was saying,' Delphine said. 'He got cracked on the head when the men stormed the hall, so his wits are likely a bit addled. Now that he's got sense enough to know he's in trouble, I think he's playing dumb in the hope we'll leave him alone.'

'She's right,' Harwin said quietly. 'I saw it, too.'

'Merciful Gods,' Torren said again. 'Do you know what this means? Do you have any idea how much we could learn from him?'

Delphine rolled her eyes. 'Yes, Torren, the thought had occurred to me.'

'I'd best take him to Presarius and the other commanders,' Torren went on, oblivious to her words. 'In the shape he's in, it won't take much to make him talk.' Torren signalled to the guards, who cut the ties that bound the prisoner's ankles and hauled him to his feet in a movement that made him cry out in pain. 'Good work, Delphi.' Torren beckoned the guards. 'Bring him,' he said, and started for the doorway.

The guards half carried, half dragged Isidro across the temple grounds to the Priests' Hall. The folk who had taken shelter there were crammed into the common room, divided by sex as they had been in the shrine. Guards armed with clubs roamed amongst them, doling out punishing blows for every murmur or movement.

The men escorting Isidro dragged him right past them and after conferring for a moment with another Akharian they shoved him into the High Priestess's chamber. The priestess herself lay on the floor, a wizened, shrunken figure crumpled into her heavy robes. Her pinched and narrow lips were blue and her watery eyes were already covered with a milky film. There wasn't a mark on her and it looked to Isidro as if she'd been taken by an apoplexy, perhaps even before the temple had fallen.

In the chamber the men shoved him to the floor, bound his feet again and left him there. There was a guard at the door but he kept his back to the chamber and paid Isidro no mind. Every so often other men would come in and deposit a heavy sack or basket onto a growing pile accumulating on the bench. As Isidro came back to his senses, he realised they were sacking the temple; he was being stored alongside looted valuables until someone could be bothered dealing with him.

The blow to his head had left him feeling queasy and the stone floor pressed painfully against his bones, but at least it was warmer here than out in the shrine. After a while he fell into a shallow and restless doze, only to be woken again when a pair of men freed his feet and marched him outside. There, he was loaded onto a sled like so much cargo and driven behind a slave-train through the darkness to the Akharian camp.

The journey was a nightmare. With his hands bound, there was nothing he could do to ease the pain in his arm or brace himself against the bouncing of the sled. Every time he moved, the Akharian guard marching alongside him would jab at him with the butt of his spear and snarl at him to be still.

At some point, he must have fainted from the pain, for when he came back to his senses, much later, Isidro found himself in a dark and sheltered place. He was lying on a bed of spruce with an old and worn fur thrown carelessly over him for a blanket. His bed, such as it was, was amid a great stack of wooden crates and trunks. His hands were still bound behind his back and when he tried to wriggle away from where he lay he found they were tied to one of the crates as well. With his head pounding and his throat parched, Isidro lay very still, listening for any sound that might give him a hint where he was. There was a stove nearby with a fire crackling within and Isidro thought he could hear the comforting hiss of a simmering kettle. The air was uncomfortably cold, but not so much that he risked hypothermia. Although it was dark he could make out the outlines of the boxes and crates to one side of him and the roof of the tent overhead, so there was *some* light nearby. The tent was made in the Mesentreian style, with a peaked roof sloping away from a central pole to meet vertical walls, all held taut with guy-ropes. Isidro could tell nothing else, not even whether it was night or day. Nothing was moving except him and he hurt too much to do much of that.

Hours passed and Isidro was dozing again when the sound of people entering the tent brought him suddenly, heart-poundingly, awake. They were speaking in Akharian with voices too low for him to make out the words, but one of them laughed as they tramped around the boxes and crates towards him. As they rounded the corner to his little enclave they paused for a moment looking down at him — two men with close-cropped hair and winter furs belted over red tunics, accompanied by a shorter man, who had the demeanour of a servant. The taller men each carried a small lantern about the size of a woman's fist; one of them wore his tied to his belt and unlit, but the other held his high to shine down on their captive. After the gloom of the tent, it was so bright Isidro had to squint and turn his head away to shield his eyes.

There was power in the air. It crawled over Isidro's skin, making his hair stand on end. Those two were mages.

'At least we don't have to go to the trouble of waking him up,' one of the men said. 'Do you suppose that wretched woman is right and he does understand us?'

The other one shrugged and reached inside his coat to produce a small sack of dark cloth. 'She's a pain in the arse, but Mage-Captain Castalior believes her. I suppose we'll find out soon enough.' He handed the sack to the servant. 'Bag him and get him on his feet.'

Blindfolded and masked, Isidro was hauled to his feet and marched out of the tent. He could hear men around him, passing by in a crunch of boots on snow as they talked and joked in a foreign tongue. It was utterly disorienting; the only familiar thing was the cold, biting through the soft indoor clothes he had been wearing after being dumped in the storage tent. By the time they brought him into another tent he was shivering so violently he had no strength to resist when they forced him to his knees and held him while they stripped him to the waist. There was a moment of murmured consternation when they discovered his splinted arm and the scars on his back, then they bound his hands together in front of him.

By the time he felt them throw a rope over something above them, Isidro was trembling uncontrollably and it had nothing to do with the cold. His heart was beating so hard it felt as if it would burst. His breath was coming fast and hard, no matter how he tried to control it. In his mind he was in another place, another time. This was how it had begun on the day he'd been brought to face Kell and Rasten. Back then he'd been calm, despite the fear. He had focussed on just one thing, keeping it firmly in his mind no matter what came — he had to hold out long enough for Cam to get away. Nothing else mattered.

Now he could only guess what they wanted from him. Moreover, both he and they knew he'd already been broken once by torture. It wouldn't take much to bring him to that point again.

They hauled on the rope, lifting his arms over his head and pulling him to his feet. The splints on his arm protected him a little, but the pressure of the rope was enough to tear a groan from his throat. He tried to support his weight and ease the pressure of the rope, but they kept hauling until only the tips of his toes were touching the ground. For a moment the blackness threatened to swallow him again, but Isidro gritted his teeth and fought his way through it, concentrating just on breathing, in and out, in and out. He'd done this once before, he suddenly remembered, under Rasten's glowing poker and then the club, only he'd forgotten it until now.

He sensed someone standing in front of him and, for an irrational moment, he feared that it *was* Rasten, come to finish what he'd begun. The sense of power prickling over his skin was the same, and Isidro could feel the scar on his back throbbing beneath the burn-marks and the healing skin — the *original* scar, the one Rasten had scored at the beginning of the ritual to suck his life-force the way a leech sucks blood.

The person facing him took hold of the mask and pulled it off in one swift movement. It wasn't Rasten — Isidro knew it couldn't be, but his mind was too overwhelmed to be rational right now — it was the mage who had taken him from the shrine. Other men were standing around the edges of the tent, arms folded as they watched in silence, or muttered to their neighbours in low voices. They were all mages, Isidro realised.

The man facing him tossed the sack aside and turned to a trestle set up along the long side of the tent. He picked up a device consisting of a two-foot rod with a leather-wrapped handle at one end and two metal prongs at the other, while wires bound a handful of jade plaques to the shaft. The mage held the prongs under Isidro's nose and somehow activated the device, sending a big blue spark buzzing and crackling between the prongs. 'Now,' the mage said in a conversational tone. 'I know you can understand me and if you can understand my tongue then you can speak it well enough. First of all, I'm going to give you a taste of what you can expect if you choose not to cooperate with us.'

He pressed the prongs of the device against Isidro's breastbone. Isidro had been on the receiving end of enough of Sierra's accidental zaps to have a vague idea of what to expect — he tried to brace himself for it.

It was not enough. If the device was kin to Sierra's power, then it was closer to one of her attacks than it was to an accidental spill of energy.

It sent such a jolt through him that it felt as if he had been picked up bodily and hurled against the ground. Every muscle in his body clenched and it knocked the wind from him in such a rush of breath that he couldn't scream when the muscles in his ruined arm twitched and clenched around the splintered bones. An awful buzzing like a swarm of wasps filled his ears and he was vaguely aware of thrashing against the ropes hard enough to make the tent shake. When the mage pulled the device away it left twin welts on his skin, livid and throbbing like the sting of a wasp. It stole what strength he had and Isidro slumped in the ropes, head hanging to the ground with sweat trickling down his brow.

'Now you know what you can expect if you try to resist,' the mage said. 'So let us begin. What do you know about the Ricalani Blood-Mages?'

He told them what they wanted to know. Of course he did — anything else would have been idiocy. While he would willingly shed blood to protect Cam or Sierra, he wouldn't sacrifice so much as a drop for Kell and Rasten.

But the Akharians were suspicious of such an easy capitulation. When he fainted they roused him with cold water and shocks. As time wore on it grew harder to make any sense of the questions they asked and he found himself talking in Ricalani or Mesentreian instead of Akharian when he tried to form a reply.

At some point they must have realised they weren't going to get any more sense out of him in this session. He was vaguely aware of the men trooping out in a swirl of cold air, leaving a single servant behind to build up the fire in the brazier and keep an eye on the prisoner. Isidro fully expected the next man through the door to cut his throat, and in his present condition he didn't much care, so long as they came soon.

When another blast of cold from outside heralded the arrival of a second group of men, Isidro realised his ordeal was far from over. His first interrogators had been warriors, lean, fit and hard, although with an air of asceticism that reminded him of the priesthood. These men were softer and rounder and the clothes beneath their winter furs were not the military uniforms of the first group. They were definitely mages, though — Isidro could feel their power prickling over his skin.

They circled around him, prodding at the burn scars and the splints on his arm as they talked to each other in low voices. Isidro was too weary to tease any meaning from their words. When one of them snapped his fingers in front of Isidro's nose in an effort to rouse him, he managed to focus enough to see the bluish splotches of ink on the Akharian's thumb and forefinger.

Then one of the mages standing behind him grasped the other, intangible scar, the one through which Rasten had drawn the power raised by his rituals. It felt as if someone had plunged a spear into his back, and took him with such surprise that Isidro couldn't bite back on a strangled cry of pain. It set him rigid and shaking in his bonds. The men around him all jumped back, just like a flock of crows that have discovered their prey might still be strong enough to fight them off. They erupted in chatter, making about as much sense as a flock of chortling birds, and all the while it felt to Isidro as if someone was trying to pull his spine out through his skin.

He was fighting to keep from sobbing with pain when he felt another awareness settle around him in a veil of power. The presence felt so strong and so real it seemed to shove the physical realm away from him, giving him room enough to breathe. *Sirri!* he gasped in relief. *Sirri, is that you?*

*Afraid not.* The voice that answered him was calm and dispassionate, dryer and deeper than Sierra's tones; while her power was tinted with the blue brilliancy of lightning, this fire was tinged with a sooty red glow. *Now hold your tongue,* Rasten said. *If they sense me here, things will go very badly for you.* For a moment Isidro saw a vision of Rasten's tent but then it vanished as he closed his eyes to concentrate on what he could see through Isidro's gaze.

There must be a way to push him out and repel this invasion, but Isidro had no idea how, and what power he had was minuscule compared to what Rasten could raise. The presence in his mind brought on such a wave of revulsion that Isidro gagged and threw himself against the ropes, not caring if the pain in his arm brought him to a faint once again. It was a reaction of pure instinct — he couldn't have stopped it if he'd wanted to — a deep, visceral response to a violation perhaps even more intimate than the ones Kell had forced Rasten to perform on him all those weeks ago. Somewhere amid that fit of panic and disgust, Isidro heard Rasten curse and then felt him withdraw. His abrupt absence brought such relief that finding himself back in the tent surrounded by chattering scholars felt like a reprieve.

It seemed to go on for some hours, as the mages first channelled power into him through the sigil engraved into his back and then stripped it away again, all the while poking and prodding him and even shocking him with the device to study his reactions. Before long Isidro gave up trying to make sense of it and simply waited for it to be over. Rasten never tried to contact him again and for that much, Isidro was grateful.

By the time the mages finished their strange examination, every bone and fibre of his body hurt and Isidro felt as though the world was spinning around him. When a pair of soldiers cut him down, he couldn't stop himself from crumpling into a heap at their feet. He could neither help nor resist as they bundled him into his coat and dragged him back to the dark storage tent where he'd woken. The moment they let him lay down, he curled up on the prickling spruce and let the blessed numbness of sleep sweep him away.

After days of hard riding, they'd narrowed Rasten's lead down to only a few hours, though it came at a cost — men and horses both were nearing the limit of their endurance.

At first Sierra had welcomed the frantic pace, hoping the weariness and exhaustion would quiet her mind and silence her worries and fears for Isidro. In reality it did no such thing. Anxiety preyed on her mind and with every breath she imagined some new torment they would inflict on him. After all, the knowledge Isidro had was his only value to them — they wouldn't hesitate to take him apart piece by piece if that was what it took to get what they wanted. Rasten believed the Akharians knew nothing about her, but if he was mistaken and they pressed on Isidro to tell them more …

She had the utmost faith in him to resist with all the strength he had, but she knew his strength was waning. At first she'd felt flashes of his experience and had seen brief glimpses of his surroundings but that had all stopped and now she couldn't feel anything. She wasn't afraid of what he would tell his captors — she was afraid of what they would do to him when he refused.

And Rasten was no help. Since their first exchange after Isidro's capture he had refused to tell her anything more about him unless she halted this chase and accepted the truce he offered. She couldn't accept his offer in a ruse, either — as anxious as she was, her control was slipping, and Sierra knew there was no way she could hide her actions from him well enough to convince him she had called the chase off.

These were the thoughts that occupied her mind when Ardamon finally called a halt in the pre-dawn gloom. The first light was beginning to stain the sky and Sierra barely noticed Mira's cousin leaning down from his saddle to talk to the scouts at the head of the line. It was only when Cam turned his horse out of line and trotted back towards her that Sierra realised they were arguing about something and gesturing to a trampled path that led off the trail they followed.

'Sirri,' Cam said, beckoning her to join him. 'There's something odd down that path. Sounds like it's something you ought to see.'

She turned her horse out of line to follow him without asking what the matter was. Right now, any distraction would be welcome.

As they reached Ardamon, he twisted around in the saddle to glare at them both. 'Is this really necessary?'

'From what your scout says, it is,' Cam replied.

One of the men Ardamon had been arguing with had a warding-stone around his neck and as Sierra came close he clutched it in his fist like a talisman. 'I think it would be best, sir,' the scout said. 'There's something cursed queer gone on there. More than just the corpse, I mean.'

That snapped Sierra out of her miserable reverie. 'Corpse?' she said. 'You're right, Cam. I'd better see it myself.'

'I'm coming, too,' Mira said. She had been riding beside Ardamon when the scouts came back and had watched the whole exchange from the periphery. 'If Rasten has been killing our people, I'll have to do whatever I can to identify them and find their kin.'

The scouts led the way down the path — or alongside it, to be more accurate, pointing out tracks and signs in the snow. 'Lord Rasten's men came this way a few hours ago — turned down this path and then back the way they'd come a short time later. But before that — probably last night — a bunch of sleds went down this way, hauled by *yaka*. They came down this way, but never went back, y'see? They made a camp up ahead. It's still standing.'

'How many bodies?' Sierra asked the scout.

'I think it's just the one, miss.' It was the man with the warding-stone who replied. 'I couldn't make meself get close enough to tell for sure. There was something in the air that set me skin to crawling ...' He reached for the stone again, as though it gave him comfort. 'Made me wonder if the apprentice had set some kind of trap.'

'And you wanted to check it out without her?' Cam said to Ardamon.

A trap was possible, Sierra thought, but unlikely. She doubted Rasten would take the risk of giving her a wounded man to feed from. He wasn't going to make things that easy for her.

When she could see the dark shape of a tent looming through leafless trees the scouts gestured for them to stop. 'You'll want to leave the horses here, sir. They'll spook if you try to take them closer.'

'As will I,' said the scout with the stone. 'I'll stay here to hold them, sir.'

When Sierra dismounted and handed him her reins he took them with care not to brush against her fingers.

The trail led to a clearing where two conical tents had been pitched and half a dozen heavily laden sleds had been left in a haphazard line. No smoke rose from the tents and the whole place felt still and abandoned.

Sierra was only a few paces into the clearing when she felt the sensation that had spooked the scout. Some residual energy from the ritual still lingered, tainting the air with a memory of pain and terror. It made the air feel somehow greasy and scratched at her throat like smoke.

Cam matched her stride with his thumbs hooked into his belt and showed no sign of apprehension until they rounded the line of tents and saw the circle of blood-stained snow and the great heap of raw and bloody meat at the centre.

'By the Black Sun,' he swore.

Sierra sighed. 'You'd best wait here. I'll make sure Rasten hasn't left us any surprises.'

He didn't argue and reached for Ardamon's arm to make sure he hung back as well.

Sierra created a globe of light and tossed it into the air to float over her head.

Not long ago the heap of cooling meat had been a man. A calm detachment settled over her as she picked out the detail of yellow bone and silvery muscle membrane, all covered now with a fine hoar of frost. The body had been flayed. The little scraps of skin looked oddly pale and flabby and in some places bore a thatch of coarse hair. The dead man had Mesentreian blood, then. Ricalani men generally lacked the body hair common among southerners.

Sierra turned back to the others. 'There's no trap. You can come closer. If you want to.'

'The scout was just squeamish, then?' Ardamon said as he strode across the snow.

'I didn't say that.'

Ardamon gazed down at the corpse. A muscle in his jaw twitched with the effort of containing himself. 'How long ago?'

She closed her eyes and opened her other senses to the lingering energy. 'Not long. An hour, perhaps.'

'He knows we're gaining on him, then. Well, his men and his horses must be tiring badly by now.'

Mira came closer, covering her mouth with her hand.

'Mira, you should stay back,' Cam said, gently.

'No, I need to see it for myself. I've heard so much about him … but it's not real until you've seen it with your own eyes.'

'I'm surprised the scavengers haven't come for him yet,' Ardamon said.

'They will,' Sierra told him. 'The power has kept them away, but it's fading quickly.' She stepped into the circle to peer at a small red lump that lay a few feet away from the body.

'What is that?' Cam said, circling around for a closer look.

'A tongue. He probably begged for mercy. Rasten hates it when they do that.'

'They must have had beasts to pull their sleds,' Cam said. 'Look, there's a broken tether-line over there.' He pointed to a pair of trees at the edge of the clearing.

'They probably bolted during the ritual,' Sierra said. 'He can't have been camping here alone.'

'No,' Cam agreed. 'Did the others run off, do you think?'

'No. Rasten kept them.' Sierra felt ill, but it was nothing to do with the remains at her feet. 'Can you find out how many there were?'

'I'll check the tents.'

Ardamon called his men down from the road to help and with ruthless efficiency the tents and all the sleds were pulled apart in search of evidence of their previous owners.

293

While she waited for the news Sierra turned away, shuffling through the snow to the far edge of the clearing. She felt cold all over, despite her heavy fur. It was only when she cupped her hands over her face to warm it that she realised she was shaking. Rasten was close, so very close … and he had a full charge of power. She'd felt nothing from the ritual — he'd shielded it carefully from her — and all she had to call upon was the little that had come to her from the assorted aches and pains of Ardamon's men. She'd been on a fast since the night Isidro had been taken prisoner, and here Rasten had gorged himself to full.

'Sirri!' Cam called, waving her over. 'They're smugglers, not a family of trappers as we first thought.'

He was relieved. Sierra was not. Rasten wouldn't work on children unless he had no choice, but grown men, on the other hand …

Ardamon was examining a mark stamped into a bit of harness. 'Look,' he said, showing it to Mira. 'That's the sigil of Lord Endrian of Therasford.'

'Endrian?' Cam said. 'He's been bribing the Raiders to leave his villages alone for months now. It looks as though Rasten stumbled across some of his messengers.'

'But why would he slaughter them? If they're in Endrian's hire, then ultimately they're on the side of the king.'

'That means nothing to Rasten,' Sierra said. 'How many?'

'Eight, judging from the bedding in there,' Ardamon said, jerking his head towards the tents. 'Seven, minus the one out here. Why? What does it matter?'

Sierra felt the blood drain from her face so quickly that for a moment she swayed on her feet.

Cam grabbed her by the arm to steady her. 'What is it, Sirri?'

'Seven! Spirit of Storm, defend us! When he only had the men of his escort to feed on, we had a chance,' she said. 'He's wounded, so it's harder for him to raise and hold power. He would have needed to charge in preparation for a battle. We could have harried him and pulled back over and over, and he'd've had to burn through his own men in order to keep his power up, until they mutinied or deserted, or they were all dead.' Sierra raked her hair back from her face and began to pace across the clearing. 'But now he's got seven sacrifices to draw on. His own men won't care what happens to them, not the way they would if it was one of their own.' She turned to Cam. 'We can't go on. It would be suicide.'

'What in the hells are you talking about?' Ardamon demanded. 'You want us to break off the chase now? When we're only an hour behind?'

'He's right,' Cam said. 'We can't turn back. We'll never get this chance again.'

'No!' Sierra shouted. 'How in the Black Sun's name do you expect me to face him? He'll be full to bursting and I've got no power to fight him with!'

'I should have known it would come to this,' Ardamon snarled, turning to Cam. 'Your great sorcerer is nothing more than a coward.'

'What would you have me do?' Sierra yelled at him. 'Do you want me to choose the man to go under the knife? Will you volunteer yourself, or order one of your men to do what you're not willing to? Perhaps you can find a condemned criminal to sacrifice?'

'Calm down, you're scaring the horses,' Cam snapped. 'What do you need? I'll do it if that's what it takes to kill Rasten.'

She shook her head. 'Cam —'

'I mean it, Sirri.'

'You don't know what you're talking about! That man — ' she pointed at the frost-rimed corpse, 'was skinned alive, piece by piece, and then jointed like a beast for the pot. What they did to Isidro? That was gentle handling so he'd live long enough to be executed — and it still cursed near killed him. Rasten left that as a message, to show us all what to expect if this comes to a battle. I'm not prepared to do what it would take to counter him — not under any circumstances. Do you hear me? I won't.'

'Sirri …' Cam came closer and rested his hands on her shoulders.

'I *won't*,' she whispered. 'If I did, you'd have to kill me. I'd be no better than them.'

'If we let him go, Sierra, this will never be over.'

'Killing him wouldn't change anything anyway,' she said. 'You and Isidro will still be hunted. Kell will still move heavens and earth to get me back.' No doubt Kell would find someone else eager to take on the task of breaking her down to an empty shell.

Cam turned to Ardamon. 'You know this land best. What's Rasten's fastest route to safety?'

Ardamon scowled, jamming his fists against his belt. 'From here? Through Horrock's Pass. The base of it is only a few hours' ride away.'

'Is it even open at this time of year? I'd have thought it'd be buried under snow.'

'That doesn't matter to Rasten,' Sierra said. 'He can blast his way through and he'll bury us if we try to stop him.'

'Can't you do something about that?' Ardamon asked.

Sierra stared at him. 'Just how many of your men are you planning to sacrifice? Cam, this is stupidity.'

'Ardamon, I agree,' Mira said. 'We have to turn back.'

Ardamon turned on her with fury in his eyes. '*Now* you believe her! Just days ago you were saying you'd never trust a sorcerer!'

'Yes, I believe her, when she's telling us directly that this is a battle she can't win. Do you want your grave to be under an avalanche, or in the firepit where Kell disposes of his refuse?'

'But this is our only chance!' Ardamon roared. 'We'll never get another! Why in the hells did you agree to this if only to back down now?'

'I told you in the first place that the plan was madness,' Sierra told him. 'Rasten has ten years of training on me and he's not afraid to sacrifice every last one of his men if that's what it takes. Forgive me if I'm not the monster you hoped I was!'

'Sierra, isn't there any way we can make this happen?' Cam said. 'What if every man here takes a cut, or a burn?'

Sierra shook her head. 'It won't be enough.'

'Are you sure?'

She met his gaze. 'No. But is that a chance you want to take?'

A thread of power brushed against her mind and Sierra closed her eyes with a silent prayer to the Black Sun. *Not now, please, not him.*

Rasten chuckled within her skull. *At last, Little Crow, you're beginning to understand what it will cost you to follow this path. If you want them to live, their only hope is for you to turn yourself in.*

The vision through his eyes was crisp and clear — he made no effort to conceal it from her. He was at the foot of the pass, gazing up at a switchback trail that marched up a rocky cliff face, a natural boundary marking the southern edge of the Wolf Lands. Power hummed beneath his skin, drowning out the ache of the wound in his back. In her mind's eye he glowed like a hot coal.

*Come after me if you wish, Little Crow, but if you're going to end up in my hands anyway, you may as well leave those poor souls behind to eke out another year or two.*

*Get. Out. Of. My. Head.* She severed the contact with a wrench that left her dizzy.

'Sirri?' Once again, Cam clapped a hand on her shoulder to steady her.

'It's nothing,' she muttered. 'I'm alright.'

'Ardamon, I've made up my mind, and the order is mine to give,' Mira said. 'Tell the men we're turning back.'

# Chapter 23

He couldn't go on like this. The pain was too much. Not just the physical pain, although that was bad enough, but the anguish of knowing he was helpless. If he'd been whole and able-bodied he might have held out hope of escape, but now? It wouldn't have mattered if they'd left him unchained, Isidro doubted he had the strength even to make it to the edge of the camp. If he merely waited passively while his captors did as they wished to him this would go on for days, weeks, or maybe for the rest of his life. Presumably the interrogations would eventually come to an end. After all, there was only so much he could tell them about Rasten and Kell, but the other mages and the strange experiment they'd performed ...

Isidro shuddered at the memory, pressing his face into the crook of his arm to hide the sudden sob. He couldn't bear it, not again. While Kell had subjected him to every humiliation he could contrive, Isidro had been able to cling to the knowledge that *he'd still won*. He'd saved Cam. Nothing could change that, and it was the only thing that mattered at that point. But here he was utterly powerless. What they wanted from him they would simply take and there was nothing he could do about it. He would be subjected to that awful violation again and again, until they had all they wanted and simply threw him away.

When the day rolled around to the evening and they brought him food and drink, Isidro had made up his mind. He wouldn't — he couldn't — go on like this.

His reserves were spent and the fever that had been fought down under Jorgen's care was flaring up again, thickening his lungs and burning on his cheeks. If he was to have any chance of recovering he would need warmth and rest, good food and clean water. Well, warmth and rest had already been denied him. If he could find the strength to refuse to eat or drink, then within another day or two he would be too far gone for even the best physician to halt his decline.

It was the mage who had led the interrogation who came to him, the one called Torren. He was accompanied by a Ricalani slave, a skinny young woman of about Sierra's age with tangled hair and old bruises on her face. She carried a tray with a pair of bowls on it and when her master gave her a shove in Isidro's direction he couldn't help but pity the girl. Her master would punish her if she failed to feed him, but Isidro was determined not to let anything pass his lips. Either way, this would go badly for her, but he couldn't afford to weaken his resolve.

She set the tray down on a trunk and cautiously approached with a bowl in her hand. Isidro gathered what strength he had and heaved himself up into a sitting position, leaning his back against a crate. The insubstantial scar hovering over his spine throbbed like a fresh burn. It felt as though it should sting at the contact but of course it passed through the rough wood as though there was nothing there.

When they'd returned him to this tent, they'd locked a manacle around the wrist of his good arm and strung the chain fastened to it through a metal ring bolted to one of the crates, before anchoring the end of it well out of his reach. There was enough slack in the chain to let him lift his hand to his mouth, but that was all — it would not have let him stand, had he the strength to do so.

The girl offered him the bowl. Isidro made no move to take it. She cast a nervous glance to her master, who gestured impatiently. 'Get on with it,' he said in Akharian.

With a glare at him for making her life more difficult she crouched down and tried to press the bowl to his lips. It held some kind of thin and watery gruel. Isidro turned his head away.

With a curse, Torren reached into his coat and produced a Slaver's club. The sight of it made Isidro begin to sweat, but he forced down the memories and the fear. With a growl Torren jammed a knee against Isidro's chest to hold him still, laid the club against his throat, and took a handful of Isidro's hair to wrench his head around and keep him from turning away. Back when he'd been a warrior, Isidro had kept his black hair short for that reason, but since he'd been injured no one had bothered to trim it.

'Go on, then,' Torren snapped at the girl. She tried pressing the bowl to his lips again and this time Isidro lashed out with his good hand. He knocked the bowl from her grip, sending it flying across the narrow aisle. The gruel spilled, splattering over crates and dripping through the spruce. The bowl struck a trunk opposite and shattered and the girl jumped back with a small cry, cowering away from his fist. Cursing, Torren backhanded Isidro across the face and pressed down on the club across his throat to hold him still. Choking, Isidro clawed at the wood and at the mage's gloved fingers, but he'd spent what strength he had. His vision was turning black when Torren finally eased up and backed away, still seething and furious.

'You want to starve yourself, you wretched dog?' he rasped. 'Fine.' He grabbed the other bowl and tipped the water out through the spruce. 'You'll eat when you're hungry enough.' He grabbed the slave-girl by the shoulder and shoved her towards the ground. 'Pick those up.'

She did as he said, gathering up the larger fragments of the bowl and then scrambled along to the end of the aisle to pile them all on the tray. Still cursing, Torren strode past her and she hurried after him with her small burden, casting a dark look behind her at Isidro as she left.

Gasping for breath, Isidro watched them go. It was only once he heard them crunching away through the snow outside that he turned his attention to the scratch on the trunk where the bowl had hit and broken.

She hadn't gathered up all the fragments. He could see one pointed shard lying on the green carpet of spruce at the base of the trunk.

One small shard of pottery, half buried amid the greenery.

He couldn't reach it with his good hand. Instead, he had to squirm around quietly to take off his boots and his socks, moving cautiously in case the sound of him shuffling around and drawing sharp breaths when his battered and cramping muscles protested let someone know he was up to something.

Any small items that fell on a spruce floor could quickly work their way through the twigs and needles to be lost in the snow beneath. If anyone dropped a button or a small coin everyone in the tent had to remain still until it was found, or else the wretched thing would be lost forever — even pulling up the floor was no guarantee of finding it. If he didn't pick up the shard on his first attempt it would slip beneath the twigs and out of his reach.

Isidro reached for his prize with his bare toes and closed them over the fragment. It was cold and hard against his cooling skin. He was braced for the sting of a cut — shards from a glazed pot could be razor-sharp if

300

it fractured the right way — but no cut came. Holding his breath, he picked up the shard with his toes.

It fell from his grip before he could bring it within reach of his hand, but at last he could get a good look at it. There was no sharply angled edge to provide a neat cutting surface, but the shard was triangular, roughly the shape of a spear-head. A sharp edge would have helped, but no matter. It would serve.

He kicked it closer, but even by straining against the chain on his wrist Isidro could barely get his fingertips on it. Just one fraction of an inch closer — his fingertips scrabbled over the smooth glaze — and he had it in his grip.

It wasn't sharp. He knew how much force it took to pierce flesh with a weapon that was designed for the task, let alone a blunt shard. It wouldn't be easy, but strangely he felt no fear, only a kind of calm resolve.

*Black Sun, I don't want to die, but I can't live like this.* It was the only power he had, the only way he could make the pain stop. The thought of Cam troubled him — Isidro was breaking his promise, but he knew Cam would understand. And Sierra ... well, his chances of ever seeing her again had never been very great. She needed to keep moving to be safe and he could never have kept up with her. She would know when it happened; she would tell Cam and then he wouldn't have to worry about Isidro any more. He would no longer be burdened by the need to provide for his crippled brother, when the two of them had barely been able to provide for themselves.

Cam would forgive him.

There was no use in waiting. Isidro set the blunt point of the shard against his neck, braced the heel of his palm against the butt and thrust it in, gouging through skin and flesh as he gritted his teeth against the pain.

There was a rush of sound in his head like the roar of a waterfall and then Rasten was there. *What in the Black Sun's name are you doing?*

Isidro didn't reply. He'd broken the skin and could feel the hot trickle of blood dripping down to his shoulder, but there was a lot of muscle to go through and the shard was so blunt it forced the fibres apart rather than cutting through them.

Rasten reached for the sigil carved into his back. His touch bit hard and deep and Isidro shuddered so violently his fingers slipped over the shard, now sticky with blood.

*What do you think Sierra is going to do if you die?* Rasten snarled in his ear. *If she tries to take revenge on the Akharians now, they'll kill her!*

Isidro faltered. He hadn't considered that. *She wouldn't ...*

*She will! She loves you, you worthless cripple! I don't know why, but she does, and I won't let you drive her to throw her life away for your sake.* Through that insubstantial scar, Rasten had a hand buried right in the depths of him and through that grasp he flooded Isidro with power.

It roared through him like a flood of golden light, striking swifter and deeper than any drug. All his aches and fatigue were swept away by that rush and the chill in his bones vanished like smoke in the wind.

Sierra had told him about this — that rush of power buried all the cares of this world, she'd said. Under the full flood of it she hadn't cared what they'd done to her or to whichever poor soul was trapped in the chains, although by that point they were one and the same as Sierra could feel everything that was inflicted upon them. That rising tide of power had saved her sanity — otherwise she would have gone utterly mad as she experienced being tortured to death again and again. She'd tried to describe it but he had never really understood until now.

Isidro fought to keep his will and his mind together under the assault of that flood. He could *just* feel the shard in his hand and the blunt throb of the wound on his neck. The power was giving him strength to resist the pain — if he could just hold on to his awareness for a little longer, he would be able to finish the job and it would all be over — no more pain, no more fear, just peace.

Somewhere, he felt hands close around his wrist. Through the golden roar of the power, he could hear someone shouting in rage and fury. He fought against it, and the power lent him strength, but it wasn't enough. Something struck him across the head — he could see shadowy forms standing over him, but they were thin and insubstantial, mere shadows of the physical world. *NO!* Isidro howled as he felt them winning, pulling his hand away. There were too many of them and they had power — he could feel it battering against the energy Rasten had fed to him — and *they* knew how to use it. It was already leaking away from him, pouring like water from a sprung barrel. Isidro fought and struggled and howled, but his chance — his one chance to end it all here and now — was gone.

He was helpless once again.

# Chapter 24

Delphine trudged through the snow back towards the Collegium quarter. The lantern dangling from her fist was enough for the soldiers to recognise her as a mage and step aside to let her pass, but Delphine barely noticed them.

Visiting the slave camps always left her depressed. Back in Akhara when she'd first put her name in for this expedition she'd never imagined just how bad it would be. She simply couldn't shake the thought that until a few days ago these folk had been living happy and free and had probably never spared the empire a moment's thought.

Slaves were the lifeblood of the empire. Without them the crops would go unplanted, the grain would not be cut, no quarries would be dug, no roads built, no ore hauled from the mines or smelted into metal. Without slaves, the empire would collapse and all five million souls who lived within her borders would be defenceless against the barbarians who envied their rich lands and their wealth.

The problem with slaves was that the empire needed a constant supply. A certain number could be bred at home, of course, and those house-born slaves, raised to know their place, were always in demand. But for the most part, raising a worker from infancy to a useful age was simply too expensive to be feasible, so slaves had to be brought in from elsewhere. Unpleasant, yes; regrettable, certainly; but it was a necessary fact of life.

Delphine simply couldn't shake the feeling that it was *all her fault*.

*It's not as though I could have stopped it*, she told herself. Five years ago when a group of students looking for a research project had found Barranecour's old log and brought it to show her, it wouldn't have mattered if she'd sent them away. If she hadn't shoved aside the stack of papers she was supposed to be grading to open the musty, mouldering tome, someone else would have. When the world turns everyone on this earth moves with it. Only a fool believes he can hold back the forces of history.

Back then all she knew about Ricalan was that it lay in the north and was buried under snow for six months of each year. But that book had changed everything. Her utter absorption in it had ultimately led to her divorce, the scandal of which had nearly ruined her career. It had driven her to stake everything she valued on a theory and had brought her out here to this Gods-forsaken wilderness of ice and cold.

And now, after all that work, it was looking like a gamble she was going to lose.

Nearly a hundred years ago a man called Caltoreas Barranecour had launched an expedition to Ricalan. At the time it had been regarded as a fool's errand, a waste of time and money. The fact that Ricalan had powerful mages was widely known at that time. Akhara had contributed most of them due to the laws that required any mage trained by the empire to repay the debt of his or her education. Some ornery-minded folk insisted such an arrangement was no different than slavery and rather than submit to it they fled the empire's borders to seek their fortune elsewhere.

There were only a handful of places they could go. Mesentreia did not tolerate mages. Five centuries earlier they had driven all their mages out, an action that was singularly responsible for Akhara's founding, as a handful of land-starved nobles had gone with them and established a colony on the continent west of the Mesentreian Islands. In modern times there were now other nations on the continent further west again, where such disenfranchised mages could try to carve a life for themselves, but they were primitive places and Blood-Mages were common there. That left Ricalan, which at least had the benefit of being close enough for some trade with Akhara and Mesentreia, and where the savage natives could be impressed by the trappings of civilisation — or so the exiled mages believed.

The reality wasn't quite so neat. Ricalan had society and mages of its own and they had become accustomed to Akharian exiles trespassing on to their lands, fully expecting to be treated like Gods. Many of them were no doubt killed, but a few were able to carve places for themselves in Ricalani society and once a toehold was established it was a small matter for newcomers to buy places there for themselves.

And then in a fit of madness, the Ricalani people had turned on their mages in a long and bloody war. One of these Akharian exiles, deciding he preferred life and service in civilisation to death in the snow, had somehow got word to his cousin Barranecour, and told him there was profit to be had in the north. Barranecour raised the money and sailed there only to learn his relative had been killed shortly after the message had left Ricalan. The native clans were burning every book and record of mage-craft they could find and slaughtering any mage unlucky enough to fall into their hands. Faced with the prospect of returning home empty-handed, Barranecour set about collecting every piece of mage-lore he could get his hands on, in an attempt to preserve the knowledge before it was lost forever.

While this was an interesting footnote of history for an academic, a century on it was all of very minor importance. It would have remained buried and forgotten if it weren't for Barranecour's log, which had been unearthed by her students one rainy afternoon in Akhara. At the same time as Barranecour was attempting to collect the dying knowledge, a Ricalani mage was succeeding. This was the man who came to be known in Ricalan as the Last Great Mage, or to his enemies as the Demon Vasant.

The scholars of the Collegium, along with the Battle-Mages who served in the empire's army, had long scoffed at the idea that the empire had anything to learn from the mages of a barbarian country, until Mesentreian ships began raiding the Akharian coast. Ricalanis had kept the Mesentreian Raiders away for centuries and, although no one alive today knew quite how they achieved it, there was no doubt they'd had some method of defence — one that didn't rely on having a battle-trained mage at hand.

When she got right down to it, Delphine could only say she was to blame. Most likely the invasion would have happened regardless; the only way they could halt the raids was by sacking and burning the harbours that sheltered the raiding ships. But while the main Akharian force was concentrating on that goal, General Boreas was leading two legions into the peaceful tribal lands to the east, pillaging and enslaving villagers who were barely even aware of the empire's existence, so the Collegium could find the hidden treasure of books and knowledge hidden by the Last Great Mage.

The other mages on the expedition were certain Barranecour's records were all they needed and that his maps and directions would be enough to lead them to the hoards. If Akharian mages were among the scholars who assembled the libraries, they argued, then the texts must surely be written in Akharian, as theirs was the language of scholarship, and the mages of the Collegium the world's pre-eminent. If barbarian mage-craft had achieved even a fraction of the greatness implied by the tales, then it must have been Akharian mages who drove the progress.

Delphine doubted the fates would be so kind to them. Every record she found indicated that the Ricalani mages distrusted the Akharian exiles and regarded them as troublemakers. She could see no reason why they would have let a foreign tongue dominate their craft in the face of their own long history of scholarship. All the books Barranecour had collected were in Ricalani and he must have been able to read the language, because he'd left notes here and there in the margins. There wasn't one person in Akhara, however, who knew the language. Delphine had tracked down the descendants of slaves taken from the northern lands but not one of them had ever been taught the barbarian tongue. What use was it here in a civilised society?

The solution seemed a simple one. After every raid, once the reality of their situation had descended upon the captives, Delphine took one of her books through the slave tents with their miserable, chained occupants, searching for anyone who could read the text and speak enough Akharian or Mesentreian to serve as a translator.

So far she'd had no success. There was no doubt that she'd found folk who could read Ricalani but none of them spoke more than a smattering of Mesentreian and couldn't read any at all. She had found slaves who could speak and read Mesentreian, mostly merchants who had ventured here from the south, but none of them knew more than a few words of Ricalani. Perhaps in the south they would have more success, but reaching it and subduing the coastal towns would take months, and the treasure they sought wasn't down on the coast, but here in the northern foothills. It could take years.

It had grown dark by the time Delphine gave up the search and returned to the Collegium quarter. The next day they would be on the march again and the slaves would be shuffled around in their camps, so she had made an effort to question all of them today. They had taken a temple this time and she had hopes for the priests, but once again her search had been fruitless. Delphine was thinking only of her warm tent and a bowl of tea when a tall figure loomed in front of her. 'Delphine! Where in the hells have you been? I've been looking for you for hours!'

He had his hood pulled forward far enough to hide his face but Delphine recognised the voice. 'I've been in the slave camps, Torren. Didn't my girls tell you?' Her two students had offered to help but they were too young to be subjected to the suffering of the new captives.

Torren swept his hood back to glare at her. 'I don't like the idea of you traipsing around among the barbarians on your own, Delphi.'

'Oh really, Torren, I'm still a mage — I can deal with chained and terrified barbarians. If I took a guard along with me I doubt they'd speak to me at all.'

'Find anything useful?' Torren asked.

Delphine frowned. Torren didn't usually ask after her work. In fact, ever since her divorce he treated everything she did as a mortal embarrassment. 'No,' she said, abruptly. 'Even the priests don't speak more than a smattering of Mesentreian. Why?' She narrowed her eyes. 'Is this about that slave I picked out? Are you finally going to let me talk to him?'

'Well ...' Torren said, and fumbled around in his sash. 'As a matter of fact something did turn up ...' He pulled out a little slip of parchment and handed it to her.

It was a ragged little offcut, the sort left over after the hides have been trimmed into pages. In the gloom all Delphine could see on it was a dark smear of ink until she held it up to her lantern; she bit her lip.

'That's Ricalani script, isn't it?' Torren said.

'Torren, you son of a bitch! How long have you had this?'

'Delphi!' he snapped, shocked. 'Watch your language! I only found it a few hours ago, I swear —'

'A few *hours*!'

'The slave was carrying it in his clothes. I didn't even notice it at the time. One of the clerks recording the interrogation found it and showed it to me and I've been looking for you ever since!'

'So are you finally going to let me question him?' Delphine said.

'Well ... there's been something of a problem.'

She followed Torren to the Battle-Mages' quarter. The military mages were far too important to do their own cooking and laundry, or even heat their own water. There were servants scattered through the quarter, supplied with tents where they did the work and stored their goods. The tents were kept warm to dry the laundry: it was in one of these, isolated behind a stack of boxes and crates, that the prisoner was being kept.

Delphine could feel him long before she saw him. 'What in the hells has been going on here, Torren?' The slave ached all over. She could feel it like pins and needles tingling right through her limbs.

'He tried to kill himself,' Torren admitted. 'Damn near succeeded, too. What's cursed odd is how we found out about it. Someone flooded him with power. We all sensed it and came running just in time to stop him.'

'Someone? Who in the hells could … *Oh*.'

'Right,' Torren said. 'It wasn't anyone around here. It had to be one of the Blood-Mages.'

Delphine peered around the edge of the crates, raising her lantern to lift the shadows.

The prisoner was slumped with his back against the crates and his arms bound outstretched to either side of him. A rough bandage had been tied around his throat and he hung limply in his bonds with his head bowed and his chin on his chest.

'So why have you brought me here?' Delphine said. 'Blood-Mages are your department, Torren, not mine. I'm just a scholar.'

'He won't eat,' Torren said. 'He won't drink. We tried holding his nose and forcing him but he just spits it out again. The physician says he's got a fever. He's willing himself to die, Delphi, and … well, I thought of your father and I thought that if anyone had an idea of how to stop it, you would.'

Delphine just stared at him. 'You want me to play nursemaid to a barbarian slave? You, Torren? You're the one always going on about propriety and fit behaviour for a lady of my station.'

'Delphi, please! I need your help! Presarius assigned the slave to me and you know what he's like. If the slave dies I'll take the blame and I can kiss any chance of a promotion goodbye. I know Ballenar lost the will to live after his friend was killed. You nursed him right up till the end, Delphi, and all the Gods know you've got a knack for getting people to do what you want.'

Delphine sighed. He just had to bring her father into this.

Her mother, Jasenia, and Torren's father had been siblings. Jasenia had run away from her noble home rather than enter an arranged marriage and had chosen a hiding place so infamous it ensured her family would never force her to return to them. She'd hidden in the Sympath's Palace as a pleasure-girl, where she'd met Delphine's father Ballenar and fallen pregnant by him.

Delphine had always regretted that she'd never had a chance to know her mother. Jasenia sounded like the sort of woman she would have liked to meet, but she had died in childbirth and her family had never acknowledged their grandchild. Ballenar had been her only kin for most of her life, until Torren became head of the family and made contact with her again. Bringing her back into the family had been his idea, but the results had proved contrary to both their expectations. Delphine had been raised as a Collegium brat and her ideas and attitudes were vastly different from those of the noble family her mother had fled.

Delphine peered around the crates again. The prisoner hadn't moved. She wasn't sure if he was even aware of their presence. *Curse you, Torren*, she thought. Now that he had mentioned it, she did see something of her father in him. It was no physical resemblance. Ballenar, dark-skinned and merry, had run to fat in his later life, as did so many Sympaths — he had been worlds away from this gaunt and broken warrior. What reminded her of him was the hopelessness, the utter dejection and the sense of wilful withdrawal from this world, to actively seek out the next.

In his younger years Ballenar had taken myriad lovers but as he grew older he'd settled down with just one — a man, much to the consternation of the staid Collegium governors. One day while out in the city Galwin had been knocked down by a runaway wagon and seriously injured. It had taken him days to die and Ballenar had been unable to see him even long enough to say a brief goodbye. While Sympaths shared the pleasure of those around them, they were also sensitive to the suffering of those nearby. Instead of deriving power from it, the suffering of others aroused a sympathetic agony that could, over time, cripple their powers and turn a Sympath into a twisted, dangerous creature, as vicious as any Blood-Mage. Even if the Collegium governors had allowed him to risk himself in Galwin's presence in those final days, Ballenar wouldn't have been able to physically stand it.

After Galwin's death Ballenar had lost his will to live and entered a steady decline. Years of indulgence had eroded his health and, despite Delphine's efforts to coax him out of his overwhelming grief, he had wasted away over a matter of weeks.

Studying the chained prisoner, Delphine doubted this one would take anything like as long to die.

'Look, Delphi, will you just try?'

Delphine pulled out the slip of parchment again. She'd spent months looking for a prisoner who could read Ricalani. Of course she had hoped to find an ageing priest, someone long past any thoughts of resistance or escape, someone she wouldn't have to watch around her girls the way she'd watch a dog rumoured to be vicious. But he was all she had. 'Alright. I can't promise anything but I'll try.' She turned to Torren with a frown. 'But only if you guarantee I'll get access to him as a translator.'

'I can't promise anything,' he said, 'but I'll try.'

'Oh, very funny,' she said with a roll of her eyes. 'Do you have transcripts of the interrogation? I'll need to see them.'

A delicious scent tickled his nose on a waft of steam. Isidro lifted his head with a groan. Even while his mind had been too muddled to think clearly, that scent had gone straight to the most visceral part of him and made his mouth water.

A rustle of paper made him look up. His eyes were blurred and with his arms still chained outstretched he couldn't wipe his face on his shoulder or his sleeve. All he could do was try to blink them clear.

A woman was sitting across from him, perched on one of the crates with her legs crossed and her head bent over a sheaf of papers. One of those small, flameless lanterns hung from the ridge-pole near her head.

The wound on his neck stung and the muscles of his back and shoulders protested at being forced to hold this unnatural posture. Isidro tried to shift his position but between his weakness and the chains he could barely move an inch.

The woman glanced up from her papers. 'Ah! The sleeper awakes.' She had nut-brown skin and dark, wavy hair pulled back into a braid, though small strands had escaped to frame her face in a frizzy haze. Her features reminded him of Rhia's, although her colouring was quite different.

That delicious scent was still teasing him. Isidro twisted around until he found the source. A bowl, wooden this time, was resting on the crate to which he was bound. It would have been within arm's reach had he been free to reach for it. From the scent it was a good meat broth, plain and wholesome, the sort that wouldn't upset a starved and empty stomach.

'I've been reading about you,' the woman said, waving the papers at him. 'It seems you've been through the wars. Captured by Blood-Mages, tortured and rescued only to be taken by Slavers. After what you've been through, despair would seem the only reasonable option.' She turned back to the page, holding it up to the light to read through to the end. Isidro guessed she was a little older than him, but it was hard to tell. The skin of her face and hands was fine and unlined, not roughened by the weather. The only thing that gave her age away were the strands of silver in her dark curls. Some of them gleamed red, dyed with henna, but nearer the scalp they were untouched. She was definitely a mage. He could sense the power in her and when she lifted a hand to brush back a strand of hair he saw a blotch of ink staining her sleeve. Perhaps a scholar as well.

'What I don't understand,' she said, 'is why on earth this Blood-Mage is trying to keep you alive. He must know we can use you against him. Did you know that? You had a slight touch of talent before they got to you, a Sensitive, I'd say, but by blasting through you the way they did, they've expanded your capacity significantly. Fascinating really, to know that you can turn a weak mage into a more powerful one just by raping and torturing him, but somehow I doubt it'll catch on. Of course it's a bit late for you to learn how to use it, but we can still teach you to spy on them and perhaps use you to weaken them enough to bring them down. So I can understand why a Blood-Mage would want you dead. What I can't understand is, if you are so determined to kill yourself that you'd rip your own throat out with a bit of broken pot, *why in the hells would he try to stop you?*'

She paused for a moment, giving him a chance to speak, but Isidro held his tongue and she continued with a shrug. 'I have to say,' she said, leafing through the papers again, 'this fellow Rasten seems a fascinating case.'

Isidro cursed himself silently. He couldn't remember what he had or hadn't told the men who'd interrogated him. At first he'd tried to hold

311

back some of the details but they'd gone over his tale again and again and his mind had been too overwhelmed with pain and shock to remember what he'd admitted from one recital to the next. The one thing he was certain of was that he'd left Sierra out of it.

'You said his master took him as an apprentice when Rasten was just a boy. Can you imagine what it would have been like for the poor lad? In a way,' she said, leaning forward, 'it's a little like what has happened to you, only worse. He saw his family slaughtered, then he was taken prisoner and made the plaything of a vile old man who brutalised him until he relented to brutalise others to spare his own hide. You said he has been with his master for ten years. Ten years! Can you imagine it? You've been here only a few days and already you're fighting like a wild beast caught in a snare. Ten years and he's still alive. By the Good Goddess, imagine how much he hates his master. What do you think he would do if he happened to be here in your place? Do you think he'd try to kill himself, or would he see this as an opportunity to take revenge on the one who tortured him? It looks to me as if he's stronger than you are. What else would you think when one man survives a decade of torture and another is prepared to kill himself after just a day?'

Something shifted within his mind. Isidro knew that sensation by now and squeezed his eyes shut, wishing to the Black Sun he had some way of repelling that touch. He hadn't felt Rasten's awareness settle over him, so Rasten must have been there, silent, since before Isidro woke.

*You know,* the Blood-Mage whispered into his mind, *the Akharian bitch has a point.*

'Rasten's a monster,' Isidro rasped in Akharian. 'He has no conscience. He'll turn on anyone his master tells him to.'

*That's ... only* partially *true,* came Rasten's measured response.

'That's right,' the woman said, unfolding herself from her perch. She slipped off the crate and crouched down beside him. 'But you're not like that. You're an honourable man. I can see that from what you went through to protect your brother. Why should Rasten thrive and a man like you starve himself to death in chains? Especially when you can help us destroy him and his master and make sure they can't do this to anyone else?'

*Why* did *you save my life?* Isidro asked Rasten.

*I'll tell you later. Once she's gone,* Rasten replied.

312

The woman stepped delicately over his long, sprawled legs and loosened the end of the cord binding his broken arm. As it dropped from the horizontal the rush of blood back into the limb was painful enough that he thumped his head back against the crate, fighting not to cry out. The sound of it and the sudden movement startled the woman. He felt her power pulse and for a brief moment there was a violet flicker of light between them as she cast a shield over herself. It vanished again when she realised there was no threat, but she watched him carefully as she went to the end of the chain attached to his good arm and loosened that as well. 'The broth is good,' she told him. 'I had a bowl of it myself. Drink it, leave it, or tip it through the twigs. No one but you will ever know.' She gathered up her papers and unhooked the lantern from the ridge-pole. 'I'll be back to speak to you again in the morning. Try to get some rest.'

When she left Isidro was still pressing his back against the crate, gritting his teeth as he waited for the pain to subside.

The tickle in his head came again. *Leave me alone!* he snarled at Rasten.

*Issey?* It wasn't Rasten's voice he heard, but Sierra's. The voice was faint and distant but it was undoubtedly her.

*Sirri?* He sounded as querulous as a child and hated himself for it.

*Yes, it's me. I'm talking through Rasten. I'm sorry, Issey, but it's the only way. He says if I reach for you directly the Akharian mages might sense it.*

*She doesn't have enough control,* Rasten broke in. *She might spill over. They already know about me, but I don't want them finding out about her.*

Well that was one thing they could agree on, even if the thought of sharing *anything* with Rasten repulsed him.

*Issey, I swear by the Black Sun we'll get you back. We'll find a way …*

*No! This place is crawling with mages. They can do things we've never dreamed of.*

*I don't care! We'll find a way, even if I have to come to Akhara to find you!*

*If you die she'll want revenge,* Rasten interrupted. *She's not ready for this yet. She might be able to handle a few of them, but if the Akharian mages corner her they'll kill her. Is that what you want?*

Isidro swallowed hard. He didn't want to admit this in front of Rasten but pride was a luxury he could no longer afford. *Sirri, I don't know if I can take this.*

*I ... I understand.*

*What?* Rasten demanded. *I went to all the trouble of saving his worthless life and now you're giving him permission to kill himself?*

*Shut up, Rasten! It's not a matter of permission! It's a matter of forgiveness. I can't ask him to do something I'm not prepared to do myself ... If you have to do it then I understand, but please try to survive. For Cam's sake, if not for mine.*

Isidro was braced for Rasten's scorn but to his surprise Rasten remained silent. This peculiar connection shared more than just a person's words — it gave the same sense of mood and demeanour as talking to someone in person would. He was expecting contempt from Rasten, but what he sensed instead was puzzlement, and perhaps a little envy. Of course — there was no one Rasten cared about and no one who cared about him, except perhaps Sierra. If he was willing to endanger himself to protect her, then he must have some degree of care for her.

If he died, Isidro realised, it would mean Sierra had one less ally against Rasten's voice whispering in her ear.

*Issey, please ...*

*I'll try,* he told her. *I can't promise, but I'll try.*

*That's all I ask. We'll find a way to free you, I promise.*

The bowl was empty when Delphine returned the next morning. Isidro was curled up beneath the blanket and dozing when she rapped her knuckles on a crate to wake him. He saw a young girl with her when he lifted his head blearily, blinking in the lamplight. She was about fourteen with honey-coloured skin and hair the hue of sun-bleached straw. She held a cloth-wrapped parcel to her chest and stared at him with wide eyes.

As he sat up slowly, moving carefully because of his stiff and bruised muscles, Delphine tossed something to the ground beside him.

It was an oblong plaque of jade as long as his palm and half the width, carved with an abstract motif. After a moment Isidro realised it held an enchantment. The power tickled against the back of his hand like a cool breeze.

'Well, Master Sensitive, what do you make of that?' Delphine said.

He reached for it gingerly. Most of the enchantments he had contact with were unpleasant, like the warding-stones or Sierra's punishment bands. When he laid his fingertips against the jade it felt warm and comfortable and seemed to buzz slightly in his grasp.

Delphine perched on the crate again, with her legs stretched out in front of her and crossed at the ankle. The girl hovered in the background. 'Close your eyes,' Delphine told him gently. 'Think of an empty bowl, on a shelf in a dark room. The bowl is your mind. It is quiet and still, just waiting. You can feel the enchantment fluttering against your palm. Open your mind and let it in. What do you see?'

He didn't know why he obeyed her. Perhaps it was because she was the only person who had showed him a little human kindness, or perhaps it was out of simple shock that the only time he was able to learn anything about mage-craft was after he had been made a slave. Exactly why he did it Isidro never knew, but he closed his hand over the plaque and did as she requested.

The image flickered through his mind for just an instant before he lost it in surprise. He had the impression of warmth and movement, a jerky, swaying motion that made him momentarily dizzy.

'What do you see?' she asked him softly.

'Something's moving. Swaying, really. And it's warm.'

'Really? Well, you are a curious one, aren't you?' She gestured to him to move back against the crates. 'Lift your arms. I'm going to fasten the chains again so Alameda can try out her device.'

If he didn't cooperate, Isidro suspected, she was quite capable of forcing him to obey. Lifting his right arm was agony and he had to support it with his left hand until she tightened the rope to take some of the weight. She frowned at him as he pressed his back against the rough wood and tried to breathe through it. 'It's painful, isn't it? Well, we'll soon see if there's anything to be done about it.'

She tightened the other chain so he was once again pinned and helpless. Isidro began to sweat. His subconscious mind associated it with unpleasant things and he couldn't keep the dark memories at bay.

Delphine never lifted her gaze from him as she gestured to the girl, Alameda, to come around the crates and into his small prison. Watching him shyly from beneath her lashes she ducked behind her teacher as she unwrapped the parcel she carried.

At first glance the device she revealed looked like a kind of tray. It was a flat sheet of translucent stone, two hand-spans wide and a little over one span high, with holes drilled around the edges and wrapped with copper wire. There were handles fixed to each of the short sides and the girl grasped these as she raised it and held it over Isidro's broken arm.

He felt a pulse of power wash over him as she activated the device and began to tremble uncontrollably. It was too close to the other times he'd been helpless under an assault of power.

Alameda glanced up at her teacher. 'Madame —'

'Be still,' Delphine urged him. 'It won't hurt, I promise.'

He couldn't even speak to reply. Delphine assessed his distress with a glance and slipped one hand under his elbow to support it and the other under his splinted wrist. 'Does that help?' she murmured to the girl. With her support the pain eased and he was able to breathe again.

Alameda peered at the stone. 'Ahh … yes! Look, madame, it works! You see there are the splints and the finger bones …' Her voice trailed off and for a moment they were both silent.

Isidro glanced over. The device gave off green light which played over their faces. Curiosity pricked him and he craned his head trying to see what was on the sheet of stone.

A tracery of green light illuminated the shape of the bones buried beneath flesh and bandages. The hand itself was whole, but the wrist and the forearm were a jumbled mess of spurs and fragments of bone.

'That's enough, Alameda,' Delphine said to the girl. 'Loosen the end of the rope and then go back to the end of the passage.'

The girl loosened the knot and then scrambled back out of the way. Gently Delphine lowered his ruined arm and loosened the other chain. Once he was free to move again Isidro cradled the ruined limb to his chest and focussed on breathing deeply until the pain passed.

'I have need of a translator,' Delphine said after a moment. 'But I doubt you'll ever have enough use of that hand to hold a pen. I don't suppose you're left-handed?'

Isidro shook his head. 'I don't suppose you can heal the wretched arm'

'No,' she said. 'You can't manipulate living matter that way, only dead stuff like stone and water. Still, you can learn to write with the left. Your Akharian is passable. Tell me, do you write it as well?'

'A little,' Isidro gasped. All he wanted was for her to go away and leave him alone and answering her questions seemed to be the easiest way to reach that end.

'What about Mesentreian?' she asked, in that language.

'Yes,' he replied.

'As well as you know Akharian?'

'Better.'

She gazed down at him thoughtfully with her arms folded over her narrow chest. 'Have you ever heard of a man called Vasant?'

Isidro went very still and slowly lifted his gaze to meet hers.

'He was a great mage of your people.'

'The last,' Isidro said. 'The Last Great Mage.'

'In the war when your people destroyed their mages, while the others were fighting, Vasant gathered up all the recorded knowledge of the Ricalani mages and hid the books. Have you heard the tale?'

He nodded.

'Well, we've come here to find them. You must have wondered what your life would have been like if there were people who'd recognised your talent when you were still young enough to learn how to use it. They stole your potential when they killed the last of the mages. Aren't you curious to see what might have been?'

'You want me to help you find Vasant's lost treasure?'

'Yes,' Delphine said. 'We would most likely find them with or without you, but I need a translator.'

Isidro tipped his head back against the crate and closed his eyes. Last night it had all seemed so simple, but now ... What he'd thought was a clear path had become a maze.

He was a fool to let her words from the night before weaken his resolve, but he couldn't deny she was right. Rasten had survived a decade of this treatment. Was he really going to give up after just a few days? If it was only himself he had to worry about, then perhaps the question would be easier to answer, but there was the matter of Sierra and Cam, as well. If Kell took Sierra back and succeeded in turning her into an obedient weapon, Cam would be doomed. Sierra's best hope for freedom was to master her powers independent of Rasten and Kell. Vasant's books, if they existed, would be her best chance of that. If he only considered himself, the choice was simple, but escaping this pain-filled existence

317

was a purely selfish solution. He could do more good if he stayed. If he could bring himself to stay.

Just the thought of it made him cringe. His soul-destroying despair wouldn't respond to logic or rational thought. If this was the path he chose it would likely be the longest and hardest-fought battle of his life.

'I'll let you think it over,' Delphine said. 'I'm not interested in compelling obedience from a recalcitrant and rebellious slave. If you come with me I expect you to do as I say willingly. I'll see you are treated well. You'll have decent food and a warm place to sleep.'

'What about the interrogations?' Isidro said. 'The experiments. I had the impression they're just getting warmed up.'

'Those will continue,' Delphine said with a toss of her head. 'The information you have is valuable. We've never had a survivor of the Blood-Mages' rituals to study before. Once you've demonstrated you're willing to cooperate, they will be easier on you. If you work with us you'll probably end up as a Collegium slave and there are far worse fates for a man in your position. I'll come and see you again in the evening and you can tell me what you've decided.' She turned to go, but then hesitated and came back to retrieve the enchantment she'd given him.

It was lying on the spruce where Isidro had dropped it when she tightened the chains. He picked it up and handed it to her. 'What is it?'

She frowned at him. 'You should address a free woman as madame and a man as sir. As for the enchantment, I've no idea. This place has given us a whole world of puzzles to solve — this is just one of them.'

The Akharian army broke camp that day, moving on from the temple and its village, which had been stripped of valuables and reduced to rubble, so that none who escaped the raid could find shelter there. It was past midwinter, but the days were so short the army set out while it was still dark and made camp well after sunset. Their route had been chosen to take them along the path Barranecour had theorised that Vasant took, and while she waited in the pre-dawn gloom for the last of the gear to be loaded onto the slave-hauled sleds, Delphine pulled her well-worn notes out of her satchel to study them again.

'Any progress, Delphi?'

'Hmm?' She turned to see Harwin coming towards her with his slave-girl Lucia trotting behind him, leading the pony Harwin would ride.

318

Delphine shook the papers to dislodge the scatter of snow that had settled over them. It was open to the map that had been copied from Barranecour's log. 'Just wondering if this whole cursed mission is nothing but a wild goose chase. A very expensive, drawn-out, painfully slow and miserably cold wild goose chase. I'm beginning to wonder if I shouldn't have burned that wretched book the day Darius dumped it on my desk.'

'Oh come now, Delphi, it's not that bad. Maybe we haven't found Barranecour's treasure yet, but we've found enough abandoned and forgotten devices in the temples to keep us busy for a while. And just think of the tales you'll be able to tell your children.'

'Children? I think I've lost my chance for that, Harwin.'

'Then you could write about it instead. When we first set out you were talking about how you were going to write of your experiences in the barbarian lands.'

Delphine sighed and Harwin cocked his head to one side, regarding her with concern. 'What's the matter? Is that slave of your cousin's getting to you?'

'Ah, ye Gods, Harwin, I've never seen man or beast so wretched. But it's not just him — it's all of them. We've torn their lives apart and we have nothing to show for it. Oh, I know it would have happened even if I hadn't written that cursed paper on Barranecour's expedition. It's just … it's weighing me down. I'm trying to hide it from the girls but it's getting harder and harder.'

'So forget about this slave. He's Torren's problem, not yours.'

Delphine shook her head. 'I thought about it. But he's the closest thing to a translator we have. By the Good Goddess, a young barbarian male is not what I had hoped for, but at least in his condition he's not going to give us trouble. No, I can't give up on him, not when he's the best chance we have of finding and using the relics. And if we can do that, I can at least convince myself that all this has been worthwhile. If he hasn't come around by this evening, then the next interrogation will do it, I'm sure.'

Delphine intended to look in on the slave again once the camp was pitched and her students were safely settled to their work for the evening, but Torren sent for her almost as soon as the general sounded the halt.

The slave had been secured on a sled for the day's march and wrapped in blankets and furs to keep him from freezing. Despite those precautions he was so thoroughly chilled his lips were tinged with blue. His clothes were drenched with sweat and there was a flush of fever on his cheeks. When Delphine spoke to him and waved a hand in front of his eyes he made only a brief effort to focus on her before retreating to whatever fevered dream was lurking within his mind.

'Do you know his name?' Delphine said to Torren.

'Of course not,' Torren said. Captives were never permitted to keep the names they had borne as free men or women and no one would assign them a new one unless it was needed. His old name might have been enough to reach him, lost in the feverish haze as he was, but no slave-name would have the power to call to him.

'It looks bad,' Delphine told him, wrapping her arms around herself against the chill. She wanted to be in the familiar surroundings of her tent, warming her hands and her belly with a bowl of hot tea, not standing around in the Battle-Mages' quarter. 'Have you had a physician look at him?'

'The slave-doctor's been around once or twice.'

'Slave-doctor? Torren, I wouldn't trust one of those fools to treat a dog for fleas. Look, even I can tell he's feverish and he must be in pain from that arm bouncing around on a sled all day. He needs willow-bark at the very least and probably tincture of poppy as well. Call the cursed physician or you're going to lose him. It might already be too late.'

'Presarius won't authorise the budget for it,' Torren said. 'He's just a slave and a cripple to boot. I can't justify the expense.'

Delphine shifted the satchel slung over her shoulder to ease the weight on the strap. She'd been planning to show the slave one of the Ricalani texts Barranecour had collected, hoping it would tempt him to accept her offer. She doubted he would be able to make out the words in his current state but as she shifted the bag around she felt the lumpy tangle of stones and leather harness she'd had Alameda construct. The girl would be disappointed if she didn't get the chance to find out if the device acted as they'd hoped. 'Don't you have some supplies of your own, Torren?'

'You want me to waste them on a slave who's likely to die anyway?'

'Just give him a dose. If it lifts the fever and the pain enough to make him lucid I'll see if he can read enough to be useful to me. If you sign him over to me I'll pay for the physician myself if I have to — but I want him for a translator, Torren.'

'I can't, Delphi,' Torren said. 'Presarius assigned him to me.'

'Because he knew he was likely to die! Presarius wants to knock you down a peg. How do you know he hasn't set you up for this? Of course he won't survive if you keep treating him like this. Even a slave needs something to live for and you've set it up so he has nothing. Pass him over to me and then when you come to interrogate him he'll be so afraid of being pulled out of his comfortable position you won't even have to rough him up. He'll be happy to cooperate.'

Torren snorted. 'He's a warrior, Delphi, or at least, he was. Not some milksop coward of a priest.'

'He was, Torren, but he's not now. Pain changes a man. I know, I saw it happen to my father. In any case, what do you stand to lose? He'll die if you do nothing.'

Torren stared at the trampled snow for a long moment and then cursed. 'Demons take the wretched boy. Alright, Delphi, have it your way. Come to my tent and I'll mix the dose myself. If we leave it to that lazy cow of mine she'll either spill it all or poison him in the process.'

He was too harsh on the girl, but Delphine had to admit she wouldn't trust Torren's slave with anything important either. There were fresh bruises on the girl's sullen face and behind her master's back she watched him with thinly disguised hatred. Delphine told herself it didn't mean he had earned that look. The bruises could have come from an accident after all, and the fact that she'd been taken from her kin was enough to justify her hostility. It sickened her to think of any other explanation. Under the law Torren could do whatever he liked to his slave and if she tried to tell him otherwise he would simply laugh in her face. For the sake of peace between them it was better if she pretended not to see.

Once the draught was ready she and Torren gave it to the slave themselves, Delphine tipping it down his throat while Torren clamped hands over his mouth and his nose to keep him from spitting it out or breathing in again until he had swallowed it. Then while the servants brought their evening meal to the service tent for them they sat back to wait for the drugs to take effect.

They wouldn't let him sleep. Now that the pain had retreated, even if it was only a small respite and not the icy numbness that Sierra gave him, all Isidro wanted was to close his eyes and escape this world, but they were always there, poking and prodding him and refusing to let him rest.

In the end, it was the frigid touch of the metal prongs that finally roused him to their satisfaction.

'Go on, Delphine, give him a zap. It's the only thing these savages understand. Don't you know how to use it? Here, give it to me then.'

'By the Good Goddess, Torren, get out of my way! I know what I'm doing, curse you. Just back off and let me do it!'

The woman, Delphine, was kneeling by his head and looking down at him with concern. She held the stinger against his chest, still covered with welts from the last time they had used it on him, but she held it by the shaft and not the handle.

'No, stay awake,' she said, jogging his shoulder when his eyes began to drift closed again. 'I have something to show you. Here, look at this.' She pressed something cold and hard into his good hand. More enchantments, bound into plaques of jade. It was hard to focus, but for one brief moment he thought he sensed the power bound within them. He sensed stillness and calm.

'Alameda made those for you,' Delphine said. 'Can you guess what it does? Here, I'll show you …' She reached for his splinted arm. Isidro would have pulled away but his reactions were sluggish and by the time he'd gathered himself she had one small hand wrapped around his ruined wrist. He lifted his head off the prickling spruce just enough to see her wrapping leather thongs over the bandages and splints. 'All that bumping and jolting on a sled must be unpleasant. Well, these will help. They'll dampen the movement so the bones won't grate every time you hit a bump. Now if you come and work for me I'll let you keep it and I'll give you more poppy when you need it. So what do you say?'

'By all the Gods, Delphi, don't *ask* him, *tell* him. He's a slave, dammit. He'll do as he's told.'

'Torren, shut up. I'm not interested in having to beat the work out of him. Do you understand that, boy? You'll either do as I say willingly or you can go on like this. What's it to be?'

If he went on like this he'd be dead within days. At that moment Isidro wanted it more than he'd wanted anything in his life. He craved that release, craved an end to the pain, the fear and the uncertainty. But if he took that path, then what? Perhaps Cam would be better off without a crippled, tainted brother to worry about and care for, but if he believed that he'd failed Isidro, the prince would spend the rest of his life suffering because of it. And Sierra? Despite what she had said — or perhaps because of it — he wasn't at all certain she would let him die unavenged. And once he was gone, then she would have one less ally to turn to when Rasten came whispering in her ear. Isidro could bear the cost of it to himself, but what of the price to them? Just suppose there was a world beyond this one, as the priests said. Could he bear to watch their suffering, all because he had been too weak to go on? There was no way of knowing what would arise in the weeks and months to come, or what he could do to turn those events in their favour. It was a small hope to be sure, but it was still hope. No matter how much he wanted to escape, he knew that choosing death was the same as abandoning them.

'I'll do it,' he said, burying the shame he felt at the surrender. He was betraying his people to save his kin. 'I'll do what you ask.'

# Chapter 25

Sierra scowled at the cracked and burnt-out stove sitting on the flagstones at the centre of the chamber.

After the argument at the smuggler's camp Ardamon and Mira had decided to retreat to the village of Terundel, where War-Leader Dremman and his men were due to meet up with the second muster of warriors on their march to face the Akharian invaders. The village usually housed only a few hundred souls but had swelled to more than a thousand while they waited for Dremman. When Sierra had asked Mira to find her a place to practise, she had expected to be sent some distance from the village. Instead Mira had arranged for her to have the use of an empty barn, even though it meant shuffling the beasts that had been stabled there among the other households. Since Mira had also stationed a couple of men to see she was not disturbed, it meant she could work in relative privacy.

Given that everything she had tried so far had resulted in complete and utter failure, Sierra was grateful she had been spared an audience.

The ancient stove clinked at her as it cooled.

Sierra jammed her fists against her hips. 'Alright,' she muttered. 'Let's try this again.'

She gathered her power and wrapped it around the hulk of metal, attempting to lift the massive weight of iron off the flagstones. As her power touched it, the stove erupted with Black Sun's Fire, giving off a shimmering veil of light. Miniature bolts of lightning writhed over its surface and quested to the ground around it. The stove had barely had a chance to cool from her last attempt and within seconds it was glowing a bright, cherry red. A few wisps of straw lying on the ground nearby smoked briefly then burst into flames. With a silent snarl Sierra pulled her power back and stamped the flames out with the thick felt sole of her boot. 'Son of a bitch!' she shouted at the stove. 'Why won't you move?'

There was no response but the *clink* of cooling metal.

Sierra raked her hair back from her face and fought the urge to kick Kell's book across the room. She was too tired for this. They had ridden all day to reach Terundel, yet she couldn't bring herself to admit such a simple task had defeated her. If she did, it could only mean that Rasten was right — she did need him to teach her how to master her power.

Just the thought of being back in that place made her sick with panic and terror. It forced her into action and she began to pace, circling the warm and smoky chamber while fine strands of lightning coursed over her skin and through her hair. She had spent whole nights pacing like this, confined in her cell in Kell's dungeons.

What if he was right? That was the question that had plagued her for days now. All her instincts told her to run as far and fast as she could from Kell and hope that he would never find her, but she knew that was no solution. The only way to end it was to kill him. But how could she achieve that, when she couldn't even master a mage's most basic skill? How could she hope to take Isidro back from the Slavers when even the weakest of their mages knew more of the craft than she?

'Right,' Sierra growled at the lump of dull iron. 'One more time.'

Ardamon sat with his head in his hands, a half-empty bottle beside him and a sticky bowl at his elbow. 'Cammarian, I don't think you understand the full impact of the situation. We are doomed. Our clan would have been able to negotiate a way back from this rebellion before all this, but now the only recompense the king will accept is one which includes our heads!'

'I understand that,' Cam said. 'I'm just saying that sitting around and moaning about it isn't going to achieve anything.'

Ardamon lifted his head enough to glower at him. 'If you can see a way out of this, Prince Cammarian, then please enlighten us,' he growled.

'Ardamon, please,' Mira said, covering her eyes with a hand. 'Cam's right, this is getting us nowhere.'

'That's because there's nowhere to go. There is no way out of this situation. We had our chance and we failed miserably. The Black Sun would have done the world a favour if She had taken the wretched girl at birth.'

Mira shook her head. 'That's a bit harsh.'

'Harsh?' Ardamon said as he poured himself another measure of brandy. 'It's the truth! She's a coward! She's nothing but a liability to us and I see no reason to saddle ourselves with her any further.'

'Oh, by the Black Sun, will you listen to yourself? If she says that going on would have been suicide, what reason do we have to doubt her?'

Ardamon glared at her. 'Well, you *have* changed your tune, cousin. You were the one who set men on her trail, remember?'

'I'm aware of that,' Mira said with a toss of her braids. 'It was a hasty decision and one I now regret. But try for a moment to see all of this from her point of view. No doubt the poor girl is absolutely terrified of being sent back to Kell.'

'Well, that's not going to happen,' Ardamon muttered. 'She might be as useless as tits on a bull but she's still too cursed dangerous to be handed back to him. Here, that physician of yours, Rhia, she seems to have a well-stocked store of medicines. Surely she's got something that would knock her out for a few hours and five minutes with a pillow over her face would see her out of our hair for good. History tells us that mages are always more trouble than they're worth.'

'Hold your tongue, you sot,' Mira said, coldly. 'What kind of fool makes the same mistake twice?'

'There is the small matter of the Akharian Raiders,' Cam said. 'Rumour has it they have mages of their own and from what I know of them it's entirely possible. She's our one weapon against them.'

'And what makes you think she'll be any more use against them than she was against Rasten?' Ardamon asked bitterly.

'At the moment perhaps not,' Mira said. 'But in the future? Do you expect a boy to learn all he needs to know about being a warrior by playing with sticks? She needs time.'

'Well then, it's a pity we have none to spare and no one to teach her. And why is that again? Oh, yes, because our ancestors and the Gods themselves decided mages do more harm than good!'

With a sigh, Mira reached across the table to grasp the bottle, and took a swig from it herself. 'The head of the village militia wants to take all the men here and march after them.'

'And what does the fool think he's going to achieve with a few hundred trappers and herders against professional soldiers? Fires Below, we don't have so much as a vague idea of their numbers.'

'I've told them to wait for the war-leader to arrive,' Mira said. 'Uncle was due days ago, so they should be here at any moment.'

'In the meantime there are some preparations we should make,' Cam said. 'I suppose the captain of the militia has posted sentries?'

Mira frowned. 'He said something about nightly patrols —'

'Not good enough,' Cam said. 'If the Akharians raided Drysprings, then they're closer than we thought. We need sentries posted all around the village, far enough out that we'll get some warning before they're on our doorstep. The village folk should sleep with their weapons near at hand and they ought to have gear packed so they can grab it and go if we need to evacuate —'

'Now see here!' Ardamon said. 'I'm in command, not you!'

'You should blasted well have thought of that before you got yourself drunk!' Mira said. She turned to Cam. 'I'll send for the head of the militia so you can tell him what needs to be done. You have far more experience in these matters than I do.'

Room had been found for them in the blacksmith's house, the finest one in the village. The head of the militia was one of the blacksmith's brothers, a burly man with frost-scarred cheeks. He considered himself a loyal subject of the Wolf Clan and didn't take kindly to being given orders by an outsider, especially one with as much Mesentreian blood as Cam. But with Mira standing at his shoulder and nodding her approval of the orders he could not object and grudgingly showed them around the village while Cam organised a roster of sentries.

By the time they returned Ardamon was asleep and snoring in his furs. Mira nudged him with her boot until he rolled over with a snort. 'He's not usually like this,' she whispered to Cam. 'All that's happening is weighing on his mind.'

'On all our minds, I think,' Cam replied.

'Where's Sierra?'

Her furs were laid out but empty. 'She must still be studying,' Cam snapped. 'If she'd put this much effort in *before* we reached the pass …'

'Don't tell me you blame her for this, as well.' She went to lay a hand on his arm but Cam turned away.

'She wouldn't even try. It was our *only* chance to get rid of Rasten and she was too afraid of him to make the attempt.'

'She did say right at the start that she didn't think we would succeed,' Mira said. 'And she knows better than any of us what he's capable of. How can you blame her for acknowledging her limitations? Would you rather have her lead us all to our deaths?'

Cam turned to her. 'What's made you change your mind so drastically?'

'It's what she said when we found the body,' Mira said. 'Rasten wouldn't hesitate to torture one of his own men but she flatly refused to use ours — not that we'd have let her. That and ... some other things. I have misjudged her badly. I just hope she'll forgive me for it.'

Cam grunted and turned way.

'Do you think I'm wrong?'

'No, it's not that. It's just ...' He sighed, and sat on a bench to bury his face in his hands. 'I wanted to be able to tell Isidro that Rasten is dead. After all he gave up for me I wanted to do that one thing for him. It was our only chance, Mira, and it's gone. And now Isidro is too ...'

Mira sat beside him and took his hand. 'We will free him, Cam. I promise —'

'Don't,' he growled. 'Don't make promises you can't keep. He's only a liability to your clan. They won't fight for him.'

'They will,' Mira said. 'I'll make them. I'll find a way to convince them ... I swear by everything I hold dear, I'll find a way.'


It was late when Sierra came back to the chamber with the tome under one arm and a tiny bead of light cupped in her hand to guide her way. She'd fallen asleep rather than admit defeat and had awoken cold and stiff with her head pillowed on her arms beside the book.

When she closed the door behind her one of the lumps beneath the blankets stirred. Sierra quickly shielded her light in her fist but not before she saw the red braids shake free of the fur.

'Sierra?' Mira whispered from across the room. 'Is that you?'

*Fires Below*, Sierra cursed inwardly. 'Yes. Did I wake you? Sorry.'

'Oh, never mind that. I wanted to talk to you.'

Sierra set the book down on her bed and led Mira back into the other room where they wouldn't disturb the men or Mira's servants, who were also curled in their furs. There she created a larger globe of light and fixed it to a nail in the wall so it wouldn't bob and float away.

Mira stared at it, wide eyed.

Sierra cleared her throat. 'So, what do we do now?'

Mira jumped. 'Oh … we'll wait here until Dremman and his men arrive. We don't have enough men to face the Akharians.'

'And what about Rasten?'

Mira shrugged and looked away. 'There's nothing we can do at this point. I wanted to ask you what *you* intend to do now. I realise that I … we … treated you unfairly. I'll extend the truce we agreed indefinitely, but if you wish to leave I'll find a horse and gear for you —'

'Will your cousin consent to any of that?'

'Ardamon? He's just frightened and too proud to admit it. We need a plan. Things will be better when we know what path we're on but I need to know if you're with us or not.'

'I'd rather stay,' Sierra said. 'I want to see Isidro safe again. I don't know what help I'll be — ' She broke off with a whoosh of breath as a sudden spear of pain lanced through her gut.

Mira grabbed her shoulders to keep her from falling to the floor. 'What's wrong? Are you alright?'

Clamping her arms across her belly, Sierra looked down, half expecting to see blood on her hands. She felt for all the world as if she'd been sliced open.

She realised it was an echo of sensation just as something else struck her neck, slicing from ear to collarbone. A moment later, she felt an arrow between her ribs. Her legs buckled and the globe of light fixed to the wall pulsated and flickered with colour until it burned a bright and unnatural blue, giving off miniature bolts of lightning as long as her hand.

Her rising power swept away the echoed sensation, just as Mira reached the door and yanked it open to scream for Cam and Ardamon.

By the time they came running Sierra was back on her feet with power shimmering and singing in her head. 'You posted sentries?' she said to Cam when he appeared in the doorway.

'Yes, we —'

'They're dying,' Sierra said.

# Chapter 26

The village headman and the senior militia men assembled in the main hall of the blacksmith's house to hear Cam's orders. Ardamon, still affected by all he'd had to drink that evening, had turned command over to him. Neither Ardamon's second nor the headman were happy about it, but there was no time to argue.

While the men gathered round, the women of the household were waking the children and bundling them up against the cold as they prepared to take shelter.

'The Akharians have done this many times by now,' Cam said as he buckled himself into his coat-of-scale. 'They'll have a standard set of tactics and they'll follow that unless we give them a reason to do otherwise.'

'How do we know it's the Slavers and not just some band of outlaws?' one of the men called out.

'Charzic doesn't have enough men to risk attacking a village this size,' Cam replied.

'And how can we be certain they're all coming from the same direction?' the blacksmith asked. 'We could be sending the women and children into more danger.'

Cam glanced at Sierra and hesitated.

'Only the sentries to the east are dying,' she said. 'The ones to the west are fine.'

'The best we can hope for now is that they haven't yet faced a village that wasn't taken by surprise, so they won't know what to expect when we fight back,' Cam said. 'Tell your men to leave their whites behind. We will be fighting between the buildings and dark colours will serve us better for camouflage. Our archers and sling-men should be up on the roofs and the walkways by now and they'll be aiming for men in white.'

He called them sling-men but Sierra knew that they would most likely be women and adolescents. Aside from a handful of warriors assigned to guard the children and the women who couldn't fight, everyone else who had any skill with a weapon would be on the ground between the houses, waiting in ambush.

'Go pass these orders on,' Cam said. 'Bar the doors when you leave your homes. We don't want the Slavers taking shelter inside. Gather your people against the end walls of the houses along the village square. We want to stop them there so the arrows and the sling-shots can pick them off. Go quickly. We will have only a few minutes to get in place.'

As the men trooped out Ardamon turned to Mira. 'You head across and take shelter with the others,' he ordered as he settled his helmet in place.

'Fires Below, Ardamon, I can fight better than most of the women who will be standing out there with you!'

'They are not heirs to the clan! You've been trained to defend yourself, Mira, but there's a difference between that and being a warrior,' Ardamon said.

'But you're still drunk!'

'I'm sobering up with every moment,' Ardamon said. 'Now, Sierra —'

'She'll stay with us,' Cam said. 'She can tell us how the battle is going.'

'I can tell you where people are dying,' Sierra said. 'I can't tell you if they are ours or not.'

'Knowing where the fighting is thickest is still useful,' Cam said. 'Put your coat on.'

'It's easier to hold my power in if I'm cold,' Sierra said.

'But you'll stand out,' Cam said. 'If the Akharians have mages of their own, I don't want them singling you out. Wear the coat and carry a spear. You don't have to use it, but you'll blend in.'

Sierra didn't argue. The power pulsing through her was warring with her nerves and humming inside her head, demanding all of her attention. It called to her with a siren song, promising to wash all her cares and fears away in a golden tide. She longed to let it go to quell the anxiety and fear already gripping her, but she was afraid of what else that would bring. Kell had always made sure she was kept well away from any fighting. To date, the largest battle she had been involved in was the one

331

that had killed Garzen and then fewer than a dozen men had died to fuel her power.

Here there were nearly a thousand souls in the village, including all the men who had come to join the Wolf Clan's army, and the Black Sun only knew how many among the attackers. The power pulsing beneath her skin was controllable now but there was no way of knowing what might happen if she was pushed over the edge.

Cam wrapped his coat over the armour and buckled his sword belt on over that. 'Alright then,' he said, pulling his gloves on and working his fingers to settle them in place. 'Let's go.'

They trooped out into the central aisle that separated the dwelling half of the house from the barn on the other side. The non-combatant women and children were just leaving. The older children were silent and frightened but the younger, too little to understand what was going on, squalled and fussed in their bundled furs. With a dark look for her cousin, Mira joined them with her two serving-women and Rhia, who was hefting the pack with her medicines onto her shoulders.

'If the battle goes badly lead them out into the forest to the west,' Cam told Mira. 'They will chase you, but if you scatter some of you will escape.'

Turning pale, Mira nodded and left with the others.

Outside, Sierra could see a stream of people heading to the western side of the village. The only evidence they had that the attack would come from the east was that that was where she had felt the sentries die. If she were wrong then the women and children would be caught in the thick of the fighting

She felt nothing from them now. The last of the sentries had died. With no way of knowing how many men there were or how far away, she felt as though she had been blinded. Her power was throbbing against her skin, spurred on by her unease, and Sierra dreaded what would happen next. If it was fighting her control now, what would happen when the battle began, with people injured and dying all around her?

Cam glanced at her, one eyebrow raised. 'Sirri?'

'Nothing yet.'

He must have read her unease because he beckoned her closer and pointed at the roof of the house opposite. She could just make out a dark shape huddled within the shadows of the chimney. 'The archers have been told to hold off until the Slavers get to this point,' he said, indicating a line from the end of one building to its neighbour. 'They won't be able to fall back without abandoning the attack. There's no shelter for them in there. If they stay close to the wall on one side they'll be in full view of the archers on the next roof. All they can do is try to rush through without being hit. If we can stop them there the archers will be able to rip through them as long as their arrows hold out.'

Sierra nodded. Inter-clan warfare was rare these days but prior to the alliance with Mesentreia it had been common and villages were still laid out with an eye for defence.

This one was built around a cat's-eye lobe of open ground that served as a gathering space and village market in fair weather. The houses were all built along the edges of this open ground with their short sides facing on to it and their long sides parallel. If circumstances allowed, barricades could be built around the outside, but even in a surprise attack the aisles between the houses could be made deadly for any attackers. Of course an assault could come from the narrower end of the village to the north or south, but in that case the villagers could flee from the far end. The attacker would still have to face the danger of archers as the open ground was never more than a bow-shot wide. In order to take the village swiftly the attackers had to attack from the broadest side.

A shuffle and scrape from the roof above startled Sierra so badly she jumped, a quick, jittery ripple of blue sparking and swarming over her skin before she wrenched it back again. The men gathered around her quickly pulled away but Cam stayed where he was and craned his head back to look up at the roof of the building above. A hooded figure was leaning over the edge and waving some signal Sierra couldn't quite make out.

Cam waved back in acknowledgement and the figure withdrew. 'That's it,' Cam murmured. 'They're coming.'

A murmur sprang up around him until Ardamon growled in an undertone, 'Hold your tongues, you mangy dogs! Do you want them to know we're here?' Silence ensued and Sierra heard the soft crunch of snow under approaching feet. She clenched her fists and scrunched her eyes closed, waiting for the first arrow to *thunk* its way into a target. She had waited like this countless times when Kell had a new victim chained to his slab. She felt as if she had spent half her life waiting for the first spark and blossom of pain.

The first shot was a good one. She felt it punch into the centre of her back dead between her shoulderblades and felt the man who had been struck drop to his knees with a strangled cry.

That gargled moan of pain was a signal to the defenders. Shouting defiance, they charged out from their places of concealment and fell upon the attackers, just as the archers and the sling-throwers above let loose their deadly hail.

The initial wave of pain drove Sierra to her knees and for a moment she thought she would pass out. Blackness swelled and overtook her vision and she seemed to be viewing the world through a tunnel while the blood roared and pounded in her ears. She took one deep, shuddering breath and by the time her lungs were full the blackness and the pain had receded, replaced by a shimmering, golden flood of power.

It seemed as though she floated to her feet. With the power singing inside her head she glided out to the middle of the aisle where Cam and the villagers were standing shoulder to shoulder, shields locked together as they braced against the onslaught of men fighting for their lives as arrows and stones rained down around them. The same scene was being staged all along the eastern side of the village. Men were falling all around her, but it seemed utterly unimportant.

Then in the aisle ahead of her a pale green veil of light boiled out of the air to form a shield that stretched from rooftop to rooftop across the aisle, protecting the soldiers below. A strand of light reached out of it to grope along the ice-covered shingles. Sierra heard the sound of scrambling feet and then a scream as one of the sling-throwers was plucked off the roof and hoisted over the aisle in a strand of light.

Suddenly the scene around her snapped back into perspective. These were *her* men and women, *her* archers and sling-throwers. 'The Black Sun take you,' Sierra snarled and pushed her way through the line of defenders.

She felt someone grab for her shoulder but she cast a shield around herself and the hand slipped away as the shield-wall closed behind her. An Akharian soldier was staring at her, his eyes the only part of him visible between the white cowl over his mouth and nose and the knitted cap pulled down to his eyebrows. She saw his eyes widen and then he tried to stab her.

With a flick of her hand she snapped the blade of his sword and then she snapped his neck.

The mage was standing in the very centre of the aisle staring up at the youth he held in a coil of power. He had another shield around him but other than that he paid no attention to anything on the ground, as though he were utterly certain that nothing in this village could threaten him.

That was a mistake.

With a spike of power Sierra shattered his shield and turned her power loose. It swept over him in a furious crackling wave that stabbed through flesh and bone. The shield overhead vanished, evaporating as quickly as it had come and the youth he had held suspended fell and hit the ground with a sickening crack. There was no burst of power from him, though. The boy was already dead. He was no more than fourteen.

There was no hope of reining in her power now. It fed off her fury and her sudden thirst for revenge and slowly tore the mage apart, savouring every drop of the golden flood of power it sent roaring through her.

It was only when the flow stopped that she noticed the men around her. They couldn't penetrate her shield and all she saw was a circle of flailing weapons, glowing blue with Black Sun's fire and trailing minute bolts of lightning. Over their shouts and bellows she thought she heard someone yelling her name.

Cam.

She felt a flash of irritation. He should know that she could take care herself. But he had sworn to look after her, so she would go and show him she was unharmed.

Slavers blocked her way. Sierra prepared to shove her way through them, but she underestimated her own strength. She meant to clear a path but instead she hurled them away from her and slammed them against the stout log walls to either side. She felt the *crunch* of breaking bones and the slicing wounds as men were hurled against the weapons of their comrades. The cries and screams of dying men echoed in her head and another swell of power made her feel as though she could take flight.

The shield wall ahead of her broke open and Cam shoved his way through, grabbing her by the arm and dragging her back to the safe side of the wall. A swarm of light covered them both and the other men shied away from her, but Ardamon bellowed and shouted at them to form up again.

Cam wrenched his hood back. Beneath it his face was pale. 'By all the Gods, Sirri —'

She shrugged his hand away. 'I should help the others.' The fighting had slackened off in this aisle. The attackers had seen her destroy the mage and they must have diverted the men elsewhere while they tried to plan a counter-attack. The men on the other aisles were facing a fiercer battle than here. Over the rooftops she could see the glow of another shield.

Cam saw it too. 'Ardamon has control of the men here. I'll come along in case these folk panic at the sight of you ...' They had gone only a few steps when the glow vanished.

Cam stopped in his tracks. 'What happened? Did they kill him?'

Sierra shook her head. 'No. Only another mage could ... oh, Fires Below ...' Only another mage could kill a mage. The Akharians had seen one of their mages die, therefore they knew there was a mage here in the village.

She hurried back to the aisle where she had killed the man. Perhaps she could do more good by killing foot soldiers. She could kill hundreds of their men while they chased her through the aisles, but without her there to defend the shield-walls against them they would rip through her men just as quickly.

'Sirri, wait!' Cam grabbed for her arm and pulled her back. 'Can you do this? If you couldn't face Rasten ...'

'Even Rasten wouldn't face me in the middle of a battle,' Sierra shouted back. 'You worry about the soldiers. Leave the mages to me.' She felt something stir at the end of the aisle, a prickle of energy that skittered along the edge of her senses. She gathered up her power, now too great to hold in. It covered her in a writhing, flashing veil of lights. When she stepped up to the shield wall again this time they parted to let her through.

A trio of men stood at the far end, heads together and conversing. As she stepped out of the ranks their heads snapped up and as one they cast shields around themselves. She could tell at once that it was a more complex structure than the one that had failed to protect the mage she had killed. There was a lot of power held between them and they felt ... *different.*

336

The only other mages she had had any contact with were Kell and Rasten and their power was tainted by the method they used to raise it. Their energy always felt greasy and unclean but this was as hot and fierce as flame and it felt somehow cleaner. It didn't set her nerves on edge or make her skin crawl the way Kell and his rituals did.

There was a sudden hum in her head and Sierra felt Rasten's awareness settle around her. For a moment her vision was doubled with a view of a dark chamber hung all around with tapestries and hangings, but then he closed his eyes to spare her the distraction. *What are you up to, Little Crow?*

*Akharian mages,* she told him. *What do you know about them?*

*Battle-Mages or civilians?* he said.

*This is a battle, so I'm guessing the former. I've killed one but there are three more I can see here. Is there anything I should know?*

She felt rather than heard him chuckle. *Only that no mage in his right mind would chose to face a Sympath on a battlefield. They don't know what you are, Little Crow. This is going to be fun.*

People were still dying all around. The battle raged on in the other aisles and at the edges of the village as well. This was the only place spared the carnage. Sierra was sure now that these three were the only other mages the Akharians had here. Everywhere else the archers and the sling-throwers were hard at work. All the arrows and stones, the blows and cuts had all run together and melded with the golden hum of power to fill her body with fire. It burned within her in a sensation too harsh to be called pleasurable but wasn't exactly painful, either. It made her want to climb out of her skin, to leave the husk behind and become a being of pure energy.

Then the mages struck. Acting as one they sent a spike of power against her shield. It actually hurt and that surprised her. She felt it as a line of fire across her body, a searing heat, quickly quenched as her power rushed in to shore up her shields. Her power surged with a fierce heat of its own. Between their spear and her defence she could see the struggle in the air between them as the power stained the night sky with a vivid glow, rippling and pulsing like the northern lights.

The power was fighting and thrashing against the controls she placed on it. She could feel it slipping away, like water pouring between her fingers.

Flames were licking along the edge of the buildings to either side of her and water from melting ice dripped and pattered from the eaves. The packed snow beneath her feet shifted, reminding her of the tipping of the ice on the river. All around her little jets of steam erupted from the ground. Elsewhere, wicked spears of ice pierced through the snow, glistening in the firelight.

Her power was fighting to break free and Sierra could feel her control slipping. She felt it tearing at her skin from the inside, fighting like a wild beast caught in a net. The Akharian mages were increasing their attack but she could do nothing to respond, not without setting all this power loose. *Help me!* she cried to Rasten.

*I can't, Little Crow. The beast is out of its cage now and you won't be able to coax it back in until it's sated. If you want those who call themselves your allies to survive, you had best tell them to flee now, before it's too late.*

'Cam!' she screamed, her voice rising like a bird's shriek over the crackling of power and flame.

He pushed his way towards her, battling through the maelstrom of power like a man forcing his way through a storm.

'Cam, you have to sound the retreat!' Sierra said. 'I ... I don't think I can hold it any longer.'

'Sirri —'

'Just do it, Cam!'

'I can't! If we turn tail and run, they'll slaughter us! We're only barely holding our own as it is.'

'If you stay here you'll all die!'

*You need to make a barricade*, Rasten said.

*How?*

*Pull the houses down on top of them.*

Sierra went cold at the thought. The attackers would be trapped under the rubble — injured, not dead, but unable to flee. They would slowly die in a rising storm of power. That spike of power would take her further than she'd ever been before. There was no telling what the consequences would be.

*It won't help. My people will still die.*

*You will have to shield to keep the worst of it off them. You should be able to hold it for a few minutes. If they're quick they'll be able to get away. Most of them will, anyway. It's the only choice you have if you want them to live.*

*And why should I trust you? It would suit your purpose if they all died and left me alone.*

*Perhaps*, Rasten said. *But I'm trying to show you that you can trust me and that's not going to happen if I trick you into killing them. These allies of yours are an annoyance, but the way they're going they'll get themselves killed soon enough, and without any help from me.*

He was right about one thing. She had no other choice. 'Alright,' she said to Cam. 'Get the archers down off the roofs and tell the men to be ready to run. I'm not sure how long I'll be able to give them. Tell the women and children to flee as well.'

He hesitated for just a moment and then nodded. 'It'll take a few moments for the orders to reach everyone. I'll tell you when they're ready.'

Sierra nodded and turned her attention back to the mages as they renewed their attack against her shields. They worried her less than the power she was struggling to contain, which clawed and fought and wrenched at her.

*If you were a mage like them you would be growing weaker by now, not stronger*, Rasten murmured to her. *They're beginning to realise they've strolled into an Akharian mage's worst nightmare.*

Behind her, Cam shouted that the men were ready. Sierra squeezed her eyes shut and sent a silent prayer to the Bright Sun, begging forgiveness for what she was about to do.

Then she loosed the bonds on her power and unleashed all her pent-up fury on the houses strewn along this side of the village.

For a moment there was peace and the sort of relief one felt upon setting down a burden. Sierra felt hands of pure energy take hold of each of those buildings, sturdy constructions of wood and stone and iron, built to last a hundred years or more of the harsh northern winter. Under those insubstantial hands they cracked open like eggs. Setting it loose eased the pain of holding all that power in and she breathed a sigh of release as the wood splintered and tore and the houses toppled down into the aisles, crushing the attackers below.

*Your shield, Sirri, get your shield up!* Rasten barked at her and she had just enough wit and will left to respond before the great tide of power hit her and lifted her up beyond the reach of any care for the physical world. For a moment she felt as though she was dying as the sensation of hundreds of souls with broken bones, twisted limbs and vital organs damaged beyond repair all washed over her. Then in the next instant she was flying as the world around her erupted into an inferno of flame and destruction, a beautiful, terrible vision of light and power that boiled away the ice and snow and consumed everything else that remained, blazing like the birth of a new sun.

And then all that Sierra remembered was the golden song of the power echoing through the night.

# Chapter 27

Cam signalled the men to slow as the Akharian camp loomed ahead of them. It was surrounded by a ditch and wall dug from snow and topped by a palisade of wooden stakes. Beyond it there was no movement in the camp and no sound other than the distant crackle of a fire, the gleam of which he could see over the wall.

'Halt,' Cam ordered. 'I want some volunteers to skirt around the outside and see if there is anything to be seen. But for the love of life stay beyond bow-shot of that wall. If you see any tracks or signs of life report back at once.'

A few of the men and women had whites. They'd had foresight enough to tuck them inside their coats in case they were needed. The darker browns and greys of worn and smoke-cured leather which had camouflaged them in the village made them targets on the barren snow.

'The rest of you form up in a shield wall,' Ardamon bellowed. 'It looks quiet enough, but I wouldn't put it past them to stage a ruse. Stay on your guard.'

It was possible, Cam conceded, but unlikely. The time it had taken the villagers to regroup and then find the Akharian camp was more than enough to allow the Slavers to retreat in some semblance of order. The tracks they had left were littered with the dead and dying, but only the most grievously wounded had been left behind. He had organised a group to check them as they passed for any who could be interrogated.

The village was some way behind them but Cam could see the ground where it had stood when he turned to the west. It was covered by a flickering, seething storm of power just visible over the tops of the trees that stood between the Akharian camp and the village. Flame and lightning seemed to be warring with each other beneath a black and oily pall of smoke. Sheer terror at the sight of it had made them take a longer way around it than they probably needed, but if that meant the Akharians had had more time to retreat, Cam was in no mind to complain.

If they had regrouped he didn't like to consider the fate of this rag-tag militia of hunters and herders against an army of professional soldiers, even one stinging from the defeat they'd taken in the village.

Once they were sure there was no threat awaiting them, he and Ardamon led the men into the abandoned camp. What he saw confirmed that the Akharians had taken heavy casualties and were retreating as fast as they could go. The camp was a shambles. The survivors had taken what they could carry and could not live without and attempted to render the rest unusable. Tents had been cut down and dragged into piles, contents and all, doused with oil and set alight. Stoves that had been heated in preparation for the soldiers' return had been toppled, still hot and sizzling, onto the ice and snow so the brittle iron would crack from the cold. Sleds had been hastily chopped and hacked to render them unusable and sacks of food and other supplies had been slashed open, spilling out onto the snow and splashed with oil and other substances in an attempt to spoil them.

'You lot,' Ardamon roared, indicating a few dozen defenders with a sweep of his arm, 'set up a perimeter. We don't want any more surprises. The rest of you pull those fires apart. Let's see what we can salvage.'

The tents were made from a stout woollen cloth and though the ones on top were scorched badly, the ones beneath were untouched. Some of the supplies were ruined either from the flames or from the oil poured over them but more could be salvaged. 'Looks like they were in too much of a hurry to make a proper job of it,' Cam said to Ardamon.

'I suppose that's one stroke of luck,' Ardamon said. 'I wasn't looking forward to telling these folks that we'd saved their lives only for them to starve to death. I doubt there'll be anything left to recover from the village.' Ardamon shook himself. 'I'll send word back to Mira and the others to make their way here. The Akharians made this camp defensible, so we may as well make use of it. The horses we have had better go back with them, to help carry the wounded.'

It was entirely due to Mira's quick thinking that they had any horses or medicinal supplies, other than what Rhia had carried in her bag. Even before Cam had sent her the message to flee, she had the women ready any horses or oxen in their barns and gather whatever supplies they had, and prepare to turn their herds loose rather than leave them to be captured. The women and children had fled the western half of the village in a much more orderly fashion than the fighters, who had only moments to get clear once Sierra's shields went up.

The next few hours passed in a frenzy of activity as they set up the Akharian tents and lit the stoves to heat them. Even the cracked ones were put to use, and as the survivors trooped up to the Akharian camp the tents were soon crammed with the wounded and those too weak to go without shelter, the elderly and the very young. Mira recruited an army of assistants for Rhia and set a score of them to search the abandoned gear for any medicines they could find. There was none left among the spilled and scattered supplies; but Cam knew that any dedicated soldier would keep a small stock for himself and sure enough, the searcher party soon assembled a cache of cleansers, astringents, clean bandages and medicinal herbs.

Aside from guards posted to watch for any further attack, all those who were able were set to work. Salvaged tents were erected to ease the crowding and give Rhia and her assistants more room to work. While the fighters took on the dangerous task of venturing into the forest to round up whatever animals they could find, as well as seeking out survivors lost during the retreat, the women and children set to salvaging supplies and providing wood and water to the camp.

Cam had no idea of the hour when Mira sought him out and found him at the eastern gate of the camp. Staring out in the direction the Akharians had left, he wondered if they were gone for good or if they had reinforcements nearby and would return with more men and more mages. The warring lights over the village had faded but they still flickered over the trees like a distant storm and he had no idea how long it would be before Sierra returned.

'Cam!' Mira called to him and beckoned him towards the growing row of tents. 'There's some news you should hear.'

He followed her to a tent at the end of a row, away from the cries and moans of the wounded. 'Any word on how many we've lost?'

'So far there are about three hundred unaccounted for, but there are still survivors trickling in,' Mira said. 'Of the wounded, Rhia thinks a dozen or so won't live to this evening, but the rest of them have minor injuries for the most part. Most of the folk who were hurt badly weren't able to make it out of the village before ...' She trailed off and glanced to the west. Perhaps once people would have known how to speak of such things, but the vocabulary had been lost along with the craft of the mages, when Vasant and his followers had died.

He and Mira reached the tent just as Ardamon came out, followed by a grizzled fellow in winter whites who wore the Wolf Clan's colours in the sash binding his coat. Cam was weary enough for it to take him a few moments to realise the man wasn't one of Mira's escorts, but someone he hadn't seen before.

'Cam, this is Hassarec, one of my uncle's trusted men,' Mira said. 'Hassarec, this is Cam.'

Hassarec nodded to him and began to pull his outer gloves on as Ardamon signalled to a boy, who led the man's horse over.

'We thought Dremman and his men must be close,' Mira said. 'It turns out they were only a day's march from us. The sentries saw the light from Sierra's ... well, from the village, and they're heading towards us. Dremman sent some scouts on ahead and some of the men searching for stock ran into them and sent them here.'

'How far away?' Cam asked.

'Commander Dremman should be here by sunrise with a thousand men,' Hassarec said. 'They are travelling light. The rest of the men should arrive by sunset.'

Cam breathed a sigh of relief. As near as he could tell from the size of the camp and the amount of gear left behind, the Akharians had lost fully half their men and perhaps a little more. Nevertheless, the number of men they had left even without reinforcements would still be enough to give their depleted band of defenders trouble, especially without Sierra directly on hand.

'Hassarec's riding back now to report to my uncle about what's happened here,' Mira said.

Cam nodded. 'May the Gods grant you a safe journey.'

'From what I hear there should be no one left in these hills to give me any trouble, my lord,' Hassarec said. He saluted Mira with a gloved fist. 'My lady, my lords, with your leave ...'

Mira nodded her permission and Hassarec wheeled his horse and kicked it towards the gate while the villagers scattered out of his way.

'Was there nothing you wanted to pass on about Sierra?' Mira asked Cam.

'Not through a messenger,' Cam said. 'I would rather speak to Commander Dremman face to face.' Frowning, he turned towards the village. 'I'd better go down there and see if I can find her. It's probably best not to let her walk unprepared into a camp full of strangers.'

'I'll go with you,' Mira said. 'But first have something to eat, Cam. There's fresh bannock and hot tea inside.'

Cam half turned towards the men who were standing a miserable sentry duty at the gate. 'The other men should eat first —'

'Theirs will already be on its way.'

She ushered him into the tent, where two covered bowls, one of tea and one of shredded bannock, were waiting on a salvaged trestle table. As Cam sat down to eat Mira poured herself another bowl of tea and sat across from him. She swept the knitted cap from her head to press her fingers to her temples. Her hands and the sleeves of her jacket were stained with dried blood from where she'd been helping Rhia with the wounded. Her face was smudged with soot and grime and her shoulders slumped with weariness. 'Do you think she's alright?'

'Sierra?'

Mira nodded.

'It's hard to see how any harm could come to her in the middle of all that.'

'What about the village? Will there be anything left?'

Cam shook his head. 'I don't know, Mira. But there's only one way to find out.'

Sierra stood on scorched and blackened rubble, unable to tell if she was awake or dreaming. The golden song of the power still hummed and chimed in her head, but it was in the background now, not filling and overwhelming her as it had before.

There was no snow, but her breath misted in the air. She didn't feel cold, even though she seemed to have lost her coat and her gloves. The ground had been blasted back to bare earth and there were patches where even that had melted to an opaque black glass, which crazed and shattered when it cooled, leaving edges as sharp as one of Rasten's knives.

Of the houses that had stood in the village, very little remained. The stone foundations were blackened and cracked and the stove-walls that had marked the heart of each house had toppled, leaving behind, if anything, only a few spindly fragments of what had been massive and sturdy structures. Everything else was gone.

All Sierra could remember following that ecstatic release was a hazy vision of beauty and wonder, of brilliant lights and shifting colours. While the entrancing song of power filled her mind it never once occurred to her that her vision was an inferno of destruction. It seemed impossible that she was the one who had turned this place into such a strange and barren wasteland. Once her power faded enough to let her think clearly she felt ill at the thought of how many had died here — not just died — destroyed completely, leaving no trace of their existence. There were no bones lying on the blasted earth, only dozens of strange milk-white nodules littering the ground, hard like stone but warm to the touch.

Nothing else moved in this strange, blasted landscape, but Sierra could see snow in the distance marking a crisp, defining line between the ruined village and the world beyond. Cam and the others would be waiting out there somewhere, or so she hoped. If Rasten had lied to her ... No, that was too terrible to think about. Perhaps it had been foolish of her to trust him, but she'd had no one else to turn to. Soon she would have to venture out to find them, but not just yet. There would be wounded and though her power was winding down she couldn't trust it not to spring up again with fresh blood to feed it.

In the end, Cam found her. She heard him calling her name as she was lying on a fallen portion of wall studded with white crystals like a constellation of stars. 'Over here, Cam,' she called to him and sat up, giving off a shower of blue sparks.

When he found her, she was surprised to see he was not alone. Mira was at his side, staring wide-eyed at the ruin all around her.

Sierra suddenly didn't know what to say. She stared at them for a moment, bundled up in their heavy furs while she stood there, wearing soft indoor clothes in which anyone else would have frozen to death by now. 'Um ...' Sierra said, feeling foolish beyond words. 'Is everyone alright?'

'There are some wounded, but Rhia's seeing to them,' Cam said. 'The Akharians abandoned their camp and fled so we've taken it over. We've got shelter and enough supplies to keep us for a little while.'

'I have your pack, too,' Mira chimed in. 'One of my women grabbed it when we sounded the evacuation.'

'Oh,' Sierra said, surprised. 'Thank you.' She'd assumed her gear was gone, and the wretched book and Kell's enchantments along with it. Now she wasn't sure if she was relieved or disappointed. 'Do you have any water?'

Mira unbuckled a water-skin she was carrying beneath her coat and passed it over.

'Dremman and his men are finally here,' Cam said as Sierra drank greedily. 'They were close enough to see something was happening and they're marching through the night to reach us. According to their scouts they're not far away. Are you ready to head back to the camp? We can go and find a coat for you first if you need it.'

Sierra shook her head. 'I can manage 'til we get there. I don't know what happened to mine. I looked but I couldn't find it.'

'I'm sure we'll be able to find you a spare,' Mira said.

They spoke of small things as Cam led the way back, although later Sierra couldn't remember what. The power, which still filled her mind with its languorous hum, seemed to chase all other thoughts from her head.

At the edge of the blasted land, the snow was piled up in a huge drift encircling the village: a blast of great force had thrown it there. Cam had brought an extra pair of snowshoes for her; they trudged back along the path and Sierra felt her head clear as the cold began to assert itself and the energy she still held was diverted to keeping her warm.

They reached the camp just as a long line of horsemen emerged from the trees at a canter. 'By the Black Sun, they made good time,' Cam said as he squinted through the gloom. 'But that's a good deal fewer than a thousand men.'

'Just an advance party,' Mira agreed. 'They must have split again when Hassarec reached them to pass on the news.'

As they reached the gate one of the men hailed her as Lady Mirasada and the line halted to let them pass through. Close up Sierra could see that each of the men wore a sash in the Wolf Clan's colours and the horse-gear was all stamped with their emblem. Cam and Mira flanked her as they entered the camp and Sierra saw heads turn to follow her as she passed by. A sudden flash of nerves saw her power rise and Sierra didn't bother to quell it, letting the blue sparks spill and writhe over her skin. She could feel the wounded nearby feeding her power with every heartbeat, and after the events of this night she didn't care to speculate on what might happen if she tried to suppress it again.

By the time they reached the centre of the camp, Ardamon was waiting for them alongside a powerfully built man with thick black hair and a close-cropped beard, both streaked with grey. His eyes flickered over Sierra before he turned to Mira. 'Mirasada.'

'Uncle,' Mira said and bowed.

'And Cammarian. Every time I see you, boy, you look more like your mother.'

'Sir.' Cam made him a bow but from the stiffness of his posture Sierra could tell he wasn't pleased.

'Hmph,' Dremman said. 'I suppose I shouldn't call a man of your years "boy".'

'Just Cam will do, sir, if you don't mind.'

'Good to see you don't take after Valeria in temperament.'

'I believe I have my foster-father to thank for that, sir.'

'No doubt.' Dremman turned back to Sierra.

She returned his gaze with her hands clasped behind her back. He was a man accustomed to the deference due his rank, she judged, and saw in him the same arrogance that had irritated her in Mira and Ardamon. It reminded her of Kell's supercilious air and the way he expected everyone to fawn and tremble before him.

'And here, at last, is our fugitive sorcerer,' Dremman said. 'Miss Sierra, how do you fare?'

'Well enough, sir,' Sierra said. She didn't want to repeat the same mistakes that had put her and Mira at each other's throats, but she'd be cursed if she would humble herself and beg for shelter. Sierra wasn't sure exactly what it was that had changed Mira's attitude, but she was willing to wager Dremman shared his clan's distrust of anything associated with mage-craft.

'On my authority as war-leader and on behalf of the Wolf Clan, let me welcome you as an honoured guest of my clan, Miss Sierra. I understand this evening has been very taxing for you. While there is much to discuss I see no reason to burden you with it. I'm sure my son can find adequate quarters for you ... You there,' he said, gesturing to a pair of warriors who were awaiting orders off to one side. 'Escort the lady to the lodgings Ardamon selects and make sure she is not disturbed.'

'My lord uncle, it's only thanks to Sierra that we weren't slaughtered or enslaved,' Mira said, but Dremman waved her to silence.

'Do not imagine this is an insult, child,' Dremman said. 'Common folk and soldiers both are a superstitious lot and in our current situation I would not tempt the wrath of the Gods by permitting harm to come to an honoured guest. Until the rest of my men arrive and everyone here understands the situation it would be better for the lady to remain out of sight.'

Sierra felt a chill creep over her flesh as he spoke, but she knew it was pointless to object. Arguing would get her nowhere and flexing her power right now would risk a repeat of what had happened in the village. She wouldn't do that when this camp and its abandoned gear was the only shelter available to those she had made homeless.

'I understand, sir,' she said. 'But I will need my gear brought to me. There are ... certain items in my packs that I took from Kell which would be dangerous if handled incorrectly. You had best advise your people not to meddle with them.'

'I'll see to it, Uncle, if you please,' Mira said.

Dremman nodded with the appearance of magnanimous acceptance, but Sierra couldn't tell if it was genuine or if he had taken her words as a warning.

With a bow Mira hurried away, signalling her serving-women to follow her. Only Cam remained, and as Sierra followed Ardamon away she heard him say through gritted teeth, 'If I may have your permission to withdraw, sir, I'd like to have a quick word with Sierra.'

'I'm glad you recognise that if you wish to remain here you must place yourself under my command, Cammarian,' Dremman said. 'You may have a few moments but return here quickly. There is much to be done.'

Ardamon showed her to an empty tent so newly erected that the floor of salvaged spruce hadn't yet been laid out over the trampled snow.

Cam followed her in, ducking through the flap as the guards took up position outside. 'Sirri, for the love of life, don't do anything hasty —'

'What kind of a fool do you take me for?' Her power snapped as she turned around. A thick worm of light leapt from her shoulder to the ground, shifting restlessly as it hummed through the air. 'The only way to free Isidro is with the help of the Wolf Clan and their men. Do you think I'd endanger that?'

'After this night I'm not sure what you'll do. Fires Below, Sirri, each time you loose your power it's bigger than the last. Will it keep growing like this, escalating each time?'

Sierra looked away. 'I don't know. I didn't expect it to happen like that.'

There was silence for a long moment, broken at last as Mira came in carrying Sierra's pack. 'I brought it myself so you can be sure everything is there. I've set my women to finding a new coat for you and rounding up some things to make this place more comfortable. I'll see what I can do to make sure we sleep here too, so you don't have to spend all your time alone ...'

'Thank you,' Sierra said. 'And can you get a message to Rhia? Tell her I'll help with the wounded if she wants.'

'I will, and I'll work on Uncle, too. It might take a few days, though ...' Looking harried, Mira ducked out again.

'So you're not upset about this?' Cam said to her.

'I wouldn't say that, but I *am* tired and I could use a few hours' rest. And although I may not have demonstrated it particularly well, I do know how to bide my time. This is all a game, but I'm prepared to play along with it for now.'

'Alright then,' Cam said, hooking his thumbs into his sash. 'I'll do what I can to keep you informed of what's going on.'

'Thank you.'

Mira was true to her word — within half an hour her women had the tent set up with a stove, hot water, a basic kitchen kit and bedding. They also brought lanterns but Sierra didn't bother to light them. Once they had left she created a light of her own and pulled out two of the white stones she'd collected while wandering the ruined village. She rattled them in her palm and wished she had Isidro's sensitivity to the delicate network of power that made up an enchantment. Her own power was too crude and heavy a tool for such fine work, but she was certain these stones had some affinity for power.

*Rasten?* she said, casting the thought out into the air.

He was there instantly in a flood of relief. *Sierra! I've been waiting for you to call me again. What happened?*

*Oh, we won. The Akharians who survived it fled. Now Dremman is here.*

He gave the psychic equivalent of an indrawn breath. *You want to watch out for that one,* Rasten said. *He's as mercenary as they come.*

*I can handle him,* she said. *There was something else I wanted to talk to you about. A while ago you said that you would teach me how to use my power.*

*Yes,* he said.

Sierra stared at the plain walls of the tent. It smelled of men and sweat. She had a new fur hanging from the ridge-pole to air. It still smelled of its last owner, one of the men who had died. It was the only place a spare could have come from after the village burned.

Dremman wouldn't want to keep her around, not once he'd seen what she could do if pushed into action. The question was, would he sell her back to Kell or would he dream up some other fate for her?

*When can we begin?* she asked.

*Whenever you wish.*

# Chapter 28

*Six weeks later*

Isidro was reaching for the flap of the tent when he heard a girl's voice sound from within in a cry of surprise.

'Tigers take him,' he muttered in Ricalani and dropped the bag he was carrying to unhook the mage-lantern from the tip of the ridge-pole. Holding it in front of him he ducked through the opening. 'What's going on here?' he said in Akharian, doing his best to suppress his Ricalani accent and mimic Harwin's manner of speech.

One of the teamsters had cornered Lucia against the back of the tent, where she had been laying down an armful of spruce for the tent floor.

The mage-lantern was brighter than any candle or oil-lamp. As the light streamed over him the teamster flinched and paused in the act of untying his sash. He turned with wide eyes and then narrowed them again when he saw it was a slave who had interrupted him and not the girl's owner.

In his moment of inattention Lucia tried to dodge past him but the teamster grabbed her arm and hauled her back. He was short like most Akharians, but he was used to loading and unloading sleds and dealing with baulky oxen day in and day out. One gangly fifteen-year-old was no match for him.

'The girl has work to do, sir,' Isidro said. 'As do you, I'm sure.'

Lucia scowled and shifted her stance. She was in perfect range to knee the teamster in the balls, but if she struck a free man Harwin would have no choice but to have her flogged. Technically the teamster had no right to lay hands on another man's property, but if he claimed innocence the testimony of two slaves would be worthless against him.

The teamster fumbled in his sash and pulled out a coin, which he flipped in Isidro's direction. 'This is none of your business, boy. Go find something else to do for a few minutes.'

The coin landed at his feet. Isidro ignored it. He hooked the lantern to the chain already hanging from the ridge-pole and swept the tent flap back.

He had intended it only so that anyone passing by would be able to see in and maybe act as witnesses if Lucia did shove his balls into his belly for him. Instead he pulled the flap open to reveal Delphine striding up to the tent. She hesitated for a moment, then narrowed her eyes and strode in. 'Get away from him, Lucia, you don't know where he's been. And as for you,' she said, fixing her gaze on the teamster, 'if you damage Professor Harwin's slave he'll take the value of her out of your salary. Now come with me. There's a trunk of books I need brought into the tent.'

Glowering, the teamster shoved Lucia away, sending her sprawling onto the pile of spruce. Isidro stepped out of the way before the teamster could blunder into him and jolt his broken arm. 'Don't forget your coin, sir,' he said and, red-faced, the man stooped to snatch it up.

'I believe you are familiar with my tent,' Delphine told him. 'My students will tell you which trunk we require.' She watched him go and once he was out of earshot turned to Lucia with a shake of her head. 'Are you hurt, girl? No? Well then I suppose there's no harm done. If this keeps up your master's going to have to find you a chastity belt.'

'That teamster's been sniffing around her for days, madame,' Isidro said.

'Has he? I'll mention it to Harwin. If he makes a complaint he might be able to get the wretched fellow reassigned. Here, Aleksar, tell Professor Harwin I will bring my girls here for dinner so we can make an early start on the evening's work. There's a lot that must be done before we reach Milksprings.'

Aleksar was the slave-name she had given him. 'Yes, madame,' he said. She gave him a narrow look and left before he could work out if she was amused by his courtesy or suspicious of it.

Once she was gone Lucia sniffed and wiped her face on her sleeve.

'Are you alright?' Isidro asked.

Lucia just shrugged. 'I had worse in the slave camps before Harwin picked me out. It's better now that you're around all the time. I'd best get those stakes in to hold the stove, but then will you help me carry it in?'

353

With only one good hand he was of limited help to her in setting up the tent but since she had to do all the work on her own before he came, Lucia was happy for any help at all.

'I've been hearing tales about you,' she told him in an undertone as they settled the heavy stove onto the three green-wood stakes she had driven into the snow.

'Oh?' he said.

'The women who brought the wood told me,' Lucia said. The camp needed a phenomenal amount of fuel and the Akharians usually gave the task of cutting it to women with young children or nurselings, who they believed were less likely to try to escape or to turn the axes against their captors. 'They said you were bedding a sorcerer back at Drysprings.'

Isidro held his breath, listening for the sound of boots in the snow outside. Since they were alone and no one was here to forbid it, they were speaking in Ricalani, but that was no guarantee of safety.

'Folk have been saying she's the one who drove that legion off,' Lucia said. 'I told 'em you said it was the Bloodletter's Apprentice, but they just laughed and said I should ask you about her.'

'This is a dangerous topic of conversation, Lucia,' Isidro said. 'Did anyone hear you talking about this? There must have been guards watching them.'

'Oh, we were talking Ricalani. They can't understand us.'

'Are you sure of that? You know Harwin and Delphine have picked up a bit of our language. What makes you think the other men haven't done the same?'

Lucia frowned. 'B-but the other women weren't worried about that —'

'Then they're fools,' Isidro said. 'Do you have any idea what the Slavers would do if they thought there was another mage in Ricalan and we had information about her?' He ran a hand over his splinted arm. 'I thought you would have seen enough of torture to learn some caution.'

Lucia's eyes widened. 'So it's true, then?'

'That's not what I said. Fires Below, Lucia, what do you think they would do to a girl like you if they thought you had information they wanted? This is too dangerous for idle gossip, do you understand?'

'That's what one of the women said. But then someone else said you were a traitor. She said we should tell the guards about you and that other mage to punish you for being a turncoat. The other women told her to keep her mouth shut and if the other mage could kill half a legion

354

she might be able to help us — and it wasn't worth the risk to punish you. They said I should ask you about it.'

'Tell them this,' Isidro said. 'If there is another mage out there who might help us, then the most important thing we can do is keep the Akharians from finding out about her. And by the Black Sun, tell them to cursed well stop talking about it or sooner or later someone will sell the information to the Akharians for an extra fur or a crust of bread.'

The girl nodded, eyes as wide as saucers.

Of course it might not help at all. If the Akharians found out about Sierra and that Isidro had information about her, things would get very ugly. They would do anything to make him talk and Rasten would do anything to keep him silent. It was the only situation Isidro could imagine in which he and Rasten would have the same goal.

'If there is another mage ... she'll need Vasant's books, won't she?' Lucia said. 'But the Akharians are going to find them first. Everyone is saying so.'

'Maybe,' Isidro said. 'We won't know until we get to Well-of-Poisons.'

Harwin returned just as they were bringing in the last of the gear and once he heard the tale he insisted on examining Lucia's arm himself, though there was nothing more than a fading red mark where the teamster had grabbed her. Harwin treated his slaves with the same fond indulgence he would show a pet and, although he was a perfectionist who insisted that everything be done to his minute specifications, the worst punishment he delivered was an extensive rant of invective that was beyond Lucia's limited grasp of Akharian. Harwin had no interest in sharing his furs with women, an orientation considered scandalous at best and criminal at worst. He had chosen Lucia as much for a decoy as for a servant, but most of the men in the camp knew this was the case.

Delphine had told Isidro all this when she'd brought him to the Collegium quarter on the night he had agreed to be her translator. Delphine couldn't accommodate him herself. She shared her tent with her two young students and a slave-girl of her own and housing a male slave was simply out of the question. Since the black pall of despair still overtook him at times she refused to leave him unsupervised in one of the Collegium's storage tents and had talked Harwin into watching over him instead. She had warned him of Harwin's preferences, only to reassure him that Harwin was not the sort to force himself on anyone.

That was the first evidence Isidro had seen of Delphine's keen powers of observation. Isidro knew he couldn't defend himself against a mage, even one as soft and mild as Harwin, and he couldn't predict how he would react if someone tried to use him as Rasten had. Just thinking about it threatened to bring the memories back and overwhelm him with a helpless fury and despair.

Delphine and her two students arrived for the evening meal, making the tent bright and cosy with the warmth of many bodies. Along with bright and sunny Alameda, there was dark-haired and studious Fontaine, who had made it her task to improve Isidro's Akharian. Lucia knew how to make herself agreeable and served them all with bows and smiles before dishing up food for herself and Isidro and joining him in the slaves' place in the draught by the door. Once the meal was eaten, she busied herself with cleaning up, while the rest of them got to work.

Translating was a tedious business. Isidro didn't speak Akharian well enough to transcribe directly from Ricalani. Instead he translated it into Mesentreian which, thanks to Cam and his father, he spoke like a mother tongue. Then Delphine's students translated from Mesentreian to Akharian, before she or Harwin went through it with him to compare the new text with the original and make sure the translation was accurate.

The texts he was translating were the books and records the Akharian mage, Caltoreas Barranecour, had collected during the War of the Mages, as well as the various texts and chronicles the Akharians had captured in temple raids. The latter had proved as fruitless as Isidro had predicted when Delphine explained she wanted him to search for any mention of Vasant or the other Ricalani mages. The history books had all been expunged of any flattering mention of mage-craft following Leandra's victory. Only her version of events had been recorded in Ricalan, but Barranecour's records held more information. It was a fascinating glimpse of history for Isidro, who had only ever heard the official account, but there was little there that Delphine hadn't already gleaned from other sources.

Isidro was just settling down with Delphine to go through the latest translation when someone rang the bell that hung from the ridge-pole outside to allow visitors to announce themselves. Lucia bounced to her feet to unlace the door flap and bowed deeply as the visitor stooped to enter. Isidro's stomach lurched at the flash of red uniform and the close-cropped hair customary among the Battle-Mages. He knew who it was even before he saw the man's face — Delphine's cousin, Torren.

'Delphi, I need your slave for the evening,' Torren said, brushing snow from his shoulders and onto the spruce floor.

Delphine closed her waxed tablet with a snap. 'Torren, we've talked about this. I have work to do, too, you know. I would appreciate a little notice.'

'And I've given it to you when I can, but this is important. It's about the legion that was wiped out in the south.'

Delphine sighed and fluffed her dark curls. 'Oh, very well then, but try not to keep him out all night. The general says we'll be at the temple within a week and I have a lot to do before then.' To Isidro, she said, 'Get your coat.'

'Yes, madame.'

Torren waited impatiently while Isidro pulled on his fur, his mittens and his boots, then snapped the manacle of a slave-chain around his wrist, blindfolded him and led him out into the cold.

The metal was warm and it hummed faintly against his skin. That was an invention of Alameda's, who was skilled with enchantments despite her youth. She'd invented it after one of these trips had frozen the metal to his skin, and Torren, too impatient to let it warm and come loose on its own, had simply pulled it free and taken a layer of skin with it. Now at least he didn't risk frostbite every time the Battle-Mages wished to question him.

He was allowed some limited freedoms in the Collegium quarter but he was never taken out of the academics' little enclave without being masked. The Akharians were still very much aware of the fact that Rasten could invade his mind at any time and use him to spy on them. In this way, information such as the layout of the Akharian camp and the number of their troops was hidden from him.

The interrogations had slackened after the first week or so of his enslavement, but had begun all over again following the rout in the south. They always began the same way, with the mage collecting him from Harwin's tent, then leading him on a disorienting and chilling march through the camp. In the early days that alone had left him exhausted and in pain, but the good food and rest Delphine had promised had let him regain some strength and the enchantments Alameda had made finally let the shattered bones begin to heal, even if the harsher interrogations periodically set him back. He still moved cautiously, but one bad step was no longer enough to bring him to a faint. Physically he was the strongest he'd been since the duke had captured him in the village.

He recognised the atmosphere of the interrogation tent the moment they led him through the door. It was warmer within and heady with the smell of spruce and smoke. When rough hands shoved him to the floor he was ready for it, and fought to keep himself from tensing as they stripped his coat from him and bound his hands behind his back again, wrapping the ropes over the splints and stones that supported his broken arm. It was always the same, and familiarity had given him the means to deal with the powerlessness and the fear. When they hauled him up onto his knees Isidro already felt as though he was watching all this from some remote point, a detached and dispassionate observer.

Torren gazed down at him, pulling on a pair of fine leather gloves. There was a brazier in the tent that gave just enough heat to keep hypothermia at bay, while still leaving the air chilled enough to be uncomfortable.

Torren wasn't a true sadist — this was only a job to him. He would carry it out to the best of his abilities but he didn't savour the task as others might, or spend the hours in between thinking of new and varied tactics to increase his pleasure in these moments. Isidro supposed it was something to be grateful for, but it disturbed him that he had become such a connoisseur of sadism.

'I have received new information from the survivors of the Seventh Legion,' Torren said. 'Let me ask you this again, boy. How many Blood-Mages are there in Ricalan?'

'Two that I know of, sir,' Isidro said. 'Kell and his apprentice, Rasten.'

'And you're sure of this?'

'I can only speak of my own experience, sir, but in that respect yes, I'm sure.'

'How then do you explain the fact that survivors of the massacre of the Seventh Legion have reported seeing another mage, a female, before the inferno struck?'

He had been waiting for this. 'Sir, in a village under attack anyone capable of taking up arms would have been fighting, women among them. Perhaps they were confused as to what they saw.'

'Are you saying these men lied?'

'No, sir. They must have been mistaken. Kell does not permit other mages to exist in Ricalan outside of his control.'

'You have heard nothing of a female mage in Ricalan?'

'No, sir,' Isidro said.

'No rumours, no whispered tales?'

'No, sir.' It was a gamble to deny it entirely. For all he knew one of the slaves had already sold the information, or their whisperings had been overheard by one of their guards. But if he so much as admitted the possibility, his captors would press him for more information. Outright denial was safer than making up some story.

'Then what explanation do you have for what our men saw?'

'As I said, sir, they must have been mistaken,' Isidro said.

Torren struck him across the face with the back of his hand. 'Don't you dare insult your masters! You halfwit natives wouldn't know a mage if she had you by the balls, but Akharian men know one when they see one. No mage capable of something like that would be able to pass herself off as a normal person. You have heard something about her, I know it, and we will get it out of you. Who was behind that massacre?'

'It had to be Lord Rasten, sir. It's the only explanation.'

'Horseshit.' Torren gestured to a pair of aides who waited silently beside the brazier. 'String him to the ridge-pole,' he said and turned to a table set along one of the walls. He pulled back a cloth to reveal a two-foot rod with a leather-wrapped handle at one end and two metal prongs at the other. The Stinger.

Isidro closed his eyes and murmured a silent prayer to the Black Sun. Perhaps it would have been better to come up with some story, but it was too late now. He had made his denial and he had to stick with it. Admitting to anything else would be the crack they needed to break him.

His shirt was damp and clammy by the time the aides stepped back, leaving him with his wrists bound to the pole overhead and stretched so that only the tips of his toes touched the floor. He flinched as the icy metal of the prongs brushed against his prickling skin.

'Well, boy?'

'There's nothing more I can tell you, sir.'

'Well, we'll soon see about that, won't we?'

It was hours later when Torren delivered him back to Harwin's tent, numb with cold and stumbling with exhaustion.

Delphine's students had long gone back to their tent, presumably, but Delphine was perched on the edge of the bed while Harwin lounged in the leather-slung chair. Both of them were drinking bowls of hot tea.

Torren shoved Isidro to the floor before unfastening his manacles and then stood over him, slapping the chain against the hem of his coat in irritation.

'Well, Torren, I hope you got something useful out of him,' Delphine said. 'He'll be no good at all to me for the next few days.'

'Watch your tongue, Delphi! I've half a mind to take him back to the storage tents and see if a few days of cold and hunger will loosen his tongue.'

'This is about that business with the Seventh, isn't it, Mage-Captain Castalior?' Harwin said. 'What makes you so sure he knows anything about it? Surely it could have been a natural mage. Statistically, there must be some folk among the natives with enough power to be able to use it even without formal training.'

'There were four Battle-Mages with the Seventh,' Torren said. 'I knew them all. I even trained with one of them. No unschooled mage could kill four Akharian Battle-Mages. No, that bitch has to be a Blood-Mage. And this wretch — ' he gave Isidro a kick to the ribs '— still insists this man Kell and his apprentice are the only Blood-Mages in Ricalan.'

'Well, maybe that's all he knows,' Harwin said. 'I can't see the slave taking any risks to protect the ones who crippled him.'

'You know, Torren, there is another possibility,' Delphine said. 'This other mage could be a Sympath.'

'Don't even joke about that, Delphi!' Torren snapped. 'And as for you,' he said to Isidro. 'I know you're holding out on me. When I get proof, I'll make you wish you were back with the Blood-Mages. You hear me?' With another kick and a curse he slung the slave-chain over his shoulder and strode out into the night.

With a sigh Delphine drained her bowl and handed it to Lucia. 'Take this, girl, and help him get cleaned up and bedded down for the night.' She frowned down at Isidro, who was still on his knees, too weak and shaky to stand just yet. 'He's going to keep this up until you find something to tell him, you know.'

'Yes, madame?' he said.

She recognised it for the useless platitude it was and scowled at him.

'Are you sure you haven't heard anything? No gossip or rumours? It will go easier on you if you find something to tell him.'

Behind her, Lucia looked stricken.

'Perhaps, madame, but then he would want to know who I heard it from. How could I subject someone else to that? The survivors from the Seventh must be mistaken. Kell would never tolerate a rival mage in Ricalan. There must be some other explanation.'

Delphine just sighed and reached for her coat. 'You are too cursed high-minded for your own good, Aleksar. Harwin, I'm turning in. See you in the morning.'

When she left, Harwin waited for Lucia to lace the doors closed again before he ordered Isidro to open his shirt and show him the damage. He winced at the welts the Stinger had left and rummaged in a trunk for a pot of salve. 'Here, this will soothe them. I'll mix you a sleeping draught, too. I know you always sleep poorly on nights like this …'

That was putting it mildly. Even though the interrogations left him exhausted, Isidro knew from experience he wouldn't be able to sleep without waking hourly from nightmares of being back in Kell's domain. Harwin knew all about it — he was woken by them, too, and often roused Isidro himself, seeming so concerned Isidro wondered what noises he made before he broke free of the visions. 'If you don't mind, sir, I'd rather sit up and try to get some work done. Perhaps I'll sleep better on the sled tomorrow.'

'If you wish,' Harwin said with a shrug.

Before he retired, Harwin locked a manacle around Isidro's good wrist. It tethered him to a few feet of chain that was padlocked to a trunk full of books. On some nights he was given a little more freedom but after these sessions with Torren, Harwin always made sure he was in no position to do himself harm.

While Lucia settled down in her post by the stove, Isidro reached for the book he had been working on, the page marked with a leather thong bearing the fat round bead of a lantern-stone. He hung the cord around his neck, took the stone in his fist and activated the enchantment with a moment of concentration. Between Rasten and the other mages who continued their strange experiments on an irregular basis, he had been prey to odd fluctuations of power until Delphine had taught him the basics of controlling them. As a side-effect he'd gained enough skill to activate the small enchantments the mages used on a daily basis. The lantern-bead was no bigger than the first joint of his thumb but it gave enough light to let him read and write. With his back to Harwin to hide the light, Isidro opened the book on his lap but simply sat there for a while, gazing at the page without reading a line.

*When I get proof,* Torren had said.

The interrogations were a strain both physically and mentally, but he could handle them for now. He knew what to expect and he knew he could withstand it. But if Torren found hard evidence that Isidro was lying to him then the game would be stepped up. They had wrung enough information out of him to tell them how to break him down if they had reason to do so. He was useful to Delphine and the academic mages but not valuable enough to be spared harsher methods. Even if they wanted to, Delphine and Harwin could not protect him.

'Can you explain something for me, madame?' Isidro said. 'What is a Sympath?'

Delphine gazed down at him from the saddle, her lips pursed thoughtfully. 'Where did you hear that term? Oh, of course, the other night ...'

'I've come across it in books, too, madame, but I've found no explanation for the word.'

It had taken him a day or so to recover from the latest interrogation. The Stinger left no marks other than the welts that still stung on his chest, but it left him feeling as though he'd been beaten with sticks. At first he had been left incapacitated for days afterwards, but since Delphine had offered him her patronage, his health and his strength had been steadily improving. He could now spend all day on his feet and keep up with the pace of the march, although Delphine made sure there was a sled available for him if he needed to rest. Most wondrous of all, his arm was finally healing.

Once a week, Alameda examined it with that peculiar device that could see through flesh and bandages to the bones beneath, and sketched the changes under Delphine's guidance. It confirmed he would never have use of the arm or the hand, as the bones were healing ragged and crooked, but at last the pain was diminishing.

Sometimes Isidro slept on the march, wrapped in furs and riding on a sled if he had worked through the night before, but the return of his strength was such a welcome sensation that he savoured the activity and the weariness it brought. Delphine often had him walk beside her, leading her pony or carrying her lantern while they travelled in the dark. As the Akharians reckoned these things, entrusting him with the responsibility was a mark of her favour.

'Well,' Delphine said, 'there are several classes of mages. The first are ones like yourself, Sensitives, born with a modicum of talent. If they are identified young enough and trained with rigour they can become competent low-level mages. This level of talent is tolerable in slaves, as without training their power tends to atrophy and they are essentially harmless. Once trained to competence they are generally employed in the more menial divisions of mage-craft, mostly charging mage-lights for the emperor's household and the administration and for anyone else wealthy enough to keep a mage on retainer. Generally, when one speaks of mages it is not this class we are referring to, but the ones above them.

'The next class are those we call "born into power", although that is something of a misnomer. The talent usually manifests sometime between the child's fifth year and the time they reach puberty, although it can happen earlier — this indicates a very powerful mage. Like Sensitives, these mages are born with an internal store of power, but they also have an instinctive knowledge of how to cultivate this power, how to keep it from leaking away and how to replenish it once used. Some scholars have posited that the only difference between Sensitives and those born into power is the possession of this instinctive knowledge. This level of ability cannot be tolerated in slaves, as they will inevitably pose a danger to their masters and to society as a whole.

'There are grades of ability within this classification but it is demonstrably possible for a born mage of the lowest capacity to progress through the ranks to the highest level, given enough discipline and work. A Sensitive, however, can never progress higher than the lowest few ranks. It is only the born mages who are powerful enough to become Battle-Mages, but technically they are a different class again. There are not that many mages who can shut out the chaos and confusion of a battle well enough to retain the calm and focus necessary to control their power and be useful on a battlefield. Mages who do not enter the military have the choice of either entering the Collegium as scholars, or entering private or public industry. Either way, all mages trained by the Collegium are required to spend a certain amount of time each year in the service of the empire, to repay the debt incurred by their extensive training.'

'I've heard of this, madame,' Isidro said. 'I must be confused. It seems as though mages are treated as slaves of the empire.'

Delphine sighed. 'There are some who hold such views, but it is a ridiculous notion. Mages cannot be bought and sold. We have the right to marry, to hold property and enter into contracts, even to vote, should the occasion arise. If anything the arrangement is more akin to a tax than to slavery. And here,' she glared at him from under her hood, then looked away, 'you have drawn me off topic.'

'My apologies, madame.'

'Oh, hush,' she said and gave him a sidelong glance. In trying to adopt what the Akharians thought the proper demeanour for a slave, Isidro had drawn upon his father's teachings of courtly manner and appropriate conduct around one's superiors. So far it had stood him in good stead, but Delphine seemed to be always suspicious he was mocking her. 'Now, where was I? Ah, yes. Sympaths. While born mages have an instinctive knowledge of how to generate and raise their power, Sympaths have an innate ability so strong they can't help but gather power. In some ways it's something of a deformity. Any characteristic, even a desirable one, can be taken to such extremes that it becomes a liability. Sympaths are capable of deriving power from the world around them in such vast quantities they are physically incapable of holding it in. They often cause general havoc until they are identified and brought under control.'

'Control, madame?' Isidro said.

'Oh, it's not as ominous as it sounds. Sympaths are immensely valuable to the empire. Large works — bridges, dams, aqueducts and the like — can be built in a matter of weeks with a Sympath providing the raw power for their construction. If built by hand, they can take years or even decades. An ordinary mage can assist but they are still limited by the rate at which they can generate power. A Sympath, however, removes that constraint from the equation. There seems to be no real limit on the amount of power a Sympath can generate. The constraining factor appears to be simply the level of energy of the participants.'

'Participants?' Isidro said. 'I'm afraid I don't understand.'

Delphine laughed in a puff of mist. 'In Akhara this is considered a most indelicate subject. Certainly not fit for discussion between a mistress and her slave. But I doubt you native folk would see it the same way, given your marriage traditions. Sympaths feed off sensation. They generate power from sexual energy and activity. In Akhara they have a residence attached to the Collegium. To us it is the House of the Sympaths, but everyone just calls it The Palace. It's a den of licentiousness and fornication — quite endearingly so, actually — given over to the pleasures of the flesh. There are generally several hundred inhabitants whose only duties are to eat good food, to give and receive innumerable forms of pampering and to participate in ... other various activities. It's all perfectly scandalous, you realise. Everyone in polite society pretends to be quite horrified by it all, while they secretly wish they could join in, if just for a little while.'

Trudging through the snow beside Delphine's pony, Isidro tried to imagine such a place — tried to imagine Sierra at its heart — and simply could not understand how such a place could work. 'Are the participants slaves, madame?'

'Actually, no. Most people imagine it as simply a glorified brothel, but that's very far from the truth. Most of the girls in a brothel *are* slaves. They never chose to be there and that would be utterly intolerable in The Palace. Sympaths feed off pleasure but they are exquisitely sensitive to pain. If any of the participants were not enjoying it or didn't want to be there, the Sympaths would sense it. Not only would they be unable to draw any power from it, but the sensation of suffering is damaging to them. Sympaths are far too valuable to allow anything of the sort to happen, so participants are screened very carefully before they are admitted. Some of them are slaves of course, and participants with a modicum of talent are often preferred, but they are never forced to enter or to remain and are often granted their freedom in return for service.'

'It must cost a fortune ...' Isidro mused.

'Oh, it does, but it's worth the price to have a constant supply of power. The Sympaths can travel with a suitable entourage to provide power on hand for major construction outside of Akhara.

'Other than supplying power, they are quite limited. No Sympath has ever become a great mage. Power comes to them so easily they never have to learn the discipline necessary to hone their skills. A Sympath is a little like the queen of an ant nest — essential to the survival of the colony but ultimately helpless on her own and dependent on others to care for her and supply her needs.'

Isidro bowed his head, staring at his feet as he trudged on so that Delphine couldn't read his thoughts in his face. This news simply did not add up with what he already knew. 'So ... a Sympath can *only* feed from pleasurable sensation?'

'That's correct.'

'But ... I'm certain I've read of Sympaths being stalked by Blood-Mages, and the other night, madame, you suggested a Sympath might have been involved in the rout of the Seventh. How is that possible?'

'It is possible for a Sympath to be ... corrupted,' Delphine admitted. 'That's one of the reasons why unenthusiastic participants at The Palace are evicted. As I said, prolonged exposure to suffering is damaging to a Sympath. We believe Sympaths are very rare, but it's possible there are more of them born than we realise and it's just that some of them are, well, crippled by early exposure to pain and suffering. They experience an echo of the sensations that feed them power, so in these cases many of them simply shut down their talent entirely and are left with no more power than an ordinary person.

'Unfortunately, that isn't always the case. The power brings a certain pleasure of its own and for some that's enough to outweigh the echo of pain. If corrupted thoroughly enough a Sympath can lose the ability to derive power from pleasure all together. Or perhaps they simply choose not to. There's a limit to how long a body can experience mind-numbing pleasure, after all, but there are no such limits on how long a man can be kept in pain, as you have experienced for yourself.'

'So a corrupted Sympath is a Blood-Mage, madame?'

'Not quite. What Blood-Mages do with their rituals is an attempt to do artificially what Sympaths — corrupted Sympaths, I mean — do naturally. Given the opportunity, a Blood-Mage will enslave a Sympath to boost his or her own power. It is difficult to achieve, as a Sympath will usually close off his or her power in self-defence, but if they do manage it the Blood-Mage is well-nigh unstoppable. Sympaths will likely never gain enough control of their power to challenge and kill their masters. If that happened it would be a disaster of epic proportions, but realistically? I think it highly unlikely in a nation as primitive as this for a Sympath to survive with his powers intact for long enough to be captured by a Blood-Mage.'

Delphine shifted in her saddle. It was considered beneath the dignity of a mage and a member of the elite to walk like a slave or a servant, but Isidro knew from experience she would be cold from inactivity and he didn't envy her the privilege. 'Why all the questions?' she asked. 'Have you even heard of a Sympath other than that night?'

He had an answer ready for her. 'There was a mention of a Sympath in one of the texts Barranecour collected. Apparently there was a Sympath in Ricalan prior to the War of the Mages. One of the factions had a Blood-Mage and it seems he set out to capture the Sympath, but she committed suicide rather than be enslaved.'

'Ah, yes. I read of that in one of Barranecour's translations. It seems to be something of a tradition among your folk,' Delphine said dryly. 'But there you have a classic example of the class. Sympaths are quite incapable of defending themselves. Barranecour noted his intention to offer the woman shelter in Akhara, but he was unable to get word to her in time. To be honest it strikes me as unlikely she would have accepted, given the information she would have had about the empire. The point you raised earlier is one that many have raised before, Aleksar. There are folk who find the service required to repay their education onerous and who choose exile instead. It requires a certain kind of personality to make such a choice, and the tales the Ricalani mages would have heard of the empire and how it treats its mages undoubtedly had a rather skewed perspective. I have no doubt the Ricalani mages viewed the exiles as troublemakers, likely with good reason.'

'Yes, madame.'

Isidro had now been a slave for longer than the span of time between his rescue from the king's men and the morning Cam and the others had left him behind in Drysprings to heal. It struck him as a supreme irony that in that time he'd learned more about Ricalani mage-craft and the war that had destroyed it than he had learned in all his previous quarter-century of years. Every Ricalani child knew the story of Well-of-Poisons, but now Isidro had read the contemporary accounts compiled by Barranecour in the log that had brought the Akharians here to the north in search of Vasant's treasure.

Milksprings was a hot spring housed in a system of caves carved from the rock by millennia of flowing water. Like all hot springs it was considered a sacred place and became a temple, named for the colour of the water. For centuries it was renowned as an oracle and a place of healing.

That had all changed in the early days of the War, following the first battle Queen Leandra had led to avenge the death of her daughter. One faction of mages, led jointly by a Ricalani woman named Sofera and an Akharian exile, Delcarion, had swept in and taken control of the temple, driving out or killing the priests who lived there. The temple was in the lands of the Marten Clan, but Sofera and Delcarion declared the surrounding land now belonged to Milksprings and claimed the folk living there as serfs. When the clan objected, the mages simply slaughtered them.

Taking control of Milksprings had been a measured decision. The caves were unbreachable, especially when defended by mages. Leandra had realised this at once and turned her attention to other factions without wasting her men. Instead she set about cultivating allies among the folk who were now beholden to the temple and was eventually able to place an agent within Milksprings itself, supplied with a quantity of poison.

On the night of a celebratory feast attended by most of the mages under Sofera and Delcarion's command, Leandra's agent spread the poison into everything he could reach, the food, the wine, even the springs itself. Nearly every mage in the temple was struck down, along with many of the slaves and servants. The poison was a slow-acting one, however; and once they realised they were dying Delcarian went on a rampage, killing serfs and servants he blamed for the betrayal, while Sofera wrung the story from Leandra's spy.

Leandra and her followers rode in a few days later to find the caves full of the rotting dead. They hauled the bodies out and burned them, except for the few mages who had survived the initial dose and were too weak to leave the caves or to fight back. Leandra had them chained within sight of food and clean water and then filled in the entrance of the caves with rubble, leaving them to starve in the darkness and the silence. Afterwards, it was known throughout Ricalan as Well-of-Poisons.

The history Isidro had been taught described Vasant as the greatest villain of them all, a mastermind who tricked the other mage factions into fighting Leandra and her allies while he himself sought some means to escape his doom. The reality, he discovered from Barranecour's records, was quite different.

For most of the war Leandra had barely been aware of Vasant's existence. He had been part of a small school of mages devoted to scholarship and seemed to have no interest in politics at all, until the situation grew so severe he was forced to acknowledge it. While Sofera and Delcarion lay dying, Vasant was already gathering the books and records Leandra's followers had set out to destroy. A few months after Leandra's men filled in the entrance to Milksprings, Vasant and his followers opened it again, and spent months sequestered there while they came up with a plan to preserve the knowledge Leandra and her allies were so determined to destroy.

The version of history Isidro had been taught said Vasant had tried to escape Ricalan, but he knew now that this was untrue. Vasant had had the opportunity to leave. He'd certainly been aware Barranecour was in Ricalan and would have known that a life of comfortable exile in Akhara was his for the taking, but Vasant had chosen to stay, even though it would mean his death.

For all their power, mages could no more survive alone in those days than they could now. Life in Ricalan depended on other people and Leandra had slowly but inexorably turned the common folk against the sorcerers. The actions of Sofera and Delcarion were held up as just one example of the demands and depredations mages made against the common folk, who were helpless to resist them.

After leaving Well-of-Poisons Vasant and his followers set out for the other great sanctuary of the north, the place now known as Demon's Spire. He had spent so long here in the caves there was no doubt he had left some form of treasure there. Even Barranecour had been certain of it.

After Vasant fell, Leandra searched the caves. Isidro had always been told she found the books and destroyed them, but then she could hardly admit the Last Great Mage had defeated her from the afterlife. Afterwards she sealed the caves up again with rubble and rock. Why would she have done that if the books had been found?

In all the weeks since he had agreed to help Delphine as the price of his sanity and his life, Isidro wasn't sure just what he hoped to find. Though Delphine was pleased to finally have a translator, he hadn't yet provided them with anything of value. He could still decide that aiding the enemies of his nation was too high a price to pay. He could perhaps still escape this situation with his honour intact, but that choice would be beyond his reach once they found the mouth of the caves.

The Akharians didn't know precisely where Milksprings was located. They had started out with Barranecour's century-old map, scrawled in a page of his notebook and based on information gleaned from various guides and informants. Once in Ricalan, temple raids had given them native-drawn maps, but they were difficult for foreigners to interpret. Rivers and watercourses shifted from year to year and were of dubious value as landmarks, so instead Ricalani mapmakers relied heavily on cliffs, hills and outcrops.

Still, the maps gave the Akharians a rough idea of where to look. Under the general's orders a camp was established near the base of the long ridge of cliff face said to hold the caves, and teams of Collegium scholars and Battle-Mages set out to begin the search.

All the records said Leandra had taken pains to conceal the entrance to the caves and at this time of year it would be hidden under snow. Isidro was mystified as to how the Akharians would find it without waiting for the thaw, until Alameda mentioned a device that was being carried along the top of the cliff with a rota of mages to power it, which could apparently sense the open space of a cave beneath. When the search began, Harwin and Delphine and her students were part of that rota, and spent so many hours at their duties that they returned to the camp only to eat and sleep.

For Isidro it meant days of waiting in Harwin's tent with nothing but the books to distract him. When Delphine or Harwin were there to supervise him, he was often left unchained, but with both of them absent

Delphine locked the manacle around his wrist early each morning and set Lucia to watch over him until they returned. She and Harwin never directly spoke of his attempt to kill himself, but the healing scar on his neck was all the reminder they needed. Lucia had never dared ask him about it, but Isidro sometimes caught her studying it when she thought he couldn't see.

In preparation for their long absence, Delphine had also gone through his meagre assortment of gear to make sure he hadn't acquired anything he could use to harm himself. There was pitifully little of it in the sack that now held all his worldly possessions. He had a set of bedding and a change of clothing, which Lucia laundered along with her master's garments. Delphine had given him a leather satchel so he could carry things while still leaving his one good hand free and in it there was a motley assortment of waxed tablets and a handful of battered old styluses for writing in the wax.

She had taken one of those away: a slender rod of a very hard and fine-grained wood, which Isidro had to concede could be used as a weapon in a pinch. Of the rest of the odds and ends that had been bestowed upon him by his masters, the only thing of any value was the lantern-stone strung on a leather cord he wore around his neck and, as no slave was permitted to own a magical device, it technically still belonged to Delphine.

In her master's absence and without the daily work of striking and setting up the tent, Lucia saw this time as a chance to rest. Once her daily chores of washing and cooking were completed she had nothing to do with her time but eat and doze in the warmth of the stove. After the first half-day of being imprisoned in the tent had passed, Isidro envied her the escape.

Since agreeing to serve Delphine he had thrown himself into the work with a vigour bordering on obsession. Perhaps in part it was a response to feeling so powerless, but he had set himself the task of learning all he could about the Akharian mages and their craft, as well as piecing together the true history of Vasant and the War of the Mages. If he was ever able to see Cam and Sierra again, the knowledge he was able to assemble now might be the most valuable thing he could offer them. It became his driving force and he would work until his vision grew too blurred to focus on the letters.

When he could work no more he practised the exercises Delphine had set him. The Akharian mages were still puzzled by his peculiar reaction to power, but it seemed the strange experiments they performed on him didn't produce the results they had expected — they lost interest in him after a week or so of those exhausting sessions. Delphine was the only one still curious about him; she had set him the same training exercises that were given to novice mages to teach them how to raise and focus their power.

So far the drills had taught him only one thing: the trick of activating the enchantments the mages used in their lanterns. This puzzled Delphine, as he shouldn't have been able to do it without first mastering the basics, and she ordered him to practice the meditations and visualisations for an hour each day. Isidro willingly complied in the hope that one day he would be able to make contact with Sierra, when he did have information valuable enough to pass on.

For two days he applied himself to the tasks, but on the third he fell back into the black pall of despair welling up around him. When he read the same page of the book three times without taking in a word of it, he set the text aside and lay back on his furs. Instead of emptying his mind to begin the first of the meditations, he simply stared at the roof and wondered what sort of life awaited him if Sierra and Cam could find no way to free him and he was taken back to Akhara with the rest of the slaves.

He was idly studying the ridge-pole and wondering if it would take his weight when the sound of boots crunching in the snow outside brought him out of his thoughts and back to the present. Someone was approaching the tent.

His first thought was of the teamster, come to harass Lucia again now there was no one here to prevent it, but he soon realised these steps were too light and quick.

There was a pause as the person stooped to pull the cord that freed the lacing and then shouldered her way into the tent. It was Delphine, with a dusting of snow clinging to her shoulders and her hood. When she straightened she looked him over with a narrow eye as Isidro forced himself to sit up and he wondered if she could read his black mood on his face. If she did, she didn't mention it.

'Alright, my lad,' she said as she pulled off her mittens and her gloves. 'On your feet. Give me your hand. The Gods must be smiling on you today. We've found Milksprings and there's something there I want you to see.'

For the sake of speed he was allowed to ride to the temple, although one of the soldiers who had escorted Delphine back to the camp held the reins and led his horse. Delphine studiously ignored him, but he was used to that. With only Harwin and her students as witnesses, she permitted a certain degree of familiarity, but around strangers she spoke to him no more than was necessary and with a distinct and chilly formality. By now, Isidro knew enough of Akharian society to understand why. No one cared what a man did with his slaves, but for a woman the same degree of intimacy was not just scandalous, but criminal. If the wrong impression was given, Isidro was certain the consequences would be bad for both of them, so he remained silent.

The weather was worsening and the soldiers led them through a pall of driving snow that limited visibility to within a few hundred feet. Once they were beyond the perimeter of the camp Isidro surreptitiously glanced behind, trying to get a rough idea of how many men were under the general's command but the soldier leading his horse growled a warning to keep his eyes ahead. He needn't have bothered. The camp was already lost to the weather and Isidro couldn't make out any more than a portion of it.

The snow also hid the cave and it wasn't until they were nearly on top of it that Isidro realised they had arrived. A dark scar of rubble and earth excavated from within had been dumped to stain the slope below the jagged crevice of the cave mouth, but already a scatter of snow was covering it. Once there must have been a proper path leading up to the entrance but now there was just a switchback track trampled into the snow, its twists and turns marked with mage-lights and flags of red cloth.

As the soldiers led the horses away to a rough windbreak that sheltered them and the men watching over them, Delphine beckoned Isidro with an imperious gesture. 'Attend, Aleksar,' she said and started up the slope without looking around to see if he followed.

Even with his improved condition the path was still a challenge for him. It was steep and narrow, threatening to crumble at the edges, and had been trampled by so many feet that the packed surface offered no grip to the felt soles of his boots. A rope strung between the marker posts tempted him with a hand-hold, but he had no way of knowing how deep the posts had been sunk and whether it would hold his weight. Delphine took pity on him and paused at each of the turns to give him a chance to rest, while pretending it was she who needed to catch her breath.

When they reached the cave entrance at the top of the path Isidro paused to look out over the valley, shrouded beneath a thick haze of snow. Vasant had stood here, as had Cam's ancestor, Leandra the Great; as had Sofera and Delcarion and countless others from a world that was now lost.

'Come along,' Delphine scolded him, but she entered the cave slowly, giving him a chance to absorb the sight.

When clear the passage would have been wide enough to lead four horses abreast, although the edges of it were still choked with rubble. From outside the mouth of the cave appeared to be a natural feature, but within a few lengths the interior seemed more like a man-made structure than anything carved by nature. The natural caves Isidro had seen never conformed so conveniently to man's dimensions. They were usually low and wide, more easily traversed on hands and knees than on two feet, and with floors that were a jumble of rock fallen from the cavern roof. This passage had a high ceiling and was more square in cross-section than oval. The walls were suspiciously smooth and upright, but it was the floor that was the least natural. It had been smoothed flat, then etched with a crosshatch of grooves that would give grip to smooth-soled boots, though these were currently filled in with grit and windblown snow.

'The first thirty paces of this passage was filled with rock and rubble,' Delphine informed him. 'Some of the rocks were as big as an ox and they'd been fitted together like a stone wall. It must have taken months to fill it in without power to speed the work.'

And yet the Akharian mages had cleared it in less than half a day.

The days were growing longer as the seasons shifted towards spring, but the heavy clouds outside had turned the daylight dim and within twenty paces of the entrance the passage was as dark as night. Delphine pulled her lantern out of her satchel and set it glowing and Isidro did the same with the tiny lantern-stone he wore around his neck. The stone cast a pale yellow light around him, enough to let him avoid the cobbles and rocks still littering the floor.

Thirty paces past the entrance the passage was clear as Delphine had said, except for a wooden trunk shoved against one wall. The wood was damp and crusted with what Isidro took at first glance to be salt, but something had been painted onto the lid and was still visible beneath the crust — a few lines of Ricalani script.

'This is why I brought you here,' Delphine said. 'What does it say?'

'"Searcher, here is what you seek,"' Isidro said. '"Vasant's books are gone to ashes. Here is all that remains." There's a name underneath it — "Leandra, first of that name, Queen of all the North."' He turned to Delphine. 'What's inside, madame?'

'Take a look,' she said, standing back with her arms folded across her chest.

Isidro knelt down to lift the lid. The wood was soft and spongy under his hands. The air inside the caves was different, moist and humid. Before the blockage had been cleared and allowed the dry air of winter to mix in from outside it must have been even more so. The trunk had been made from one of the species of wood that resisted rot, but even so it was slowly decaying.

The trunk was full of blackened and corroded shards of metal. Isidro lifted one out and held it up to the light. It was a thin shaft of green and crumbling bronze. He could make out the remains of decorative scrollwork and an oval fitting that would hold a cabochon stone. This one held nothing in the setting but others had the cracked and chalky remains of stones, which crumbled to powder at a touch; some of them bore flecks of gold amid the corroded metal. They had been the sort of metal fittings that would be affixed to the covers of valuable books and from the looks of it some had borne enchantments as well.

'They burned them,' Isidro said.

'Or at least that's what they wanted us to think,' Delphine said. 'Why would they close off the caves if they knew the books had been burned?'

The unnaturally smooth and regular passage curved away from them into the rock. 'This passage is mage-crafted,' Isidro said. 'Leandra wouldn't have wanted future generations to speculate on what else mages could do.' He turned the corroded fitting over in his hand and then placed it back with the others. 'Even his enemies said Vasant was a brilliant man.'

'So how could he have been stupid enough to leave his treasures where people of no talent at all would be able to find and destroy them?'

'A decoy?' Isidro said. There were soldiers standing guard at the entrance huddled in furs as they stood around a brazier. Delphine paid them no mind. She was too absorbed now to care what observers might think. There were men deeper in the caves, too. Their voices echoed along the passage, too diffuse to be understood but undoubtedly there. The Akharians hadn't come all this way to be so easily discouraged.

'I imagine a queen would be able to read Ricalani script,' Delphine said. 'Or her retainers could, if she was illiterate.'

'A member of a ruling clan would know how to read,' Isidro said.

'So she wouldn't have been fooled if Vasant had put the covers on other books,' Delphine said.

'Not necessarily,' Isidro said, thinking of the book Sierra had stolen from Kell. 'Maybe there were enchantments locking them shut.'

'Ah,' Delphine said, with a faint smile. 'Perhaps. Or perhaps the queen felt it was all too easy. Vasant could have concealed the books where none but another mage would have been able to find them. She must have been suspicious that she was able to get hold of them so easily. But she left the remains here anyway, to discourage anyone who did make it through that wall.'

The voices in the passage were heading their way. Isidro gazed hungrily into the darkness. He wanted desperately to explore this place, but he knew it was now a privilege beyond his station.

Harwin appeared around the curve of the passage holding his lantern high and raised his free hand in greeting when he saw them. 'Delphi, you're back. Good. They've found another one and they're about to try and open it.'

'Another one, sir?' Isidro said.

'We've found chambers hidden behind the walls,' Delphine said. 'If Vasant was as clever as they say he must have been smart enough not to put all his eggs in one basket. We may as well go and watch, but I'm not sure what we'll find. The air in here is so damp I hate to imagine what state a book would be in after five years, let alone a hundred.'

'Madame, aren't there enchantments that can be used to prevent mould?'

'By drying the air, you mean? There are, but they only last for a few days at most before needing to be renewed. Even if the Ricalani mages had some other technique I can't imagine it would be so far ahead of ours that it could go without maintenance for a century. The cold would help preserve them, but unless they're frozen solid this dampness would have reduced them to pulp by now ...'

The air was growing more humid as she led him deeper, insulated from the cold outside. It was likely the hot spring never froze over and constantly fed steam into the air trapped in the caves. Isidro tried to put himself in Vasant's place and imagine his reasoning behind using these caves, when both of his enemies knew he'd spent so much time here. Surely he would have been better off concealing the books elsewhere?

But where in Ricalan could one possibly leave something so fragile and vulnerable to the elements?

Despite the thick blanket of snow and ice covering the land, winter was the driest time in Ricalan. The spring thaw brought floods and the summer brought rain. Folk had such a struggle keeping the things they used every day free of mould and mildew that winter cold and snow were something of a relief. Perhaps this was simply the best Vasant could come up with in the time he had.

So, Vasant left books here for Leandra to find and let her believe she had destroyed the treasure. But she wasn't the only one he expected to seek this place out — if he'd known of Barranecour then he had to have suspected the Akharians would be back one day. If he had left a decoy here to mislead Leandra, then surely he would have done the same for the imperial mages. Or perhaps something more than just a diversion, given that they intended to steal away the legacy he had left for his own people.

Isidro stopped in his tracks. 'By the Black Sun, it's the bait in a trap.'

Harwin and Delphine both turned to him. 'What did you say?' Delphine said.

For a moment Isidro froze with indecision and cursed himself for speaking without thinking. The Akharians considered it the duty of a slave to protect his masters from harm, but given time to think about it Isidro doubted he would go to any effort to keep his captors from harm.

But here he had done just that and blurted it out without a thought. The very fact that he had done such a thing suggested he was beginning to think of his captors as comrades. That realisation filled him with a sudden loathing and disgust. He was a traitor.

'A trap?' Delphine said. 'What do you mean?'

The words had been said and there was no calling them back. 'Vasant knew people would come to search for the books. He left some for Leandra to find and he knew Barranecour meant to seek them out. Perhaps he left a decoy for your people as well?'

'What sort of decoy?' Harwin said. 'He intended those books to be preserved. He wanted them to be found. There's no point hiding them otherwise.'

'Preserved, yes, but for Ricalani mages,' Isidro said. 'Vasant knew Barranecour would give him refuge and he chose to stay and die instead. He must have known the Akharians would be back. He didn't go to all this effort just to have the spoils taken by Slavers.'

Delphine frowned with a haughty lift of her chin. Isidro knew he had strayed perilously close to insolence but thankfully she was more concerned with his disclosure than his impertinence. 'What sort of trap? How could he be sure it would be Akharians who set it off and not a fledgling Ricalani mage?'

Before he could reply Isidro felt a pulse of power ripple through his body. Harwin and Delphine felt it too. They turned to the north and Harwin frowned while Delphine hissed a curse.

'They were about to open one of them when I came to find you, Delphi,' Harwin said.

'By the Good Goddess! We need to stop them until we can investigate this more thoroughly!'

She turned to the deeper reaches of the cave and broke into a run with Harwin on her heels, but they had gone only a few paces when another deep thrum of power reverberated through and around them.

To Isidro it felt like being inside a bell when it was struck. The power filled his head and overwhelmed his mind and senses. His thoughts scattered like leaves in the wind; it sent a pulse of energy along his nerves ending in a burst of sensation that echoed back through him like, and yet completely unlike, one of Sierra's shocks.

Isidro stumbled and fell to his knees with bruising force. The lantern-stone around his neck flared like a falling star then died, along with the mages' lanterns. For a moment they were in total and utter darkness, darker even than the most clouded night.

In the passage ahead a light flared in the darkness. It began as a blossom of flame but within the space of a heartbeat it swelled and burst into a great jet of fire. It roared along the passage towards them, and through the ruddy light Isidro glimpsed dark shapes at its heart. Men cowered away from the flames, and the blast lifted them from their feet and hurled them against the walls. Amid the great roar of flame and power he heard human screams cut short at the moment of impact.

The jet of flame seemed to bounce off the stone. Channelled by the cave walls, it cascaded towards them, as fast as a waterfall. Dazed by the power still echoing around his skull, Isidro could do nothing but watch, but the mages were quicker to act. Delphine and Harwin each cast a hasty shield across the tunnel.

The jet of flame slammed against it with an impact that shook the rock around them. The shields bowed like a sheet in the wind. The mages, strained and grimacing with the effort, held them steady, pouring all their power into it.

Then the flame vanished as quickly as it had come. Harwin let the shield drop and slumped against the preternaturally smooth wall, groping for a handhold that didn't exist, as he slid in an ungainly heap to the floor. Delphine merely folded where she stood, crumpling limp and exhausted. They were both gasping as though they had been winded, but as the last of the shield evaporated Isidro could no longer see them. The cave had once again been plunged into absolute darkness.

'Light!' Delphine croaked. 'Where is that Gods-be-damned lantern?'

In the passage ahead of them someone was coughing and choking and a low voice lifted in a ragged call for help.

Isidro felt for the cord around his neck and groped along it to the lantern-stone at the end. The bead always felt slick and warm with the fluttering tickle of power like the beat of a moth's wings against his palm. Now it seemed dry and dead and left a fine film of powder on his hand.

'Aleksar!' Delphine demanded. 'Where's your lantern-stone?'

'It's dead, madame,' he said. There was no sense of enchantment within the stone. He tried to activate it anyway, in case he was mistaken, but reaching for it was like reaching for something that wasn't there. He was flailing in empty space.

There was a stream of green-gold light off to his left. Harwin had created a globe of light like the ones Sierra often used, cupping it between his hands with shafts of light streaming through his fingers. A pall of dust and smoke hung in the air, and there was a revolting, sickly scent that Isidro found all too familiar. He pressed his hand over his mouth, fighting the urge to gag and retch. It was the smell of burning skin and hair. It took him back to Kell's tent with Rasten standing over him with the hot poker reeking from the scorched skin of Isidro's back.

In the passage up ahead, someone began to scream.

It only made his memories worse. Isidro turned away and tried to focus on something, anything to convince himself of the reality of the present and let him drive away the past. But his heart was pounding against his ribs and his throat was so tight he could hardly breathe.

'Here,' he heard Harwin say from somewhere very far away. 'What's wrong with the slave?' He felt a hand on his shoulder and tensed as the healed scars on his back throbbed in sympathy. 'Are you alright, man?'

'Leave him be, Harwin. He is in shock. That blast probably rattled him like dice in a cup. Here, let's move him out of the way.' Together, they manoeuvred him to the edge of the passage, against the wall. Delphine crouched down to peer into his face. 'Stay here,' she ordered him. 'Do not move until I return, or I'll tan your hide. Do you understand me?'

He thought he tried to nod but he couldn't be certain. A moment later Harwin and Delphine were gone, heading into the deeper regions of the cave to give what help they could to the wounded.

An age seemed to pass before Isidro was able to force those memories down and anchor himself firmly in the present, leaving him shaken, drained and exhausted. He wasn't sure if he should be ashamed he had frozen up so badly in a crisis, or relieved he hadn't been forced to help save the lives of the people who had enslaved him. He hadn't felt this useless since he was a stripling boy who had just learned of his father's death. Would it always be like this when small sensations could overwhelm him and sweep him back into those awful days? If so, then Rasten had crippled him twice over.

Isidro waited for some hours while others dealt with the crisis. He watched in silence as the wounded and the dead were ferried out on makeshift stretchers. The ordinary soldiers had been defenceless against the blast unless they happened to be close to a mage who was able to shield them. A few mages who hadn't been as quick or as focussed as Delphine and Harwin had failed to protect even themselves. Isidro heard later one Battle-Mage had died, probably knocked unconscious by the initial blast before he succumbed to the flames.

When Delphine finally returned for him she was drawn and weary and beckoned him to his feet with an exhausted flap of her hand. Isidro was chilled and stiff, so drained that a wave of dizziness swept over him when he struggled to his feet.

'You were right,' she said. 'It was a trap. A cursed vicious trap. We'll be leaving the place under guard tonight and in the morning the academics will be working with the Battle-Mages to disarm the others. It looks like there could be as many as four or five of them scattered through these caves. Maybe more.' She frowned, wrapping a strand of dark hair thoughtfully around her finger. 'Are they all traps, do you think?'

'I couldn't say, madame.'

'There were books in there. Now they're nothing but ash. I tried to find some fragments but they crumble the moment you touch them. Do ... do you think Vasant meant to destroy all of them rather than let them fall into the Slavers' hands? Isn't that what you call us Akharians?'

He was too weary to play games with words. 'Yes, madame.'

'Hmm. Well, you will likely be coming back here with us in the morning. If *any* of these caches were meant to be found by Ricalani mages you might be able to sense the difference between them and the traps.'

Isidro dozed in the saddle as they rode back to the camp only to dream of heat and flames and wake with a start that made his horse baulk and toss its head.

At the edge of the camp Delphine dismounted and handed the reins over to one of the men escorting them. 'Thank you, soldier. I will manage the slave on my own from here,' she said as Isidro carefully slipped down to the snow.

'Pardon me, madame, but didn't anyone tell you?' the soldier said. 'Mage-Captain Castalior wants to see you and the slave both. He has ordered us to bring you to him as soon as you returned to the camp.'

'Oh, by all the Gods, can't it wait?'

'Sorry, madame, but those are our orders. This way, if you please.'

A knot grew in Isidro's belly as the soldier led them through the neat and orderly rows of tents to the Battle-Mages' quarter. His nerves were already frayed and he wasn't sure he had the strength to face this on top of everything else.

The tent the soldiers brought them to was the one Torren usually used for the interrogations. The soldier ordered Isidro to kneel and then stood guard over him while a servant was dispatched to find the captain. Delphine paced and fumed at the delay.

When Torren arrived scowling and sombre, Delphine pounced on him. 'Is this really necessary? It has been a long day and the boy is exhausted. I need him tomorrow and I cannot have him shaking and puking all day.'

'This is more important.' Torren had brought a pair of aides with him. He gestured to Isidro and the aides set about the usual preparations for an interrogation, stripping him to the waist and binding his hands, while Delphine watched in shock. While she had seen the aftermath many times, she had never been privy to the process of an interrogation before.

'Torren,' Delphine began with a scowl, but before she could launch on a tirade, Torren shoved a sheaf of papers in her direction.

'Here. Read.'

She snatched the pages from his hand and held them up to the light. After a moment her eyes grew wide and Isidro's heart sank. 'When did you get this?' Delphine demanded.

'The messenger carrying it arrived this afternoon. This wretch has been lying to us from the moment he arrived here.'

'Torren, no. There must be some other explanation. The slave has never given me reason to think him untrustworthy. He has never been the slightest bit of trouble or shown any tendency towards rebellion …'

Torren shook his head with a low chuckle. 'I know you've lived a sheltered life, but think about what you just said. Doesn't it strike you as strange that an unseasoned barbarian slave, one who used to be a warrior at that, has bowed his head to service so readily? I've seen enough of this fellow to know he's no coward, despite the way he shakes and trembles when we bring him in here. He's hiding something. I'm certain of it.'

She shoved the papers back to him. 'I don't believe it!' she snapped. 'You're just trying to renege on our deal now that I've nursed him back to health for you!'

'Fine, then. I'll prove it.' Torren turned to Isidro, his eyes tight with anger. Isidro almost drew in a sharp breath out of reflex. It usually took the Battle-Mage some time to work himself up into a state of such anger. Depending on what proof he had, this could be a very long night.

'Tell me again, slave,' Torren said. 'How many apprentices does the Blood-Mage Kell have?'

This time Isidro kept his eyes fixed on the Battle-Mage's face. It did not matter what the papers said. He had to keep to the story he'd told. Admitting to a lie now would only make things worse. 'Just one, sir, a man named Rasten.'

'And how long were you kept as a prisoner of the Blood-Mage?'

'About a week, sir, as near as I can remember.'

Delphine shuffled her feet and gave a short, sharp sigh.

'Then perhaps you can explain, slave, why a number of captured Mesentreian soldiers have all sworn that Kell had a second apprentice, a woman. They say she escaped during a blizzard some weeks ago and fled to the east. Well? What do you say to that?'

'Nothing, sir,' Isidro said. 'I don't know anything about it.'

'Oh, so you're saying imperial interrogators are incompetent?' Torren turned on his heel and struck him with the back of his hand. Bound and kneeling, Isidro could do nothing to deflect the blow. It knocked him sprawling and the aides stepped in to haul him up again. 'The lies are written on your face as plain as day. Why else would all these men have the same tale to tell?'

'Sir, rumours spread like wildfire through a camp,' Isidro said. 'Kell has no interest in women, but Rasten does and his master supplies them for him. Having mage-talent is a capital offence under Mesentreian law. It's likely that a woman with mage-talent was captured and given to Kell to dispose of. If she lingered a while and was seen around Kell's camp, it might have given rise to rumours. I know little about mages, sir, but I know Kell would sooner cut out his own heart than train a woman to be his equal in power.'

'Torren,' Delphine said.

'Be quiet, Delphi!'

'The hell I will! He is telling the truth —'

'He is not! Another mage wiped out the Seventh, not the one who massacred the scouting party all those weeks ago. The manifestation of power is quite different. This wretch knows something. The tale of his rescue from the Blood-Mage's men doesn't ring true. How could a handful of desperate fugitives wipe out an escort of the king's Guard? They must have had help. He knows something about this. Either he's trying to protect someone or he's hoping to somehow draw us into facing this third mage.'

He signalled one of the aides. 'You, strip him and string him up. And you,' he gestured to the other servant. 'Escort Madame Castalior back to her tent. This is about to become unfit for a lady's sight. I'm going to get to the heart of this, no matter what it takes.'

# Chapter 29

It proved to be a very long night, but Isidro survived it. From time to time he felt Rasten looking in on him with a clinical, assessing eye, but he never spoke or did anything other than simply observe.

Torren lacked the talent for cruelty Kell possessed and cultivated in his apprentice. He lacked the stomach to delve right to the depths of a man's soul, to identify the pillars he built himself around and set about cutting them away. There had been no broken bones this night, no sodomy or excision. It left Isidro aching and exhausted, but with his secret and his will intact, for the moment at least.

When Torren gave up in disgust he had Isidro chained in the storage tent once more with his back to a crate and his arms outstretched, taking no chances this time that he would find a way to end his life. Torren had ordered he be given no food or water in the hope that privation would loosen his tongue, where pain had not.

Isidro dozed for a while despite the discomfort. He woke once, when Rasten looked in on him again, pushing his way into Isidro's awareness like a man shouldering open a door.

*Why is it you can do that now, but you didn't know I was alive after Cam killed your men?* Isidro demanded of him.

*They were the king's men, not ours,* Rasten corrected him. *And you were close to death then. Your life-force was running low.*

*That makes a difference?*

Inside his head, Rasten snorted. *Of course. The connection was tenuous, too, but then you went and fucked Sierra and burned it deeper.*

It made a vague sort of sense, he supposed. Or at least, what passed for sense in Rasten's mind. *Any advice?* He asked Rasten. It still felt decidedly odd to realise they both wanted the same thing here, even if only in part.

*I never thought I'd be thankful for your strength of will*, Rasten said. *You'll manage so long as you stay lucid. Once you start raving from thirst or cold, it will be a different matter*. Rasten took one last look around and left with Isidro no more able to halt his departure than he was to obstruct his arrival. Alone again, Isidro hung his head with a sigh. For a while he tried to contact Sierra, just to hear her voice and maybe ask her to pass a message on to Cam. But he had no real idea how to go about it, even if he'd had the power to reach that far. His crude attempts felt as though he was shouting into an empty well. In the end he gave up and just sat, silent and still. There was nothing to do now but wait.

There was no way to measure the passage of time. When Isidro heard someone fumbling with the cords that bound the door of the tent he couldn't tell if he'd been there a few hours or for most of a day. He went tense as he listened, certain it was Torren come to fetch him for another session, but the Battle-Mage usually burst through the door with a confident stride. These people were tugging tentatively at the cords and he could just make out a low conversation held in fierce whispers on the other side of the leather and canvas.

The flap opened in a brief spill of daylight made murky by heavy clouds.

'Delphi, this is madness! You'll be court-martialled!'

'Oh, don't be ridiculous. I'm not going to set him free or anything stupid. And anyway, it's always better to ask forgiveness than permission.'

'Always, Delphi? Really?' There was a rustle of fabric and leather, then the warm yellow light of a mage-lantern streamed around the edges of the crates stacked in front of him. Delphine came around the pile and Isidro winced away from the glare with a mumbled curse.

'Well,' Delphine said. 'What have you got yourself into, Aleksar?'

'Dear Gods,' Harwin said from behind her. Delphine may have had a nasty streak but Harwin was a gentle soul and he stared with horror at the fresh welts on Isidro's chest and his bruised and battered face.

'Hold this,' Delphine said to Harwin, thrusting the lantern into his hands. She marched across to Isidro and unlocked the manacles one by one then glared down at him with her hands on her hips while he tried to work the blood back into his arms.

'Now tell me the truth. What is the story with this girl, Aleksar?'

'There is no girl, madame.'

She rolled her eyes. 'Of course there's a girl. You're far too clever to delude yourself into thinking you can nudge an army as large as this one into danger, so you must be protecting someone. You've done it before, after all. You young men and your romantic notions ...'

It was rich for her to be calling him young. She was his elder by only a handful of years and had spent all her life sheltered by the Collegium's walls. But Isidro held his tongue.

'Anyway,' Delphine went on. 'I'm not going to let Torren back out on our deal now, not when we're so cursed close. I want you to give me your word you won't try anything stupid, like running away.'

Isidro sighed and held up his splinted arm. 'Where would I go? It's not as though I could survive on my own in the snow.'

'I'm glad you realise that.' She disappeared behind the wall of crates and returned with a rough bundle of his clothing, which she dropped into his lap. 'Get dressed, quickly now. I want to get you to the caves before anyone realises you're gone.'

He hesitated before pulling on his undervest and shirt. If they were stopped it would be him who was punished. It would make no difference that Delphine had ordered him. Technically she had no authority over him now, but he knew she wouldn't take no for an answer. And really, what difference did it make? There was nothing they would do to him in punishment they wouldn't eventually try in order to make him talk. He pulled the knitted vest over his head. 'May I ask where we're going, madame?'

'There's something in the caves I want you to see,' Delphine said. 'And I'm not saying anything else until we get there.'

The soldiers Delphine found to escort them back to the caves didn't so much as blink at Isidro's presence. This time he was allowed to guide his horse himself, although he was flanked by a pair of soldiers for the entire journey.

When they dismounted at the mouth of the cave and the soldiers led the horses away, Delphine jammed her fists against her belt and scowled up at the dark crevice in the rock. 'Harwin, you go in first and find my girls. Torren's in there somewhere and if he sees us there's going to be a nasty scene. Find him and keep him away from the main passage as if your life depends on it. Once the coast is clear, send the girls out here to find me. When we've passed the main passages and are on our way to the springs you can come and join us.'

'It's not my life I'm worried about, Delphi, it's my career,' Harwin grumbled. 'But I suppose we may as well be hung for a sheep as a lamb.' He trudged up the switchback path while Delphine and Isidro followed more slowly behind.

'Madame, wouldn't it be simpler just to have him tell you when the passage is clear?' Isidro said.

Delphine gave him a strange look. 'But Harwin won't be here,' she said carefully, as though talking to a child. 'He'll be where Torren is. How would I talk to him?'

'You can't talk to him mind to mind?' Isidro cursed himself silently. It hadn't occurred to him that the Akharians didn't have that particular skill, although perhaps it should have, given it had taken Torren this long to receive the report of the Mesentreian soldiers' interrogation.

Delphine frowned. 'No. How do you even know about that? It can be done, of course, but it's far too difficult to be used for anything other than an emergency. So what do you know of it?'

'The Blood-Mages communicate in that manner, madame.' If they didn't know about it, then they couldn't have guessed that Rasten had been in contact with him. So either Rasten was mistaken in thinking the Akharians could overhear any such communications or he didn't want the Akharians to know he and Kell could remain in contact without relying on a slow and vulnerable messenger.

'Fascinating!' Delphine said. 'I suppose it must be a hold-over from the power-transfer rituals.'

'It never happens between Akharian mages?' Isidro asked.

'No ...' Delphine said. 'And if it had ever been reported you can bet it would have been studied by now. That sort of communication would revolutionise the army. Well, it can't simply involve sexual contact — mages are always marrying or having affairs with other mages. And it can't just be power-transfer; Sympaths do that all the time, often with folk with some base level of talent, and they've never reported anything like it either. Then again, Sympaths aren't exactly known for their discipline and ability to focus. It's a fascinating bit of information, though, and something we will have to investigate further when we're back in Akhara. You're going to love it in the Collegium, Aleksar. A man with your mind will do well there.'

Isidro looked away, trying to conceal a sudden rush of anger and despair. The way things were going it seemed there would be nothing he could do to keep from being taken to the heart of the empire to spend the rest of his life in servitude.

Delphine gave him a none-too-gentle thump on the arm to bring his attention back to her. 'Oh, don't get all morose again. You don't have to be a slave forever. If you put your mind to it and work hard you could earn your freedom in ten years or so. With your knowledge of languages you could have a position for life in the Collegium. They'll even find you a wife. You could have a family and your children will be Akharian citizens.'

'Really, madame?' Isidro couldn't keep the disbelief from his voice. 'Even with Mage-Captain Castalior howling for my blood?'

'Oh, you're far too valuable to be cast aside once he's finished with you,' Delphine said. 'And the Collegium is full of ex-slaves. Just look at Alameda. She was a slave once. I identified her myself when I was serving as a talent scout. She was only six years old. The Collegium found fostering for her until she was old enough to begin her training.'

Isidro straightened with surprise. He had heard that slave-children with talent were taken to be trained, but he hadn't realised it meant being plucked from the lowest ranks of society and elevated to one of the highest. 'What happened to her family?' he said.

Delphine shrugged. 'Who knows? She doesn't remember her mother and she has a new family now anyway, the folk who fostered her. And you've seen how brilliant she is with enchantments — that girl has a great future ahead of her. I know it must be hard to leave all the people you knew behind, but you have to grieve for them and let them go and get on with life as it is.'

Isidro knew children were sold away from their mothers every day in the slave markets. The grief of loss would have been no less sharp than if Alameda was sent to the auction block, but at least this way her mother would have known the girl was going to a better future than she could ever have provided.

He wondered if Delphine had any idea how callous she was, but doubted it. This desensitisation probably began in the cradle.

They waited in silence a few minutes more, standing just inside the entrance of the cave before Alameda and Fontaine came trotting down the passage to find them. 'There you are, madame!' Alameda said breathlessly. 'Mage-Captain Castalior is with the men trying to dismantle one of the traps. They will be at it for hours the way they're going, so we have a clear run.'

'Professor Harwin is keeping an eye on him just in case,' Fontaine said as she tucked a strand of dark hair back behind her ear.

'Right, then,' Delphine said. 'Let's get moving before someone comes along who knows Torren tried to take the slave back.'

Delphine had a new lantern, as her old one had been destroyed the day before. Her students also had their own. Isidro was the only one without one since his hadn't yet been replaced. In order to see where he was putting his feet he had to keep pace with the others, who went quickly through the gloomy caverns. Keeping up with their shorter strides was no challenge with his long legs, even after the night he'd had, but he desperately wanted to explore. From what he knew of the wall of rubble that had sealed the entrance, no Ricalani had set foot in these caves since Leandra's day.

The caves were a priceless relic of the age when mages had still been a force in the land. Everywhere he looked there were more details of life in those times: side-passages that branched off the main tunnels, each with a signpost in Ricalani script engraved into the stone; crumbling stumps of metal sunk into the walls at regular intervals at the prefect height to hold lanterns, with the carvings around them stained green from the corroding metal; great murals carved into the walls, some painted, some bare, and in varying degrees of repair.

A few seemed to be untouched since Leandra's day, but others looked as if someone had taken a sledgehammer to them and were so badly damaged that only a few fragments of the relief remained. Occasionally he saw an abandoned basket, damp and mouldering in the humid air, and wondered if it had been dropped and forgotten in the chaos of the night Sofera and Delcarion had been poisoned, or if Vasant's followers had left it there before heading north to their doom.

Whenever he tried to slow or stop for a closer look Delphine would urge him on. Harwin joined them once they had passed six or seven of the side passages and from that point Delphine drove them to go even faster.

Isidro counted twelve branches in all before the form and finish of the cave began to change. The wide, spacious passages grew narrower, more ragged and irregular, coming to resemble the walls of a natural cave. The floor also changed, becoming sandy and uneven as the passage twisted and turned, rising and then descending until Isidro lost track of east and west and the only directions he could be certain of were up and down.

The air grew steadily warmer and more humid. When Delphine called a stop to let them pull off their winter coats Isidro realised he hadn't seen a lamppost for some time. The only way anyone would find their way in this narrow passage was with a hand-held light.

There were more murals, lurking unexpected around corners or watching from the roof. Most of them were animals — Clan Totems. Isidro spotted his Owl gliding near the roof, with flared wing-tip feathers depicted in exquisite detail. A little further on he saw Cam's Lion, prowling against one wall. He knew the cat only from legends as the beasts' homeland was on the plains in the west of the empire. Lions had come to Ricalan only as a talisman of Cam's distant ancestors.

Deeper still came enormous reliefs of the Twin Suns coupling with their Consorts, the Bright Sun and the Bear, the Black Sun and the Tiger, carved over such length in the narrow passage that those going past could see only bits of it at once. They made the girls giggle, hiding behind their hands; even Delphine blushed and looked away, turning so that the lantern cast that part of the wall in shadow.

Isidro saw no sign they were nearing their destination. There was no noise down here, nothing but their breathing and the dull shuffle of boots on the sandy floor. There was nothing to herald their arrival either; Delphine simply led them around one last bend in the passage and the cave opened up into a vast cavern, a perfect bubble of beauty buried deep with the rock.

The roof was several man-heights above Isidro's head, but the cavern was many times wider than it was tall. They had entered from one end and the void swept away into the distance ahead of them as Delphine's lamplight faded away to nothing in the gloom.

A great pool of water filled most of the floor. It was as white as milk and as smooth as a sheet of ice formed on a cold still morning before the wind stirred the water. There was no ice, though — the surface of the water steamed gently, forming a haze of mist.

Rippling curtains and massive pillars of stone dripped from the ceiling, following contours in the rock overhead. At some point in the long-distant past a portion of the roof had fallen, but the rubble had long since been covered by flowstone like a sheet of molten wax, forming a smooth and undulating slope down to the water's edge.

Another rockfall had provided the stone that formed the path at their feet. It hugged the wall, creating a ledge along the edge of the water, drawing them deeper into the cavern.

Delphine reached into her satchel and pulled out a spare lantern, which she handed to Isidro. '*Now* you can go explore,' she said, moving to one side of the path and gesturing him past.

He hesitated for a moment before taking the lantern from her. Delphine had always taken pains to make sure he knew his place in her world. She had told him it was for his own good, as a slave with thoughts above his station would always draw trouble. The fact she was giving him free rein here instead of insisting he remain at her heel made him wonder exactly what she thought he was going to find.

He moved away from them before lighting the lantern and followed the path around a wrinkle in the cavern wall that hid the deeper reaches from sight. He could hear Delphine and the others following him, but they all remained silent. At the point where a pillar of stone blocked the light from behind and cast the void ahead in shadow, Isidro nestled the lantern in the crook of his broken arm to pry the little window open and reach inside and activate the stone.

As the enchantment pulsed beneath his fingertips, he felt another surge of energy nearby, but not from the Akharian mages behind him. It came from overhead. As the lantern flared so did myriad points of light in the ceiling of the cavern.

Faint at first but growing stronger, they glowed like the stars on a clear night. They pulsed once in the space of a heartbeat and then dwindled and died again like a spark fallen on barren stone. Even though the light had gone Isidro could still feel the energy throbbing overhead. There were hundreds, perhaps thousands of stones embedded in the roof of the cavern. They had been untouched for nearly a hundred years but the power contained within them hadn't wasted away.

With the lantern forgotten Isidro craned his head back to gaze up at the ceiling. The stones were the same milky colour as the limestone of the cave and the white water of the spring. If he could touch them he might be able to find out more about them, but they were well beyond his reach. Even if he had two good hands with which to climb, the walls here were too smooth and sheer to scale.

He glanced back at Delphine, but she said nothing and merely watched him with her lips pursed thoughtfully. The Akharians were silent, waiting to see how he reacted before they ventured any thoughts of their own.

Holding the lantern in his good hand, Isidro followed the path around the edge of the pool. After a dozen or so strides it crossed the pool in a bridge of scattered stepping stones that led to another path on the far side.

Since the cavern was broken by several dog-leg turns Isidro was halfway across before he saw the massive statue carved from a pillar of stone. It was a woman seated cross-legged on a plinth, with one hand raised in welcome and the other touching the earth beneath her. She was naked with only thick braids of hair cascading over her shoulders for raiment and greeted those who approached with a calm and serene smile.

He moved a few stones further across the pool and saw opposite the seated Goddess a little platform up near the roof with the dark maw of a passage behind it.

The path led along the far wall for only a short distance before it crossed the pool again. A few stepping stones led a small diversion to the Goddess's island to allow the priests to tend to her and for offerings to be placed at her feet. Isidro turned his back on her for now and followed the path over several more crossings. He had to traverse nearly the whole length of the vast cavern before he found a passage leading off into the rock. It was on the opposite side of the pool to the little platform he was aiming for, but he could see no other branches leading from the chamber. Once, it seemed, the passage had been closed off with a wall of stone but now there was just a sheet of gravel underfoot. Isidro turned to Delphine, who was following him silently. 'Was it like this when you first came here?'

'No,' she said. 'The passage was closed off. Harwin and I opened it up ourselves.'

'Does it lead up there?' he said, gesturing to the platform with his lantern. She nodded.

The walls of the narrow passage looked more like marble than limestone. They were smooth and polished and the lamp reflected off them in a dizzying, shifting flash of light.

The tunnel led into the wall for a short distance before descending in a tight spiral. The steps were as smooth as the walls and his felt-soled boots offered little grip. There were no hand-holds, but they wouldn't have done Isidro any good — he needed his one good hand for the lantern. He descended cautiously while the Akharians followed him, still in silence.

The stairs ended in a narrow horizontal shaft Isidro guessed led under the chamber above. There was a slow, steady drip of water somewhere down here, and a channel had been cut into the floor to drain it away into another crevice in the stone. The air was humid, but distinctly colder than that of the chamber above.

At the far end of the shaft another spiral stair led up again. Isidro wanted to hurry but the deeper passage had dampened the soles of his boots and he had to be even more cautious on the ascent. The featureless walls gave no indication of how far the stairs climbed. The only sign he had that he was getting anywhere at all was when the deep chill of the depths gave way to warmth and steam once again.

The stairs opened out onto the small landing overlooking the water and the seated Goddess. It was big enough for perhaps three people to stand in comfort but there was just enough space for the five of them. Isidro was grateful for the rail around the edge, a sturdy balustrade to prevent anyone from slipping off and falling to the water and the rocks below.

He could feel the stones overhead throbbing with power. There was a cluster right at the edge of the platform, little milky nodules the size of an infant's fist, shaped like a skewed cube with each of its faces bowed outwards as though it was under pressure from within. Now he was closer to the ceiling and without the haze of steam impeding his vision he could see the other stones were all the same, spread across the ceiling in an irregular grid.

He set his lantern down on the flat top of the rail around the platform and reached up to touch the stone, to gain a sense of the enchantment it carried.

With one touch he felt *all* the stones throb, as though he was in contact with all of them, not just one. It was warm to the touch and hummed like the string of a musical instrument.

Isidro closed his eyes and tried to empty his mind. Most of the enchantments he had seen were simple things. The mage-lanterns were either on or off. The locks that kept him imprisoned were either fastened or loose. The most complex enchantments he had seen were the ones housed in the rubies Sierra had been wearing when she made her escape, which would flash to a punishing heat whenever her power spilled, but not when Kell or Rasten used their power around her.

This was many times more complex. A searing flurry of images and sensations flashed across his vision. For a moment he glimpsed this chamber full of people standing on scaffolding made of saplings and bamboo as they set the stones into the ceiling. He saw a man, tall and skinny with a large nose and a shock of red hair, standing beside him on the platform, while a woman perched on the railing, her head thrown back in laughter. He saw people packed onto the paths and the stepping stones, crammed in as tight as space would allow, all staring up at this platform. He saw the cavern dark except for a strange blue light radiating down from the ceiling, casting a complex pattern on the milky surface of the water.

They were images from the creation of the enchantment. It happened that way sometimes. He occasionally caught a glimpse of the one who had created the device but it had never struck him so thick or so fierce before. Now they were swept away in a burst of sensation from the enchantment itself. He smelled ancient paper and parchment, the glue that bound it and the stiff leather of the covers. He saw page after page of crabbed, cramped script and diagrams as fine and as intricate as a spider's web, all flickering past his vision too fast to make out any detail.

The hum of the power filled his head, echoing around and around like a bell tolling within his skull. It grew to a crescendo, more than he could bear, and yet he couldn't pull away. He felt as though he was drowning in a sea of power and information. It was pouring down his throat and filling his lungs, dragging him down to a depth where he would forget who he was, forget his own name …

With a wrench he was lifted out of that ocean of power. Isidro came back to himself sitting on the cold stone with his back to a wall and Delphine crouched in front of him, patting his cheek with one small, chill hand. 'Ah,' she said, 'there you are. Just take deep, slow breaths. Put your head between your knees if you think you're going to heave.'

His heart was racing and his lungs cried out for air. 'What in the hells was that?' he said. He had forgotten his manners. It was about all he could do to remember to speak in Akharian.

'You've never come across a really powerful enchantment before, have you? It probably wouldn't have been so bad if they hadn't blasted your channels open. It seems to have heightened your perception of power as well. What a shame we never had a chance to measure your abilities before they got to you …'

'Madame,' Isidro said, trying to draw her back to the matter at hand and rolled his eyes to the ceiling. 'What is that thing?'

'We're not sure,' she said. 'Harwin and I found this place this morning. We couldn't get anything from the enchantment. I surmise it was created for a Ricalani mage and you are the closest thing we have to one of them. Do you think you can stand now? You should try to activate it —'

'Madame?' Fontaine interrupted her. She was leaning over the rail to peer along the cavern towards the entrance. Isidro realised he could hear voices approaching and the heavy tread of hurrying feet. 'Madame, I think we have a problem. Mage-Captain Castalior is coming!'

Torren held Isidro by the throat and shoved him back against the railing. Delphine had cast a shield to keep him from going over. Isidro conceded it was better to have a wall at his back than to be held out over the empty air, but the reality was that it gave Torren another surface to slam him against.

His instincts were howling at him to break the mage's nose or gouge at his eyes. Isidro knew that would only make the situation many times worse, but it still took all of his willpower to resist his warrior's training and keep from striking back.

'Torren, you fool! Let him go! You're not going to drop him over the rail and everyone knows it, so you may as well stop this useless charade!'

Torren turned to Delphine with a wordless snarl of fury. While Akharian tradition made him the head of Delphine's household, his legal authority over her was disputable, as they were related through the female line and his family had disowned her mother anyway. In addition, she was a mage of no mean power. Torren couldn't lay a hand on her, Battle-Mage or not.

No one, however, would dispute his right to discipline a slave and Torren had turned the fury of his thwarted will onto Isidro.

There came a shout from the cavern below and Torren cursed, slamming Isidro against the insubstantial wall again. Isidro couldn't see who was coming their way, but concern mingled with relief on Delphine's face. When Torren had appeared in the cavern below she had sent Harwin for help. Apparently it had arrived, but perhaps not in the form that she had hoped.

It was a long, interminable moment before the sound of approaching feet echoed up the stairway leading to this little platform. Isidro didn't recognise the man who emerged but he had been among the Akharians long enough to understand the significance of the gilded insignia pinned to the man's collar. 'Mage-Captain Castalior, stand down! You too, madame, sheath your power. That is an order! Just what in the hells is going on here? Captain, why are you attacking a Collegium slave?'

With another snarl Torren shoved Isidro to the floor. 'He's not a Collegium slave, commander. He's *my* slave. He was assigned to the Battle-Mages as an informant and Mage-Commander Presarius placed him in my charge. This ungrateful bitch,' he glared at Delphine, 'has stolen him from the tent I placed him in.'

'Oh?' The officer turned to Delphine with one eyebrow raised.

'Sir, "stole" is a strong word,' Delphine said. 'I merely borrowed the slave. As you can see he's in perfectly sound condition —'

'That's not the point! This is tantamount to treason!'

'Oh, don't be ridiculous. We had a deal —'

'And I reserved the right to end it at any time. Sir, the slave has information about a Ricalani mage he is refusing to reveal. Delphine lacks the firmness to instil proper discipline, so I had him placed in solitary confinement. Madame Castalior waited until I was away from the camp and sneaked in to steal him!'

The officer turned to Delphine. 'Madame, this is a serious accusation. Is it true?'

Delphine shuffled her feet. 'Well, perhaps, in a manner of speaking. But sir, the empire has spent a fortune sending the army into the middle of this Gods-forsaken wilderness for one specific reason. I'm not convinced the slave has the information Captain Castalior claims but I do believe he is essential to our mission. Tell me, Torren, have you found anything of note in the outer regions of the cave?'

Torren didn't answer and the officer frowned. 'Well, captain? I heard your team had succeeded in disarming the trap. What did you find behind the wall?'

Torren shoved Isidro to his knees and stepped back. He was still furious but his fury was under control as he turned to the commander. 'Nothing, sir. There were some books there but they are nothing but mould and pulp.'

Isidro slumped to the floor, his head pounding for want of air. But even as he gasped for breath, his mind was racing. Vasant wouldn't have left his books in an airless cavern to moulder and rot. If the books weren't hidden behind the walls in the outer passages, where else could they be?

Even his enemies had been forced to admit Vasant was a genius. He must have found some way to keep the books here in a form that couldn't be stolen or destroyed. Precisely what he had done Isidro couldn't imagine, but he was certain it had something to do with the vast and complex enchantment overhead.

Momentarily forgotten while Delphine and Torren both argued their cases to the increasingly impatient commander, Isidro heaved himself to his feet with the support of the railing.

There were three paths laid out before him. He could do nothing. He could refuse to help them decipher this enchantment and deny them the treasure they sought. But the Akharians might well untangle it without his help and then his captors would have no reason to spare him from harsh treatment. Isidro had already broken once under torture. He had no faith in his ability to hold out a second time, despite Torren's relative restraint.

Another option was the void before him. Delphine's shield was gone and there was nothing to stop him from throwing himself from the platform and down onto the rocks below ...

Except perhaps that it would make Sierra believe there was nothing for her here and leave her with no one but Rasten to teach her. And there was Cam to consider. How would he survive if Rasten convinced Sierra to return to him? With Sierra to supply them with power, the king wouldn't need the warriors the Wolf Clan could provide. The clan would need to pay a hefty price to buy forgiveness for their rebellion. Mira's sentiment for Cam had kept him safe so far, but how long would it take for the Wolf Elders to realise that handing Cam back to the king and his mother would turn the bargaining in their favour? Cam would be safe so long as his alliance with Sierra held. She was his last true ally and if that alliance broke Cam would have nothing to fall back on.

He couldn't do it to them. No matter how he longed for release from a life that had spun out of his control, a release from the pain and the fear and this awful sensation of helplessness, he couldn't abandon them. His conscience would not allow it.

That left one option. He could activate the enchantment. Just what it would do, Isidro couldn't know. That path was a blank and he couldn't imagine the consequences. To take it would be a gamble but if the other choices were equally untenable then there was no decision to make.

Seemingly of its own accord, his hand reached for the stone overhead. This time there was no welter of images. The part of him that sensed power knew the enchantment now and in turn it seemed to recognise him. The power pulsed beneath his fingertips, waiting for his command.

*Show me*, he said inside his head — and activated the device.

A ripple of power ran through the network of stones and they pulsed in a flash of vivid violet blue. Glowing like stars in a clear sky they radiated light down onto the steaming pool, illuminating the haze of steam in the air like sunlight breaking through clouds.

When he removed his hand from the stone the light remained, tracing an intricate pattern in the air. Behind him the Akharians had fallen silent, their argument forgotten as Isidro stepped to the edge of the platform and laid his hand on the railing.

The beams of light traced lines and lines of text on the flat, mirror-like surface of the water below. For a moment, all Isidro could do was stare at them dumbly. It took him a long moment to recognise they were the titles of books, arranged in two neat columns. Another thrum of power beneath his hand drew his attention to the railing, where more lights had appeared beneath the broad, flat surface of marble-like stone. He touched one hesitantly and the image traced onto the water changed, showing two more columns different from the first.

His knees felt weak and for a moment Isidro thought they might give way altogether and send him sprawling to the stone. Vasant was a genius. When he'd come to these caves he'd been faced with a hopeless situation. Even if he did find a way to preserve the books, there was no way he could hide them so that an untrained Ricalani mage could find them and the best mages the Akharian Collegium had to offer could not.

So instead of trying to win an unwinnable battle, Vasant had changed the game.

The points of light within the railing let him navigate through titles. Isidro selected one at random and it glowed a little brighter while the others dimmed. When another light pulsed within the railing he touched that, and the image projected onto the water changed again, displaying a double page of text.

The books weren't hidden in some damp cache. They were in the enchantment. Somehow Vasant had captured an image of every page in every book his followers had salvaged and locked it into that grid of stone. Isidro couldn't comprehend just how it had been done, the hours it must have taken and the problems that must be solved, the mind that could invent such a solution … but as he flicked through the pages with a touch of his fingers he was overcome with awe.

The books couldn't be stolen. They couldn't be destroyed. A powerful mage could stop up the spring that fed the pool, but Isidro suspected that trying to do so would be like trying to stop the tide. The roof of the cave could be collapsed, but not without burying a mage who tried to do so. The best Leandra and her contemporaries could do was to seal the cavern with its secrets and hope it would be forgotten.

Now they had found it, the Akharians couldn't take the books away. They couldn't risk excavating the stones and dismantling the grid. Doing so could destroy the very thing they had come so far to find. By projecting the text onto such a vast canvas the purpose of the enchantment could not be concealed. Anyone who was in the cavern when the enchantment was activated would see what Vasant had wrought. Trying to keep it hidden would be a nightmare.

Behind him Delphine gave a whoop of triumph while the commander began to curse. 'In the name of all that's holy, what is that?'

'It's what we came here for, commander!' Delphine cried. 'It's Vasant's treasure. By the Good Goddess, I've never seen anything like it!'

'What in the hells does it say?'

'I've no idea, commander! But we'll know soon enough. We have a translator now, after all.'

Isidro was still too shocked to react when Torren grabbed him by the shoulder and hauled him back from the rail to shove him against the wall.

'Don't you imagine for one moment that this is over, you barbarian dog,' Torren snarled. 'I still know you're hiding something from me. I'll get the truth if I have to wring it from you myself!'

'Don't be ridiculous,' Delphine said. She was examining the lights within the railing and spared them only the briefest of glances as the text changed again. 'There must be nearly a hundred books here and at the moment he's the only translator we've got. The general's not going to risk him to torture now.'

With another snarl Torren slammed Isidro into the wall again, then released him and stalked down the stairs into the darkness and out of sight.

Isidro pressed his back against the smooth stone and closed his eyes. *Spirit of Storm defend us and Black Sun have mercy.*

Delphine was right. With one act he'd made himself indispensable to the Akharian Empire. These books were all in Ricalani. They were useless to the empire without someone to translate the text or teach them the language themselves.

It made him safe from torture. The Akharians wouldn't risk him when he was the only translator they had. But how long would it be before they found another? Any member of a ruling clan would speak Mesentreian as well as him and could translate as effectively.

It had won him safety, true, but for how long? And in the meantime he would be as closely guarded as any other captured valuable. If the legions were attacked they wouldn't give him up unless they stood to be wiped out. If his chances of rescue had been slim before, now it was infinitesimally remote.

Faced with just such a dilemma, Vasant had changed the game not just for himself, but for Isidro as well. Since he had made his choice to become Delphine's servant he had been clinging to the hope that one day he would be able to present Vasant's books to Sierra and give her the means to free herself from Kell and Rasten's influence. But Vasant's treasure was as immovable as the earth itself. Now Isidro's last hope to help the people he loved had been snuffed out like the flame of a candle.

He had gambled and he had lost. With one act he had sealed his fate. He was a prisoner for life.

His legs gave way with shock and he slid heavily to the floor. Delphine must have heard, for a moment later she was crouched beside him, pressing a cool hand to his forehead. 'What is it, Aleksar? Did he hurt your arm?' He opened his eyes to find her frowning at him in concern.

'Curse Torren for leaving you tied up in the cold all night. You are feverish again. Well, don't worry about him. Don't worry about a thing.' She gave him a brilliant smile of pure and honest joy. 'You have earned yourself a place for life with this day's work! It will never be the same after this. Just wait and see!'

# Chapter 30

Sierra sat on her snowshoes with her feet buried in the powdery snow at the edge of the churned up circle. Since she had finished her training session and the light and the noise had stopped, a grey squirrel had emerged and was digging stored food out from hiding places beneath the snow. Usually watching such a creature's antics brought a smile to Sierra's face, but tonight it wasn't enough to lift her spirits. *These rituals are stupid*, she said. *This makes no sense.*

*I know,* Rasten said. *I felt the same way.*

*Then why teach us this rubbish?* She shrugged deeper into her furs and shivered. Dremman's scouts always sought out the deepest valleys they could find for her training sessions, to hide the light from any Akharian scouts who might be around. The deepest valleys were also the coldest and, though her power kept her warm when it ran high, at the end of the lesson, when her strength was running down, the cold inexorably took its toll. *This is a waste of time*, she told Rasten. *I'm getting nowhere.*

*You're not trying hard enough.*

*The rituals don't work for me!*

*They will! It's when your concentration wavers that your power breaks out and the working falls apart. You need to work on your focus. And I did tell you at the start of this that there's a limit to what I can teach you from a distance.*

Sierra sighed in a huff of mist and said nothing. The problem was that Rasten had never learned to use his power any other way. He'd had Kell's undivided attention during his training and Kell had made sure Rasten only ever worked using the rituals, a specific set of actions learned by rote to shape and direct his power. Before Kell had inadvertently crippled his Sympathic powers Rasten must have worked instinctively, like her, but early on in his training Kell had forbidden it and insisted he only use Kell's method.

It held him back as effectively as a set of mental shackles. Rasten's workings took longer and were less flexible and more constrained than Kell's. From the moment he had taken Rasten, Kell had the foresight to ensure his apprentice would never be capable of challenging him.

Even though she could see the issue, Sierra was too far beneath Rasten in skill to be able to challenge him. The rituals only weakened his potential. They didn't mean *he* was weak, but it meant his training would instil those same flaws in her. As she saw it, there were two possibilities ahead of her — she could either follow his training and hope she didn't lose her ability to work outside of the rituals, or she could work with him to try to find a middle ground, combining enough of both techniques to minimise the flaws. If she succeeded in the latter, however, then Rasten would be learning this new skill alongside her — and when the time came for them to face off against each other he would be a stronger opponent because of it.

*If only Isidro were here!* She would welcome his advice. His power might be weak but his instinctive understanding of it, along with his sharp mind, gave him insights she would never find on her own.

*What about Vasant's books?* she asked Rasten. *Surely there must be something in them that would help us?*

*Well, maybe,* he said, grudgingly. *But even if they find them, how would you get your hands on them? I know you don't want to hear this, but I don't think you're going to make much more progress on your own. There are some things that can only be taught in person.*

*You keep saying that!*

*Because it's the truth! I know you're frightened, but it's not that bad. If I could survive it, you can. There's nothing like the prospect of the rack for teaching you how to focus —*

Sierra stood, brushing the snow from her coat. *That's enough for today, Rasten. I'm cold and hungry and I'm going back to the camp.*

*Wait. Before you go there's something I need to tell you.*

Sierra glanced up to where her escort waited above on the valley slope, where the air was warmer. Cam had seen her stand and was starting down towards her. *Can't it wait until morning?*

*Oh, believe me, you don't want that. Your friend Dremman has sent me a messenger.*

*He's not my friend*, Sierra snapped. A knot formed in her belly. *What does he want?*

*He's intending to sell you back to Kell.*

For a moment she couldn't breathe. *Why tell me?* she demanded. *Isn't that what you want?*

*I told you, I don't want to fight you again.*

*Then why go along with it? Tell him you're not interested.*

*And have him realise I'm playing a different game entirely? Why would I do that? He thinks he can use you to his profit, Little Crow. When he finds out he can't, he may well decide it's easier just to get rid of you. Watch your back, Sierra.*

*For what? What has he planned?*

*That I don't know — and there's no reason for him to tell me. All his messages have said is to stand by to take possession of you. So don't say you weren't warned.*

He severed the contact just as Cam reached the foot of the slope and crunched across the snow towards her. 'Done for the evening?' he asked, covering a yawn with one hand. Then he came close enough to see her stricken expression and frowned. 'What's the matter?'

She glanced at the men on the slope. Even with the way sound carried in cold air she judged they were far enough away for her to speak in privacy. 'Rasten said Dremman's planning to sell me back to Kell.'

Cam sighed. 'Well, of course he would say that. He's trying to scare you.'

'Dremman doesn't like having me around —'

'No, he doesn't, but he's also not fool enough to try something so stupid.'

Sierra steepled her hands together over her face and turned away. Ever since that night in Terundel the tension in the camp had been unrelenting. To some of the men she was a gift from the Gods; to others she was a demon in the flesh. There were eyes upon her everywhere she went. Men spat to ward off bad luck as she passed and dark whispers followed her through the camp. The only peace she had was in Mira's tent or here during her daily lessons.

'Oh, Sirri, come here,' Cam said, moving towards her. 'By the Fires Below, it's wise to be wary ... Did he give you any details?'

'Only that Dremman's messengers said he should be ready to take charge of me at any time.'

'Look, even if Dremman means to hand you back it makes no sense to do it now. You don't hand over a bargaining chip before you've made your deal. He would have no leverage once he's passed you over. It's more likely that Rasten's lying to you. Or maybe Dremman is playing *him*.'

Sierra shook herself. 'You must be right. It makes no sense.' She glanced up at the sky, half hidden behind the smoky haze that had accumulated from her breath and the stirred-up snow. 'It's late. We should head back.'

He leaned close, peering at her face. 'You have frost.'

Sierra quickly raised a hand to her cheek, feeling for the numb and icy patch that was the first sign of frost-nip. She held the furred back of her mitten against her cheek to warm it. 'It gets cursed cold down here once I stop using power.'

'I'll say. Do you have something to eat?'

Sierra shook her head. She'd kept a chunk of bannock back from the noon meal so she'd have something to eat on the ride back to camp, but she'd been hungry enough to eat it before the lesson.

Cam pulled a parcel out from the front of his coat and handed it to her.

'Oh, Cam, I can't. I've already kept you from your evening meal ...'

'But I've been sitting in front of a fire drinking hot tea while you've been working down here in the cold,' Cam said. 'I kept it for you anyway. Take it.'

With a small sigh, she accepted the parcel. 'Thanks.'

'When we get back I'll talk to Mira about having some spare rations sent along for these evening sessions. If you're working yourself to the bone for the army's sake, it's the least they can do.'

Once they got back to the camp, however, Mira was nowhere to be found. Instead Ardamon met them at the door of the tent. 'There you are,' he said. 'Come on, Dremman wants to see you. There's news. The scouts we sent north have returned and they've brought an escaped prisoner with them. Mira's tending to him at the moment. The Akharians are camped at Well-of-Poisons and, well ... it's not good. Hannomar's about to deliver the report to Father's captains. I've convinced him the pair of you should be admitted as well.'

Ardamon led them to Dremman's tent, a large, sprawling structure formed from several conical frames linked together. Inside, the officers were gathered at one end of the tent while Dremman and a few others were poring over a set of maps. At the sight of them Dremman muttered a few words to his companions and turned to the other end of the tent, beckoning them to follow with a jerk of his head.

When they were far enough away from the others to speak with a little privacy, Dremman said to Cam, 'I'm afraid there's some bad news for you, lad. The scouts found a fellow who escaped from the Akharian slave camps. He had some word of your brother.'

Sierra felt her breath catch in her throat. How bad could the news be? If it were something awful surely she would have known of it long before this?

'When it became clear the Akharians were heading for Well-of-Poisons I was afraid they were searching for the Demon Vasant's books,' Dremman said. 'According to this man Elomar they have found it — and Isidro Balorica was the one who led them to it.'

Sierra felt a rush of elation, quickly tempered by unease. She was probably the only person in the camp to whom this was anything other than the worst possible news.

'I understand word of this is already spreading,' Dremman said. 'I didn't want you to hear it through camp gossip.'

She could see the muscles in Cam's neck grow tense as he fought to control himself. 'Thank you, sir,' he said.

'If it's any comfort, I doubt any man of sense would hold your brother responsible for this,' Dremman said. 'A man broken once by torture cannot be expected to withstand it again. When the time comes for the Gods to judge him for this betrayal I'm sure they will be merciful. The common folk will denounce him of course, but don't take it to heart, eh, lad? All this business of sorcerers has got them on edge and it's best not to make things worse.' He clapped a hand briefly on Cam's shoulder. 'You have a few moments before the briefing begins. I'm sorry, lad.'

'Sir,' Cam said stiffly.

Dremman went back to his maps and Ardamon turned away, demonstrating a consideration of which Sierra hadn't thought him capable. Cam didn't move and when Sierra laid a hand on his arm he was as tense as a bowstring.

'Insufferable pig,' she hissed once Dremman was out of earshot.

'I suppose he means well.'

'The Black Sun take him,' Sierra hissed. 'He means to tell us not to defend Isidro, that's all.'

Cam turned to her. 'He's doing this for you. Nothing else would make him aid our enemies.'

She could feel a flush creeping over her cheeks. 'I know.'

'Once people see what you can do they'll understand why he did it. It'll be difficult for a while, but they'll come around.'

'I'm sure they will,' Sierra said.

Cam shook himself like a dog. 'We'd best go listen to this report.'

'The Akharian force encamped at Well-of-Poisons has near four thousand warriors and nearly a thousand captives,' Hannomar said to the assembled officers. 'Their camp is well fortified with ditch and palisade and, were it not for the need for fuel, they could withstand a siege very well. The slaves are spread through the camp so that their numbers are not great enough in any one place to turn on their captors. The supply lines reach west across Wolf Lands and then through the pass. They constitute a weak point, but the raids on villages and farmsteads mean the Akharian force can go some time between resupplies without feeling the pinch. According to the escaped prisoner, slave-gangs are regularly taken from the camp and marched west along the supply routes en route to the slave markets in Akhara. This keeps the slaves with the army within controllable numbers.

'It seems certain now that the Akharians have come east for the sole purpose of seeking out the Demon's Hoard. From the rumours Elomar heard in the slave camp, now that they have found the treasure at Well-of-Poisons, they are marching next to find the cache at Demon's Spire.

'In addition to the larger force it seems there are several smaller groups of warriors operating as raiding and foraging parties: it was one of these patrols that attacked Terundel. As of yet we don't know how many of these raiding parties there are, or where they might be located, but our prisoners taken from the Terundel raid have indicated there might be as many as six thousand imperial soldiers in the Wolf Clan's lands alone. If these numbers are correct — and we have no reason to doubt them — then it is clear that we will not be able to drive the Slavers from our lands without aid from the king.'

A murmur of surprise went through the assembled men at the number and it turned to a dark mutter at the mention of the king.

'How are your men going to take the news that they have followed their war-leader into rebellion only to see him turn around and beg Severian for forgiveness?' Cam asked Ardamon in a low voice.

'We never intended to depose the king,' Ardamon replied. 'Letting the Akharians ravage our lands was a power play. The Crown must have known we would hear of it and act. No doubt the king rues that decision now. He can't make a show of denouncing Dremman because he can't spare the men it would take to punish him. It would only make him look weak to the other clans. Father is wagering that the king will have to overlook it and I don't see that he has any other choice.'

'Perhaps,' Cam said. 'It strikes me as odd that Valeria let him be put in such a position.'

Sierra stole a glance at Cam's face. His voice and expression were utterly devoid of emotion when he spoke his mother's name.

'The clan elders were concerned about that, too,' Ardamon said. 'People were wondering if keeping the Wolf men away from our lands was an idea cooked up between King Severian and Duke Osebian as an attempt to weaken the clan. If so it was carried out without the queen's knowledge.'

'It's possible,' Cam conceded. 'Valeria will be livid. Has there been any mention of breaking Mira's betrothal to Osebian?'

'None,' Ardamon said. 'The way things are going it will be their only hope of regaining any control over the clan. The only thing that's holding the other clans under the king's command is the knowledge that if they pulled out now the Akharians would sweep over the lot of them. Even if we do win this war the king will find himself weakened and the clans will finally have some power again. It's the best way to defend our people. We simply don't have the power to cast off Mesentreian rule.'

*Not while Kell's at the king's side*, Sierra thought.

'If we win?' Cam said. 'That's a big if. If the Akharians can send six thousand soldiers into the Wolf Lands alone how many do they have to throw into the west?'

'It's the Mesentreian harbours they're bent on burning,' Ardamon said. 'Once they've got what they want from Vasant's relics I imagine they'll head west again. There's not enough loot to keep them here. Our goal should be to keep them from taking all their captives with them.'

'You think they'll burn the towns and leave?' Cam said. 'The Mesentreians will set the next boat-load of settlers to rebuilding them.

There will be new hulls laid within a year. What if the empire decides there's wealth enough in Ricalan to justify staying — and so ensuring the Mesentreians don't start raiding again? We would be exchanging one overlord for another and we'll be facing the new one when we've already been bled white.'

'We'll deal with that when we come to it,' Ardamon muttered. 'I'm sure the war-leader has a plan. Here, Hannomar's talking again. We'd best listen.'

Hannomar had broken off to discuss something with Dremman and now he cleared his throat to continue. 'The Akharian forces would win if we met them in open battle. Their numbers and the presence of their mages leaves no doubt of that. Once the king sends aid it will be a different matter, but that will take months —'

'If we're lucky,' Cam muttered. 'Winter is nearly over. We have maybe a month left before the Thaw. Once the rains start I wouldn't be surprised if it takes half a year.'

'In the meantime we must fight them alone,' Hannomar said. 'With such great numbers and the need to keep their slaves in check they will be an easy target. With small detachments we'll ambush and harry them along the route, striking quickly and retreating before they have time to launch a counter-attack. Scouts and foraging parties will be particular targets, as will slave-teams. By killing the Slavers and arming the freed captives with their weapons we will strengthen our numbers while weakening theirs.'

'Then it will only be a matter of time before they start sending mages out with them,' Sierra said under her breath.

'That's where you come in,' Ardamon whispered back.

'The Slavers will no doubt respond by sending detachments of men after our warriors. If they are foolish enough to follow us too far they will meet up with the rest of our men, who will be following a small distance behind. While the Akharians are too great in number to be defeated, they cannot commit such a great number to the chase without leaving those who stay behind vulnerable to a slave uprising. In this way we will harass and weaken their forces until they have no choice but to take the prizes they have and quit the Wolf Lands.

'In the short term, however, we can expect the Slavers to respond by choosing routes that provide little cover for ambush. This will slow them down while offering them only a minor degree of protection. They cannot avoid wooded areas completely, given the amount of fuel required by so many men. And once the Thaw begins, they will have no choice in the matter.'

The broad, treeless routes of ice and packed snow that allowed the armies to move freely would cease to exist in a month or so. Once the seasons turned and the Thaw began, those frozen rivers would become raging torrents of water and ice. Then the rains would start and whatever open land that wasn't lost beneath the flooding waters would soon become a sticky quagmire of mud. Furs that kept one warm in the dry air of winter could be soaked in moments in a spring downpour. Frostbite and hypothermia were no less of a threat when the days grew longer.

'Even if their informants have warned the Slavers what to expect, it is unlikely they will be prepared,' Hannomar said. 'The search for good footing will force them into wooded areas ripe for ambush. What's more, as foreigners in their first Ricalani spring, they will suffer badly from the miasma and spring fevers. By the time the king's reinforcements get here the Slavers should be thoroughly demoralised and weak enough for us to wipe them out in one last battle. This matter should be well and truly settled by the first snowfall of next winter.'

Ardamon was obliged to stay a little longer at his father's side but Sierra and Cam headed back to Mira's tent.

'There's been no mention of any role for me in all this,' Sierra said once they were alone. 'There must be something I can do.'

'It's hard to factor your powers into their tactics when they don't know what you can do,' Cam said. 'It's also unwise to rely upon you when you'll have to hide away once Dremman makes contact with the king.'

Sierra sighed as they stopped at the doorway. 'I suppose you're right,' she said. 'But this plan of Dremman's … it won't free Isidro.'

'No,' Cam said. 'If he's with the civilian mages he won't be freed unless the whole legion is wiped out.'

'But once these mages have found what they're searching for they aren't likely to wait around for us to drive them off, are they? They'll take their prizes back to Akhara and Isidro with them.'

Cam looked away over the field of conical tents stretched around them. 'That's right.'

'But he won't just accept that, will he?'

'You think he'll try to escape? He's a cripple now, Sirri. Some things just aren't possible any more.' He turned and ducked into the warmth of the tent.

Inside they found Mira standing by the stove and peering into a pot simmering on the hob. 'Oh,' she said. 'There you are. Is the briefing finished?'

'Just now,' Cam said. 'I was surprised you weren't there.'

'The war-leader had me taking a detailed account from the escaped slave, Elomar, to send back to Ruhavera. Rhia's still with him. It looks as if the poor fellow will lose half his fingers to frostbite.' She lifted a spoon from the pot, tasted it and winced. 'Dremman's steward must have prepared this. That man's always had a heavy hand on the spice jar, but I'm too cursed hungry to care right now. Pass me those bowls, will you?'

It was well past the middle of the night before Rhia left her patient's side. The camp was still as she trudged her way back through the rows towards Mira's tent. When she saw another figure stalking towards her through the darkness, she immediately went tense and checked her stride. The years she had spent as a slave had made her wary of unfamiliar men, especially ones as tall as these Ricalani warriors, who all towered head and shoulders above her.

'Rhia!' he hailed her softly and she relaxed a little when she recognised the voice.

'Lord Ardamon,' she replied with a brief bow of her head.

'What are you doing up at this hour?'

'I was attending to the escaped prisoner, sir, and I've only just been released from duty.'

'Oh, yes? Well, there's another one on short sleep tonight. I think half the camp has been up dancing attendance on my father in one way or another.' At the doorway of the tent he lifted the flap and waved her inside.

The interior was dark and markedly cold. It wasn't as cold as outside, but neither was it as warm as it should have been. There was a distinct, familiar smell in the air, the sour tang of vomit.

'Faugh, what a stink! What's been going on here?' Ardamon said as he followed her in and let the flap fall.

'If someone comes in late usually the others leave a lamp burning,' Rhia said. 'Something is wrong.'

It was pitch black inside the tent. Without even a glow around the stove door to guide her, Rhia struck out for where she thought the stove should be, feeling her way with the sleeves of her coat over her hands to protect them. When she found it, the coals inside were blanketed with a thick layer of ash. By the time she stirred it into life again, Ardamon had found a lamp and Rhia lit it with a splint.

Once the flame steadied he lifted it up to cast a meagre light over the interior of the tent. 'Mira's not here.'

Cam lay curled on the bare spruce, unconscious and with a pool of vomit beside him. Mira's furs were empty. So were Sierra's. Both the servants were huddled in their place near the door but neither of them had stirred and Rhia and Ardamon had made no effort to be quiet.

Rhia knelt by Cam's side. 'Bring light,' Rhia said to Ardamon, digging her fingers into Cam's neck below the line of his jaw. His pulse was there, but slow, and his skin was clammy. There was a half-eaten bowl of stew beside him with a spoon in the congealing mess, as though he'd set it down for a moment but never picked it up again.

'Is he alright?' Ardamon said.

'He lives.' She left him for a moment to check Mira's women. Both of them were sleeping deeply with slow but steady pulses and were warm beneath their furs. She went back to Cam. 'He is cold. Help me get him to his furs.' The trampled spruce made a warm and fresh-smelling floor for a tent, but the needles were sharp. No one would choose to lie on a spruce floor when there were blankets and bedding available.

Together, she and Ardamon lifted Cam onto his furs. The movement seemed to rouse him and he stirred with a slight moan and began to gag.

'Fires Below, he's going to heave again,' Ardamon said as Rhia rolled Cam onto his side.

'Bring me a bucket, bowl, something,' she told him. 'Quickly!'

He brought her a basin from the kitchen kit and stood well back while she held Cam's head over it. He was partially awake and making an effort to support himself, but she had to hold him steady.

'I'll wake one of the women to help you,' Ardamon said, turning towards the servants.

'They will not wake. They have been drugged. Cam too. More light, please, Ardamon.'

He stared at her. 'Drugged? Where's Mira? Where's Sierra?'

'I don't know. Lamps, please, my lord. I need more light.'

He did as she asked while Rhia tested the kettle on the stove. It was lukewarm. She splashed some into a bowl, found a clean rag and wiped Cam's face.

'Mira?' he said.

'No, Cam, it is Rhia.'

'Where … where's Sirri?'

'I don't know, Cam. Can you tell me what happened?'

He didn't respond, even when she patted and pinched his cheek.

Rhia turned to the bowl that had been sitting beside him. She stirred the congealed mess around, sniffed it, and dipped a cautious finger in to taste it. Then to Ardamon's disgust she sniffed the vomit she'd collected in the basin as well.

'Poppy,' she said. 'They used spices to cover the taste. By all the demons in hell, Cam could have died if he had been lying on his back.'

'Why did it make him sick and not the others?'

'It takes some people that way. I'll give him a purge to make sure there's none left in his belly.'

'We should raise the alarm. Someone must have seen something! Mira and Sierra couldn't have been stolen away from beneath the war-leader's nose. *Someone* has to know …' He trailed off.

'I am sure someone does know,' Rhia said. She opened the lid of the chest that held her supplies and broke off, staring at what should have been a neat arrangement of baskets and parcels. It had all been disrupted, pulled apart and riffled through and then shoved back in disarray, the lid crammed down over the mess.

'They have taken something,' Rhia said. 'Why else would there be such a mess?' She would have to go through it carefully to find out what was missing but right now it was more important to make sure the dose Cam had been given wouldn't make him any sicker.

Ardamon frowned down at the mess. 'I'm going to go and find out just what in the Black Sun's name has been going on here,' he said. 'Do you need anything? I can find someone to assist you if you like.'

'No. I will see to Cam myself.'

'Alright. When he wakes, tell him I swear on the honour of my clan that I'm going to get to the bottom of this.'

Dremman's manservant showed Ardamon through to the war-leader's private quarters, a corner of the tent partitioned by a blanket strung up for a curtain. Dremman lounged in a folding chair honing his belt-knife with a small oilstone. 'I thought I might be seeing you again, lad,' he said.

'Mira's gone,' Ardamon said. 'Sierra, too. Cam's been drugged.'

Dremman glanced up at him and then turned back to his knife. 'That's quite a tale, lad. Who else have you told it to?'

'You already know? Where's Mira? What in the Black Sun's name is going on here?'

'Mira's gone back to Ruhavera. Spring is coming and it's time she began preparations for her marriage. She's been getting far too involved in matters here.'

'So you had her drugged and bundled away like a load of baggage on a sled?'

Dremman shrugged. 'It was easier this way. This betrothal isn't popular and there's enough division among the men without bringing that up for question. And given our current situation, having her arrive at Lathayan with her belly swollen wouldn't be a good idea. This way there'll be time enough to take care of things if necessary.'

'So she doesn't know about this?'

'Her escort will tell her what she needs to know.'

'What about Sierra?'

Dremman put the oilstone aside and began cleaning his fingernails with the tip of the freshly honed knife. 'What about her?'

'Where is she?'

'I have no idea, my boy. Perhaps she has deserted. Mages are dangerous, fickle creatures. We're better off without her.'

'Don't treat me like a fool, Father —'

'Then stop acting like one! The girl is gone and we're well rid of her. That little show she put on at the village came cursed close to ruining everything. The common folk have less sense than a flock of sheep. One show of light and noise and they're prepared to kneel down and worship her as a Goddess. Never once did it occur to them she could wipe them out just as easily.'

'But we need her, sir. The Akharians —'

'Once they've taken what they want the Akharians will leave,' Dremman said. 'They're not cut out to live in the north and they know it. Thanks to young Balorica they'll find what they want and be gone by next spring. The Akharians are not our problem, Ardamon. It's the king's pet sorcerer we must be wary of. How long do you think it took for word of what happened at the village to reach him? How long before he knew his lost pet had found a home?'

'But —'

'Our little rebellion was only a game, Ardamon, thought up by Severian and Osebian to weaken our clan before the wedding. If Valeria had known about it she would never have let it happen. The king can't punish us for disobeying his orders. If he did, he knows we would lead the clans in revolt, and without us the Akharians will crush the Mesentreian lords and their men. We've got them over a barrel — and Valeria sewed the marriage contract up so tight there's no way out of it. We had them exactly where we wanted them, right up until that little sorcerer came along.

'Suddenly it's not the king and the duke we're playing, it's Kell himself. The king wanted to control our clan, not destroy it. So long as he thought he had the chance to regain the upper hand he'd keep Kell and Rasten in check, but if we turn that madman's pet against him? He'd take Ruhavera back to the bedrock. He'd wipe out every last branch of the Wolf's bloodline. We'd be looking at a slaughter worse than the Demon's Last Stand. We had to be rid of her.'

'But without her we are defenceless against the Akharians!'

'Defenceless? I taught you better than that, boy! Just how much use do you think a single mage is against dozens?'

'But she's not like them! She's not an ordinary mage — she's a Child of the Black Sun!'

'What cursed difference does that make? She's still only one person, who can only be in one place at a time. And in the heat of a battle she's as likely to slaughter our men as she is theirs. They will either overwhelm and kill her and then slaughter us, or she'll lose her grip and save them the trouble by reducing our men to ash. In any case, we don't need her! Our strategies were invented by men who fought against mages and, while folk might have forgotten why we drove the demons out, at least we haven't forgotten how to fight them. On an open battlefield against men in fixed positions with nowhere to retreat and no cover they would ruin us. But in a forest, taken by ambush? They're as blind and confused as any other man. By the time they gather their wits and separate friend from foe we'll already be falling back and beyond their reach. We will whittle them down until they snap, boy, and we don't need a mage to do it.'

Ardamon sat heavily on the ground at his father's feet. 'So ... If I may ask, sir, what have you done with her?'

'The only thing we could do. We've sold her back to the king as the price of forgiving our rebellion and maintaining Mira's betrothal. We've been in contact with Lord Rasten and the men are handing her over to him tomorrow.'

'But ... Lord Rasten? Have you lost your mind? If she's dangerous when she's on our side what manner of demon do you think she'll be when Kell has turned her into a weapon for the king?'

'Now you're the one taking me for a fool, boy!' Dremman barked. 'All I said was that we've sold her back. Keeping her there and keeping her alive is their problem.'

Ardamon blinked. 'The safest way to kill a mage is with poison,' he said.

'No, lad, best of all is to let them kill each other. From what I hear she came cursed close to finishing Rasten the last time, but she lacked the guts to try again. If that fails, then poison is the next choice. We have a man going along with them, posing as my messenger to the king. He has a supply of poison we took from that Mesentreian physician's gear —'

'*Akharian*,' Ardamon said. 'Rhia is Akharian, not Mesentreian.'

'Whatever,' Dremman said. 'My physician swears it will be enough to kill the whole cursed party.'

'Both of them?' Ardamon said. 'You mean to kill both Rasten and Sierra?'

'Well, of course, boy! Bringing one sorcerer down won't do us much good. But the two of them ... Kell is an old man. I doubt he has it in him to train another apprentice and he'll be tied to the king's army until the Akharians either go home or turn their own mages against them.'

Ardamon scrubbed his hands over his face. The thought of Mira being treated like a bale of goods frankly sickened him, but having her

safe in Ruhavera was surely worth it. As for Sierra, well, her fate was unfortunate but unavoidable. Power such as hers was an intolerable threat. 'What
about Cam?'

'What about him?'

'What do you intend to do with him? And what do I tell him about this?'

'Tell him nothing except to keep his mouth shut. I've given orders he is to be confined to the tent, but if he gives any trouble I'll have him put in chains as well.'

'You don't mean to kill him, then?'

'Kill him? Why would we do that? He's the last of Leandra's line and we might still need him to father Mira's children.'

'The drug your men gave him has made him sick,' Ardamon said.

'Good. It'll keep him quiet for a while.' Dremman wiped the blade of his knife down with a scrap of oily wool and slid it into the sheath. 'Go to bed, Ardamon. In the morning we'll let it be known that our little sorcerer has deserted us. Tomorrow is likely to be a long day.'

Cam was sitting up and sipping tea when Ardamon returned to the tent. His face was deathly pale and his hands shook as they cupped the bowl.

Numb with weariness, Ardamon stamped the snow from his boots, stripped off his fur and hung it from a peg driven into the tent post.

'Well?' Rhia said to him. 'What news? Is there to be a search? They have only been gone a few hours. They might still be in the camp.'

Ardamon tried to speak but then broke off with a shake of his head. He went to the stove and poured himself a bowl of tea.

'No search,' Cam said with a rasp. 'Tell him what was missing from your supplies, Rhia.'

Rhia frowned as she glanced at her trunk. 'Thessalet. I brought it with me from Mesentreia. It is a powerful drug and one that does not grow in Ricalan. It kills in hours if it is not administered correctly. An unpleasant death.'

'No doubt your clan's physicians know that,' Cam said. 'If the drug is identified as the one that killed them Rhia will be named as the one who supplied it. She's a foreigner after all, with no ties here and no one to be angered when she's made a scapegoat.'

Ardamon drained the bowl and slammed it down on Mira's table.

'What have they done with Mira?' Cam said.

'She is safely on her way to Ruhavera. She's better off behind those walls than she is here with the Slavers so close.'

'And Sierra?'

'She deserted in the middle of the night,' Ardamon said. 'No doubt the witnesses are already primed and ready to tell of how she slipped past the sentries.'

'And what have they done with her? There's no blood here. If they cut her throat while she was sleeping it was done elsewhere ...'

Ardamon shook his head. 'Not that.'

'Then what? Where —' Cam suddenly broke off and went very still. 'Spirit of Storm defend us and Black Sun have mercy. He was telling the truth.' Cam set the bowl down and tried to stand. His legs, however, wouldn't support his weight. He was as unsteady as a newborn foal.

Rhia grabbed him by the arm and pulled him back down to the furs. 'Cam, sit! Or you will fall into the stove —'

'Fires below, Rhia, let me go! When she finds out the Gods only know what she'll do! I have to catch up with them ...'

'Cam!'

'Who?' Ardamon demanded. 'Who was telling the truth?'

After a brief struggle Cam lost what strength he had and sat heavily on the furs, his eyes hazy and unfocussed as he swayed gently from side to side.

'For the love of life, Cam, I swear I never heard of this before tonight,' Ardamon said. 'My father has sold her back to Kell but he doesn't intend her to reach him. He's planning to kill her and the apprentice both. Who knew of this? Who tried to warn you?'

'Rasten,' Cam said. 'Rasten told her the Wolf Clan was plotting against her. She refused to believe him.' He doubled over with a choking sound. Rhia held the basin under his nose again, but Cam pushed it away though his shoulders were heaving and a harsh, grating sound came from his throat.

'Cam!' Rhia grabbed his shoulders. 'Cam, what is wrong?'

He was laughing. 'Ah, my aunt, the dear departed Queen Leandra, who was murdered by a Mesentreian sorcerer ... she used to say that the Gods have a sick sense of humour.'

Ardamon turned to Rhia. 'That drug they put in the food. Does it drive people mad?'

'Just listen, you fool!' Cam said. 'Sierra forgave Mira, but she never trusted your clan. Rasten's been talking to her. He didn't want to risk another fight. After your father put her under guard she asked him to train her and he warned her that your clan was plotting something. When she finds out he was telling the truth ...' Cam raked his hand through his hair. 'I have to go after her.'

'Cam, you cannot stand, let alone ride after them in the dark and the snow!' Rhia pleaded with him.

'And Dremman has ordered you be confined to this tent,' Ardamon said. 'What good would it do anyway? There are a dozen men with her and they won't listen to anyone but my father.'

'The men will be dead before Rasten ever gets there,' Cam said. 'Were they planning to keep her drugged until the hand-over?'

'I suppose so,' Ardamon said. 'Father didn't tell me the details.'

'They would have to. Even the warding-stones won't hold her any more. They might find she wakes up a little earlier than they intended. You see, she wasn't that hungry when we came back to the tent. Mira and I were ravenous, but Sierra ate after her lesson. While Mira and I were stuffing ourselves, she only had half a bowl. Unless they're watching her very closely they're in for a nasty surprise. She'll wake up alone, confused and surrounded by enemies and with Rasten there ready to whisper in her ear ...'

'Surely she will not listen to him?' Rhia said, but there was a note of uncertainty in her voice.

'I don't know what she'll do,' Cam said. 'This is the second time the Wolf Clan has betrayed her. Why would she let you try for a third?'

'For you,' Ardamon said. 'She'd come back here for you.'

'Then help me ride after her!'

Ardamon reached for his fur. 'Rhia's right. You wouldn't make it. I'll go. I'll tell her everything.' He pulled on his coat and wrapped his sword-belt around it.

'Ardamon!' Cam called after him as he swung open the door. 'Don't push your horse too hard. If you get there before she wakes she'll probably kill you as well.'

# Chapter 31

Sierra only realised her world was in motion when it bumped to a stop. For a while now she had been growing steadily more aware of a pounding in her head and a foul, sickly taste in her mouth. It was only at the sudden cessation of movement that these sensations coalesced into coherent thoughts.

She was uncomfortable, lying half on her side and half on her belly, with her arm twisted awkwardly beneath her, but when she tried to move, she couldn't. Her fingers, exploring, found only rough cloth. Her hands seemed to be close together but she couldn't find the fingers of one hand with the other. Her feet could not be separated.

Blankets and furs were wrapped around her in a dense cocoon but she was chilled despite them. She lay on something hard and unyielding and as she tried to work out just what it was she felt a cord lashed across her shoulders pull tight and then come loose.

She was lying on a sled, lashed down like a piece of cargo. As the lashings were loosened the blankets over her shifted a little and then were pulled aside in a sudden blinding flash of sunlight.

'See that?' a voice said from somewhere above her head. 'She flinched. I reckon she's waking up. Time for another dose, I'd say.'

'I still think we ought to wait till she's stirring proper. The physician said she'd be out for hours yet. She's a slight little thing and I'd hate to give her too much. The king's man's expecting a fine live calf. He's not going to accept a load of dead meat instead.'

'Do you want her to wake up, you fool? Just fetch the cursed flask.'

There was some rustling of clothing and snow around her. It took all of Sierra's willpower not to move. She heard a trickle of liquid and then a voice, directly over her head this time, said, 'Hold her nose so she'll open her mouth. Get ready to put your hand over it once she's got the dose. This stuff tastes so foul folk will spit it out even in their sleep.'

Rough, coarse hands pressed against her face. Sierra forced herself to remain limp, resisting the rush of fury that came at the touch. At any other time her power would have been arcing over her skin by now but the drugged sleep had drained her reserves and there was no one here in enough discomfort to feed her.

She had to fight not to let the muscles of her jaw tense as massive fingers pinched her nostrils shut and another hand fumbled to pry open her mouth. When a calloused finger brushed against her lips, Sierra sank her teeth into his fingertip.

The man let out a shriek and threw himself back, thrashing and fighting like a calf at the first touch of a rope on its neck. He tasted foul, of dirt and grease and blood. Sierra opened her eyes to see faces and bodies of half a dozen men looming over her with many hands holding her down while others tried to pry her jaw apart. She held on for as long as she could, soaking up power until one of the men cuffed her across the face hard enough to dislodge her grip.

The beast within her roared into life, woken by the blow. It was a weak thing compared to her normal strength but sheer fury gave it an edge that bit deep. It swarmed over the men in a flickering net of light that tore through them like venom and filled her with a golden rush of power.

At the very first touch of it a searing line of fire bloomed around one of her wrists, scorching like hot metal. It dragged a cry of pain from her throat and the rippling threads of lightning flared red with pain as she tried to choke the power off.

Nearby, a horse squealed in fright. From her prone position Sierra saw it rear and then it bolted, yanking the sled beneath her into sudden, violent motion. For a moment the straps held her in place but when the horse veered in a few panicked strides the movement threw her out and sent her tumbling into the soft, deep snow.

She was wearing only soft indoor clothes but the sudden slap of the cold seemed distant and unimportant, buffered by the shield the power gave her. Sierra landed face down and spat out a mouthful of snow and blood. She still couldn't move, but it only then occurred to her it was because her hands and feet were bound.

Her wrists stung and throbbed. She knew that sensation and was in no hurry to invite it again. Sierra groped with hands bound behind her back but could get no purchase on anything. She could feel nothing, in fact, but the thick cloth that encased them. Mittens had been bound over them, she realised, before her wrists were tied with a cord. Her captors, whoever they were, were relying on Kell's old enchantments to contain her. With no time to repair them they must have merely tied them around her wrists and used the mittens so she couldn't get her fingers under them and wrench them free.

Sierra gritted her teeth and summoned her power. With a single slash she cut through cords, fabric, everything, and the cold touched her hands just as the punishment band flared again in a searing flash of heat that made her grunt in pain. With her hands free she sat up and tore the remains of the mittens away. Kell's old bracelets were there. The suppression stones were no longer strong enough to restrain her but the rubies gleamed at her darkly, wet now with the fluid from burst blisters. Sierra slipped her fingers under them and snapped the cords, dropping them into the snow. Then she freed her feet, slashing the cord with a quick lash of power.

She stood, sinking past her knees in the soft snow. The men who had been guarding her were running towards her with weapons in their hands. Their leader slowed when he saw the expression on her face and shifted his grip on the sword. 'Now then, miss,' he said. 'There's no need for all this. Just you do as you're told, and come quietly, or things will go cursed hard on you and your friends.'

Sierra let her power flare and surround her with a crackling nimbus of blue light. '*Make* me.'

Most of the men died when they tried to corner her and bring her back under control. What had possessed them to even try it Sierra couldn't say, but this time she didn't hesitate to kill them. She'd learned her lesson when Rasten had come to her on the riverbank.

When it was over, she felt drained. Not of power — power spilled over with every movement, leaving a trail of sparks crackling in the air — she simply felt empty and utterly alone. Nothing moved but the tips of the branches of the trees all around her, gently swaying in the air. The only sound was the wind moaning through the needles.

A few of them had tried to escape, fleeing on their panicked horses or in one case on foot. That was the one Sierra had followed, hoping to learn why they had brought her here and where 'here' even was.

But the fellow had heard her coming. The moment she had worked out his location was the instant he cut his own throat. She found him staring blankly up at the sky with the knife fallen from his hand and blood sheeting down his chest. He had blinked at her once, rolled his eyes and then died with one last rattle of breath.

If she could catch one of the spooked horses maybe she could follow the others, but in their place she would be riding as if all the demons of the underworld were after her. Her chance of catching up with them was small.

With a sigh, Sierra laid the dead man face down on the snow to strip off his coat, boots and any other gear she would need once her power calmed enough to let her feel the cold.

She was just setting the snowgoggles over her face when she heard the shuffling cadence of a horse trotting in snowshoes. Pulling the goggles down to hang around her neck, she moved away from the body lying in a smear of frozen red and let her scavenged war-coat conceal her as she hunkered against a drift of snow.

A man on horseback came into sight a few moments later. The horse was weary but skittish and it baulked as its rider urged it towards the crumpled corpse. Sierra now knew enough to recognise it as a finer beast than the scruffy ponies assigned to the rank and file of the warriors.

When the horse refused to move any closer the rider dismounted and with the reins in one hand crouched down to turn the body over.

Sierra clenched and unclenched her hands, working hard to keep her power in check.

With a shake of his head the figure stood, pushing his hood back and tugging down his goggles. Sierra narrowed her eyes when she saw his face. Ardamon.

He muttered a curse as he looked around, squinting in the sunlight and the glare. Then he looked down at the snow, just as she remembered her tracks would lead him to her. She tensed, readying her power, but Ardamon didn't move. In fact he held himself very still.

'Sierra?' he called quietly. It was cold enough that even a conversational tone would carry a long way. 'Sierra, I know you're here.

I've come to help you. I … Well, Cam sent me. I swear on what honour my clan has left that I had no part in this.'

'Why should I believe you?' she said, and stepped out from behind the trees, power ready to cast a shield. 'If Cam had something to tell me he would come and find me himself.'

'He's sick,' Ardamon said. 'They fed him the same thing they used to drug you and Mira, only he had a bad reaction to it. He couldn't stand, let alone ride. Rhia says he'll be alright in a day or so.'

'Mira?' Sierra said. 'What's happened to her?'

'Dremman sent her back to Ruhavera.'

'And what was the plan for me? Was he going to sell me back to Kell?'

Ardamon twisted the reins between his hands. 'Yes.'

'Tigers take him,' Sierra snarled. The burn around her wrist throbbed and tears stung her eyes. She blinked them back and turned her face up to the brilliant sky. 'He was telling the truth.'

'You mean Rasten?' Ardamon said. 'Cam told me.'

Sierra gritted her teeth, unsure whether or not she could believe him. She hadn't had time to take in the faces of the men gathered around her when she lay on the sled and there might well have been others who had hung back. She couldn't be sure Ardamon hadn't been among them. 'Why would you come to help me? You've never thought me to be anything more than a nuisance and a threat.'

Ardamon shifted his weight uncomfortably. 'I can't deny that. And I have no proof to offer you. Look, Lord Rasten was due to meet my father's men but I don't know when or where. Cam told me you might wake earlier than expected. All I could do was hope he was right and that I found you before they met to hand you over.'

Sierra hissed and turned on her heel to survey the surrounding land. Of course Rasten would be out here. Her mind was still addled by the drugs and the rush from the power she had gained was more a hindrance there than a help. The slowness of her wits frightened her.

'We should head back before Rasten realises something's gone wrong,' Ardamon said. 'My horse can carry two until we can track down one of the others from the escort —'

Sierra pressed the heel of her hand against her forehead. 'Wait! Wait just a moment.'

'There's no time.' He started towards her, leading the weary and reluctant horse after him. 'Get on. I'll ride behind you —'

Sierra backed away, raising one hand to warn him off. 'Just why in the Black Sun's name should I trust you?' she snapped. 'For all I know Dremman sent you here in case this all went wrong —'

'Fires Below, girl, just do as I say! For the love of life, there's no telling how close Lord Rasten and his men may be — ' Ardamon reached for her arm and Sierra slapped his hand away. She was tense enough that her power spilled over with the movement and a twisting strand of energy leapt up and stung him like a hornet. Ardamon stiffened with a grunt of pain and Sierra hastily called it back in while the horse danced and snorted at the end of the reins. It was pure luck that Ardamon kept enough of a grip on them to keep the beast from bolting.

'I have no reason to trust you,' Sierra said, while Ardamon swore and flexed his throbbing hand.

'On the honour of my clan!'

'What honour?' she spat.

He flushed and spluttered under her narrow gaze. He was as arrogant as only one of the noble-born could be. She had seen the same in Cam and Isidro on occasion, but the hard life they had led had beaten most of it out of them. Ardamon had always rubbed her the wrong way and now she couldn't be sure whether this was merely more of the same, or if her instincts were telling her something to which she ought to listen.

'Listen to me, you daft chit,' Ardamon said. 'We can sort this out when we get back to camp. Right now we have to move. If Lord Rasten catches up with us —'

'If he does, I'd rather it happened when I'm awake and full of power, not drugged into a stupor,' Sierra said. 'For that matter, why wait? He can't be far away. *Rasten!*' she shouted, and echoed the cry within her own mind, summoning him with power as well. Ardamon blanched and staggered back a few steps while his horse began to spook and plunge all over again.

*I'm here, Little Crow. I wondered when you'd get around to calling me. Look to the ridge to your south.*

She turned to see a flare of red light shoot up through the trees.

While her attention was diverted Ardamon came up behind her and clapped a hand on her shoulder, but then he, too, saw the light; she felt his hand tremble. 'You little fool,' he said hoarsely.

They had to wait only a few minutes until Rasten emerged from the trees, mounted on a fine black horse. At a distance of fifty yards or so he dismounted and approached on foot. 'Well, Sirri, do you believe me now?' he called as he led the horse over.

Sierra had moved out into the clearing to meet him. Behind her the remains of the men she'd killed lay scattered over the snow between the trees. Ardamon stood a little way back and to her left, where she could keep watch on him from the corner of her eye.

'Are you here to tell me you told me so?' Sierra said.

Rasten pushed his hood back, tugged his snowgoggles down and grinned at her, displaying a mouthful of neat white teeth as though this were the best joke he'd heard in an age.

'You could have warned me,' Sierra snarled at him.

'I told you everything I knew.'

He *had* told her. She'd just chosen not to believe him. Sierra folded her arms. 'Just what did you plan to do when Dremman's men handed me over?'

'Well, my sweet, I was going to keep them there until you woke up and let you decide what to do with them. Then I intended to give you a horse and whatever gear you wanted and send you on your way. I meant what I said, Sierra. I don't want to fight you again.'

Her power was surging with every nervous beat of her heart and swarming over her skin in a crackling pulse. She wasn't sure if Ardamon had noticed it but Rasten definitely had. She could sense his own power held quiescent in a way she hadn't yet mastered herself.

'Then why make the deal with Dremman?' Ardamon said.

'Hold your tongue, lordling, or I'll cut it out and feed it to the dogs,' Rasten said. 'Well? What are you going to do, Little Crow?'

Sierra watched him carefully. 'I have to go back.' She was prepared for him to react with anger and frustration but he just nodded, as though he'd expected as much.

'And what do you think Dremman will try next?'

She shuffled her feet in her too-large boots. Dremman wouldn't deal with Rasten again, not when he knew Rasten was playing an entirely different game. But he couldn't sell her directly to Kell, either. She was too powerful a weapon to be put into his hands. If Dremman could get no value from her he would likely find a way to kill her. If he resorted to poison it wouldn't be just her at risk, but Cam as well. All of this, even overlooking the danger to the pair of them, only lessened their chances of ever freeing Isidro from slavery. 'I have no choice,' she told him. 'I can't leave Cam and Isidro where they are. They're only in this mess because of me.'

'Getting caught up with them has made you weak,' Rasten said. 'They're a distraction.'

'No one survives out here alone.'

'Maybe not, but you didn't need to become bosom friends with them. Now those who wish you harm will turn on them instead. You can't protect them, Sierra. But if you come with me now, no one will ever threaten them to get at you.'

'I can't leave them. Not yet.'

'Not yet? But you're beginning to understand what I've been saying, aren't you? This is the only way you will ever be free.'

Sierra turned her face away. The thought of what he was suggesting terrified her. She knew what Kell's training would involve. 'I can't,' she said. 'I will not!'

'You will have to, Little Crow. I know you don't believe me, but your power is still growing. When it reaches its peak, you will understand.'

If he was right, there was no way Cam would stand by and let her go back — or Isidro, if he were in a position to stop it. But Isidro was beyond her reach and Dremman, once he saw what fruit his plans had borne, could well decide his next step ought to be to separate her from Cam. If that happened she would be alone again but for Rasten's voice whispering in her ear.

'I have to go,' Sierra whispered and took a step away from him.

'Then go,' Rasten said. 'But here, take my horse. He's used to carrying a sorcerer and he won't spook under you. The lordling's wretched beast won't carry the two of you far and my men will have rounded up all the others by now.' He held the reins out in one gloved hand.

Sierra had to summon all the courage she had to take the reins from his fingertips. When his fingers brushed hers she felt herself tremble. With the reins in her grip she backed away sharply, leading the horse with her. It tossed its head, snorting once in mild surprise, but then came with her meekly enough. Sierra turned it in a circle and swung up into the saddle in one quick motion, trying to keep Rasten in her sights as she did so. Some part of her couldn't believe he would let her go so easily, but Rasten did not move.

'I'll be here when you need me, Little Crow,' he said.

Sierra and Ardamon rode in an uncomfortable silence as they followed the tracks back to Dremman's camp. It took some hours, but they didn't exchange anything more than the most necessary words until Ardamon called a halt to let his weary horse rest.

They startled a small herd of white-tailed deer, which scattered at their approach, and Ardamon's mount didn't even nuzzle around the snow they had disturbed, but merely stood where he had let it stop, with one hind hoof cocked on its tip and its head down by its knees.

Sierra had eaten nothing since the night before and the few mouthfuls of snow she'd snatched along the way only made her thirst worse. While Ardamon stamped some warmth back into his feet, she hunted through the saddlebags to see what, if anything, Rasten sent with her. In one side she found a water-bag in a double-furred pouch. The water must have been hot when he set out, but now it had cooled to a slurry of ice. Sierra only took a few mouthfuls before replacing the stopper and putting the bag away. It might wet her throat, but it would chill her from the inside out. There was also a package of emergency rations, thick slabs of pemmican made by mixing ground dried meat and dried berries with rendered fat. There was nothing else in the saddlebags, a fact that further convinced her Rasten had always intended to let her have the horse. He had known she wouldn't return with him.

She broke off a piece of pemmican and offered it to the horse, trusting the beast's sense of smell, which was more acute than any human's. When the horse lipped it up from her palm she broke off a larger piece for herself and offered it to Ardamon as well, while he watched the whole affair. Rather grudgingly he took a piece and glared at it suspiciously.

'Why would you trust anything that creature gives you?'

'Because I know *he* wants me alive,' she said, checking the other saddlebag, which held more pemmican and nothing else. It would make a monotonous diet, but the fat would keep her warm and it needed no cooking. There was enough for a week or more and at least it was food she could trust.

Sierra considered Ardamon as they each gnawed on the bars, stiff and hard with the cold. 'Tell me,' she said at last. 'If you thought your father's plan was going to work, what would you have done? Would you have ridden after me anyway?'

Ardamon turned his glare on her. 'Do you understand what it means to be cast out by your clan?'

'To live as an outcast with no kin and no safe haven to turn to? Yes, Ardamon, I believe I do.'

'It's not as though I could have done anything. The men escorting you took their orders from my father. They wouldn't have listened to me if I countermanded him. Now you tell me. What would you have done if you'd woken up and found yourself in Rasten's camp?'

'Panicked, probably,' Sierra said.

'Would you have ridden away if he let you?'

'I couldn't leave Cam where he is.'

'Why not? Rasten was right about one thing. He's in danger as long as you stay with him.'

Sierra looked down at the snow. 'I couldn't walk away from Isidro.'

'And just what in the Black Sun's name can you do to help him? He's a slave now! He's beyond our reach. This is all fucked beyond repair, Sierra. I don't know what you're going to do now but you're mad if you stay in my father's camp.'

He looked haggard. *Of course*, she thought, *he's been riding all night while I at least slept for a few hours on the sled.*

'Why would Rasten think for a moment that you'd choose to go with him?' Ardamon demanded.

'He wants me to help him destroy Kell,' Sierra said with a shrug. 'What will you tell your father?'

'I'll tell him I rode after you because Cam was sure you'd wake early. Beyond that, I don't know.'

She had never got along with Ardamon, but for all his faults he was unfailingly honest, which seemed to be a rare quality among his clan. Sierra's instincts told her he was telling the truth. 'What do you think I should do?'

'I have no idea,' he said with a weary shake of his head. 'You should talk to Cam. He's had more experience in these things than I do.'

'Do you want me gone?'

'I won't lie. I'd have been happier if I had never laid eyes on you. But from what I've heard from that man Elomar about the raid on his village, I don't like the idea of facing the Akharian mages without any way to counter them. If it were my choice I would keep you here. But it's not up to me.'

The outer ring of sentries were puzzled to see them, but the men waved Ardamon through without question. As they approached the camp itself a man hailed Ardamon by name and came running to meet them. Sierra tensed but the fellow, wearing the badge of a camp aide, paid her no attention.

'Lord Ardamon, thank the Gods you've returned. Commander Dremman has been asking for you. There's been some dreadful news. Lady Mira and her escort were attacked by Akharian Raiders. The lady has been taken prisoner!'

'What?' Ardamon snapped. 'How? When did this happen?'

'Some hours ago this morning, my lord, but the rider who brought the news only returned an hour ago. Commander Dremman has had us searching the camp for you ever since.'

'I had best go see him,' Ardamon said and beckoned Sierra with an imperious flick of his hand. 'Stay close behind me,' he said and, as the aide leapt out of the way, he kicked his horse into a canter through the wide avenue between the tents while men on foot scattered from his path. Sierra turned Rasten's horse to follow.

The news was still spreading through the camp. Sierra could see groups of men huddled together, anxious and gesticulating. Shouts rose up around them as she followed Ardamon through the aisles. They were moving too quickly to hear any more than a few words, but Sierra caught a few sour looks turned her way and heard curses spat in her wake. Mira was popular and well respected and Sierra was a sorcerer, a herald of misfortune. Of course it was her fault this disaster had come to pass.

Dremman was standing outside his tent with fists jammed against his belt and his face red with fury as he barked orders. Mira's tent still stood in its usual place but her banner no longer flapped at the front and two men stood guard at the entrance, which had been laced shut from the outside.

Someone at the edge of the crowd spotted Ardamon and shouted his name. The cry ran ahead of them, and by the time he drew his horse to a halt in a shower of loose snow the crowd around Dremman had parted to let them approach.

'Where in the Black Sun's name have you been, boy?' Dremman snapped as his eyes raked over Ardamon and his trembling, weary horse. 'Your cousin —' Then his gaze fell on Sierra and his voice faltered.

She met his eyes and held the contact for a moment before turning away to dismount. A soldier came to lead the beast away but she made him wait for her to take the saddlebags off and sling them over her shoulder.

'Your cousin,' Dremman said to Ardamon, 'my dear niece, has been taken prisoner by the Slavers.'

'So I've been told,' Ardamon said. 'How could this happen, Father? Why was she put in such danger?'

'A messenger arrived from Ruhavera early this morning. One of Lady Mira's cousins was taken ill and Mira insisted she return at once to Ruhavera to care for her. I sent her with an escort of fifty men. Our scouts were certain the route was clear.'

Ardamon was turning white with anger, his lips bloodless as he clamped them down over his teeth. 'And what is to be done about it?' he said through clenched teeth.

'I've sent a detachment of three hundred riders to recover her under the command of Captain Hannomar. If you had been here, my boy, I would have sent them under you. You had better have a cursed good explanation for disappearing like this.'

'I do, Father. Perhaps in private ...'

Dremman glowered at him. 'In my tent, boy. You there,' he said, pointing to a nearby soldier. 'Escort Miss Sierra to her quarters and see she is not disturbed.'

The soldier bowed and Sierra let him usher her away from Dremman towards the familiar tent. She held a shield beneath her coat just in case.

The guards at the entrance bowed to her impassively before untying the cords that bound it. If they knew the circumstances in which she'd been spirited away during the night they showed no sign of it.

When she appeared in the opening Cam was sitting on his furs with a blanket around his shoulders and a bowl of tea in his hands. Rhia was tending the stove. At the sight of her they both stood.

When the flap fell closed behind her she heard the rustle of toggles and ties as they fastened it again. She refused to let the thought of being closed in bother her. After all, they could leave any time they liked. If only they had somewhere to go.

'Sirri — ' Cam said and crossed the tent in a few strides to enfold her in his arms.

'By the Bright Sun, Cam,' she said, returning the embrace for a moment before taking his face between her hands to get a proper look at him. His skin was pale, his eyes bloodshot. 'Ardamon said you were sick?'

'I'm fine,' he said, gruffly. 'What about you? What happened out there?' He took hold of her hands and she flinched when his grip pressed against the fresh burns. 'You're hurt,' he said and Rhia looked up sharply in the gloom. 'Tell me.'

'In a moment,' she said, setting the saddlebags down and shrugging off her coat. Cam took it from her to hang it up and she could tell from the way he looked it over that he realised it wasn't the one she usually wore. 'Have you heard the news about Mira?'

He paused with the coat still in his hands. 'What news?'

Ardamon returned just as Rhia was tying off the fresh bandages around Sierra's wrists. Cam was pacing back and forth across the cramped confines of the tent while on the stove a small pot of stew bubbled. Cam and Rhia had cooked it in anticipation of Sierra's return so they would have a meal they could be certain was unadulterated. None of them had much appetite now but if they left it unattended they would have to discard it and start over again.

Ardamon lifted the flap and hesitated for a moment while cold air and drifting snow swirled in around his shoulders. 'My father is here to speak to you,' he said at last and came inside while another soldier held the flap up for Dremman.

Sierra searched the war-leader's face for any hint of shame or guilt. Not for what he had tried to do to her, she expected no regret for that, but for what his actions had done to Mira. The cold gaze he turned on Sierra seemed to indicate he blamed *her* for what had come to pass.

'Miss Sierra,' he said. 'You have my apologies for this unfortunate incident. It seems agents of the king who had been planted among my

433

men were responsible for your abduction. I am most relieved their plot came to nothing.'

'You are?' Sierra said. 'Perhaps you can tell me, War-Leader, did this occur before or after Mira decided to return to Ruhavera?'

'After, of course,' Dremman said. 'If you were not here when Mira left your absence would have been noticed and the alarm raised. My men think it most likely that some of these fellows crept in here once Mirasada had departed and drugged you while you slept. Unfortunately we cannot be sure we have discovered all the king's spies. It would be best for you to remain here in Mirasada's tent. I will leave the guards in place, for your safety, of course. It would be best not to make much fuss over this little incident. There are those among my men who distrust your kind and if rumours were to spread that you made an attempt to desert and return to your former master, the mood of my men could turn dangerous very quickly.'

'Oh, I understand *perfectly*, War-Leader,' Sierra said. 'But you may rest assured, if I detect any other threat towards me or my friends I will make every effort to keep the culprits alive so they can face the clan's justice.'

'Quite so,' Dremman said, with a smile that had every appearance of warmth. 'Well then, Miss Sierra, I will leave you to rest and recover from your ordeal. If you need anything don't hesitate to ask one of your guards. They will supply you with anything you require.'

Once he left Sierra went over to the entrance to listen as the guards took up their positions again. No doubt Dremman had ordered them to report on any conversations they could hear. The rest of the tent was tightly sewn from reindeer hides with water and windproof seams. The doorway was the one weak point where they might be able to overhear what was said. It was too bad Mira was gone. The strumming of her setar would have made their conversation unintelligible but perhaps a crackling fire and the hiss of a simmering kettle would be enough, so long as they kept their voices down.

'How much did you tell your father?' she said quietly to Ardamon, who had seated himself in Mira's chair with his chin resting on his fist.

'Only that Cam convinced me you would wake early. He accepted I made the right choice.'

'Didn't he want to know why you didn't come and tell him that before riding off?' Cam said.

'It would have taken too long. I only just reached her in time as it was.'

'And does he know I know the truth of what happened?' Sierra asked him.

'Probably. I only told him you were suspicious. He wouldn't have believed anything less.'

'And what about Rasten?' Cam said.

'I told him nothing of that. If he knew he would be making plans to have you killed without delay.'

'Oh, yes,' Sierra said with a toss of her head. 'The only thing worse than a sorcerer is a sorcerer you know cursed well you can't control. What's his next move?'

'How in the hells should I know? Look, you arrogant little chit! I've spent this entire day running around like a servant for your sake! And if it wasn't bad enough that my cousin was hauled away like a cow to the market, the only reason my father seems to care is because of the trouble it's going to make when we postpone the betrothal. Am I the only one who cares one jot what's going to happen to Mira?'

'You're not,' Cam said. 'But there's nothing we can do about that right now.'

Ardamon hurled his tea-bowl against the stove, where it shattered in a clatter of pottery shards. 'How dare you?'

'It was true when we learned Isidro had been taken and it's true now,' Cam said. 'We'll get her back. We *will*. But for the moment we have a more pressing concern.'

Ardamon clenched his fists with a snarl.

'We need a plan *now*,' Cam said, ignoring his anger. 'And we need to know if we can trust you.'

Ardamon clenched his hands around the arms of the chair and rolled his head back with a sound halfway between a roar and a moan. 'Black Sun take you, you son of a bitch! Do you think I would do that to Mira? This … this sorcerer of yours.' He pointed one long finger at Sierra. 'She may be as flighty as a yearling filly but she's the best chance we have of taking Mira back. Just what kind of man do you think I am that I would abandon her like that?'

'I think you're a man who is loyal to his kin and his clan,' Cam said. 'Dremman isn't going to sit back and pick at his teeth because his plan failed. No doubt he's already concocting another way to get rid of Sirri.

If you're serious about helping us you're going to have to lie to his face. If you can't do that then you had better leave now.'

'I'll keep your secrets,' Ardamon said through clenched teeth. 'I'd swear it on the honour of my clan but I doubt that you would accept that oath.'

'No,' Sierra said. 'Swear it on your cousin's life. That, I will accept.'

'On Mira's life, I swear,' Ardamon said and then buried his face in his hands.

While they spoke Rhia had been mixing a blend of herbs in a bowl. She poured water onto them and carried it around the stove to press it into Ardamon's hands. 'You are distraught,' she told him gently. 'Drink this. It will help clear your mind.'

Ardamon roused himself with a shudder and glared at Rhia as though he wanted to throw the bowl in her face, but he calmed himself with a deep breath and took it from her with a bow of his head.

'Alright,' Cam said. 'I've had all day to think this over and I think we can keep you safe, Sirri. We will cook for ourselves and Rhia and I can be food-tasters for you. With the four of us we can keep a watch through the night without going too short on sleep —'

'No,' Sierra said, shaking her head. 'It's not going to work.'

'Sirri, we can do it. It won't be easy —'

'No, we can't. Dremman will work out what we're doing, then what do you think he'll do next? The whole point of food-tasters is that they're *expendable* and have less value to the one they're protecting than they do to his enemies. He'll poison you both. It would be a death sentence.'

Cam sighed and bowed his head in defeat. 'What do you suggest, then?'

'I don't know,' Sierra said, raking her hands through her tangled hair. 'Striking out on our own isn't feasible. We tried that and we failed.'

'Agreed,' Cam said. 'What other options are there?'

Sierra sat down on the spruce floor. She felt grimy and filthy and she wanted a bath, a hot meal, and hours of dreamless sleep in her furs. 'What if … what if I reached an agreement with Rasten?'

'That's out of the question!' Cam snapped.

'Wait — just hear me out. We need to get Isidro and Mira back. That's our first priority, isn't it?'

436

Cam hooked his thumbs into his belt and scowled. 'Yes, but it won't change anything with Dremman and Kell. Our situation here will be the same.'

'I realise that,' Sierra said. 'I doubt there's anything that will change Dremman's view of me. I'm a threat to his clan's power, as the other mages were. He has to be rid of me. But if I do what Rasten wants and join him to destroy Kell … Well, that would change things. It would change everything.'

'Forgive me for not understanding this brilliant plan,' Ardamon drawled. 'Which, if I'm not mistaken, is the very same thing those men died this morning to prevent. But how in the Black Sun's name is turning you over to Rasten supposed to help Mira?'

'I could make a deal with him,' Sierra said. 'I could surrender in return for troops to wipe out the Slavers and Rasten's help against the Akharian mages. When Isidro and Mira are free I would turn myself in.' She was trying to maintain the appearance of calm but on the final words her voice cracked and betrayed her.

'Sirri,' Cam said. She could feel his eyes upon her. 'You told me you'd rather die than go back. You said you surrendered once and it was the worst decision you ever made.'

Tears were stinging her eyes. She tried her best not to let them spill. 'It was the wrong decision then. But I can't sit back and watch the people I care about die. Not again.'

'No,' Rhia said, breaking into the discussion for the first time. 'Do not do this, Sierra. You would be choosing a life of slavery and I know what happens to a woman who is made a slave. There must be another way.'

'But I don't know what else to do!' Sierra wailed. 'I can't stay here and I can't go! What other choice is left to me?'

The very moment when the words left her mouth a possibility came to her. She felt herself go very still.

There *was* one other place she could go. A place where she would be beyond the reach of both Rasten and Dremman. A place where even Kell couldn't touch her.

She sensed rather than saw Cam looming over her. She was still frozen to the spot when he asked, 'What is it?'

'The Slavers,' she whispered. 'The Akharians and their mages …'

437

'What of them?' he said, puzzled, and then went still, just as she had. 'The books. Vasant's books! Isidro's already found some of them. They would teach you what you need to know. You wouldn't need Rasten to guide you. You could go after Kell on your own terms.'

Sierra had no faith in her ability to learn from books alone. Studying Kell's book had taught her nothing. It was only once she had begun her lessons with Rasten that her abilities had grown. Isidro had suspected that the book was deliberately written to be confusing so an apprentice couldn't learn without his master's direction. Surely Vasant's books would be different. They were *meant* to pass the knowledge down, not hoard it like a miser.

'What are you talking about?' Ardamon demanded.

'I could let myself be captured by the Akharians,' Sierra said. 'Neither Rasten nor Dremman could reach me in the Slavers' camp. If I can wipe out their mages it will go a long way towards evening the odds against your father's men.'

'But isn't there a small matter you're forgetting?' Ardamon said. 'The Akharians check their slaves for mage-talent. What makes you think you can get past their sentries?'

'And what about your power?' Rhia said. 'The life of a slave is a difficult one. There will be people suffering all around you. You already have trouble keeping your power in check and I promise you it will be much, much worse in there. And that is not all you must consider. You are young and beautiful. You will be raped, probably many times. I know this. I was a slave myself.'

Sierra nodded. 'It's a possibility I know, but —'

'A possibility? You're not taking this seriously — ' Cam shouted.

'Of course I am!' Sierra said. 'But it's not exactly a new threat, is it? I lived with it for two years in Kell's dungeons. Every day I thought this would be the day Kell would let Rasten have me. And then there were the rituals ...' She could feel the spruce beneath her but for a moment all she could see was the grey stone and the flickering shadows and all she could hear were sobs of pain, mingled with the tormentors' breathy grunts of sadistic pleasure.

Cam's voice startled her out of it. 'You said they never touched you —'

'Not *me*, not *my* flesh and blood, but everyone else who came into Kell's dungeons was given the treatment. I felt the echo, until the power rose to drown it out ...' When it did, she retreated into it willingly, grateful for the refuge.

'Everyone?' Ardamon scoffed. 'Every woman, you mean.'

'No,' Sierra said. '*Everyone*. Rasten wants only women but Kell prefers men and Rasten does as he says. Kell likes pain and humiliation, whatever the flavour.'

'You mean ... Isidro —' Ardamon fell abruptly silent when Cam turned on him a glare so hard and vicious it turned Sierra cold.

'As I said,' she broke the silence, 'it's a possibility. But if I went back to Kell it would be a certainty. Among the Slavers I'll at least have a chance to defend myself.'

'Without giving yourself away?' Cam's voice was calm but Sierra could see the tightness around his eyes that showed he was holding himself under rigid control. 'How?'

'I'm not sure,' Sierra said. 'I ... I'll need to talk to Rasten. If there's a way, he'll help me find it. He'd rather keep me for himself.'

Cam frowned at her. 'Are you sure about this?'

'I don't see any other choice.'

He sighed and bowed his head. 'Alright, then,' he said. 'Rhia, make a list. If we're seriously going to consider this, there are a number of things we need to decide.'

# Chapter 32

The new book still stank of the glue used in the bindings, but to Delphine it was almost a comfort, the scent of home. Fontaine wrinkled her nose, but Alameda didn't seem to care as she bent close to peer at the diagrams and the odd, unfamiliar script, while Harwin leafed through the pages. The scribes had been working day and night to copy the text from the steaming surface of the water and this was the first fruit of that harvest.

When Harwin lost interest in the incomprehensible text and signalled to Lucia to pour him a bowl of tea, Delphine decided her girls had been distracted enough. 'Pass it to me, Alameda,' she said. 'It's no good to you until you learn the letters, so you had best attend to your lessons.' Alameda pouted but didn't argue as she closed the heavy tome and handed it to her teacher.

The book was plain and hastily constructed, lacking even the most basic metal fittings to hold the enchantments protecting the pages from fire and mould. The stones had merely been pushed into crude pockets sewn to the leather covers. Back in Akhara they would be rebound with sturdier end-pieces, but now time was more important than presentation. As soon as the ink was dry on the last page the army would be on the move again, marching for the place known as Demon's Spire.

The days until then were an opportunity Delphine could not afford to waste. Torren still hadn't forgiven her for spiriting the slave away and he wasn't the only one working against her. The other academics resented her for swooping in and discovering the device while they had been occupied with the decoy caches. Noises were being made about the propriety of allowing a woman to work so closely with a barbarian male and some muttered that her investigations of Aleksar's peculiar manifestations of mage-talent were straying perilously close to the crime of teaching mage-craft to a slave.

The fact that it was she who had discovered the device had bought her some grace, but unless she quickly followed the discovery with some tangible results, those whisperers would win and she would lose possession of the slave. Delphine desperately needed every hour the scribes spent scribbling away in the dark.

With the heavy book in her arms Delphine turned to the rear of the tent, where Aleksar was tethered once again to one of Harwin's trunks. He sat in utter silence with his back pressed against the wood, his elbows propped on his knees and his head hanging low.

Delphine bit her lip. It was becoming harder to ignore his grief. Until that day in the caves he had merely been trying to survive, but now she suspected it had finally struck him that he would never see his loved ones and his kin again.

She ought to be able to dismiss his despair. He was a slave after all, and she a free woman. A slave was a walking, talking tool, nothing more. What he thought and felt should have been utterly irrelevant to her. She knew she ought not to concern herself with it, but she simply couldn't block it out any longer. There were few enough people in the world that she loved, and the idea of being stolen away without hope of ever seeing them again was enough to bring her half to tears.

Delphine perched on a corner of the chest and laid her hand on his shoulder. He stiffened at her touch and lifted his head, craning it back to meet her gaze. 'Madame?' he murmured.

His eyes were such a dark brown as to be almost black. Now that she had grown used to his barbarian features, the high cheekbones and the wide-set eyes with the epicanthal fold, Delphine was willing to concede he was quite handsome. Or at least he would be, if he ever smiled. Not that she could ever admit to such a thing.

She had tried ignoring his grief. She had tried jollying him along or badgering him out of it, but all to no avail. Now she knew there was nothing she could do but let it pass, although she could perhaps offer him some distraction in the meantime. She only hoped it would be enough to draw him out of his bleak despair. If she failed to make him produce the information the Collegium and the general demanded, he would be taken from her and she would no longer be able to protect him from the Battle-Mages and their interrogations.

441

'Here,' she said and passed him the book. 'Before we reach Demon's Spire we must compile a catalogue of the books from Milksprings. I will need you to read through this as best you can in the next day or so and then write a brief report of its contents before the scribes deliver the next one. There is a great deal of information to go through, Aleksar. You're about to take a very intensive course in Ricalani mage-craft.'

He looked so weary that for a moment she thought he would set the book aside, but then, almost with reluctance, he opened the cover and began leafing through the pages. After a long moment, the lure of knowledge drew him in as she had hoped. He sat up a little straighter and fumbled inside his shirt for the lantern-stone around his neck.

Delphine had work of her own awaiting her, but she stayed where she was and watched as he leafed through the pages. She ought to be studying the Ricalani syllabary she had made him write out, or working to find another translator, but she couldn't bring herself to do either, not if it meant that Aleksar would be free to face Torren's interrogations again. She didn't want to see him bruised and bloody from another session, or worse, broken down as he had been when she first saw him chained like a dog in the supply tent. He deserved better.

'Don't sit up with it all night,' she told Aleksar and with a final pat of his shoulder she stood and stretched just as someone rang the bell on the ridge-pole outside. Hiding a yawn behind her hand, Lucia scrambled up to open the door.

'Is Madame Castalior in this tent?' a man outside said. Delphine had been half afraid it would be Torren, but instead it was one of the general's functionaries.

'I am she,' she said, heading to the door. 'Who is asking for me?'

'The general requests your attendance, madame,' the messenger said. 'Along with your translator. The general has come into possession of a high-ranking captive and he wants your slave to question her.'

Isidro's worst fears were confirmed when he saw the bright red flash of Mira's hair.

At first he had been irrationally afraid it would be Sierra, but he knew that fear was absurd. She would never be foolish enough to allow herself to be taken by the Slavers. Still, he couldn't imagine how Mira had been in a position to be captured — she ought to be miles away, safely ensconced within the Wolf Clan's army.

She was kneeling on the floor of the general's tent with her braids in disarray and her hands bound behind her back as she glared furiously at the spruce beneath her. She was dressed in a clanswoman's finery: a jacket with full, wide sleeves intricately decorated with layers of coloured fabric and a shirt woven with a fine pattern of coloured threads. Each of her braids was tipped with a golden bead and she wore wide bracelets on her wrists and a necklace at her throat. Isidro couldn't imagine why she would be dressed in such a manner out here in the war-torn north.

He tried to guard his expression, but Delphine was nothing if not observant. While they were still at the back of the crowd that had gathered in the general's tent she caught his arm and held him back. 'Who is she?'

He warred for a moment over telling the truth. If he lied and said she was of no importance it would put Mira in a terrible position. A slave woman was free game to any man who wanted her and Mira's exotic looks meant she would catch many eyes. He couldn't subject her to that, not if there was anything he could do to prevent it. 'She's heir to the Wolf Clan, the family that rules this region. I have no idea what she was doing out here, to be captured by your men.'

'Really?' Delphine breathed, her eyes wide. 'A tribal princess?'

'I suppose so,' Isidro said. There was a cluster of men standing behind Mira. In the warmth of the tent they had stripped off their outer furs and the insignia on their uniforms were not the same as the ones he had grown familiar with. 'Madame, may I ask, who are those men with her?'

She stood on her toes in an attempt to see them. 'It looks as if they're from the Seventeenth! How interesting!'

'Madame?'

'The commander of the Seventeenth married the general's daughter. Actually, she ran off with him after the general promised her to a friend of his. It was an awful scandal and Boreas tried to have the marriage annulled, but they reached some sort of agreement in the end and now Druseus, that's the commander, must be trying to repair some bridges by sending such a valuable prize to his father-in-law. My, she's a pretty thing. Such a shame. She's a noblewoman, you say?'

Delphine had sidled around so she could see Mira in profile. As her voice came closer Mira glanced up furtively and her eyes fell on Isidro. She registered no surprise on seeing him, giving him a glare full of venom and disgust.

Delphine went very still and turned to him with a frown. 'A noblewoman. Your nobles all speak Mesentreian, do they not?'

Isidro felt ill. Mira could translate from Ricalani to Mesentreian as well as he could. She wouldn't willingly help her captors, but the Akharians would have no hesitation in doling out the sort of treatment that would bend her to their will. If the rapes and beatings were enough to make her capitulate then *he* would be freed to face Torren's interrogations again.

Delphine grabbed his arm, her fingers clenching tight, and she pulled him down until she could whisper in his ear. 'Don't mention a word of it,' she hissed. 'I will not have you sent back to Torren to be tortured. And that girl — do you know her? You must do if you were noble-born yourself.'

Isidro held himself still, wondering if he dared trust her. It would give her something to hold over him, but what did that matter? She held near-total power over him anyway. He nodded his head, moving just a fraction of an inch.

'Well,' she said. 'I'll see what can be done to protect her, but I can't promise anything. Now, stand at my heel and don't speak unless you're spoken to.'

He fell into step behind her as she shoved her way through the crowd to the head of the tent to await the general.

When General Boreas finally arrived, he tramped through the entrance without bothering to stamp the snow from his boots. 'Now then, what is this all about?'

'A gift from Commander Druseus, sir,' the leader of the newcomers proffered. 'This barbarian noblewoman was captured by his men this morning and he presents her to you with his compliments.'

'Yes? And what exactly am I supposed to do with her?'

Isidro studied Mira's reactions while the men talked over her. The Akharian language was close kin to Mesentreian so she may have been able to pick out a word here and there but probably not enough to understand what was being said.

444

'General, my slave tells me this woman is the daughter of a clan chieftain,' Delphine said, once the men from the Seventeenth had said their piece.

'Really?' The general was a short, bullish man with a shaved head and a close cropped beard. He looked more like a labourer than a soldier, but his eyes were sharp and intelligent and Isidro had seen enough of the man to suspect he had earned his command. 'Well, she looks the part, I suppose,' Boreas said. 'What in the hells is she doing all the way out here?'

'With your permission, sir, I will have the slave ask her.'

Boreas gave his assent with a wave and sat himself down in his fur-swathed chair.

Delphine motioned for Isidro to step forward. As a slave he was required to kneel before speaking to his superiors and at her gesture he sank to the ground beside Mira. In Ricalani, he said, 'Lady, they want to know what you are doing out here and where you were going when you were captured.'

'I'll tell you nothing, traitor,' Mira snapped and she spat in his face.

It happened so quickly Isidro didn't have time to flinch. The tent erupted with laughter as he wiped the spittle away with his sleeve.

'Well, we need no translator for that,' Druseus's man said with a grin. 'What do you think, sir? Is your cripple a match for a barbarian girl or should we give him a hand?'

'Well, Madame Castalior?' Boreas said. 'Is your servant up to the task?'

'I suggest we let him get on with it, sir,' Delphine said, keeping her expression severe and unamused.

Isidro leaned towards Mira. 'Don't be a fool,' he told her. 'They'll get what they want one way or another. It's in your best interest to cooperate. Why were you out here in the north?'

'Why don't you tell them yourself, traitor?' she hissed.

'How would I know?' he said. 'I was nothing but a destitute cripple sheltering in a temple,' he said. 'I have no idea why a clanswoman would be out here in the wilderness. They want an explanation, but whatever you do don't let them know you speak Mesentreian.'

She closed her mouth with a snap and Isidro shoved down the urge to shake her. She'd had hours in which to come up with a story and he knew Mira was clever enough to know she ought to have one ready.

445

'I was on a pilgrimage to prepare for my betrothal,' she said, grudgingly. 'In the bad weather my escort must have travelled off course.'

He repeated her words to the general.

'Betrothal?' Boreas said. 'Isn't she a little old to be a bride?'

'Sir?'

'Ricalani girls marry later than Akharians do, sir,' Delphine broke in. 'And it's not uncommon for the noble-born to hold out for an alliance that suits them. Does she come from a wealthy clan, Aleksar?'

'Yes, madame, one of the wealthiest. Her family would pay a fine ransom for her return. More than she would fetch on the block in Akhara.'

Boreas chuckled. 'I think you underestimate what Akharians will pay for a barbarian princess. What ransom could a Ricalani tribe possibly pay that would be valuable to civilised man?'

'Furs, sir?' Isidro said. 'I am told that sable and mink fetch a high price in Akhara. Her clan would pay you several hundred-weight of each. Then there's the matter of gold and jewels. The northern ground is rich with both. You could use her as a bargaining chip, too, to keep her clan from attacking your men. But she is worth more to them if she's untouched and in fair condition. They will not want to break the betrothal.'

Boreas stroked his bristling chin. 'Well then ... perhaps this *is* a matter worth considering.' With a flick of his fingers he signalled his men to come and take charge of her. 'I'll think it over. In the meantime take her to the slave camps but put her in with the women and children and let it be known that I want her untouched. If any man trifles with her and lessens her value I'll take the difference out of his pay.'

When Delphine was dismissed a short time later Isidro followed her in a miserable silence as she led the way back to the Collegium quarters. 'You did a good thing there, Aleksar,' she told him. 'You have spared that poor girl a great deal of misery. You should be pleased with yourself.'

'I'll be pleased when she's back with her family,' he said. 'I don't want to see her sold into a brothel in Akhara.'

'Oh, she's far too pretty for a brothel. They only buy ugly women. They're cheaper. Brothels make their money on quantity, not quality. The good-looking ones end up in rich men's households.' She glanced at his face and grimaced. 'I'm not helping, am I? Well, come on, then, it's time I let you get back to your work.'

It was in the early hours of the morning that Sierra stood motionless by the door of the tent, trying to sense the world on the other side of the hide. She could vaguely feel the men, who seemed to have been chosen so as not to feed her any power, but the rest of it was a blank void to her senses.

Rasten could pick up an object on the other side of a locked door. He would be able to find the thongs that bound the door closed and untie them with a touch, but she could do no such thing.

Standing behind her she heard Ardamon fidget and Cam hissed at him to be still. She wanted to yell at them both to be silent, but instead with a mental curse she simply slashed through the flap, aiming for where she remembered the ties to be and slicing through leather and fur indiscriminately.

She threw the door open and before the men standing guard could do more than turn in surprise, she grabbed them by the arms and dropped them with a bolt of power. Then she turned to the men warming themselves by the fire.

They were on their feet and reaching for their weapons when Sierra dropped them, too. With her power riled up like a dog expecting a hunt, it took her several moments to bring it back under control, while Cam and Ardamon picked up the fallen men and carried them into the tent where they would be safe from frostbite and hypothermia.

'Right then,' Cam said to Ardamon. 'How long are you going to give us?'

'Half an hour or a bit more if I can manage it,' Ardamon said. 'You had best move quickly. I'll have a small group of men with me. Dremman won't hear of me riding off alone, but it shouldn't be hard to convince him she'll react badly if she sees a troop of warriors charging after her.'

The way he spoke about her as if she weren't present still put Sierra's teeth on edge, but she now believed Ardamon was on their side, convinced by his genuine fury over what had happened to Mira.

The plan, when Cam and Ardamon returned to camp without her, was for them to spread the word that she was too wary of more spies to remain in the camp and had gone to infiltrate the Akharian camp and to strike at them as she had in the village.

Cam wrapped his sword-belt over his coat and picked up the light packs that were all he and Sierra would be carrying. His contained only the most minimal of supplies but Sierra's held a small tent and a tiny brazier. She hadn't wanted to carry that much until Cam had pointed out that any warrior worth his salt would be suspicious of a captive taken without even the most basic gear for survival.

With their gear, she and Cam walked swiftly through the camp, heading for the tether-lines. Several times they had to duck between the tents to avoid early-morning wanderers but at this hour the camp was mostly quiet and still.

There were two men standing watch over the horses. Sierra felt guilty when she dropped them both with a bolt of power and made sure their coats were well wrapped to protect them from the cold before she went to help Cam with the horses. He had already saddled Rasten's black, which tugged at her sleeve with velvet lips and eagerly snuffled a piece of bannock she offered from her palm. The horse lifted its feet obediently when she knelt to fasten the snowshoes around its hooves and offered no protest as she turned its head away from its herd-mates and nudged it out into the night.

'I wish we had another day to think this over,' Cam said once they were far enough away to speak in safety.

'I thought you were the impulsive one and it was Isidro who devised the plans and strategies.'

'It used to be that way,' Cam said. 'But everything is different now. Are you sure you're prepared for this, Sirri?'

'Rasten said he had solutions for all our concerns,' she said. 'He wouldn't be agreeing to this if he thought I would end up dead.' Sierra knew it didn't quite answer Cam's question, but she wasn't prepared to discuss it. From this point on she would have to keep her power under rigorous control and focussing on her fears and worries now would only result in it rising up again. *I've learned so much in the last two months*, Sierra told herself yet again. *I'll be able to control it this time. I know I will.*

They met Rasten just after dawn. His escort waited some distance away, gathered in plain sight. Rasten strode out to meet them alone with his coat open and swinging from his shoulders and his hands clasped behind his back. Since they'd set out Sierra had been wondering what mood they would find him in and once they drew close enough for her to make out his eyes, she sighed in resignation. His good humour of the day before was gone. Today his face was tight and hard and he watched Cam with a narrow gaze as they approached.

'Good morning, Little Crow,' Rasten said to her as she reined in and dismounted, dropping her mount's reins to make him stand. 'Do you mean to hand the gelding over to the Akharians, too?'

'Cam will take him back for me,' she said.

Rasten shrugged and Sierra relaxed a little. Perhaps his mood wasn't as dark as she had thought. 'And so you are set on this course, Little Crow? There's nothing I can say to change your mind?'

'Nothing,' Sierra said. 'Until Isidro is safe I can't consider anything else.'

'I don't suppose it has occurred to you that Balorica's better off where he is? The Collegium won't care if he's crippled so long as his mind is sharp enough to serve, and he'll be beyond Kell's reach. Valeria's, too.' Rasten turned his gaze to Cam. 'This one would be wise to join him. He would survive longer in an Akharian mine than he will when Dremman realises he is working against him.'

'I've made up my mind, Rasten,' Sierra said.

He sighed. 'So you have. I ought to be glad of it. You would be no good to me if your spirit was broken. Tell me, Sierra, have you ever heard the tale of the prisoner in the tower who tamed the birds that lived in the rafters and watched their flight? It's a load of horseshit, of course. Any jailer who knew his business would have poisoned the birds. But you're my bird, Little Crow, and I won't stop you from flying.'

Cam shuffled his feet in the snow. 'Sirri,' he said in an undertone. 'We have a time limit here.'

Rasten swung around to glare at him with undisguised hostility. 'So you have,' he said and reached into his pocket to pull out a pair of milky-white stones. For a moment Sierra stared at them in sheer surprise. They were identical to the ones that had littered the scorched ruins of the village.

Rasten held one up to show to her. 'Oh, they're yours, sure enough. I had some men ride out there to gather them. This one is for you,' he said, holding it out to her. 'You'll have to keep it hidden. At least you have a choice as to where. If I had a cunt I'd choose that over the other option.'

That made Cam choke a little and when Rasten turned his gaze back to him Sierra cursed inwardly. She had been hoping to keep Rasten's attention fixed on her. To drag him back she stepped closer and took the stone from his hand, letting her fingers brush against his. It worked. Rasten turned back to her and held her gaze as she slowly stepped back again.

'Of course if they find it on you they'll know you're playing them,' Rasten said. 'If any man takes a shine to you, you will have to deal with it quickly.'

Sierra nodded and focussed on the stone in her hand, trying to make sure it was the communication device she and Rasten had agreed upon, and nothing more.

'That's it?' Cam said. 'You know how the Akharians treat their slave-women and *that's* the extent of your concern for her?'

'Cam —' Sierra said, her heart sinking as Rasten's head snapped around to focus on him again. *By the Black Sun, why couldn't he leave well enough alone?*

'You think I should be concerned?' Rasten said. 'I would be happier if no other man ever touched her, but that's not within my control. She knows what she's letting herself in for. Better than you do, I'd imagine, although your brother could no doubt tell you a thing or two about it.'

Cam recoiled and began to snarl a reply and as Rasten threw his head back in a peal of laughter Sierra grabbed Cam by the arm, prepared to use power to restrain him if she had to.

'You son of a bitch —' Cam began as Sierra dug her fingers into his arm.

'Don't let him bait you,' she hissed.

Rasten was watching them both with mild interest. 'It's such a little thing,' he said. 'At worst it's a few unpleasant hours, but it's inevitable and at the end of it all what difference does it make?'

'If you really think that way,' Cam said, 'why is it so important for you to kill your master?'

Rasten's face turned flat. He started towards Cam but Sierra pushed herself between them. 'Rasten! We have other things to attend to.'

'That fool of a prince —'

'*He doesn't understand*, Rasten.' She caught Cam's eye with a warning glare. 'He doesn't know what he's talking about.'

'Oh, I think I do,' Cam said. 'I'm talking about total and utter hypocrisy. You claim to care about her, Rasten, and yet you don't blink an eye when there's every chance that she'll be passed around a camp full of soldiers —'

'What's your point?' Rasten said. 'It's just fucking.'

'Rasten! I told you, he doesn't understand.' She placed both hands on his chest and felt his power pulsing beneath his skin, hotter than blood.

'If I ever get the chance, princeling, I'll *make* you understand,' Rasten said. 'That's a promise.'

'Rasten, what about the other stone?' Sierra said, desperate to bring him back on track. She could fight him here if she had to but the display it would create would undoubtedly draw notice and it would delay their plans by days at least.

'The other one is for him,' Rasten said. 'Since he doesn't have so much as a spark of power we'll have to seal it to him with a ritual so he can use it.'

'A ritual?' Sierra said. 'You didn't mention that.'

Rasten shrugged. 'You wanted some way to communicate. There aren't many options when one of you has as much talent as a lump of coal.'

'Alright, then,' Sierra said, 'but *I'll* do it.' If Rasten did the working, he would have a permanent link with Cam. Since Cam had no talent at all it would be of limited use, but it was still something Sierra would far rather avoid. 'You'll have to walk me through it. Give me the stone.'

He handed it over and turned to Cam. 'We're going to need some blood. Strip.'

'What?' Cam said. 'Sirri —'

'Just to the waist will do,' Sierra said. 'Sorry, Cam, I should have guessed it would need this. I should have warned you.'

'But it's cursed cold out here!'

'I can cast a shield to keep you warm. It will only take a few minutes.'

'Will he hold still, or do you want to tie him up?' Rasten asked her.

'He'll stand,' Sierra said.

Cam made no move to take off his coat. 'How do you know this thing is even going to work for me if I'm not a mage?'

'It's an enchantment,' Sierra explained. 'The work lies in its creation. The problem here is that you need to be able to use it, not just wear it, which is why we need the ritual. It'll be using your life force to fuel itself, but we'll only need it for a few months, so it shouldn't do you any real harm.'

'Just don't take it off,' Rasten said. 'Or it'll run down and die and you'll need another mage to restart it.'

'Sirri —' Cam began.

'It only needs a little cut. Best to get it over with.' She summoned her power and with a gesture cast an encircling shield that surrounded the three of them in a bubble of warm air. It immediately began to fill with mist as the trapped moisture from their breath condensed into fog. Her shield manifested as a net of flickering lightning and Rasten turned his face up to watch it fade into the mist.

'Pretty,' he remarked.

Cam took off his belt, laying his sword at his feet, and quickly stripped off his coat, jacket, shirt and undershirt. He immediately began to shiver. The temperature inside the bubble was only a little above freezing. It was warm enough that he wouldn't get frostbite, but hardly a comfortable temperature to be standing around half naked. Any warmer however, would soon have them standing in a pool of freezing slush.

'You have a knife or do you want mine?' Rasten asked Sierra.

'I'll use my own,' she said, baring her hands and pulling out the little belt-knife Mira had given her.

'Alright. You do it like this.'

Rasten explained the ritual to her once before they began and then again as she followed his instructions step by step. Sierra had never made an enchantment. Her lessons with Rasten had focussed on offensive and defensive techniques, not the minute precision and control required to secure a working within the crystalline matrix of a stone. She followed Rasten's instructions by rote as she nicked a tiny cut on Cam's chest, just over his breast bone amid the downy fuzz of fine, pale hair that marked his foreign blood.

When she smeared a drop of his blood on the milky surface of the stone she felt the enchantment inside uncoil and awaken, latching onto him like a leech. Cam didn't flinch at the touch of the blade, but when the enchantment sank its teeth into him he gasped and bent double as though someone had taken him by surprise with a punch to the gut.

Sierra grabbed his shoulder, forgetting that her fingertips were smeared with blood and left sticky streaks on his skin. 'Cam?'

'Ah … Fires Below, you might have warned me.' It felt like a fish-hook snagged beneath his heart — Sierra sensed it, too, for an instant before the pain was washed away in a tide of warmth. Part of her wanted to close her eyes and bask in it while the rest of her wanted to wilt in shame that she could take such pleasure in her friend's pain.

'You'll forget all about it in a couple of days,' Rasten said. Sierra felt him come to stand behind her and he laid a hand on the back of her neck. It made her shudder. She wanted to slap him away but she made herself hold still, unsure how he would react if she did. Her power reared up and surged at the repression, though, and he surely felt it bite at him through her skin.

Cam must have felt her go very still. He looked up with an expression of pure hatred in his eyes and encircled her arm with his hand. He took a step back, drawing her with him.

'I'll find something to bandage that cut,' she said to him.

'Don't bother. It's no more than a scratch. It will stop on its own.' He pulled his clothing on again and took the bloody stone from her fingers. 'Does the wretched thing actually work after all that?'

*Well, let's test it and see*, she thought to him. *Can you hear me?*

He recoiled as though she'd slapped him. 'By the Black Sun herself …' *How … like this?*

*Yes. Just picture me and imagine you're saying the words.*

Rasten watched them with his lips pressed together. He was jealous, Sierra knew, but she couldn't bring herself to move away from Cam to placate him. 'There's one more thing to be dealt with,' she said. 'I still can't keep my power from peaking —'

'I've noticed,' he said dryly. 'We don't have time to teach you to control it properly so we'll have to do it the roundabout way. I can take the excess from you but you'll have to lower your shields and let me in. If you fight me in the middle of an Akharian camp their mages will know at once just what is hiding among their slaves.'

'I can do that,' Sierra said. She was familiar with the procedure. Raising and supplying power had been Kell's main use for her. Early on, the suppression stones had been enough to prevent her from fighting him and later the heat of the punishment bands had forced her to submit.

'You're making a mistake allying yourself with these people,' he said to Sierra.

'But you think she should go back to Kell with you?' Cam said. 'You, who doesn't care what she might go though in the slave camps? Why would she ever choose to go with you over staying with people who care about her for who she is, not what she can do for them? But of course you wouldn't say anything against it. It's what you have in mind for her, after all, if she were ever fool enough to turn herself in.'

Rasten stared at Cam blankly, as though he'd spoken in an unfamiliar language. Then he turned to Sierra. 'You're right. He doesn't understand.'

'I tried to tell you,' Sierra said.

'Look, princeling,' Rasten said. 'She's higher above you than you could possibly imagine and she is still growing. She's not like you at all.' To Sierra, he said, 'You're starting to feel it, aren't you? It's getting harder and harder to remember that you're supposed to share their little hurts and struggles. To pretend you're human. Well, this is only the beginning, Little Crow. That night at the village wasn't an aberration, a freak moment you can put to the back of your mind and forget all about. That's what the world is really like. At the moment you think these insects will help you, that they will keep you warm and safe and share what you're going through, but when they see the real you they'll run screaming.

'I know you think I've forgotten, but I do remember what it was like to have a family, and so I know what I'm talking about. You'll destroy them if they don't abandon you first. I want to spare you that pain … but you'll fly where you will, Little Crow, and I can't stop you.'

He dispelled her shield with a flick of his hand, breaking it so sharply the power returned to Sierra in a stinging smack of energy that rippled and crackled over her skin before arcing down to earth itself in the ground.

'When the time comes, call me. I'll be nearby.'

He turned and stalked away across the bright swathe of snow. In the distance a man started out from his waiting riders, trotting closer with a riderless horse in tow.

Sierra turned away, leaning towards Cam as he slipped an arm around her shoulders. She leaned close, taking comfort in his warmth and the trickle of power that still flowed from the cut on his chest.

'He's mad, isn't he?' Cam said. 'Totally and utterly mad.'

'I tried to tell you,' Sierra said.

# Epilogue

Cam made her a makeshift toboggan by cutting a forked limb from a tree with the two long branches to form the base and a short, upwardly curved stem on which to affix the traces. They disturbed a moose feeding in the stand of trees where he cut the branch. The beast peered down its long nose as it stamped and pawed at the snow and rather than risk goading it into a charge they took the branch elsewhere to finish the job.

Sierra lashed a hide to the forked branches with the fur side down to provide a slick base, then tied her meagre supplies to it. She hoped it would be enough to convince anyone who came across her that she had been travelling alone in the wilderness for some time.

When it was all ready Sierra slipped her feet into the thongs of her snowshoes and slung the sled-rope across her shoulder. 'Well,' she said, 'I suppose this is it.'

'Do you have your magic rock?' he said with a straight face.

'Cam!' She went to prod him with her forefinger but he stepped back out of her reach with a grin. The humour was short-lived. They could hear the sound of axes echoing over the hillside.

'Will you be alright?' he asked her one last time.

'They can't do anything to me unless I let them. I'm more worried about you, getting past Rasten first, and then dealing with Dremman.'

Cam shrugged. 'Ardamon won't be far behind us. I'll wait with him until you send word that everything has gone as expected.'

Sierra shook her head. 'I'd rather not use it unless it's absolutely necessary. There's always the chance that one of the Akharian mages will overhear. Just go, Cam. If anything goes wrong, I'll deal with it and tell you afterwards. But if Rasten gives you any trouble, call me, and I'll deal with him.'

He turned away with a grimace. 'I'm the warrior here, I should be protecting *you*.' He scrubbed a hand through his hair and sighed. 'Well, at the rate the Akharians have been travelling they should reach Demon's Spire within a month. So long as the Thaw holds off, anyway.' He looked away over the valley. 'He was only saying those things to scare you.'

'I know.'

'You won't need his help once you get your hands on Vasant's books.'

'I'm sure you're right.'

He wrapped his arms around her. Sierra shut her eyes against the sting of tears. She'd hugged her mothers and fathers before walking down the hill to surrender to Kell. They'd begged her not to go, but they hadn't tried to stop her.

'You're shaking,' he said.

'I'm just a little nervous.'

'You don't have to do this.'

'Yes, I do. There's nowhere else I can go, remember?' She shook her hood back and let the cold air brace her. 'I'd best go.'

'Sirri, tell Isidro ... tell him I'll see him soon. And tell Mira I'll bring her the head of any man who hurts her. Starting with her uncle if she wants.'

'I will. Be well, Cam.'

'Spirit of Storm watch over you, Sirri.'

Sierra left him in the cover of the trees, dragging the awkward and unbalanced sled behind her as she descended into the valley. The one time she let herself look back she couldn't see him at all.

She followed the sound of the axes. If she were really a wandering traveller living hand-to-mouth in the thin and hungry end of winter, she might be desperate enough not to care that the sound was as much a threat as it was an offer of safety. If she was desperate enough she would take the chance.

They must have seen her coming as she crossed the open valley, for they were waiting for her at the edge of the trees. The first she knew of them was a shout of warning in a strange-yet-familiar language and then a rapid bellow of orders as they fanned out from the trees to surround her with spears and bows. She recognised few words from their rapid babble but the meaning was clear enough. She let the sled-rope fall and dropped to her knees, raising her hands in surrender. A moment later they'd shoved her face down onto the snow while they bound her hands behind her back. She couldn't have resisted if she'd wanted to. She was too busy trying to keep her power contained beneath her skin.

They kept her there with the snow melting and seeping into her clothes while they sorted through the gear on her sled and discarded it all as worthless. Between Kell and Rhia she'd learned just enough Akharian to tease some meaning from the conversation going on over her head: *What do you reckon, sir? She looks like a young 'un under all those furs.*

*Ye Gods and demons, man, d'you think I'm going to stand around here in the cold waiting for you to get your end away while there's a hot meal waiting for me back at the camp? I don't care how desperate you are to get frostbite on your tackle, you can do it on your own cursed time. Get her on her feet.*

One of the men hauled her up and shoved her towards the sound of the axes.

As she let them march her away Sierra heard Rasten's voice drifting over the snow-covered hills.

*I'll be waiting for your call, Little Crow.*

Printed by RR Donnelley at Glasgow, UK